John Timb

Historic Ninepins

Salzwasser

John Timbs

Historic Ninepins

1. Auflage | ISBN: 978-3-84605-156-6

Erscheinungsort: Frankfurt, Deutschland

Erscheinungsjahr: 2020

Salzwasser Verlag GmbH

Reprint of the original, first published in 1869.

HISTORIC NINEPINS.

A BOOK OF CURIOSITIES, WHERE OLD AND YOUNG
MAY READ STRANGE MATTERS:

CONTAINING

CHARACTERS AND CHRONICLES.
DOUBTS AND DIFFICULTIES.
FICTIONS AND FABULOUS HISTORIES.
IFS AND INCREDIBILIA.
LEGENDARY STORIES.
MARVELS AND MISREPRESENTATIONS.
MYTHS AND MYTHOLOGIES.
PARALLELS AND PERIODS.

POPULAR ERRORS.
PROPHECIES AND GUESSES.
PRÆ-HISTORIC TIMES.
RECKONINGS AND REFUTATIONS.
TALES AND TRADITIONS.
UNIVERSAL HISTORY: READINGS, WITH
   NEW LIGHTS.

By JOHN TIMBS,

AUTHOR OF

"THINGS NOT GENERALLY KNOWN,"
"NOTABLE THINGS OF OUR OWN TIME," ETC.

LONDON:

LOCKWOOD & CO., STATIONERS' HALL COURT.

MDCCCLXIX.

LONDON :

SAVILL, EDWARDS AND CO., PRINTERS, CHANDOS STREET,
COVENT GARDEN.

TO THE READER.

THE Art of Writing History has, of late years, received many aids and accessions from the most accredited sources of truth, which, as Horace Walpole has remarked, is "the essence of History." The value of these gains has, however, been variously estimated. "We think," says a popular writer, "the existing generation is not favourable to the production of durable impartial history. Ours is an age of discovery; we do not now mean scientific discovery. For a century or so the habit had prevailed of receiving implicitly the traditions and records of past times, assuming them to have been substantiated at the date of their publication. This style of constructing history consisted merely in breaking up and rearranging stereotype blocks. Recently, the worthlessness of such a mode of proceeding has become apparent, and now the opposite error has come strongly into vogue—that of leaping back to contemporaneous neglected documents, and, on their evidence, reversing the settled deliberate verdict of past centuries. Thus, Cromwell and Mary of Scotland, and George of England (we don't mean him of the Dragon) get new characters;—nay, to such an extent is this carried, that, following the example of a learned prelate, we have a worthy man presenting us with 'historic doubts' relative to the existence of Shakspeare—a writer of plays; and this style of thing is creeping into science."

It is not proposed in the present volume to treat of these historic studies in all their bearings; our object in quoting the above passage being to show the extent and variety which they have assumed.

In France and Germany these inquiries have long occupied public attention very largely, and have had a corresponding influence upon historical works published contemporaneously in England A vigorous offshoot of this widely-extended object we have now had in this country for nineteen years, in the valuable *Notes and Queries*, a "Medium of Intercommunication" which has much of the historic element in its pages.

Within the present year has appeared a volume, displaying much learning and research, by Dr. Octave Delepierre, entitled *Historical Difficulties and Contested Events*, in the introduction to which, the author points out "a great many so-called historical facts, which are perfectly familiar even to the ignorant, and yet which never happened." The

Historic Difficulties comprise twelve histories, ranging from the ancient world, B. C. 306, to Galileo Galilei, 1620.

We had long observed the public taste for this species of corrective reading, extended to modern times, and inquiries of a more popular and practical character than those of the antique world. In 1841, we published a volume of *Popular Errors Explained and Illustrated*, which, though successful, did not attain an extraordinary sale. Readers were not then ready for such inquiries; but, in 1858, we reproduced this work in an entirely new form; taking Sir Thomas Browne's *Vulgar Errors* as the text book for the older portion of the work, in great part re-written. Of this improved edition of *Popular Errors* several thousand copies have been sold, and the Work is kept in print.

The present volume—HISTORIC NINEPINS—an eccentric title, by the way—seeks to supply the requirements of a large class of readers, and in such plain words "that he may run who readeth." The work is divided into eleven sections, which collectively contain more than three hundred articles. We have termed it "A Book for Old and Young," inasmuch as, besides the Wonders of Classic Fable and Popular Fiction, those in our Early History extend beyond the limits of mere abstracts; such are the Stories of English Life, which are the delight of our early years—indeed, of all ages. To the leading events of our history, proportionate attention is paid, in such a manner, as by their concentration, to point with warmth and quickness upon the reader's comprehension.

Meanwhile, a contemporaneous interest attaches to the HISTORIC NINEPINS, for its "Historico-Political Information," by way of annotation; and here we have specially to acknowledge our obligation to "the Fourth Estate," which affords a faithful and eloquent reflex of "the very age and body of the time." The annexed Table of Contents and copious Index will, however, best bespeak the variety as well as general character of the work, which has been prepared with due regard to accredited authorities, as well as attractiveness of narration.

In such an assemblage of Names, Dates, and Facts, as the present volume contains, it would be presumptuous to promise freedom from error; but the reader is assured that no pains have been spared to insure accuracy.

December, 1868.

CONTENTS.

The General Subject.

Ancient History.

Myths and Popular Fictions.

Great Events from Little Causes.

British History.

British History—*continued.*

British History—*continued.*

French History.

Historico-Political Information.

Ecclesiastical History.

Retributive Justice.

Science applied to the Arts.

Books, Phrases, etc.

Appendix.

⁎ THE "IFS" OF HISTORY, pp. 3—6, omitted to be acknowledged,—Abridged from an able paper in the *Saturday Review.*

HISTORIC NINEPINS.

The General Subject.

CHANCES OF HISTORY.

NATIONS will more readily part with the essentials than with the forms of liberty; and Napoleon might have died an emperor in reality, if he had been contented to have lived a consul in name. Had Cromwell displayed his hankerings for royalty somewhat sooner than he did, it is probable that he would have survived his power. Mr. Pitt gained a supremacy in this country, which none of his predecessors dared to hope, and which none of his successors will, we trust, attempt to attain. For twenty years he was "*de facto*," not "*de jure*," a king. But he was wise in his generation, and took care to confine the swelling stream of his ambition to channels that were *constitutional*; and with respect to the impurity, the filth, and the corruption of those channels, he trusted to the vast means he possessed of alarming the weak, blinding the acute, bribing the mercenary, and intimidating the bold: confiding his own individual security, to that selfishness inherent in our nature, which dictates to the most efficient mind, to have too much respect for itself to become a Catiline, and too little esteem for others to become a Cato. There was a short period in the Roman history, when that nation enjoyed as much liberty as is compatible with the infirmities of humanity. Their neighbours the Athenians, had much of the form, but little of the substance, of freedom; disputers about this rich inheritance rather than enjoyers of it, the Athenians treated liberty, as schismatics religion, where the true benefits of both have been respectively lost to each by their rancorous contentions about them.

GREAT RULERS IN HISTORY.

Lord Macaulay, in his admirable paper on the great Lord Clive, has the following remarks upon the rules for judging the conduct of eminent rulers:—"Ordinary criminal justice knows nothing of set-off. The greatest desert cannot be pleaded in answer to a charge of the slightest transgression. If a man has sold beer on Sunday morning, it is no defence that he has saved the life of a fellow-creature at the risk of his own. If he has harnessed a Newfoundland dog to his little child's carriage, it is no defence that he was wounded at Waterloo. But it is not in this way that we ought to deal with men who, raised far above ordinary restraints, and tried by far more than ordinary temptations, are entitled to a more than ordinary measure of indulgence. Such men should be judged by their contemporaries as they will be judged by posterity. Their bad actions ought not, indeed, to be called good ; but their good and bad actions ought to be fairly weighed; and if, on the whole, the good preponderate, the sentence ought to be one, not merely of acquittal, but of approbation. Not a single great ruler in history can be absolved by a judge who fixes his eye inexorably on one or two unjustifiable acts. Bruce, the deliverer of Scotland ; Maurice, the deliverer of Germany; William, the deliverer of Holland; his great descendant, the deliverer of England; Murray, the good Regent; Cosmo, the father of his country; Henry the Fourth of France; Peter the Great of Russia—how would the best of them pass such a scrutiny ? History takes wider views; and the best tribunal for great political cases is the tribunal which anticipates the verdict of history."

CHARACTERS OF KINGS.

Horace Walpole writes to Sir Horace Mann, in 1764:—" Count Poniatowski, with whom I was acquainted when he was here, is King of Poland, and calls himself Stanislaus the Second. This is the sole instance, I believe, upon record, of a second of a name being on the throne while the first was living, without having contributed to dethrone him. Old Stanislaus lives to see a line of successors, like Macbeth in the cave of the witches. So much for Poland ! Don't let us go farther north ; we shall find there Alecto herself. I have almost wept for poor Ivan. [The deposed Czar Ivan, attempting to make his escape, had been murdered ; but it is very doubtful whether the Czarina could be privy to his death.] I shall soon begin to believe that Richard III. murdered as many folks as the Lancastrians say he did. I expect that this Fury will poison her son next, lest Semiramis should have the bloody honour of having been more unnatural. As Voltaire has poisoned so many persons of former ages, methinks he ought to do as much for the present time, and assure posterity that there never was such a lamb as Catherine the Second, and that, so far from assassinating her own husband and Czar Ivan, she wept over every chicken that she had for dinner. How crimes, like fashions, flit from clime to clime! Murder reigns under the State, while you, who are in the very town where Catherine de' Medici was born, and within a stone's-throw of Rome, where Borgia and his holy father sent cardinals to the other world by hecatombs, are surprised to hear that there is such an instrument as a stiletto.

" I have no more monarchs to chat over; all the rest are the most Catholic or most Christian, or most something or other that is divine ; and you know one can never talk long about folks that are only excellent. One can say no more about Stanislaus *the First* than that he is the best of beings. I mean, unless they do not deserve it, and then their flatterers can hold forth upon their virtues by the hour."

THE MORAL OF MONARCHY.

"A man may read a sermon," says Jeremy Taylor, "the best and most passionate that ever man preached, if he shall but enter into the sepulchres of kings. In the same Escurial where the Spanish princes live in greatness and power, and decree war or peace, they have wisely placed a cemetery where their ashes and their glory shall sleep till time shall be no more: and where *our* kings have been crowned, their ancestors lie interred, and they must walk over their grandsire's head to take his crown. There is an acre sown with royal seed, the copy of the greatest change, from rich to naked, from ceiled roofs to arched coffins, from living like gods to die like men. There is enough to cool the flames of lust, to abate the height of pride, to appease the itch of covetous desires, to sully and dash out the dissembling colours of a lustful, artificial, and imaginary beauty. There the warlike and the peaceful, the fortunate and the miserable, the beloved and the despised princes mingle their dust, and lay down their symbol of mortality, and tell all the world, that when we die our ashes shall be equal to kings, and our accounts shall be easier, and our pains for our crimes shall be less. To my apprehension, it is a sad record which is left by Athenæus, concerning Ninus, the great Assyrian monarch, whose life and death is summed up in these words: ' Ninus, the Assyrian, had an ocean of gold, and other riches more than the sand in the Caspian Sea ; he never saw the stars, and perhaps he never desired it ; he never stirred up the holy fire among the Magi, nor touched his God with the sacred rod, according to the laws; he never offered sacrifice, nor worshipped the Deity, nor administered justice, nor spake to the people, nor numbered them; but he was most valiant to eat and drink, and having mingled his wines, he threw the rest upon the stones. This man is dead: behold his sepulchre, and now hear where Ninus is. *Sometime I was Ninus, and drew the breath of a living man, but now am nothing but clay. I have nothing but what I did eat, and what I served to myself in lust is all my portion : the wealth with which I was blest, my enemies meeting together shall carry away, as the mad Thyades carry a raw goat. I am gone to Hell; and when I went thither, I carried neither gold nor horses, nor a silver chariot. I that wore a mitre, am now a little heap of dust !*''

THE "IFS" OF HISTORY.

If something had happened which didn't happen, what would have happened afterwards? is a kind of speculation which is now much in fashion. Of course, no one can answer positively the above inquiry. Yet, in looking back upon the course of history, it is impossible not to dwell for a moment upon some of the more important crises, and to remark how small a difference might have made an incalculable change. We know the usual sayings about the decisive battles of the world. If Themistocles had lost the battle of Salamis, if Asdrubal had won the battle of the Metaurus, if Charles Martel had been beaten by the

Saracens, would not the subsequent history of Europe and the world have been altered, and a great many fine philosophical theories have been destroyed before their birth?

Even the strictest believer in universal causation may admit without prejudice to his opinions that the most trivial circumstances may be of cardinal importance. The reluctance to admit the doctrine about great events springing from trivial causes results from another consequence of the theory. Where the fate of a few persons is concerned, no one cares to dispute it. When Noah was in the Ark, the most trifling error of steering might (in the absence of providential interference) have shipwrecked the whole human race. Now the logical difficulties raised by Necessitarians apply just as much to a party of twenty as to twenty millions. The importance of small cases does not affect their theory more in one case than the other. But philosophers are unwilling to allow that the fate of whole countries and many generations can depend upon these petty accidents, because it would obviously render all prediction impossible, and at least leave the future of mankind dependent upon the chance of the necessary hero arising at the critical moment.

It is impossible here to discuss so large a question as the frequency with which those historical crises occur in which the merest trifle may turn the balance, or to inquire whether they ever occur at all. But we may notice shortly two or three conditions of the argument which are frequently overlooked, and which make most of these discussions eminently unsatisfactory. Thus, for example, the believers in decisive battles very seldom take the trouble even to argue the real difficulty of the question. The defeat of Napoleon at Leipzig, or perhaps at Waterloo, it has been said, changed the history of Europe. It may be so; but the fact that a particular battle was the most crushing, or the final blow which he received, does not even tend to prove that a different result would have been equally decisive the other way. On the contrary, a victory might probably have been the next worst thing to a defeat. The battles in which the Saracens or the Hungarians received the final check to their advance are in the same way reckoned as decisive of history. But, to make this out, we should have to prove that which is at first sight opposed to all probability—that, in the event of a victory, they could have permanently held their conquests; and afterwards that, if they had held them, they would not have been absorbed by the conquered population. When Canute rebuked his courtiers, he happened to select a time at which the tide was rising. If, by a little management, they had induced him to give the order just as the tide turned, they might perhaps have persuaded him that his order was the cause of the change. A good many historical heroes seem to have been Canutes who issued their commands precisely at the turn of the tide, and historical writers have been crying out ever since that, if it had not been for this marvellous Canute, the tide would have swelled until the whole country had been engulphed. The analogy is, of course, imperfect; for the historical tide is really affected in some degree by the hero who opposes its progress at the proper moment, only he has a wonderful advantage if he happens to strike just at the fortunate epoch.—*Saturday Review.*

The absurdity of a series of "*ifs*" has also been thus shown. " If this did not happen, then something else must have happened, and the whole course of subsequent events must have been altered." It is one of those far-fetched explanations which we can produce at will to account for any phenomenon. We might say, for instance, that the prophet Jonah is the cause of American slavery. If he had not preached, Nineveh would not have repented ; if Nineveh had not repented, it would have been overthrown ; if it had been overthrown, who knows the consequences? The whole course of empire would have been changed, and America might still be a forest.

Mr. Phillimore, in his *History of England in the Reign of George III.*, describes the difficulty of writing modern history, and laments that in modern times we have no Herodotus nor Thucydides, no Livy nor Tacitus. He says, that if these Greek and Roman historians lived in our day—if they saw this, and if they saw that, if they were acquainted with India, if they were acquainted with America, and if they knew a great number of other things besides—the result, the grand result, the astonishing result, would be that they would have known more than they knew, and would have told us more.

In Whitaker's *Vindication of Mary Queen of Scots*, that curious writer thus speculates in the true spirit of this paper. When dependence was made upon Elizabeth's dying without issue, the Countess of Shrewsbury had her son purposely residing in London, with two good and able horses continually ready, to give the earliest intelligence of the sick Elizabeth's death to the imprisoned Mary. On this the historian observes, " And had this *not improbable event actually taken place, what a different complexion would our history have assumed from what it wears at present !* Mary would have been carried from a prison to a throne. Her wise conduct in prison would have been applauded by all. From Tutbury, from Sheffield, and from Chatsworth, she would have been said to have touched with a gentle and masterly hand the springs that actuated all the nation, against the death of her tyrannical cousin," &c. So ductile is history in the hands of man ! and so peculiarly does it bend to the force of success, and warp with the warmth of prosperity !

" If Mary had lived a little longer, or Elizabeth died sooner," says Mr. Mill, "the Reformation would have been crushed in England. People who believe in a steady development of human thought, are naturally unwilling to allow that the spread of new ideas may be arrested or made possible by the accident of a single woman's life ; for, on the same principles, we can have no certainty that in a few years hence we may not all be Roman Catholics, or Mormons, or followers of Comte."

It is always a question among military writers how far the pause of Hannibal was compulsory—a question not likely now to be solved, unless Pompeii yields us further literary treasures. As far as one can decide at such a distance of time and of scene, it seems all but certain that the rapid advance of Hannibal on Rome after the battle of Cannæ, that of Henry of Navarre on Paris after the battle of Ivry, or that of Charles Stuart on London after penetrating as far as Derby, would have changed the course of human history.—*Builder,* 1868.

"THE MUSE OF HISTORY."

In an able review of Mr. Froude's *History of England*, vols. v. and vi., the writer thus reproves a fashion of writing history in the present day, which is unsound and misrepresentative. "History," says the critic, "is one of those pursuits which have been blest with a Muse, and for the love of this excellent lady, historians are continually aiming at the heroic. They select a theme—the life of a nation within a particular century. They represent this life as actuated by the sublimest motives which they can invent. The heroes are patriots fighting for the independence of their homes, or citizens resisting the encroachments of tyranny, or believers animated by the ardours of a religious struggle. There is an epic grandeur in the action. The men are giants; their motives are divine, and the result is sacred. The history of our own times is paltry in comparison. In writing contemporary history, we are obliged to confine ourselves to the facts before us; and what are these facts? That statesmanship in its last analysis is reduced to a question of finance; that Cocker is the greatest of our Ministers; that the resumption of cash payments, the repeal of a duty, the discovery of a gold mine, the accident of a potato-blight, the sale of opium, and the state of the Three per Cents. are the dominant elements of our political life; and that, however we may prate of Church and State, life and liberty, most of the leading questions of the day reduce themselves by a very simple process to the old eternal question of the big loaf, the little loaf, and the payment of the piper. By way of contrast, look at any history of the Tudor reigns, including even the work of Mr. Froude. We at once leap to the conclusion that there were people of simple faith and noble aspirations in those days, who were raised high above the petty concerns which trouble nations now. They thought more of the remission of sins than of the reduction of taxes. They were more interested in the mass than in their daily bread. The Bible supplied the place of Consols in public regard. The rate of wages and the price of mutton were matters of indifference; but the sermon preached at Paul's Cross and the last bull from the Pope were affairs of the greatest moment. Whether the revenue of the year was short and the expenditure of the country was excessive, were inquiries completely overshadowed by questions relating to the religious nurture of the boy-King, or the religious sentiments of the Queen's betrothed. We observe that the whole nation is intent on mighty speculations as to fate and free will, the real presence, the Pope's authority, and justification by faith; and it is only when we come to the appendix that we find huddled together a few scraps of information as to the state of the currency, the price of wheat, and the amount of the public income. We have surely had quite enough of this highflying style of history. We would say nothing disrespectful of the Muse who has inspired some very pretty histories in her time. We only wish that historians would give her a holyday for a little while, and come down to the sober level of facts. Human nature is pretty much the same all the world over, and the nature of nations has a wonderful similarity from age to age. That 300 years ago a nation which now grovels in pursuit of gain, and aims at physical perfection, was all for romance and spiritual profit, is a fallacy which we leave to the poets, but deny to the historian. With regard to our own history, and with regard to a period of it not very far removed from the present time, a purifying criticism is required similar to that which the German scholars have applied to the early legends of Greece and Rome. The history of England during the sixteenth century, which witnessed the revival of letters and the reform of religion, has a legendary tone about it from which even Mr. Froude's volumes are not entirely free.—*Times*, 1860.

WORTH OF HISTORICAL AUTHORITIES.

Among the various kinds of original authorities, some form the main staple of our knowledge of one age, and some of another. For old Greek and Roman history, we have to rely mainly on literary evidence—the direct statements of historians, and the incidental allusions of other writers. Of strictly documentary evidence we have none, except what may be found in coins and inscriptions. This is of course partly the result of the destruction of documents, but it is far more extensively owing to their original paucity. The Greeks not only had no printing, but they were incomparably more chary of writing than our forefathers of the Middle Ages. This was owing to several causes—to their general out-door life, to the publicity of everything in so many of their governments, and to the awkward and costly nature of their writing materials. Public documents took the form of inscriptions on brass or stone; when the state of things which they expressed ceased to exist, the visible memorial of that state of things was often taken away. If Athens and Sparta made a treaty, its terms were graven on a pillar; the next time war broke out, the pillar was taken away. The best chance of a document surviving the state of things which it described was if some historian like Thucydides or Polybius thought fit to insert it bodily in his text. And this not only confines modern inquirers almost wholly to literary sources; it gives a peculiar character to the literary sources themselves. If Mr. Kinglake sits down nowadays to write the history of the Crimean war, besides his personal knwledge and the oral reports of eye-witnesses, he has before him vast masses of literary material. Thucydides, in writing the history of his own contemporaries, Herodotus, in writing the history of his father's contemporaries, could have got nearly all their information by word of mouth. This was not wholly a disadvantage; for there can be no doubt that, where there are few artificial helps to memory, the memory itself becomes much stronger and clearer. When people read so much about everything as we do now, and read it, too, for the most part, so very hastily and superficially, it is wonderful how fast they forget things. Altogether, though the old writers had to trust mainly to oral information, yet the oral information to which they had to trust must have been of a much higher kind than most oral information now. And one can hardly doubt that the sort of reflexion and inquiry thus needed, the necessity of personal recollection for many things and of

personal intercourse with actors for others, had something to do in producing that peculiar and unapproachable character which distinguishes the best of the old Greek histories from all other human writings.—
. *Abridged from the Saturday Review.*

WORTH OF ANTIQUARIANISM.

Antiquarianism has been pronounced, by high authority, to be "an indispensable element in history." Unquestionably it is so. Yet nothing is more certain than that histories of steady popularity and considerable renown have been written without it. In one sense, indeed, it is of very modern growth and culture. Real antiquarianism, defined as a lively knowledge of the past, comprehending the spirit of a period through the details of its customs, events, and institutions, may of course be exercised in any direction; in Athens and Attica, or at Stonehenge and Sarum. There is as much antiquarianism in Arnold's *Thucydides*, or Mitchell's *Aristophanes*, as in any cubic foot of the *Gentleman's Magazine*. And there are few generations without individual examples of this spirit. But the conventional import of the term is a particular and circumstantial knowledge of the men, manners, and events of the Middle Ages, a knowledge in which the writers of the last century could hardly have been otherwise than deficient, since they openly treated it with contempt. Hume considers it a singular proof of Horace Walpole's eloquence, that he succeeded in attracting attention to so obsolete a subject as the reign of Richard III. The judgments of these writers have accordingly been liable to reversal, and their misstatements to exposure. Whether the opinions of later generations may have gone too far in an opposite direction, is a point which we shall not here discuss; but the change of sentiment has certainly been for the advantage of mediæval history. One remarkable improvement is in the circumstantial detail of the narrative. Compare the return of Edward IV., or the reign of Edward V., in Turner, with the like portions in Hume, and the contrast will be most striking. It is by this method of proceeding, by entering into the spirit of an age, by living for a while in the language of its writers, by handling its relics, by contemplating the monuments of its sciences and its arts, and by concentrating upon one object the numberless rays of light which are thus procurable, that the modern historian of the Middle Ages must hope to supply the deficiency of a contemporary authority.—*Quarterly Review.*

ANCIENT AND MODERN ESTIMATE OF ORATORY.

There are no potentates of modern times that would imitate Philip, and offer a town containing ten thousand inhabitants for an orator. The ancients were a gossiping and a listening rather than a writing or a reading set. This circumstance gave an orator great opportunities of display; for the tongue effects that for thoughts that the Press does for words; but the tongue confers on them a much shorter existence, and produces them in a far less tangible shape—two circumstances that are often not unfavourable to the speechifier. An ancient demagogue said that so long as the people had ears, he would rather that they should be without understandings. All good things here below have their drawbacks, and all evil things their compensations. The drawback of the advantage of printing is, that it enables coxcombs to deluge us with dulness; and the compensation for the want of that art was this, that if blockheads wrote nonsense, no one else would transcribe it: neither could they take their trash to the market, when it cost so much time and labour to multiply the copies. Booksellers are like horse-dealers in one respect, and, if they buy the devil, they must also sell the devil; but the misfortune is, that a bookseller seldom understands the merits of a book so thoroughly as the horsedealer the merits of a horse, and reads with far less judgment than the other rides. But to return to the speechifiers. An orator who, like Demosthenes, appeals to the head rather than the heart, who resorts to argument, not to sophistry, who has no sounding words, unsupported by strong conceptions, who would rather convince without persuading than persuade without convincing, is an exception to all rules, and would succeed in all periods. When the Roman people had listened to the loud, diffuse, and polished discourses of Cicero, they departed, saying to one another, what a splendid speech our orator has made; but when the Athenians heard Demosthenes, he so filled them with the subject-matter of his oration, that they quite forgot the orator, but left him at the finish of his harangue, breathing revenge, and exclaiming, " Let us go and fight against Philip. — Colton's *Lacon.*

CHARTERS SIGNED WITH THE CROSS.

The practice of affixing the sign of the Cross proceeded from the inability of the signers to write: this is honestly avowed by Caedwalla, a Saxon king, at the end of one of his charters. A similar circumstance is related of the Emperor Justin in the East, and Theodore, king of the Goths in Italy. Procopius, in his *Historiæ Arcana*, says: " Justin, not being able to write his name, had a thin, smooth piece of board, through which were cut the four letters of his name, J. V. S. T., which, laid on the paper, served to direct the point of his pen, his hand being guided by another. Possibly this may likewise have given the hint to the first of our card-makers, who paint their cards in the same manner, by plates of pewter or copper, or only pasteboard, with slits in them in form of the figures that are to be painted on the cards." (*Philosophical Transactions*, vol. xl. p. 393.) This is the art of stencil, which has been applied, in our time, to decorating the walls of rooms, as well as to the marking of linen.

Charlemagne used his monogram for his signature, for which Eginhard gives this as the reason: namely, that Charlemagne could not write; and, having attempted in vain to learn in his grown age, he was reduced to the necessity of signing with his monogram.

The probable reason why the Cross was always used in the Middle Ages in the testing of ecclesiastical charters, was not only that it was a sacred symbol, but that Justinian had decreed it should have the strength of an oath.

WRITING HISTORY.

Many writers, including now an Imperial historian, have attempted to weigh and measure the share that individual men and accidents have in the course of human affairs. How far has the world really been affected by Alexander, or by the cold bath that cut him off in his very youth; by the day's march of Claudius Nero, that drove the Carthaginians out of Italy, and led to the ruin of their State; by the mighty genius, or the assassination, of Julius Cæsar; by the arrow that pierced Harold, or the bullet that killed Charles XII., of Sweden; by the passions of our Henry VIII., by the obstinacy of Charles I., or by the religious convictions of James II.; by the cold *ragout* which is said to have deprived Napoleon of one victory, or the timely arrival of the Prussians, which extinguished all hope of another? History must deal with persons and things, and it must also clothe them with dramatic interest and importance, but philosophers are apt to think them only the superficial indications of an irresistible current below. A despot is murdered, but the despotism remains. A great soldier falls, but the nation is not less warlike.—*Times' journal.*

When, after the victory of Aumale, in which Henry IV. was wounded, he called his generals round his bed, to give him an account of what had occurred subsequently to his leaving the field, no two could agree on the course of the very events in which they had been actors; and the king, struck with the difficulty of ascertaining facts so evident and recent, exclaimed, "*Voilà ce que c'est l'histoire !*"—" What, then, is history!"

" Give me my liar," was the phrase in which Charles V. was used to call for a volume of history; and certainly no man can attentively examine any important period of our annals without remarking that almost every incident admits of two handles, almost every character of two interpretations; and that by a judicious packing of facts the historian may make his picture assume nearly what form he pleases without any direct violation of truth.—*Quarterly Review,* 1832.

WORTH OF HERALDRY.

The only individuals who affect to sneer at Heraldic pursuits and studies are those of apocryphal gentility, or whose ancestral reminiscences are associated with the rope sinister, or some such distinctive badge. Heraldry is, however, a branch of the hieroglyphical language, and the only branch which has been handed down to us with a recognised key. It in many cases represents the very names of persons, their birth, family, and alliances; in others, it illustrates their ranks and titles; and in all *is*, or rather *was*, a faithful record of their illustrious deeds, represented by signs imitative and conventional. Taking this view of the question, it is evident that it is capable of vast improvements: in fact, a well-emblazoned shield might be made practically to represent, at a single glance, a synopsis of biography, chronology, and history. Insignia of individuals and races, which are of a kindred character with heraldry, at least in its original form and design, may be recognised among the nations of antiquity, and may perhaps be carried back to the primeval ages of Egyptian history. The Israelites, from their long captivity familiarized with such objects, naturally adopted them as distinguishing characteristics; and Sir William Drummond believed that the twelve tribes adopted the signs of the zodiac as their respective ensigns; " nor," as has been observed, " does the supposed allusion to those signs by Jacob imply anything impious, magical, or offensive to the Deity."

The heraldry (?) of the heroic ages may be traced in the pages of Homer and Æschylus; and in the succeeding generations we have testimony of the adoption of a sort of armorial bearings by the princes of Greece. Omitting Nicias, Lamachus, Alcibiades, and others on record, we will merely observe that the arms of Niochorus, who slew Lysander, were a dragon, thus realizing the prediction of the oracle,

> Fly from Oplites' watery strand ;
> The earth-born serpent, too, beware.

Nor were mottoes by any means unfrequent. The shield which Demosthenes so pusillanimously threw away was inscribed "To good Fortune."

The animals which are frequently represented within shields on the Roman vases sufficiently establish the fact, that this usage was common amongst that great people; and the striking example of a goat on a specimen in the British Museum, might by analogy, without any great stretch of imagination, be ascribed to the family of *Caprus !*

Students of heraldry are commonly great enthusiasts; so that, in its pursuit, they are apt to depreciate more important subjects. We remember to have heard an amateur herald painter, who had filled all his windows with arms of his own painting, condemn Mr. Salt's collection of Egyptian Antiquities in terms of unmistakeable contempt!— *Knowledge for the Time*, 1864, p. 85.

WRITING HISTORY FOR THE STAGE.

Sheridan's popular play of *Pizarro* owes much of its success to its sentiments, chiefly made up by Sheridan from his speeches on the trial of Warren Hastings, and on the subject of the invasion. The most objectionable point in the original arrangement of the piece is the ill-contrived and almost ludicrous manner in which retributive justice is dealt on Pizarro, who, after being bullied through five acts by Alonzo, Elvira, and Rolla in succession, is killed unfairly in the end, as Porson commemorates in his amusing parody :—

> Four acts are tol, lol ; but the fifth's my delight ;
> Where history's trac'd with the pen of a Varro ;
> And Elvira in black, and Alonzo in white,
> Put an end to the piece by killing Pizarro.

It is but just to the memory of Kotzebue to remark, that this gross departure from historical fact was a gratuitous interpretation by Sheridan. Every schoolboy might have known and remembered that Pizarro lived to conquer Peru, and was finally assassinated in his vice-regal palace at Lima by the son and friend of his early associate, Almagro, whom he executed some years before.

The inflated, false sentiments of the play have received this chastisement from a contemporary critic:—"It is observable and not a little edifying to observe, that when those who excel in a spirit of satire above everything else come to attempt serious specimens of the poetry and romance whose exaggerations they ridicule, they make ridiculous mistakes of their own, and of the very same kind,—so allied is the habitual want of faith with want of all higher power."

TRAVELS OF ANACHARSIS.

This popular work of the Abbé Barthélemy, first published in 1788, is a strange admixture of fiction with real facts, which is not very favourable to historical accuracy. Barthélemy supposes a young Scythian, of the name of Anacharsis, acquainted with the language of the Greeks, to have made a journey into Greece in search of information, and to have resided many years in its principal cities, between 363 and 337 B.C. The greater part of this period corresponds with the reign of Philip of Macedonia till the battle of Cheronæa, after which Anacharsis is made finally to leave Greece and return to Scythia, where he is supposed to have compiled a narrative of his travels and observations in Greece. Barthélemy's object in writing the *Anacharsis* was to revive among the people of his age the taste for ancient erudition, to vindicate it from the supercilious contempt of the philosophers of the day, and to show the utility of such studies. "In this work the Abbé enlightens us on the memorable battle of Thermopylæ, where Leonidas, instead of resisting the Persians with three hundred men, commanded, according to Diodorus, at least seven thousand, or even twelve thousand, if we may believe Pausanias."—See Delepierre's *Historical Difficulties and Contested Events*, p. 8.

Horace Walpole criticises Barthélemy with much *verve*. In a letter to the Countess of Ossory, he writes:—"I am reading the *Anacharsis* of the Abbé Barthélemy, four most corpulent quartos, into which he has amassed, and, indeed, very ingeniously arranged, every passage I believe (for aught I know) that is extant in any Greek or Latin author, which gives any account of Greece, and all and every part of it; but, alas! I have not yet waded through the second volume—a sure sign that the appetite of my eyes has decayed. I can read now but for amusement. It is not at all necessary to improve one's self for the next world, especially as one's knowledge will probably not prove standard there. The Abbé is, besides, a little too partial to the Grecian accounts of their own virtues, and, as Dr. Pauw and Dr. Gillies have lately unhinged their scale of merits, a rehabilitation is no business of mine." In another letter to the Countess, Walpole writes :—"The Abbé's book is extremely well described *by a Mosaic compound all-bits of truth ;* but, alas ! the pavement is a fiction, and not slippery enough to make one slide over it. It is, as Mrs. Damer says, a vision—a dream about truths ; in short, it is an excellent work for a man of twenty-five, just fresh from the classics, and would range them most compendiously in his head, and he would know where to find any parcel he should want on occasion ; but for me, I have not been able to wade to the end of the second volume. I cannot gulp again the reveries of the old philosophers on the origin of the world, and still less the foolish romances of Herodotus, such as that of the patriotic courtier who cut off his own nose and ears in order to betray Babylon to Darius. *Iron tears may fall down Pluto's cheek* when he sees Nebuchadnezzar come to himself; yet even that I should not believe at the distance of two thousand years ! Then, having just read Dr. Gillies and Mr. Pauw, I cannot for the life of me admire the Lacedemonians again, nor listen gravely to the legend of Lycurgus, when Mr. Pauw has proved it very doubtful whether any such person existed. If there did, he only refined savages into greater barbarism. I will tell your Ladyship an additional observation that I made just as I broke off with *Anacharsis.* We are told that Lycurgus allowed theft, and enjoined community of goods. I beg to know where was the use of stealing where there was no individual property ? Does stealth consist in filching what is your own as much as any other man's ? It would be like Mr. Cumberland, who steals from himself."

Again : " I allow all the merit of Anacharsis, and do believe your Ladyship reads it ; but I know that its great vogue at Paris, on its first appearance, was during the first fortnight, when, to be sure, nobody had got through thirty pages of the first volume. I penetrated a great way, and, though I was tired of it, it was not from any faults I found, but it did not interest me in the least. Mrs. Damer is a convert, and is now reading it. I broke off at the Lacedemonians, whom I abhor, though I allow the merit your Ladyship so justly admires in them— their brevity."

Voltaire's *Universal History* was a favourite book of Walpole's. He thought it Voltaire's *chef-d'œuvre.* "It is a marvellous mass both of genius and sagacity, and the quintessence of political wisdom as well as of history. Any one chapter on a single reign, as those of Philip II., Henry IV., Richelieu, Elizabeth, Cromwell, is a complete picture of their characters and of their times. Whatever may be said of his incorrectness in some facts, his observations and inferences are always just and profound. . . . . The story of the whole modern world is comprised in less space than that of the three centuries of diminutive Greece in the tedious travels of Anacharsis, who makes you remember rather than reflect."

Ancient History.

THE DEUCALIONAL DELUGE.

DEUCALION, in Grecian legend, is the person specially saved at the general deluge; and he is the father of Hellen, the great eponym of the Hellenic race. The enormous iniquity, as Apollodorus says, of the then existing brazen race, or, as others say, of the fifty monstrous sons of Lycaon—provoked Zeus to send a general deluge. An unremitting and terrible rain laid the whole of Greece under water, except the highest mountain tops, whereon a few stragglers found refuge. Deucalion was saved in a chest or ark, which he had been forewarned by his father, Prometheus, to construct. After floating for nine days on the water, he at length landed on the summit of Mount Parnassus. He then prayed that men and companions might be sent to him in his solitude, when Zeus directed both him and Pyrrha, his wife, to cast stones over their heads: those cast by Pyrrha became woman, those by Deucalion men. And thus "the stony race of men came to tenant the soil of Greece."

The reality of this deluge was firmly believed throughout the historical ages of Greece: the chronologers, reckoning up by genealogies, assigned the exact date to it, and placed it at the same time as the conflagration of the world, by the rashness of Phaeton. The meteorological work ascribed to Aristotle, places Mount Pindus near Dodona, and the river Achelous: he treats it as a physical phenomenon, the result of periodical cycles in the atmosphere, thus departing from the religious character of the old legend, which described it as a judgment inflicted by Zeus upon a wicked race. Statements founded upon this event were in circulation throughout Greece to a very late date. The Megarians affirmed that Megaros, their hero, son of Zeus by a local nymph, had found safety from the waters on the lofty summit of their mountain Geranei, which had not been completely submerged; and in the magnificent temple of the Olympian Zeus, at Athens (according to the Parian marble, founded by Deucalion), a cavity in the earth was shown, through which it was affirmed the waters of the deluge had retired: even in the time of Pausanias, the priests poured into this cavity holy offerings of meal and honey.—*Abridged from Grote's Hist. Greece*, vol. i.

EGYPT: ITS MONUMENTS AND HISTORY.

Egypt has been under many dynasties, none of which sprang originally from her own soil. Indeed, to those who take pleasure in observing historical retribution, it must be a striking reflection that this country has been subject to foreign powers, or to dominant races unassimilated with the original stock, ever since the days of those mighty kings who were wont from time to time to oppress the children of Israel. It is true that subjection to a foreign race has become the normal condition of many Eastern countries; but there is, perhaps, no region in which ancient splendour and long-continued modern degradation are so harshly contrasted as in the land of the Pharaohs.—(*Athenæum*.) Canon Trevor puts this strikingly:—

"It is hardly possible to imagine a greater contrast than is presented between the *Monuments* and the *History* of Egypt. The monuments tell of a native monarchy flourishing among the great empires of the East; its kings little less than demi-gods; its priesthood endued with a sanctity revered in distant lands; its chariots and horses pouring out to battle under the banners of a thousand gods; the nations of the earth bringing tribute; and art and luxury carried to an extent only possible to a numerous population, with abundant material resources and a high mental development. On the date and duration of this splendid period the monuments are dumb. They witness what Ancient Egypt was; they know nothing of her rise, progress, or decay. Their testimony is confirmed by the position of Egypt in the Holy Scriptures, where her rulers are found showing hospitality to the father of the faithful, or reducing his descendants into bondage. Still, we only know that Egypt was a great power before Israel was a nation. It gleams out of a remote antiquity with a splendour that cannot be denied; but the splendour is a pre-historic memory, separated from authentic chronology by a gulf, which nothing but the Bible can span. All that we know of it is, that it existed before Moses, and perished about the close of the Old Testament. With the first page of secular history Ancient Egypt is already dead. The Pharaohs have become a tradition, the temples and altars are shrouded in mystery, the fleets and armies have disappeared, the people are reduced to inexorable servitude."

PLATO SOLD AS A SLAVE.

When Dionysius received, at Syracuse, the visit of Plato (who came to Sicily to see Mount Etna, 388 B.C.), he discoursed eloquently upon justice and virtue, enforcing his doctrine that wicked men were inevitably miserable, that true happiness belonged only to the virtuous, and that despots could not lay claim to the merit of courage. This pleased not Dionysius, who took a deep-rooted dislike to Plato, whom, according to Diodorus, the despot caused to be seized, taken to the Syracusan slave-market, and put up for sale as a slave, at the price of twenty minæ; which his friends subscribed to pay, and thus released him. Plato then left Syracuse in a trireme which was about to convey home the Lacedæmonian envoy, Pollio. But Dionysius secretly entreated Pollio to cause him to be slain on the voyage—or at least to sell him as a slave. Plato was accordingly landed at Ægina, and there sold; but, being re-purchased, he was sent back to Athens: but it is certain that Plato was really sold, and became for a moment a slave!—*Abridged from Grote's Hist. Greece*, vol. xi.

HOW DEMOSTHENES BECAME AN ORATOR.

Demosthenes, when a youth, corrected his defective elocution by speaking with pebbles in his mouth; he prepared himself to overcome the noise of the assembly by declaiming in stormy weather on the sea-shore of the Phalerum; he opened his lungs by running, and extended the power of holding breath by pronouncing sentences in marching up-hill; he sometimes passed two or three months without interruption in a subterranean chamber, practising night and day, either in composition or declamation, and shaving one-half of his beard in order to disqualify himself from going abroad. In his unremitting private practice, he acquired a graceful action by keeping watch on all his movements while declaiming before a tall looking-glass. More details are given by Plutarch, from Demetrius, the Phalerean, who heard them himself from Demosthenes; and the subterranean chamber where he practised was shown at Athens, even in the time of Plutarch.

THE HOMERIC POEMS.

Mr. Froude, the historian, loves Homeric masterpieces; and he has traced with a fine and cunning hand the moral creed of the great poet, the state of society described by him, the power and grand simplicity of his manner, his sympathy with what is noble and beautiful. We quote his very striking reflections on the moral differences between the *Iliad* and *Odyssey:*

" In the *Iliad*, in spite of the gloom of Achilles, and his complaint of the double urn, the sense of life, on the whole, is sunny and cheerful. There is no yearning for anything beyond—nothing vague, nothing mystical. The earth, the men, the gods, have all a palpable reality about them. From first to last, we know where we are, and what we are about. In the *Odyssey*, we are breathing another atmosphere. The speculations on the moral mysteries of our being hang like a mist over us from the beginning to the end, and the cloud, from time to time, descends on the actors, and envelopes them in a preternatural halo. . . We never know as we go on, so fast we pass from one to the other, when we are among mere human beings, and when among the spiritual and mystical. Those sea-nymphs, those cannibals, those enchantresses, if intended to be real, are neither mortal nor divine; at any rate, like nothing divine which we had seen in Olympus or on the plains of Ilium; and at times there is a strangeness seen in the hero himself. Sometimes it is Ulysses painfully toiling his way home across the unknown ocean; sometimes it is we that are Ulysses, and that unknown ocean is the life across which we are wandering with too many Circes and Sirens, and Isles of Error in our path. In the same spirit death is no longer the end, and on every side long vistas seem to stretch away into the infinite, peopled with shadowy forms."

The candour and integrity of Homer, in an historical point of view, have been so impugned as to be set beneath the authority of Geoffrey of Monmouth. One of the latest Homeric theories is that by Mr. James Hutchinson, of Cape Town, Cape of Good Hope, who points out remarkable resemblances in the *Iliad* of Homer and the *Rámáyana* of Valmiki. He contends that the rape of Helen and the siege of Troy are really but the carrying off of Sitá and the capture of Lanka done into Greek verse. He goes further, and asserts his conviction that Homer not only worshipped the same deities as the Hindus, but was himself a Hindu.

Dr. August Jacob, after six years' study of the ancient Greek epics, has constructed a theory of Homer, according to which there was really a singer, or bard, named Homer, who, somewhere about the tenth century B.C., flourished on the western coast of Asia Minor, or in the islands hard by. The wrath of Achilles, and the return of Odysseus, formed the subjects of his songs, which, for a long time, were not written down, but preserved by oral tradition. But Homer had predecessors, contemporaries, and successors, who celebrated the fall of Troy. All the lays, Homeric and others, were altered from time to time; and were edited by Pisistratus, who presented them to the Athenians in the same order in which they now appear. Dr. Jacob points out the ancient songs or stories, examines the whole of the *Iliad* and *Odyssey* book by book, and makes his citations in German.

HOMER'S BATTLES, AND HIS IMITATORS.

The first great poet whose works have come down to us sang of war long before war became a science or a trade. If, in his time, there was enmity between two little Greek towns, each poured forth its crowd of citizens, ignorant of discipline, and armed with implements of labour rudely turned into weapons. On each side appeared conspicuous a few chiefs, whose wealth had enabled them to procure good armour, horses, and chariots, and whose leisure had enabled them to practise military exercises. One such chief, if he were a man of great strength, agility, and courage, would, probably, be more formidable than twenty common men; and the force and dexterity with which he flung his spear might have no inconsiderable share in deciding the event of the day. Such were, probably, the Battles with which Homer was familiar. But Homer related the actions of men of a former generation, of men who sprang from the gods, and communed with the Gods face to face, one of whom could with ease hurl rocks, which two sturdy hinds of a later period would be unable even to lift. He therefore naturally represented their martial exploits as resembling in kind, but far surpassing in magnitude, those of the stoutest and most expert combatants of his own age! Achilles, clad in celestial armour, drawn by celestial coursers, grasping

c

his spear which none but himself could raise, driving all Troy and Lycia before him, and choking the Scamander with dead, was only a magnificent exaggeration of the real hero, who, strong, fearless, accustomed to the use of weapons, guarded by a shield and helmet of the best Sidonian fabric, and whirled along by horses of Thessalian breed, struck down with his right arm, foe after foe. In all rude societies, similar notions are found. There are at this day countries where the Life-guardsman, Shaw, would be considered as a much greater warrior than the Duke of Wellington. Buonaparte loved to describe the astonishment with which the Mamelukes looked at his diminutive figure. Mourad Bey, distinguished above all his fellows by his bodily strength, and by the skill with which he managed his horse and his sabre, could not believe that a man who was scarcely five feet high, and rode like a butcher, could be the greatest soldier in Europe.

Homer's description of war had, therefore, as much truth as poetry requires. But truth was altogether wanting to the performances of those who, writing about battles which had scarcely anything in common with the battles of his times, servilely imitated his manner. The folly of Silius Italicus, in particular, is positively nauseous. He undertook to record in verse the vicissitudes of a great struggle between generals of the first order; and his narrative is made up of the hideous wounds which these generals inflicted with their own hands. Asdrubal flings a spear which grazes the shoulder of the consul Nero; but Nero sends his spear into Asdrubal's side. Fabius slays Thuris and Butes and Maris and Arses, and the long-haired Adherbes, and the gigantic Thylis, and Sapharus, and Monæsus, and the trumpeter Morinus. Hannibal runs Perusinus through the groin with a stake, and breaks the backbone of Telesinus with a huge stone. This detestable fashion was copied in modern times, and continued to prevail down to the age of Addison. Several versifiers had described William turning thousands to flight by his single prowess, and dyeing the Boyne with Irish blood. Nay, so estimable a writer as John Philips, the author of the *Splendid Shilling*, represented Marlborough as having won the battle of Blenheim merely by strength of muscle and skill in fence.—*Macaulay.*

FABULOUS LOCALITIES OF CLASSIC HISTORY.

Mr. Grote, at the opening of his valuable *History of Greece*, gives this very interesting *précis* of certain classic localities, the existence of which has been disproved by the extension of geographical discovery:—

" Many of these fabulous localities are to be found in Homer and Hesiod, and the other Greek poets and topographers,—Erytheia, the garden of the Hesperides, the garden of Phœbus, to which Boreas transported the Attic maiden Orithya, the delicious country of the Hyperboreans, the Elysian plain, the floating island of Æolus, Trinakria, the country of the Æthiopians, the Læstrygones, the Cyclopes, the Lotophagi, the Sirens, the Cimmerians, and the Gorgons, &c. These are places which (to use the expression of Pindar respecting the Hyperboreans) you cannot approach either by sea or by land : the wings of the poet alone can bring you there. . . . .

" In the present advanced state of geographical knowledge, the story of that man who, after reading *Gulliver's Travels*, went to look in his map for Lilliput, appears an absurdity ; but those who fixed the exact locality of the floating island of Æolus on the rocks of the Sirens did much the same ; and with their ignorance of geography and imperfect appreciation of historical evidence, the error was hardly to be avoided. The ancient belief which fixed the Sirens on the island of Sireneuse off the coast of Naples ; the Cyclopes, Erytheia, and the Læstrygones in Sicily ; the Lotophagi on the island of Meninx, near the Lesser Syrtis ; the Phæacians at Corcyra, and the goddess Circe at the promontory of Circeium, took its rise at a time when these regions were first Hellenized, and comparatively little visited."

COLOSSAL ANTS PRODUCING GOLD.

This extravagant fable is related by the Greeks, and repeated by travellers of the Middle Ages, of ants as big as foxes producing gold. The passage states that the tribes who dwell between the Meru and Mandara mountains brought lumps of the paipilika, or ant-gold,—so named because it was dug out by the common large ant, or paipilika. Professor Wilson explains this absurdity, by observing that it was believed that the native gold found on the surface of some of the auriferous deserts of Northern India had been laid bare by the action of these insects,—an idea by no means irrational, although erroneous, but which grew up, in its progress westward, into a monstrous fable. The native country of these tribes is that described by the Greeks—the mountains between Hindostan and Thibet ; and the names are those of barbarous races still found there.

GREEK A NEW LANGUAGE !

In the *Quarterly Review*, vol. xxxix. p. 477, we are told that Conrad, a monk of Heresbach, had pronounced, in presence of an assembly, an anathema against Greek, saying that " a new language had been discovered, called Greek, against which it was necessary to guard, as this language engendered every species of heresy ; just as all they who learned Hebrew infallibly became Jews."

M. Delepierre, in correction, says :—" The real fact is, that Conrad of Heresbach had never been a monk, but was a confidential councillor of the Duke of Cleves, and that, far from prohibiting the study of the ancient languages, he was one of the *savans* of the sixteenth century who showed the greatest zeal in encouraging a taste for their culture. It is he himself who, in order to expose the ignorance of the clergy of that period, relates that he heard a monk from the pulpit pronounce the anathema on the Greek language mentioned above. So easy is it, by distorting facts, to make or mar a reputation !"—*Historical Difficulties*, 1868, pp. 5, 6.

THE DEATH OF ÆSCHYLUS.

Æschylus, the celebrated Athenian tragic poet, spent the latter part of his life in Sicily, where he died. For this change of residence, at an advanced period of life, no certain reason has been transmitted by ancient authors. It has been recorded that a prophet informed him of the day on which he would be killed by something falling upon his head; and, in order to avoid an accident of that kind, he quitted the town, and retired to the fields, where an eagle dropped a tortoise on his head, probably mistaking it for a stone, as he was very bald. This stroke instantly deprived the poet of life. Pliny and Valerius Maximus narrate the account of the death of Æschylus with all the gravity of truth; and, however improbable it may appear, there can be little doubt but both believed in the accuracy of what they stated. Plutarch has, in his writings, mentioned a number of particulars of the life of Æschylus, which would require to be confirmed by other testimony before they are admitted as authentic history.

THE BATTLE OF ARBELA.

Mr. Rawlinson, in the closing volume of his *Five Great Monarchies of the Eastern World*, makes the following remarks on the battle of Arbela, and its effects on the Persian Empire:—

"Arbela was not, like Issus, won by mere fighting. It was the leader's victory, rather than the soldiers'. Alexander's diagonal advance, the confusion which it caused, the break in the Persian line, and its prompt occupation by some of the best cavalry and a portion of the phalanx, are the turning-points of the engagement. All the rest followed as a matter of course. Far too much importance has been assigned to Darius's flight, which was the effect rather than the cause of victory. When the centre of an Asiatic army is so deeply penetrated that the person of the monarch is exposed and his near attendants begin to fall, the battle is won. Darius did not—indeed, he could not—'set the example of flight.' Hemmed in by vast masses of troops, it was not until their falling away from him on his left flank at once exposed him to the enemy and gave him room to escape, that he could extricate himself from the *mêlée*. No doubt it would have been nobler, finer, more heroic, had the Persian monarch, seeing that all was lost, and that the Empire of the Persians was over, resolved not to outlive the independence of his country. Had he died in the thick of the fight, a halo of glory would have surrounded him. But because he lacked, in common with many other great kings and commanders, the quality of heroism, we are not justified in affixing to his memory the stigma of personal cowardice. Like Pompey, like Napoleon, he yielded in the crisis of his fate to the instinct of self-preservation. He fled from the field where he had lost his crown, not to organize a new army, not to renew the contest, but to prolong for a few weeks a life which had ceased to have any public value. It is needless to pursue further the dissolution of the Empire. The fatal blow was struck at Arbela—all the rest was but the long death-agony. At Arbela the crown of Cyrus passed to the Macedonian; the Fifth Monarchy came to an end. The *he-goat*, with the notable horn between his eyes, had come from the west to the ram which had two horns, and had run into him with the fury of his power. He had come close to him, and, moved with choler, had smitten the ram, and broken his two horns—there was no power in the ram to stand before him, but he had cast him down to the ground and stamped upon him—and there was none to deliver the ram out of his hand."*

ALEXANDER THE GREAT, AND HIS HORSE BUCEPHALUS.

The fame of Alexander and his steed, Bucephalus, are built up together. The latter was named from his head resembling that of an ox. Alexander was the first to break in this famous horse, and thus fulfil the condition stated by an oracle as necessary for gaining the crown of Macedon. Aulus Gellius† has given a minute account of Bucephalus, and records that, after he had been killed in battle, Alexander built, in honour of his horse, a city in India, which, from him, he called Bucephale. To this day, the burial-place of Bucephalus is pointed out by the natives, and the tomb erected to his memory by Alexander stands in the centre of a large plain, between Jelam and Chenab rivers, in the Punjab. It is formed of earth, breasted with marble; the base extends 100 paces, and diminishes at the top to thirty, to which you ascend by a flight of stone steps, fifty-five in number. In the centre, at the top, which is quite flat, is a square draw-well, faced with stone; a tree grows a few yards from the mouth of the well, and under its shade sits a faquier (a monk or mendicant). We gather these details from the letter of an officer of the 41st Regiment, who was, a few years since, encamped close to the tomb in his campaign.

---

* Le Brun has painted the Battle of Arbela, which we remember to have seen engraved upon a glass vase, by a Bohemian artist: as a modern intaglio engraving, this vase was unrivalled. It was long in the possession of Mr. Apsley Pellatt, who has engraved it in his *Curiosities of Glass-making*, 1849.

† Aulus Gellius (or, according to some writers, Agellius), the author of the *Noctes Atticæ*, was born at Rome, early in the second century, and died at the beginning of the reign of the Emperor Marcus Aurelius. The *Noctes Atticæ* was written, as he informs us in the preface to the work, during the winter evenings in Attica, to amuse his children in their hours of relaxation. It appears from his own account, that he had been accustomed to keep a commonplace book, in which he entered whatever he heard in conversation, or met with in his private reading that appeared worthy of memory. There is no attempt at classification or arrangement in the work, which contains anecdotes and arguments, scraps of history and pieces of poetry, and dissertations on various points, its philosophy, geometry, and grammar. Amidst much that is trifling and puerile, we obtain information upon many subjects relating to antiquity, of which we must otherwise have been ignorant. The work was printed for the first time at Rome in 1469; it was translated into English by Beloe, 1795.

The name Bucephalus has been applied to a beautiful animal of
the gazelle tribe, as well as generally to a showy steed.   Sheridan,
in his Prologue to *Pizarro*, sings of the Sunday equestrian in Hyde
Park :—

> Anxious—yet timorous too !—his steed to show,
> The hack Bucephalus of Rotten Row.

HERODOTUS, THE FATHER OF HISTORY.

Herodotus, the author of the most ancient history which has been
transmitted to modern times, was born at Halicarnassus about 484 B.C.
If the passages in his own History (i. 30, iii. 15) were written by himself,
he was probably alive 408 B.C.   To obtain authentic and abundant
materials for writing his History, he visited Asia, spent some time in
Egypt, crossed to Greece, and afterwards to Italy.   To the Egyptian
priests he, probably, owed the greatest obligations.   He presents himself
as a traveller and observer, and as an historian.   The story of his reading
his work at the Olympic Games has been disproved, and is not even
alluded to by Plutarch, in his Treatise on the malignity of Herodotus.
He makes no display of the extent of his travels ; but his details are surprising: he describes an object as standing behind the door, or on the
right hand, as you enter a temple ; or he was told something by a person in a particular place ; or he uses other words equally significant.
The sketches of the various people and countries are among the most
valuable parts of the work of Herodotus, throwing a clear and steady
light over ancient history.   When he has any doubt about the authenticity
of his information, Herodotus always uses qualifying expressions ; but
his statements made without doubt or hesitation may be relied on.   His
digressions elevate him to the rank of an intelligent traveller, who com-
bines in harmonious union with a great historical work, designed to per-
petuate the glories of his own nation, so endless a variety of matter collected
from the general history of mankind.   He chose for his subjects a series of
events which concerned the universal Greek nation, and not them only, but
the whole civilized world ; and by his execution of his great undertaking,
he was called by Cicero the Father of History.   He was not fully appreci-
ated by all his countrymen ; and in modern times his wonderful stories have
been the subject of merriment to the half-learned, who measure his experience by their own ignorance.   The incidental confirmations of his
veracity have been accumulating of late years on all sides, and our more
exact knowledge of the countries which he visited enable us to appreciate
him better than many of the Greeks themselves could do.   His style is
simple, pleasing, and generally perspicuous ; but with evident marks of
defective composition.

Forty years ago, it was remarked in the *Edinburgh Review* :—
" Few persons are aware how often they imitate the Father of History.
Thus, children and servants are remarkably 'Herodotean' in their style
of narration.   They tell everything dramatically.   Their ' says he ' and

'says shes' are proverbial. Every person who has had to settle their disputes, knows that, even when they have no intention to deceive, their reports of conversation always require to be carefully sifted. If an educated man were giving an account of a certain change of administration, he would say: 'Lord John Russell resigned, and the Queen, in consequence, sent for Sir Robert Peel.' A porter would tell the story as if he had been behind the curtains of the Royal bed at Buckingham Palace. 'So Lord John Russell says, " I cannot manage this business, I must go out." So the Queen says, " Well, then, I must send for Sir Robert Peel, that's all." This is the very manner of the Father of History.

" Herodotus has been most unblushingly mis-quoted, by great men, too: Denon, the traveller in Egypt, several times quotes Herodotus for what is not in that author. But this is so common even with people who have claims to scholarship, that it has become almost a fashion to say that anything is in Herodotus."

In a review of Wheeler's *Geography of Herodotus*, in the *Literary Gazette*, 1854, we find this summary of his present status:—

" The fame of Herodotus brightens as time advances. After all the assaults upon his veracity as a traveller and his credibility as a historian, the substantial truth and value of his writings are more and more acknowledged. The researches of the most learned scholars and the discoveries of the most recent travellers are ever bringing to light new proofs of the authenticity of his narrative. That he admitted into his history many doubtful traditions, and that along with the record of what he himself saw he gave many idle tales related to him by others, is understood by every reader. But the historian himself made no pretension to an exact and systematic narrative of events. His work was intended not for philosophical but for popular use, and he set down all that he thought might prove generally interesting. Sometimes he warns his readers against receiving his statements as facts, as in the account of the clerk of the temple at Elephantina, when, recording the reply to his inquiry about the course of the Nile, he adds, 'the man, however, seemed to me to be jesting.' He frankly tells the sources of his information, and makes no concealment of his being frequently a mere compiler and reporter of tales, as well as an eyewitness and narrator of events. For the purposes of his work, he did not think it necessary to exercise the strict discrimination between fact and fiction which is now expected in every historian. It is not fair, therefore, to judge him according to the ideas of modern criticism, as has been done by the commentator on Herodotus, Mr. Blakesley, in the introduction to the recently published edition of his history. He repeats the old charge, that much of the narrative of ' the Father of History' is a mere bundle of stories, imposed upon his credulity by ' Egyptian priests ' and 'ancient mariners;' and he even renews the discussion as to whether Herodotus really did accomplish those travels which have been generally ascribed to him. The criticisms and arguments of the learned commentator may serve to induce increased caution and discrimination in regard to the details of the writings of Herodotus, but we do not think they injure his general reputation either as a historian or as a geographer. Notwithstanding Mr. Blakesley's scepticism, and that of all previous critics, from Plutarch to Voltaire, we still turn with confidence to the pages of the old ' Homer of History,' believing that there we find much true and valuable information as to the nations of antiquity which no other work contains, and that we there have a striking and, on the whole, a faithful picture of the ancient world as it appeared to a Greek traveller five centuries before the Christian era."

DIOGENES: HIS SAYINGS AND DOINGS.

Diogenes was a native of Sinope, in Pontus, which he and his father, who was a banker, were compelled to quit, for coining false money. On settling at Athens, he studied philosophy under Antisthenes. From his writings being lost, the extent of his information and his discoveries in science are unknown. That he had the reputation of being a great genius seems undeniable ; although much of his celebrity may be referred to the strictness of his tenets, contempt of comfort, and oddity of manner. It must not be inferred that because he despised riches he cultivated humility : on the contrary, he looked down with scorn upon the whole world, censured with the dignity of a magistrate all mankind, and considered every philosopher as greatly his inferior. Extreme poverty, the result of his despising riches, obliged him to beg—a state to which his raiment was not superior ; yet, when Alexander the Great offered him riches, he spurned at the proposal, and said, " All I ask is, do not stand between me and the sun." In after-life, Diogenes was taken by pirates, who carried him into Crete, and sold him to Xeniades, a Corinthian, in whose family he lived as tutor, and refused to be ransomed by his friends, giving as a reason, that " a lion was not the servant of his feeders, but their master." He died in the same year, and, according to one account, on the same day, with Alexander the Great (323 B.C.), at the age of ninety years. Of him Plato may be said to have given a just character in a few words, that "he was Socrates run mad." His dress was a coarse double robe, which served him as a cloak by day and a coverlet by night, and carried a wallet to receive alms of food. His abode was a cask in the temple of Cybele. In the summer he rolled himself upon the burning sand, and in the winter clung to the images in the street covered with snow, in order that he might accustom himself to endure all kinds of weather.

The smart things and witty repartees of Diogenes were collected by his kinsman, Diogenes Laertius ; and of them Professor de Morgan has, in the *Athenæum*, collected some specimens.

"Diogenes is not a *Cynic* : that is a name for the snapping school which he raised into fame, nominally founded by Antisthenes. He is as much more than a Cynic as Plato is more than a Platonist. 'I am Alexander the great king.—And I am Diogenes the Dog (κύων).' The school frequented the Cynosargus at Athens ; whence some thought the name was derived. Very likely ; and in this way : dirty mendicants haunting a place so called would be called dogs, and philosophic pride would adopt the name.

" Diogenes, like R. B. Sheridan, must have every stray joke sworn to him. But the genuine stock is in Laertius. He was asked why gold is so pale, and he replied, Because so many are lying in wait for it. Very likely the querist expected Diogenes to answer that he did not know, and would then have answered his own question with—Because it is afraid you and your father will put a wrong stamp on it. For Icesias and Son were bankers at Sinope, and were driven away for operations on the coinage. When Diogenes was afterwards reproached with this, his answer was—I was once what you are now ; what I am now you never will be.

" When should a man dine? If rich, said Diogenes, when he likes ; if poor, when he can.

" Why, said some one, who wanted to be very smart upon the poor tub-tenant who lived by his wit, do people give cheerfully to the lame and blind, but not to philosophers ? Because said Diogenes, people feel they may (ἐλπίζουσι) become lame and blind themselves, but they have no fear of becoming philosophers. He begged of a stingy man who was very slow about producing anything: My friend ! said he, what I ask for is to feed me, not to bury me.

" The well-known house, or bed, in which the sage lived—when at Athens, at least ; no doubt Xeniades found him a better lodging—has produced a comparison. Cranger said that the large hoop-apparatus which the ladies wore in hi day was no more a petticoat than Diogenes's tub was his breeches. Would they now let Diogenes, tuo and all, into an omnibus ?

" The humility of Diogenes was of that kind which is 'aped by pride,' and is, perhaps, the best understood point of his enigmatical character. It did not impose upon Plato, whose repartee is equally well known. Byron embodies it in one of the stanzas of Don Juan :—

> Trampling on Plato's pride, with greater pride,
>   As did the cynic on some like occasion :
> Deeming the sage would be much mortified,
>   Or thrown into a philosophic passion,
> For a spoilt carpet—but the "Attic bee.
> Was much consoled by his own repartee."

The same idea is illustrated in a different way by Sir Thomas Browne : " Diogenes I hold to be the most vain inglorious man of his time, and more ambitious in refusing all honours than Alexander in rejecting none."—*Religio Medici.*

The tub story has been demolished : "And why?" says De Morgan. "Because it is not mentioned by Cicero, Plutarch, Arrian, and Valerius Maximus; only by Lucian, Laertius, Juvenal, and Seneca."

Diogenes desired to be buried head downwards, feeling sure, he said, that things would soon be topsy-turvy: this was an allusion to the growth of Macedonia. Diogenes was imitated by the eccentric Major Labellière, who was buried on the most north-western brow of Box Hill, in Surrey, with his head downwards, in order, he said, that "as the world was turned topsy-turvy, it was fit he should be buried so, that he might be *right at last.*"

XERXES AND HIS EXPLOITS.

Ancient authors differ respecting the number of the army under Xerxes in his invasion of Greece. Justinus makes it consist of 700,000 native troops and 300,000 auxiliaries, adding that it had not been improperly recorded that *rivers had been drunk up by his armies*, and that his fleet consisted of 14,000 ships. That historian says: " His army wanted a commander: that, in considering the king, you may praise his wealth, but see him as a general: that he was first in flight, last in war, timid in perils, and puffed up when not in personal danger. Before he made trial of war, from confidence of his strength, he seemed the lord of nature itself, levelled mountains, filled up valleys, covered certain seas with bridges, and contributed to the advantage of navigation by the invention of shorter methods. His entrance into Greece was as terrible as his retreat was dishonourable. When he came down upon Greece, Leonidas, with 4000 men, guarded the Straits of Thermopylæ for three days against the whole army of Xerxes, and would probably have successfully repelled the invaders (though, according to Diodorus, there were at least 7000, or even 12,000, if we may believe Pausanias), had not the enemy, by the treachery of a Grecian, been conducted to the top of a hill which overhangs the pass. The obstinate bravery of Leonidas and his men had nearly proved fatal to the king himself, who, in his retreat, crossed the Hellespont in a fishing-boat, traversing the space in thirty days, and returned to Persia; traversing a space in thirty days over which it took six months to march with his army. Such mortality prevailed among the troops who accompanied him, that the birds of prey marked his track, and feasted on the bodies of the Persians. Before the naval engagement, Xerxes sent 4000 armed men to plunder Delphi, who fell by showers and lightning. He made war a second time on Greece, and was defeated by Cimon, son of Miltiades, both by land and sea. These unsuccessful attacks on Greece rendered Xerxes contemptible in the eyes of his own subjects; and Artabanus, his prefect, put him to death, in order to procure the crown for himself.

THE PLAINS OF TROY.

The histories of the Troad and the city of Troy are either mythical or entirely lost to us. Of the latter, although it was one of the most celebrated cities of antiquity, its site has been the subject of much discussion in modern times by travellers and antiquaries. Some have denied the existence of ancient Troy altogether, or have declared it to be a useless task to investigate its site, since it was totally destroyed by the Greeks, and abandoned by its inhabitants. But this last opinion is too sweeping; since, although Troy may have been destroyed by the Greeks, Homer, who cannot have been mistaken on this point, clearly suggests, and is borne out by Strabo, that after the calamity that befel Troy in the reign of Priam, it continued, at least for some time, to be ruled over by the Æneadæ, a branch of the house of Priam. The city of Troy, which

Xerxes (Herodotus) and afterwards Alexander the Great visited, may have been of later origin, but it is nevertheless attested that it was built on the site of the ancient Troy. This town gradually decayed after the time of Alexander, and a new town of the same name was built, which the Romans regarded and treated as the genuine ancient Troy, from which they derived their descent.

After a siege of nine years, the Greeks took and destroyed the city of Troy, about the year 1184 B.C. Thenceforth, the history of Troy, which, until then, is thoroughly mythical, is completely lost to us; although, as indicated above, it must have continued for a considerable time afterwards. At the time of the Trojan war, the inhabitants of the Troad had reached a higher state of prosperity than their opponents, the Achæans. There seems, however, to have been no considerable town in the district, except the capital, Ilium or Troy: the cities mentioned by Homer would seem, from the ease with which they were taken, to have been nothing more than villages.

The strength and resources of Troy baffled the united efforts of all Greece for nine years. Catullus has beautifully described the enormous carnage of its bloody siege in a single line:—"Iniquitous Troy, the common grave of Europe and Asia." The Trojan walls were built by Neptune and Apollo for a certain sum, which they were to receive from Laomedon, but out of which he defrauded them.

Webster, who visited the plains of Troy in 1830, describes them as now barren and desolate. The classic Scamander is but a muddy stream, winding through an uncultivated plain, covered with stunted oaks, underwood, and rushes. At the opposite extremity of the plain, stood the tombs of Hector and Achilles; that of the latter near the Hellespont, where the Greek fleet was moored. Near is the grave of his friend Patroclus. Thus, Athenian glories are now reduced to a few tumuli about thirty feet high.

SOLIMAN "THE MAGNIFICENT."

Here is a specimen of the barbarity with which this historical butcher treated his fellow-creatures:—

Among the many distinctions of Soliman's reign must be noticed the increased diplomatic intercourse with European nations. Three years after the capture of Rhodes appeared the first French ambassador at the Ottoman Porte: he received a robe of honour, a present of two hundred ducats, and, what was more to his purpose, a promise of a campaign in Hungary, which should engage on that side the army of Charles and his brother, Ferdinand. Soliman kept his promise. At the head of 100,000 men and 300 pieces of artillery, he commenced this memorable campaign. On the fatal field of Mohacs the fate of Hungary was decided, in the year 1526, in an unequal fight. Louis II., as he fled from the Turkish sabres, was drowned in a morass. The next day the Sultan received in state the compliments of his officers. The heads of 2000 of the slain, including those of seven bishops, and many of the nobility, were piled up as a trophy before his tent. Seven days after the battle a tumultuous cry arose in the camp to massacre the prisoners and peasants, and, in consequence, 10,000 men were put to the sword. The keys of Buda were sent to the conqueror, who celebrated the feast of Bairam in the Castle of the Hungarian Kings. Fourteen days afterwards he began to retire, bloodshed and devastation marking the course of his army. To Maroth, belonging to the Bishop of Gran, many thousands of the people had fled with their property, relying on the strength of the castle. The Turkish artillery, however, soon levelled it, and the wretched fugitives were indiscriminately butchered. No less than 25,000 fell here; and the whole number of the Hungarians destroyed in the barbarous warfare of this single campaign amounted to at least 200,000 souls.

HISTORY OF EARLY ROME.

The early history of Rome has undergone some strange ups and downs within the memory of man. A generation which is hardly yet extinct, believed it as it stood. Niebuhr taught us to disbelieve the old history; he gave a history of his own making to believe instead of it; though his statements too often rested not on any tangible evidence, but on a power of "divination" vested in Niebuhr himself. Much that Niebuhr had rejected, Mr. Newman believed. The last history of Rome, that of Mommsen, like Niebuhr's, pulls down and builds up, but never quotes authorities. Meanwhile, Sir George Cornewall Lewis assailed Niebuhr's whole system, scoffed at the power of divination, denied the right of any man to assert anything which he could not prove, and maintained that next to nothing could be proved as to the times embraced in the first Decade of Livy. Yet, Sir G. C. Lewis did not deny that many of the leading events in earlier times had a real historical groundwork; and he only laid it down, that without contemporary evidence it is impossible to distinguish the truth from falsehood, while he did infinite service in utterly discrediting the wild notion of "divination," and in exposing the reckless dogmatism with which Niebuhr had imposed upon the world statements unsupported by a shadow of evidence. The result of Sir G. C. Lewis's labours is, in effect, to wipe Niebuhr out altogether, and to leave the early books of Livy as a beautiful story, a sort of prose *Iliad*, which we may read and enjoy, without believing it. For history, he would send us to the later days of Rome; to those mighty struggles with Hannibal and Philip, which have been so strangely neglected for myths about Romulus and Coriolanus. The one fact of early Roman history for which real contemporary evidence can be shown, is the fact that Rome was taken by the Gauls. Roman history, in the highest and fullest sense of the word, begins only with the war with Pyrrhus. Up to the invasion, all is chaos; all records have perished; we can be sure of nothing. The political history of Rome, if we like to believe it, begins with Romulus and Tatius. That Romulus made a treaty with Tatius is in itself more credible than that he was suckled by a wolf; but there is no more historical evidence for one story than the other. Except two or three notices of Polybius, we have nothing earlier than Livy and Dionysius, though they were but copyists of copyists.—*Selected and abridged from the Saturday Review.*

HOW THE CAPITOL OF ROME WAS SAVED BY THE CACKLING OF GEESE.

The goose appears to have been much maligned by the moderns, who term it a "stupid bird," and even the trustworthiness of modern history has been impeached in support of this imputation. Every one recollects the story in Livy of the geese of Juno saving the Roman Capitol. The historical credit of this story depends in great measure upon the vigilant habits of the bird, and its superiority to the dog as a guardian.

The alertness and watchfulness of the Wild Goose, which have made its chase proverbially difficult, appear, from the following testimony, to be characteristic of the bird in its domesticated state. The establishment of this fact we have in the following evidence, by Professor Owen, from Richmond Park:—

"Opposite the cottage where I live is a pond, which is frequented during the summer by two brood-flocks of Geese belonging to the keepers. These geese take up their quarters for the night along the margin of the pond, into which they are ready to plunge at a moment's notice. Several times when I have been up late, or wakeful, I have heard the old gander sound the alarm, which is immediately taken up, and has been sometimes followed by a simultaneous plunge of the flock into the pool. On mentioning this to the keeper, he, quite aware of the characteristic readiness of the Geese to sound an alarm in the night, attributed it to a foumart, or other predatory vermin. On other occasions the cackling has seemed to be caused by a deer stalking near the flock. But often has the old Roman anecdote occurred to me, when I have been awoke by the midnight alarm-notes of my anserine neighbours; and more than once I have noticed, when the cause of alarm has been such as to excite the dogs of the next-door keeper, that the Geese were beforehand in giving loud warning of the strange steps.

"I have never had the smallest sympathy with the sceptics as to Livy's statement: it is not a likely one to be feigned; it is in exact accordance with the characteristic acuteness of sight and hearing, watchfulness and power, and instinct to utter alarm-cries, of the goose."

The Gray Lag Goose, identical with the domestic goose of our farmyards, is the *Anser* of the Romans—the same that saved the Capitol by its vigilance, and was cherished accordingly. Pliny (lib. x., c. xxii.) speaks of this bird at much length, stating how they were driven from a distance on foot to Rome; he mentions the value of the feathers of the white ones, and relates that in some places they were plucked twice a year. In the *Palazzo de' Conservatori*, fifth room, are "two *Ducks*, in bronze, said to have been found in the Tarpeian Rock, and to be the representation of those ducks which saved the Capitol."—*Starke.*

The liver of the goose seems to have been a favourite morsel with epicures in all ages, and their invention appears to have been active in exercising the means of increasing the volume of that organ.   The *pâte de foie d'oie de Strasburg* is not more in request now than were the great goose-livers in the time of the Romans.—See Pliny, *Hist.* lib. x. c. 22, &c.

The Egyptian goose, which appears to be the *Chelanopex* of the Greeks, was much prized on account of its eggs, second only to those of the peacock.   Ælian notices this bird, and speaks of its cunning.   But it is Herodotus who draws our attention to the bird as one of those held sacred by the Egyptians; and the researches of modern travellers have fully shown that it was at least a favourite dish with the priests.   It is impossible to look at the paintings and sculptures—many will be found in the British Museum, and many more copied in Rocellini's, and other works of the same kind—without being struck with the frequent occurrence of geese represented both alive and plucked, and prepared for the table.   That some of these represent the *Chelanopex* there can be no doubt. It is of frequent occurrence on the sculptures in the British Museum, though it was not a sacred bird; unless it may have some claims to that honour from having been a luxurious article of food for the priests.   A place in Upper Egypt had its name Chenoboscion, or Chenoboscia (goose-pens), from these animals being fed there, probably for sale; though there may have been sacred geese, for the goose, we are told, was a bird under the care of Isis.

The tame goose is very long-lived.   " A certain friend of ours," says Willoughby, " of undoubted fidelity, told us that his father had once a goose that was known to be eighty years old, which, for aught he knew, might have lived another eighty years, had he not been constrained to kill it for its mischievousness in beating and destroying the younger geese."   Dr. Buckland describes and figures from the clay in which the remains of elephant and rhinoceros are so often found, the humerus of a bird in size and shape nearly resembling that of a goose, which, says Dr. Buckland, " is the first example within my knowledge of the bones of birds being noticed in the diluvium of England."   The name of gooseberry has been most probably applied from the fruit being made into a sauce and used for young or green geese.

ROME, THE MISTRESS OF THE WORLD.

An achievement almost unrivalled in military annals was the strategic march by Nero, which deceived Hannibal, and defeated Asdrubal.   The first intelligence of Nero's return to Carthage, was the sight of Asdrubal's head thrown into his camp.   When Hannibal saw this, he exclaimed, with a sigh, that " Rome would now be the mistress of the world."   And yet, to this victory of Nero's it might be owing that his imperial namesake reigned at all.   But the infamy of the one has eclipsed the glory of the other. When the name of Nero is heard, who thinks of the consul? But such are human things!—Lord Byron: *Notes to the Island.*

The virtues of Hannibal were counterbalanced by vices of equal magnitude: inhuman cruelty, perfidy beyond that of a Carthaginian, no regard for truth, no sense of religious obligations, no fear of the gods, and no respect for an oath. Livy ascribes to him actions which the reader is unwilling to believe of so great a man, such as making bridges and ramparts of the bodies of the dead, and even teaching his men to feed on human flesh! During the sixteen years he was in Italy, he destroyed 400 towns, and killed 300,000 men in battle. After his submission to Rome, he was persecuted by the Romans with rancour disgraceful to their national character. After wandering about destitute and forlorn, he sought the protection of Prusias, king of Bithynia, whom, however, the Romans compelled to surrender the aged and excited Hannibal a sacrifice to their vengeance, and being beset in his fort by armed men, he swallowed poison, and expired, in 185 B.C.; but other accounts of his death are given.

EXTENT OF THE ROMAN EMPIRE.

We are sometimes under a little delusion in the estimates we form of the magnitude of the Roman Empire, or the multitude of troops that it maintained. Russia surpasses it in extent of territory, and maintains an army considerably more numerous. France and Austria, who rank next to Russia in the number of their standing armies, could singly bring into the field a much larger force than the whole Roman Empire. The military force of the Pagan Empire is here estimated at 450,000 men; the Christian monarchies of France and Austria are each of them reputed to maintain an army of 650,000 men. And when we reflect upon the invention of gunpowder, and the enormous force of artillery, it is evident that any one of the first-rate powers of modern Europe could bring into the field a destructive force that would sweep from the face of the earth the thirty legions of Adrian. The very division of Europe into a number of States involves this increase of soldiery. In the old Roman Empire, the great Mediterranean Sea lay peaceful as a lake, and the Roman ships had nothing to dread but the winds and the waves; whereas in modern Europe many quite artificial boundaries have to be guarded by an array of soldiers. " Belgium defends her flats with a hundred thousand men, and the marshes of Holland are secured by sixty thousand Dutch."—*Blackwood's Edinburgh Magazine.*

CHARACTER OF CATO.

Dr. Mommsen, in his *History of Rome,* gives the following depreciatory and unjust character of this " noble Roman":—

" Cato was anything but a great man; but with all that shortsightedness, that perversity, that dry prolixity, and those spurious phrases which have stamped him, for his own and for all time, as the ideal of unreflecting republicanism, and the favourite of all who make it their hobby, he was yet the only man who honourably and courageously defended in the last struggles the great system doomed to destruction. It only elevates the deep and tragic significance of his death, that he was himself a fool; in truth, it is just because Don Quixote is a fool that he is a tragic feature. It is an affecting fact, that on that world stage on which so many great and wise men had moved and acted, the fool was destined to give the epilogue. His greatest title to respect is the involuntary homage which Cæsar rendered to him when he made an exception to the contemptuous clemency with which he was wont to treat his opponents, Pompeians as well as Republicans, in the case of Cato alone."

CÆSAR'S CONQUEST OF GAUL.

Dr. Mommsen, in his *History of Rome*, does not conceal the atrocities committed by Cæsar in this war, nor yet the carnage of the vanquished nation; nor does he dwell with too much emphasis on Cæsar's clemency in pacifying Gaul, or extol too highly his settlement of the province. He knows that a solitude may be called peace, and he is perfectly aware to what account the great Proconsul turned his conquest. But he tries to make us forget these deeds in contemplating the glorious results so far as regards the safety of Rome, and he persists not only in describing Cæsar as conquering Gaul in the interests of humanity, but he thinks him entitled to claim credit for all that ever flowed from the conquest. This, the merest fallacy of hero-worship, is thus exemplified :—

" What the Gothic Theodoric achieved was nearly effected by Ariovistus. Had it so happened, our civilization would have hardly stood in any more intimate relation to the Romano-Greek than to the Indian and Assyrian culture. That there is a bridge connecting the past story of Hellas and Rome with the prouder fabric of modern history; that Western Europe is Romanic and Germanic Europe classic; that the names of Themistocles and Scipio have to us a very different sound from those of Asoka and Salmanassar; that Homer and Sophocles are not merely like the Vedas and Kalidasa, attractive to the literary botanist, but bloom for us in our own garden—all this is the work of Cæsar; and while the creation of his great antagonist in the East has been almost reduced to ruin by the tempests of the Middle Ages, the structure of Cæsar has outlasted these thousands of years, and stands erect for what we may term perpetuity."

MIDDLETON'S LIFE OF CICERO.

Macaulay has observed that the fanaticism of the devout worshipper of genius is proof against all evidence and all argument. The character of his idol is matter of faith; and the province of faith is not to be invaded by reason. He maintains his superstition with a credulity as boundless and a zeal as unscrupulous as can be found in the most ardent partisans of religious or political factions. The most decisive proofs are rejected; the plainest rules of morality are explained away; extensive and important portions of history are completely distorted The enthusiast represents facts with all the effrontery of an advocate, and confounds right and wrong with all the dexterity of a Jesuit; and all this only in order that some man who has been in his grave many ages may have a fairer character than he deserves.

"Middleton's *Life of Cicero* is a striking instance of the influence of this sort of partiality. Never was there a character which it was easier to read than that of Cicero. Never was there a mind keener or more critical than that of Middleton. Had the biographer brought to his examination of his favourite statesman's conduct but a very small part of the acuteness and sense which he displayed when he was engaged in investigating the high pretensions of Epiphanius and Justin Martyr, he could not have failed to produce a most valuable history of a most interesting portion of time; but this most ingenious and learned man, though

> So wary held and wise,
> That, as 'twas said, he scarce received
> For gospel what the church believed,

had a superstition of his own. The great Iconoclast was himself an idolater. The great *Avvocato del Diavolo*, while he disputed, with no small ability, the claims of Cyprian and Athanasius to a place in the calendar, was himself composing a lying legend in honour of St. Tully. He was holding up as a model of every virtue a man whose talents and acquirements, indeed, can never be too highly extolled, and who was by no means destitute of amiable qualities, but whose whole soul was under the dominion of a girlish vanity and a craven fear. Actions for which Cicero himself, the most eloquent and skilful of advocates, could conceive no excuse, actions which in his confidential correspondence he mentioned with remorse and shame, are represented by his biographer as wise, virtuous, heroic. The whole history of the great revolution which overthrew the Roman aristocracy, the whole state of parties, the character of every public man, is elaborately misrepresented, in order to make out something which may look like a defence of one most eloquent and accomplished trimmer.

We are not surprised that the Emperor of the French, in his *Life of Julius Cæsar*, should have made the most of the weakness of Cicero, and should have glossed over his eminent qualities, for, unluckily, Cicero's view of Cæsar contradicts that of his imperial admirer. Every schoolboy can appreciate the vanity of the accomplished philosopher and rhetorician; and we quite admit that on some occasions he seems to have been timid and vacillating, that he tried to keep well with both parties in the State, and that he was a lukewarm adherent, as well as a placable antagonist. But Cicero displayed consummate ability in overwhelming the conspiracy of Catiline; his civil and even his military services in his provincial government were conspicuous; and, by his example and his noble eloquence, he endeavoured to raise the standard of statesmen, and to oppose political tyranny and corruption. These great merits defy detraction; and even the trimming tendencies of Cicero, placed by the Emperor in harsher relief than by Lord Macaulay, may not have been caused by moral cowardice. His pure, scrupulous, and upright character seems to have shrunk from taking a decided course in an age of revolution and disorder; and he shaped his way between hostile parties, and leaders ready to overwhelm the State, not so much to advance his own interests, as from a desire to moderate and to conciliate, and a strong dislike to extreme measures. We cannot forget the remark of Thucydides, that in times such as those of Cicero, the wise and the good are ever denounced as wanting in downrightness and zeal, and seem to oscillate between opposite factions.

THE ALEXANDRIAN LIBRARY.

This celebrated collection of books was formed and maintained by the first Ptolemy, King of Egypt, and his successors. Eusebius states the number of volumes at 100,000; though Josephus sets it at 200,000. Orosius tells us 400,000 volumes, when burnt with the fleet by Julius Cæsar. It is not, however, generally known that the rolls (*volumina*) here spoken of contained far less than a printed volume: for instance, the *Metamorphoses* of Ovid, in fifteen books, would make fifteen volumes; and one Didymus is said by Athenæus to have written 3500 volumes. This consideration will bring the number assigned at least within the bounds of credibility.

After the siege of Alexandria, the library was re-established, and continued to increase for four centuries, when it was dispersed. It was again re-established, until Alexandria was conquered by the Arabs, A.D. 640. The collection was then distributed in the various baths of Alexandria, to be burnt in the stoves; and, after six months, not a vestige of them remained; so says a Syriac chronicle. D'Herbelot tells there were then 4000 baths in Alexandria, which were heated by the burning for six months! Renaudot discredits this as an Eastern tale. At any rate, Amrou, who had, for centuries, been set down as guilty of burning the Alexandrian Library, is now exonerated from that unenviable distinction.

We read, however, of other destruction of prodigious numbers of books. At the taking of Bagdad by Halagon, the Tartars threw the books belonging to the colleges of this city into the river Euphrates, when, we are told, the number was so great, that they formed a bridge, across which went foot-passengers and horsemen!

ROME UNDER THE OLIGARCHY.

It was a dark and disastrous era when the sword of Sulla restored order, and having, after atrocious crimes, put an end to the struggles of the democracy, and covered Italy with blood and ashes, he handed over the dominion of the world to the reorganized but corrupt Senate, invested by him with absolute power. We may judge from Dr. Mommsen's description of the most respectable members of this body what was the nature of its meaner elements:—

" Even the better aristocrats were not much less remiss and short-sighted than the average senators of the time. In presence of an outward foe the more eminent among them, doubtless, proved themselves useful and brave; but no one of them evinced the desire or the skill to solve the problems of politics proper, and to guide the vessel of the State through the stormy seas of intrigue and faction with the hand of a true pilot. Their political wisdom was limited to a sincere belief in the oligarchy as the sole means of salvation, and to a cordial hatred and courageous execration of demagogism, as well as of every individual authority seeking to emancipate itself. Their petty ambition was contented with little. . . . . . They were content when they had gained, not favour and influence, but the consulship and a triumph, and a place of honour in the Senate; and at the very time when, with right ambition, they would have first begun to be truly useful to their country and their party, they retired from the political stage to spend their days in princely luxury. . . . . . . The traditional aptitude and the individual self-denial in which all oligarchic government is based were lost in the decayed and artificially restored Roman aristocracy of this age."

The provinces ruined by a succession of harpies, Italy partly disfranchised and largely unpeopled, and the vast capital, corrupt yet supreme, with its frightful contrasts of power and misery, form a spectacle possibly too darkly painted, but of remarkable and appalling interest. Dr. Mommsen has this frightful reflection on Rome:—

" It is a dreadful picture, this picture of Italy under the oligarchy. There was nothing to bridge over or soften the fatal contrast between the world of beggars and the world of the rich. The more clearly and painfully this contrast was felt on both sides—the giddier the height to which riches rose, the deeper the abyss of poverty yawned—the more frequently, amid that changeful world of speculation and playing at hazard, were individuals tossed from the bottom to the top, and again from the top to the bottom. The wider the chasm by which the two worlds were externally divided, the more completely they coincided in the like annihilation of family life—which is yet the germ and core of all nationality—in the like laziness and luxury, the like unsubstantial economy, the like unmanly dependence, the like corruption differing only in its scale, the like demoralization of criminals, the like longing to begin the war with property. Riches and misery in close league drove the Italians out of Italy, and filled the peninsula partly with swarms of slaves, partly with awful silence. It is a terrible picture, but not one peculiar to Italy; wherever the government of capitalists in a Slave State has fully developed itself, it has desolated God's fair world in the same way. As rivers glisten in different colours, but a common sewer everywhere looks like itself, so the Italy of the Ciceronian epoch resembles substantially the Hellas of Polybius, and still more decidedly the Carthage of Hannibal's time."

CRUELTIES OF HANNO AND THE CARTHAGINIANS.

Mr. Saxe Bannister, in his *Records of British Enterprise beyond Sea,* says in a note:—" The first nomade tribe the voyagers reached was friendly, and furnished Hanno with *interpreters.* At length they discovered a nation *whose language was unknown to the interpreters.* These strangers they attempted to seize, and, upon their resistance, they took three of the women, whom they put to death, and carried their skins to Carthage."—(*Geogr. Græci Minores,* Paris, 1826, p. 115.)

" Hanno obtained interpreters from a people who dwelt on the banks of a large river, called the Lixus, and supposed to be the modern St. Cyprian. Having sailed thence for several days, and touched at different places, planting a colony in one of them, he came to a mountainous country, inhabited by savages, who wore the skins of wild beasts. At a distance of twelve days' sail he came to some Ethiopians, who could not endure the Carthaginians, and who spoke unintelligibly even to the Lixite interpreters. These are the people whose women Mr. Bannister says they killed. Hanno sailed from this inhospitable coast fifteen days, and came to the gulf South Horn. Here was an island containing a lake, and in this another island full of wild men, but the women were much more numerous, with hairy bodies. The voyagers pursued the men, who, flying to the precipices, defended themselves with stones, and could not be taken. Three women, who bit and scratched their leaders, would not follow them. Having killed them, the voyagers brought their skins to Carthage." Here it is not intimated that the creatures who defended themselves spoke any language; while the description of the behaviour of the men, and the bodies of the women, is not repugnant to the supposition that they were *large apes, baboons, or ourang-outangs* common to this part of Africa. At all events, the voyagers do not say that they flayed a people having the faculty of speech. In the *History of Maritime Discovery,* it is stated that these *Gorillæ* were probably some species of *ourang-outang.*" Purchas says they might be the *baboons* or *Pongos* of those parts. Ramusio gathered from a Portuguese pilot some particulars of this *Gorgon Island full of hairy men and women*—judged to be Fernando Po.

Gosselin, also, speaking of this part of Hanno's voyage, says:— "Hanno encountered a troop of *ourang-outangs,* which he took for savages, because these animals walk erect, often having a staff in their hands to support themselves, as well as for attack or defence; and they throw stones when they are pursued. They are the satyrs, and the Argipani, with which Pliny says Atlas was peopled. It would be useless to say more on this subject, as it is avowed *by all the modern commentators of the Periplus.*"

Upon this, says Mr. S. W. Singer (*Notes and Queries,* No. 26), " the relation we have here is evidently only an abridgment or summary, made by some Greek studious of Carthaginian affairs, long subsequent to the time of Hanno; and, judging from a passage in Pliny (l. ii. c. 67), it appears that the ancients were acquainted with other extracts from the original; yet, though its authenticity has been doubted by Strabo and others, there seems little reason to question that it is a correct *outline* of the voyage. That the Carthaginians were oppressors of the people they subjugated may be probable; yet we must not, on such slender grounds as this narration affords, presume that they would wantonly kill and flay *human beings* to possess themselves of their skins."

HANNIBAL'S VINEGAR PASSAGE THROUGH THE ALPS.

The passage of Hannibal across the Alps has been a matter of much dispute. Whitaker, in a work published in 1794, maintains that the passage was made over the Great St. Bernard. Our inquiry is, however, not as to the route, but the means by which this great exploit was accomplished. Having gained the summit of the Alpine range, on the top of the highest eminence he pitched his camp, and continued for two days to recruit the exhausted strength both of men and beasts: to make a way down the rock, through which it was necessary to effect a passage, he felled a number of trees which stood near, raised a vast pile of timber, which he set on fire as soon as a strong wind arose, and, when the stone was violently heated, he *poured vinegar upon it, which made it either crumble in pieces or rend.* Through the rock disjointed by the power of heat, he opened a way with iron instruments, and made the descent so gentle that both the beasts of burden and the elephants could be brought down. Such is the account of Livy, 1st book, 3rd decade.

Sir Thomas Browne is content to class the above with his *Vulgar Errors*, as follows:—"That Hannibal ate or brake through the Alps with vinegar may be too grossly taken, and the author of the Life annexed unto Plutarch affirmeth only he used this artifice upon the tops of some of the highest mountains. For as it is vulgarly understood that he cut a passage for his army through these mighty mountains, it may seem incredible not only in the greatness of the effect, but the quantity of the efficient, and such as behold them may think an ocean of vinegar too little for that effect."

Upon this Dr. (Sir Christopher) Wren notes : " There needed not more than some few hogsheads of vinegar ; for, having hewed down the woods of fir growing there, and with the huge piles thereof calcined the tops of some cliffes which stood in his waye, a small quantity of vinegar poured on the fire-glowing rocks would make them cleave in sunder, as is manifest in calcined flints, which being often burned, and as often quencht in vinegar, will in fine turn into an impalpable powder, as is truly experimented, and is dayly manifest in the lime-kilnes."

Dr. M'Keevor (*Annals of Philosophy*, N. S., vol. v.) discusses this question, and considers the expansive operation of the fire on the water percolating through the fissures of the rocks, may have led to the detachment of large portions by explosions, just as masses are detached from cliffs, by a similar physical cause ; and icebergs, with summer-heat, break away.   Or perhaps the only vinegar employed might be the pyroligneous acid produced by the combustion of the wood.   But Mr. Brayley, the chemist, supposes Hannibal might have used vinegar to dissolve a particular mass of impeding limestone.

An ingenious commentator, less credulous than either of the foregoing, observes :—"The vinegar of the Ancients must have been, beyond all comparison, greatly more potent than any of modern times, for if all that is recorded of it be true, it could not only dissolve pearls, but melt mountains.   I must confess, however, to having been always exceedingly and incurably sceptical as to the story of Hannibal having made a way for his army across and through the Alps by such a *coup-de-main* of scientific skill as well as generalship, as enabled him to mollify the solid rock.   He and each of his soldiers must have been provided with more than a cruet-ful of vinegar.   An ingenious friend of mine, who has made such matters his study, assures me that even 22,000,000,000 gallons of vinegar, or even aquafortis, would make scarcely the slightest perceptible impression on the Alps, except as so much water would do ; in fact, the story of Hannibal's winning his way over the Alps with vinegar is one of those puzzling problems in history which will never be solved satisfactorily."

CORRUPT HISTORY OF THE MIDDLE AGES.

The literature of Europe, shortly before the final dissolution of the Roman Empire, fell entirely into the hands of the clergy, who were long venerated as the sole instructors of mankind.   For several centuries, it was extremely rare to meet with a layman who could read or write ; and, of course, it was still rarer to meet with one able to compose a work.   There was nothing men were unwilling to believe. Nothing came amiss to their greedy and credulous ears.   Histories of omens, prodigies, apparitions, strange portents, monstrous appearances in the heavens, the wildest and most incoherent absurdities, were repeated from mouth to mouth, and copied from book to book, with as much care as if they were the choicest treasures of human wisdom.   Hence the history of Europe became corrupted to an extent for which we can find no parallel in any other period.   There was, properly speaking, no history ;   and, unhappily, men, not satisfied with the absence of truth, supplied its place by the invention of falsehood, especially regarding the origin of different nations.   During many centuries it was believed by every people that they were directly descended from ancestors who had been present at the siege of Troy.   This was a proposition which no one thought of doubting.   The descent of the Kings of France from the Trojans was universally believed before the sixteenth century. Polydore Vergil, who died in the middle of the sixteenth century, attacked this opinion in regard to England, and thereby made his history unpopular : he discarded Brute as an unreal personage.   Matthew of Westminster describes the descent of the Britons from Priam and Æneas ; and at the beginning of the fourteenth century, their Trojan.

origin was stated as a notorious fact. In a letter written to Pope Boniface, by Edward I., and signed by the English nobility, it was admitted that the French were descended from Francus, whom everybody knew to be the son of Hector; and it was also known that the Britons came from Brutus, whose father was no other than Æneas himself, though some historians affirmed that he was the great-grandson.

The great historians of the Middle Ages usually begin their history at a very remote period; and the events relating to their subject are often traced back, in an unbroken series, from the moment when Noah left the ark, or even when Adam passed the gates of Paradise. William of Malmesbury traces the genealogies of the Saxon kings back to Adam; the Spanish chroniclers present an uninterrupted succession of Spanish kings from Tubal, a grandson of Noah. And in the *Notes to a Chronicle of London* from 1089 to 1483, edition 4to, 1827, there is a pedigree, in which the history of the Bishops of London is traced back, not only to the migration of Brutus from Troy, but also to Noah and Adam.

The Middle Age historians likewise say that the capital of France is called after Paris, the son of Priam, because he fled there when Troy was overthrown. Monteil, in his curious book, *Histoire des divers Etats*, mentions the old belief that the Parisians are from the blood of the kings of the ancient Trojans, by Paris, son of Priam; even in the seventeenth century this idea was not extinct; and Coryat, who travelled in France in 1608, gives another version of it: he says, "As for her name of Paris, she hath it (as some write) from Paris, the eighteenth King of Gallia Celtica, whom some write to have been lineally descended from Japhet, one of the three sons of Noah, and to have founded this city."

They also mention that Tours owed its name to being the burial-place of Turonus, one of the Trojans, while the City of Troyes was actually built by the Trojans, as its etymology clearly proves. It was well ascertained that Nuremberg was called after the Emperor Nero, and Monconys, who was at Nuremberg in 1663, found this opinion still held there, and he seems himself half inclined to believe it. Jerusalem, it was held, was called after King Jebus, a man of vast celebrity in the Middle Ages, but whose existence later historians have not been able to verify. The river Humber received its name because in ancient times a king of the Huns had been drowned in it. The Gauls derived their origin, according to some, from Galathia, a female descendant of Japhet; according to others, from Gomer, the son of Japhet; and these two opinions long divided the learned world. Prussia was called after Prussus, a brother of Augustus. This was remarkably modern, but Silesia had its name from the prophet Elisha, from whom, indeed, the Silesians descended; while as to the city of Zurich, its exact date was a matter of dispute, but it was unquestionably built in the time of Abraham, as Coryat when at Zurich, in 1608, was told by the learned Hospinian. It was likewise from Abraham and Sarah that the Gipsies immediately sprung—their "seuls enfans légitimes." The blood of the Saracens was less pure, since they were only descended from Sarah, in what way is not mentioned. At all events, the Scotch certainly came from Egypt, for they were originally the issue of Scota, who was a daughter of Pharaoh, and who bequeathed to them her name; stated in a letter to the Pope, early in the fourteenth century, as a well-known historical fact.

On sundry similar matters the Middle Ages possessed information equally valuable. It was well known that the city of Naples was founded on eggs; and it was also known that the Order of St. Michael was instituted in person by the archangel, who was himself the first knight, and to whom, in fact, chivalry owes its origin. (See Mills's *Chivalry*). In regard to Tartary, that people, of course, proceeded from Tartarus, ascribed to the piety of St. Louis. Since the thirteenth century the subject has attracted the attention of English divines; and the celebrated theologian Whiston, mentions: " My last famous discovery, or rather my revival of Dr. Giles Fletcher's famous discovery, that the Tartars are no other than the ten tribes of Israel which have been so long sought for in vain." Then the Turks were identical with the Tartars, and it was notorious that since the cross had fallen into Turkish hands all Christian children had ten teeth less than formerly; an universal calamity, which there seemed to be no means of repairing.[*]

ABELARD AND ELOISA.

Abelard died long before Eloisa; and the hour never arrived for *him* of which with such tenderness she says,—

> It will be *then* no crime to gaze on me.

But another anticipation *has* been fulfilled in a degree that he could hardly have contemplated, the anticipation, namely,—

> That ages hence, when all her woes were o'er,
> And that rebellious heart should beat no more,

wandering feet should be attracted from afar,

> To Paraclete's white walls and silver springs.

as the common resting-place and everlasting marriage-bed of Abelard and Eloisa. They were buried in the same grave; Abelard dying first by a few weeks more than twenty-one years; his tomb was opened to admit the coffin of Eloisa; and the tradition at Quincy, the parish near Nogent-sur-Seine, in which the monastery of the Paraclete is situated, was —that at the moment of interment Abelard *opened his arms* to receive the impassioned creature that once had loved *him* so frantically, and whom *he* loved with a romance so memorable. In the last century, six hundred years after their departure from earth, there was placed over their common remains a Latin inscription, singularly solemn in its brief simplicity, considering that it came from Paris, and from Academic wits. The epitaph is thus Englished:—" Here, under the same marble slab, lie the founder of this Monastery, Peter Abelard, and its earliest Abbess, Heloisa, once united in studies, in love, and in their unhappy nuptial engagements, and in penitential sorrow; but now, our hope is reunited for ever in bliss."

---

* Selected and abridged from Buckle's *History of Civilisation in England*, vol. i. pp. 282—288.

Myths and Popular Fictions.

"INCREDIBILIA" OF THE ANCIENTS.

SIR THOMAS BROWNE shows from Palæphatus's book "concerning Incredible Tales"—

"That the fable of Orpheus by his music making woods and trees to follow him, is founded upon a crew of mad women retired unto a mountain being pacified by his music, and caused to descend with boughs in their hands: whence the magic of Orpheus's harp, and its power to attract the senseless trees about it.

"That Medea, the famous sorceress, could renew youth, and make old men young again; being nothing else but that from the knowledge of simples she had a receipt to make white hair black, and reduce old heads into the tincture of youth again.

"The fable of Geryon and Cerberus with three heads was this: Geryon was of the city of Tricarinia (Trinacria), that is, of three heads; and Cerberus, of the same place, was one of his dogs, which, running into a cave in pursuit of his master's oxen, Hercules perforce drew him out of that place: from whence the conceits of those days affirmed no less than that Hercules descended into hell, and brought up Cerberus into the habitation of the living.

"Upon the like ground was raised the figment of Briareus, who dwelling in a city called Hekatoncheira, the fancies of those times assigned him a hundred hands.

"That Niobe weeping over her children was turned into a stone, was nothing else but that during her life she erected over their sepulchres a marble tomb of her own.

"When Actæon had undone himself with dogs and the prodigal attendants of hunting, they made a solemn story of how he was devoured by his hounds. And upon the like grounds was raised the anthropophagie of Diomedes his horses.

"Diodorus plainly delivereth that the famous fable of Charon had this nativity: who, being no other but the common ferryman of Egypt that wafted over the dead bodies from Memphis, was made by the Greeks to be the ferryman of hell, and solemn stories raised after of him.

"The Centaurs were a body of young men from Thessaly, who first trained and mounted horses for repelling a herd of wild bulls belonging to Ixion, king of the Lapithæ. They pursued these wild bulls on horseback, and pierced them with their spears, thus acquiring both the name of prickers, and the imputed attribute of joint body with the horse.

"The Dragon whom Cadmus killed at Thebes was in reality Draco, king of Thebes; and the dragon's teeth which he is said to have sown, and from whence sprung a crop of armed men, were in point of fact elephant's teeth which Cadmus as a rich Phœnician had brought over with him. The sons of Draco sold these elephants' teeth, and employed the proceeds to levy troops against Cadmus.

" Dædalus, instead of flying across the sea on wings, had escaped from Crete in a sailing-boat, under a violent storm. Kottus, Briareus, and Gyges, were not persons with one hundred hands, but inhabitants of the village of Hekatoncheira in Upper Macedonia, who warred with the inhabitants of Mount Olympus against the Titans. Scylla, whom Odysseus so narrowly escaped, was a fast-sailing piratical vessel; as was also Pegasus, the alleged winged horse of Bellerophon.

" Again, Gal and Westermann, like Palæphatus, interpret Scylla as a beautiful woman surrounded with abominable parasites. She ensnared and ruined the companions of Odysseus, though he himself was prudent enough to escape her. Atlas was a great astronomer. Pasiphae fell in love with a youth named Taurus. The monster called the Chimæra was in reality a ferocious queen, who had two brothers named Leo and Draco. The ram which carried Phryxus and Helle across the Ægean was a boatman named Krius.

" Plutarch, however, in one of his treatises, accepts minotaurs, sphinxes, centaurs, &c., as realities; and Dr. Delany, in his *Life of David*, produces some ingenious arguments to prove that Orpheus was in reality, the same person with David."

THE WANDERING JEW.

Of the many myths which diverge from every little incident of Our Saviour's career, the legend of Ahasuerus, the Wandering Jew, is certainly the most striking and widely distributed. According to the old ballad, in Percy's collection:

> He hath past through many a foreign place :
> Arabia, Egypt, Africa,
> Greece, Syria, and great Thrace,
> And throughout all Hungaria.

All the nations of the Seven Champions have it in some shape or other, and it is amusing to note the way in which the story adapts itself to the exigencies of time and place. In Germany, where he appeared A.D. 1547, he was a kind of Polyglot errant, battling professors and divines with the accumulated learning of fifteen centuries. In Paris, he heralded the advent of Cagliostro and Mesmer, cured diseases, and astounded the *salons* by his prodigious stories. He remembered seeing Nero standing on a hill to enjoy the flames of his capital; and was a particular crony of Mahomet's father at Ormus. It was here, too, he anticipated the coming scepticism, by declaring, from personal experience, that all history was a tissue of lies. In Italy the myth has become interwoven with the national art lore. When he came to Venice, he brought with him a fine cabinet of choice pictures, including his own portrait by Titian, taken some two centuries before. In England John Bull has endowed him with the commercial spirit of his stationary brethren, and, to complete his certificate of naturalization, made him always thirsty! But the Jew of Quarter Sessions' Reports, who is always getting into scrapes, is not the Jew of the rural popular legends; in which he is invariably represented as a purely benevolent being, whose crime has been long since expiated by his cruel punishment, and therefore entitled to the help of every good Christian. When on the weary way to Golgotha, Christ fainting, and overcome under the burden of the cross, asked him, as he was standing at his door, for a cup of water to cool his parched throat, he spurned the supplication, and bade him on the faster. "I go," said the Saviour, "but thou shalt thirst, and tarry till I come." And ever since then, by day and night, through the long centuries, he has been doomed to wander about the earth, ever craving for water, and ever expecting the day of judgment which shall end his toils.

Sometimes, during the cold winter nights, the lonely cottager will be awoke by a plaintive demand for "Water, good Christian! water for the love of God!" And if he looks out into the moonlight, he will see a venerable old man in antique raiment, with grey flowing beard and a tall staff, who beseeches his charity with the most earnest gesture. Woe to the churl who refuses him water or shelter. If, on the contrary, you treat him well, and refrain from indelicate inquiries respecting his age— on which point he is very touchy—his visit is sure to bring good luck. Perhaps years afterwards, when you are on your death-bed, he may happen to be passing; and if he *should*, you are safe; for three knocks with his staff will make you hale, and he never forgets any kindnesses. Many stories are current of his wonderful cures.[*]

In the *Athenæum*, No. 2036, it is ingeniously remarked: "When it is remembered that these Wandering Jews were received at great men's tables, and were kept as guests as long as they had any wild story to tell (they all grew old till they were a hundred, and then began again, at the age at which Christ found them) it is simply astonishing that we do not hear more of these clever and erratic parasites." The writer then relates the last on the mysterious roll.

"From the year 1818 (perhaps earlier) to about 1830, a handsomely-featured Jew, in semi-eastern costume, fair-haired, bare-headed, his eyes intently fixed on a little ancient book he held in both hands, might be seen gliding through the streets of London, but was never seen to issue from or to enter a house, or to pause upon his way. He was popularly known as "the Wandering Jew," but there was something so dignified and anxious in his look, that he was never known to suffer the slightest molestation. Young and old looked silently on him as he passed, and shook their heads pitifully when he had gone by. He disappeared, was seen again in London some ten years later, still young, fair-haired, bare-headed, his eyes bent on his book, his feet going steadily forward as he

---

[*] This able *précis* is from *Notes and Queries*, No. 322.

went straight on; and men again whispered as he glided through our streets for the last time, 'The Wandering Jew!' There were many who believed that he was the very man to whom had been uttered the awful words, 'Tarry thou till I come!'"

Roger of Wendover, a monk of St. Albans, and Matthew Paris, a Benedictine monk of Clugny and likewise of St. Albans, give the oldest traditions of the Wandering Jew. According to Menzel (*History of German Poetry*) the whole tradition is but an allegory, symbolizing heathenism. M. Lacroix suggests that it represents the Hebrew race dispersed and wandering throughout the earth, but not destroyed. In Germany, the tradition of the Wandering Jew became connected with John Bultadæus, a real person, said to have been at Antwerp in the 13th century, again in the 15th, and a third time in the 16th, with every appearance of age and decrepitude. His last recorded apparition was at Brussels, in April, 1774. Southey, in his *Curse of Kehama*, and Croly, in his *Salathiel*, trace the course of the Wandering Jew, but in violation of the whole legend; and Eugene Sue adopted the name as the title of one of his most popular and most immoral novels (*Le Juif Errant*), though the Jew scarcely figures at all in the work. (Wheeler's *Noted Names of Fiction.*)

There is a well-known English ballad on the Wandering Jew, perhaps of the time of Elizabeth. It relates to the Jew's appearance in Germany in the sixteenth century. The first stanza is,—

Whereas in fair Jerusalem,
Our Saviour Christ did live,
And for the sins of all the world
His own dear life did give:
The wicked Jews, with scoff and scorn,
Did dailye him molest,
That never till he left his life
Our Saviour could not rest.

THE FOUNDING OF CARTHAGE.

Most ancient writers agree in following an old tradition, that Carthage was founded about a hundred years before Rome, by Dido or Elissa, upon her arrival in Africa, after her flight from Tyre; when the wily Queen purchased as much land of the natives of the former place as she could cover, or rather enclose, with an ox's hide; and thereupon cut the hide into thongs, and thus included a much larger space than the sellers expected. Now, the place which afterwards became the citadel of Carthage was called Betzura, or Bosra—*i.e.*, the castle; a name which the Greeks altered into Byrsa, a hide, from the shape of the peninsula resembling an ox-hide. This tale, which is either related or alluded to by Appian and Dionysius the geographer amongst the Greeks, and by Justin, Virgil, Silius Italicus, and others of the Latins, has been applied by later writers. Thus, Sigebert, monk of Gemblours, in 1100, relates that Hengist, the first Saxon king of Kent, purchased of the British king, and enclosed, a site called *Castellum Corrigiæ*, or the *Castle of the Thong;* but there being several more edifices named *Thong,* or *Tong,* in England, as in Kent, Lincolnshire, Shropshire, and Yorkshire (Doncaster being written in Saxon *Thongceaster*), the story has been applied to most, if not all of them. It is true that Sigebert knew nothing of the Greek authors, but he was well acquainted with Justin and Virgil, and Geoffrey of Monmouth, 1159, who has the same story. Again, Saxo Grammaticus, in 1170, applied the tale to Ivarus, who, by the thong artifice in respect of Hella, got a footing in Britain. The like story has travelled to the East Indies. "There is a tradition," says Hamilton, "that the Portuguese circumvented the King of Guzerat, as Dido did the Africans, when they gave her leave to build Carthage, by describing no more ground than could be circumscribed in an ox's hide, which having obtained, they cut a fine thong of a great length," &c. Now, the Indians knew nothing of the Greek or Latin authors, nor probably did the Portuguese, who first made the settlement at Din; though it may have been carried there as a tradition by missionaries from Europe. (*Gentleman's Magazine,* 1771.)

This legend seems to have gone round the world. Hassun Subah, the chief of the Assassins, is said to have acquired in the same manner the hill-fort of Allahamowt. The Persians maintain that the British got Calcutta in the same way; and it is somewhere stated, that this was the mode by which one of our colonies in America obtained their land of the Indians. An English tradition avers that it was by a similar trick Hengist and Horsa got a settlement in the Isle of Thanet.

To the legend of Dido's expiatory sacrifice upon a vast funeral pile Virgil has given a new colour by interweaving the adventures of Æneas, and thus connecting the foundation legends of Carthage and Rome, careless of his deviation from the received mythical chronology. Dido was worshipped as a goddess at Carthage until the destruction of the city; she is, with some probability, imagined to be identical with Astarte, the divine patroness under whose auspices the colony was originally established; the tale of the funeral pile and self-burning appearing in the religious ceremonies of other Cilician and Syrian towns.

Napoleon I. used to compare our countrymen to the Carthaginians; both being distinguished by their success in commerce, their command of the sea, and their numerous colonies; and he predicted that a similar fate, originating in similar causes, would overtake his great rival. But the comparison is imperfect; the reputation of the Carthaginians was not equal to that of their country, and the reproach of Punic Faith still adhered to their crafty and subtle character.

———◆———

SAINT GEORGE AND THE DRAGON.

It has been strangely asserted that Alban Butler identifies St. George the Martyr with George, the infamous Arian; whereas he settles the question as follows:—"Certain ancient heretics forged false acts of St.

George, which the learned Pope Gelasius condemned in 494. Calvin and the centuriators call him an imaginary saint; but their slander is confuted by most authentic titles and monuments. Jurien, Reynolds, and Ischard, blush not to confound him with George, the Arian usurper of the see of Alexandria, the infamous persecutor of St. Athanasius and the Catholics, whom he endeavoured to dragoon into Arianism by butchering great numbers, banishing their bishops, plundering the homes of orphans and widows, and outraging the nuns with the utmost barbarity, till the Gentiles, exasperated by his cruelties and scandalous behaviour, massacred him, under Julian. The stories of the combat of St. George with the magician Athanasius, and the like trumpery, came from the mint of the Arians; and we find them rejected by Pope Gelasius and the other Catholics, who were too well acquainted with the Arian wolf, whose acts they condemned, to confound him with the illustrious martyr of Christ; though the forgeries of the heretics have been so blended with the truth in the history of this holy martyr, that, as we have it, there is no means of separating the sterling from the counterfeit."

Again, as to the dragon of St. George, the learned Pettingall shows that the symbol is merely a relic of the ancient amulets, invented by Oriental nations to express the virtues of Mithra, the sun, and the confidence which they reposed in that great luminary. From the Pagans he says, "The use of these charms passed to the Basilidians, and in their Abraxas, the traces of the ancient Mithras and the more modern St. George, are equally visible. In the dark ages, the Christians borrowed their superstitions from the heretics, but they disguised the origin of them, and transformed into the saint the sun of the Persians and the archangel of the Gnostics."

Still, this is one of the class of minor historic doubts which seems least likely to be ever satisfactorily disposed of. Between the disparaging estimate of Gibbon and the more flattering one of Alban Butler it is next to impossible to strike the balance. The fairest course with the reader doubtless is to state what few facts rest upon actual testimony. Whether we elect to pin our belief upon the fraudulent contractor of Cappadocia, with his loose semi-Arian tendencies, or upon the orthodox champion of the Romish martyrology, the oddest thing about both these rival hypotheses is that neither of them can be said to affect appreciably the real point of interest—why, that is, St. George ever came to be the special patron of Englishmen at all. The view of Butler and the Bollandists, in other respects the weakest of the two, gives, at all events, the go-by to the notion that the special *cultus* of the saint arose out of his favour to the national arms during the Crusades. In vain is it urged that St. George first fought for the host of Godfrey at Antioch, or presaged to Cœur de Lion the victory of Acre, when it is known that even before the Conquest, his name had its place in Saxon martyrologies. The true key to this difficulty is to be sought, we are persuaded, through a closer study of the relations between the early British Church and the Greek communions in the East—a subject strangely neglected by our ecclesiastical historians. The name of St. George forms a text for some curious particulars upon dragon worship, and the legendary lore connected with those singular monsters in the mythology of the middle ages. In many instances, there is no doubt that the ravages of floods have been " emblematized as the malevolent deeds of dragons* ":—

" In the seventh century, St. Romanus is said to have delivered the city of Rouen from one of those monsters. The feat was accomplished in this very simple manner. On Ascension day, Romanus, taking a condemned criminal out of prison, ordered him to go and fetch the dragon. The criminal obeyed, and the dragon following him into the city, walked into a blazing fire that had previously been prepared, and was burned to death. To commemorate the event, King Dagobert gave the clergy of Rouen the annual privilege of pardoning a condemned criminal on Ascension day ; a right exercised with many ceremonies, till the period of the first Revolution. This dragon, named Gargouille (a water-spout), lived in the river Seine ; and as Romanus is said to have constructed embankments to defend Rouen from the overflowing of that river, the story seems to explain itself. The legends of Tarasque, the dragon of the Rhone, destroyed by St. Martha, and the dragon of the Garonne, killed by St. Martial at Bordeaux, admit of a similar explanation. The winding rivers resembling the convolutions of a serpent, are frequently found to take the name of that animal in common language, as well as in poetical metaphor. The river Draco, in Bithynia, is so called from its numerous windings, and in Italy and Germany there are rivers deriving their names from the same cause. In Switzerland the word *drach* has been frequently given to impetuous mountain torrents, which, suddenly breaking out, descend like avalanches on the lower country. Thus we can easily account for such local names as *Drachenlok*, the dragon's hole ; *Drachenreid*, the dragon's march ; and the legends of Struth, of Winkelreid, and other Swiss dragon-slayers."—*Chambers's Book of Days.*

SAINT DUNSTAN AND HIS MIRACLES.

Dunstan, "the arch miracle-monger," as Southey styles him, was in every way a remarkable man. At Mayfield, in Sussex, is a well called St. Dunstan's, which is thought to be that referred to in the legends of him, which say that wherever he struck his staff fountains of limpid water burst forth. Dunstan built the original church of wood at Mayfield, and its orientation not being accurate, was made so by an application of his shoulder to one of the angles, which caused it to slue round to its proper point, to the amazement of all present !

In his retreat at Glastonbury, he employed himself in such manual arts as were useful to the service of the Church, as a worker in metals, and in the formation of crosses, censers, &c. Here, to escape from unholy thoughts, he almost destroyed himself with fasting and labouring at his forge. Osborn relates a story of this period of his life, which has become one of the best known of monkish legends. The devil used to annoy the young saint by paying him untoward visits, in the form of a bear, or serpent, or other noxious animal; but one night, as he was hammering at his forge, Satan came in a human form, as a woman, and looking in at his window, began to tempt him with improper conversation. Dunstan bore it till he had heated his pincers sufficiently, and then, with the red-hot instrument, seized his visitor by the nose. So, at least, he is reported to have told his neighbours in the morning, when they inquired what those horrible cries were which had startled them from their sleep during the previous night.

St. Dunstan was chosen patron saint of the Goldsmiths' Company, whose noble Hall, in Foster-lane, Cheapside, contains several interesting memorials of the holy man. Their second Hall was hung with Flemish tapestry, representing the history of the saint. In the court-room of the present Hall hangs a large painting of St. Dunstan in rich robes, and crozier in hand; while in the background the saint is taking the devil by the nose with a pair of tongs, the heavenly host appearing above. Their list of splendid jewellery is remarkable, as tending to show the antiquity, as well as traditionary propriety, of the goldsmiths adopting St. Dunstan as their patron, since it specifies among the articles, " a gold ring with a sapphire, of the workmanship of St. Dunstan," thus described in a Wardrobe Account of Edward I.

Great honours have been paid by the Company to this saint. His image, of silver gilt, set with gems, adorned the screen of the second Hall; and his memory was drunk, at particular times, from a great cup, equally rich, called " St. Dunstan's Cup," which was surmounted by another image of the saint. At the Reformation, by entries in the Company's books, "the Image of Seynt Dunstan," and "the grete Standyng Cup," were "broken and turned into other plate." The Company had also their "St. Dunstan's Light" in St. John Zachary Church; and their chapel of St. Dunstan, with a second image of him, in St. Paul's Cathedral. The style given him in their books is—" Seynt Dunstan, our blessed patron, protector, and founder."[*]

St. Dunstan is also said to have built the palace at Mayfield, when he was Archbishop of Canterbury, for the residence of the See; and this was made the scene of his reputed contest with the devil, though others place it at Glastonbury. As though that was not sufficiently marvellous, tradition has added a clincher. After holding the evil spirit with his tongs for some time, the saint let him go, when he leaped at one bound to Tunbridge Wells, where plunging his nose into the spring, he imparted to the water its chalybeate qualities; another version attributes the chalybeate to St. Dunstan himself, who, finding that the enemy's nose had imparted an unusual heat to his tongs, cooled them in the water at this place. Mayfield Palace is in part an ivied ruin; here are preserved St. Dunstan's forge, and anvil, and tongs.

Walter Gale, the Sussex schoolmaster, records, that in 1749, " there

---

* *Curiosities of London*, new edit., 1868, p. 403.

was at Mayfield a pair of tongs, which, the inhabitants affirmed, *and many believed*, to be that with which St. Dunstan " pinched the devil by the nose."

SAINT LUKE NOT A PAINTER.

Little is recorded of St. Luke in Scripture, but from a passage in the Epistle to the Colossians, we infer that he had been bred a physician. He is also stated, by ecclesiastical writers, to have practised as a painter, and some ancient pictures of the Virgin, still extant, are ascribed to his pencil. In consequence of this belief, which, however, rests on very uncertain foundations, St. Luke has been regarded as the patron of painters and the fine arts. The mulatto or black Madonnas, which go by St. Luke's name, were not painted by him, but by Signor Luco, who flourished in the fifteenth century ; whose works were, by a " pious fraud " of the monks, attributed to the saint, as more likely to command the reverence of the ignorant, who were also taught to regard the pictures as " miraculous." (See the *Private Diary of the Duke of Buckingham.*)

In May, 1868, Sir George Bowyer sent to the Archæological Institute a photograph of the picture of our Blessed Lady of Philermos, attributed to St. Luke, and removed from Malta to St. Petersburg by the Emperor of Russia on its surrender to the French Republic. This was one of the Black Madonnas which it was the fashion for a certain period to paint. Its attribution, with that of other pictures, to St. Luke the Evangelist, was owing to there having been a famous artist in the eleventh century named Luke. The example shown was probably of the twelfth or thirteenth century ; a point which caused some discussion, in the course of which Mr. Waller read an extract from Molanus, to show that St. Luke was not considered a painter. Raphael's famous picture of Luke painting the portrait of the Virgin, has, doubtless, fostered the above popular error. He is commonly represented in a seated position, writing or painting, whilst behind him appears the head of an ox, frequently winged. The Academy of St. Luke, at Rome, for painters and sculptors, would also foster the error. St. Luke would be more appropriately the patron of hospitals, from his having been bred a physician.

FRIAR BACON'S BRAZEN HEAD.

This widely-known legend has little to do with the veritable history of Roger or Friar Bacon, the greatest of English philosophers before the time of his celebrated namesake ; though he, Roger Bacon, is more popularly known by this fictitious name than by his real merit. In a rare tract, entitled *The Famous Historie of Friar Bacon*, 4to, London, 1652, it is pretended he discovered, "after great study,' that if he could succeed in making a head of brass, which should speak, and hear it when it spoke, he might be able to surround all England with a wall of brass. By the assistance of Friar Bungay, and a devil likewise called into the consultation, Bacon accomplished his object, but with this drawback—the head, when finished, was warranted to speak in the course of one month ; but it was quite uncertain when ; and if they heard it not before it had done speaking, all their labour would be lost. After watching for three weeks, fatigue got the mastery over them, and Bacon set his man Miles to watch, with strict injunctions to awake them if the head should speak. The fellow heard the head at the end of one half-hour say, "Time is ;" at the end of another, "Time was;" and at the end of another half-hour, "Time's past ;" when down it fell! with a tremendous crash, but the blockhead of a servant thought that his master would be angry if he disturbed him for such trifles ! "And hereof came it," says the excellent Robert Recorde, "that fryer Bacon was accompted so greate a necromancier, whiche never used that arte (by any conjecture that I can finde), but was in geometrie and other mathematicall sciences so experte that he coulde doe by them suche thynges as were wonderful in the sight of most people."

Bacon died at Oxford in 1292, where existed, nearly until our own times, a traditional memorial of "the wonderful doctor," as he was styled by some of his contemporaries. On Grandpont, or the Old Folly Bridge, at the southern entrance into Oxford, stood a tower called "Friar Bacon's Study," from a belief that the philosopher was accustomed to ascend this building in the night, and "study the stars." It was entirely demolished in 1778. Of the bridge, Wood says: "No record can resolve its precise beginning."

"The mind of Roger Bacon," says Hallam, "was strangely compounded of almost prophetic gleams of the future course of science, and the best principles of the inductive philosophy, with more than a sacred credulity in the superstitions of his own time. Some have deemed him overrated by the nationality of the English. But if we have sometimes given him credit for the discoveries to which he had only borne testimony, there can be no doubt of the originality of his genius." He bears a singular resemblance to Francis Bacon, not only in the character of his philosophy, but in several coincidences of expression ; and the latter has even been charged with having borrowed much from Roger Bacon without having acknowledged his obligations.

COLUMBUS AND THE EGG.

Among the popular errors of the day is the story of Columbus, who, finding it impossible to make an egg stand on its end, crushed in the basis, and thus made it stand. The goldfish of Charles II. was accepted as imponderable by many wise heads without experiment (if, indeed, it ever had a being), and the story of Columbus and the egg is supposed to be based on the physical axiom that it is *impossible* to make an egg stand on its end. Yet, five minutes' careful balancing will convince any dexterous experimenter that an egg may be made to stand, and remain balanced on its end, without breaking the shell. All that is required is steadiness of hand, and perhaps a little patience. And M. Delepierre mentions that " the fable of the egg that he is said to have broken, in order to make it stand upright, has been disproved by M. de Humboldt, in his *Examen Critique de l'Histoire de la Géographie.*" Hogarth, it will be recollected, has made " Columbus and the Egg" the subject of one of his admirable illustrative prints.

Now, if Vasari is to be credited, the Florentine architect, Brunelleschi, many years before Columbus was born, performed the egg feat relative to his intended cupola for the Church of Santa Maria del Fiore, in Florence. The other architects desired that Filippo should explain his purpose minutely, and show his model, as they had done theirs. This he would not do, but proposed to all the masters, foreigners and compatriots, that he who could make an egg stand upright on a piece of smooth marble should be appointed to build the cupola, since in doing that his genius should be made manifest. They took an egg accordingly, and all those masters did their best to make it stand upright, but none discovered the method of doing so. Wherefore, Filippo being told that he might make it stand himself, took it daintily into his hand, gave the end of it a blow on the plane of the marble, and made it stand upright. Beholding this, the artists loudly protested, exclaiming that they could all have done the same ; but Filippo replied, laughing, that they might also know how to construct the cupola if they had seen the model and the design. This occurred about A.D. 1420.

WILLIAM TELL: A FABLE.

Delepierre shows there to be four different views existing of this tradition of William Tell. 1. The authenticity of the legend, in all its details, as it is believed in the canton of Uri. 2. The existence of Tell, his refusal to do homage to the hat, his voyage on the lake, and the tragical end of Gessler, but rejects the story of the apple. 3. William Tell is believed to have existed, and to have made himself remarkable by some daring exploit ; but this exploit was not connected with the plans of the conspirators, and consequently exercised no influence over the formation of the Swiss Confederation. 4. The tradition of William Tell, a mere fable, an after-thought, unworthy of being inserted in any history of Switzerland. In 1760 Uriel Frendenberger created a terrible disturbance in Berne by publishing a small volume in Latin, entitled *William Tell; a Danish Fable.* The canton of Uri condemned the author to be burned with his book. In 1727 Isaac Christ. Iselin, in his large historical dictionary, doubted the story, because Olaus Magnus has related the same adventure of a certain Toko, in the reign of Harold, King of Denmark. The two stories are so similar that one is supposed to have been copied from the other.

In 1840 M. Hausser, in answer to a proposition from the University of Heidelberg, obtained a prize for his essay, showing—1. There is nothing to justify the historical importance that is commonly attached to William Tell. He has no right to the title of Deliverer of Switzerland, seeing that he took no active part in the freedom of Waldstätter. 2. The existence of a Swiss named William Tell, is without doubt, but not in any way connected with the history of the Confederation. 3. The tradition, as preserved in ballads and chronicles, is a pure invention : the apple shot from the head of the child is of Scandinavian origin. (See Hiseley's *Recherches Critiques*, 1843.) Ideler (Berlin, 1836) says :— " There exists no record of incontestable authenticity referring to the romantic incident of Tell's life. The chapel near Flüelen, on the borders of the lake, was only constructed in 1388; the chapel at Burglen, on the spot where Tell's house formerly stood, dates back to the same time ; and there is no written document to prove that they were built to commemorate any share taken by Tell in the emancipation of Switzerland. The stone fountain at Altdorf, which bore the name of Tell, and above which was seen the statue of Tell, and of his son with an apple placed upon his head, was only constructed in 1786, when the tradition had already been invalidated by critical researches. The fountain was taken down in 1861. Tell's lime-tree in the market-place at Altdorf, and his crossbow, preserved in the arsenal at Zurich, are not more valid proof than the pieces of the true cross which are exhibited in a thousand places. In conclusion, M. Delepierre relates the corresponding apple legends. Altogether this is one of the most interesting of his *Historical Difficulties.*

THE TULIPOMANIA.

With the marvels of this madness, as told in books of wonders, the world is tolerably familiar. The gardens of Haarlem are still famous for their luxuriant flowers; but the trade in tulips is not carried on as in the days of the Tulipomania, and 100 florins is now a very large sum for a root. Beckmann states, on Dutch authorities, that 400 *perits* in weight (something less than a grain), of the bulb of a tulip named *Admiral Leifken*, cost 4400 florins ; and 200 of another, named *Semper Augustus*, 2000 florins. Of this last, he tells us, it once happened there were only two roots to be had, the one at Amsterdam, the other at Haarlem ; and that, for one of these, were offered 4600 florins, a new carriage, two grey horses, and a complete set of harness ; and that another person offered 12 acres of land. It is almost impossible to give credence to such madness. *The real truth of the story is that these tulip roots were never bought or sold*, but they became the medium of a systematized species of gambling. The bulbs, and their division into *perits*, became like the different stocks in our public funds, and were bought and sold at different prices from day to day, the parties settling their amount at fixed periods, the innocent tulips all the while never once appearing in the transaction. " Before the tulip mania was over," says Beckmann, " more roots were sold and purchased, bespoke and promised to be delivered, than in all probability were to be found in the gardens of Holland ; and when *Semper Augustus* was not to be had anywhere, which happened twice, no species perhaps was oftener purchased and sold." This kind of sheer gambling reached at length to such a height that the Government found it necessary to interfere and put a stop to it. Still, the enormous prices that were actually given for real tulip-bulbs of particular kinds, formed but a small fraction of the extent to which the mercantile transactions in this gaudy flower were carried.

THE NINE WORTHIES.

These are famous personages, often alluded to, and classed together rather in an arbitrary manner, like the Seven Wonders of the World, &c.

The number have been thus counted up as the *Nine Worthies of the World* by Richard Burton, in a book published in 1687:—

Three Gentiles	1. Hector, son of Priam.
	2. Alexander the Great.
	3. Julius Cæsar.
Three Jews	4. Joshua, conqueror of Canaan.
	5. David, king of Israel.
	6. Judas Maccabæus.
Three Christians	7. Arthur, king of Britain.
	8. Charles the Great, or Charlemagne.
	9. Godfrey of Bullen [Bouillon].

London had also Nine Worthies of her own, according to a pamphlet by Richard Johnson, author of the famous *History of the Seven Champions*. These worthies are: 1. Sir William Walworth, fishmonger; 2. Sir Henry Pritchard, vintner; 3. Sir William Sevenoake, grocer; 4. Sir Thomas White, merchant-tailor; 5. Sir John Bonham, mercer; 6. Sir Christopher Croker, vintner; 7. Sir John Hawkwood, merchant-tailor; 8. Sir Hugh Calvert, silk-weaver; 9. Sir Henry Maleverer, grocer. Sir Thomas White seems to have been the only quite peaceable worthy among them, whose fame lives in St. John's College, Oxford, and Merchant Taylors' School, London, which school he founded.

From the fame of these personages, Butler formed his curious title of *Nine-worthiness*, meaning, it is presumed, that his hero (Hudibras) was equal in valour to any or all of the nine.

THE LABYRINTH OF CRETE.

. The Labyrinth of Crete is noticed by most of the ancient authors who have treated of the fabled history of the Minotaur or of Crete. Homer is, however, silent upon it, unless the passage in the *Iliad*, book 2, has reference to it, as some think. The early coins of Gnossus, indeed, represent it; but they cannot date further back than the 6th or 7th century B.C., if so early, and were consequently struck when only the tradition existed of such a labyrinth; and how vague even then was the idea of this labyrinth is shown by the varied representations of it upon these Cretan coins—some representing its passages in circular convolutions, others square, and also different in coins of different times. But Plutarch, in his *Life of Theseus*, gives a more natural explanation of the object of the Labyrinth than the story of the mythical Minotaur, and says it was a prison for the tributary youths of Athens. . . . . . That there was, therefore, something of a labyrinth, which might serve as a foundation for that which was attributed to the great master of art, Dædalus, is thus more than simply probable. " What, then, do we find in Crete to explain it ? Is there a labyrinth of any kind ?" is the natural inquiry. There is ; yet not at Gnossus, but at Gortyna ; and not a building, but a subterranean excavation resembling a quarry, or more properly the galleries of a mine, and penetrating horizontally, in labyrinthine courses, no one knows how far, into one of the roots of Mount Ida lying behind Gortyna, and in which I myself spent nearly two hours in tracing some of its courses, as far as they are now penetrable ; for the Cretans have long since walled or stopped up its inner and unknown extremes, so as not to be lost in its inner intricacies. —Captain Spratt's *Crete.*

THE COLOSSUS OF RHODES.

Rhodes was famous of old for its brazen colossal statue, the remains of whose pedestal Mr. Newton thinks he has discovered. Everybody is supposed to know, yet somebody may be glad to be reminded, that the Colossus was one of the Seven Wonders of the World, was 105 feet high, and was thrown down by an earthquake B.C. 224. In the seventh century the Saracens sold it as old brass to a Jew for 36,000*l.*

Dr. C. F. Lüders, professor at the Johanneum at Hamburg, has published a critical and historical treatise on the Colossus. According to his researches, this wonder of the world is reduced to nothing more than a colossal statue, standing on terra firma, like the Bavaria at Munich, but near the harbour, and dedicated to Phœbus Apollo. He insists upon it that its standing open-legged across the mouth of the harbour, and being used as a lighthouse, is a pure invention, and an emanation of fancy from later writers.

Rhodes is renowned for its occupation in the Middle Ages by the Knights of St. John, numerous traces of whose handiwork still exist. No European city can show a street so little changed since the 15th century as the Strada dei Cavalieri.

COMMON ORIGIN OF POPULAR FICTIONS.

Dr. Leyden is inclined to connect the history of popular narrative with ancient romance, as he has overlooked the mythological basis of the system. " In the repetition of an unskilful reciter," says the Doctor, " the metrical romance or fabliau seems often to have degenerated into a popular story ; and it is a curious fact that the subjects of some of the popular stories which I have heard repeated in Scotland, do not differ essentially from those of some of the ancient Norman fabliaux, presented to the public in an elegant form by Le Grand. Thus, when I first perused the fabliaux of the 'Poor Scholar,' the 'Three Thieves,' and the 'Sexton of China,' I was surprised to recognise the popular stories I had often heard repeated in infancy; and which I had often repeated myself when the song or the tale repeated by turns, amused the tedious evening of winter. From this circumstance I am inclined to think that many of the Scottish popular stories may have been common to the Norman-French. Whether these tales be derived immediately from the French during their long and intimate intercourse with the Scottish nation, or whether both nations borrowed them from the Celtic, may admit of some doubt."

In ascribing a common origin to the popular fictions of our island and the Continent, we cannot be far from the truth; but since the people of England and the Scottish Lowlands are undoubtedly offsets and grafts from the Teutonic stock, it is probable that our popular fables are chiefly of Teutonic origin. These idle stories boast a higher antiquity than romances and poems of much greater pretensions. Our proud baronial families can trace their line only up to Battle Abbey Roll; whilst the yeomen and franklins of Essex and Sussex and Kent, the *Spongs* and the *Pungs*, and the *Wapshotts* and the *Eppses*, bear in their names the evidence of their descent from the Saxon and Danish conquerors of Britain; and even the knights of the romance of the Round Table, in their present forms, are mere striplings when compared to the acquaintances of our early childhood, who troop along by the side of the go-cart, and help to rock the cradle. Jack, commonly called the Giant Killer, and Thomas Thumb landed in England from the very same keels and warships which conveyed Hengist and Horsa, and Ebba the Saxon.

THE STORY OF JACK THE GIANT-KILLER.

In Jack's memoirs may be traced indubitable resemblances to the fictions of the Edda. Jack, as we are told, having got a little money, travelled into Flintshire, and came to a large house in a lonesome place; here, by reason of his present necessity, he took courage to knock at the gate, when, to his amazement, there came forth a monstrous Giant with *two* heads, yet he did not seem so fiery as the former Giants, for he was a Welsh Giant, rendered less fiery than he would naturally have been, in consequence of "breakfasting," as the story says, "on a great bowl of hasty pudding," instead of keeping to the warm, invigorating national diet, toasted cheese. To this low feeding we also attribute the want of sagacity which enabled Jack "to outwit him," notwithstanding his two heads. The history states that Jack undressed himself, and as the Giant was walking towards another apartment, Jack heard him say to himself—

Though here you lodge with me this night,
You shall not see the morning light,
My club shall dash your brains out quite.

"Say you so," says Jack; "is that one of your Welsh tricks? I hope to be as cunning as you." Then, getting out of bed, he found a thick billet, and laid it in the bed in his stead, and hid himself in a dark corner of the room. In the dead of the night came the Giant with his club, and struck several blows with his club on the bed where Jack had laid the billet, and then returned to his own room, supposing that "he had broken all Jack's bones." In the morning early, came Jack to thank him for his lodging. "Oh!" said the Giant, "how have you rested? did you see anything last night?" "No," said Jack, "but a rat gave me three or four slaps with his tail."

Although the *locus in quo* is placed in Flintshire by the English writer, we find a parallel in the device practised by the Giant Skrimner, when he and Thor journeyed to Skrimner's Castle of Utgaard, as related in the Edda of Snorro. At midnight, the mighty son of earth laid himself to sleep beneath an oak, and snored aloud. Thor, the giant-killer, resolved to rid himself of his unsuspicious companion, and struck him with his tremendous hammer. "*Hath a leaf fallen upon me from the tree?*" exclaimed the awakened Giant. The Giant soon slept again, and "snored," the Edda says, "as loudly as if it had thundered in the forest." Thor struck the Giant again, and, as he thought, the hammer made a mortal indentation in his forehead. "What is the matter?" quoth Skrimner; "*hath an acorn fallen on my head?*" A third time the potent Giant snored, and a third time did the hammer descend "with huge two-handed sway," and with such force that Thor believed the iron had buried itself in Skrimner's temple. "*Methinks,*" quoth Skrimner, rubbing his cheek, "*some moss has fallen on my face.*" Thor might be well amazed at the escape of the Giant, but Skrimner, acting exactly like Jack, had outwitted his enemy by placing an immense rock on the leafy couch where Thor supposed he was sleeping, and which received the blows of the hammer in his stead.

Next, we have, in the fictions of the North and East, Jack's robbery of his cousin, a Giant with three heads, and who would beat five hundred men in armour. Jack terrified his three-headed cousin out of all his wits, by telling him that the king's son was coming. The Giant hid himself in a large vault underground; and in the morning, when Jack let his cousin out, the Giant asked what he would give him for his care, seeing that his castle was not demolished. "Why," answered Jack, "I desire nothing but your *old rusty sword*, the *coat* in the closet, and the *cap* and the *shoes* which you keep at the bed's-head." "With all my heart," said the Giant, "and be sure to keep them for my sake, for they are things of excellent use: the coat will keep you *invisible*, the cap will furnish you with *knowledge*, the sword cuts asunder *whatever you strike*, and the *shoes* are of *extraordinary swiftness*." These wonderful articles have been stolen out of the Great Northern treasury. The coat is the magic garment known in ancient German by the equivalent denomination of the "*Nebel Kappe*," or *cloud cloak*, fabled to belong to King Alberich, and the other dwarfs of the Teutonic cycle of romance, who, clad therein, could walk invisible. To them also belongs the Tarn hat, or hat of darkness, possessing the same virtue. Veleut, the cunning smith of the Edda of Sæmund, wrought Jack's "sword of sharpness," which, in the Wilkina Saga bears the name of *Balmung*. So keen was its edge, that when Veleut cleft his rival Æmilius through the middle with the wondrous weapon, it merely seemed to Æmilius as though cold water had glided down him. "Shake thyself," said Veleut. Æmilius shook himself, and fell dead into two halves, one on each side of his chair. That the story of Veleut's skill was known in this country is evinced by the Auchinleck text of the Geste of King Horn, where he is called Weland.

Jack's *shoes of swiftness* were once worn by *Loke* when he escaped from Valhalla. In the Calmuck romance of Ssidi Kur, the Chan steals a similar pair of seven-league *boots* from the Tchadkurrs, or evil spirits, by means of the *cap* which made him invisible, which he won from certain quarrelling children, or dwarfs, whom he encounters in the middle of a forest. Are these merely incidental coincidences between the superstitions and fictions of the followers of Buddha, and those of Odin ?

In the history of *Jack and the Bean Stalk*, the consistency of the character is still finely preserved. The awful distich put into the mouth of the Jette or Ettin, the principal agent in this romance,

> Snouk but, snouk ben,
> I find the smell of earthly men,

is scarcely inferior to the "fee-faw-fum" of the keen-scented anthropophaginian of the other. The bean-stalk, "the top whereof, when Jack looked upwards he could not discern, as it appeared lost in the clouds," has grown in fanciful imitation of the ash *Yadraid*, reaching, according to the Edda, from hell to heaven. As to the beautiful harp, which "played of its own accord," and which Jack stole from the Giant, we must find a parallel for it in the wonderful harp made of the breast-bone of the King's daughter, and which sang so sweetly to the miller, "Binnorie, oh, Binnorie," and in old Dunstan's harp, which sounded without hands, when hanging in the vale.

Most of these Giants rest upon good romance authority; or, to speak more correctly, Jack's history is a popular and degraded version of the traditions upon which our earliest romances are founded. "The Mount of Cornwall," which was kept by a large and monstrous Giant, is St. Michael's Mount; and the Giant Cormoran, whom Jack despatched there, and who was eighteen feet high, and *about* three yards round, is the same who figures in the romance of Tristem. It was by killing this Cormoran (the Corinæus, probably, of Geoffrey of Monmouth, and the Brut), that Jack acquired his triumphal epithet of the Giant-killer. Care should be taken not to confound "the History of Jack and the Giants," with "The History of the Giants." These works differ essentially in merit; and although the latter begins with the history of Goliath, the champion of the Philistines, yet the adventures contained in the remainder of the work, and particularly all those which relate to the Giants Trapsaca and Trandello, are, as the Irish Bishop observed of *Gulliver's Travels*, exceedingly incredible.—*Abridged from the Quarterly Review*, No. 41.

THE STORY OF TOM HICKATHRIFT.

Hearne has identified Sir Thomas Hickathrift, "the famous champion," with the far less celebrated Sir Frederick de Tylney, Baron of Tylney, in Norfolk, the ancestor of the Tylney family, who was killed at Acon, in Syria, in the reign of Richard Cœur de Lion: " *Hycophric,* or *Hycothrift,*" as the mister-wight observes, " being a corruption of Frederick;"—Hearne having here adopted a hint from Le Neve, of the College of Arms. Their conjectures, however, accord but slightly with the traditions given by the accurate Spelman, in his *Icenia.* From the most remote antiquity the fables and achievements of *Hickifric* have been obstinately credited by the inhabitants of the township of Tylney. " *Hickifric* " is venerated by them as the asserter of the rights and liberties of their ancestors. The "monstrous giant" who guarded the March, was, in truth, no other than the tyrannical lord of the manor, who attempted to keep his copy-holders out of the common field, called *Tylney Smeeth;* but who was driven away, with his retainers, by the prowess of Tom, armed with only his axletree and cart-wheel. Spelman tells the story in good Latin.

The pranks which Tom performed when his "natural strength, which exceeded twenty common men," became manifest, were correctly Scandinavian. Similar were the achievements of the great northern champion, Greter, when he kept geese upon the common, as told in his Saga. Tom's youth retraces the tales of the prowess of the youthful Siegfrid, detailed in the Niflunga Saga, and in the Book of Heroes. The supposed axtletree, with the superincumbent wheel, was represented on "Hycothrift's " grave-stone, in Tylney churchyard, in the shape of a cross. This is the form in which all the Runic monuments represent the celebrated hammer, or thunderbolt of the son of Odin, which shattered the skulls and scattered the brains of so many luckless giants. How far this surmise may be supported by Tom's skill in throwing the hammer, we will not pretend to decide. The common people have a faculty of seeing whatever they choose to believe, and of refusing to see things in which they disbelieve. It may, therefore, be supposed that the rude sculpture which the Tylneyites used to call the offensive and defensive arms of their champion, was nothing more than a cross, of which the upper part is inscribed in a circle, a figure often found on ancient sepulchres.

THE STORY OF TOM THUMB.

Tom Hearne would almost have sworn that Tom Thumb, the fairy knight, was " King Edgar's page." On ballad authority, we learn that "Tomalyn was a Scotsman born." Now Tom Hearne and the ballad are both in the wrong ; for Tomaline, otherwise Tamlane, is no other than Tom Thumb himself, who was originally a dwarf or droergar of Scandinavian descent, being the *Thum Lin—i.e., Little Thumb—*of the

Northmen. Drayton, who introduces both these heroes in his *Nymphidia*, seems to have suspected their identity.

The German "Daumerling," that is, little Thumb, is degraded to the son of a tailor; he has not much in common with Tom Thumb the Great, except the misfortune of being swallowed by the dun cow, which took place in Germany, just as it did in England.* This is a traditionary story of the Germans; but there is a little book in the Danish language, analysed by Professor Nierup, of the University of Copenhagen, who censures it, and perhaps with some degree of justice, as "a very childish history." It treats of "Swain Tomling, a man no bigger than a thumb, who would be married to a woman three ells and three-quarters long." The Danish title-page enumerates other of Tomling's adventures which are not found in the "History of his Marvellous Acts of Manhood," as preserved in England; the manhood, however, which emboldened the Swain to venture on a wife of "three ells and three-quarters" in length, is yet commemorated in the ancient rhyme which begins "I had a little husband no bigger than my thumb."

According to popular tradition, Tom Thumb died at Lincoln, which it may be recollected was one of the five Danish towns of England; we do not, however, therefore, intend to insist that the story was handed down by the northern invaders. There was a little blue flag-stone in the pavement of the Minster "which was shown as 'Tom Thumb's monument, and the country-folks never failed to marvel at it when they came to church on the Assize-Sunday: but during some of the modern repairs which have been inflicted on that venerable building, the flag-stone has been displaced and lost, to the great discomfiture of the holiday visitor.

In the Bodleian Library is a work with this title: "Tom Thumb, his Life and Death, wherein is declared many maruailous acts of manhood, full of wonder and strange merriments. Which little Knight lived in King Arthur's time, and famous in the Court of Great Brittaine. London: Printed for John Wright, 1630." It begins thus:

> In Arthur's court, *Tom Thumbe* did liue,
> A man of mickle might,
> The best of all the Table Round,
> And eke a doughty knight.

> His stature but an inch in height,
> Or quarter of a span :
> Then thinke you not this little knight
> Was prou'd a valiant man ?

---

* Tom Thumb, it is conjectured, if the truth should be discovered, would be found to be a mythological personage. His adventure bears a near analogy to the right of adoption into the Brahminical order, a ceremony which still exists in India, and to which the Rajah of Tanjore submitted many years ago. In Dubois's work there is an account of a diminutive deity, whose person and character are analogous to those of Tom Thumb. He, too, was not originally a Brahmin, but became one by adoption, like some of the worthies in the Ramayana. Compare the multiplicity of Tom Thumb's metamorphoses with those of Taliesin, as quoted by Davies, we shall then see that this diminutive per-

The prose history of Tom Thumb is manufactured from the ballad; and by the introduction of the fairy queen at his birth, and certain poetical touches which it yet exhibits, we are led to suppose that it is a *rifacciamento* of an earlier and better original. One of Tom's sports deserves note: it is when, in order to be revenged on his playmates, he

> took in pleasant game
> Black pots and glasses which he hung
> Upon a bright sunbeam.
>
> The other boys to do the same,
> In pieces broke them quite;
> For which they were most soundly whipt,
> At which he laught outright.

This "pleasant game" is borrowed from the pseudo-hagiography of the Middle Ages. It is found not only in one of the spurious Gospels, but also in the Legend of St. Columbanus, who, as we are told, performed a similar miracle by hanging his garments on a sunbeam.

LEGEND OF THE CROSS.[*]

The Rev. Baring Gould, in the second series of his *Curious Myths of the Middle Ages*, considers Thor's hammer or fylfot, a cross cramponnée, one of the earlier forms of the Cross, through which, according to the Discipline of the Secret, it passed more or less dissembled before it could be exhibited openly—that is, about the fourth or fifth century—in places remote from Rome. In the picture erected by Constantine, in the Palatine, we see the Knight with the Cross upon his helmet, warring with a dragon, as related by Eusebius. Mr. Gould finds the material origin of the use of the Cross before Christianity in the use of two sticks used for lighting fire, and discovers that under every system it was a symbol of life and regeneration by water, " a portion of the primeval religion, traces of which exist over the whole world, among every people, trust in the Cross, a part of the ancient faith which taught men to believe in a Trinity, in a war in Heaven, a Paradise from which man fell, a Flood, and a Babel, a faith which was deeply impressed with a conviction that a Virgin should conceive and bear a Son, that the Dragon's head should be bruised, and that through shedding of blood should come remission. The shadow of the Cross was cast back into the night of ages."

---

sonage is a slender but distinct thread of communication between the Brahminical and Druidical superstitions. Even independent of the analogy between his transformations and those of Taliesin, his station in the court of King Arthur (evidently the mythological Arthur), mark him as a person of the highest fabulous antiquity in this island; while the adventure of the cow, to which there is nothing analogous in Celtic mythology, appears to connect him with India.

[*] See the History of the Holy Cross, *Curiosities of History*, pp. 5—7.

Great Events from Little Causes.

N wandering through the highways and byeways of History, how curious it is to seek out the springs which have set the world in motion, and to read how the most trivial circumstances have occasioned the subversion of empires, and erected new ones in their stead; in a word, how the most important events frequently came to pass from very inconsiderable causes. A few instances, though at random strung, may be interesting.

The story of Semiramis shall be our first instance. How this beautiful heroine, by her charms and her valour, won the heart and crown of Ninus, King of Assyria, history doth tell. Enamoured of his bride, one unlucky morning, he resolved on the pleasure of seeing all Asia subject to the will of one who had possession of his heart: he, therefore, gave her absolute authority for the space of one day, and ordered all his subjects to execute the commands of Semiramis. A wise and prudent woman would, doubtless, have made use of this frolic to tell Ninus of his faults; not so, however, Semiramis: she consulted her ambition and her cruelty, for as soon as Ninus had placed this power in her hands, she employed it in causing him to be assassinated. The traitors whom she employed for this vile purpose, reported that the king had given up the reins of the empire to his wife, because he found his end approaching; this the people believed, and readily acknowledged Semiramis as their sovereign. How she used her newly-acquired power by building the city of Babylon, employing two millions of men; how she extended the Assyrian empire by levelling mountains, turning the course of rivers, and building vast cities; and how she failed in her attempted conquest of India, and was, in consequence, privately put to death by her son Ninias, history doth narrate; we have told enough to prove how a little cause produced a great effect.

"In most naval fights," says Sir Thomas Browne, "some notable advantage, error, or unexpected occurrence hath determined the victory. The great fleet of Xerxes was overthrown by the disadvantage of a narrow plain for battle. In the encounter of Duillius, the Roman, with the Carthaginian fleet, a new invention of the iron *corvi* (beak to the ships), made a decision of the battle on the Roman side. The unexpected falling off of the galleys of Cleopatra lost the battle of Actium. Even in the battle of Lepanto, if Caracoza had given the Turks orders not to narrow on account of the number of the Christian galleys, they had in all probability, declined the adventure of a battle ; and even when they came to fight the unknown force, an advantage of the eight Venetian galliasses gave the main stroke unto the victory."

Archimedes, we know, set fire to the ships of Marcellus at a considerable distance, by burning-glasses; yet, this philosopher, who had offered to move the world with a lever, was taken off in a very unseemly manner; for he was killed by a soldier who knew him not, while intent upon some geometrical figures, which he had drawn upon the sand.

Antoninus Commodus, the Roman Emperor, of a very different stamp, was killed through a child playing with a paper which he had found in the emperor's chamber: the little boy had been reared in the palace, had followed Commodus into his apartment, and staying there after his departure, took up a paper, and went out of doors, playing with it as he walked through the streets; the child was met by a woman, who, taking the document out of his hand, found it to be the sentence for her own death, as well as some other persons; they together saved their own lives by first poisoning, and then strangling the imperial tyrant.

Belisarius, one of the greatest captains in history, after having conquered the Persians, and subdued Africa and Italy, was deprived of all his honours and dignities for having very properly reproached his worthless wife. She being a *confidante* of the Empress, persuaded the latter to get up a charge of revolt against Belisarius, and then instigated Justinian to confiscate the soldier's estate and goods, and degrade him. " Before Belisarius's disgrace," says the account, somewhat naïvely, " every person thought it an honour to be in his company; but, after his misfortune, none dared to speak to him, compassionate him, or even mention his name. True friends are rarely met with among the great."

Placidia, the mother of Valentinian III., Emperor of the West, brought up her daughter, Honoria, so severely, that the young princess, who was a forward vixen, to get rid of the maternal restraint, wrote a letter to Attila, King of the Huns, offering him her hand, and as a pledge of her faith, sent him half a ring. Attila, who only wanted a pretext for ravaging the West, took advantage of Honoria's offer, and wrote to the Emperor Valentinian, that Honoria was his wife; desired that he would send her to him, and likewise cede to him the moiety of the empire which was to be her portion. Valentinian, of course, refused these unreasonable demands, which so enraged Attila, that he ravaged all Gaul and Italy, and drove some of the inhabitants of the latter to the point of the Adriatic Gulf, where they built themselves cottages, and thus commenced the city of Venice.

Valentinian III. was a reckless gambler, and whilst Rome was falling to pieces for the second time, this emperor was playing at dice with his ministers, and cheating them whenever he could; and Maximus preserved the friendship of this weak emperor only by gaming with him. One day, when they had both played very deeply, Maximus lost a considerable sum; and, as he had not the amount with him, the emperor compelled him to leave his ring with him as security. Through the base use which Valentinian made of the ring, he was assassinated in a conspiracy formed by Maximus, who succeeded to the imperial throne, and then compelled Eudoxia, the widow of Valentinian, to accept his hand. She soon became disgusted at his cruelty, and invited the Vandals from Africa to come to her aid; Genseric caught at this opportunity of gratifying the desire he had of pillaging Italy: he soon landed with a large army, advanced to Rome, and entered the city sword in hand and pillaged it for fourteen days. He then returned to Carthage, carrying with him the Empress Eudoxia, and the principal personages of Rome, loaded with chains; in the meantime, the people, enraged at Maximus, tore him to pieces. Thus we see how the inability of a gambler to pay a loss immediately led to the sacking of the mistress of the world.

Many a war has been caused by the most trifling circumstance: here is an instance. About the middle of the thirteenth century, the two republics of Genoa and Venice were at the height of their prosperity, and had establishments in all parts of the world. They had a considerable one in the city of Acre, on the coast of Syria, where they lived, subject to the laws of their respective countries, in perfect union. Their peace was, however, destroyed by a mere accident. One day, two porters, one a Genoese, and the other a Venetian, fell out about a bale of goods which was to be carried. From words they fell to blows; the merchants, who at first gathered round them only by way of amusement to see the battle, at length took part in the quarrel, each assisting his countryman; and much blood was spilt on both sides. Complaints were soon carried to Genoa and Venice; and the magistrates of each republic agreed that satisfaction should be made for the damage, by arbitration. The Genoese had the greater sum to pay, which they failed to do; when the Venetians, by way of retribution, set on fire all the Genoese vessels which were then in the port of Acre. A sanguinary battle ensued; and the account says, Genoa and Venice resolved to support their merchants, and each fitted out a considerable fleet; the Genoese were beaten, and compelled to abandon their settlements at Acre, when the Venetians rased their houses and forts, and destroyed their magazines. The Genoese, irritated at their defeat, refitted their fleet, and every citizen offered to venture his person and fortune to revenge the outrage on his country. Meanwhile, the Venetians were equally active. The sea was covered with the ships of the rival republics; an engagement ensued, much blood was spilt, and many brave citizens were lost on both sides. In fine, after a long and cruel war, in which the two republics reaped nothing but shame, they made peace.

Towards the middle of the fourteenth century, the Genoese became disgusted with the tyranny of their nobility, and sighed for change. The populace wished to elect an *Abbé*, whose authority should keep in check the captains, who were then the magistrates of the republic. A large and tumultuous meeting was accordingly held for the election of an *Abbé of the People*. The tumult increased, the people grew warm, and were about to proceed to blows; when a shoemaker, who had just come out of a wine-house, mixed among the crowd, and getting upon an elevation, emboldened by the fumes of wine, he bawled out, "Fellow-citizens, will you hearken to me?" The Genoese, who were about to tear each other to pieces, burst into a hearty laugh. Some told the shoemaker to be quiet; others encouraged him to speak; but some threw dirt at him. The orator was nowise disconcerted, and shouted out: "You ought to nominate to the dignity of *Abbé of the People* an honest man; and I know of none more so than Simon Boccanegra; you ought to appoint him." Now, Simon was a good man, and was much esteemed both by the nobility and the people; and he was, moreover, a man of good family. In short, his merits occasioned the people to attend to the shoemaker's recommendation: they elected Simon to be *Abbé*, and presented him with a sword, as the mark of his dignity; this, however, he returned, thanking the people for the goodwill they had shown him, but declining to be the first *Abbé*; but, availing himself of the shoemaker's speech, he soon attained the lead in the republic. The people soon shouted, "Boccanegra, Lord of Genoa." The ambitious man then said he was ready to submit to the will of the people; to be *Abbé*, or *Lord*, as they should ordain. This feigned humility pleased the people, as he had calculated: they shouted, "Lord Boccanegra!" and he was proclaimed perpetual Doge! So that, the speech of a drunken shoemaker caused the government of Genoa to be transferred from the nobles to the people, and enabled a single man to become sole master in the State.

How the Genoese fell under the Austrian yoke we need not particularize: they freed themselves from it through a very trifling occurrence. On December 5, 1746, the Genoese were compelled to assist in drawing the artillery of their city, to aid their conquerors in an expedition against Provence. In drawing one of the mortars through a narrow street, the carriage broke; a crowd assembled, in the midst of which an Austrian officer struck with his cane a Genoese, who was slow at his work. The exasperated republican drew his knife, and stabbed the officer; the whole crowd of Genoese became excited; they broke open the armourers' shops, demolished the gates of the arsenal and of the powder magazines, fell upon the Austrians, and drove them out of the city; the peasantry poured in, and joined the citizens, and thus they drove the enemy entirely from the state of Genoa. The Genoese celebrated, with great rejoicing, the recovery of their liberty: with great solemnity they drew through the streets the mortar which had occasioned this revolution. The Austrian army, destined for the expedition against Provence, marched to, and blocked up, Genoa; but France sent the citizens aid—the Duke de Richelieu saved the republic, and the senate erected a statue in honour of him.

A window was once the cause of a war, and very oddly, too. When the palace of Trianon was building for Louis XIV., at the end of the park, at Versailles, the king, one day, went to inspect it, accompanied by Louvois, secretary at war, and superintendent of the building. The sovereign and the minister were walking together, when the king remarked that one of the windows was out of shape, and smaller than the rest; this Louvois denied, asserting that he could not perceive the least difference. Louis had it measured, and finding that he was right in his observation, treated Louvois with contumely before the whole court. This so incensed the minister, that when he reached home he was heard to say he would find better employment for a sovereign than that of insulting his favourites: Louvois was as good as his word; for by his haughtiness and ill-temper, he insulted the other leading powers of Europe, and occasioned the sanguinary war, begun in 1688 by France against Holland, England, Germany, and Spain, the parties to the league of Augsburg (1686) and the Grand Alliance (1689). The Treaty of Ryswick, in 1697, terminated the war, by which Louis gained nothing; acknowledged William III. as lawful king of Great Britain, and engaged not to furnish any succour to the deposed king James II. Louis also consented to the re-establishment of the Duke of Lorraine. The Treaty was signed in a house, the site of which is now marked by an obelisk.

In the cathedral of Modena, in the marble tower called "La Ghirlandina," is kept the old worm-eaten wooden bucket which was the cause of the civil war, or rather affray, between the Modenese and Bolognese, in the time of Frederic II., Nov. 15, 1325. It was long suspended by the chain which fastened the gate of Bologna, through which the Modenese forced their passage, and seized the prize, which was deposited in the cathedral by the victors, the Geminiani, as a trophy of the defeat of the Petronii, with wonderful triumph. The event is the subject of Tassoni's *Secchia Rapita, or Rape of the Bucket*, the first modern mock-heroic poem.

The Mission of St. Augustine is one of the most striking instances in all history of the vast results which may flow from a very small beginning,—of the immense effects produced by a single thought in the heart of a single man, carried out conscientiously, deliberately, and fearlessly. Nothing in itself could seem more trivial than the meeting of Gregory with the three Yorkshire boys in the market-place at Rome; yet this roused a feeling in his mind which he never lost; and through all the obstacles which were thrown first in his own way, and then in that of Augustine, his highest desire concerning it was more than realized. From Canterbury, the first English Christian city—from Kent, the first English Christian kingdom—has by degrees arisen the whole constitution of Church and State in England, which now binds together the whole British empire. And from the Christianity here established has flowed, by direct consequences, first, the Christianity of Germany—then, after a long interval, of North America—and, lastly, we may trust, in time, of all India and all Australasia.—Dean Stanley's *Historical Memorials of Canterbury*.

The Discovery of America is referred to by Humboldt as a "wonderful concatenation of trivial circumstances which undeniably exercised an influence on the course of the world's destiny. These circumstances are, "Washington Irving has justly observed, that if Columbus had resisted the counsel of Martin Alonzo Pinzon, and continued to steer westward, he would have entered the Gulf Stream and been borne to Florida, and from thence, probably, to Cape Hatteras and Virginia,—a circumstance of incalculable importance, since it might have been the means of giving to the United States of North America a Catholic Spanish population, in the place of the Protestant English one by which those regions were subsequently colonized. 'It seems to me like an inspiration,' said Pinzon to the Admiral, 'that my heart dictates to me that we ought to steer in a different direction.' It was on the strength

F

of this circumstance that in the celebrated lawsuit which Pinzon carried on against the heirs of Columbus, between 1513 and 1515, he maintained that the discovery of America was alone due to him. This inspiration Pinzon owed, as related by an old sailor of Moguez, at the same trial, to *the flight of a flock of parrots* which he had observed in the evening flying towards the south-west, in order, as he might well have conjectured, to roost on trees on the land. *Never has a flight of birds been attended by more important results.* It may even be said that it has decided the first colonization in the New Continent, and the original of the Roman and Germanic races of men."

An instance pregnant with mightier results could not, perhaps, be quoted than the following:—When many Puritans emigrated, or were about to emigrate, to America, in 1637, Cromwell, either despairing of his fortunes at home, or indignant at the rule of government which prevailed, resolved to quit his native country, in search of those civil and religious privileges of which he could freely partake in the New World. Eight ships were lying in the Thames, ready to sail: in one of them, says Hume (quoting Mather and other authorities), were embarked Hazelrig, Hampden, Pym, and Cromwell. A proclamation was issued, and the vessels were detained by Order in Council. The King had, indeed, cause to rue the exercise of his authority. In the same year, Hampden's memorable trial—the great cause of Ship-money—occurred. What events rapidly followed!

Great changes have been decided by *Casting Votes*. At the beginning of the reign of Elizabeth, when the Protestant religion was restored, the question whether there should be Saints' Days in the Calendar was considered by the Convocation, and sharply and fully debated. The Saints' Days were carried only by a single vote; 59 members voted for Saints' Days, 58 for omitting them.—*Literary Remains of H. Fynes Clinton.*

Bishop Burnet relates that the Habeas Corpus Act passed by a mere mistake; that one peer was counted for ten, and that made a majority for the measure.—*Earl Stanhope's Speech,* 1856.

Sir Arthur Owen, Bart., of Orielton, in the county of Pembroke, is the individual who is asserted to have given the casting vote which placed the Brunswick dynasty on the throne of England. A lady, in 1856, residing at Haverfordwest, remembered her grandmother, who was staying at Orielton, at the time when Sir Arthur Owen rode to London on *horseback*, for the purpose of recording his vote: he arrived at the precise juncture when his single vote caused the scale to preponderate in favour of the descendants of the Electress Sophia (*Notes and Queries,* 2nd S., No. 313). Another account states that Sir Arthur Owen made the number even, and that it was Mr. Griffith Rice, M.P. for Carmarthenshire, who gave the *casting vote.* (See Debrett's *Baronetage,* 1824.)

The Act to recharter the first Bank of the United States was defeated yb the casting vote of Vice-President Clinton (*ex-officio* President of the Senate), and the Tariff Act of 1846 was ordered to be engrossed by the casting vote of Vice-President Dallas.

"If the nose of Cleopatra had been shorter," said Pascal, in his epigrammatic and brilliant manner, "the condition of the world would have been different." The Mahomedans have a tradition, that when their prophet concealed himself in Mount Shur, his pursuers were deceived by a spider's web, which covered the mouth of the cave. Luther might have been a lawyer, had his friend and companion escaped the thunder-storm at Erfurt. Scotland had wanted her stern reformer, if the appeal of the preacher had not startled him in the chapel of St. Andrew's Castle. And if Mr. Grenville had not carried, in 1764, his memorable resolution as to the expediency of charging "certain Stamp-Duties" on the plantations in America, the western world might still have bowed to the British sceptre. Cowley might never have been a poet, if he had not found the *Faëry Queen* in his mother's parlour. Opie might have perished in mute obscurity, if he had not looked over the shoulder of his young companion, Mark Otes, while he was drawing a butterfly. Giotto, one of the early Florentine painters, might have continued a rude shepherd-boy, if a sheep drawn by him upon a stone had not attracted the notice of Cimabue as he went that way.

Cromwell was near being strangled in his cradle by a monkey: here was this wretched ape wielding in his paws the destinies of nations. Charles Wesley refuses to go with his wealthy namesake to Ireland; and the inheritance which would have been his, goes to build up the fortunes of a Wellesley instead of a Wesley; and to this decision of a schoolboy (as Mr. Southey observes) Methodism may owe its existence, and England its military—and we trust we may now add, its civil and political—glory.—*Quarterly Review*.

The possibility of a great change being brought about by very slight beginnings may be illustrated by the tale which Lockman tells of a vizier who, having offended his master, was condemned to perpetual captivity in a lofty tower. At night his wife came to weep below his window. "Cease your grief," said the sage; "go home for the present, and return thither when you have procured a live black-beetle, together with a little *ghee* (or buffalo's butter), three clews, one of the finest silk, another of stout pack-thread, and another of whipcord; finally, a stout coil of rope." When she again came to the foot of the tower, provided according to her husband's commands, he directed her to touch the head of the beetle with a little of the *ghee*, to tie one end of the silk around him, and to place the beetle on the wall of the tower. Attracted by the smell of the butter, which he conceived to be in store somewhere above him, the beetle continued to ascend till he reached the top, and thus put the vizier in possession of the end of the silk thread, who drew up the pack-thread by means of the silk, the small cord by means of the pack-thread, and by means of the cord a stout rope capable of sustaining his whole weight; and so, at last, escaped from the place of his duresse.

Many a writer, for want of attention to the soundness of his premises, arrives at a "most lame and impotent conclusion." So long as the first is taken for granted, the latter passes muster; but disturb the one, and down topples the other. Colton, in the second volume of his *Lacon*, in illustrating "great events from small causes," has fallen into an error of this class when he tells us that " If a private country gentleman in Cheshire about the year 1730 had not been overturned in his carriage, it is extremely probable that America, instead of being a free republic at this moment, would have continued a dependent colony of England. This country gentleman happened to be Augustus Washington, Esquire, who was thus accidentally *thrown into* the company of a lady who afterwards became his wife, who emigrated with him to America, and in the year 1732, at Virginia, became the envied mother of George Washington the Great." Many thousand copies of *Lacon* had been published before the authenticity of this anecdote was questioned, in *Notes and Queries* in 1858, when it was found to be at variance with the facts of Washington's biography, as pointed out by Dr. Doran: "the father of George Washington (*Augustin*, not Augustus) was born in America, where his family had been settled since the year 1657. It was, at least, about that time that the brothers, John and Lawrence Washington, emigrated from England to Virginia. Both of them married. John had two sons; Lawrence had one daughter and two sons, John and Augustin. This Augustin was twice married, and the great George Washington (born in 1732) was the eldest son of the second marriage."

The failure of men who have embarked in literature as a profession is a favourite subject with those authors who are men of the world as well as men of letters. Still, their estimates are not unfrequently grounded in error, and the lessons they convey are fabulous and faulty. Mr. Blanchard Jerrold, in his nicely-written life of his father, instances " the most unhappy mistake made by all men who have dwelt upon the life of Laman Blanchard. It has been said by Sir Edward Lytton, as by lesser commentators, that Mr. Blanchard passed a life of intense anxiety—of war with the world, that only very slowly consented to exchange the fruits of his graceful genius for its solid comforts. No statement could be further from the truth. After a very short struggle in London, it was Mr. Blanchard's good fortune to have one or two powerful friends who were inclined to give a hearing to his tender and eloquent voice. He was for some time Resident Secretary to the Zoological Society in Bruton-street, an institution founded chiefly through the exertions of his brother-in-law, N. A. Vigors, M.P. for Carlow ; and hence he went direct from good appointment to good appointment to the end of his days. He edited, among other papers, the *Courier*, the *True Sun*, and the *Court Journal*. He was sub-editor of the *Examiner* when he died, and he long enjoyed the ripe fruits of a large popularity as a most gracefully-humorous magazine writer. If he had a disappointment, it must have been the neglect with which the world received the poetic gems that oozed from him—a neglect that has yet to be made good."

British History.

WHY WAS BRITAIN CALLED ALBION?

ECAUSE of its lofty white cliffs (Lat. *albus*, white) on the southern coast. Others trace the word to the Celtic *alb*, *alp*, high. In the fabulous history of England, it is related that the first inhabitants were subdued by *Albion*, a giant, and a son of Neptune, who called the island after his own name, and ruled it forty-four years. Another legend derives the name from a certain *Albina*, the eldest of fifty daughters of " a strange Dioclesian king of Syria," who, having murdered their husbands on their marriage-night, one only excepted, whom his wife's loyalty saved, were by him, at the suit of his wife, their sister, not put to death, but turned out to sea in a ship unmanned, and who, as the tale goes, were driven on this island, where they had issue by the inhabitants—none but devils, as some write or others report, a lawless crew, without head or governor. Milton characterizes these stories as "too absurd and too unconscionably gross" for credence; but he remarks: "Sure enough we are that Britain hath been anciently termed *Albion*, both by Greeks and Romans." Coleridge has:—

> Not yet enslav'd, not wholly vile,
> O Albion, O my mother isle !

The name of " Albion " was probably given to England by the Gaels of the opposite coast, who could not fail to be struck with the chalky cliffs that characterize the nearest part of Kent. Settlers from Gaul probably came over to Britain, and their descendants, as we presume the Gaels of Scotland to be, though now confined to the northern part of the island, still retain among them the name of Albina, by which the whole country was once designated. (See *Thoughts on the Origin, &c.,* *of the Gael*, by James Grant, of Carimony.)

THE ENGLISH CONQUEST OF BRITAIN.

Both Englishmen and Welshmen are in the habit of calling every object which they do not understand by the name " Druidical," which for the most part is simply an excuse for ignorance. At the same time, the mass of Englishmen fail to have any rational view of a matter so simple in its main outline (though so perplexing in its details) as the English conquest of Britain. People look upon the " Ancient Britons " as their ancestors, while they sometimes wonder why the modern Britons do not speak English. Men read of the English Conquest as if it were analogous to the Norman Conquest. Not one man in ten realizes that

Hengest and Horsa, Ælla and Cissa, were his own kinsmen, and that the Vortigern or the Arthur with whom he sympathizes, were not his kinsmen, but the enemies of his kinsmen. We believe that one great source of all this confusion is our fatal habit of calling all Englishmen who lived before 1066 Saxons. We all, like George III., "glory in the name of Briton," while, unless we are very affected indeed, we do not nowadays call ourselves Anglo-Saxons. Hence we naturally identify ourselves with the "ancient Briton," and forget that our own ancestor is to be looked for in the invading "Saxon." The plain fact is that, in 858 just as in 1858, and probably for four centuries before 858, the Englishman called himself an Englishman, while his Welsh neighbour called him a Saxon. The name "Saxon," to express the whole united nation of Angles, Saxons, and Jutes, is absolutely unknown to our early writers. It was the Anglian, not the Saxon branch which gave its name to the whole. Among all Dr. Guest's many contributions to our early history, none was more valuable than his daring to call things by their right names, and to speak of "the Early English Settlements" in Britain.

When people, then, have realized the plain fact that the Welsh or Britons were the earlier inhabitants, while the English were the intruding conquerors, the question naturally follows, What vestiges, ·n blood, language, or anything else, have the Celtic races left in that part of Britain which is now occupied by the English? The question involves a host of others, as to the exact relations existing between the Celtic inhabitants of different parts of Britain, and as to the possibility of earlier Teutonic settlements before the great English Conquest. Thoroughly to answer it requires a most rare familiarity alike with the written documents and with the existing phenomena of our land. It requires a union of Celtic and Teutonic scholarship, and an acquaintance with Celtic and Teutonic history, combined with the most diligent personal examination of the natural features, the artificial remains, the local nomenclature, and the local dialects of the whole island.—*Saturday Review.*

DOMESDAY BOOK AND ITS PARTIALITIES.

Domesday has been well characterized as a wonder, almost a miracle. The work had never been done before, and, in the ages that have passed, it has never been done so thoroughly again. The record is anything but dry and lifeless. As might be expected, Domesday takes a very decided line in politics. In its view King William was the lawful and immediate successor of King Eadward. He undoubtedly had to come from foreign parts to take possession of his kingdom; we read how "Rex Willelmus venit in Angliam," but this might be said of George the First, of Charles the Second, or of that sanctified person King Jeames himself. It is only by little hints here and there that we find out that there was any more armed opposition to his coming than there was in the other three cases. We hear ever and anon how the former owners of certain lands died in the " bellum apud Hastinges." In one case a man of Essex (Essex f. 14) is recorded to have gone out to fight by sea against King William. He came back, seemingly wounded, and gave a lordship to Saint Peter of Westminster, and we are significantly told how St. Peter kept it without any kind of authority from King William, "postquam Rex venit in istam terram." That there ever was a King Harold is implicitly denied throughout the book. Norman chroniclers, even those most bitter against Harold, do not scruple to give a king *de facto* the title of " Rex." The Survey, as becomes a legal document, is more precise. We might as soon expect an Act of Charles the Second to recognise His Highness the Lord Protector. " Heraldus Comes" is constantly spoken of, but " Heraldus Rex" never. Once only, or rather twice in one page, do we find something like the titles of royalty given to the usurper. To be sure he is not called King, but it oozes out that he somehow or other reigned. One Loman in Hampshire (fol. 38) seems to have had his lands confiscated to the Crown in Harold's reign. Throughout Domesday runs an anxiety to put every act of Harold's in an unfavourable light. Harold, like every other eminent man of his time, was involved in controversies about lands with churches and religious houses. The charters and local histories are full of such stories about everybody— not only about sinners like Godwine and Harold, but about holy men like Leofric, Waltheof, Saint Eadward himself. All of them appear, in this or that story, as robbers of the Church. That is to say, the monks or other churchmen told the story their own way, and of course in the way unfavourable to the layman. It is only here and there that we get the layman's version, which enables us to see that there are two sides to the story. Plenty of such disputes are spoken of in Domesday, but it is only when Harold is concerned that the transaction is invariably and pointedly spoken of as unjust. We hear of Harold in Domesday, as we hear in the Worcester Cartulary of Eadward, seizing church lands by violence; but the chances are that the Founder of Waltham and the Founder of Westminster would each have had something to say for himself. In one case we distinctly find that the supposed act of violence was really an exchange. Harold gave the churchmen a " commutatio," but Domesday takes care to tell us that it was an " iniqua commutatio." —Selected and abridged from the *Saturday Review*.

DISPERSION OF ANCIENT MANUSCRIPTS.

Fortunately, the spirit of antiquarianism awoke at the moment when monastic vanity or love of hoarding could protect no more the monuments of the past. Men like Lord Burghley, notes in whose handwriting Mr. Hardy has discovered on manuscripts, and Selden, sheltered many a homeless volume. So high did the passion for collecting rise that a devotee of this new sect, when he thought the guardian of one of his adored relics undeserving of the trust, would steal it even from a friend, to the latter's grief, unmixed, however, with anything like con-

tempt. Thus, one manuscript seems to have been purloined on a pretext of exchange—gold for brass—for printed copies of the same work. Mr. Hardy quotes Bishop Gibson's letter to the Master of University College on the subject:—
"Sir John Marsham's collection must be considerable. There is a curious *Ingulphus* in your library, which, as his family says, Obadiah Walker stole from him. I told him what they lay to his charge. His answer was, that Sir John gave it to him, and that, as an acknowledgment, he presented him with some copies of the *Ingulphus* printed at Oxford. It is very probable, though, Sir John did not design to part with the book; nay, he used to be complaining of Mr. Walker for using him so unkindly; but the old gentleman has too much the spirit of an antiquary and a great scholar to think stealing a manuscript any sin. He has ordered me not to discover where it is lodged."

With all these occasional eccentricities in the antiquarian code of honour, the general taste awakened by such zealots has saved much ancient learning to us. And yet how much has managed to sip into oblivion! Some works have been cast up on shore wanting an author, some authors without their works. Giraldus's *Itinerarium Cambriæ* has lost its invaluable maps; nothing is left, but a description, of Queen Christina's copy, the solitary one, of the *Draco Normannicus;* posterity is indebted to Bishop Fitz Nigel himself for the information that his *Liber Tricolumnus* is a work likely to be " useful" to it, as well as " agreeable reading" to the bishop's contemporaries; and Lelard interrupted the rats and beetles of Abingdon only in time to learn that they had been feasting on Joseph of Exeter's grand epic, the *Bellun Antiochenum.* Sometimes a manuscript has been spirited away even in these days of printed catalogues, making its appearance in the lists of a cathedral library, but when searched for gone, perhaps the prey of some kleptomaniacal antiquarian, perhaps only mislaid, or bound up by mistake with another work. In a few exceptional cases, even modern guardians and owners have themselves proved unfaithful, like the Arras librarian, commemorated by Dr. Giles, who mutilated a valuable copy of Herbert of Bosham's *Life of Becket* for the value of the vellum; and like the authorities of the same city, who refused to redeem the missing leaves from Sir Thomas Phillipps, who had rescued them from a tailor, at the price of old parchment.—*Times journal.*

Aubrey, in his *Natural History of Wiltshire,* gives this curious "digression" upon the dispersion of MSS. in his time:—" Anno 1633, I entered into my grammar at the Latin school at Yatton-Keynel, in the church, where the curate, Mr. Hart, taught the eldest boys Virgil, Ovid, Cicero, &c. The fashion then was to save the forses of the bookes with a false cover of parchment, &c., old manuscript which I [could not] was too young to understand; but I was pleased with the elegancy of the writing and the coloured initiall letters. I remember the rector here, Mr. Wm. Stump, gr.-son of St. the cloathier of Malmesbury, had severall manuscripts of the abbey. He was a proper man and a good fellow; and when he brewed a barrell of spec all ale, his use was to stop the bunghole, under the clay, with a sheet of manuscript;

he sayd nothing did it so well, which sore thought did grieve me then to see. Afterwards I went to schoole to Mr. Latimer at Leigh-delamer, the next parish, where was the like use of covering of books. In my grandfather's dayes the manuscripts flew about like butterflies. All musick bookes, account bookes, copie bookes, &c., were covered with old manuscripts, as wee cover them now with blew paper or marbled paper; and the glover at Malmesbury made great havock of them, and gloves were wrapt up, no doubt, in many good pieces of antiquity. Before the late warres, a world of rare manuscripts perished hereabout; for within half a dozen miles of this place was the abbey of Malmesbury, where it may be presumed the library was as well furnished with choice copies as most libraries of England; and, perhaps, in this library we might have found a correct Plinie's *Naturall History*, which Camitus, a monk here, did abridge for King Henry the Second. . . . . One may also perceive, by the binding of old bookes, how the old manuscripts went to wrack in those dayes. Anno 1647, I went to Parson Stump out of curiosity to see his manuscripts, whereof I had seen some in my childhood; but by that time they were lost and disperst. His sons were gunners and souldiers, and scoured their gunnes with them; but he shewed me severall old deedes granted by the Lords Abbotts, with their seales annexed."

WHO WAS GILDAS?

According to some authorities, a British historian, who flourished in the first half of the sixth century. But, in 1839, a paper was read to the Royal Society of Literature, the commencement of the *Biographia Literaria Britannica*, by Mr. Thomas Wright, M.A., wherein is an entire overthrow of all the previous opinions of this writer, showing that, in all probability, *such a person never existed*, and that his history was a forgery. Archbishop Ussher, to solve the chronological difficulties, has supposed that there were two persons of this name; but this conjecture, Mr. Wright shows, involves greater absurdities; and he adds, that some, to reconcile all of it, "have supposed that there were six or seven." Gildas is supposed to have been the son of a British king, and the most ancient historian of Britain before the arrival of the Saxons. He bears a most forcible testimony to the vices of the British kings at the above period. He is often quoted by Horsley, in his *Britannia Romana*.

Gibbon gave to Gildas the title of "the British Jeremiah;" and in the *Edinburgh Review* we find this exquisite bit of satire upon his pretensions:—"The British Jeremiah . . . . is so pleased to find, or so determined to invent, topics for declamatory lamentation or praise, that it is difficult to distinguish the basis of truth from the fantastic superstructure of exaggeration and falsehood with which he has overloaded it."

In Mr. Douce's copy of Tanner, in the Bodleian, there is the following note in Ritson's handwriting on the numerous surnames given to Gildas:—"1. Gildas was called *Albanius*, from his being born in Albany, now Scotland; 2. *Aldanus*, a nonentity, forged by T. Dempster; 3. *Badonicus*, from his having mentioned the battle of Badon, or being born in that year; 4. *Cambrius*, as being a Briton; 5. *Hibernus*, as sometime residing in Ireland; 6. *Quartus*, from an absurd fancy that there were three of yᵉ name before him; 7. *Sapiens*, from his writeings, real or imaginary.

"There were no less than five Gildases made out of one, each of whom is the author of books that never existed." *

INGULF OF CROYLAND AND WILLIAM OF MALMESBURY.

The *soi-disant* Ingulf of Croyland's chronicle is now known—though apparently Savile, and Spelman, and other giants of antiquarianism did not know it—to have been framed with a dishonest object, and to be from first to last a monkish forgery, with its charters composed in the scriptorium, its general history a patchwork of piracies, and its special anecdotes fictions. The compilers of such narratives, whether retained advocates—for authorship was now become a profession—or patriotic believers in the abstract justice of their society's claims, and in the duty of all pious brethren to repair unlucky legal flaws, had their appointed task—viz., to arrange, not to select, materials, and to make out as good a case as possible from them. The name of William of Malmesbury himself, prefixed to works of this order, is no guarantee of good faith. His critical scepticism may perhaps be seen struggling occasionally, as in his *Glastonbury Chronicle*; but in the end, as servilely, though with more semblance of squeamishness than the pseudo-Ingulf, "pure fable" and "forged charters" are all obediently copied by him and stamped with the authority of his name.

The History of Ingulphus is a clever but undoubted fiction of the fourteenth and fifteenth centuries, an impudent fabrication, to all appearance, by the Croyland monks for patching up a defective title. The genuineness and authenticity were first questioned more than a century ago; and in the last ten or twelve years the subject has received increased attention. In the *Archæological Journal* for March, 1862, both the history and charters of Ingulphus have been dissected at considerable length; and though in some parts an interesting compilation, the book, as an historical authority, is altogether worthless.—*Athenæum.*†

HISTORIC MISREPRESENTATIONS.

We have been accustomed of late to very remarkable disturbances in the atmosphere of history. We have been told that Richard the Third

---

* *A Manual of British Historians*, 1845.
† In the same journal, No. 2121, we read of Giraldus's *Itinerarium*, being "stuffed full of stupendously impossible things that are gravely described as facts."

did not kill his nephews, and that Henry the Eighth was rather a tender husband; but we were not prepared for Major Murray's discovery that the Black Prince, and not Henry the Fifth, won the great day at Agincourt. Surely this transfer of glory from Lancaster to Plantagenet is a little unjust to the former! Would it be fair if we were to maintain that Sir Cloudesley Shovel gained the battle of Trafalgar or that Marlborough won the victory of 1815 at Waterloo? If this be the method by which the Major registers the glories of the Scottish regiments, we may well be doubtful of the few he does chronicle amid the masses of fine writing, droll logic, and of his oracular remarks, which remind us of the words of the poet:—

> To observations which ourselves we make,
> We grow more partial for th' observer's sake.

Again, as if to render undoubted the right of the Black Prince to the glory of being the victor at Agincourt, the Major calls Poitiers, Agincourt, and Cressy *successive defeats*. If you allow that young Edward at fifteen or sixteen gained the last of these fields in 1346, the Major supposes, it would seem, that he, incontestably, carried off the glory of Agincourt some years previously—Agincourt having been fought in 1415! and that the young hero commenced his career of invincibility at Poitiers, which *we* used to think was fought ten years after Cressy—namely, in 1356.—*Athenæum.*

THE QUEENS OF ENGLAND.

The principle of female succession seems to have been indigenous in Britain. Tacitus mentions it as a peculiarity of this nation: "*neque sexum in imperiis discrimerunt;*" and though Blackstone is under a slight error in considering Boadicea, who was the *widow* and not the *daughter* of the last King, as an instance of hereditary succession, it is clear that the British crown was in those days inheritable by females.

Our English annals afford a curious and lamentable anomaly on this subject; for, while the *principle* of female succession has never been denied, it has so happened in *practice* that from the Conquest to the accession of Queen Mary I.—nearly 500 years—there is not a single instance in which the female heir was not violently deprived of her regal rights, and generally by the next heir male. Matilda, the only surviving child of Henry I., was dispossessed by Stephen, and, after his death, passed over by her own son. Philippa of Clarence and her issue, heirs to the Crown, on the death of Richard II., were excluded by the usurpation of the next male, Henry IV. and his descendants, which produced those bloody and protracted struggles called somewhat inaccurately the contest of the Houses of *York* and Lancaster, for the Duke of York's only title was as the son of Anne, the daughter of Philippa of *Clarence*. Elizabeth, only surviving child of Edward IV., was set aside by the next male, her uncle, Richard III., and subsequently by Henry VII., who, though he was glad to repair his own illegitimate title by an union with her, never acknowledged her separate rights, and affected to transmit the crown to their son, Henry VIII., as the heir of the *Lancastrian* branch, though his real right was as the descendant, through three females and two males, of Lionel of *Clarence*.

Fortunately for England, there existed at the death of Edward VI. no one who could advance any claim to the Crown to the exclusion of heirs female; and in the person of Mary was the first time brought into *practice* a principle which was coeval with the monarchy. The disturbances which she and her sister successively met with, arose from questions not of her *sex*, but of her *legitimacy*; for they were advanced by persons pretending to be *heirs female*, like themselves, and were easily put down. How it might have been if there had been a male competitor may be doubted, though it is probable that the severe lessons inflicted on the nation by the War of the Roses would have taught them to acquiesce in the legitimate line of succession; and that first step being made in the case of Mary, the vigour, glory, and duration of Elizabeth's reign may be said to have fixed and consecrated the ancient theory of the Constitution.—*Quarterly Review.*

TEST OF HISTORIC TRUTH.

Without attempting to press the reader into the meshes of minute historic investigation, we ask him to accept the following as a useful hint of ready practical application:—

An acute critic in the *Quarterly Review*, writing of the constitutional history of the Anglo-Saxons, maintains that so beset is the subject with enigmas, that no labour or sagacity can entirely unravel them. We can only proceed by the comparison of probabilities; an approximation to the truth is all that can be effected or desired, and the fitness of the hypothesis must be judged, not only from its application to the particular page or chapter, but from its conformity to the entire system. The right exposition of the Anglo-Saxon laws may become an object of interest, not merely to the antiquary or the historian, but to the practical lawyer. Many questions of vital importance in our present form of government can only be decided by reference to laws or usages which have prevailed since the time "whereof the memory of man runneth not to the contrary." The rights of the electors of a borough may depend upon the exposition of the most obsolete passages in the laws of King Canute. Such cases have occurred. Should they be mooted again, the truth of the most ingenious theory by which the zealous, learned, and laborious advocate attempts to deduce universal suffrage from the Anglo-Saxon or Anglo-Norman free-pledge, may be put to an easy and certain test by simply inquiring how far this political equality was possible, according to the general frame of the Anglo-Saxon or Anglo-Norman commonwealth. *When any historical theory does not agree with the general structure of the Constitution, we may safely pronounce it to be unfounded.* We may discover the error in the same manner that Linnæus detected the ingenuity of his students, who produced to him a shrub composed of different plants so nicely adapted together, that the eye failed to discern the junction of the parts. But the factitious origin of the compound was immediately perceptible to the mind which saw that the functions, united by art, could never have been co-existent in living nature.

DECAY OF LOCAL TRADITION.

It has been frequently remarked that the general decay of local tradition, or the difficulty of obtaining particulars of events, or the sites of the most remarkable passages of history, is, year by year, becoming more evident. The great destroyer of tradition is, no doubt, the engine which also embalms it and records its value—the destroyer, because it is the renovator of so much else—the printing press. The narrator is silent before the writer and the reader, as the rhapsodist gave way to the scribe of antiquity. Yet, still we might expect that in the vicinity of great transactions among a rude and ignorant peasantry we should find more frequent vestiges of the one memorable action which made their locality famous, and it is astonishing to find how often these are completely obliterated.

Let the traveller in quest of tradition make, for example, a pilgrimage to the several sites of the great actions of our civil wars—let him question the peasantry about Newbury, Naseby, Edgehill, Marston Moor, &c., and we incline to the belief, from the little that has been thus obtained, that there is little more forthcoming or in existence. Yet it is probable that among those living near these spots are the lineal descendants of spectators of these very battles. There are no families in the British islands more ancient than many of those which are to be found among our yeomanry and peasantry. Every now and then some proof comes to light of an antiquity of tenure on the part of such families far exceeding that of the Stanleys or Howards. The Duke of York, for example, ejected from a farm at Chertsey a certain Mr. Wapshott, who claimed lineal and accredited descent from Reginald Wapshott, the armour-bearer of Alfred, who is said to have established Reginald in this very farm. This personage was an example of the tenacity with which tradition might be thus preserved, for his family version of their origin derived them from Wapshott, the warrener, and not the armour-bearer of Alfred.* Again, we have recovered of late a series of instances which show how few individuals not uncommonly intervene between ourselves and the eyewitnesses of remarkable men or actions. The Countess of Desmond is a well-known example, and our contemporaries of *Notes and Queries* have been bringing to light a series of others. King William IV. had spoken to a butcher at Windsor who had conversed with Charles II. What is still more remarkable, a person living in 1786 conversed with a man who knew a man who knew a man that fought at Flodden Field.—*Times journal.*

---

* This tradition is of very questionable worth (See page 91.)

AN ENGLISHMAN'S KNOWLEDGE OF HIS COUNTRY'S HISTORY.

Sir James Stephen, in the examinations for the Indian Civil Service, was astonished to find how badly the candidates generally acquitted themselves in English history. The fact points to a defect in the routine education of our schools. As a general rule, all that a boy knows, when he leaves school, of English history, has been derived from Goldsmith or some other abridgment, aided by the light thrown on particular periods by some historical novels. When, as a young man, he begins to think that really he must obtain some more profound knowledge, he sets down resolutely to Hume and Smollett. Let us suppose him to have "got up" these carefully: we much doubt whether he would have been able to answer more than one or two of Sir James Stephen's questions. But let him have given the same attention to Hallam's two great works, and we will answer for it the professor would not have had to complain of his ignorance. The pernicious influence of Hume on English history was discussed some years ago in the *Quarterly Review*, in an article written, we believe, by Sir Francis Palgrave, a most competent authority. It is to this influence must be referred the remarkable fact that accomplished Englishmen, who have mastered the history of other nations—who know all about the Fronde, and can discourse ably on Guelf and Ghibelin, white and black—who are even somewhat deep in the hardy institutions of Castile and Aragon, have so little real knowledge of the history of their own country. Hume has splendid passages; but he omits almost as much as he tells. Lingard is able, acute, and singularly laborious—in fact, his history is admirable; but then we are rather afraid of him. The subjects for English composition proposed by Sir J. Stephen—the problem in Strafford's case as to penalties of death by retrospective acts of the Legislature, the dialogue in 1674 between Clarendon and Burnet, and the letter of the Jacobite agent in London to his friend in the country on the receipt of the news of the Pretender's arrival at Derby—are excellent; but we think many of Mr. Temple's questions objectionable. For instance, " Compare the character of Shylock with that of Barabbas in Marlow's *Jew of Malta*." We will undertake to say that Mr. Temple himself never commenced his study of the old dramatists until after he had taken his degree. To put such a question to young men fresh from college, was to suppose that they had been substituting a peculiar and remote kind of reading for their proper studies, whether voluntary or prescribed. Again, " Compare the *Utopia* of Sir T. More with the *Nova Atalantis* of Bacon." We should like to how many young men have read the *Utopia*, except by accident. The notice of the book in Sir J. Mackintosh's *Life of More* is sufficiently full to enable a candidate to make some kind of answer to the question; and perhaps an eccentric college tutor, as an out-of-the-way kind of exercise, may have given passages to his pupils, in order that they might convert this Erasmian Latin into pure Ciceronian ; but this sort of second-hand knowledge of the book was, we are certain, never contemplated by Mr. Temple. He probably is as much opposed as his colleagues to "shabby superficiality." We must also object to what may be called the astronomical parts of Milton being offered for the explanation of candidates; and we do not greatly admire the encouragement given to such books as *Elegant Extracts,* by calling on young men "to write out Johnson's celebrated comparison of Dryden and Pope."

HUME'S HISTORY OF ENGLAND.

Though Hume's authority as a text-book is growing weaker and weaker, he has still a classic status on our bookshelves; and his style will probably keep him, as it has kept him hitherto, in tolerable repute. But for a faithful presentment of history, apart from his scepticism and his inveterate antipathy to the popular elements of our progress, he has been in great measure superseded by the lapse of time and by the infinite accretions to our knowledge which time has brought to light. No one refers with confidence to his narrative of our earlier kings since the researches of Hallam and others into our institutions during the Middle Ages. His knowledge of the Tudor sovereigns is equally meagre beside that of Mr. Froude, Mr. Bruce, and various modern contributors. Godwin, Guizot, Forster, Carlyle, Sandford, and others have materially damaged his presentation of Charles I. and of the Commonwealth; and his whole history of the Stuarts is now seen to be an inadequate statement even of the facts, irrespective of its unwarrantable bias, in which it has been counterbalanced by the eloquent exaggerations of Macaulay. In short, not only is Hume the reverse of popular in his aim and predilections, but his narrative, in the presence of our better information, is imperfect as a mere record of the incidents which constitute the History of England.

PERSONAL MOTIVES AND PRETENDED PATRIOTISM.

Could we sometimes discover the motives of those who first head political revolutions, we should find how greatly personal hatreds have actuated them in deeds which have come down to us in the form of patriotism, and how often the revolutionary spirit disguises its private passions by its public conduct. In illustration of this principle, Disraeli takes two very notorious politicians—Wat Tyler and Sir William Walworth. "Wat, when in servitude, had been beaten by his master, a great merchant of wines, and a sheriff of London. His chastisement, working on an evil disposition, appears never to have been forgiven; and when this Radical assumed his short-lived dominion, he had his old master beheaded, and his head carried before him on the point of a spear! So Grafton tells us, to the eternal obloquy of this arch-Jacobin, who 'was a crafty fellow, and an excellent wit, but wanting grace.' I would not sully the glory of the patriotic blow which ended the rebellion with the rebel; yet there are secrets in history! Sir William Walworth, 'the ever-famous mayor of London,' as Stow designates him, has left the immortality of his name to one of our suburbs; but when I discovered in Stow's Survey, that Bankside, which he farmed out to the Dutch *vrows*, and which Wat had pulled down, I am inclined to suspect that private feeling first knocked down the saucy ribald, and then thrust him through and through with his dagger; and that there was as much of personal vengeance as patriotism, which raised his arm to crush the demolisher of so much valuable property!"—*Curiosities of Literature*, p. 550, note.   Edit. 1867.

WHITEWASHING REPUTATIONS.

It was the shrewd remark of Dr. Johnson, that when the world think long about a matter, they generally think right; and this may be one reason why attempts to *whitewash* the received villains or tyrants of history have been commonly attended with but indifferent success. The ugly features of Robespierre's character look positively more repulsive through the varnish of sophistry which M. Louis Blanc has spread over them. The new light thrown by Mr. Carlyle on the domestic and political career of Frederic William of Prussia, the collector of giants, simply exhibits him as the closest approximation to a downright brute or madman that was ever long tolerated as the ruler of a civilized community. Despite of Mr. Froude's indefatigable research, skilful arrangement of materials, and attractive style, Henry VIII. is still the Royal Bluebeard, who spared neither man in his anger nor woman in his lust; and hardly any perceptible change has been effected in the popular impression of Richard III., although since 1621 (the date of Buck's *History*), it has continued an open question whether he was really guilty of more than a small fraction of the crimes imputed to him.

Walpole's *Historic Doubts* are described by Sir Walter Scott as "an acute and curious example how minute antiquarian research may shake our faith in the facts most pointedly averred by general history. It is remarkable also to observe how, in defending a system, which was, probably, at first adopted as a mere literary exercise, Mr. Walpole's doubts acquired in his own eyes the respectability of certainties, in which he could not brook controversy." Yet, no part of this remarkable essay is freshly remembered, except an incidental reference (on which the ingenious author laid little stress) to the apocryphal testimony of the Countess of Desmond, who had danced with Richard in her youth, and declared him to be the handsomest man at court except his brother Edward, confessedly the handsomest man of his day. Mr. Sharon Turner's learned and conscientious recapitulation of the good measures, enlightened views, and kindly actions of Richard, has proved equally inoperative to stem the current of obloquy. Why is all this? why do we thus cling to a judgment which, we are assured, has been ill considered, to the extent of uniformly opposing a deaf ear to motions for a new trial? Is it because the numerical majority of the English public are in the same predicament as the great Duke of Marlborough, who boldly avowed Shakspeare to be the only History of England he ever read? because the ground once occupied by creative genius is thenceforth unapproachable by realities and unassailable by proofs.—(Abridged from the *Edinburgh Review*, No. 234.) The paper has this *naïve* conclusion : " Polydore Vergil speaks of Richard's ' horrible vigilance and celerity.' It was the old story of the sword wearing out the scabbard ; and the chances are that *he would not long have survived Bosworth Field had he come off unscathed the conqueror.*"

———◆———

THE CELTS AND THE IRISH COMPARED.

Dr. Mommsen, in his *History of Rome*, vol. iv., vividly describes the Celtic race in Gaul, with their loose septs, their impressionable nature, their sense of nationality without its power, their superstition, idleness, and vanity, and adds the following comparison :—

" On the eve of parting from this remarkable nation we may be allowed to call attention to the fact that in the accounts of the ancients, as to the Celts on the Loire and Seine, we find almost every one of the characteristic traits which we are accustomed to recognise as marking the Irish. Every feature reappears: the laziness in the culture of the fields; the delight in tippling and brawling ; the ostentation ; the language, full of comparisons and hyperboles, of allusions and quaint terms; the droll humour, the hearty delight in singing and reciting the deeds of past ages, and the most decided talent for rhetoric and poetry ; the curiosity and the extravagant credulity ; the childlike piety which sees in a priest a father and asks for his advice in all things ; the unsurpassed power of national feeling ; and the closeness with which those who are fellow-countrymen cling together, almost like one family, in opposition to the stranger ; the inclination to rise in revolt under the first chance leader, but, at the same time, the utter incapacity to preserve a self-reliant courage, to perceive the right time for waiting and for striking, to attain or even to tolerate any organization, any sort of fixed military or political discipline. It is, and remains, at all times and places the same indolent and poetical, irresolute and fervid, inquisitive, credulous, amiable, clever, but, in a political point of view, thoroughly useless nation."

———◆———

THE CELTIC POPULATION OF BRITAIN.

In the *History of England during the Early and Middle Ages*, Mr. Pearson, in his chapter on " the Saxon Conquest," thus ably confutes a notion which has hitherto been prevalent. The Celtic race in this country, never a dense population, became fused and soon lost sight of, among the hordes that from the fourth century, if not from an earlier date, in ever-increasing numbers, were descending upon the British coasts. " The common belief (says Mr. Pearson) that the Celtic population of Britain was exterminated or driven into Wales or Brittany by the Saxons, has absolutely no foundation in history. It probably originated with the Welsh, who confounded the position of their ancestors, as premier tribe under Vortigern, with the occupation of the island. The mistake is as if we should suppose that the Silures, under Caractacus, were the whole British people. . . . We hear of great slaughters by the Saxons on their bloody battle-fields, but no massacres after the fight, except in the single case of Anderida. . . . We know, by the complaints of Welsh poets, that a race of Romanized Britons, whom they called Loegrians, took part with the invaders against their Celtic kinsmen ; and we cannot suppose that the Saxons would cut the throats of their allies after the war. The object of the races who broke up the Roman Empire was not to settle in a desert, but to live at ease, as an aristocracy of soldiers, drawing rent from a peaceful population of tenants. Moreover, coming in small and narrow skiffs, the conquerors could not bring their families with them, and must in most cases have taken wives from the women of the country. . . . These probabilities are confirmed by facts that meet us on every side. The political division of hundreds belonged to the Germans, in the time of the earliest Frank kings, and probably indicates in England what number of Saxons settled in a conquered district. Now here we find as a rule that the number is always greatest in maritime countries, and smaller as we advance inland and westward. Sixty-six in Kent and seventy-two in Sussex contrast strongly with six in Lancashire, five in Staffordshire, and seven in Leicestershire. . . . Evidently the sea-rovers settled chiefly in the parts which the sea washed, and which they had first fought for and won, leaving the heart of the country to a more gradual process of military colonization by their sons.'

PRÆ-HISTORIC KINGS OF BRITAIN.

Dr. Latham, in a paper read by him to the Royal Society of Literature, has pointed out the remarkable repetition of the same names noticeable in the earliest accounts of English history; and has shown " (1) That many of the early names may be accounted for by the effort so natural in all early nations to invent an *Eponymus* from which the different districts were supposed to have taken their names: thus Debbon was assumed as the ancestor (so to speak) of Devon ; Corindus of Cornwall ; Canute of Kent. (2) That the whole story of these rulers must be considered, not as legend, not as the offspring of mere fancy, but rather as inferential—with some slight book-learning intermixed; when, however, this occurs, it is altogether incorrect. (3) That the early story of Britain repeats itself in that of Prussia. Thus the ancient name of that country is Prothenia, and so we find a Prothenius as its *Eponymus*. In the same way, we find the three sons of Brutus, Locrine, Albanac, and Camber, respectively as the eponymi of Luggris (the Welsh part of England), of Albion, and of Cambria. Besides these, some names occur which cannot be connected with any particular places, such as Madan, Membricius, and Maguild. These last are possibly of German origin, alliteration being common in the German genealogies. Again, such names as Ebroin and Brunehild are clearly historical, and refer, the latter to a Queen of the Franks in the fifth century, and contemporary with King Arthur (see Gregory of Tours), the former, to a well-known Chamberlain. Then, we find a set of names (such as Reval, Dunwa', Cassival) who agree in the termination *val* which is common to all of them ; of these Cassival, probably, has some connexion with the well-known Cassivelaunus. In the same way, it is possible that Gorboduc and Vigent may be modifications of Caractacus and Fulgentius. Generally, much of this legendary story must be looked upon rather as a misrepresentation of real history—a portion, in fact, of true history repeated and distorted, with an entire absence of any poetry or imagination. In all, we probably have before us a reflexion of the way in which the true history struck different hearers with reference, in some instances, to the conflict between the British and Saxon Church, and a representation of speculations which would be not unnatural to the period and to the disciples of St. Columbanus."

THE BRITONS IN THE TIME OF CÆSAR.

Mr. Craufurd, F.R.S., has written an able critical dissertation on "Cæsar's Account of Britain and its Inhabitants in reference to Ethnology." The facts stated and opinions put forward by the Roman General are minutely examined by the light of the knowledge since acquired, and the accounts of barbarous countries visited for the first time in our own day. "The conclusion," said Mr. Craufurd, "to which we must, I think, come from the perusal of Cæsar's account of such of the Britons as he saw is, that although they were certainly barbarians, they were very far from being savages. They were in possession of nearly all the domestic animals known to the Greeks, Romans, and Egyptians. They possessed the art of making malleable iron, and they mixed and melted, and exported tin. They had a fixed money, although a very rude one. In war they had an infantry, a cavalry, and chariots. There can be no doubt that they possessed the art of manufacturing pottery ; and I think it most probable that they had the art of weaving the wool into a coarse fabric, and perhaps of dyeing this fabric with woad. We may, then, safely pronounce our forefathers to have been a more advanced people than were the Mexicans and Peruvians when first seen by Europeans, 1600 years after the time of Cæsar. They encountered the first invader of their country with far more courage and even military prowess than did the Mexicans the Spaniards, or than did even the Hindoos the Greeks and Macedonians of Alexander ; but these last results were more an affair of race than of civilization. Such were the Britons whom Cæsar saw, and assuredly he saw no savages."

CANNIBALISM IN EUROPE.

Mr. Craufurd states that the only European nation against whom a charge of cannibalism has been brought are the Caledonians, and more especially the ancient Scots, the accusation being made by Jerome. Mr. Craufurd, however, seems to have overlooked what is said by Diodorus Siculus and by Strabo. The former says (Book v. c. 32), speaking of the Gauls,—" But the most savage being those dwelling under the north and those who border on Scythia. They say that some eat men, as also of the Britons, those that inhabit Iris as it is called."

Strabo says (Book iv. sec. 4),—" Now, there are also other islands about Britain, small ones, but one large one, Ierne, extended along it towards the north, long, but having greater width. About which we have nothing to say positively, except that the inhabitants are more savage than the Britons, being both man-eaters and much-eaters, and thinking it right to devour their fathers when they have died, and openly to do acts of incest. And this, however, we say thus, as not having (for it) faithworthy witnesses. Yet as to the man-eating, it is said to be also a Scythian practice, and in the necessities of sieges, the Celti too, and the Iberes, and others besides, are said to have done this. But about Thule the account is still more indistinct, because of the remoteness, for they place it the northernmost of the lands that have names."

THE TWO ARTHURS AND THE ROUND TABLE.

The semi-mythical British chieftain, who defeated the heathen Saxons in twelve pitched battles, and the supposed discovery of whose bones at Glastonbury in the time of Henry the Second, is recorded by Giraldus Cambrensis, is quite another being from the son of Uther Pendragon, who instituted the famous Round Table, and whose knights went in adventurous quest of the Holy Grayl. What though the good bishop of St. Asaph, Geoffrey of Monmouth, was denounced as an impudent liar by his contemporary William of Newburgh, whose notions of history were more sober and prosaic? He has created for us Arthur as we know him now, excepting those finer and higher touches of character that are due to the creative power of Tennyson. Arthur is the most mythical of all those who are known as " The Nine Worthies." Whether Arthur was or was not a real personage, matters not the least to the readers of Sir Thomas Malory's romance, *Morte d'Arthur*, originally printed by Caxton, and prepared for reprinting in the edition of 1817, by William Upcott, who supplied in one place seventeen pages, without any hint to that effect. For fifty years the interpolations have passed as genuine among learned critics, who have quoted from them passages wholly spurious as Caxton's genuine text. Mr. Upcott's has been traced to the first edition by Wynkyn de Worde, from which it was ingeniously adapted, not without certain alterations that disguised the interpolation, and made it appear uniform with the rest. There is, however, a peculiar charm about Malory's romance which endears it to us and gives it a real value. He does not describe to us our most remote ancestors, the Britons (whom their Saxon conquerors did *not*, after all, wholly exterminate from that portion of the country in which they themselves settled), but he presents us with life-like pictures of our Norman forefathers, the chivalrous knights and stately dames of England, from the time of Henry the Second downwards. The whole compilation, though from numerous sources, is instinct with the spirit of chivalry, and the same adventurous daring that impelled the Knights of the Round Table to set off in quest of the Sangreal, actually possessed the living knights who went a-crusading in very earnest, and who considered no duty more binding than the redemption of the Holy Land from the infidels. There is Sir Gawayne, whose sad death Malory passes over much too slightly, but who was so tenderly lamented by King Arthur, in the beautiful words of the old alliterative romance—

> Dear cousin by kind, in care am I left,
> For now my worship is went, and my war ended ;
> Here is the hope of my health, my happing of arms !
> My heart and my heartiness, whole in him lingered,
> My counsel, my comfort, that keepèd my heart ;
> Of all knights the king that under Christ lived !

There are Merlin the Magician, King Mark the treasonable, Sir Tristram and La Beale Isoud, Sir Galahad " without fear and without reproach," Sir Bors, Sir Perceval, Sir Ector, Sir Bedevere, and a host of other familiar names ; and at last the drama draws to its dark, sad close, where the names meet us of Sir Mordred, whom Layamon calls wickedest of kings, and of her whom the same old poet describes as

> Wenhaver the queen, most miserable of women !

And it is to Layamon that we owe the first description of Arthur's departure to the Isle of Avilion : " There approached from the sea a short boat, floating with the waves ; and two women therein, wondrously formed ; and they took Arthur anon, and bare him quickly to the boat, and laid him softly down, and forth they gan depart. Then was it accomplished that Merlin whilom said, that mickle care should be of Arthur's departure. The Britons believe that he is yet alive, and dwelleth in Avalun with the fairest of all elves ; and the Britons ever yet expect when Arthur shall return."—(Abridged from the *Athenæum*.)

The true history of King Arthur has been overlaid with so many absurd fictions by the monkish chroniclers and mediæval poets and romancers, that many have erroneously regarded him as altogether a mythical personage.

The *Round Table* is described as of marble, and modelled after one established by Joseph of Arimathea, in imitation of that which Jesus had used at the Last Supper. The existing representative Round Table is, however, of wood, and is preserved at Winchester, and hangs upon the interior eastern wall of the County Hall. The decorations of the table indicate a date not later nor much earlier than the reign of

Henry VIII., and the figure of Arthur has been repainted within the time of living memory.

Mr. Buckle gives the following version of this semi-mythic history: In the Middle Ages different accounts had been circulated of this celebrated king, when Geoffrey of Monmouth, in his *History of the Britons*, ascertained that after the capture of Troy Ascanius fled from the city, and begat a son, who became father to Brutus. In those days England was peopled by giants, all of whom were slain by Brutus, who, having extirpated the entire race, built London, settled the affairs of the country, and called it after himself by the name of Britain. Geoffrey then relates the actions of a long line of kings who succeeded Brutus, and that during the government of Rivallo it rained blood for three consecutive days; and when Morvidus was on the throne the coasts were infested by a horrid sea-monster, which, having devoured innumerable persons, at length swallowed the king himself.

Geoffrey and his friend, Walter of Oxford, then state that King Arthur owed his existence to a magical contrivance of Merlin, the celebrated wizard. The subsequent actions of Arthur did not belie his supernatural origin. His might nothing was able to withstand. He slew an immense number of Saxons; he overran Norway, invaded Gaul, fixed his court at Paris, and made preparations to effect the conquest of all Europe. He engaged two giants in single combat, and killed them both. One of these giants, who inhabited the Mount of St. Michael, was the terror of the whole country, and destroyed all the soldiers sent against him, except those he took prisoners in order to eat them while they were yet alive. But he fell a victim to the prowess of Arthur; as also did another giant, named Ritho, who was, if possible, still more formidable. For Ritho, not content with warring on men of the meaner sort, actually clothed himself in furs, which were entirely made of the beards of the kings he had killed.

The work which contains these statements, which, under the name of history, was laid before the world in the twelfth century, was considered so important a contribution to the national literature, that its principal author was raised to the bishopric of Asaph. Within a century from its first publication it was generally adopted by writers on English history; and for several centuries only one or two persons ventured to speak against its veracity. Polydore Vergil, early in the 16th century, repudiated this strange work, for which he was considered almost as a man deprived of reason; and in the next century Boyle classed together "the fabulous labours of Hercules and exploits of Arthur of Britain." The industrious Sharon Turner has collected a great deal of evidence respecting Arthur, "of whose existence," says Mr. Buckle, "he, of course, entertains no doubt. Indeed, at p. 292 (*Hist. England*, vol. i.) he gives an account of the discovery, in the twelfth century, of Arthur's body!"—(Selected and abridged from Buckle's *History of Civilization in England*, pp. 294-298.)

ALFRED'S TIME-CANDLES.

In the *Life of Alfred*, by Asser, we read that before the invention of clocks, Alfred caused six tapers to be made for his daily use; each taper containing twelve pennyweights of wax, was twelve inches long, and of proportionate breadth. The whole length was divided into twelve parts or inches, of which three would burn for one hour, so that each taper would be consumed in four hours; and the six tapers being lighted one after the other, lasted for twenty-four hours. But the wind blowing through the windows and doors and the chinks of the walls of the chapel, or through the cloth of his tent in which they were burning, wasted these tapers, and, consequently, they burnt with no regularity. He therefore designed a lantern made of ox or cow horn, cut into thin plates, in which he inclosed the tapers, and thus protecting them from the wind, the period of their burning became a matter of certainty.

This is an amusing and oft-quoted story; but, like many other old stories, it lacks authenticity. The work of Asser, there is reason to believe, is not genuine. (See the arguments in Wright's *Biog. Brit. Lit.*, vol. i. pp. 408-412.) It moreover appears that some of the institutions popularly ascribed to Alfred existed before his time.—(Kemble's *Saxons in England.*)

Alfred's acquirements have been variously estimated. His zeal for learning was great, but the results unsatisfactory. Mr. Pearson, in his *History of the Early and Middle Ages*, represents Alfred as "probably unable to read or write to his last days, though he repeatedly put himself under masters, and perhaps got so far as to attach a certain sense to the words in the little book of prayers which he carried about him;" yet, in the next page, this historian represents Alfred to have attained great proficiency. "Above all," he says, "Alfred served in the great army of learning himself as a translator. His translations do not pretend to servile accuracy: sometimes he expands to explain a difficulty, or inserts a fuller account from his own knowledge or from the report of travellers at his court; more often he epitomises, as if he were giving the pith of a paragraph that had just been read out to him." It is added that "the historical and ethical character of the king's mind is apparent in his choice of authors. A translation of Gregory's *Pastoral Care* was executed by the king in partnership with his bishops."

BURIAL-PLACE OF HAROLD.

Concerning the much vexed question of the burial-place of Harold, there exists among the authorities of the time a good deal of uncertainty and contradiction. We find three distinct statements:—

First. Harold escaped from Hastings, and died long after at Chester or elsewhere.

Second. He was buried on the seashore.

Third. He was buried at Waltham.

The first is wretched fable. Florence tells us the true tale in words speaking straight from the heart of England's grief—"Heu, ipsemet occidit crepusculi tempore." The son of Godwin died, as such king and hero should die, helm on head and battle-axe in hand, striking the last blow for his crown and people, with the Holy Rood of Waltham the last cry rising from his lips and ringing in his ears. Disabled by the Norman arrow, cut down by the Norman sword, he died beneath the standard of England, side by side with his brothers in blood and valour. What then was the fate of the lifeless relics which alone came into the power of the Conqueror?

There is, however, strong contemporary, or nearly contemporary, evidence in favour of both the second and third accounts, and Mr. Freeman, in his account of Waltham Abbey (*Trans. Essex Archæolog. Soc.*), makes an ingenious attempt to reconcile them. "The contemporary Norman evidence seems certainly in favour of the belief that Harold was buried on the seashore," to "guard the land and sea," as the Conqueror is reported to have said in mockery. But there is also strong evidence in favour of his burial at Waltham. Even the "Vita Haroldi," which adopts the story of his survival, acknowledges that he was supposed to be buried at Waltham immediately after the battle, and, in order to reconcile these two conflicting statements, conceives that a wrong body was buried there in his stead.

William of Malmesbury is the first writer who speaks of Harold's burial at Waltham. Later annalists narrate details of his burial there, with regal honours, in the presence of many Norman nobles and gentlemen. The supposition that a disinterment took place after Harold had been buried in this county is one which there appears no reason for discrediting, although some are of opinion that the story is merely traditionary, and that it originated in the desire of the monks of Waltham to attract visitors to their shrine.

We quote the above from a paper by the Rev. F. H. Arnold, in the *Sussex Archæological Collections*, vol. 19, to which is appended the following note:—"Sir Francis Palgrave asks the question, 'Was not the tomb at Waltham an empty one?' On the Bayeux tapestry we see Harold falling to the ground, and read the words, '*Hic Harold interfectus est.*' In history his burial succeeds, and then there is usually an account of his living long afterwards. Aelred of Rievaulx hints at Harold's surviving Senlac or Hastings, and Giraldus Cambrensis, in his *Itinerary*, mentions that the Saxons long cherished a belief that their king was alive. According to him, a hermit deeply scarred and blinded in his left eye, long dwelt in a cell near the Abbey of St. John at Chester. He was visited by Henry I., who had a protracted private discourse with him. On his deathbed the King declared that the recluse was Harold. The tradition that he was dragged from among the slain, and carried off alive, is repeated by Bromton and Knyghton. Sir F. Palgrave observes:—"If we compare the different narratives concerning the inhumation of Harold, we shall find the most remarkable discrepancies. The escape of Harold would solve the difficulty; the tale, though romantic, is not incredible, and the circumstances may easily be reconciled with probability. But of ,this story it may be asked, in the words of Fuller, where is the grain of probability to season it? It is well known how fondly a vanquished people will embrace any supposition of escape for a popular and native king:

> View not that corpse mistrustfully,
> Defaced and mangled though it be,
> Nor cherish hope in vain.

After Flodden the idea was long entertained that James IV. survived. So was it with respect to Don Sebastian of Portugal; Frederick, Emperor of Germany, and the Greek Emperor, Baldwin of Flanders; and with such delusions may be classed the supposed escape of Harold."

ENGLAND, FROM THE ROMAN PERIOD TO THE NORMAN INVASION.

From the Descriptive Catalogue of materials prepared by the Deputy Keeper of the Public Records, we learn that the prevalent diseases were gout, fever, plague and yellow plague, king's evil, leprosy, imposthume, and epilepsy, and exceptional cases such as hydrophobia. We learn also what were the various methods of cure, medicine, bleeding, cupping, plasters, fomentations, and ointments; the use of anæsthetics and an operation in lithotomy. St. Erkenwald had a two-wheeled car constructed after he lost the use of his legs, and among other instances of surgical mechanism, we read of a copper foot and a silver hand made to supply the loss of the natural members. In one part we are introduced to St. Hugh, carrying his hod while engaged in building Lincoln Minster; and St. Wilfrid, rearing at Hexham a church with four apses turned to the cardinal points. We are enabled to trace the progress of the architecture from the modest fabric of wicker, and the jealousy towards Irish workmen shown by cutting off the head of a clever carpenter of that nation; we then find the church of stone, still later the introduction of a leaden roof, and lastly the employment of English marbles, cloth of gold and embroidery for altars, and the ornamentation of walls with pictures of saints on parchment; shrines of silver, sculptured plates of gold, dainty MSS. written on purple vellum in letters of the same precious metal by the fair fingers of devout ladies, organs and bells, stained glass, and decorative painting, and quaint models of limbs made in wax as votive offerings.

The great and noble were buried in stone, the humbler dead were laid below the turf in coffins of wood; the northern side of a cemetery was an object of dislike, and economical folks set aside Roman sarcophagi for their own interment. We meet with descriptions of the grotesque carving common in churches, the miracle play acted round the cemetery cross, the importation of marble from Rome for pavements; of Caen stone for Westminster Palace and St. Augustine's, Canterbury, in vessels having only one mast and one sail, and covered with tanned hides, unloading at Bramber. When an Anglo-Saxon noble entertained a bishop, he hung his hall with shields of gold, strewed his courtyard and door-steps with roses and lilies, furnished horns of mead and barrels of wine innumerable, and placed him on the couch with his own hands and cherished his feet in his bosom.

Bells and sea-banks, drainage and brewing, the use of marl to improve land, ordeals, penal punishments, the plays of children, are all incidentally commemorated, while from these unpromising sources we learn two historical facts nowhere else recorded, that many Anglo-Saxon nobles went into exile after the Norman invasion and took service there in preference to servility at home, and that Dunstan collected the few fragments of Anglo-Saxon MSS. which remained after the wholesale destruction of the monastic libraries by the Danes.

DID WILLIAM THE CONQUEROR DEPOPULATE THE NEW FOREST ?

It is very difficult to look at the New Forest without feeling inclined to question the justice of the popular opinion about the devastations laid to the charge of William the Conqueror. An immense proportion of the ground is utterly worthless for any purpose whatever, even in the present day. Large tracts of it are more profitable as woodland than they would be in any other shape, and it is altogether inconceivable that it should ever have been otherwise than a very barren region. The whole population of England is supposed at the time of the Conquest to have been under rather than over 2,000,000, and it is impossible to suppose that when it was so thin elsewhere, it can have been dense in that particular spot. Besides this, it would not appear, from the best authorities upon the subject, that the Norman forests were mere wildernesses. We have a very curious and complete account of their organization in Manwood's work on the *Laws of the Forest*. Some of his authorities claim, truly or not, to be as ancient as the days of Canute. It is impossible not to infer from many parts of the book that the forests anciently supported a considerable population, for there was a complete judicial and executive system for their especial use. The Courts of Swanimote and Justice Seat were attended by those who lived in the forest, much as the Courts Baron and Courts Leet were attended by the men of manors and hundreds. The various rights of agistment, pannage, and the like which are minutely specified, and the obligation under which the rangers were placed of making "drifts"—that is, of driving off all cattle depasturing in the forest—at certain periods of the year, imply the existence of a pretty numerous population, supported principally by cattle-breeding within the forest bounds. Indeed, some considerable part of the soil over which the king held forestal rights was—subject to those rights—the property of private persons. For these reasons, we should be inclined to suppose that the hardship inflicted by William the Conqueror consisted rather in the strictness and harshness of his system of forest administration than in a depopulation which would have been both needless and cruel, not to say impossible.— *Saturday Review.*

The remains of the Conqueror have been most indecorously treated by his posterity, as if in derision of his conventional greatness. His burial, in the Church of St. Stephen, at Caen, with its strange combination of awful, ludicrous, and disgusting incidents, is an often-told tale. The tomb was destroyed by the Huguenots, and the remains of William were as thoroughly scattered to the winds as those of Harold or Waltheof. A single bone was recovered at the Restoration, for which a new tomb was made, and which has again been destroyed and repaired more than once. The present plain slab is, it is believed, merely a cenotaph.

DEATH OF WILLIAM RUFUS.

"King William, notwithstanding forewarned by many signs of some great disaster towards him, would need the day after Lammas, go hunting in the New Forest; yet, something relenting the many passages, he stayed within all the afternoon. About dinner-time, an artificer brought him six cross-bow arrows, very strong and sharp; whereof four he kept himself, and the other two he delivered to Sir Walter Tyrrell, a knight of Normandy, his bow-bearer, saying, "Here, Tyrrell, take you two, for you know how to shoot them to purpose. And so, having at dinner drank more liberally than his custom, as it were in contempt of presages, out he rode unto the New Forest, where Sir Walter Tyrrell shooting at a deer, at a place called Charingham (where since a chapel hath been erected), the arrow glanced against a tree, or, as some write, grazed upon the back of the deer, and flying forward, hit the King upon the breast; with which he instantly fell down dead. Thus it is delivered by common consent of all: only one Sugerus, a writer who lived at that time, and was a familiar acquaintance of Tyrrell's, against the current of all writers, affirms that he hath often heard the said Walter swear that he was not in the forest with the King all that day." "I have been," adds Sir R. Baker, "longer upon this point, because a more pregnant example of God's judgment remains not anywhere upon record. For not only this King, at this time, but before this, a brother of his named Richard, a young prince of great hope, and also a nephew of his, came all in this place to violent deaths; that although King William, the founder of the forest, escaped the punishment in his own person, yet it was doubled and trebled upon him in his issue.

"Thus died King William Rufus, in the forty-third year of his age, and twelfth and some months of his reign. His body was drawn in a collier's cart, with one horse, to the city of Winchester, where the day following it was buried in the cathedral church of St. Swithern, and was laid there in the choir, under a marble stone, till afterwards it was translated, and laid by King Canute's bones."

Baker's description of the King's "Personage and Condition" is as follows: "He was but of mean stature, thick and square-bodied, his belly swelling somewhat round; his face was red, his hair deep yellow, wherefore he was called *Rufus*; his forehead four-square like a window;

his eyes spotted, and not one like another; his speech unpleasant and stammering, especially when he was moved with anger. Concerning the qualities of his mind, they may best be known by looking upon the actions of his life; in which we shall find that he never was more assured than when he was least sure; never less dejected than when in most extremity; being like a cube, that which way soever he fell, he was still upon his bottom. For his delight to pass the time, there was none in more request with him than hunting, a delight hereditary to him; which was the cause that as his father had begun the great New Forest, so he enlarged it to a far greater extent. Other delights of his we find not any, unless we shall reckon his wars for delights, for though they were oftentimes forced upon him, when he could not avoid them, yet sometimes he entered into them when he needed not but for his pleasure. And in general it may be said one of his greatest virtues was that which is one of the greatest virtues—magnanimity; and his worst vice was that which is the worst of vices—irreligion."

In the year 1806, the spot in the new forest where Rufus was killed was visited by Mr. (subsequently Sir Richard) Phillips. Desirous of inquiring after local tradition on the subject, he applied at a cottage about 100 yards distant, and the only dwelling in sight, when, to his astonishment, he found that the family living in it bore the name of Purkis, the same as that of the charcoal-burner, who, in 1100, lived on the same spot, and conveyed the king's body in his cart to Winchester. On further inquiry, he learned that they were the same family, and had, from that time, not only lived on the same site, but to that day, pursued the same occupation of making charcoal, and conveying it by a cart to Southampton and other towns. It appeared, also, that till within two or three years they had preserved a wheel of the cart in which Rufus was conveyed; but the then possessor having quarrelled with the next heir, came home one evening, much intoxicated, and burnt the wheel.

Pursuing his inquiries, Sir Richard learned that the family still possessed the bridle which was on the king's horse, and which, on the king's fall, and on the flight of Tyrrell and his attendants, fell into Purkis's hands; but as the then master of the dwelling had endeavoured to destroy the bridle, his wife concealed it, and described it as lost. Sir Richard purchased the bridle, which is true Norman, and of the same fashion as the ornamented bridles still in use in the northern provinces of France.

Upon the site of the king's fall in the forest there was set up a memorial stone in the year 1744; but this becoming mutilated, it was cased over with fresh stone, which bears these inscriptions:—

On one side: "Here stood the oak-tree, on which an arrow, shot by sir Walter Tyrrel at a stag, glanced, and struck king William the Second, surnamed Rufus, on the breast: of which he instantly died, on the 2nd day of August, 1100." On the second side are these words : "King William the Second, surnamed Rufus, being slain, as before related, was laid in a cart belonging to one Purkis, and drawn from hence to Winchester, and buried in the cathedral church of that city." On the third side : "That the spot where an event so memorable might not hereafter be forgotten, the enclosed stone was set up by John lord Delaware, who had seen the tree grow in this place." " This stone having been much mutilated, and the inscriptions on each of the three sides defaced, this more durable memorial, with the original inscriptions, was erected in the year 1844." The memorial stone is about six feet high : it may be seen by looking on the top of the present monument : there were bars of iron laid across, through the openings between which can be seen the top of the original stone.

THE KNIGHT TEMPLARS.

The historical treatment of the noble fraternity of the Temple is by no means creditable to its writers. They are reviled by way of record, as they were tortured by their cruel persecutors. The order was instituted about 1117 or 1118, and they were called Templers, says an heraldic manuscript in the British Museum, " for that they were placed in a house adjoining to, or near to, the Temple of Jerusalem, by vow and profession, to bear and wage war against the pagans and infidels, and keep from spoil and profanation the sacred sepulchre of our Lord and Saviour Jesus Christ, attempted by Turks, Saracens, and Argarins, and other barbarous miscreants, pursuing with malice and hostility Christians, and infesting Palestine, or the Holy Land, with cruelty, homicide, and bloodshed." The fraternity was instituted by two crusaders, who were at first joined by seven other persons only; but eventually the brotherhood increased to such a degree, and became so renowned for valour, that the most illustrious nobility in Christendom deemed it an honour to be admitted to their order. Matthew Paris must not, however, be numbered with their friends, for he states that although they at first lived upon alms, and were so poor that *one horse served two of them* (as was apparent from their seal), yet they suddenly waxed so insolent that they disdained other orders, and sorted themselves with noblemen.

Mills observes, in a note to his *History of Chivalry* :—" The Templars find no favour in the eyes of the author of *Ivanhoe* and *Tales of the Crusaders*. He has imbibed all the vulgar prejudices of the order, and when he wants a villain to form the shadow of his scene, he as regularly and unscrupulously resorts to the fraternity of the Temple as other novelists refer to the Church or to Italy for a similar purpose." So much for the tendency of historical romance-writing.

THE WAPSHOTTS OF CHERTSEY.

Near Saint Anne's Hill, in Surrey, is Almners' Barns, which name is supposed to have been derived from the former appropriation of this estate to the *Almoners* of Chertsey Abbey, it having belonged to that foundation. For a long series of years this property was occupied by the Wapshott family, both as tenants to the Abbots of Chertsey and to the Crown. It has indeed been said, but certainly on very questionable grounds, that " they continued to cultivate the same spot of earth from generation to generation, ever since the reign of Alfred, by whom the farm on which they lived was granted to Reginald Wapshott, their ancestor." We believe there to be no authority for this long holding; but that the Wapshotts were actually resident here some centuries ago is traditionally acknowledged; and a document was shown by the solicitor of Sir Joseph Mawbey, to Mr. John Wapshott, of Chertsey, their descendant, who had to give up his farm in 1828, proving their occupation of Almners' Barns upwards of 500 years previously. The common story, often repeated, sets their tenancy at one thousand years. There are in the county some existing instances of ancient holdings. Thus, the Marquis of Winchester and Lord Bolton, the descendants of Hugh Part, still hold manors in Hampshire, which during eight centuries have never been severed from the family, to which also Sir St John Mildmay belongs. The manor of Nunwell is still in the possession of the Oglanders, the first of whom, Richard de Okelander, came over with William I. from Caen, and reduced the Isle of Wight.

CHARACTER OF OUR NORMAN KINGS.

We must not class the Normans amongst barbarians, since they came to us after they had been somewhat civilized and Christianized in France. General report gives them credit for being somewhat more civilized than the Saxons whom they conquered. But if we read the pages of the industrious Lappenberg, we shall not rise from his *History of our Norman Kings* with any great respect for the civilization of the Normans. The gold cup, the suit of armour, the robe of state, they knew how to purloin and appropriate; they set others to build for them; whether we are absolutely indebted to them for anything that really advances the civilization of a country, seems doubtful. Their only art of government was to conquer and subdue, and keep as much power as possible in one single hand. There is a period in the life of nations, when the establishment of this harsh dominion is very serviceable. In this light the Norman Conquest may have been beneficial, tending to unite the people into one strong nation. So far as personal influence was concerned, we were indebted only to such men as Anselm and Lanfranc, Italians by birth, but who may be called Norman bishops. "Anselm," says Lappenberg, "was one of those heroes of love and humility which Christianity has produced in every age." Lanfranc reminds us of his successor in a subsequent century, Cranmer; honest and good in the main, but having something of the wisdom of the serpent. Both Anselm and Lanfranc were amongst the most learned men of their respective ages. For the Norman kings, they seem to have had no virtue but bravery, and an occasional generosity in giving with one hand what they pillaged with the other. Richard I., the most popular of the series, was, as Sismondi tersely says, " a bad son, a bad husband, a bad brother, and a bad king;" but he was the bravest of knights, and his companions in arms loved him with a kind of idolatry. Mr. White does not spare any of them:—" They were sensual, cruel,

and unprincipled to a degree unusual even in those ages of rude manners
and undeveloped conscience. Their personal appearance itself was an
index of the ungovernable passions within. Fat, broad-shouldered, low-
statured, red-haired, loud-voiced, they were frightful to look upon,
even in their calmest moods; but when the Conqueror stormed, no
feeling of ruth or reverence stood in his way. When he was refused
the daughter of the Count of Boulogne, he forced his way into the
chamber of the Countess, seized her by the hair of her head, dragged
her round the room, and stamped on her with his feet; Robert, his son,
was of the same uninviting exterior; William Rufus was little and very
stout [no great harm in that]; Henry II. was gluttonous and de-
bauched; Richard the Lionheart was cruel as the animal that gave him
name; and John was the most debased and contemptible of mankind."*

THE STORY OF FAIR ROSAMOND.

Rosamond, the fayre daughter of Walter, Lord Clifford, concubine
of Henry II., poisoned by Queen Eleanor, as some have thought, died
at Woodstock, in 1177, where King Henry had made for her a home of
wonderful working, so that no man or woman might come to her, but
he that was intrusted by the King, or such as were right secret with him
touching the matter. This " house " was a *Maze*, consisting of vaults
underground, arched and walled with brick and stone.

Miss Strickland, in her *Lives of the Queens of England*, has this interesting note upon the Maze. " As to the labyrinth, or maze at Woodstock, it most likely existed before the time of Rosamond, and remained
after her death, since all pleasances or gardens in the Middle Ages were
contrived with this adjunct. Traces of them exist to this day in the
names of places near royal palaces : witness, Maize-hill, Greenwich, near
the site of the maze or labyrinth of Greenwich Palace; also the Maze
in Southwark, once part of the garden of the Princess Mary Tudor's
palace." We have evidence that Edward III., (between whom and the
death of Rosamond little more than a century intervened), familiarly called
a structure pertaining to Woodstock Palace, " Rosamond's Chamber,"
the locality of which is minutely described in the *Fœdera*, vol. i. p. 269.
In this document he directs William de Montacute " to order various
repairs at his Manor of Woodstock; and that the house *beyond the
gate in the new wall* be built again, and that same chamber called
Rosamond's chamber, be restored as before, and crystal plates, and
marble, and lead to be provided for it." Here is an indisputable proof
that there was a structure called Rosamond's chamber, distinct from
Woodstock Palace, yet belonging to its domain, being a building situated
beyond the park-wall. Edward III. passed the first years of his marriage principally at Woodstock, therefore he well knew the localities,
which will agree with the old chroniclers, if we suppose Rosamond's
residence was approached by a tunnel under the park-wall.

---

* *Eighteen Christian Centuries.*

It was commonly said that "the Queen came to Rosamond by a clue of threidde or silke, and so dealt with her that she lived not long after." It is observable, however, that none of the old writers attribute Rosamond's death to poison (Stow merely mentions it as a slight conjecture) ; they only give us to understand that the queen treated her harshly; with furious menaces and sharp expostulations, we may suppose, but used neither dagger nor bowl. Brompton says, "she lived with Henry a long time after he had imprisoned Eleanor;" and Carte, in his *History of England*, vol. i. p. 659, goes far to prove that Rosamond was not poisoned by the queen (which popular legend was based on no other authority than an old ballad) ; but, that through grief at the defection of her royal admirer, she retired from the world, and became a nun at Godstow, where she lived twenty years.

How the queen gained admittance into Rosamond's bower is differently related. Holinshed speaks of it as the common report of the people, that "the queene found hir out by a silken thridde, which the kinge had drawne after him out of hir chamber with his foote, and dealt with her in such sharpe and cruell wise that she lived not long after. Brompton says, that one day Queen Eleanor saw the king walking in the pleasance of Woodstock, with the end of a ball of floss silk attached to his spur; coming near him unperceived, she took up the ball, and the king walking on, the silk unwound, and thus the queen traced him to a thicket in the labyrinth or maze of the park, where he disappeared. She kept the matter a secret, often revolving in her own mind in what company he could meet with balls of silk. Soon after the king left Woodstock for a distant journey; then Queen Eleanor, bearing her discovery in mind, searched the thicket in the park, and discovered a low door cunningly concealed; this door she forced, and found it was the entrance to a winding subterranean path, which led out at a distance to a sylvan lodge in the most retired part of the adjacent forest."

Speed, on the other hand, tells us that the jealous queen found Rosamond out by "a clewe of silke" fallen from her lap, as she sat taking air, and suddenly fleeing from the sight of the searcher, the end of the clewe still unwinding, remained behind, which the Queen followed till she found what she sought, and upon Rosamond so vented her spleen that she did not live long after. Another story, in a popular ballad, is that the clue was gained by surprise from the knight who was left to guard the bower.

Rosamond was buried at Godstow, "in a house of nunnes, beside Oxford," with these verses upon her tombe :—

> Hic jacet in tumba, Rosa mundi, non Rosa munda ;
> Non redolet, sed olet, quæ redolere solet.

Stow's Annals, ed. 1631, p. 154.

> This tomb doth here enclose the world's most beauteous rose,
> Rose passing sweet erewhile—now nought but odour vile.

Speed.

Her body was buried in the middle of the choir in the chapel of the nunnery, at Godstow, in which place it remained until the year 1191, when Hugh, Bishop of Lincoln, caused it to be removed.

Stow thus relates the circumstances. "When Hugh, Bishop of Lin-colne, had entered the church to pray, he saw a tombe in the middle of the quire, covered with a pall of silke, and set about with lights of waxe; and demanding whose tombe it was, he was answered, that it was the tombe of Rosamond, that was some time lemman to Henry II. . . . who for the love of her had done much good to that church. Then, quoth the bishop, take out of this place the harlot, and bury her without the church, lest Christian religion should grow in contempt, to the end that, through example of her, other women being made afraid, may beware and keepe themselves from unlawful and adventurous company with men."

The body was then buried in the chapter-house, or in the cloisters (historians differ on this point), and though after her removal there were not the same ornaments about her as before, yet the nuns inclosed the bones in a perfumed leather bag, which they afterwards inclosed in a leaden coffin, over which a tomb different from the former was laid, being a fair large stone, I suppose in form of a coffin, agreeable to those times; on which was put this inscription, Tumba Rosamundæ; thus it continued till about the time of the Dissolution, when it was taken up and broken to pieces. The remains of the tomb are still to be seen in the old ruined chapel of the nunnery, of which a view is given in Grose's *Antiquities*. Thus wrote Dugdale, in his *Monasticon*.

In the *French Chronicle of London*[*] we find, however, another legend of Rosamond's death. The Queen had her taken, and stripped all naked, and made her sit between two great fires, in a chamber quite closed, so that this very beauteous damsel was quite terrified, for she thought for certain she should be burnt, and began to be in great sorrow by reason thereof.

"And in the meantime the Queen had caused a bath to be prepared, and then made the beauteous damsel enter therein; and forthwith she made a wicked old hag beat this beauteous damsel upon both her arms with a staff; and then, so soon as ever the blood gushed forth, there came another execrable sorceress, and brought two frightful toads upon a trowel, and put them upon the breasts of the gentle damsel; whereupon they immediately seized her breasts and began to suck. Two other old hags held her arms stretched out, so that the beauteous damsel might not be able to sink down into the water until all the blood that was in her body had run out. And all the time that the filthy toads were sucking her breasts, the Queen laughed, and mocked her, and had great joy in her heart in being thus revenged upon Rosamund. And when she was dead, the queen had the body taken and buried in a filthy ditch, and with the body the toads.

"But when the King heard how the Queen had acted towards the damsel he so greatly loved, he made great lamentation: 'Alas! for my grief; what shall I do for the most beauteous Rosamond? For never was her peer found for beauty, disposition, and courtliness.' The King

---

[*] Translation, by Riley, 1863.

H

desired to know what had become of the body; he caused one of the wicked sorceresses to be seized, and had her put into great straights, that she might tell him all the truth as to what they had done with the gentle damsel; and he swore by Almighty God that if she should lie in any word she should have as shocking a sentence as man could devise.

"Then the old hag told the King all the truth, and where the body could be found. And in the meantime, the queen had the body of the most beauteous damsel taken up, and commanded the body to be carried to a house of religion which has 'Godestowe' for name, near Oxenforde, at a distance of two leagues therefrom; and had the body of Rosamonde there buried, to colour her evil deeds, so that no one might perceive the horrid and too shameful deeds which the Queen had done, and she might exculpate herself from the death of this most gentle damsel.

"And then King Henry began to ride towards Wodestocke, where Rosamonde, whom he loved so much at heart, was so treacherously murdered by the Queen. And, as the King was riding towards Wodestocke, he met the dead body of Rosamonde, strongly enclosed within a chest, that was well and strongly bound with iron. And the King forthwith demanded whose corpse it was. Then they made answer to him, that it was the corpse of the most beauteous Rosamond. And when King Henry heard this, he instantly ordered them to open the chest, that he might behold the body that had been so vilely martyred. Immediately thereupon, they did the King's command, and showed him the corpse of Rosamond, who was so hideously put to death. And when King Henry saw the whole truth thereof, through great grief, he fell fainting to the ground, and lay there in a swoon for a long time before any one could have converse with him.

"And when the King awoke from his swoon, he spoke, and he swore a great oath, that he would take full vengeance for the most horrid felony which, for great spite, had upon the gentle damsel been committed. Then began the King to lament and to give way to great sorrow for the most beauteous Rosamond, whom he loved so much at heart. 'Alas! for my grief,' said he. 'Sweet Rosamond, never was thy peer, never so sweet, nor so beauteous a creature to be found; may then the sweet God, who abides in Trinity, on the soul of sweet Rosamond have mercy, and may He pardon her all her misdeeds; very God Almighty, Thou who art the end and the beginning, suffer not now that this soul shall in horrible torment come to perish, and grant unto her true remission for all her sins, for Thy great mercy's sake.'

"And when he had thus prayed, he commanded them forthwith to ride straight on to Godestowe, with the body of the lady, and there had her burial celebrated in that religious home of nuns; and there did he appoint thirteen chaplains to sing for the soul of the said Rosamonde, so long as the world shall last. In this religious house of Godestowe, I tell you for truth, lieth the fair Rosamonde burried. May very God Almighty of her soul have mercy. Amen."

In the old ballad the death of Rosamond is attributed to the Queen:

But nothing could this furious queen
    Therewith appeased bee ;
The cup of deadlye poyson stronge,
    As she knelt on her knee,

She gave this comelye dame to drinke ;
    Who took it in her hand,
And from her bended knee arose
    And on her feet did stand.

And casting up her eyes to heaven,
    She did for mercye calle ;
And drinking up the poyson stronge,
    Her life she lost withalle.

And when that death through every limbe
    Had showde its greatest spite,
Her chiefest foes did plaine confesse
    She was a glorious wight.

Her body then they did entomb,
    When life was fled away,
At Godstowe, neare to Oxford towne,
    As may be seen this day.

Of the nunnery at Godstow only a small chapel with a portion of the outward walls remain.

STORY OF THE LION KING.

Richard I., the most barbarous of our princes, was known to his contemporaries as *The Lion ;* an appellation conferred upon him on account of his fearlessness, and the ferocity of his temper. Hence it was said that he had the heart of a lion ; and the title *Cœur de Lion* not only became indissolubly connected with his name, but actually gave rise to a story, repeated by innumerable writers, according to which he slew a lion in single combat. The name gave rise to the story ; the story confirmed the name ; and another fiction was added to that long series of falsehoods of which history mainly consisted during the Middle Ages. The chronicler of Richard's crusade says that he was called Lion on account of his never pardoning an offence. Some of the Egyptian kings received the name of Lion " from their heroic exploits." I should not be surprised if the story of Alexander and the Lion (*Thirlwall's History of Greece*, vol. i. p. 305) were equally fabulous.

Richard's reign is remarkable also for the absence of other superior men. Short as it was, it did not witness the declining glories of the statesmen of Henry, nor form a school of training for those who were to resist King John. The former were spent and worn out in the very beginning of it. Of the latter it would be difficult, says Mr. Stubbs, (in the *Chronicles and Memorials,* edited from a MS. in the library of Corpus Christi, Cambridge) to mention any, except William Marshall, who occupy even a secondary place of interest in the reign of Richard. It has its warriors and politicians all to itself, and the roll of the latter is not a long one. Hubert Walter, William Longchamp, Walter of

Coutances, Geoffrey of Fitzpeter, and William Marshall were about all. In the class of warriors the king himself throws all others into the second rank. Few of his companions were native Englishmen, or even Anglicized Normans. The chief field of their exploits was too remote, and the time of their adventure too short for them to produce any effect on the national character, and that produced by the character of Richard himself was neither immediate nor direct. The siege of Acre used up the brave men that his father had left him, and his French wars those whom he had himself formed in the triumphs and troubles of the Holy Land. He was the creation and impersonation of his own age ; and that, though full of character and adventure, was short and transitory in its very essence.

Still, the interest of Richard's reign does not consist exclusively of the mere details of adventure or character. The reader who will follow him will be brought into contact with a variety of men and complications of polities unequalled in interest by those of many longer and more important reigns. The crusade brings east and west together. The family connexions of the king involve him in the conflicting interests of Italy, France, Germany, and Spain. His personal adventures open up the whole political history of the age. The dominions in which he exercised real or nominal sway were more diversified in character and circumstances than those of any prince of his time; from Scotland to Cyprus, and from Normandy to Palestine. In his continental dominions, confronted by an unwearied enemy in Philip of France ; in Sicily involved in quarrels with both the Norman Tancred and the German Henry; in Cyprus, not only startling the fitful lethargy of the Eastern Empire, which almost thought that the yellow-haired King of the West was coming, before whom the golden gate of Constantinople was to open of its own accord, but affording a ground of accusation to enemies who might be thought far enough removed from the interest of the Comneni ; drawing on himself envy in Palestine by his superior prowess, or by his utter want of tact alienating the good-will of every Prince of East or West with whom he had to do ; with no policy abroad any more than at home, and his foreign relations as anomalous and unquiet as his domestic ones ; such opportunities and hazards surrounded him with an energetic circle of notables who were either his friends or foes, but mostly his foes. And with all this, besides the undoubted influence which his personal character gave him in his own dominions, he had power to place one of his nephews on the throne of Godfrey of Bouillon, and another on the throne of Charles the Great.

Great interest has been concentrated on Richard from these divers points of view. We know what Englishman, Norman, Frenchman, German, Greek, and Mussulman thought about him; and it is no wonder, considering the number of princes whom he either outshone by his exploits, or offended by his pride, or injured by active aggression, or who, having injured him, hated him with the pertinacity of injustice, that his character has fared badly in the hands of foreign chroniclers.

The German historians describe Richard as a monster of pride and arrogance; the French as the most perfidious of men. " *Anglicanam itaque perfidiam detestantes,"* says Otto of St. Blaise, a partisan of the Emperor and Duke Leopold, after the surrender of Acre, on the insult offered to the Duke's flag. And Ansbert, though with more moderation, says, *"dominium sibi super omnes usurpabat. . . . Rex Angliæ Ricbardus, qui gloria omnes anteire conavit, et omnium indignationem meruit."* But the Germans have envenomed their calumny with a hatred that is absent altogether from the French historians, and, what is more to the point, they look upon him as an Englishman, and involve his country in his condemnation.—Abridged from *The Times.*

THE CRUSADES AND CHIVALRY.

It has been well remarked, with respect to the historic field of the Crusades and Chivalry, that poetry, or mere works of imagination, may have a great effect on the real manners of an age. In chivalry we have an instance how a quite ideal picture of manners may be imitated to some degree, and thus the fictitious history of a past time produce a real history bearing some faint resemblance to it. Sismondi has observed, that the more we look into this matter the more clearly shall we perceive that the system of chivalry is an invention almost entirely poetical. "It is always represented," he shrewdly observes, "as distant from us both in time and place; and whilst the contemporary historian gives us a clear, detailed, and complete account of the vices of the court and the great, of the ferocity or corruption of the nobles, and of the servility of the people, we are astonished to find the poets, after a long lapse of time, adorning the very same ages with the most splendid fictions of grace, virtue, and loyalty." The romance-writers of the twelfth century placed the age of chivalry in the time of Charlemagne. This very age of the twelfth century was pointed to with envy by Francis I. Times nearer our own have thought that chivalry flourished in the persons of Du Guesclin and Bayard. But though, if we examine any of these periods, we shall certainly not find the ideal of chivalry, we shall find in some of them an influence of this ideal on the manners of the age. When our Edward the Black Prince treated his royal prisoner with ostentatious respect and deference, he was probably translating fiction, as well as he could, into reality. Amongst the multitude of powers, lay and spiritual, that are seen in action throughout the Europe of the middle ages, let the poet, too, have his place.

Mr. Kingsley gives us this new view of Chivalry. The ideal of knighthood arose, he says, to supply the defects of the ideal of Monkhood. "It asserted the possibility of consecrating the whole manhood, and not merely a few faculties thereof, to God: and it thus contained the first germ of that Protestantism which conquered at the Reformation."

KING JOHN VINDICATED.

John exacted great sums of money from the Jews, with great cruelty. There was one Jew who would not be ransomed, till the king caused every one of his great teeth to be pulled out by the space of seven days, and then he was content to give the king 10,000 marks of silver, that no more might be pulled out, for he had but one tooth left!—Baker's *Chronicle*.

Mr. Chadwick, who has written a volume in vindication of King John, refutes this charge by quoting a number of charters in which the king forgives to various persons the debts they owe to the Jews. This Mr. Chadwick strangely takes as proving his hero's special kindness to the Hebrew race. He seems at any rate to fancy that John paid the Jews himself. The truth of course is that the Jews and all their goods were the king's property; what they held they held by his sufferance; he could seize their goods when he pleased; a debt, then, owing to a Jew was really a debt owing to the king; the king could therefore forgive such a debt, and the Jew had to go without his money.—*Saturday Review*.

Sir Richard Baker, in giving the "Personage and Condition" of King John, has made him as little disreputable as he well could. He tells us that "he was of stature indifferent tall, and something fat, of a sour and angry countenance. Concerning his conditions, it may be said that his nature and his fortune did not well agree; for naturally he loved his ease, yet his fortune was to be ever in action. He won more of his enemies by surprises than by battles, which shows that he had more of lightning in him than of thunder. He was never so true of his word as when he threatened, because he meant always as cruelly as he spake, not always as graciously; and he that would have known what it was he never meant to perform, must have looked upon his promises. He was neither fit for prosperity nor adversity; for prosperity made him insolent, and adversity dejected; a mean fortune would have suited best with him. He was all that he was by fits: sometimes doing nothing without deliberation, and sometimes doing all upon a sudden; sometimes very religious, and sometimes scarce a Christian. His unsatiableness of money was not so much, as that no man knew what he did with it; gotten with much noise but spent in silence. He was but intemperate in his best temper, but when distempered most of all, as appeared at his last; when, being in a fever, he would needs be eating of raw peaches, and drinking of sweet ale. If we look upon his works, we must needs think him a worthy prince, but, if upon his actions, nothing less; for his works of piety were very many; but, as for his actions, he neither came to the crown by justice, nor held it with honour, nor left it with peace. Yet, having had many good parts in him, and especially having his royal posterity continued to this day, we can do no less but honour his memory."

Such is Baker's character of the monarch. In his defence, it has been urged that "if a sensible writer chose to sit down to show that King John was not the fool or the coward which he is generally described, we think it is very likely that he might in some degree succeed. John became so early an object of traditional dislike that there is every probability that the popular picture of him is an exaggerated one. And there are contradictions about his character as generally drawn; some actions of his life do not at all agree with the notion of his mere folly and cowardice. Some of the popular stories about him come from late and untrustworthy writers, and some of the details of the contemporary writers can be shown to be inaccurate by the evidence of records. Here, then, is really some ground to go upon; it would probably not be very difficult to show that King John was not quite so black as he is painted. But to show this is a very different matter from setting up John as a perfect sovereign, and loading Stephen Langton with every possible epithet of abuse. To upset the Great Charter, to show that its authors were rogues and the Charter itself waste paper, requires a very strong hand indeed.

" In truth it is too late in the day for any man to try to show that the Great Charter was all humbug. Oliver Cromwell spoke irreverently of it only because it stood in the way of some of his own doings. Roger of Wendover certainly calls the leaders of the barons 'principales hujus *pestis* incentores,' a form which Matthew Paris alters to the gentler ' præsumptionis.' But even Roger does not speak disrespectfully of the charter itself."—*Saturday Review.*

ORIGIN OF THE ENGLISH ARISTOCRACY.—MAGNA CHARTA.

Soon after the middle of the eleventh century, and therefore while the Aristocracy was in the process of formation, England was conquered by the Duke of Normandy, who naturally introduced the policy existing in his own country. But in his hands it underwent a modification suitable to the new circumstances in which he was placed. He, being in a foreign country, the general of a successful army, composed partly of mercenaries, was able to dispense with some of those feudal usages which were customary in France. The great Norman lords, thrown as strangers into the midst of a hostile population, were glad to accept estates from the crown on almost any terms that would guarantee their own security. Of this William naturally availed himself. For, by granting baronies on conditions favourable to the crown, he prevented the barons from possessing that power which they exercised in France, and which, but for this, they would have exercised in England. The result was that the most powerful of our nobles became amenable to the law, or, at all events, to the authority of the king. Indeed, to such an extent was this carried, that William, shortly before his death, obliged all the landowners to render their fealty to him; thus entirely neglecting that peculiarity of feudalism, according to which each vassal was separately dependent on his own lord.

But in France the course of affairs was very different. In that country the great nobles held their lands not so much by grant as by prescription. A character of antiquity was thus thrown over their rights; which, when added to the weakness of the crown, enabled them to exercise on their own estates all the functions of independent Sovereigns. Even when they received their first great check, under Philip Augustus, they, in his reign, and indeed, long after, wielded a power quite unknown in England. Thus, to give only two instances: the right of coining money, which has always been regarded as an attribute of sovereignty, was never allowed in England, even to the greatest nobles. But in France it was exercised by many persons, independently of the crown, and was not abrogated until the sixteenth century. A similar remark holds good of what was called the right of private war; by virtue of which the nobles were allowed to attack each other, and disturb the peace of the country with the prosecution of their private feuds. In England, the aristocracy was never strong enough to have this admitted as a right, though they too often exercised it as a practice. But in France it became a part of the established law; it was incorporated into the text-books of feudalism, and it was distinctly recognised by Louis IX. and Philip the Fair, two kings of considerable energy, who did everything in their power to curtail the enormous authority of the nobles.

Out of this difference between the aristocratic power of France and England, there followed many consequences of great importance. In our country, the nobles being too feeble to contend with the crown, were compelled, in self-defence, to ally themselves with the people; an important consequence, which Sir Francis Palgrave omits to notice, in attempting to estimate the results produced by the Norman conquest. About a hundred years after this great event, the Normans and Saxons amalgamated, and both parties united against the king, in order to uphold their common rights.[*] The Magna Charta, which John was forced to yield, contained concessions to the aristocracy; but its most important stipulations were those in favour of "all classes of freemen."[†] Within half a century fresh contests broke out; the barons were again associated with the people, and again there followed the same results,—the extension of popular privileges being each time the condition and the consequence of this singular alliance.

The English aristocracy being thus forced, by their own weakness, to rely on the people, it naturally followed that the people imbibed that tone of independence, and that lofty bearing, of which our civil and political institutions are the consequence, rather than the cause. It is to this, and not to any fanciful superiority of race, that we owe the sturdy and enterprising spirit for which the inhabitants of this island have long been remarkable. It is this which has enabled us to baffle all the arts of

---

[*] Of this amalgamation of races we have three distinct kinds of evidence: 1. Towards the end of the twelfth century, a new language began to be formed by blending Norman with Saxon; and English literature, properly so called, dates from the commencement of the thirteenth century. 2. We have the specific statement of this admixture of races by a writer in the reign of Henry II. 3. Before the thirteenth century had passed away, the difference of dress, which, in that state of society would survive many other differences, was no longer observed, and the distinctive peculiarities of Norman and Saxon attire had disappeared.

[†] "An equal distribution of civil rights to all classes of freemen forms the peculiar beauty of the charter." (*Hallam's Middle Ages*, vol. ii. p. 108.) This is very finely noticed in one of Lord Chatham's great speeches.—*Parliamentary Hist.* vol. xvi. p. 662.

oppression, and to maintain for centuries liberties which no other nation ever possessed. And it is this which has fostered and upheld those great municipal privileges, which, whatever be their faults, have at least the invaluable merit of accustoming freemen to the exercise of power, giving to citizens the management of their own city, and perpetuating the idea of independence by preserving it in a living type, and by enlisting in its support the interest and affections of individual men.— Abridged from Buckle's *Hist. Civilization,* vol. i. pp. 563—567.

WHAT IS ARISTOCRACY ?

Professor Kingsley contrasts strongly Aristocracy with Caste, and taking an enlarged view of aristocracy, he attributes its creation and maintenance to the possession of superior merit rather than to superior wealth. It would be an evil day for this country were the aristocracy destroyed ; and in his *beau ideal* of such an institution it should include every one who is by his deeds noble and meritorious, and should extirpate from its ranks all who are base and ignoble ; though he fears it would be many years before that opinion is generally accepted and acted on. He repudiates the notion of equality, as being contrary to experience and common sense, and at some length shows how, even on the assumption of the unity of the human race—which he is not inclined to dispute— differences would arise which would place some men and some classes of men above others. Thus, for example, the invention of the bow and arrow would give immense advantage to those who first possessed it ; and he considers the invention of riding on horseback to have been of equal importance in its time to the invention of locomotion on railways in modern days. The consequences resulting from it he points out in many ways, showing how the people who rode on horseback had conquered and ruled over nations numerically much more powerful. The invention of breaking-in horses to draw, and the construction of carts with wheels, are also noticed as giving governing power to those who first contrived those appliances ; and in this manner the growth of aristocracies is traced to its elementary principles.

ORIGIN OF THE HOUSE OF COMMONS.

When Simon de Montfort, Earl of Leicester, raised a rebellion against Henry III., he found his own party too weak to make head against the Crown. He therefore applied to the people ; and it is to him that our House of Commons owes its origin ; since he, in 1264, set the first example of issuing writs to cities and boroughs ; thus calling upon citizens and burgesses to take their places in what had hitherto been a Parliament composed entirely of priests and nobles. Some writers suppose that burgesses were summoned before the reign of Henry III., but this assertion is not only unsupported by evidence, but is in itself improbable ;

because, at an earlier period, the citizens, though rapidly increasing in power, were hardly important enough to warrant such a step being taken. The best authorities are now agreed to refer the origin of the House of Commons to the above period. The notion of tracing this to the Wittenagemot is as absurd as finding the origin of Juries in the system of Compurgators, both of which were favourite errors in the 17th and even in the 18th century. In regard to the Wittenagemot, this idea still lingers among antiquaries; but in regard to the Compurgators, even they have abandoned the old ground; and it is now well understood that even Trial by Jury did not exist till long after the Conquest. There are few things in our history so irrational as the admiration expressed by a certain class of writers for the institutions of our barbarous Anglo-Saxon ancestors.—Buckle's *Hist. Civilization*, vol. i. pp. 566-7, *note.*

WHO WAS ROBIN HOOD?

Great and long has been the discussion about Robin Hood,—whether he was a myth or a real personage. There exists in the handwriting of Dr. Stukeley, the antiquary, a very long pedigree of Robin Hood, in which his descent is traced from Raff Raby, Earl of Northumberland, to Waltheof, the great earl of that name, who married Judith, Countess of Huntingdon, the Conqueror's niece, from whom the pedigree states Robert Fitzooth, commonly called Robin Hood, the pretended Earl of Huntingdon, was descended, and that he died in 1274. This pedigree is far more elaborate in its genealogical tracings than that inserted by Mr. Ritson in his edition of the *Robin Hood Ballads*, 1795, vol. i. p. xxi. Latimer, in his sixth sermon before Edward VI., tells a story about wishing to preach at a country church, when he found the door locked, and the people gone abroad to gather for Robin Hood. He then adds: "Under the pretence of gathering for Robin Hood, a *traitor* and a *thief*, to put out a preacher." This may corroborate Mr. Hunter's view of the renowned personage, to be noticed presently.

Ireland, too, is associated with the fame of this renowned wood-ranger. "In the year 1189," writes Holinshed, "there ranged three robbers and outlaws in England, among which 'Robert' Hood and Little John were chieftains, of all thieves doubtless the most courteous. Robert, being betrayed at a nunnery in Scotland called Bricklies, the remnant of the 'crue' was scattered, and every man forced to shift for himself; whereupon Little John was fain *to flee the realm* by sailing into Ireland, where he sojourned for a few days at Dublin. The citizens being 'doone' to understand the wandering outcast to be an excellent archer, requested him heartily to try how far he could shoot at random, who, yielding to their behest, stood on the bridge of Dublin, and shot to a hillock in Oxmantown, thereafter called Little John's shot, leaving behind him a monument, rather by posterity to be wondered than possibly by any man living to be counterscored."—(*Description of Ireland*, fol., p. 24.) The danger, however, of being taken, drove

Little John thence to Scotland, where, adds the annalist, "he died at a town or village called Moravia."

In the *Vision of Piers Ploughman* are two remarkable passages, in which mention is made of "Robberd the Robber," and of "Roberdes knaves." In a note Mr. Wright quotes a statute of Edward III., in which certain malefactors are classed together, one of which is *Roberdesmen*, and he adds two curious instances, in which the name is applied in a similar manner—one from a Latin song of the reign of Henry III. It seems not impossible that we have in these passages a trace of some forgotten mythical personage. "Whitaker," says Mr. Wright, "supposes, without any reason, the 'Roberde's knaves' to be Robin Hood's men. It is singular enough, however, that as early as the time of Henry III., we find the term 'comaro Roberto' applied generally, as designating any common thief or robber; and without asserting that there is any direct allusion to "Robin Hood's men" in the expression "Roberdes knaves," one is tempted to ask whence the hero of Sherwood got his own name? Grimm has suggested that Robin Hood may be connected with an equally famous namesake, Robin Goodfellow; and that he may have been so called from the hood or hoodikin, which is a well-known characteristic of the mischievous doer. We believe, however, it is now generally admitted that "Robin Hood" is a corruption of "Robin o' th' Wood," equivalent to 'silvaticus' or 'wild man,' a term which, as we learn from Ordericus, was generally given to those Saxons who fled to the woods and morasses, and long held them against their Norman enemies. Whether Robin Goodfellow and his German brother, "Knecht Ruprecht," are at all connected with Robin Hood, seems very doubtful. The plants which, both in England and in Germany, are thus named, appear to belong to the elf rather than the outlaw. The wild geranium, called 'Herb Robert' in Gerarde's time, is known in Germany as "Ruprecht's Kraut;" "Poor Robin," "Ragged Robin," and "Robin in the House," probably all commemorate the same "merry wanderer of the night."—R. J. King, *Notes and Queries*, No. 51.

The ballads in honour of the Bold Robin were, for centuries, popular over our isle, the most valuable belonging to Nottinghamshire, Lancashire, Derbyshire, and Yorkshire. They are full of incident and of human character; they reflect the manner and feelings of remote times; they delineate much that the painter has not touched, and the historian forgotten; they express, but without acrimony, a sense of public injury or of private wrong; nay, they sometimes venture into the regions of fancy, and give pictures in the spirit of romance. He, Robin, was no lover of blood: nay, he delighted in sparing those who sought his life when they fell into his power; and he was beyond all example, even of knighthood, tender and thoughtful about women. Next to the ladies he loved the yeomanry of England; he molested no herd at the plough, no thresher in the barn, no shepherd with his flocks; he was the friend and protector of the husbandman and hind, and woe to the priest who fleeced, or the noble who oppressed them. The widow, too, and the fatherless, he looked upon as under his care, and wheresoever he

went some old woman was ready to do him a kindness for a saved son
or a rescued husband. The personal character of Robin Hood stands
high in the pages both of history and poetry. Fordun, a priest, extols
his piety; Maijor pronounced him the most humane of robbers; and
Camden, a more judicious authority, calls him "the gentlest of thieves."
Festivals were once annually held, and sylvan games celebrated in his
honour in Scotland as well as in England. The grave where he lies has
still its pilgrims; the well out of which he drank still retains his name;
and his bow, and some of his broad arrows, were, within this century, to
be seen in Fountains Abbey, a place memorable by his adventure with
the curtal friar. The choice of his grave is thus told in the ballad:—

> "Give me my bent bow in my hand,
>   And a broad arrow I'll let flee;
> And where this arrow is taken up,
>   There shall my grave digg'd be.

> "Lay me a green sod under my head,
>   And another at my feet,
> And lay my bent bow by my side,
>   Which was my music sweet,
> And make my grave of gravel and green,
>   Which is most right and meet.

> "Let me have length and breadth enough,
>   With a green sod under my head,
> That they may say, when I am dead,
>   Here lies bold Robin Hood."

> These words they readily promised him,
>   Which did bold Robin please,
> And there they buried bold Robin Hood,
>   Near to the fair Kirkleys.

Little John, it is said, survived but to see his master buried: his grave
is claimed by Scotland as well as England, but tradition inclines to the
grave in the churchyard of Hathersage.

The fictitious pedigree, and numerous other fanciful conjectures, concerning the origin and family of Robin Hood, are now swept away by
the Rev. Joseph Hunter's discovery of documents in our national
archives, by which he proves Robin Hood to have been a yeoman in the
time of Edward II.; that he fell into the king's power, when he was
freeing his forest from the marauders of that day; that the king, pursuing a more lenient policy towards his refractory subjects, took Robin
Hood into his service, made him one of his *Vaellets, porteurs de la chambre*, in his household; and Mr. Hunter has discovered the exact amount of
wages that was paid him, and other circumstances, establishing the
veritable existence of this hero of our childhood.

A Correspondent of *Notes and Queries*, No. 165, thus briefly sums up
what, he shows, there are good grounds for inferring:

" 1. The name of Robin Hood was no patronymic, but a purely descriptive name. 2. It was the name of the ideal personification of a class—
the outlaws of former times. 3. Robin's fame has extended through-

out England, Scotland, and France; and so far as can at present be seen, it seems to have pertained equally to these three countries. 4. Though men of the name of Robin Hood have existed in England, that of itself would afford no ground for inferring that one of them was the Robin Hood of romantic tradition; but any pretence for such a supposition is taken away by the strong evidence, both Scotch and French, now adduced in support of the opposite view."

Robin Hood appears to have become the general name for a chieftain of archers; for in Stow's account of King Henry VIII. going to Shooter's Hill-wood to fetch may, in the year 1511, when "the King, with Queen Catherine his wife, accompanied by many lords and ladies, rode a-maying from Greenwich to the high ground of Shooter's Hill, where, as they passed by the way, they espyed a company of tall yeomen, clothed all in greene, with greene hoods and with bowes and arrowes, to the number of 200. One being the chieftain, was called Robin Hood, who required the King and all his company to stay and see his men shoot; whereunto the King granting, Robin Hood whistled, and all the 200 archers shot off, loosing all at once; and when he whistled againe, they likewise shot againe; their arrowes whistled by craft of the head, so that the noise was strange and loud, which greatly delighted the King and Queen, and their company." Afterwards, Robin Hood invited them to enter the wood, where, "in arbours made with boughs and deck't with flowers, they were set and served plentifully with venison and wine."

Shooter's Hill, named from its having been a place for the practice of archery from a very early period, became noted for the numerous robberies committed upon it. In the sixth year of Richard an order was issued by the Crown to "cut down the woods on each side the road at Shetor's Held, leading from London to Rochester, which was become very dangerous to travellers, in compliance with the statute of Edward I. for widening roads where there were woods which afforded shelter for thieves." In the reign of Henry VIII. there was a beacon on the summit of the Hill, as appears from several entries in the churchwarden's accounts of Eltham, of sums paid "for watching the beacon on Shuter's Hill." The modern triangular Tower built here is 445 feet above the level of the sea.

THE BATTLE OF SPURS.

This was the name given to the battle of Courtray, July 11, 1302, the first great engagement between the nobles and the burghers, which, with the subsequent battles of Bannockburn, Crecy, and Poitiers, decided the fate of feudalism. In this encounter the knights and gentlemen of France were entirely overthrown by the citizens of a Flemish manufacturing town. The French nobility rushed forward with loose bridles, and fell headlong, one after another, into an enormous ditch, which lay between them and their enemies. The whole army was annihilated, and when the spoils were gathered, there were found 4000 golden spurs to mark the extent of the knightly slaughter, and give a name to the engagement:—

> " I beheld the Flemish weavers, with Namur and Juliers bold,
> Marching homeward from the bloody Battle of the Spurs of Gold."
>
> *Longfellow.*

The name of the Battle of Spurs was also given to an affair at Guinegate, near Calais, August 18, 1513, in which the English troops under Henry VIII. defeated the French forces. The allusion is said to be to the unusual energy of the beaten party in riding off the field.—*Wheeler's Dictionary of the Noted Names of Fiction.*

A highly intelligent young prisoner, Louis d'Orleans, the Duke of Longueville, &c., was taken at the Battle of Spurs, and sent over to the safe keeping of Queen Catherine, who did not care for the custody of a lively French nobleman, and so recommended that he should be disposed of in the Tower. Nevertheless, he contrived to make himself agreeable, if not to Queen Catherine, certainly to the king and to Wolsey, and he was not slow in turning these advantages to the interest of Louis, and in bringing him to a more promising understanding with Henry. It was reported that Anne of Brittany had died January 9, 1514, and though the report was probably premature, it is certain that some correspondence had been going on between his master and Henry by the means of this adroit Duke of Longueville ; and with what object ? Whether for the marriage of Louis with Mary, Tudor princess, and the most beautiful woman of her time, cannot at present be ascertained ; but the result was, at all events, that Prince Charles, a sickly, melancholy boy of 14, was set aside as a worse alternative than a valetudinarian of 52, and Mary was publicly betrothed to Louis ; so that the whole course of her wooing, her love letters, the number of her dresses, her attendants, her reception at Paris, her coronation, and life at the French Court, may be read in the documents appended to Mr. Brewer's *Catalogue* of the Letters and Papers of the Reign of Henry VIII.

THE BATTLE OF THE THIRTY.

This celebrated engagement took place at a spot known as Midway Oak, halfway between the castles of Josselin and Ploermel, in France, March 27, 1351. The French General Beaumanoir, commanding the former post, being enraged by depredations committed by Bemborough, the English general occupying the latter position, challenged him to fight. Upon this, it was agreed that thirty knights of each party should meet and decide the contest. The two chiefs presented themselves at the head of their best soldiers, and the battle began in earnest. At the first onset the English were successful ; but Bemborough having been killed, the French renewed the struggle with redoubled courage, and won the victory. " This," says Wheeler, " was one of the most heroic exploits of the age, and gained such popularity that, more than a hundred years later, when speaking of a hard contest, it was usually said, " There was never such hard fighting since ' the Battle of the Thirty.' "

WHERE WAS THE FIRST PRINCE OF WALES BORN?

The title of Princes of Wales originally distinguished the native Princes of that country; and after the entire conquest of Wales and its union with England, the title was transferred to the heir-apparent of the English crown. Henry III., in the thirty-ninth year of his reign, gave to his son Edward (afterwards Edward I.) the principality of Wales and earldom of Chester, but rather as an office of trust and government than an especial title for the heir-apparent to his crown. When Edward afterwards became King, he conquered, in 1277, Llewelyn and David, the last native Princes of Wales, and united the kingdom of Wales with the crown of England. There is a tradition that Edward, to satisfy the national feelings of the Welsh people, promised to give them a prince without blemish on his honour, a Welshman by birth, and one who could not speak a word of English. In order to fulfil his promise literally, he sent the Queen Eleanor to be confined at Caernarvon Castle; and he invested with the principality her son, Edward of Caernarvon, then an infant, and caused the barons and great men to do him homage. Edward was not at the time the King's eldest son, but on the death of his brother, Alfonso, he became heir-apparent, and from that time the Prince of Wales has ever been the title of the eldest son of the King. The title, however, is not inherited, but conferred by special creation and investiture, and was not always given shortly after the birth of the heir-apparent. Edward's creation of Prince of Wales dates from the year 1301, when he was seventeen years old; his son was ten years old when he was created Prince of Wales.

It is not easy to understand what honour can attach to any spot from its being the birth-place of Edward the Second, one of the few kings of England who were deposed by Parliament for their crimes. But Caernarvon rejoices in the honour of being the birthplace of the first Prince of Wales. It is, however, difficult to understand why the inhabitants of the counties and towns of North Wales should rejoice to speak of the son of the conqueror as "the first Prince of Wales," as if they had wholly forgotten their last Llwyelyn, as if there had never been such a prince as Gruffydd, the head and shield and defender of Britons; the warrior whom it needed all the might of Harold himself to overthrow. Still, Caernarvon claims its *Castle* as the birthplace of the Prince, though this is a strange perversion of the facts of history. When, in April, 1868, the Prince of Wales visited Caernarvon, he was welcomed in the Castle "on this the anniversary of the birth within these walls of the first Prince of Wales," and reference was made to "the period in which the first Prince of Wales was presented to a reluctant population from the gates of this majestic and venerable building." Lastly, "the Prince and Princess of Wales were conducted to the Eagle Tower, the chamber in which, according to tradition, the first Prince of Wales was born." In all these words and deeds there is a flagrant falsification of history. Nothing is more certain than that Edward the Second was not born in the present Caernarvon Castle, least of all in the Eagle Tower which he himself built. And the truth of the matter is per-

fectly well known, and perfectly well known on the spot. The late
Mr. Hartshorne twice, in 1848 and in 1857, lectured to large audiences in the Castle, and explained its history. Mr. Hartshorne's discoveries are not only familiar to all antiquaries, but they are quite
familiar at Caernarvon.

Edward the Second was undoubtedly born at Caernarvon on St.
Mark's Day, 1284; but he was not born in the present castle, which
did not then exist. The only passage of any ancient writer which could
have given ground for such a belief is the expression of Nicholas Trivet:—
"Apud castrum de Karnarvan quod 'nuper Rex Angliæ fortissimum
fecerat, natus est Regi filius, ex nomine patris vocatus Edwardus." But
"castrum" may just as well mean the town as the castle, and anyhow
N. Trivet is wrong in his fact, as the first beginning of fortifications at
Caernarvon at all was made in November 1284, seven months after
Edward's birth. There is no guess-work in the matter. Mr. Hartshorne made out the date of everything from the Public Records. The
first Castle of Caernarvon was begun in November 1284, and was finished
in 1291. The town walls were built in 1296. Edward the Second was
therefore not born either in a castle or in a fortified town. And the
castle which began to be built a few months after his death is not the
castle which is now standing. The first castle was destroyed in Madoc's
revolt in 1295. Edward the First then began again, but the work was
not finished at the time of his death. The work was continued by
Edward the Second. The Eagle Tower, in which tradition says that
he was born, was built by Edward the Second himself, and was finished
in 1317. The gateway of the majestic and venerable building, at which
he was presented to a reluctant population, was also built by himself,
and was finished in 1320, when he had attained the mature age of thirty-
six years. All these are facts, resting on documentary evidence, facts
perfectly well known to every decently-informed person."—*Saturday
Review*, May 2, 1868.

Nor are these all the strange stories of the Castle. It has been
affirmed on authority, that the Castle was built in one year; and that
the Eagle Tower was named from a now shapeless figure of an eagle,
brought, it is alleged, from the ruins of Segontium; but an eagle was
one of Edward's crests. The whole edifice was repaired about twenty
years ago, at a cost of upwards of 3000l. The late Marquis of Angle-
sey was long governor of the fortress. Painful as it may be to contem-
plate the downfall of such a tradition, historic truth is of greater consequence to establish. The "first Prince of Wales" was certainly born
in the town of Caernarvon, and most probably in some building temporarily erected for the accommodation of the royal household.

EDWARD II. AND BERKELEY CASTLE.

When Horace Walpole, in 1774, visited Matson, near Gloucester,
the very mansion where King Charles I. and his two eldest sons lay
during the siege; and there are marks of the lad's hacking with his

hanger on a window,—he went to Gloucester Cathedral, and on seeing the monument of Edward II. a new historic doubt started, which, writes Walpole to Cole, " I pray you to solve. His Majesty has a longish beard; and such were certainly worn at that time. Who is the first historian that tells the story of his being shaven with cold water from a ditch, and weeping to supply warm, as he was carried to Berkeley Castle? Is not this apocryphal?" [The incident is narrated by Rapin.] In the neighbourhood Walpole found in a wretched cottage a child in an ancient oaken cradle, exactly in the form of that lately published from the cradle of Edward II. Walpole purchased it for five shillings, but doubted whether he should have fortitude enough to transport it to Strawberry Hill. He was much disappointed with Berkeley Castle, though very entire: he notes: "the room shown for the murder of Edward II., and the shrieks of an agonising king, I verily believe to be genuine. It is a dismal chamber, almost at the top of the house, quite detached, and to be approached only by a kind of footbridge, and from that descends a large flight of steps, that terminate on strong gates; exactly a situation for a *corps de garde*. In that room they show you a cast of a face, in plaster, and tell you it was taken from Edward's. I was not quite so easy of faith about that; for it is evidently the face of Charles I."

WERE CANNON USED AT CRECY?

This is a *quæstio vexata* of long standing. We find it said that in King Edward's army there were a few of those novel engines, and that the good service which they did, conduced most to his victory. On the other hand, many modern writers leave out all mention of them, not deeming the evidence of the fact strong enough. Not only our old Latin chroniclers, but our English historians also, Holinshed and Speed, are wholly silent upon this subject. Such a statement seems to rest on the one-sided authority of French writers—on Mezerai, Larrey, and others; making it a sort of palliation of this extraordinary defeat of their countrymen. The former says, "then these hitherto unknown and formidable engines induced them to believe that they were combating with devils rather than men."—*Notes and Queries*, No. 264.

The Italian writer, Villani, who died in 1348, states that the English used "bombards, which shot out balls of iron with fire, to terrify and destroy the horses of the French," and of their discharges being accompanied with "so great a shaking and noise that it seemed as if the Deity were thundering, and with a great slaying of men and horses." Mr. Sharon Turner states that Froissart says nothing about the use of cannon at this battle; but in a manuscript of Froissart, preserved in the Library of Amiens, it is distinctly stated that cannon were used by the English at Crecy. The passage referred to is quoted by the Emperor Napoleon I., in his work on Artillery, and runs thus, translated: " And the English caused to fire suddenly certain guns which they had in the battle, to astonish (or confound) the Genoese."—*Notes and Queries*, No. 270

Now Villani is the older writer of the two, for he was nearly fifty years of age when the battle of Crecy was fought, whereas Froissart was but a child of nine. The means of information which Froissart possessed were probably superior to those of Villani; yet, when Villani died, only two years after the battle, the intelligence upon which he built his notice of it must have been fresh.

There is a story of cannon-balls being found in the field of Crecy; but this is not authenticated. Some have even gone so far as to present us with actual drawings of the very guns used on that occasion. Major Mitchell distinctly states that artillery was not used at Crecy, and the only foundation for the mis-statement is a passage in the *Grandes Chroniques de France,* which is the only book on the battle in which the faintest allusion is made to cannon. There it is stated, indeed, that the English "jettèrent trois canons;" and this has been taken to mean that they had artillery. The preceding sentence, however, explains the meaning of the statement in a very different manner. We read that "the English threw so many arrows that they looked like flakes of drifting snow—ils en jettèrent trois canons; they threw three quivers full of them, the word canon being generally used at the period for tube or quiver."

In some public accounts of the reign of Edward III., wherein are specified the names of the persons employed in the manufacture of gunpowder (out of saltpetre and "quick sulphur," without any mention of charcoal), with the quantities supplied to King Edward, just previously to his expedition to France, in June or July, 1346, the records show that a considerable weight had been supplied to the English army subsequently to its landing at La Hogue, and previously to the battle of Crecy; and that before Edward III. engaged in the siege of Calais, he issued an order to the proper officers in England, requiring them to purchase as much saltpetre and sulphur as they could procure.

THE ORDER OF THE GARTER.

It is contended by the best modern authorities that the celebrated Order of the Garter was instituted in 1348, by the chivalrous Edward III. Some years before this date he had gone some way in forming an Order of the Round Table, in commemoration of the legend of King Arthur; and in January, 1344, had caused an actual *Round Table* of two hundred feet diameter to be constructed in Windsor Castle, where the knights were entertained at his expense. Before the above date a turn had been given to the views of the King, leading him to adopt a totally different idea for the basis of the Order. "The popular idea is, that during a festival at Court, a lady happened to drop her garter, which was taken up by King Edward, who, observing a significant smile among the bystanders, exclaimed with some displeasure, 'Honi soit qui mal y pense!'—Shame to him who thinks ill of it! In the spirit of gallantry which belonged no less to the age than his own disposition, conformably with the action of wearing a lady's favour, and perhaps to prevent any further impertinence, the King is said to have placed the garter round his own knee."—Tighe and Davis's *Annals of Windsor.*

It is commonly said that the fair owner of the Garter was the Countess of Salisbury; but this is doubtful, and some consider the whole story fabulous. It is to be remarked that the tale is far from being modern. It is stated by Polydore Vergil as early as the reign of Henry VII.

Although the Order is believed to have been not founded before June 24, 1348, it is certain that the Garter itself was become an object of some note at Court in the autumn of the preceding year, when at a great tournament, held in honour of the King's return from France, "Garters with the motto of the Order embroidered thereon, and robes and other habiliments, as well as banners and couches, ornamented with the same ensign, were issued from the great wardrobe at the charge of the Sovereign."—(Beltz's *Memorials of the Order of the Garter,* 1841.) The royal mind was evidently by this time deeply interested in the Garter. A surcoat furnished in 1348 for a spear-play or hastilude at Canterbury, was covered with Garters. At the same time the youthful Prince of Wales presented twenty-four garters to the Knights of the Society.

EUSTACHE DE ST. PIERRE AND THE BURGESSES OF CALAIS.

With the siege of Calais, and its surrender to Edward III. in 1347, is associated the name of Eustache de Saint Pierre, whose loyalty and disinterestedness have been immortalized by the historian, and commemorated by the artist's pencil. The subject of Queen Philippa's intercession on behalf of Eustache and his brave companions, is familiar: the stern demeanour of the king; the tears and supplicating attitude of the Queen Philippa; and the humiliating position of the burgesses of Calais, &c. But what if Eustache de St. Pierre had been bought over by King Edward? For, without going the length of pronouncing the scene of the worthy citizens, with halters round their necks, to have been a "got up" affair, there is, however, some reason to doubt whether the boasted loyalty of Eustache de St. Pierre was such as was represented. In one of the volumes of the *Documens inédits sur l'Histoire de France* is a statement founded on a memoir by M. de Berquigny, that Eustache de St. Pierre became a pensioner of King Edward, after the taking of Calais, on condition of his maintaining good order, and of his preserving it to England. Even in Froissart there is nothing to prove that Edward designed to put these men (the citizens) to death. On the contrary, he takes notice that the king's refusal of mercy was accompanied with a wink to his attendants, which, if it meant anything, must have meant that he was not acting seriously.—*Lingard,* 3rd edit, 1825, vol. iv. note 85.

Again, in Hume, "the story of the six burgesses of Calais, like all extraordinary stories, is somewhat to be suspected; and so much the more, as Avesbury, who is particular in his narrative of the surrender of Calais, says nothing of it, and on the contrary, extols in general the king's generosity and lenity to the inhabitants."—*Hume*, 8vo, 1807, vol. ii. note H.

Both Hume and Lingard mention that Edward expelled the natives of Calais, and repeopled the place with Englishmen ; but they say nothing as to Eustache de St. Pierre becoming a pensioner of the king's.

Miss Strickland likewise gives the story as related by Froissart, but mentions the fact of Queen Philippa taking possession of Jean d'Arc's property, and the doubt cast upon Eustache's loyalty ; and she would appear to justify him by reason of King Philip's abandoning the brave Calisians to their fate. However this may be, documents exist proving that the inhabitants of Calais were indemnified for their losses ; and, whether or not the family of Eustache de St. Pierre approved his conduct, so much is certain, that, on the death of the latter, the property which had been granted to him by King Edward was confiscated, because they would not acknowledge their allegiance to the English.—*Notes and Queries*, No. 166.

THE PRINCE OF WALES'S FEATHERS.

The origin and history of the badge and mottoes of the Prince of Wales—the ostrich feathers, "Ich Dien," and "Houmout," have exercised the ingenuity of antiquaries and genealogists for the last three centuries. Old Randall Holmes solved the question by roundly asserting that the triple plume was the blazon on the war-banner of the Ancient Britons ; but the only resemblance traceable in ancient British heraldry is stated to be three lions' tails, their tips falling like the graceful bend of the feathers in the Prince's badge.

The earliest known appearance of feathers, worn in this fashion, is on a seal appended to a grant of Prince Edward to his brother, John of Gaunt, dated 1370, *twenty-four years after the battle of Cressy*, where Edward is seen seated on a throne, a Sovereign Prince of Aquitaine, with a *single* feather and a *blank* scroll on each side of him ; and the same badge occurs again upon the seal to another grant, in 1374. The popular tradition ascribes the assumption of the *three* feathers to Edward the Black Prince, who took this crest, arms, or badge from John, King of Bohemia, slain at the battle of Cressy ; but, until recently, this tradition was not traceable to any credible authority. It is first mentioned by Camden (Clarencieux), who, in his *Remains*, says :— " The victorious Black Prince, his (Edward III.'s) sonne, used sometimes one feather, sometimes three, in token, as some say, of his speedy execution in all his services ; as the Posts, in the Roman times, were *Pteropbori*, and wore feathers to signify their flying post-haste." In the *first* edition of the " Remains " Camden states, the *tradition* is that the Prince won them (the feathers) at the battle of Poictiers ; but, in the second edition, Camden states, " the *truth* is, that he wonne them at the battle of Cressy, from John, King of Bohemia, whom he there slew !" The change from the *tradition* to the *truth* would be important, did Camden add his authority, which he fails to do ; and neither Froissart,

Walsingham, Knighton, nor any contemporary historian, alludes to so interesting an incident. Barnes, in his "Life of Edward III.," quotes Sandford's "Genealogical History;" Sandford quotes Camden, and Camden quotes *nobody*; but admits that even in his time it was a disputed point.

Mr. Planché, in his *History of British Costume*, considers there to be no reason for Edward's selecting the German motto, "Ich Diene," ("I serve,") to express his own service to his father, as surmised. Again, the crest of John of Bohemia, was the *entire* wing or pinion of an eagle, apparently from its shape (as may be seen on his seal, engraved in Olivarius Veredius), and not one or three distinct ostrich feathers. Then, it is suggested that the feathers may have been plucked from the crest of the King of Bohemia, as a symbol of triumph, and granted as an heraldic distinction by King Edward III. to his gallant son; but the feathers are henceforth borne *singly* by all the descendants of Edward III.; they are clearly those of the ostrich, and not those of the eagle, such as we see in the helmet of John, King of Bohemia, and the seals in Olivarius Veredius. In that distant age the ostrich feather may have been assumed by the Prince as emblematic of his warlike propensities, from the reputed powers of the ostrich to digest both iron and steel; so that the badge may have been merely a quaint conceit. The motto, "Ich Dien," probably had no connexion with the badge. The feathers singly appear, with blank scrolls, upon the seals or tombs of nearly all the Princes of the houses of York and Lancaster, down to Arthur, Prince of Wales, son of Henry VII., upon whose monument at Worcester they first appear as a plume in a coronet, as well as singly. It may here be stated that a writer in the *Quarterly Review* attributes the feathers to the *banner* of the King of Bohemia, "and not to the helmet, as is generally supposed."

Sir Harris Nicolas, in the *Archæologia*, xxxi. 350-384, minutely examines all the contemporary and other early evidence on the subject, from written statements, seals, and paintings. Sir Harris states that the first time the feathers are mentioned in any record is in an indenture (not hitherto known) of "the Queen's Plate, date after 1369, which is an alms-dish, marked with a sable escutcheon, charged with ostrich feathers, believed to have belonged to Queen Philippa, either as a badge of her family or as arms borne in right of some territories appertaining to her house." On this piece of plate the feathers are found for the first time.

The next and most remarkable notices of the ostrich feathers occur in the will of the Black Prince, directing that his body should be buried in Canterbury Cathedral, and that in six of the escutcheons on his tomb should be placed ostrich feathers, as well as a banner and a pennon with ostrich feathers. The Prince also bequeaths to the church of Canterbury his hangings of ostrich feathers of black tapestry; he desires that his chapel should be ornamented "with our badge of ostrich feathers," and he mentions "a blue vestment with gold roses and ostrich feathers," also "arras, embroidered with ostrich feathers," &c. Mr. Willement, from the Lansdowne MS., 932, states there were formerly in the church of St. Katherine, near the Tower, two shields, one charged with six ostrich feathers erect, each fixed on a scroll inscribed Ich Dien; and that a shield, similarly charged, once stood in a window of St. Olave's Church, in the Old Jewry.

Although the Prince directs in his will "Houmout" as a motto, it occurs only over the shields containing his arms, and over the shields with ostrich feathers is placed "Ich Dien," as well as in a scroll upon the quill of each feather. That the Black Prince did use the motto Ich Diene as well as Houmout is placed beyond dispute by evidence which Sir H. Nicolas published for the first time.

In further refutation of the Cressy tradition, Sir H. Nicolas shows that the crest of the King· of Bohemia was two wings of a *vulture* semée of linden-leaves of gold expanded, and not a plume of ostrich feathers. An ostrich is said to have been the badge of the Emperor Charles IV., King of Bohemia, son of John, King of Bohemia, who was slain at Cressy ; and it was undoubtedly the badge of his daughter Anne, consort of King Richard II. Queen Philippa's grandmother was the sister of Henry, Count of Luxemburg, great-grandfather of the Emperor Charles IV. ; and if, as there is reason to suppose, an ostrich was the ancient badge of that house, the ostrich feathers borne by Queen Philippa and her sons may have been derived from that source.

Sir H. Nicolas adds, in a note :—" Queen Anne, the first consort of Richard II., is represented on her tomb in Westminster Abbey wearing a dress richly embroidered with ostriches." An ostrich was also worn pendent to the collar of the Queen's livery. Mr. John Gough Nichols's hypothesis respecting the ostrich feathers is as follows :—

That the Bohemian King, who was a relation of Queen Anne no more distant than her paternal grandfather, may very probably have used the badge of an ostrich, as well as his son the Emperor Charles, the Queen's father; and that the Prince, upon his victory over this monarch, who, from such a badge would be called the ostrich, possibly adopted the conceit that the feathers of the conquered bird formed an emblematical trophy very significant of his success. Such a conjecture may be the more acceptable from accommodating itself with the received tradition respecting the field of Cressy ; and may therefore be adopted, unless it should appear that the feather (which we also find borne by the brothers of the Black Prince) was used by our English Princes before that event, which, I confess, I think not improbable.

The only other contemporary evidence of the usage of the feathers in the reign of Edward III. is upon seals. The feather is only to be found upon one seal of this monarch. Sir H. Nicolas then describes eight of the Prince's seals; from which it appears that the feathers were omitted on some of the Prince of Wales's seals which were engraved after the year 1346; whereas no inference in favour of the supposed connexion of the badge with the battle of Cressy can be drawn from the omission of the feathers on a seal which was certainly engraved before that event.

It is next shown that the ostrich feathers were borne, with a slight difference, by some other, if not by all, of the sons of King Edward III., besides the Prince of Wales. And the Prince's widow, Joan, Princess of Wales, by her will in 1385, bequeathed to her son, Prince Richard, a new bed of red velvet, *embroidered with ostrich feathers of silver*, and leopards' heads of gold, with branches and sleeves of silver. Sir H. Nicolas proceeds with examples to the ostrich feathers borne by Arthur Prince of Wales, son of Henry VII.; and the feathers and motto, in a novel but picturesque form, as they occur on stained glass of the time of Henry VIII., in the Porter's Lodge, in the Tower of London.

The badge seems thenceforth to have been considered to belong exclusively to the Sovereign's eldest son; but Prince Edward (afterwards King Edward VI., but who was never Prince of Wales) used it in an unprecedented manner. In old St. Dunstan's Church, Fleet-street, were the arms of Henry VIII., having on the dexter side one of his badges; and on the other a roundel, per pale, sanguine, and azure, within a leaf composed of leaves and roses, and charged with the letters E. P. Between the letters was a plume of *three ostrich feathers argent, penned, or*, passing through a label inscribed *Ich Dien*, the feathers being surmounted by the Prince's coronet. Another, but somewhat similar example, occurs on a piece of glass which is supposed to have come from Reynold's Place, Horton Kirby, in Kent.

Henry, Prince of Wales, son of King James I., sometimes bore the feathers like his predecessor, Arthur Prince of Wales; and on other occasions he placed the feathers on a sun. Since that period the usual manner of bearing the feathers is as a plume encircled by a coronet; and from ignorance of the real character of this ancient and beautiful badge it has sometimes been considered as the *crest* of the Princes of Wales.

Sir Harris says of the motto "Houmout," sometimes erroneously printed "Houmont," that it is formed of the two old German words, 'Hoogh, moed,' 'hoo moed,' or 'hoogh-moe'—i.e., magnanimous, high-spirited, and was probably adopted to express the predominant quality of the Prince's mind.

In conclusion, Sir H. Nicolas repeats his opinion that there is no truth in the tradition which assigns the badge of the ostrich feathers to the battle of Cressy, or of Poictiers; and he is strongly impressed with the belief that it was derived, as well as the mottoes, from the house of Hainault, possibly from the Comté of Ostrevant, which formed the appanage of the eldest sons of the Counts of that province.

A piece of contemporary evidence is, by some, considered to have set the question at rest: this is a manuscript of John de Ardern, physician in the time of the Black Prince; and who distinctly states that the Prince derived the feathers from the blind King of Bohemia.

CHEVY-CHASE, OR OTTERBOURNE?

The famous ballad of "Chevy Chase" has lately been proved historically worthless. The two versions, the older and the more recent, agree in stating the facts as follows:—The combat took place at Otterbourne, and was occasioned by the Percy's vow to hunt the Cheviot in spite of Douglas. The result was indecisive, 1447 out of 1500 English bowmen being killed, and 1495 out of 2000 Scotch spearmen. Douglas was shot dead by an arrow; and Percy slain by a lance-thrust. The only battle that ever took place at all near Otterbourne was contested on the one side by Douglas, with 2000 foot and 300 lances; on the other, by Harry Hotspur and Ralph, *sons of* the Percy, commanding 8000 foot and 600 spears. It was occasioned by Northumberland sending his sons to encounter the two Scotch armies which had entered England. The English attacked the enemy's camp between Otterbourne and Newcastle, and were eventually routed with the loss of 1800 men, 1000 others being wounded. The invaders lost only 100 in killed, 200 in prisoners. Douglas was slain by a spear-thrust, while Hotspur was captured. This brief summary of the fight, August 19, 1388, is from the very full narrative of Froissart, derived from two French knights who had served on the English side in the contest, and from a knight and two squires of Scotland, of the party of Earl Douglas.

It will thus be seen from this bare outline that the ballad consists of a pitifully-mangled account of the battle of Otterbourne; and the minstrel, besides openly mentioning this place as the scene, has so blended various incidents and names connected with that contest as to destroy all doubt on the subject. Nor was there any other occasion on which a Douglas was slain. Again, the composer places the event in the reign of Henry IV. and " Jamye, the Skottishe Kyng," and makes it immediately antecedent to Hombledon; but when Richard II. reigned in England the *first* " Jamye " was not *born* till ten years after, and Hombledon was not fought till 1402. The writer, therefore, must have lived a very long period subsequent to Otterbourne, or its chronicler, whose last stanza proves him to have composed his poem after 1403. The only reason for supposing a separate battle is the hunting party which gives name to the ballad; and this is conjectured to have arisen from Otterbourne being styled "The Battle of (the) *Chevachées*," that is, forays, raids over the border into an enemy's country, in one of which the Scots were engaged at this very time. The word occurs in Chaucer, during whose life Otterbourne was fought. It still exists in the French *chevauchee*, and our *chivy*.

What could be more natural than that the knightly class should style this "the Battle of (the) Chevachées," just as they spoke of the Battle of Spurs; and that the Saxon populace, ignorant of these long aristocratic French words, should construe the title into " Battle of (the) Chevy-Chase?''

Hence, then, in the belief of the writer, arose the idea that the battle of Otterbourne took place during a hunting expedition in Cheviot. The story itself furnishes corroborative testimony. The composer shows his ignorance by speaking of Otterbourne as in Cheviot, although at least a dozen miles distant. Nay, the very vow of Percy would have been unnecessary, or rather a proof of cowardice, for the Cheviots were no kss Northumbrian than Scotch, Cheviot itself clearly appertaining to England rather than Scotland. This solution of what has long been a source of serious difficulty to students of history and ballad literature, is condensed from an interesting communication to *Notes and Queries*, 3rd S., No. 294, by E. F. Nicholson, Tonbridge.

THE EARLS AND DUKES OF NORTHUMBERLAND.

There was formerly in titled life as much peril as grandeur. Take, for instance, the eighteen Earls of Northumberland. The first three were slain; the fourth, Cospatrick, from whom the Dundases are descended, died in exile; the fifth was beheaded; the sixth, who was also Bishop of Durham (Walcher), was murdered; the seventh (the Norman Alberic) was deprived, and pronounced "unfit for the dignity"; the eighth died a prisoner for treason; the ninth and tenth hardly come into the account, for they were Henry and Malcolm, princes of Scotland, who were a sort of honorary Earls of Northumberland; the eleventh earl was the old Bishop Pudsey, of Durham, who bought the earldom for 11,000*l.*, but was subsequently deprived of it and thrown into prison. Then came the Percys. The first earl of that house, but the twelfth in succession, after the death of his son, Hotspur, at Shrewsbury, was himself slain in battle; the thirteenth earl fell at St. Albans, the fourteenth at Towton, the fifteenth at Barnet, the sixteenth was murdered, the seventeenth was the first to die a natural death, and the eighteenth left no children. He, indeed, left a brother; but Sir Thomas Percy was attainted, and his honours became extinct. The son of Sir Thomas was restored in blood and title after Dudley, Duke of Northumberland, was beheaded; but the restored earl was himself beheaded in 1572. It was his nephew, Earl Henry, the husband of Dorothy, one of the sisters of Essex, who suffered fifteen years' imprisonment in the Tower, and was mulcted in a fine of 20,000*l.*, not so much because he failed to prove that he was not concerned in the Gunpowder Plot, as because the Percy who *was* actively engaged in it was his kinsman and servant. He was the last earl of his line who suffered personal constraint; and in his grandson, Josceline Percy, the male line became extinct, in 1670.

The Earl Josceline's sole child and heiress, Elizabeth, married the " proud Duke of Somerset," in which title their son, Algernon Seymour, succeeded them, with that of Earl of Northumberland added thereto. This Algernon Seymour, like Josceline Percy, had but one child, Elizabeth, sole heiress now of the Somerset and Northumberland property. This Elizabeth once expressed her surprise at a lady having refused an offer of marriage made to her by the handsome baronet, Sir Hugh Smithson, whose father is described by some writers as a London apothecary, but whose family, landed gentry in the north, from the time of the Conquest, was as *noble* as that of the Percys, and only inferior to it in the fact that the hereditary *title* of the one was higher in the scale of precedence than that of the other. Sir Hugh married the Percy heiress, and was subsequently created Duke of Northumberland in 1766. In the well-nigh hundred years that have since elapsed, there have been four dukes, Sir Hugh, his son, and two grandsons. In the later as in the earlier days, these Northumbrian nobles have had to risk their lives in battle; the fourth Duke was in Lord Exmouth's expedition to Algiers, and his father distinguished himself in America. The latter, too, came into collision with the Government of his day, as his remote predecessors had often done; but in his case with less calamitous issue, George the Third had promised him the governorship of Tynemouth; but the King broke his royal word. When he was, subsequently, asked to go out to America as "Commissioner," with a promise of the Garter on his return, he peremptorily refused; and when he was asked for the grounds of his refusal, he as promptly answered—his experience of what Court promises were!—Abridged from the *Athenæum.*

THE POET GOWER, AND THE SUTHERLAND FAMILY.

In the fine old Church of St. Saviour, Southwark, in the south transept, is the Perpendicular monument of the poet Gower, removed from the north aisle of the nave in 1832, when it was restored and coloured at the expense of the first Duke of Sutherland, a presumed collateral descendant from the poet.

"We are afraid, on the showing of Sir H. Nicolas and Dr. Pauli, that the family of the Duke of Sutherland and Lord Ellesmere must relinquish all pretension to being related to, or even descended from John Gower. They have hitherto depended solely upon the possession of a MS. of the *Confessio Amantis*, which was supposed to have been presented to an ancestor by the poet; but it now turns out, on the authority of Sir Charles Young, Garter, that it was the very copy of the work which the author laid at the feet of King Henry IV., while he was yet Harry of Hereford, Lancaster, and Derby!"—(Review of Dr. Pauli's edition of the *Confessio Amantis; Athenæum*, No. 1537, p. 468.) Sir Richard Baker is the only Chronicler who gives the date of Gower's death correctly, namely, 1408, as in his Will; most if not all other writers represent Gower as dying in 1402 or 1403.

WARS OF THE ROSES.

Never was such devastation made in the ranks of our nobility, titled and untitled, as during the English "Thirty Years' War" of the White and the Red Roses. In the thirteen battles fought between York and Lancaster, from that of St. Albans, in 1455, to that on Redmore Down, near Bosworth, in 1485,—in nine of which battles the Yorkists were victors, yet they ultimately lost the great prize at Bosworth,—there perished in fight, by murder, or under the axe, two kings, four princes, ten dukes, two marquises, one-and-twenty earls, two viscounts, and seven-and-twenty barons. To these may be added, one lord-prior, one judge, one hundred and thirty-nine knights, all noble; four hundred and forty-one esquires, the eldest sons of knights; and a body of gentlemen, or untitled nobility, of coat-armour and ancestry, the number of whom is variously stated, but which number being incorporated with the death-roll of private soldiers, swelled the great total to nearly eighty-six thousand men. Such was the cost to the country of that country's best blood, shed in a quarrel which, after all, ended in a wedding by way of compromise.—*Athenæum.*

THE PROUD SOMERSETS.

The pride of lineage was, perhaps, never more strongly displayed than by the Somersets and Seymours, who were of the same stock; and a prouder man was never seen in England than the Duke of Somerset of two centuries ago, who had the highways cleared before him, that he might not be looked upon by vulgar eyes, and who rebuked his second wife for tapping his shoulder with her fan, saying, " Madam, my first wife was a Percy, and she never took such a liberty." We may go back at once to Cardinal Beaufort, who was of the first generation of the family apart from royalty, he being the natural son of John of Gaunt. There is a better ground of pride in the family than even antiquity. Among the proud Somersets was he who, in early life, commanded a little army, raised by his father for the service of Charles I., and who, in after years, wrote the *Century of Inventions*, and first applied the condensation of steam to a practical purpose, though his invention was used only for raising water. He was the last noble who held out in his castle against Cromwell; and the stronghold was the Raglan Castle which gave his title to the Field-Marshal who, in 1854, commanded the British army in the Crimea.

WHO WAS JACK CADE ?

Mr. M. A. Lower, F.S.A., in his ingenious *Essays on English Surnames*, thus corrects an error into which most of our historians have fallen, relative to the arch-traitor Jack Cade, *temp.* Hen. VI.

They uniformly state that he was an *Irishman* by birth, but there is strong presumptive evidence that to Sussex belongs the unenviable claim of his nativity. Speed states that he had been servant to Sir Thomas Dagre. Now this Sir Thomas Dagre, or Dacre, was a Sussex knight of great eminence, who had seats at Hurstmonceaux and Heathfield, in this county. Cade has, for several centuries, been a common name about Mayfield and Heathfield, as is proved, as well by numerous entries in the parish registers, as by lands and localities designated from the family. After the defeat and dispersion of his rabble-rout of retainers, Cade is stated to have fled into the woods of Sussex, where, a price being set upon his head, he was slain by Sir Alexander Iden, sheriff of Kent. Nothing seems more probable than that he should have sought shelter from the vindictive fury of his enemies among the woods of his native county, with whose secret retreats he was, doubtless, well acquainted, and where he would have been likely to meet with friends. The daring recklessness of this villain's character is illustrated by the tradition of the district that he was engaged in the rustic game of bowls, in the garden

of a little ale-house at Heathfield, when the well-aimed arrow of the
Kentish sheriff inflicted the fatal wound.

Mr. Orridge, in his *Account of the Citizens of London and their
Rulers,* states he has reason to believe that Thomas Cooke, draper,
of the City of London, in 1450, was an ancestor of Alderman Cooke,
who was in turn an ancestor of Sir Antony Cooke. Now, this Thomas
Cooke, draper, was the friend and agent of Jack Cade; and if Mr.
Orridge's belief should turn out to be right, the friend and agent of Jack
Cade was not only the ancestor of Bacon and Cecil in Elizabeth's time,
but, among others, of our present Duke of Beaufort, our present Marquises of Exeter and Salisbury, our present Lords Fitzwilliam, Burghley,
and Cranborne.

HENRY IV. AND THE JERUSALEM CHAMBER.

Fabyan, the chronicler, relates the death of Henry IV. to have taken
place in the Jerusalem Chamber, as the fulfilment of a prediction to the
King that he should die in Jerusalem. Now, Fabyan died in 1511 or
1512: he may be supposed to have been born about 1440 or 1450, and
to have collected the materials for his history sixty or seventy years
after King Henry's death. His information, though not recent, was
doubtless obtained from persons who lived at or near the time.
Holinshed appears to have repeated the narrative of Fabyan, but to
have disbelieved the story. As Henry was about to make a pilgrimage
to Jerusalem at the time when he was attacked by his mortal disease, it
is likely that a prophecy may have been current that he would die at
Jerusalem. It may likewise have been true that when his first seizure
of illness occurred, he was carried to a room called the Jerusalem
Chamber, and that this coincidence may have been the subject of
remark. Though Fabyan states that the King died "shortly after"
his removal to the Jerusalem Chamber, yet his own narrative represents
the interval as nearly three months; that is to say, from "after the feast
of Christmas" to the 20th of March. The account of Fabyan that the
King, without any suggestion, asked if the chamber to which he was
carried had any special name, and that he immediately received the
answer that it was named Jerusalem, by which the prediction respecting
him was fulfilled, is in the highest degree improbable.—*Eironnach:
Notes and Queries,* 2nd S., No. 89. The incident is, as is well known,
verified by Shakspeare, in his play of *Henry IV.,* Second Part,
Act iv.:—

> *K. H.* Doth any name particular belong
> Unto the lodging where I first did swoon?
> *War.* 'Tis called Jerusalem, my noble lord.
> *K. H.* Laud be to God! even there my life must end.
> It hath been prophesied to me many years,
> I should not die but in Jerusalem,
> Which vainly I supposed the Holy Land.
> But bear me to that chamber, there I'll lie,
> In that Jerusalem shall Harry die.

In Capgrave's *Chronicle of England,* edited by the Rev. J. C.

Hingeston, is an account of the death of Henry IV., which may be considered as the narrative of a contemporary. Capgrave was born in 1393, and died at the age of seventy-one in 1464: he was twenty years old at the death of Henry IV. With the other authorities, he states that the King died on March 20th, and he gives the following notice of his death:—

"At his death, as was reported of full sad [*i.e.*, serious, discreet,] men, certain lords steered [*i.e.*, incited] his confessor, friar John Till, Doctor of Divinity, that he should induce the King to repent him, and do penance in special for three things. One for the death on [of] King Richard; the other for the death of Archbishop Scrope; the third for the wrong title of the crown. And his answer was this: for the two first points, I wrote unto the Pope the very truth of my conscience; and he sent me a bull, with absolution, and penance assigned, which I have fulfilled. And as for the third point, it is hard to set remedy; for my children will not suffer that the regalia go out of our lineage."

This passage implies that the King's death did not take place suddenly, but that it was foreseen; that certain exhortations of repentance were addressed to him by his Confessor at the instigation of some leading men about the court, and that he gave them a deliberate answer.

It is thought that the name Jerusalem may have been applied to a holy place, besides that in Palestine. Dean Vincent has pointed out a remarkable coincidence in a passage of Anna Comnena relating to the death of Robert Guiscard, king of Sicily, in a place called Jerusalem, at Cephalonia. In Lodge's *Devils Conjured* is a similar story of Pope Sylvester.

KING OF THE ISLE OF WIGHT.

Henry Beauchamp, Duke of Warwick, son of Richard Earl of Warwick, was crowned King of the Isle of Wight by patent 24 Henry VI., King Henry in person assisting at the ceremonial, and placing the crown on his head. Leland, in his *Itinerary*, records Henry Beauchamp "coronatus in *regem de Wighte,*" from a book in the church wherein Warwick was buried. But little notice has been taken of this singular event by our historians, and, except for some collateral evidence, the authenticity of it might be doubted; but the representation of this duke with an imperial crown on his head, and a sceptre before him, in an ancient window of the collegiate church of Warwick, leaves no doubt that such an event did take place. This honourable mark of the royal favour, however, conveyed no royal authority, the king having no power to transfer the sovereignty of any part of his dominions, as is observed by Lord Coke, in his *Institutes*, where this transaction is discussed; and there is reason to conclude that, though titular king, he did not even possess the lordship of the island, no surrender appearing from Duke Humphrey, who was then living, and had a grant for the term of his life. Selden, too, in his *Titles of Honour*, p. 29, treating of the title of

the King of Man, observes that, "it was like that of the King of the
Isle of Wight, in the great Beauchamp, Duke of Warwick, who was
crowned king under Henry VI." Henry Beauchamp was also crowned
King of Guernsey and Jersey.

STORY OF JANE SHORE AND SHOREDITCH.

The strange sad story of this "beautiful, frail, and unfortunate fair"
is one of the most curious episodes of its class in our history. It has
been told in chronicle, poem, and drama; and although its details are
unfit for readers of tender years, few narratives have been more widely
read. The materials are so abundant that we must, of necessity, restrict
ourselves to the leading incidents.

Sir Thomas More says:—"What Jane's father's name was, or where
she was born, is not certainly known." Both More and Stow tell us
she was born in London. She was, More adds, "worshipfully friended,
honestly brought up, and very well married, saving somewhat too soon;
her husband was an honest citizen, young and goodly, and of good
substance." He was by trade a goldsmith, and resided in Lombard
Street. Whether he was banker to Edward IV. is unknown. The
Shore family at this period were very opulent; and soon after this time,
Richard Shore was an alderman of London (1505), and he is thought
to have been related to Jane's husband, with whom she was not happily
allied. She lived with Shore seven years; and about 1470 she became
concubine to Edward IV. We are not told, except in legend, how the
king knew of her beauty, or when or where he first saw her. Philip
de Comines, who personally knew Edward, says:—"He was the most
beautiful prince my eyes ever beheld!" "the most beautiful man of his
time." In his resplendent court Jane delighted all by her beauty, pleasant behaviour, and proper wit, for she could "read well and write,"
which few of the highest ladies then could. "Merry in company, ready
and quick of answer, neither mute nor full of babble, sometimes taunt-
ing without displeasure, and not without disport; in whom King
Edward took special pleasure, whose favour, to say the truth, for sin it
were to belie the devil, she never abused to any man's hurt, but to many
a man's comfort and relief. When the King took displeasure, she
would mitigate and appease his mind; where men were out of favour,
she would bring them in his grace; for many that highly offended, she
obtained pardon; of great forfeitures she gat them remittance; and,
finally, in many weighty suits, she stood many men in great stead,
either for none or for very small rewards, and those rather gay than
rich; either for that she was content with the deed itself well done, or
that she delighted to be sued unto, or to show what she was able to do
with the king, or for that wanton women be not always covetous."

Such was her temper: now let us view her person. Sir Thomas
More says:—"There was nothing of her body that you would have
changed, unless you would have wished her something higher."
Drayton, in his poetical epistle from Jane to her royal lover, has noted,

by which it appears that " her stature was mean, her hair of a dark jet, her face round and full, her eyes grey, delicate harmony being between each part's proportion and each proportion's colour; her body fat, white, and smooth; her countenance cheerful, and like to her condition. Edward died at Westminster in 1482; and within two months Jane was accused by Gloucester, the usurper, of sorcery and witchcraft, who caused her to be deprived of the whole of her property, about 3000 marks, a sum now equal to about 20,000*l*.; she was then committed to the Tower, but was acquitted for want of proof of sorcery. She was next committed by the sheriffs to Ludgate prison, charged with having been the concubine of Hastings; for which she walked in penance from the cathedral to St. Paul's Cross, with a taper in her hand, wearing only her kirtle, or petticoat, in London streets; and then again committed to the prison of Ludgate, where she was kept close prisoner. Meanwhile, Lynom, the king's solicitor, would have married Jane but for the interference of King Richard. We have no account of Shore after she had left him, except that he retired from London, it is said, to Flanders. Rowe, in his drama, gives this portrait of Jane in her penance :—

> Submissive, sad, and lowly was her look;
> A burning taper in her hand she bore,
> And on her shoulders, carelessly confus'd,
> With loose neglect her lovely tresses hung;
> Upon her cheek a faintish flush was spread:
> Feeble she seem'd, and sorely smit with pain,
> While, barefoot, as she trod the flinty pavement,
> Her footsteps all along were mark'd with blood.
> Yet silent still she pass'd, and unrepining,
> Her streaming eyes bent upon the earth;
> Except, when in some bitter pang of sorrow,
> To Heav'n she seem'd in fervent zeal to raise,
> And beg that mercy man denied her here !

After the death of King Richard at Bosworth, Jane was liberated from Ludgate. She never married again, nor was her property restored to her. There is a tradition that she strewed flowers at the funeral of Henry VII. Calamitous was the rest of her life, and she died in 1533 or 1534, when more than fourscore years old; and no stone tells where her remains were deposited. Sir Thomas More says of her penury and good deeds: " At this day she beggeth of many at this day living, that at this day had begged if she had not been." For almost half a century Jane Shore was a living monitress to avoid illicit love, however fascinating; and the biographer, poet, and historian, made her so for nearly three centuries after her death.

Thomas Churchyard, who died in 1604, wrote a poem showing "How Shore's wife, King Edward the Fourth's concubine, was by King Richard despoyled of all her goods, and forced to doe open penance." Dr. Percy, in his *Reliques*, prints a ballad from a black-letter copy in the Pepys Collection. It is entitled " The Woefull Lamentation of Jane Shore, a goldsmith's wife in London, some time King Edward IV. his Concubine. To the tune of ' Live with me,' &c." Here the poet makes Jane die of hunger after doing her penance, and a man be hanged for relieving her; both of which are fictions that led to the popular error of Jane's dying of hunger in a ditch, and thus giving its name to Shoreditch, a name now proved to have been of much greater antiquity.

Shoreditch is an ancient manor and parish, extending from Norton Folgate to Old-street, and from part of Finsbury to Bethnal-green. It was originally a village on the Roman military highway, called by the Saxons Eald (*i. e.*, Old) Street. Stow declares it to have been called Soersditch more than 400 years before his time : and Weaver states it to have been named from Sir John de Soerdich, lord of the manor, *temp.* Edward III.,* and who was with that king in his wars with France. The legend of its being called after Jane Shore dying in a *ditch* in its neighbourhood, is a popular error, traceable to a black-letter ballad in the Pepys Collection, entitled, *The Woful Lamentation of Jane Shore, a Goldsmith's Wife in London, some time King Edward IV. his Concubine:*

> I could not get one bit of bread,
> Whereby my hunger might be fed ;
> Nor drink, but such as channels yield,
> Or stinking ditches in the field.
> Thus, weary of my life at lengthe,
> I yielded up my vital strength
> Within a ditch of loathsome scent,
> Where carrion dogs did much frequent :
> The which now, since my dying daye,
> Is Shoreditch call'd, as writers saye."

But this ballad is not older than the middle of the 17th century; and no mention is made of Jane so dying in a ballad by Churchyard. Dr. Percy erroneously refers *Shoreditch* to " its being a common sewer, vulgarly *shore*, or drain." It is sometimes called *Sorditch*, which is the most correct, according to the above explanation. An archer of this parish, named Barlo, was styled " Duke of Shoreditch " by Henry VIII., for having outshot his competitors in a shooting match at Windsor ; and the Captain of the Company of Archers of London was long after styled " Duke of Shoreditch." In the Beaufoy Collection are four Shoreditch tokens, one with figures of Edward IV. and his mistress; and the public-house sign of *Jane Shore* is extant in the High-street.

Fabyan's *Chronicle* gives the best account of the punishment of Jane Shore, by which it will be seen that however unjust were the charges against her, they were no other than customary measures of the times. The groundwork of the prosecution against Jane by Richard III. was that " she had bewitched the King, so that he had lost the use of his arm." The origin of this allegation we find in first of Kings, xiii. 6 (Jeroboam's hand.) Charges of witchcraft were political tricks in the, Middle Ages, to irritate the ignorant public, and prevent commiseration. The Barons seriously believed that Piers Gaveston had bewitched King Edward II.; and Fabyan writes concerning the Queen herself of Edward

---

* The same family of Soerdich, or Shordich, it is believed, possessed the manor of Ickenham, near Uxbridge, and resided at Ickenham Hall, from the reign of Edward III. to our own time. The last of this family, Paul Ricaut Shorliche, civil engineer, grandson of Michael Shordiche, of Ickenham Manor, died at Antigua, July 13th, 1865.

IV., "how the Kynge was enchaunted by the Duchesse of Bedford." Jane Shore's penance was the same as had been previously inflicted (20 Hen. VI.) upon Eleanor Cobham, first mistress, and afterwards wife, of the Duke of Gloucester, upon a similar charge of sorcery. As to the confiscation of Jane's property, this was a common measure under an impeachment of treason. In 1468 (7 Edward IV.) Sir Thomas Cooke, notwithstanding acquittal, was robbed of his property in a similar manner. As to Jane's vagrancy and destitution, "the Erle of Oxenforde remained prisoner nearly twelve years, during which time his wife was not suffered to see him; nor had she anything to live upon, but common charity, or what she might gette with her needle, or other soche cunnyng, as she exercised." Thus it appears that the sufferings of Jane were only common to her with others; and in consequence that the incidents related in the ballads are probably correct, because they are supported by analogies.

"HISTORIC DOUBTS ON RICHARD THE THIRD."

This notable work, by Horace Walpole, was published by him, Feb. 1, 1768: "twelve hundred copies were printed and sold so very fast, that a new edition was undertaken the next day of 1000 more, and published the next week."

The work is among the best of Walpole's writings. It has two plates of portraits, from the Roll at Kimbolton, which Lord Sandwich borrowed for Walpole, who writes: "It is as long as my Lord Lyttleton's History; but by what I can read of it (for it is both ill written and much decayed), it is not a roll of kings, but of all that have been possessed of, or been Earls of Warwick; or have not—for one of the first earls is Æneas. How, or wherefore, I do not know, but amongst the first is Richard the Third, in whose reign it was finished, and with whom it concludes. He is there again with his wife and son, and Edward the Fourth, and Clarence and his wife, and Edward their son (who, unluckily, is a little old man), and Margaret, Countess of Salisbury, their daughter. But why do I say with these? there is everybody else, too; and what is most meritorious, the habits of all the times are admirably well-observed from the most savage ages. Each figure is tricked with a pen, well drawn, but neither coloured nor shaded. Richard is straight, but thinner than my print; his hair short, and exactly curled in the same manner; not so handsome as mine, but what one might really believe intended for the same countenance, as drawn by a different painter, especially when so small; for the figures in general are not so long as one's finger. His Queen is ugly, and with just such a square forehead as in my print, but I cannot say like it. Nor, indeed, where forty-five figures out of fifty (I have not counted the number) must have been imaginary, can one lay great stress on the five. I shall, however, have these figures copied, especially as I know of no other image of the son."

Walpole, if he was advocating a paradox, believed it to be a truth;

K

and in the subsequent encounter with Hume, he has the advantage which thorough acquaintance with the subject must always give over the ablest antagonist, whose original views were based upon superficial knowledge.

Walpole sent a copy of his work to Voltaire, who, in his letter of acknowledgment, agrees with Walpole, that Richard was not so black as painted, and concluded thus: " Votre rose blanche et votre rose rouge avaient de terribles épines pour la nation." Those gracious kings are all a pack of rogues. " En lisant l'histoire des York et des Lancastre, et bien d'autres, on croit lire l'histoire des voleurs de grand chemin. Pour votre Henri Sept, il n'était que coupeur de bourses."

Walpole adds that the childish improbabilities in the general history of Richard place his reign on a level with the " Story of Jack the Giant Killer."

We shall not enumerate the annotators who have followed Walpole; the most recent of them, Mr. Gairdner, in the volume published by the authority of the Master of the Rolls, adduces fresh evidence, all creditable to the character of Richard. A critic, in the *Athenæum*, gives, as new to the general public: " There are documents here in London, the first portion of which seems to have been written by a clerk or secretary. The scribe, however, failing perhaps to seize the meaning of his master, lays down the pen, and the remainder of the dispatch is finished in Richard's own bold and steady hand, and subscribed thereto is the signature of his name, boldly dashed forth, yet with such grace and correctness that kings and gentlemen generally of this day might take it for an example, which, after much practice, they would probably not equal."*

Sir Thomas More, the acknowledged origin of the scandalous history, resided with Bishop Morton, the inveterate enemy of Gloucester. More's version was revived and exaggerated by the Tudor chroniclers, and copied by Shakspeare, who has merely verified the language of the early historians, who based their authority on More. Shakspeare follows Holinshed; so also does Hume; and Holinshed follows Hall,

---

* The autograph of Richard III. is of great rarity. When Dr. Dibdin was on his *Northern Tour* (published in 1839), at Whitburn, in the neighbourhood of Tynemouth, he had the good fortune to be introduced to Sir Hedworth and Lady Williamson, at a sort of manorial residence, with a good large quantity of garden and pleasure-ground, and the sea glittering at its extreme boundary. Finding Dr. Dibdin's appetite for antiquarian researches to be somewhat insatiable, Sir Hedworth was so good as to introduce the Doctor to his old trunk of *family seals*, in white and red wax ; Sir Hedworth, then one of the members for North Durham, being a descendant from an old baronetcy, and by the female line traced his ancestry to a considerably remote period. '' Much,'' writes Dr. Dibdin, ''was Sir Hedworth amused in witnessing my modified ecstasies on finding a good large seal or two of the Edwards—one in fine condition, and perhaps of the first Edward ; but when I came to examine a warrant of Richard III., then Duke of Gloucester, appointing an ancestor of mine host, of the name of Hudleston, Deputy Guardian or Warden of the West Marches, with the autograph of the duke, and a part of the seal, appended— there was no keeping my expressions of joy within moderate bounds ; as the autograph and seal of Richard, at that period, are of the most rare occurrence." Accordingly, the relic is engraved in Dr. Dibdin's ''boke.''

and Hall follows Polydore Vergil. Shakspeare's Lancastrian partialities have turned history upside down, or rather inside out.

No record of Richard's time or reign affords any foundation for the mistakes, discrepancies, and falsifications related of him, except John Rous, the recluse of Warwick, who was an avowed Lancastrian, and a bitter enemy of the line of York; and he certifies that Gloucester was "small of stature, having a short face, and uneven shoulders," which have been exaggerated into a crooked back.

Stow, who was born forty years after Richard's death, was told by some ancient men, who had seen the King, that he was "of bodily shape comely enough, only of low stature."

It seems now to be accepted that even Henry VII., its alleged vindicator in the opinion of Mr. Newdegate, put the young Earl of Warwick, son of the Duke of Clarence, out of the way, to induce the King of Spain to give his daughter Catherine to his own son, Prince Arthur. At least, this is the latest light thrown by Mr. Gairdner, under the Record Commission, on the indifference to the family principle shown by Tudors and Plantagenets in common.

Sir George Buck, the first historian who defended Richard, agrees with Philip de Comines, and with the rolls of parliament; and late researches into our ancient records, state-papers, and Parliamentary history, place Buck's history in a more credible light than could have been allowed to it some years since, and fix both him and Lord Orford as higher authorities than those who wrote professedly to please the Tudor dynasty.

The prejudiced pen of Bacon describes Richard as a "prince in military virtue approved, jealous of the honour of the English nation, and likewise a good law-maker for the ease and solace of the common people." "In no king's reign," said Sir Richard Baker, "were better laws made than in the reign of this man." And so sensible appears Bacon to have been of the injustice done to Richard, that he says: "Even his virtues themselves were conceived to be feigned."

The Chronicles of Fleetwood, a Yorkist, and Warkworth, a Lancastrian, both within about the same period, exculpate Gloucester from the charge of the murder of Edward of Lancaster. "All the other narratives," says Mr. Bruce, in his introduction to Fleetwood's Chronicles, "either emanated from partisans of the adverse faction, or were written after the subsequent triumph of the House of Lancaster."

Mr. Heneage Jesse, in *Richard III. and his Contemporaries*, is disposed to acquit Richard of the murders of King Henry and his son, and of being present and accessory to the execution of Clarence. He argues to the effect that Prince Edward was not stabbed in cold blood after the battle of Tewkesbury, but was slain in the *mêlée* as he fled with the rest of the routed Lancastrians. The evidence is scanty to prove even that Richard was present when Henry VI. was murdered in the Tower, if he was so murdered. Unquestionably Richard could not have met the Lady Anne under the circumstances described by Shakspeare; for when the corpse of Henry was on its way to Chertsey Richard was marching with his brother, King Edward, against the bastard Falconbridge; while Anne, who had fallen into the hands of Edward after the battle of Tewkesbury, was, in all probability, in close custody with her mother-in-law, Queen Margaret, in the Tower. There is reason, too, for inferring that at the time of Clarence's trial and execution Richard was quietly discharging the duties of his government in the north of England. On all these points Mr. Jesse holds to the newer lights, as also on the old question of debate whether Richard was half as deformed in person as his enemies have painted him.

More recent evidences of Richard's popularity have been brought to light by Mr. John G. Nichols, Mr. Wright, and others. Unquestionably the array of bishops at his coronation, and of those who congratulated him afterwards, such as Waynflete and Alcock, implied a remarkable indifference to "the fam'ly principle" on the part of the venerable bench; else this principle was not so exceptionally violated by the king as the Warwickshire gentlemen—the Shakspeares and Newdegates—have inferred. Rous's Roll, an authentic document, describes Richard as ruling " in his realm full commendably; punishing offenders of his laws, especially extortioners and oppressors of his commons;" and it goes on to assert that " he got great thanks of God, and love of all his subjects, rich and poor, and great laud of the people of all other lands about him."

THE BEDSTEAD OF KING RICHARD III.

The history of this assumed relic of the Plantagenet King, is thus told by Professor Babington, of St. John's College, Cambridge.

In Nichols's *History of Leicestershire* (vol. i. p. 380) the bedstead on which the King is supposed to have slept is both described and figured :— " Richard slept at the Blue Boar Inn (at Leicester). . . . . The bedstead whereon he is supposed to have slept (on the night before the battle of Bosworth) is still preserved, and its history is thus handed down."

Nichols goes on to describe at large how, in 1613, Mrs. Clark, who kept that inn, was robbed by her servant-maid and seven men, who afterwards murdered her, and were executed for the crime.[*] Mrs. Clark, it seems, had in the reign of Elizabeth discovered that the bed had a double bottom, the intermediate space being filled with gold. This treasure, left to her by her husband in the following reign, was the inciting cause of the robbery and murder. A very curious extract from Sir R. Twysden's common-place books about this may be seen in *Notes and Queries* for 1857, page 102. Nichols proceeds to add that it came afterwards into the hands of Mr. Alderman Drake. To cut matters short, after the death of my father, the Rev. Matthew Drake Babington, Rural Dean of Ackley, in Leicestershire, it came into my hands. It was examined by several antiquaries, among the rest by my learned friend Mr. M. H.

---

* It seems that the murder was committed in 1605, not 1613 ; and one woman burnt, and only one man hanged for the offence.—*Notes and Queries* for 1857, p. 154.

Bloxam, of Rugby. He was decidedly of opinion that the bed, a most beautiful piece of work, was of the age of Elizabeth. Although few people know the bed better than I do, as I have many a time struck my head against its projecting carved work, when first waking in the morning, yet it belongs to a class of antiquities about which I do not feel disposed to deliver an opinion *ex cathedrâ*. Mr. James Thompson (*Notes and Queries* for 1857, p. 154) speaks with prudent doubtfulness. After showing from Coryate's *Crudities* that the traditional bed of Richard III. was exhibited among the "Penny sights of the reign of James I." in 1611, he goes on to say, "The question yet remains doubtful whether the bedstead on which Richard III. slept was ever exhibited, and also whether he ever concealed gold in any bedstead. That he lodged in the Blue Boar, which inn was taken down about twenty years ago, I think is sufficiently established; but beyond this fact it does not appear to me safe to go on this head in the way of historical affirmation." The external evidence in favour of its genuineness is decidedly strong, and with regard to the internal evidence, the representation of the Holy Sepulchre in one of its compartments, may be thought by some to savour of the reign of Richard III. rather than of Elizabeth. Those who consider the style of carving to be manifestly of the 16th, and not of the 15th century, can, of course, enjoy their opinion, which may very probably be correct. It is certainly very specious, and I must confess that I incline to it. The bed, I may say in conclusion, is now in the possession of Mr. W. P. Herrick, of Beaumanor Park. It was with regret that I parted with it, having then no house in which to keep so large a piece of furniture; but the regret was much diminished by knowing that it would be placed in such excellent hands as those of my friend Mr. Herrick."

To this statement, the accomplished archæologist, Mr. Henry Shaw, F.S.A., has replied as follows:—" I had supposed the tradition of the old bedstead formerly preserved at the Blue Boar Inn, at Leicester, having been the one on which Richard III. slept the night before the battle of Bosworth, had been long since set at rest to the satisfaction of those who possessed only a moderate acquaintance with the archæology of architecture, as every genuine example of ancient carving carries its own chronology, within a short period, in the style of its design and the character of its execution. When I published my *Specimens of Ancient Furniture*, in the year 1836, I made most diligent search for examples of an ancient date, and was surprised to find how few remained belonging to an earlier time than the beginning of the 16th century. The oldest bed I met with then, or have heard of since, was of the time of Henry VIII., and belonged to a clergyman in the neighbourhood of Blackburn, who had bought it out of an old manor-house. The posts and back are most elaborately carved in the latest style of Gothic art, but unfortunately the cornice has disappeared.

" If, however, real specimens of ancient furniture are wanting, ivory carvings, stained glass, and more especially illuminated MSS., supply us with an abundance of examples to show the changes of fashion in those articles during the Middle Ages.

" In the earlier times beds were almost invariably mere couches. As luxury advanced they were enlarged, the counterpanes were formed of the richest materials, gorgeously embroidered with the arms and badges of their owners, and, from their great cost, bequeathed to their descendants from one generation to another. These beds were usually surmounted with testers or canopies of the richest coloured silks, edged with party-coloured fringes, and suspended from the rafters of the rooms by silken cords. The head of the bed was usually of oak, richly carved in panels. Side curtains appear, but foot posts are very rarely seen.

"The modern four-poster came into general use in the time of Elizabeth, when these features frequently assumed enormous proportions, and were almost invariably covered with the most elaborate carvings. As these embellishments are in the Renaissance style—said to have been introduced into this country by Holbein—they could not appear on a bedstead of the time of Richard III. The one removed from the Blue Boar Inn is an ordinary example of the Elizabethan type, of which many specimens still remain; one of the most beautiful, and certainly the most interesting, being the 'Great Bed at Ware,' mentioned by Shakspeare in his *Twelfth Night.*"

WAS THE DUKE OF CLARENCE DROWNED IN A BUTT OF MALMSEY?

Richard, Duke of Gloucester, is alleged to have participated in the death of Clarence, but the charge rests exclusively on a vague presumption of his having hardened the heart of King Edward, already sufficiently incensed against Clarence, and ready at all times to trample down all ties of relationship and all feelings of mercy, when his throne was in danger or his vindictiveness was roused. Clarence had joined Warwick in impeaching his title, and denying his legitimacy. Untaught by experience, he had recently indulged in intemperate language against his sovereign, who actually appeared in person as the principal accuser at the trial, which was one of the most solemn description known to the law. The Duke was found guilty by his peers, and both Houses of Parliament petitioned for his execution, and afterwards passed a Bill of attainder. He was also peculiarly obnoxious to the Queen and her friends, Rivers, Hastings, and the Greys.

"The only favour," says Hume, "which the King granted his brother after his condemnation, was to leave him the choice of his death, and he was privately drowned in a butt of malmsey in the Tower; a whimsical choice, which implies that he had an extraordinary passion for that liquor." Mr. Bayley (*History of the Tower*) suggests, that Clarence's well-known fondness for this wine was the foundation of the story, although, so far as evidence goes, the fondness for the wine is here the mother of conjecture; and we rather agree with Walpole, that "whoever can believe that a butt of wine was the engine of his death, may believe that Richard helped him into it, and kept him down till he was suffocated." Yet, this is precisely what some do believe or maintain. "After Clarence," writes Sandford, "had offered his mass-penny in the Tower of London, he was drowned in a butt of malmsey, his brother, the Duke of Gloucester, assisting thereat with his own proper hands." The most plausible solution of the enigma is suggested by Shakspeare, when he makes the First Murderer tell the second: "Take him over the costard with the hilt of thy sword, and throw him into the malmsey butt in the next room." The dialogue on Clarence awakening is,—

> *Clar.* Where art thou, keeper? Give me a cup of wine.
> *1st Murd.* You shall have wine enough, my lord, anon.

After a brief parley, the First Murderer stabs him, exclaiming,—

> Take that, and that ; if all this will not do,
> I'll drown you in the malmsey-butt within.

He carries out the body, and returns to tell his relenting comrade,—

> Well, I'll go hide the body in some hole,
> Till that the duke give order for his burial.

Clarence's groans may have been stifled in a full butt conveniently nigh, or the body may have been temporarily hidden in an empty one.—*Edinburgh Review*, No. 234.

It is conjectured that Clarence was sentenced to be poisoned, and that the fatal drug may have been conveyed to him in malmsey. All that is positively known is simply that he was put to death "secretly within the Tower."—*Chronicle of Croyland*.

THE FIRST PAPER MILL IN ENGLAND.

It was long believed that at Dartford, in Kent, paper was first made in England; but it is now proved that a paper-mill had existed in this country almost a century before the date of the mill at Dartford. In the Household Book of Henry VII. is entered:

1498. For a rewarde geven at the paper mylne, 16s. 8d.

1499. Geven in rewarde to Tate of the mylne, 6s. 8d.

And in the English translation of *Bartholomeus de Proprietatibus Rerum*, printed by Wynkyn de Worde in 1495, we read of John Tate having lately in *England* made the paper which was used for printing his book. We also gather from an early specimen of blank verse, *A Tale of Two Swannes*, written, it is believed, by a native of Ware, and printed in 1590, that the mill belonging to John Tate, was situate at Hertford; and the extract from the privy purse expenses of Henry VII. quoted above, date May 25, 1498, has reference to this particular mill, as the entry immediately preceding shows that the king went to Hertford two days before, namely, on the 23rd of May. And in Herbert's edition of Ames's *Typographical Antiquities*, we read that "this mill was where Seel or Seed Mill now is, at the end of Hertford town, towards Stevenage; and that an adjoining meadow is still called Paper Mill Mead."

Now, the paper-mill at Dartford, long reputed to have been the first in England, was established at least 110 years later than that at Hertford, in 1588, by John Spillman, jeweller to the queen, who was pleased to grant him a licence " for the sole gathering, for ten years, of all rags, &c., necessary for the making of such paper." This mill is described in a poem by Thomas Churchyard, published shortly after the foundation of the mill; the writer says:

> Then he that made for us a paper-mill,
> Is worthy well of love, a worlde's good will ;
> And though his name be *Spill*man by degree,
> Yet *Help*man now he shall be calde by mee."

Spillman was knighted by Queen Elizabeth. He was buried in the church at Dartford, beneath a sumptuous tomb, which, in 1858, was restored by " The Legal Society of Paper Makers," the funds being subscribed by the trade in d fferent parts of England, especially in the county of Kent. But we find a paper-mill mentioned by Shakspeare, in his play of Henry VI., the plot of which appears laid at least a century previously; in fact he introduces it as an additional weight to the charges which Jack Cade is made to bring against Lord Say, the passage ending with, "contrary to the king his crown and d'gnity, *thou hast built a paper-mill.*" Mr. Herring, who has written the best account of Paper-making, tells us that North Newton mill, near Banbury, in Oxfordshire, (then the property of Lord Say and Sele,) has been set down as the first paper-mill erected in this country, and that referred to by Shakspeare. Now, the first Lord Say and Sele who had property in Oxfordshire, which he acquired by marriage, was the son of the first Lord Say, to whom Shakspeare makes reference.

In some researches on Water-marks in paper, *foolscap* is traced, 1661, to the following traditional story : " When Charles I. found his revenues short, he granted several privileges amounting to monopolies ; and among these was the manufacture of paper, at which time all English paper bore in watermark the royal arms. The Parliament, under Cromwell, made jests of this law in every conceivable manner; and among other indignities to the memory of Charles, it was ordered that the royal arms be removed from the paper, and the *fool's-cap and bells* be substituted. These were also removed when the Rump Parliament was prorogued; but paper of the size of the Parliament's Journals still bears the name of *foolscap.*"

SIR WILLIAM KINGSTON'S JOCULAR CRUELTY.

In 1549 (3 Edward VI.) when sedition raged in Cornwall, among the rebels, perforce, was the Mayor of Bodmin, to whom the Provost Marshal, Sir William Kingston, sent word he would come and dine with his worship. The Mayor, accordingly, made great provision, and a little before dinner the Provost took the Mayor aside, and whispered him that an execution must be done that day in the town, and therefore required to have a pair of gallows set up against dinner should be done; the Mayor failed not of his charge. After dinner the Provost inquired for the gallows, which the Mayor having showed him, he asked his worship if he thought them strong enough ; "Yes," said the Mayor. "Well," replied the Provost, "get you up speedily, for they were provided for you." "I hope," answered the poor Mayor, "you mean not as you speak." "In faith," said the Provost, "there is no remedy, for you have been a busy rebel ;" and so, without respite or defence, he was hanged to death, a most uncourteous part for a guest to offer his host. Near Bodmin dwelt also a miller, also a busy rebel, and who, fearing the approach of the Provost, told a sturdy fellow, his servant, that he must go from home, and, if any one enquired after him, he (the servant) should say that he was the miller, and had been so for three years. So the Provost came, and called for the miller, when the servant said he was the man. "How long have you kept the mill ?" asked the Provost ; "these three years," answered the servant. Then the Provost commanded his men to lay hold on him, and hang him on the next tree. At this the fellow cried out that he was not the miller but the miller's man : "Nay," said the Provost, "I will take you at your word, and if thou bee'st the miller, thou art a busie knave ; if thou bee'st not, thou art a false, lying knave ; and however, thou can'st never do thy master better service than to hang for him ;" and so, without more ado, he was dispatched.—Baker's *Chronicle*.

SIR THOMAS MORE AND THE BUTLERSHIP OF LINCOLN'S INN.

The biographers of Sir Thomas More are almost entirely silent as to the family from which he sprung. They ascend no higher than Sir Thomas's father, Sir John More, he being no less a person than one of the superior judges for at least twelve years. That Roper is silent about the Chancellor's pedigree is surprising; seeing that he was not only Sir Thomas's son-in-law, but wrote his biography, considered as the best authority for all that is known of the private history of the family ; yet he is almost silent on this point, which must be ascribed to a delicate disinclination to expose that which he might fear would, in some minds, derogate from the respect with which the Chancellor was regarded. His great-grandson, Cresacre More, in his biography, endeavours, with a natural desire to magnify his ancestors, to show that they were of gentle descent, deriving his argument from the epitaph written by Sir Thomas, which he misquotes ; and by the arms alleged to be borne by Sir John, which he misunderstands. He cites the epitaph, "Thomas More, born of *no noble* family, but of an honest stock "; and he afterwards argues upon the word "*nobilis*," as if it occurred in the original. But no such word is really to be found there. The passage stands thus : "Thomas Morus, urbe Londinensi, familiâ non celebri, sed honestâ, natus ;" words simple enough, and which seem plainly to intimate that he could trace his pedigree little beyond his father. As to the arms, Cresacre More says : "Judge More bore arms from his birth, having his coat quartered ;" but there is no evidence that this was the case, and none of the pedigrees in the Heralds' College begin with any earlier name than that of Sir John; and who his father was no writer has yet explained. It is curious, also, that in what is told of Sir John himself, contradictory accounts are given of the Inns of Court to which he belonged, of the bench on which he sat as judge, and of the age at which he died.

It seems impossible, therefore, to come to any other conclusion than that the family was an obscure one; that John More—first the *butler*, afterwards the steward, and finally the reader of Lincoln's Inn, was the Chancellor's grandfather; and that John More, junior, who was also at one time *butler* there, was the Chancellor's father, and afterwards the judge. Not only does this descent suit precisely the "non celebri, sed honestâ, natus" in Sir Thomas More's epitaph, but it explains the silence of his biographers, and accounts for the Judge and the Chancellor attending the readings of a society with which their family had been so closely connected.

The settlement of this question is important; since it proves that at a time when the barriers between the different grades of society were far more difficult to be passed than in the present day, such a combination of talent with integrity and moral worth as distinguished the progenitors of Sir Thomas More, could overcome all the prejudices in favour of high descent which were the natural results of the feudal system.—Edward Foss, F.S.A.; *Archæologia*, vol. xxxv. pp. 27—33.

What an idea of the dismantling of our nature is conveyed by the few words which Roper, Sir Thomas More's son-in-law, relates! He had seen Henry VIII. walking round the Chancellor's garden at Chelsea, with his arm round his neck. He could not help congratulating More on being the object of so much kindness. "I thank our Lord, I find his Grace my very good lord indeed; and I believe he doth as singularly favour me as any subject in his realm. However, son Roper, I may tell thee, I have no cause to be proud thereof, for if my head would win a castle in France, it would not fail to be struck off."

ROASTING AN ABBOT.

The Earl of Cassilis, who, from his great power in Ayrshire, was usually called the King of Carrick, was desirous of obtaining certain leases and grants of feu affecting the lands of the abbey of Crossraguel, in his neighbourhood. For this purpose he entrapped the Abbot, McAllan Stewart, in the month of October, 1570, to a small tower overhanging the sea, commonly called the Black Vault of Denure. Here, when the abbot expected to be treated with a collation, he was carried to a private chamber, and, instead of wine and venison, and other good cheer, he saw only a great barred chimney with a fire beneath it. In this cell the deeds were laid before him, and he was required to execute them. So soon as he attempted to excuse himself the tragedy commenced. He was stripped naked, and stretched out on the bars of iron, to which he was secured, while the fire beneath was adjusted, so as now to burn his legs, now his shoulders, and so forth, while the Earl and his brother kept *basting him with oil.* This procedure soon removed the abbot's scruples about the alienation of the property of the Church; and when, having intimated his willingness to subscribe the deeds required, he was released from his bed of torture, his inhospitable landlord addressed him with a hypocritical impudence which is almost ludicrous. " Benedicite, Jesu Maria! you are the most obstinate man I ever saw. If I had known you would have been so stubborn, I would not for a thousand crowns have handled you in that sort. I never did so to man before you." These apologies the half-roasted abbot was compelled to receive as sufficient. The story, besides being a curious picture of the age, may serve to show that by force used or menaced, the nobles of Scotland extorted from the Catholic beneficiaries those surrenders and alienations of the Church patrimony which took place at the Reformation.

THE REIGN OF HENRY VIII.

The remarkable *History*, by Mr. Froude, presents us with what may be familiarly called an entirely new portrait of our Eighth Henry, drawn in accordance with the principle upon which the author has produced this great work. Refusing to view his subject in the light of subsequent opinions, or through the medium of modern authorities, and confining himself strictly to contemporaneous evidence, Mr. Froude has built his history upon the only basis which can satisfy the honest enquirer. Still, the results are much controverted; but his character of Henry, which follows, has been described by an able critic as " a favourable exaggeration."

" Beyond and besides the Reformation, the constitution of these islands now rests in large measure on foundations laid in this reign. Henry brought Ireland within the reach of English civilization. He absorbed Wales and the Palatinate into the general English system. He it was who raised the House of Commons from the narrow duty of voting supplies and of passing without discussion the measures of the Privy Council, and converted them into the first power in the State under the Crown. When he ascended the throne so little did the Commons care for their privileges, that their attendance at the sessions of Parliament was enforced by a law. They woke into life in 1529, and they became the right hand of the King to subdue the resistance of the House of Lords, and to force upon them a course of legislation which from their hearts they detested. Other kings, in times of difficulty, summoned their ' great councils,' composed of peers, or prelates, or municipal officials, or any persons whom they pleased to nominate. Henry VIII. broke through the ancient practice, and ever threw himself upon the representatives of the people. By the Reformation, and by the power which he forced upon them, he had so interwoven the House of Commons with the highest business of the State that the peers thenceforward sunk to be their shadow.

" Something, too, ought to be said of his individual exertions in the details of State administration. In his earlier life, though active and assiduous, he found leisure for elegant accomplishments, for splendid amusements, for relaxations, careless, extravagant, sometimes questionable. As his life drew onwards his lighter tastes disappeared, and the whole energy of his intellect was pressed into the business of the Commonwealth. Those who have examined the printed *State Papers* may form some impression of his industry from the documents, which are his own composition, and the letters which he wrote and received; but only persons who have seen the original manuscripts, who have observed the traces of his pen in side notes and corrections, and the handwritings of his secretaries in diplomatic commissions, in draughts of Acts of Parliament, in expositions and formularies, in articles of faith, in proclamations, in the countless multitudes of documents of all sorts, secular or ecclesiastical, which contain the real history of this extraordinary reign,—only they can realize the extent of labour to which he sacrificed himself, and which brought his life to a premature close. His personal faults were great, and he shared, besides them, in the errors of his age; but far deeper blemishes would be but as scars upon the features of a sovereign who, in trying times, sustained nobly the honour of the English name, and carried the Commonwealth securely through the hardest crisis in its history."

The critical writer referred to above (in the *Times*, April 8, 1858), thus sums up his objections to the work:—Mr. Froude's knowledge of constitutional law appears deficient: he has not traced out for his readers the Tudor polity, and his notions about it seem very incorrect. We dissent altogether from his theory, that formal indictments or recorded verdicts are any proof that the victims of Tudor State trials were guilty of the crimes imputed to them; and, although the real evidence in none of them is forthcoming, we think that he should have presumed against its validity when we recollect the nature and value of the testimony upon which, in better times, State prisoners were convicted. We must also protest against the conception under which he contemplates Henry VIII. and some other of the personages whom he brings before us in this history. To confound tyranny with able strength, to excuse crime on the plea of a State necessity, to represent the excesses of force or passion as the calculations of genius reluctantly compelled to work out its destiny, and to try and make us forget all moral considerations in the contemplation of power achieving great ends,—this is the leading fallacy of Mr. Froude in this conception, and must class him with the idolaters of a base hero-worship. We are bound to give this as our opinion, much as we admire the great research, the critical art, and the beautiful style of this remarkable fragment of the *History of England*.

TOURNAMENT OF THE FIELD OF CLOTH OF GOLD.

In the spring of 1830, there was exhibited in London a most superb specimen of painting on glass, the size almost amounting to stupendous, being 18 by 24 feet. The term "window" can hardly be applicable to this vast work, for there was no framework visible; but the entire picture consisted of 350 pieces, of irregular form and size, fitted into metal astragals, so contrived as to fall in the shadows, and thus to assist the appearance of an uninterrupted and unique picture upon a sheet of glass of 430 square feet.

The subject was "the Tournament of the Field of Cloth of Gold," between Henry VIII. and Francis I., in the plain of Ardres, near Calais; a scene of overwhelming gorgeousness, and in the splendour of its accessories, well suited to the brilliant effects which are the peculiar effects of painting in enamel. The stage of the event represented, was the last tourney, on June 25, 1520. The field is minutely described by Hall, the chronicler, whose details the painter had closely followed. There were artificial trees, with green damask leaves and branches and boughs, and withered leaves of cloth of gold; the trunks being also covered with cloth of gold, and intermingled with fruit and flowers of Venice gold; and "their beautie showed farre." In these trees were hung shields, emblazoned with "the Kynge of Englande's arms, within a gartier, and the French Kynge's within a collar of his Order of Saint Michael, with a close croune, with a flower de lisse in the toppe;" and around and above were the shields of the noblemen of the two courts. The two Queens were seated in a magnificent pavilion, and next to the Queen of England sat Wolsey; the judges were on stages; the heralds, in their tabards, placed at suitable points; and around were gathered the flower of the French and English nobility, to witness this closing glory of the sunset of chivalry.

The *action* of the picture is thus described:—The trumpets sounded, and the two kings and their retinues entered the field; they then put down their vizors, and rode to the encounter valiantly, or, in the words of Hall, " the ii Kynges were ready, and either of them encountered one man-of-arms, the French Kynge to the erle of Devonshire, the Kynge of England to the Mounsire Florrenges, and brake his poldron, and him disarmed, when ye strokes were stricken, this battle was departed, and was much praised."

The picture contained upwards of one hundred figures, life-size, of which forty were portraits, mostly after Holbein and other contemporary authorities. The armour of the two Kings and the challenger was very successfully painted; their coursers almost breathed chivalric fire, and the costumes and heraldic devices presented a blaze of dazzling splendour. Among the spectators, the most striking portraits were the two Queens, Wolsey, Anne Boleyn, and the Countess of Chateaubriant, Charles Brandon Duke of Suffolk, and Queen Mary Dowager of France, with the ill-fated Duke of Buckingham, whose hasty comment upon the extravagance of the tournament proved his downfall. The elaborate richness of the costumes, sparkling with gold and jewels; the fleecy, floating feathers of the champions, their burnished armour and glittering arms; the congregated glories of ermine, velvet, and cloth of gold; and the heraldic emblazonry amidst the emerald freshness of the foliage, all combined to form a scene of unparalleled sumptuousness.

The picture was executed in glass by Thomas Wilmhurst (a pupil of Muss), from a sketch by R. T. Bone; the horses by Woodward.

The work cost the artist nearly 3000*l.* It was exhibited in a first-floor at No. 15, Oxford-street; and the great picture formed one side of a room, painted for the occasion with paneling and carving of the time of Henry VIII. It proved very attractive as an exhibition; the private view was attended by the leading artists of the day; and George IV., hearing of the work, meditated a visit, but was prevented by illness. A descriptive Catalogue of the picture, of several pages, was sold to the extent of more than 50,000 copies. The writer of the Catalogue, on first seeing the picture, exclaimed, with an impulse approaching vaticination, " What, in case of a fire ! " Sad, then, to relate, in one unlucky night, January 31st, 1832, the picture and the house were entirely burnt in an accidental fire ; not even a sketch or study was saved from destruction ; and the property was wholly uninsured. As a specimen of glass-painting this work was very successful; the colours were very brilliant, and the old ruby red was all but equalled. The artistic treatment was altogether original ; the painters in no instance, borrowing from the contemporary picture of the same scene in the Hampton Court Collection.

CARDINAL WOLSEY NOT A BUTCHER'S SON.

In 1742-4, four large octavo volumes, illustrated with portraits and prints, were published under the title of *The Life and Times of Cardinall Wolsey,* by Joseph Grove, a solicitor, at Richmond, a devoted admirer of Wolsey ; and who subsequently printed eight works on the same subject, independently of eleven separate Appendices. In the last of them he tells us that, in April, 1760, he made a second journey to Ipswich, to collect materials concerning the life and actions of Mr. Robert Wolsey, the father of the famous Cardinal. He lived in St. Nicholas-street, Ipswich, where he had other estates besides his dwelling-house and property in Stoke. His lands here were partly pasture; he, after the example of other gentlemen in the kingdom, grazed great part of the pasture ; and, after the cattle were fit for market, he caused them to be sold. From thence the tale was raised of calling Wolsey's father a butcher. Mr. Grove says : " Some of our historians, when they are almost out of breath in throwing out indecent reflexions upon the Cardinall, fall at last upon this gentleman his father, calling him *a poor butcher of Ipswich;* though, at the same time, they are totally unacquainted with what he was ; whilst others have incautiously attempted to lessen his great character by insinuating that he made the pride of the English nobility stoop to *the son of a butcher of Ipswich*: when, in reality, this butcher, as they style him, was as much a gentleman, and lived as respectably, in a private manner, as any of their fathers did."

Thus far Mr. Grove, who then gives some curious details of the manner in which some of the nobility disposed of their cattle ; still it is the vulgar belief of illiterate persons that Cardinal Wolsey was the son of a poor butcher.

Robert Wolsey, and his wife Joan, were buried in St. Nicholas' Church, and their effigies, on brass, were affixed upon the stone laid down on their graves; but these brasses getting loose have been most probably sold for old metal. From a book of epitaphs in the Ipswich churches, those of St. Nicholas' parish have been torn out.

RISE AND FALL OF WOLSEY.

An acute critic has thus traced the genius of this proud Cardinal, the means by which he rose, and the false policy by which he fell:—

"Unlike his fellows in the Council, Wolsey's attention to business was not distracted by the duties of a high ecclesiastical appointment, or even the claims of large territorial estates. He held at this time no other preferment than the deanery of Lincoln. The bent of his genius was exclusively political; but it leaned more to foreign than domestic politics. It shone more conspicuous in great diplomatic combinations, for which the earlier years of the reign furnished favourable opportunities, than in domestic reforms. The more hazardous the conjuncture the higher his spirit soared to meet it. "Proud cardinal" and "proud prelate" were the terms lavished upon him by men as proud as himself, with much less reason to be proud. "He was seven times greater than the Pope himself" is no exaggeration of the Venetian Giustiniani, for he saw at his feet what no Pope had for a long time seen, and no subject before or since—princes, kings, and emperors courting his smiles. Born to command, infinitely superior in genius to those who addressed him, he was lofty and impatient. But there is not a trace throughout his correspondence of the ostentation of vulgar triumph or gratified vanity. It is remarkable how small a portion of his thoughts is occupied with domestic affairs; and with religious matters still less. Looking back upon the reign, and judging it as we do now by one great event, it appears inconceivable that a man of so much penetration and experience should have taken so little interest in the religious movements of the day, and regarded Luther and the progress of the Reformation with so little concern. He cared less for Ciceronianisms and Latin elegancies. When, therefore, questions of domestic interest became paramount, and the Sovereign and the nation were engrossed in religious discussions, he was no longer required; and so the eclipse of his greatness was inevitable. He had not surrounded himself with the support of a cordial band of younger associates, grateful to him for their advancement and dependent on him for their guidance. With the failing natural to old age, he was more willing to tax his waning strength than undertake the ungracious and unpalatable task of communicating his designs and explaining their bearings to new associates. This policy was fatal to him; it angered the King, it raised him up a host of enemies in the able and rising courtiers. It left him friendless when he most wanted friends, and the moment an opportunity offered of attacking him behind his back it was eagerly seized upon. Without any ingratitude on the part of his Sovereign, his fall was inevitable; the work and the time had outgrown him; and the expression put into his mouth by the great dramatist, '*The King has gone beyond me*,' expresses his profound conviction of the real causes of his disgrace and the utter impossibility henceforth of his restoration."—*Times.*

When Henry had decided that Wolsey should go to Asher (Esher), a house near to Hampton Court, belonging to the Bishop of Winchester, there to reside, the Cardinal delivered up all his moveables to the king's use, the greatest store and richest that ever was known, of any subject. At Asher, Wolsey and his family continued three or four weeks, without either bed, sheets, table-cloths, or dishes to eat their meat in, or money wherewith to buy any, but what he was forced to borrow of the Bishop of Carlisle!

STORY OF KATHERINE OF ARRAGON AND HER
TWO MARRIAGES.

To the *Kimbolton Papers*, published in 1864, Mr. Hepworth Dixon contributed an account of Queen Katherine, derived from some late researches among the Spanish archives, at Simancas, and the results amassed in Mr. Bergenroth's Calendar, in the Record Office, of which the following *resumé* is given in the *Times* journal:—

Katherine of Arragon is a creature of romance: it is only now, more than 300 years after her death, that we are enabled to see her as a real woman, with the weaknesses of a woman—an ardent woman, eager to marry, determined to marry Henry VIII., fond of her dinner, complaining that she could not get enough to eat, plunged in debt, deep in little plots, and apt to fib. This picture of the real woman is very curious. From facts which have been lately discovered, it appears that for 10 years before he divorced her, Henry sturdily debated with the doctors the question whether his marriage with Katherine was legitimate or not. Mr. Dixon holds that the new facts discovered prove distinctly that the marriage was illegal. But what are these facts? It is now proved that not only had Katherine gone through the religious ceremony of marriage with Arthur, the elder brother of Henry, but that after marriage she had lived with him. The Empress of the French has in her possession a letter of Henry VII.'s, addressed to Ferdinand and Isabella, in which the King states that he had sent the Prince and Princess together into Wales. The inference is that this little pair, the husband being just 15 years of age, were in the legal sense man and wife. That Katherine and Arthur had lived together may be most true; but if the proof of that fact were all that is required to show that her marriage with Arthur was in the legal sense of the term completed, it was a point easily proved three hundred years ago, and the doctors and the statesmen and the King need not have taken ten years to make up their minds as to the legality of the union between Henry and Katherine. Mr. Dixon says it was Charles V. who started the Spanish theory that the marriage between Katherine and Arthur had never been complete; but this is not the case. He himself quotes the letter of Isabella of Spain addressed to the Duke of Estrada just three months after the death of Arthur and long before the marriage of Henry, in which, alluding to Katherine, she says, " It is already known for a certainty that the said Princess of Wales, our daughter, *remains as she was here* (for so Donna Elvira has written to us)." When that letter was written Charl's V. was a mere infant. There was really a doubt about the point which probably never can be settled; and it is well understood that this doubt would have been settled in Katherine's favour if she had had a son. She had no son; the succession to the throne through a daughter was doubtful in those times of trouble; Henry consequently magnified the doubts that might be raised through the circumstances of his marriage, and he cut the knot by divorcing the Queen. In examining this tangled question, we find assertion crossing assertion with the most provoking ingenuity. It is impossible, however, to get rid of the fact that a doubt there was, and that the doubt remains. Prince Arthur was but fifteen years and a half old when he died, and at the time of his marriage it is known that his health was very delicate.

THE FIRST-BORN OF HENRY VIII. AND QUEEN KATHERINE.

With few exceptions, there was not a cloud to darken the horizon as large as a man's hand; and whatever scruples might afterwards arise, there was nothing to interfere with Henry's affection for Katherine Accounts vary as to Katherine's personal appearance, but she had all the virtues which befitted a Queen and a woman, the bluest blood of Spain, the noblest descent, and the choicest position of the proudest Court in Europe. She danced well, was a good musician, was better educated, wrote and read much better and composed in English more correctly than half the ladies of her Court. Above all, her love and admiration for Henry were unbounded. There was not such a paragon in the world. He was her hero, her Paladin. " With his health and life," she writes with affectionate solicitude to Wolsey, "nothing can come amiss to him; without him I can see no power of good thing shall fall after it." She (good pious soul!) is persuaded that the victory of Flodden and the capture of Terouenne " is all owing to the King's piety." Her greatest comfort in his absence is to hear from Wolsey of the King's health, and all the news of his proceedings. She braids his banners with a piece of King James's finery, brought from the field of Flodden by John Glyn, and she makes a pilgrimage to our Lady of Walsingham to pray for his safe return.

One great grief had redoubled her anxiety and devotion. To the inexpressible delight of the King and the nation, a Prince had been born January 1, 1511. A household and officers had been appointed for the Royal babe. His Sergeant-at-Arms and his Clerk of the Signet are immortalized in Privy Seals and in Treasury Warrants. Even the name of his nurse, Elizabeth Pointes, is recorded, and that of the Yeoman of his beds and wardrobe. A tournament in his honour was proclaimed; but, alas! the bright vision had faded before the pageant was consummated. On February 22 this desire of all eyes died; and there is to be seen in this book an entry, signed by the King and his Council, among the wages of minstrels, lords of misrule, and salaries of ambassadors, grim and emotionless as death itself, an order to pay for 432lb. of wax, which John Tomson of London, wax chandler, had made into tapers of wax of 3lb. each, and duly delivered to burn for the benefit of the "babe's" little soul, which was winging its way upwards to the other little cherubims who have not had their share of mortal comforts, but have died in their paptime without further consolations.—*Times* journal.

WHERE WAS ANNE BOLEYN BURIED?

It is stated in Miss Strickland's *Queens of England* (iv. 203), that there is a tradition at Salle in Norfolk, that the remains of Anne Boleyn were removed from the Tower, and interred at midnight, with the rites of Christian burial, in Salle church; also, that a plain black stone without any inscription is supposed to indicate the place where she was buried. Blomefield, the historian of Norfolk, does not allude to the above tradition. Lord Herbert of Cherbury, in his *History of King Henry VIII.*, does not state how or where Anne Boleyn was buried. Holinshed, Stow, and Speed say that her body, with the head, was buried in the choir of the chapel in the Tower; and Sandford, that she was buried in the chapel of St. Peter in the Tower.

Burnet, who is followed by Henry, Hume, and Lingard, says that Anne's body was thrown into an elm chest made to put arrows in, and was buried in the chapel within the Tower, before 12 o'clock. Sharon Turner, (*Hist. Henry VIII.*) cites the following from Crispin's account of Anne Boleyn's execution, written fourteen days after her death:—" Her ladies immediately took up her head and the body. They seemed to be without souls, they were so languid and extremely weak; but fearing that their mistress might be handled unworthily by inhuman men, they forced themselves to do this duty, and though almost dead, at last carried off her dead body wrapt in a white covering."

A Correspondent of the *Gentleman's Magazine*, Oct. 1815, describes "the headless remains of the departed queen as deposited in the arrow-chest, and buried in the Tower chapel, before the High Altar. Where that stood, the most sagacious antiquary, after a lapse of more than there hundred years, cannot now determine, nor is the circumstance, though related by eminent writers, clearly ascertained. In a cellar, the body of a person of short stature, without a head, not many years since was found, and supposed to be the reliques of poor Anne; but soon after reinterred in the same place, and covered with earth."

The stone in Salle church has been raised, but no remains were to be found underneath it. Miss Strickland states that a similar tradition is assigned to a black stone in the church at Thornden-on-the-Hill; but Morant, (*Hist. Essex,*) does not notice it.—*Notes and Queries*, vol. v. p. 1464.

HOW THE LADY CATHARINE PARR ESCAPED BEING BURNED FOR HERESY.

This Queen of Henry VIII., being an earnest Protestant, had many great adversaries, by whom she was accused to the King ot having heretical books found in her closet ; and this was so much aggravated against her, that her enemies prevailed with the king to sign a warran: to commit her to the Tower, with a purpose to have her *burnt for heresy*. This warrant was delivered to Wriothesley, Lord Chancellor, and he by chance, or rather, indeed, by God's providence, letting it fall from him, it was taken up, and carried to the Queen, who, having read it, went soon after to visit the King, at that time keeping his chamber, by reason of a sore leg. Being come to the King, he presently fell to talk with her about some points of religion, demanding her resolution thereon. But she knowing that his nature was not to be crossed, especially considering the case she was in, made him answer that she was a woman accompanied with many imperfections, but his Majesty was wise and judicious, of whom she must learn, as her lord and head. " Not so, by St. Mary," (said the King,) " for you are a doctor, Kate, to instruct us, and not to be instructed by us, as often we have seen heretofore." " Indeed, sir," said she, " if your Majesty have so conceived, I have been mistaken ; for if heretofore I have held talk with you touching religion, it hath been to learn of your Majesty some point whereof I stood in doubt, and sometimes that with my talk I might make you forget your present infirmity." " And is it even so, sweetheart ?" (quoth the King,)—" then we are friends ;" and so, kissing her, gave her leave to depart.

But soon after was the day appointed by the King's warrant for apprehending her, on which day the King, disposed to walk in the garden, had the Queen with him ; when suddenly, the Lord Chancellor, with forty of the guard, came into the garden with a purpose to apprehend her, whom as soon as the King saw, he stept to him, and calling him knave and fool, bid him avaunt out of his presence. The Queen, seeing the King so angry with the Chancellor, began to entreat for him, to whom the King said : " Ah, poor soul, thou little knowest what he came about ; of my word, sweetheart, he has been to thee a very knave." And thus, by God's providence, was this Queen preserved, who else had tasted of as bitter a cup as any of his former wives had done.—Baker's *Chronicle*.

SIR THOMAS WYAT'S BREAK-DOWN.

On February 3, 1553, Wyat, with an army of 3000 or 4000, came to London, but finding the bridge broken, and soldiers placed to resist him, after two days' stay in Southwark, removed to Kingston, where he found likewise the bridge broken ; yet, with great industry, suddenly repairing it, he passed over his men, and meant with all speed to get to the Court before the Queen should have notice of his coming ; and had done so, indeed, if a mischance, and an error upon that mischance, had not hindered him. For being within six miles of London, the carriage of one of his great ordnance brake, in mending whereof so much time was spent, (and Wyat by no persuasions would go forward without it,) that the time was past in which his friends at London expected his coming; which disappointment made many in those parts to fall off, and being perceived by those about him, many of them also; so that one-half of his army had suddenly gone and left him; and amongst others, Sir George Harper, the most intimate of all his council, went to the queen and discovered all his purposes. Leaving his ordnance upon a hill, with the greatest part of his army, after sundry fights with the Queen's forces (in which his success so excited Mary that she was about to take the command of the troops herself), Wyat reached Ludgate, and was denied entrance; and, then thinking to retire, he heard the Earl of Pembroke with his power was behind at Charing Cross; so that, neither able to go forward nor yet backward, he was at a stand and in amazement, and then, leaning a while upon a stall,* by the Bell-Sauvage, after a little musing, he returned towards Temple Gate, where Clarentius, the herald, meeting him, fell to persuade him to yield. The soldiers of Wyat were earnest with him to have stood it out; but Wyat, as sillily ending as he had unadvisedly began, yielded himself to Sir Maurice Berkeley, and getting up upon his horse behind him, in that manner rode to the Court, where he had not the entertainment he expected, for without more ado he was presently sent away to the Tower. The captain taken, the rest made no resistance, few fled, and of the other many were taken and laid in prison.—Baker's *Chronicle.*

CHARACTER OF QUEEN MARY.

Dr. Lingard's defence of Queen Mary will not stand, for a moment, the examination of an impartial eye. He would make Mary appear not only as the best of women, but as a good sovereign. Sir Frederick Madden has collected the best proofs of Mary's possessing some amiable qualities, which none but bigots on the other side will attempt to deny; but in removing some prejudices, he seems to contract others, and almost to fall in love with his subject. He carries most of his arguments too far, relying occasionally on the most doubtful kind of evidence, giving at other times an interpretation to words and things which they will scarcely bear, and now and then drawing conclusions directly contrary to what the premises would justify. We would scarcely attempt to defend the prejudices and minor inaccuracies of David Hume, but it seems to us that sufficient account is not made of the wonderful quickness and sagacity of that great writer and most admirable of narrators, whose intuitive penetration generally made up for his indolence in examining records and original authorities. We seldom take up any work relating, in however trifling a part, to the history of our country, without finding taunts, or sneers, or louder reproaches, against this first

---

* Baker uses the word *stall*, which means open shop (without glazed windows), such as existed to our day; and a "stall-board" is still part of the carpenter's fittings of a shop-window.

of our good historians. Hume, knowing that Mary suffered a wretched state of health, and having other evidence to go upon, describes her as being of a sour and sullen disposition. This, says Sir Frederick Madden, who classes Hume with Buchanan and Carte, as a writer of coarse invectives, (which Hume never was,) is an inaccuracy notorious to all those acquainted with the history of the period; and to support his opinion, he mentions that Mary was once seen to laugh heartily at a tumbler at Greenwich—that she kept in her service a female jester, (every King at that time kept a fool royal)—that she once had a kennel of hounds; that she was fond of music, played at cards, allowed valentines to be drawn in her household, and once lost a breakfast wagered upon a game at bowls. But the accuser of Hume's inaccuracy admits, and gives from the plainest spoken Venetian, the *broadest* account of her malady (that Mary, from the age of puberty, had suffered the most distressing of all female disorders). Ill-usage and ill-health were not likely to produce the best of tempers. But though Sir Frederick Madden may have known cheerful and light-hearted valetudinarians, we must question whether he ever knew a cheerful bigot. The disorders of her body and of her mind must have made Mary what Hume described her to be on her accession. In the minutiæ of the "Privy Purse Expenses," and incidental occurrences of court holidays, Sir Frederick Madden forgets Smithfield, and the fires that blazed in all parts of the kingdom during this *cheerful* reign.

HOW THE LADY ELIZABETH ESCAPED THE MACHINATIONS OF BISHOP GARDINER.

It is memorable what malice Bishop Gardiner bore to the Lady Elizabeth, by whose procurement not only was she kept in most hard durance (at Woodstock), but a warrant was at last framed under certain counsellors' hands to put her to death; but that Mr. Bridges, Lieutenant of the Tower, pitying her case, went to the Queen to know her pleasure, who utterly denied that she knew anything of it; by which means her life was preserved. Indeed, the Bishop would sometimes say, how they cut off boughs and branches, but as long as they let the root remain, all was nothing; and it is not unworthy remembering what trains were laid to ensnare her. The common net at that time for catching Protestants was the Real Presence, and this was used to catch Elizabeth: for being asked one day what she thought of the words of Christ, *this is my Body*, whether she thought it the true Body of Christ that was in the Sacrament, it is said that after some pausing she answered thus:—

Christ was the Word that spake it :
He took the bread, and brake it :
And what the Word did make it,
That I believe, and take it.

Which though it may seem but a slight expression, yet hath it more solidness than at first sight appears; at least, it served her turn at that time to escape the net, which by direct answer she could not have done.—Baker's *Chronicle.*

THE INVINCIBLE ARMADA.

This was the famous naval armament, or expedition, sent by Philip I. of Spain, against England, in the year 1588. It consisted of 130 vessels, 2430 great guns, 4575 quintals of powder, nearly 20,000 soldiers, above 8000 sailors, and more than 2000 volunteers. It arrived in the English Channel on the 19th of July, and was defeated the next day by Lord High Admiral Howard, who was followed by Drake, Hawkins, and Frobisher. Eight fireships having been sent into the Spanish fleet, they bore off in great disorder. Profiting by the panic the English fell upon them, and captured and destroyed a number of their ships. Admiral Howard maintained a running fight, from the 21st of July to the 27th, with such effect that the Spanish commander, despairing of success, resolved to return home; and as escape through the English Channel was prevented by contrary winds, he undertook to sail round the Orkneys; but the vessels which still remained to him were dispersed by storms, or shipwrecked among the rocks and shallows, on different parts of the Scottish and Irish coasts, and upwards of 5000 men were drowned, killed, or taken prisoners. Of the whole Armada, 53 ships only returned to Spain, and those in a wretched condition. The English lost but one ship. This great defeat was commemorated in the tapestry hangings which long adorned the old House of Lords, destroyed in the great fire of 1834. The tapestry was of Dutch workmanship, it having been woven by Francis Spearing, from the designs of Vroom, an eminent Dutch painter. It had been bespoke by Admiral Lord Howard, and was sold by him to James I. It consisted originally of ten compartments, forming separate pictures, each of which was surrounded by a wrought border, including the portraits of the officers who held commands in the English fleet. Engravings from these hangings have been made by Pine, with illustrations from charters, medals, &c. The Lord High Admiral's remains are deposited in a large vault beneath the principal chancel of the church of Reigate, in Surrey.

FRENCH PORTRAIT OF QUEEN ELIZABETH.

M. Jules Janin has drawn the following severe portrait of Elizabeth: "Daughter of a tyrant as odious and as cruel as any in history, and of a young, innocent queen, the most touching victim of the terrible Henry VIII., the young Elizabeth grew up on the steps of the scaffold which was to see so many more victims. As a child, she had the courage not to tremble before her father; she could regard the executioner of the most beautiful women and greatest men of the time without blenching. She was early accustomed to the noise of chains, locks, and the axe; and amid all these perils she could still smile. For this innocent girl, reserved for such high destiny, the reign of the bloody Mary was full of trials and dangers, and when she was fetched from the Tower and told that she was Queen, she trembled within herself at the remembrance of all the murders committed by Mary Tudor. A great day then commenced for all Protestant England, which was to live under clement laws, and, above all things under an English Queen. She was twenty-five years of age, in all the *éclat* of her youth and beauty; her head was evidently well fitted to wear a crown, and her hand to hold the golden sceptre. At her first glance she saw the greatest men in England prostrate at her feet, and ready to aid her with all their courage, their experience, and their virtue. Never did more worthy counsellors address ears better fitted to listen to them; and we, children of the Salic law, are dazzled, as it were at the sight of so much grandeur around a throne occupied by a princess of twenty-five."

SCANDAL AGAINST QUEEN ELIZABETH.

From letters to his master of Alvarez de Quadra, Bishop of Aquila, Ambassador of Philip II. in London during the first five years of the reign of Elizabeth, a man who, says Mr. Froude, would lie to any man except his master, Mr. Froude, from studying the archives of Simancas, has wrought a tale of which this is the essential part:—" From the day of her accession Elizabeth had drawn remarks on herself by the special favour which she showed to Lord Robert Dudley, the afterwards notorious Earl of Leicester. Scandal was busy with her name, and became so loud-voiced that De Quadra was led to inquire curiously into her antecedents in such matters. The result was in the main favourable. There were many stories current to her discredit; but, on the whole, the Ambassador did not believe them. She was a wilful woman, he said, and a wicked heretic, but that was the worst that could be said of her. Her regard for Dudley, however, was so palpable that it was a common subject of remark and censure from Protestants as well as Catholics. He had a wife, indeed, but the wife never appeared at court; and she was reported to have bad health, which report insisted was not altogether natural disease. Dudley himself was incautious in his language, and dropped hints from time to time of prospects which might possibly be before him.

The Queen at last was thought to be so seriously compromising herself that Cecil attempted remonstrance; and although, when Elizabeth made the advance to the Spanish Ambassador about the Archduke, Dudley and his sister were the persons through whom she communicated her wishes, the Count de Faria wrote that he doubted whether they could be trusted to act honestly. Time, however, passed on; the Scotch wars drew off public attention; Amy Robsart did not die; and the scandal was dying away, when one night, in the autumn of 1560, Cecil came secretly to De Quadra's house, and told him that all his efforts had been fruitless. The Queen was rushing upon destruction, and this time he could not save her. She had made Lord Robert Dudley " master of the government and of her own person." Dudley's wife was about to be murdered, and was at that moment with difficulty " guarding herself" against poison." Dead to honour, blind to danger, and careless to everything but the gratification of her passion, Elizabeth would be contented with nothing less than raising Dudley to the throne, and the unhappy Amy Robsart would not be long an obstacle. For himself, like a prudent mariner before a storm, he intended to retire from the public service. His interference had availed nothing; he would now only stand aside and watch the revolution which would be the instant inevitable consequence of the Queen's insanity.

While the Ambassador was cyphering this extraordinary information to his master, the news arrived in London that Amy Robsart was actually dead. She was staying (as all readers of *Kenilworth* know) at Cumnor-hall, a place about three miles from Oxford. For what purpose she had been placed there no sufficient evidence remains to show; but there she was, and there by accident, as Elizabeth assured De Quadra, she fell down a staircase and was killed. A cabinet council was immediately held. Who were present De Quadra does not say; but the chief actor was still Cecil, in whom indignation for the moment swept away all restraints of policy. It was proposed to dethrone Elizabeth and send her at once with Dudley to the Tower. The Protestants would be satisfied with the proclamation of the Queen's infamy; and out of the many claimants for the vacant throne some one could be found whom the country would agree to accept. Some one; but who was this some one to be? For many days it was uncertain how the balance would turn. Elizabeth probably knew her danger, but durst not move to defend herself. Darnley, the nominee of the Catholics, was unacceptable to Cecil; he would be a mere plaything in the hands of the reactionists. Cecil proposed to change the dynasty, to declare the Tudors usurpers, and proclaim the Earl of Huntingdon as the representative of the House of York; but the Earl of Huntingdon, as a Protestant, would be rejected by one-half the country, as Darnley would be rejected by the other. Philip, too, who would look patiently on Elizabeth's dethronement, would not countenance the substitution of a heretic. Many plans were suggested and laid aside; and among other measures taken hastily in the confusion was the secret marriage, supposed to be Cecil's work, between Lady Catherine Grey and the Earl of Hertford. But after all was said, agreement was found to be impossible. A civil war, a French invasion, and Mary Stuart seemed the certain consequence of Elizabeth's deposition; and if she could be prevented from insulting the country by the marriage, it was determined for the present to spare her. (Such, at least, seems to have been the resolution, for at this point one of De Quadra's letters is missing, and an epitome of it only remains.) At any rate there was to be no public disturbance; and if she was to remain on the throne, it was necessary to shield her honour and hush up the murder. The same veracious bishop also wrote that first Sir Henry Sidney, afterwards Dudley, afterwards Queen Elizabeth herself, brought to him offers to marry Philip, and, overthrowing the Reformation in England, "re-establish religion." Cecil alone saved the Queen. All that De Quadra writes, Mr. Froude, though he says that "he handled falsehood like a master," asks the public to believe.—*Times* journal.

DARNLEY'S MURDER, 1567.

There is a notable gap in the documents at the State Paper Office of the time of Darnley's murder. For a month before, and almost a month after it, the reports of the English agents at Edinburgh have disappeared. These had hitherto been constant and copious, with the minutest information of everything that went on. The communications upon this subject must have been numerous and important; how much so, we can judge from their graphic fulness of detail at the time of Rizzio's death. They may have been taken out to form a special collection; and, if so, their discovery will some day tell the whole of this horrid tale in its naked and minutest particulars. But what if they touched some great personage? Was it Mary? If so, their loss would be accounted for by supposing that James on his succession sought to obliterate traces of her guilt. Yet, if they had contained disclosures fatal to Mary, would Elizabeth have withheld them when she prompted and persuaded Murray and his comrades to charge her with the murder, as she undoubtedly did, when Mary was her prisoner in England—or during the long years when she wreaked her vengeance on Mary, and at last persecuted her to death? It may be that Elizabeth, in some strange fit of returning affection for Mary, might have ordered these papers to be destroyed. Or what if they touched herself? That would explain her frantic efforts for Morton, her attempt to stir up insurrection, her threats of war, her placing an army on the frontier to prevent justice being done upon him.—Caird's *Mary Stuart.*

ELIZABETH AND MARY QUEEN OF SCOTS.

Queen Elizabeth, very shortly after the condemnation of the Scots Queen, in the hall of Fotheringhay, attempted to persuade Paulet, her keeper, to put her to death privately. Her letter to that person is couched in these strange terms: " Amias, my most faithful and careful servant, God reward thee treblefold for the most troublesome charge so well discharged. If you knew, my Amias, how kindly, beside most dutifully, my grateful heart accepts and praises your spotless endeavours and faithful actions, performed in so dangerous and crafty a charge, it would ease your travail and rejoice your heart; in which I charge you to carry this most instant thought, that I cannot balance in any weight of my judgment the value that I prize you at, and suppose no treasure can countervail such a faith. And you shall condemn me in that fault that yet I never committed, if I reward not such desert; yea, let me lack when I most need it, if I acknowledge such a merit, *non omnibus datum.*"

She dares not name the crime she is wooing her faithful servant to commit. The vague language which Shakspeare puts into the mouth of King John, when persuading Hubert to murder his nephew, bears a singular resemblance to this letter:

> O my gentle Hubert,
> We owe thee much !   Within this wall of flesh
> There is a soul counts thee a creditor,
> And with advantage means to pay thy love ;
> And, my good friend, thy voluntary oath
> Lives in this bosom dearly cherished.

Paulet, a determined enemy of Mary, but an honest man, refused to take the hint, upon which Walsingham explained the meaning of the Queen somewhat sharply. " We find," he says, in a letter to Paulet, " by a speech lately made by her Majesty, that she doth note in you both a lack of that care and zeal for her service that she looketh for at your hands, in that you have not in all this time, found out some way to shorten the life of the Scots Queen, considering the great peril she is hourly subject to, so long as the said queen shall live."—*Tytler*, vol. ii. p. 319.

The final reply which Paulet returned to these nefarious proposals, must have proved a severe rebuke to Elizabeth's haughty spirit :—" Your letter of yesterday," he writes to Walsingham, "coming to my hand this day, I would not fail, according to your directions, to return my answer with all speed, which I shall deliver unto you with great grief and bitterness of mind, in that I am so unhappy as living to see this unhappy day, in which I am required, by direction of my most gracious sovereign, to do an act which God and the law forbiddeth. My goods and life are at her Majesty's disposition, and I am ready to lose them the next morrow if it shall please her. But God forbid I should make so foul a shipwreck of my conscience, or leave so great a blot to my poor posterity, as shed blood without law or warrant."

CHARACTER OF MARY QUEEN OF SCOTS.

No historical personage of the sixteenth century, much as that age abounds in illustrious names, has acquired a greater celebrity than Mary Stuart. The mother of our present race of kings, the most beautiful woman of her age, and the most unfortunate, it is not to be wondered at that the poets and painters, as well as the historians and philosophers of all countries, have rendered homage to the memory of this unhappy princess, by investing her with a degree of interest greater than that which we attach to any female name of modern annals.

Mr. Froude, in his valuable *History of England*, is the latest investigator of the history of Mary, and as the result of long studies among forgotten archives, he has thrown a flood of light on the subject. His extracts from the Simancas papers, and many of his citations from the Hatfield collection, have been made for the first time, and prove of great importance and interest ; though it must be added that Mr. Froude takes the most unfavourable view of Mary Stuart's history. An able critic in the *Churchman* thus estimates this portion of it :—

" There are only two views which can be entertained of Mary Stuart's character. Either she was the most curiously and extraordinarily unfortunate woman who ever lived, or she was a foul adulteress and murderess, who lured her husband to his death with circumstances of peculiar treachery and baseness. Mr. Froude has convinced us that the latter view is the true one. We sat down to the perusal of his volumes with an unprejudiced mind. We gave careful attention to all the points of the evidence. We compared his account with that of other historians, both favourable to Mary and adverse to her, and we rose with all doubts removed. The broad facts of the case point unquestionably to the worst conclusion. Nor can it well be denied that if Mary had been old and ugly, and had died in her bed, probably not a single voice would have been raised in her defence. The evidence against her is infinitely stronger than that which convicts John of the murder of Arthur, or Richard III. of the murder of his nephews. But it may well be replied that this is no reason against allowing their full weight to the arguments in her favour: there may be many who have been condemned by the verdict of history because no one has cared to undertake their defence.

" Her beauty, her misfortunes, the injuries which she received at the hands of her rival, and her early and tragical death, have thrown a halo of romance around her name which has raised up, and probably will always raise up, defenders of her innocence. But they have been persons led by the heart and not by the head. With the exception of Miss Strickland, there has been little difference of opinion among historians as to her guilt. Lingard, Roman Catholic as he was, though he says what he can in her defence, does not venture directly to assert her innocence; and his statement of the facts does not differ materially from that of Mr. Froude. Even Walter Scott, with all his romantic sympathies and Stuart predilections, leans to the supposition of her guilt. If any doubt remained upon the point, Mr. Froude has, in our opinion, removed it. That many will still adhere to their former belief, we doubt not. For ourselves we can only say that if Mary Stuart was innocent, no conclusion of history can be considered worthy of reliance."

It is curious to observe what pleasure the conscientious historian takes in presenting us, with a difference, some of the scenes of Scott's romance. Here is Mr. Froude's sketch of Lochleven and its castle, the scene of Mary's imprisonment :

"The castle consisted of the ordinary Scotch tower, a strong stone structure five and twenty feet square, carried up for three or four storeys. It formed one corner of a large court from 90 to 100 feet across. The basement storey was a flagged hall which served at the same time for kitchen and guardroom. The two or three rooms above it may have been set apart for the lord and lady and their female servants. . . . . In the angle opposite the castle was a round turret, entered, like the main building, from the court ; within it was something like an ordinary limekiln from seven to eight feet in diameter. This again was divided into three rooms, one above the other, the height of each may have been six feet. . . . . Here it was, in the three apartments, that the Queen of Scotland passed the long months of her imprisonment. Decency must have been difficult in such a place, and cleanliness impossible. She had happily a tough, healthy nature, which cared little for minor comforts."

Mary was elsewhere meanly lodged, as at Worksop—the house huge, and one of the magnificent works of old Bess of Hardwicke, who guarded the Queen of Scots here for some time in a wretched little bedchamber within her own lofty one.

Again, what a drawback on *beaux sentiments* and romantic ideas is presented in Pasquier's account of the execution of the Queen of Scots. He says: "The night before, knowing her body must be stripped for her shroud, she would have her feet washed, because she used ointment to one of them, which was sore." In a very old trial of Mary, which Walpole bought from Lord Oxford's collections, it is said that "she was a *large lame woman.*" Take sentiments out of their pantoufles, and reduce them to the infirmities of mortality, and what a falling off is there!

SIR WALTER RALEIGH IN THE TOWER.

Raleigh was first imprisoned in the Tower in 1592 (eight weeks) for winning the heart of Elizabeth Throgmorton, one of Queen Elizabeth's maids of honour, "not only a moral sin, but in those days a heinous political offence." Raleigh's next imprisonment was in 1603: after being first confined in his own house, he was conveyed to the Tower, next sent to Winchester gaol, returned from thence to the Tower, imprisoned for between two and three months in the Fleet, and again removed to the Tower, where he remained until his release, thirteen years afterwards, to undertake his new Expedition to Guiana. Mr. Payne Collier possesses a copy of that rare tract, *A Good Speed to Virginia*, 4to, 1609, with the autograph on the title-page, "W. Ralegh, Turr. Lond.," showing that at the time this tract was published Raleigh recorded himself as a prisoner in the Tower of London. During part of the time, Lady Raleigh resided with her husband; and here, in 1605, was born Carew, their second son. After she had been forbidden to lodge with her husband in the Tower, Lady Raleigh lived on Tower Hill. In his prison-lodging (believed to have been in the Bloody Tower), Sir Walter wrote his political discourses, and commenced his famous *History of the World*, which he published in 1614. Raleigh wrote his *History* avowedly for his patron, Prince Henry of Wales, the heir-apparent to the throne; upon whose death Sir Walter is stated to have burnt the continuation of the work, which he had written. Twelve years of his imprisonment were passed in the Bloody Tower, whither Prince Henry came to visit him; Ben Jonson and the poets also here conversed with Raleigh. Here he began a treatise on the art of conducting war by sea; made a new model of a ship; and invented his "Rare Cordial." He converted a little henhouse in the garden into a still-house, and spent whole days in distillations. It was here that in the frenzy of despair, Raleigh attempted to stab himself to the heart, after he had written to his wife the touching and pathetic letter preserved in All Souls' College, Oxford. Raleigh was also imprisoned in the Beauchamp Tower and the White Tower.

SIR WALTER RALEIGH ON THE SCAFFOLD.

The scaffold having been erected near dwelling-houses in Old Palace Yard, Westminster, Raleigh observed when he ascended it several noblemen and gentlemen, who had stationed themselves at a window of Sir Randal Crew's to witness his death, and because his voice was weak, he requested them to come out and stand on the scaffold, as he had something to say to them. When they had done as he desired, he made a short speech, the meaning of which has scarcely been preserved. What we possess under that name it is impossible he should have uttered, unless we assume the letter to James of the 5th of October, together with his examination and those of La Chêne, and all his communications with the French authorities, to be forgeries. Had he denied, as he is said to have done, that he ever saw any commission, letter, or seal, from the French king, his admission to the contrary, in his own handwriting, would doubtless have been produced on the scaffold to confound and silence him. We must, consequently, be ieve either that the documents referred to were mere fabrications, or that several gentlemen who were present at his death, and heard him deliver his farewell address to the world, either misunderstood his language or purposely misrepresented it. The reference he made to Essex's death, may have imported no more than this, that he never spontaneously sought his destruction, though the earl had fallen by the means he had been constrained to employ to preserve himself against his machinations. We quote the above from the Life of Sir Walter Raleigh, by J. A. St. John, who among other new light, shows the probability of Raleigh having sailed to the West Indies in 1578, sixteen years earlier than he is otherwise known to have visited that part of the world.

TWO TIPPLING KINGS.

In 1608, when Christian IV. of Denmark, brother of the Queen of James I., came to England to visit him, both the kings got drunk together to celebrate the meeting. Sir John Harrington, the wit, has left a most amusing account of this Court revel and carousal. He tells us that "the sports began each day in such manner and such sorte, as well nigh persuaded me of Mahomet's paradise. We had women, and indeed wine too, of such plenty, as would have astonished each beholder. Our feasts were magnificent, and the two royal guests did most lovingly embrace each other at table. I think the Dane hath strangely wrought on our good English nobles; for those whom I could never get to taste good liquor, now follow the fashion, and wallow in beastly delights. The ladies abandon their sobriety, and are seen to roll about in intoxication. In good sooth, the Parliament did kindly to provide his majestie so seasonably with money, for there have been no lack of good livinge, shews, sights, and banquetings from morn to eve.

" One day a great feast was held, and after dinner the representation of Solomon his temple, and the coming of the Queen of Sheba was made, or (as I may better say) was meant to have been made, before their majesties, by the device of the Earl of Salisbury and others. But alas! as all earthly things do fail to poor mortals in enjoyment, so did prove our presentment thereof. The lady who did play the Queen's part did carry most precious gifts to both their majesties; but forgetting the steppes arising to the canopy, overset her caskets in his Danish Majesty's lap, and fell at his feet, though I think it was rather in his face. Much was the hurry and contusion; cloths and napkins were at hand to make all clean. His Majestie then got up, and would dance with the Queen of Sheba; but he fell down and humbled himself before her, and was carried to an inner chamber, and laid on a bed of state, which was not a little defiled with the presents of the Queen, which had been bestowed on his garments; such as wine, cream, jelly, beverage, cakes, spices, and other good matters. The entertainment and show went forward, and most of the presenters went backward or fell down; wine did so occupy their upper chambers. Now did appear, in rich dress, Hope, Faith, and Charity. Hope did essay to speak, but wine rendered her endeavours so feeble that she withdrew, and hoped the King would excuse her brevity. Faith was then all alone, for I am certain she was not joyned to good works, and left the court in a staggering condition. Charity came to the King's feet, and seemed to cover the multitude of sins her sisters had committed; in some sorte she made obeysance, and brought giftes, but said she would return home again, as there was no gift which heaven had not already given his Majesty. She then returned to Hope and Faith, who were both sick . . . . in the lower hall. Next came Victory, in bright armour, and presented a rich sword to the King, who did not accept it, but put it by with his hand; and by a strange medley of versification did endeavour to make suit to the King. But Victory did not triumph long; for, after much lamentable utterance, she was led away like a silly captive, and laid to sleep in the outer steps of the ante-chamber. Now did Peace make entry, and strive to get foremost to the King; but I grieve to tell how great wrath she did discover unto those of her attendants; and much contrary to her semblance, made rudely war with her olive branch, and laid on the pates of those who did oppose her coming." *

MYSTERIOUS ROYAL DEATHS.

It has been asserted that Henry, Prince of Wales, eldest son of James I., was poisoned, and that the king was privy to the act. James did not manifest any great sorrow at the event; but it does not appear that he was in any way accessory to Henry's death, or that he had been unfairly dealt with by any person. The medical treatment might have been unskilful, but the *post mortem* examination of the body, to be found

---

* *Nugæ Antiquæ*, ed. 1804, vol. i., quoted in a note to Peyton's *Catastrophe of the Stuarts*, in the *Secret History of the Court of James I.*, vol. ii.

in the *Desiderata Curiosa*, and signed by all the medical attendants, renders it obvious that natural causes occasioned the death of that most promising young man; so, we do not perceive that there were any secrets to disclose. Yet, it is stated that at the trial of Carr, Earl of Somerset, Mrs. Turner, and others, for the poisoning of Sir Thomas Overbury, James was so fearful of the Earl's speaking of that circumstance, that two persons were provided to stand behind him with a cloak, and the moment he should utter anything reflecting on the king, he was to have been muffled therein, and hurried away; and though James most solemnly vowed to show no favour to any person that should be found guilty of Overbury's death, yet, on the conviction of the Earl and his Lady, he was pleased to grant them a lease of their lives for ninety-nine years. Had James been in any way accessory to the Prince's death, he would seem to have experienced the law of retaliation in a singular manner.

In a poem of the day, entitled, "The Duke Return'd Againe," 1627, occur these lines:—

> Or didst thou hasten headlong, to prevent
> A fruitlesse hope for needfull parliament?
> All these, noe question, with a restlesse motion
> Vext thy bespotted soule; as did thy potion
> Torture the noble Scott; whose *manes* tell
> Thy swolne ambition made his carcase swell.

The latter is an allusion to the imputed poisoning of King James I., by the Duke's means; an assertion which we shall find frequently enforced by the satirists of the day. It was broadly charged to the Duke by one of King James's physicians, Dr. George Eglisham, as well as the poisoning of the Marquis of Hamilton, in a pamphlet called the *Forerunner of Revenge*, and couched in the language of a petition to King Charles I. for justice on the Duke. A curious engraving is in existence, depicting this so-called poisoning scene in the King's bedchamber. The enemies of Buckingham and his family, and they were many, of course spread the foul tale, which was popularly credited; but the truth seems to be, that he and his mother administered a poisoned plaster and a posset of the Duke's preparation. The physicians who opened the body reported the intestines to have been very much discoloured, and his body extremely distorted. And in the charge to Sir John Eliot was "The applying of a plaister and giving of a drinke to King James in his last sicknesse, without making any of the King's sworne doctors and apothecaries acquainted therewithall, and contrary to their directions in general and particular."

In the print the King is represented in bed, one of the attendant figures is uttering "Thanks to the chymist," and another, Dr. Lambe, is standing by the bed, holding a bottle, and saying "I'll warrant you;" the portrait very much resembling that of Lambe published by Mr. Thane.

AN HISTORIC HOUSE IN FLEET-STREET.

One of the few remaining specimens of olden street architecture existing in the metropolis is the house No. 17, Fleet Street, facing Chancery Lane. In the lower portion of the house is the gateway to Inner Temple Lane, of plain Jacobean design, with a semicircular arch, and the Pegasus in the spandrils. This house was built in 1609, and was not, as inscribed, " Formerly the Palace of Henry VIII. and Cardinal Wolsey." Thither was removed in 1795, Mrs. Salmon's Waxwork Collection, celebrated before its commemoration in the *Spectator*, No. 28. Mrs. Salmon, in her advertisements, styled this house "once the Palace of Henry, Prince of Wales, son of King James I.," and so it was considered until the tenant who succeeded Mrs. Salmon gave the house its present inscription. The first-floor front-room has an enriched plaster ceiling, inscribed P. (triple plume) H., which, with part of the carved wainscoting, denote the building to be of the time of James I. Still, we do not find in the lives of Prince Henry any indication of this house as a royal palace. It appears that though never the residence of Prince Henry, it was the *office in which the Council for the Management of the Duchy of Cornwall Estates held their sittings*, in his time; and in the Calendar of State Papers, edited by Mrs. Green, we find entries dated from the Council-Chamber, in Fleet Street. The interior of the House is in the style of Inigo Jones, whose first office was Surveyor of the Works to Henry, Prince of Wales until the year 1613.—*Curiosities of London,* new edit., 1868.

It is curious to find the inscription upon this house altered from Mrs. Salmon's designation in 1795, which, though not correct, was nearer the truth than that ascribing it to Henry VIII. and Wolsey. In Hughson's *Walks through London,* 1817, we find, "The range of houses near and over the Inner Temple Gate, are of the architecture of James I., as is evident from the plume of feathers over the house to the east of the gate, intended as a compliment to Henry Prince of Wales, then the object of popular favour. The gate itself was erected in 1611, at the expense of John Benet, Esq., King's Serjeant." It may be mentioned that the former gate of the Middle Temple was erected as a fine imposed by Wolsey, which may have led to the Wolseyan celebrity wrongly attached to the house adjoining the Inner Temple Gate.

THE AGES OF ELIZABETH AND CHARLES I.

The difference between the state of mind in the reign of Elizabeth and in that of Charles I. is astonishing. In the former period there was an amazing development of power, but all connected with prudential purposes—an attempt to reconcile the moral feeling with the full exercise of the powers of the mind, and the accomplishment of certain practical ends. Thus lived Bacon, Burghley, Sir W. Raleigh, Sir Philip

Sidney, and a galaxy of great men, statesmen, lawyers, politicians, philosophers, and poets; and it is lamentable that they should have degraded their mighty powers to such base designs and purposes, dissolving the rich pearls of their great faculties in a worthless acid, to be drunken by a harlot. What was seeking the favour of a Queen, to a man like Bacon, but the mere courtship of harlotry? Compare this age with that of the Republicans; that indeed was an awful age, as compared with our own. England may be said to have then overflowed from the fulness of grand principle, from the greatness which men felt in themselves, abstracted from the prudence with which they ought to have considered whether their principles were, or were not, adapted to the condition of mankind at large. Compare the revolution then effected with that of a day not long past, when the bubbling up and overflowing was occasioned by the elevation of the dregs—when there was a total absence of all principle, when the dregs had risen from the bottom to the top, and, thus converted into scum, founded a monarchy, to be the poisonous bane and misery of the rest of mankind. It is absolutely necessary to recollect that the age in which Shakspeare lived was one of great abilities, applied to individual and prudential purposes, and not an age of high moral feeling and lofty principle, which gives a man of genius the power of thinking of all things in reference to all. If, then, we should find that Shakspeare took these materials as they were presented to him, and yet to all effectual purposes produced the same grand result as others attempted to produce in an age so much more favourable, shall we not feel and acknowledge the purity and holiness of genius—a light which, however it might shine on a dunghill, was as pure as the divine influence which created all the beauty of nature?—Coleridge's *Lectures on Shakspeare and Milton.*

QUEEN HENRIETTA MARIA, AND HER REPUTED PENANCE TO TYBURN.

Howell, in one of his letters, dated "London, 16th May, 1626," thus describes this beautiful and accomplished princess:—" We have now a most noble new Queen of England, who in true beauty, is much beyond the long-woo'd infanta. The daughter of France—this youngest branch of Bourbon, is of a more lovely and lasting complexion, a dark brown; she hath eyes that sparkle like stars; and for her physiognomy, she may be said to be a mirror of perfection. She had a rough passage in her transfretation to Dover Castle; and in Canterbury the king bedded first with her. There were a goodly number of choice ladies attended her coming upon the bowling green, at Barham Downs, upon the way, who divided themselves into two rows, and they appeared like so many constellations; but methought the country ladies outshined the courtiers.

" The Queen brought over with her two hundred thousand crowns in gold and silver, as half her portion, and the other moiety is to be paid at the year's end. Her first suite of servants (by article) are to be French; and as they die, English are to succeed. She is allowed twenty-eight ecclesiastics, of any order except Jesuits; a bishop for her almoner; and to have private exercise of her religion for herself, and for her servants.

There is another disputed event in the life of the Queen which deserves to be sifted. Sir William Waller asserts in his *Recollections*, p. 122, that the Queen's confessor once compelled her to walk in penance to Tyburn, "some say barefoot," seemingly for some kindness towards heretics. This Tyburn penance is, however, discredited. The story is conjectured to have originated with Buckingham himself, for a notable quarrel broke out between the Queen and him while this matter was discussed in council. It is evident that Charles I. believed the story; for, writing to his ambassador in France on July 12, 1626, he says: "I can no longer suffer those that I know to be about my wife any longer, which I must do if it were but for one action they made my wife do; which is to make her go to Tyburn in devotion to pray, which action can have no greater invective made against it than the relation."—Appendix to Ludlow's *Memoirs*, edit. 1771, p. 511.

The story was also credited by the King's ministers, for in the "Reply of the Commissioners of his Majesty the King of Great Britain to the proposition presented by M. le Mareschal de Bassompierre, Ambassador Extraordinary to his Most Christian Majesty," it is stated that the Bishop of Mande and his priests "abused the influence which they had acquired over the tender and religious mind of her Majesty, so far as to lead her a long way on foot through a park the gates of which had been expressly ordered by the Count de Villiers to be kept open, to go in devotion to a place (Tyburn), where it has been the custom to execute the most infamous malefactors and criminals of all sorts, exposed on the entrance of a high road; an act not only of shame and mockery towards the Queen, but of reproach and calumny of the King's predecessors of glorious memory, as accusing them of tyranny in having put to death innocent persons, whom these people look upon as martyrs; although, on the contrary, not one of them had been executed on account of religion, but for high treason. And it was this last act, above all, which provoked the royal resentment and anger of his Majesty beyond the bounds of his patience, which, until then, had enabled him to support all the rest; but he could now no longer endure to see in his house and in his kingdom people who, in the person of his dearly beloved consort, had brought such scandal upon his religion."—*Memoirs of the Embassy of the Marshal de Bassompierre*, Appendix, p. 138.

It appears, however, that the Queen herself earnestly denied this Tyburn story, and instructed Bassompierre to state to the King's council that "the Queen of Great Britain, by permission of the King, her consort, graced the jubilee at the Chapel of the Pères de l'Oratoire, at St. James's, with the devotion suitable to a great princess, so well born, and so jealous of her religion, which devotions terminated with vespers; and sometime after, the heat of the day being passed, she walked in the park of St. James's, and in the Hyde Park, which joins it—a walk she had often taken with the King, her husband; but that she made it in procession, or that she ever approached within fifty paces of the gallows, or that she made there any prayers, public or private, or that she went on her knees there, holding the crown or chaplets in her hands, is what those who impose these matters on others do not believe themselves." This is quoted from Bassompierre's *Memoirs*, p. 146, the editor of which (the late John Wilson Croker,) justly remarks, " It really requires the concurrent testimony of all writers to make us believe that the Queen of England was forced by those meddling priests to walk in procession to Tyburn, and there, on her knees, under the gibbet, glorify the blessed martyrs of the Gunpowder Plot."

D'Israeli in his *Commentaries on the Life and Reign of Charles I.*, vol. i. p. 202, edit. 1851, speaking of the "penances and mortifications" inflicted upon the Queen, says: "But the most notorious was her Majesty's pilgrimage to Tyburn, to pray under the gallows of those Jesuits who, executed as traitors to Elizabeth and James, were by the Catholics held as martyrs of faith. This incident Bassompierre, in the style of the true French Gasconade, declared that those who formed the accusation did not themselves believe it. The fact, however, seems doubtful; I find it confirmed by private accounts of the time, and afterwards sanctioned by a state paper." But D'Israeli does not give us any reference to the " private accounts of the time."

The following allusion to the incident occurs in a sermon preached in Westminster Abbey before the House of Peers, on the 24th of September, 1645, by William Gouge, one of the Members of the Assembly: " Others they either enjoyn or persuade to whip their naked backs with scourges of cords, wyers, and sharp rundalls till the bloud run down. . . . . Others must lie in shirts of haircloth. Others go barefoot and barelegged to such and such shrines. Others undertake long pilgrimages to remote lands; *nay, they stick not to send a Queen to Tyburn upon penance.*"

In one of Ellis's *Original Letters*, first series, vol. iii. p. 241-2, from the Harl. MSS. 383, we read: " No longer agon then upon St. James his day last, those hypocritical dogges made the pore Queen to walke a foot (some add barefoot,) from her house at St. James's to the gallowes at Tyborne, thereby to honour the saint of the day in visiting that holy place, where so many martyrs (forsooth!) had shed their blood in defence of the Catholic cause. Had they not also made her to dable in the dirt in a foul morning, from Somersett House to St. James's, her Luciferian Confessor riding along by her in his coach. Yea, they made her to go barefoot, to spin, to eat her meat out of tryne (treen or wooden) dishes, to wait at table and serve her servants, with many other ridiculous and absurd penances. . . . . It is hoped, after they are gone, the Queen will, by degrees, find the sweetness of liberty in being exempt from those beggarly rudiments of Popish penance."

In the *King's Cabinet Opened* there is a copy of instructions given by Charles I. to Dudley Carleton, sent in 1626, on an embassy to France to explain the reason for the dismissal of the Queen's French attendants. Charles justified the dismissal as an act "which," he says, "I must doe if it were but for one action they made my wife doe, which is, to make her go to Tiburn in devotion, to pray, which action can have no greater invective made against it than the relation."

In the *Crowle Pennant*, in the British Museum, is a German print representing the Queen kneeling in penance, the chaplets in her hands, and praying beneath the triple tree, this being the oldest existing representation in existence of the Tyburn gallows. It is moonlight, and the confessor is seated in the coach, which is drawn by six horses; at the coach-door is a servant bearing a torch. The print is of later date than the year of the reputed penance, 1628; but it is considered by print-collectors as untrustworthy as the story itself.

The ill-behaviour of the French that the Queen brought over with her, occasioned Charles the First to write the following letters to the Duke of Buckingham, which are copied from the originals in the British Museum :—

"Steenie,—I write to you by Ned Clarke, that I thought I would here cause enufe in short tyme to put away the Monsers (his wife's French servants and dependants), either by attempting to steal away my wife, or by making plots amongst my own subjects. I cannot say certainlie whether it was intended, but I am sure it is hindered. For the other, though I have good grounds to belife it, and am still hunting after it, yet seeing dailie the Malitiousness of the Monsers, by making and fomenting discontents in my wyfe, I could tarie no longer from adverticing of you, that I mean to seek of no other grounds to casier (cashier) my Monsers, having for this purpose sent you this other letter, that you may if you think good advertise the queene (Mary of Medicis, widow of Henry the Fourth,) mother with my intention.

"So I rest,
           "Your faithful constant loving friende,
                                        "Charles R."

"Steenie,—I have received your letter by Dic Greme: this is my answer—I command you to send all the French away to-morrow, out of the town, if you can by fayre means (but stike not long in disputing), otherwise force them away lyke so many wyld beastes, until ye have shipped them, and so the devil goe with them. Lett me hear no answer, but of the performance of my command.

"So I rest,
           "Your faithfull constant loving friende,
                                        "Charles R.

"Oaking, the 7th of August, 1626.
(Superscribed) "The Duke of Buckingham."

Howell, in a letter dated March 15, 1626, says :—"The French that came over with her Majesty, for their petulancies and some misdemeanors, and imposing some odd penances upon the Queen, are all cashiered this week. It was a thing suddenly done; for about one of the clock, as they were at dinner, my Lord Conway and Sir Thomas Edmondes, came with an order from the King, that they must instantly away to Somerset House, for there were barges and coaches staying for them, and there they should have all their wages paid them to a penny, and so they must be content to quit the kingdom. This sudden, undreamed-of order struck an astonishment into them all, both men and women; and running to complain to the Queen, his Majesty had taken her beforehand into his bedchamber, and locked the door upon them till he had told her how matters stood. The Queen fell into a violent passion, broke the glass window, and tore her hair, but she was cooled afterwards. Just such a destiny happened in France some years since to the Queen's Spanish servants there, who were all dismissed in like manner for some miscarriages. The like was done in Spain to the French, therefore 'tis no new thing."

"THE SADDLE LETTER" AND CHARLES I.

The long-known George and Blue Boar Inn, Holborn, which was taken down in 1864, for the site of the Inns of Court Hotel, is associated with a legendary tale, according to which here was intercepted a letter of Charles I., by which Ireton discovered it to be the King's intention to destroy him and Cromwell, which discovery brought about Charles's execution. In the Earl of Orrery's *Letters* we read: "While Cromwell was meditating how he could best 'come in' with Charles, one of his spies—of the King's bedchamber—informed him that his final doom was decreed, and that what it was might be found out by intercepting a letter sent from the King to the Queen (Henrietta Maria), wherein he declared what he would do. The letter, he said, was sewed up in the skirt of a saddle, and the bearer of it would come with the saddle upon his head, that night, to the Blue Boar Inn, in Holborn; for there he was to take horse and go to Dover with it. This messenger knew nothing of the letter in the saddle; but some persons at Dover did. Cromwell and Ireton, disguised as troopers, taking with them a trusty fellow, went to the Inn in Holborn; and this man watched at the wicket, and the troopers continued drinking beer till about ten o'clock, when the sentinel at the gate gave notice that the man with the saddle was come in. Up they got, and, as the man was leading out his horse saddled, they, with drawn swords, declared that they were to search all who went in and out there; but, as he looked like an honest man, they would only search his saddle. Upon this they ungirt the saddle and carried it into the stall where they had been drinking, and left the horseman with the sentinel; then, ripping up one of the skirts of the saddle, they found the letter, and gave back the saddle to the man, who, not knowing what he had done, went away to Dover. They then opened the letter, in which the King told the Queen that he thought he should close with the Scots. Cromwell and Ireton then took horse and went to Windsor; and, finding they were not likely to have any tolerable terms with the King, they immediately from that time forward *resolved his ruin.*"*

---

* For some notice of this veritable historical hoax of "The Saddle Letter,' see D'Israeli, *Commentaries on the Life and Reign of Charles the First*, v. 323. See also the *Gentleman's Magazine*, xxii. 204. *Notes and Queries*, 3rd series, iv. 410—7.

CHARLES THE FIRST AND HIS PARLIAMENT, 1641.

The importance of the Grand Remonstrance has not been adequately acknowledged by the ordinary historians of the Long Parliament. After the impeachment against Strafford had been carried, the Parliament found themselves in considerable danger from the lukewarmness and desertions which are almost always the consequences of success. A reaction set in against them, which in its consequences might have been most dangerous. They had to dread, on the one side, the effect of the *ad captandum* measures which Hyde was urging the King to bring forward, and on the other the employment of open force to disperse them —a possibility which was by no means too remote to cause anxious consideration. Under these circumstances, they resolved to embody in a document, to be published to all the world, their account of the grievances under which they had found the nation labouring, and of the steps which they had taken to redress them. " Declaration and Remonstrance " intended to effect this purpose was first submitted for discussion on the 8th of November, and the debates on it continued with little intermission till the 15th of December.

The Remonstrance consisted of no less than 206 articles. The great debate of all took place on the 22nd of November. The House met at ten in the morning, and the debate continued without intermission till one on the following morning. According to Clarendon, the members in favour of the Remonstrance " said very little, nor answered any reasons that were alleged to the contrary, but still called for the question, presuming their number if not their reason would serve to carry it, and after two o'clock of the morning, when many had gone home," &c. It now appears that Sir Benjamin Rudyard, Pym, and Hampden, all spoke in favour of it, as well as Denzil Holles, and Serjeant Glyn, and that hardly any one went home, inasmuch as 307 members voted on the great division, whilst only 308 and 310 voted on preceding ones on minor points. After the Remonstrance was carried, it was moved that it should be printed, and this excited a debate of a still more violent character than the motion that it should pass. It ended in the most extraordinary scene that ever occurred in Parliament. Several of the members that were in the king's interest, in pursuance of what is now proved, by a letter from Secretary Nicholas to the King, to have been a set design, claimed a right to protest against the vote of the House; and thereupon Mr. Geoffrey Palmer, who at the Restoration became Attorney-General, in the excitement of the moment declared that he did "protest for himself and all the rest." The members of his party thereupon broke into the wildest excitement. "All! all!" says D'Ewes, " was cried from side to side, and some waved their hats over their heads, and others took their swords in the scabbards out of their belts, and held them by the pummels in their hands, setting the lower part on the ground, so as, if God had not prevented it, there was very great danger that mischief might have been done." With great tact Hampden interfered, by asking Palmer how he could answer for those (of whom there might be many) who disapproved of the printing, but approved of the Remonstrance ?   His reply to the question gave time for the House to collect itself a little, and it adjourned at two in the morning, after deferring the question of the printing till another occasion.   It is very curious to contrast this, the very extreme of violence into which the House of Commons was ever hurried, with the scenes which so frequently and so deeply disgraced the sittings of the various representative Assemblies of France.—(*Saturday Review*.) The attempted Arrest of the Five Members of the House of Commons followed on the 4th of January, 1641-2, and then began our Great Civil War.

MARTYRDOM OF KING CHARLES I.

This " Anniversary " of English history is one of the darkest, the deepest, and most impressive of any age or time ; the death of Charles the First has a monumental record in our metropolis, and more than a monumental record in the heart of posterity and the memories of reading men.   There are few subjects in English history—isolated by their peculiar beauty and absorbing interest, from all meaner incidents—more noble in spirit, more touching in remembrance, more forcible in impression, and more absolutely appealing by their character to the imagination and very soul of the painter, than this of the last moments of the fated Monarch.   The associations which crowd themselves into the memory with the characters which form the grouping of the scene—the recollection of events which immediately preceded it in the awful drama of the times—the shadows of a dark history passing in pageantry before the mind, with strange contrasted forms of rebellion and fidelity, of courage and cowardice, of virtue and treachery, of piety and blasphemy, of grace, loveliness, affection, with selfishness, ferocity, and ambition : all the bad and good elements of humanity, in short, brought strikingly into play—these thoughts and memories, blending with the full inspiring awe and interest of the scene itself, lend it a pervading fervour and a deepened charm, and invest it with a sublime poetry that weaves its intense beauty not more in the grand reality of the breathing picture, than in the visions and aspirations of the gazer's mind.   The subject, too, possesses an universality, for the history of the death of Charles is one familiar to the ear of the world.   It was a life-sacrifice extorted by the rage of a people, and given by its victim without shame or fear.   Charles was, indeed, perhaps more a king upon the scaffold than in any other contingency of his disturbed, unpeaceful life   His countenance was described by the poets and historians of that and after times as wearing a look of resignation most dignified and serene :—

> No storm in his human heart,
>   No strife upon his brow,
> Where calmness, like a patient child,
>   Sits almost smiling now !
> Seems the meek Monarch, as like one
>   Whose gentle spirit sings

Its song of solace to the soul
  Before it spreads its wings !
And filling, ere it takes its flight,
  His features with a holy light !

Yet that serenest heavenly look
  Wears well its taint of earth ;
And mortal majesty retains
  The impress of its birth !   .
The lion doth not hang his mane,
  The eagle droop his wing ;
The lofty glance, the regal mien,
  Fall only with the King :
And Charles's calm, unquailing eye
Shames all who thought he feared to die !

The above grand crisis of morals, religion, and government is yet but imperfectly understood, notwithstanding so many books have been written and published in illustration of it. Coleridge attributes this labour lost to the want of genius or imagination in these works: "Not one of their authors seems to be able to throw himself back into that age: if they did, there would be less praise and less blame bestowed on both sides."

LAST WORDS OF CHARLES I.

Mr. Hargrave Jennings (*Notes and Queries*, second series, x.) has called attention to the solemn word, "Remember," the last word which Charles uttered on the scaffold ; it was addressed to Bishop Juxon. Impressed by the King's manner when he was pronouncing the word, and suspicious of what the communication should be—also actuated by some arousing private curiosity independently of any political significance to be attached to it—the officers on duty, in the first instance, and the Commissioners of the Commons afterwards, insisted on Bishop Juxon declaring what the impartment was which the king made. He only told his questioners that the king's last words were meant as a message to his son, and that the private communication, and the word "Remember," enforcing it, were only to enjoin forgiveness of his enemies, by his son, in the future time. Those who had questioned Juxon seemed to have been content with this answer.

Mr. Jennings is not satisfied that nothing lay under this solemn adjuration. "The words of the historian are: 'Charles, having taken off his cloak, delivered his 'George' to the prelate, pronouncing the word 'Remember !' In that awful moment—the last opportunity for any farther dealing on earth—when the unfortunate Charles was literally bidding adieu to the world, and standing in the presence of the Angel of Death, with, as it were, the light of the other world disclosing upon his figure, he almost seeming to have ceased to have aught to do with this state of things, Mr. Jennings thinks it not likely—nor, in the nature of probabilities, is it to be believed—that he was merely giving utterance to a common-place expression of general, unexalted forgiveness ; and he

maintains that infinitely more was under this impartment than either the
suspicions of the time seemed to have conceived, or modern ideas ever
to have speculated upon. The effect produced, on the scaffold, on the
witnesses of the execution, by this significant injunction, is proven by
the pains which were immediately taken to find out the meaning. We
have reason to conclude that Bishop Juxon was not only inquired of,
concerning it, on the scaffold, after the tragedy of the king's execution
had been consummated, but that he was sent for to Whitehall, to be
questioned by Cromwell and the king's judges. Great things—extraordinary things—wonderful things were in Charles's mind after the ex-
citements of his trial and the terrible results in condemnation. What
should be the state of a man's mind, under such circumstances, we can
only conceive. In this tumult of new sensations, and in the intense and
preternatural stretch and agony of his mind, it is very possible that he
might have achieved, in the state of exaltation well known to those who
are conversant with the *phenomena* (during paroxysms) of clairvoyant
' far-seeing,' to a real, prophetic conviction of things to happen after
him, and of the restoration of monarchy in England, and of the attainment—little as it seemed likely then—of his son to the throne. This
was a vision in the sense that we understand it of saints. But chiefest
of all in proof of these convictions regarding this interesting and hitherto
unexplained matter, is the declaration that such a vision—or supernatural,
prophetic judgment—was really experienced by the king. We hope, in
future accounts of King Charles the First, that this present little history
of a doubtful but important passage will find its proper room."

Colonel Tomlinson commanded the regiment of cavalry on guard at
the execution. They are shown in a picture made of Whitehall at
the time. In the histories Colonel Tomlinson is said to have been " converted" at the beheading of the king. Could this " conversion " consist in his belief of a miracle in the king's assurance!

John Aubrey, under the date of 1696, in his *Miscellanies*—the edition
published after his death—states, as a fact within his precise knowledge,
that :—" After King Charles the First was condemned, he did tell
Colonel Tomlinson that he ' believed the English Monarchy was now
at an end.' About half an hour after, with a radiant countenance, and
as if with a preternaturally assured manner, he affirmed to the Colonel,
positively, that his son should reign after him. This information I had
from Fabian Phillips, Esq., of the Inner Temple, who had the best
authority for the truth of it. I forget whether Mr. Phillips, who was
under some reserve, named to me the particular person. But I suspect
that it was Colonel Tomlinson himself." This divination it was that
probably " converted" Colonel Tomlinson.

THE CALVES' HEAD CLUB.

This was a pretended Society held " in ridicule of the memory of
Charles I.," first noticed in the *Secret History*, supposed to be written by
Ned Ward, attributing the formation of the Club to Milton and some

other friends of the Commonwealth, who were said to meet privately every 30th of January, with a private form of service for the day. After the Restoration they met very secretly; but in the reign of King William, in a public manner, at no fixed house, the *Secret History* states, in a blind alley near Moorfields, where an axe hung up in the club room. The bill of fare was a large dish of calves' heads, by which was represented the King and his friends; a large pike with a small one in his mouth, as an emblem of tyranny; a large cod's head representing the person of the King singly, and a boar's head with an apple in its mouth, to represent the King as bestial. After the repast the *Ikon Basilike* was burnt upon the table, anthems were sung, and the oath was sworn upon Milton's *Defensio Populi Anglicani.* The company consisted of Independents and Anabaptists; Jerry White, formerly chaplain to Oliver Cromwell, said grace, and after the removal of the table-cloth, the anniversary anthem was sung, and a calf's skull filled with wine or other liquor, and then a brimmer went about to the memory of those worthy patriots who had killed the tyrant, &c. The tract went through nine editions, but it was a literary fraud, to keep alive the calumny, there being actually no Club at all. Some thirty years after occurred a scene which seemed to give colour to the truth of the existence of the Club; some young noblemen and gentlemen met at a tavern in Suffolk-street, called themselves the Calves'-head Club, dressed up a calf's-head in a napkin, threw it upon a bonfire, dipped their napkins in red wine, and waved them out of the windows; the mob in the street had strong beer given them, but taking umbrage at some healths proposed, they broke the windows, and rushed into the house; but the guards being sent for, prevented further mischief. This outrage took place on January 30th, the fact to expiate the murder of Charles I.

To sum up, the whole affair was a hoax, kept alive by the pretended *Secret History.* An accidental riot, following a debauch on one 30th of January, has been distributed between two successive years, owing to a misapprehension of the mode of reckoning time prevalent in the early part of the last century; and there is no more reason for believing in the existence of a Calves'-head Club, in 1734-5, than there is for believing it to exist in 1868.

ROYALTY DEDUCED FROM A TUB-WOMAN.

In 1768, there appeared in the newspapers the following paragraph :—
" During the troubles of the reign of Charles I., a country girl came to London in search of a place; but not succeeding, she applied to be allowed to carry out beer from a brewhouse. These women were then called *tub-women.* The brewer, observing her to be a very good-looking girl, took her from this low situation into his house, and afterwards married her; and while she was yet a young woman, he died, and left her a large fortune. She was recommended, on giving up the brewery, to Mr. Hyde, a most able lawyer, to settle her husband's affairs ; he, in process of time, married the widow, and was made Earl of Clarendon. Of this marriage, there was a daughter, who was afterwards wife to

James II., and mother of Mary and Anne, queens of England." This statement was answered by a letter in the *London Chronicle*, December 20, 1768, proving that " Lord Clarendon married Frances, the daughter of Sir Thomas Aylesbury, knight and baronet, one of the Masters of Request to King Charles I., by whom he had four sons—viz., Henry, afterwards Earl of Clarendon ; Lawrence, afterwards Earl of Rochester; Edward, who died unmarried; and James, drowned on board the *Gloucester* frigate : also two daughters—Anne, married to the Duke of York ; and Frances, married to Thomas Keightley, of Hertingfordbury, in the county of Herts, Esq." The story appears to have been a piece of political scandal. The mother of the Protector, Oliver Cromwell, is said to have conducted with great ability the affairs of her husband's brewhouse at Huntingdon. This some republican spirit appears to have thought an indignity ; so, by way of retaliation, he determined on sinking the origin of the inheritors of the crown to the lowest possible grade —that of a *tub-woman*.

The same story has been told of the wife of Sir Thomas Aylesbury, great-grandmother of the two queens; and for anything we know yet of *her* family, it may be quite true.

CHARLES II. IN ADVERSITY AND PROSPERITY.

Happy, says John Evelyn, had it been for this sovereign, if he had demeaned himself as well in his prosperity as in his adverse fortune. The recorded facts are highly honourable to him and the companions of his exile. While Cromwell, as the Queen of Bohemia said, was the Beast in the Revelations, that all kings and nations worshipped, Charles's horses, and some of them were favourites, were sold at Brussels because he could not pay for their keep, and during the two years that he resided at Cologne he never kept a coach. So straitened were the exiles for money, that even the postage of letters between Sir Richard Browne and Hyde, was no easy burthen ; and there was a mutiny in the Ambassador's kitchen, because the maid might not be trusted with the government, and the buying of meat, in which she was thought too lavish. Hyde writes that he had not been master of a crown for many months; that he was cold for want of clothes and fire ; and for all the meat which he had eaten for three months, he was in debt to a poor woman who was no longer able to trust. "Our necessities," he says, "would be more insupportable, if we did not see the king reduced to greater distress than you can believe or imagine."

Of Charles, in prosperity, a few days before his death, Evelyn draws a fearful picture of dissipation. Writing on the day when James II. was proclaimed, he says : " I can never forget the inexpressible luxury and profaneness, gaming and all dissoluteness, and as it were, total forgetfulness of God, (it being Sunday evening,) which, this day se'nnight, I was witness of, the king sitting and toying with his concubines, Portsmouth, Cleaveland, and Mazarine, &c., a French boy singing love songs in that glorious gallery [at Whitehall] ; whilst about twenty of the great courtiers, and other dissolute persons, were at basset round a large table—a bank of at least 2000l. in gold before them ; upon which two gentlemen, who were with me, made reflexions with astonishment. Six days after, all was in the dust !"

SIR RICHARD WILLIS'S PLOT AGAINST CHARLES THE SECOND.

At No. 13, in chambers of the old courts of Lincoln's Inn, built in the reign of James I., lived John Thurloe, secretary to Oliver Cromwell, who must often have been here.   Burch, in his *Life of Thurloe*, relates that one night, early in .659, Cromwell came here for the purpose of discussing secret and important business with Thurloe.   They had conversed together for some time, when Cromwell suddenly perceived a clerk asleep at his desk.   This happened to be Mr. Morland (afterwards Sir Samuel Morland) the famous mechanist, and not unknown as a statesman.   Cromwell, it is affirmed, drew his dagger, and would have despatched him on the spot had not Thurloe, with some difficulty, prevented him.   He assured him that his intended victim was certainly sound asleep, since, to his own knowledge, he had been sitting up the two previous nights.   But Morland only feigned sleep, and overheard the conversation, which was a plot for throwing the young King Charles II., then resident at Bruges, and the Dukes of York and Gloucester, into the hands of the Protector ; Sir Richard Willis having planned that on a stated day they should pass over to a certain port in Sussex, where they would be received on landing by a body of 500 men, to be augmented on the following morning by 2000 horse. Had they fallen into the snare, it seems that all three would have been shot immediately on their reaching the shore ; but Morland disclosed the designs to the royal party, and thus frustrated the diabolical scheme.   This is a good story, but, unfortunately, it rests upon very questionable evidence.

WEARING OAK ON THE TWENTY-NINTH OF MAY.

The origin of wearing this badge is commonly believed to be to commemorate the preservation of Charles II. in the oak, on May 29.   Now, Charles fought the battle of Worcester on Wednesday, the 3rd of September 1651 ; he fled from the field, attended by Lords Derby and Wilmot, and others, and arrived early next morning at Whiteladies, about three quarters of a mile from Boscobel House.   At this place Charles secreted himself in a wood, and in a tree (from the king's own account, a pollard oak), since termed " the royal oak ;" and at night Boscobel House was his place of refuge.   At Whiteladies he exchanged his habiliments for those of the faithful Penderell.   Subsequently he embarked at Shoreham on the 15th of October, and landed next day at Fescamp in Normandy.   On his return to England, Charles entered London on his birthday, the 29th of May, when the Royalists displayed the branch of oak, from that tree having been instrumental in the king's restoration: hence the custom of wearing oak on this day, and not from Charles being then concealed in the oak. It may be added, that the oak could scarcely have been in sufficient leaf in May to have concealed the king. Boscobel House is situated near Bridgnorth, Salop, 140 miles from the metropolis; and that part of it which rendered such essential service to the sovereign is still shown. The oak has long been removed; but another, presumed to have been a seedling from it, occupies its place, and is walled round for preservation.

GENERAL MONK'S MARRIAGE.

The most curious portion of Monk's private history is his marriage to Ann, daughter of John Clarges, a farrier, in the Savoy, in the Strand. She was first married to Thomas Radford, farrier. She sold washballs, powder, gloves, &c., at the New Exchange, Strand, and she taught plain work to girls. In 1647, she and her husband fell out and separated; no certificate of any parish register appears recording his burial. In 1652, she was married at the Church of St. George, Southwark, to General Monk, though it is said her first husband was living at the time. In the following year she was delivered of a son, Christopher, who was suckled by Honour Mills, who sold apples, herbs, oysters, &c. Nan's mother was one of *Five Women Barbers*, celebrated in her time. Nan is described by Clarendon as a person "of the lowest extraction, without either wit or beauty;" and Aubrey says, "she was not at all handsome nor cleanly," and that she was seamstress to Monk when he was imprisoned in the Tower. She is known to have had great control and authority over him. Upon his being raised to a dukedom, and her becoming Duchess of Albemarle, her father, the farrier (who had his forge upon the site of No. 317, on the north side of the Strand,) is said here to have raised a Maypole to commemorate his daughter's good fortune. She died a few days after the Duke, and is interred by his side, in Henry the Seventh's Chapel, Westminster Abbey. The Duke was succeeded by his son, Christopher, who married Lady Elizabeth Cavendish, grand-daughter of the Duke of Newcastle, and who died childless. The Duchess' brother, Thomas Clarges, became a physician of note, and was created a baronet in 1674, after whose son, Sir Thomas Clarges, was named Clarges-street, Piccadilly, built about 1717.

LA CLOCHE, THE SON OF CHARLES II.

The existence of this son has hitherto entirely escaped the knowledge of the biographers of Charles; and, indeed, the only notices of him even still attainable are derived from the papers published by Boero, the letters of his father, and the entries in the records of the noviciate of St. Andrew at Rome. Charles himself, in one of his letters to the general of the Jesuits, states that his boy was born to him "in the island of Jersey, when he was little more than sixteen or seventeen years old, of a young lady of one of the noblest families in his dominions." He was brought up as a Protestant in Holland, whence in 1665 he was removed secretly to London, but soon afterwards, feeling unhappy on account of the equivocal position which he there held, he appears to have returned of his own accord to the Continent in 1667, bearing with him a formal acknowledgment of his parentage, signed by the king, and authenticated by the Royal seal, to which was afterwards added a deed of settlement assigning to him a pension of 500*l.* A few months after his return to the Continent he was received into the Roman Catholic Church at Hamburg, under the inspiration, it would seem, of Queen Christina of Sweden, then in the first fervour of her zeal for her new faith ; and in the latter part of the same year he entered the noviciate of the Jesuit Society at Rome, under the name of James La Cloche (which, by the way, was the name of his mother's family), his real name being kept secret from all, with the single exception of his confessor ; even the general of the order himself was not informed of it. —*The Gentleman's Magazine.*

WHO BUILT CHELSEA HOSPITAL?

The founder of the Holland family, Stephen Fox, who was a singing-boy in Salisbury choir. He subsequently obtained a situation in the royal household of the exiled Stuart family ; and on the Restoration was appointed army paymaster, in which situation he amassed enormous wealth by discounting soldiers' bills. In connexion with the history of this, the first Lord Holland, a popular error falls to the ground. The general belief holds that Nell Gwyn caused Charles II. to establish Chelsea Hospital, but there is no doubt that its foundation was owing mainly to Fox, who, as some men build churches to expiate their crimes, devoted a large sum out of his enormous gains at the expense of the army to create this asylum for aged and decayed soldiers, previously reduced to constant street beggary. It is said that he built to the extent of 20,000*l.* of this college, as it is termed ; and that he endowed it with 5,000*l.* per annum as maintenance.

THE FIRST DUKE OF ST. ALBAN'S.

The first Duke, the reader need scarcely be told, was Charles Beauclerk, illegitimate son of Charles II., by his Majesty's celebrated mistress, Eleanor Gwyn. [The family motto, *Auspicium melioris ævi,* (a pledge of better times,) is a strange conceit.] The tradition of his first elevation to the Peerage is not so well known. Charles one day going to see Nelly Gwyn, and the little boy being in the room, the king wanted to speak to him. His mother called to him, " Come hither, you little bastard, and speak to your father." " Nay, Nelly," said the King, " do not give the child such a name." " Your Majesty," replied Nelly, " has given me no other name by which I may call him !" Upon this the

King conferred on him the name of Beauclerk, and created him Earl of Burford; and shortly before his death made him Duke of St. Alban's. He served for some years in the Imperial armies, and gained great honour by his gallantry at the assault of Belgrade in 1688. He afterwards served under King William, who made him Captain of the band of Gentlemen Pensioners, and a Lord of the Bedchamber. Queen Anne continued him in these posts till the Tory ministry came in, when he resigned. He was, however, restored to them by George I., who also gave him the Garter. He died at the age of fifty-five, May 11th, 1726; having married Diana, heiress of Aubrey de Vere, last Earl of Oxford.

HOUSES IN WHICH NELL GWYN IS SAID TO HAVE LIVED.

"There are more houses pointed out," says Mr. Peter Cunningham, in his piquant *Story*, " in which Nell Gwyn is said to have lived, than sites of palaces belonging to King John, hunting-lodges believed to have sheltered Queen Elizabeth, or mansions and sporting-houses in which Oliver Cromwell resided or put up. She is said by some to have been born at Hereford; by others, at London; and Oxford, it is found, has a fair claim to be considered as her birthplace. But the houses in which she is said to have lived far exceed in number the cities contending for the honour of her birth. She is believed by some to have lived at Chelsea, by others at Bagnigge Wells; Highgate, and Walworth, and Filberts, near Windsor, are added to the list of reputed localities. A staring inscription in the Strand, in London, instructs the curious passenger that a house at the upper end of a narrow court was 'formerly a dairy of Nell Gwyn.' I have been willing to believe in one and all of these conjectural residences, but after a long and careful inquiry, I am obliged to reject them all. Her early life was spent in Drury-lane and Lincoln's-inn-Fields; her latter life in Pall Mall, and in Burford House, in the town of Windsor. ["The Prince of Wales is lodged (at Windsor) in the Princess of Denmark's house, which was Mrs. Ellen Gwyn's." *Letter, Aug.* 14, 1688, *Ellis Corresp.* ii. 118.] The rate-books of the parish of St. Martin's-in-the-Fields record her residence in Pall Mall from 1670 to her death; and the site of her house in Windsor may be established, if other evidence were wanting, by the large engraving after Knyff."

WAS CHARLES II. POISONED?

It was the belief of many at the time that Charles II. was poisoned. It was common then and in the preceding age to attribute the sudden death of any great man to poison; but in Charles's case the suspicions are not without authority. Sheffield, Duke of Buckingham, says: "The most knowing and the most deserving of all his physicians did not only believe him poisoned, but thought himself so too, not long after, for having declared his opinions a little too boldly." (Buckingham's *Works*, vol. ii.) Bishop Patrick (*Autobiography*,) strengthens the supposition from the testimony of Sir Thomas Mellington, who sat with the King for three days, and never went to bed for three nights. Lord Chesterfield (*Letter; to his Son*), the grandson to the Earl of Chesterfield, who was with Charles at his death, states positively that the King was poisoned. The Duchess of Portsmouth, when in England in 1699, is said to have told Lord Chancellor Cowper that Charles II. was poisoned at her house by one of her footmen in a dish of chocolate; and Fox had heard a somewhat similar report from the family of his mother, who was grand-daughter to the Duchess.

This historical evidence is, however, invalidated by more recent investigation. Charles II., according to the account of his physician, Sir C. Scarborough, had just risen from his bed when he experienced an unusual sensation in his head, shortly after which he fell down speechless, and without power of motion. An army surgeon, who happened to be at hand, bled him to the extent of 16 ounces; after which, on the arrival of the royal physician, his Majesty was cupped, and other remedies used—such as an emetic, purgatives, &c.; but he expired on the fourth day. Had there been safety in a multitude of councillors, the King's life must have been preserved, for Sir Henry Halford found the signatures of no less than fourteen physicians to one of the prescriptions. Among the remedies prescribed when the King was sinking was the *spiritus cranii humani*, 25 drops, which certainly has been improved upon in our modern preparations of ammonia.

Buckingham and Halifax, the two men who, perhaps, were best acquainted with Charles II., both declared he was a deist. "His subsequent conversion to Catholicism," says Buckle, "is exactly analogous to the increased devotion of Louis XIV. during the later years of his life. In both cases, superstition was the natural refuge of a worn-out and discontented libertine, who had exhausted all the resources of the lowest and most grovelling pleasures."

On examining King Charles's head, a copious effusion of lymph was found in the ventricles and at the base of the cranium, from which Sir Henry Halford was disposed to think that the King might have been still further bled with advantage. It is quite evident from Sir Henry's account that Charles II. died of apoplexy—the only too probable consequence of his excesses—and consequently, that his indifference to the solicitations of those about him on religious matters can only, with charity, be attributed to the effects of his disease.

STRANGE FORTUNES OF THE HOUSE OF STUART.

Since the days of the great Theban and Pelopid Houses of Greece, whose wars formed the staple of Athenian tragedy, there has been no family occupying or allied to a throne so incessantly haunted by calamity as the House of Stuart. Yet the last lineal heir of this doomed race was a peaceable, inoffensive gentleman, who attained almost to

Priam's age with but few of Priam's infelicities. Henry Benedict Maria Clement was the second and youngest son of "the old Pretender." He was born in March, 1725, and died in June, 1807. Almost without a metaphor he may be said to have pertained to two different worlds, since he had nearly attained to the Psalmist's span of life when the crowning misfortune of his life overtook him, and meanwhile witnessed the final acts of the Europe which the French Revolution swept away. His Memoirs read like those of an antediluvian. In July, 1740, the poet Gray saw him at Florence, then in his sixteenth year, dancing incessantly all night long at a ball given by the Count Patrizii, and describes him as having "more spirit than his elder brother." He was no further concerned with the events of 1745 than "in joining the troops assembled at Dunkirk to support his brother's operations in Scotland." Two years later, both his dancing and his active life came to an end, since he was then invested with a Cardinal's hat by Pope Benedict XIV., and passed the next fifty years of his life in the performance of the duties of religion. On the death of his brother Charles, in 1788, the only step which he took to assert his right to the British throne was to cause a paper to be drawn up, in which his rightful claims were insisted on ; while at the same time he ordered a medal to be struck, with the inscription—" Henricus Nonus, Angliæ Rex " on the obverse ; and the pathetic words " Dei Gratia, Sed Non Voluntate Hominum on the reverse."

But this titular king was not destined to entire exemption from the woes of his race. He had impaired his once ample means by aiding Pius VI. to make up the sum levied on him by Napoleon. This, however, was only the beginning of sorrows. In 1798, the French attacked his palace in the neighbourhood of Rome, and compelled him to fly, an infirm and almost destitute man, at first to Padua, and subsequently to Venice. His necessities were relieved in 1800 by the occupant of his throne ; and in a letter, breathing both Christian resignation and Royal dignity, he acknowledges that Henry the Ninth accepted from the hands of George III. an annual pension of 4000*l.* In return, the Cardinal bequeathed to George IV., then Prince of Wales, the crown jewels which, one hundred and twenty years before, his grandfather had carried off with him in his flight from England. Among these relics was the "George," which his great-grandfather had consigned to Bishop Juxon on the scaffold, uttering the valedictory "Remember." And so departed from earth and its troubles the last scion of the House of Stuart.—*Saturday Review.*

ENGLISH ADHERENTS OF THE HOUSE OF STUART.

A Correspondent of *Notes and Queries*, 3rd S.,No. 294, observes that the English adherents of the House of Stuart have been underrated in their services in favour of the Scotch and Irish followers of the same noble house. One may instance General Monk's great service in restoring King Charles II. Next in order comes the Duke of Berwick, whose successful enterprise in setting the crown of Spain on the rightful claimant's head, the Duke of Anjou, the grandson of Louis XIV., made the Bourbon family compact possible. Then Lord Chatham's (who, under the name of patriot, was, no doubt, a concealed Jacobite; his frequent attacks upon the employment of Hanoverian troops in this country show his leaning) measure in attacking Canada, and taking it from the French, resulted in France and Spain joining to support American independence, and wrested the American Colonies—now the fine country of the United States—out of the hands of the House of Hanover. "Washington was the descendant of a royalist who fought for King Charles I.; and Lord Mahon mentions in his *History of England*, that when the Scotch in the neighbourhood of New York, offered to raise the Standard of Prince Charles Edward Stuart, a paper among the Stuart papers states, that his answer was for them 'to mind their own business'—that is, that the then representative of the Stuart family wished them to side with Washington, which no doubt they did.

"And lastly, let us not forget Dean Swift, whose *Drapier Letters to the People of Ireland*, kept them from a useless insurrection, and paved the way, with William Pitt's Union of England and Ireland, to the measure, afterwards carried by Daniel O'Connell, of Catholic Emancipation; seating the Irish Catholic members in the English House of Commons, thus creating a powerful body of Irish Catholic members in support of the English Catholics, always great adherents of the House of Stuart. This measure (the Catholic Emancipation) would have been of no use if William Pitt, the worthy son of Lord Chatham, had not, by the Union of Ireland with England, abolished the Irish Parliament, because Ireland was commanded by the English Fleet."

KINGS AND PRETENDERS.

A King by Act of Parliament, however essential to the liberties of a nation, is a prosaic sort of being; but a king by Right Divine presents much that is attractive to persons who weigh events and characters in the scales of sentiment. Apollo himself would have failed had he composed ballads in honour of a German Elector, stricken in years and dressed in snuff-coloured broadcloth; while even the bellman's verses rang well when a young Prince in plaid and bonnet was their theme. Had Charles I. not been drawn by Vandyke, or had he died before the raising of the standard at Nottingham, it is possible that we should esteem him a very commonplace person. His address was embarrassed, his figure was puny, he was slightly lame, and his manner was sullen and ungracious. But Charles in armour, belted and plumed, and surrounded by the gallant gentlemen of his realm, riding in triumph to Barnet, or reviewing his squadrons on the morning of Marston Moor, becomes an object of interest even to those who lean to Oliver and his Ironsides; and it needed only a tragic fate to convert this long unpopular Prince into a hero and a martyr. A similar fortune, in various degrees, attended his posterity, enthroned or exiled. There was, indeed, little enough romance in the voluptuary, his successor. Yet as an exile, he was an object of compassion to many who would have been content with a Cromwell dynasty; and after his restoration, "the first gentleman of the day" won the hearts of the crowd by his popular manners and exquisite urbanity. Two members only of the English Stuart family were devoid of personal attractions—the first and second James. The former, with some worth and considerable learning, was a low comedian, shuffled by chance upon a throne; the other, bating a kind of bull-dog insensibility to danger, at least in his earlier years, possessed no popular merit whatever. He was a dull, abject creature, who neither inspired respect while in authority nor excited pity when in affliction. In the characters of the Old and Young Pretender, apart from their adventures, there was little to awaken or justify enthusiasm. The elder one was as prosaic as his sire, and was qualified by nature for no higher post than that of gold or silver stick in his own household. When he reviewed the Highland clans at Perth, in 1715, these doughty warriors could hardly be made to believe that they looked on a king's son. "He carried his sword like a dancer," shivered in the keen air of Scotland "like a sick girl," and could with difficulty be induced to accost the chiefs who were risking life and lands in his cause. Charles Edward was cast in a more heroic mould. He had not been wholly educated by priests; he bore some resemblance to his chivalrous ancestor James IV.; he could wield a claymore, breast the elements, dance reels admirably, and was winning and affable in manner, like his great-uncle Charles. But, after "the '45," his prestige passed away rapidly. In a few years the free use of the bottle converted "the young Chevalier" into a stout and red-nosed man, who beat his wife, and (report said) was in turn himself beaten by his mistresses—who, when half sober was dangerously irascible, and when wholly drunk was plundered and reviled by his own buffoons.—*Saturday Review.*

SIR RICHARD BAKER'S CHRONICLE OF THE KINGS OF ENGLAND.

Sir Richard Baker, of whom Fuller speaks in his *English Worthies*, was a native of Oxfordshire. He was descended from Sir John Baker, Chancellor of the Exchequer to Henry VIII.; was educated at the University of Oxford, and knighted in 1603. He married and settled in his native country before the year 1620. Having got into difficulties, as it should seem, soon after his marriage, he was thrown into the Fleet Prison, where he spent the remaining years of his life, and died in the year 1644-5, in a state of extreme poverty.* It was during his imprisonment, and as a means of subsistence, that he wrote his *Chronicle,* and

* Sir Richard Baker, according to the rate-books of St. Clement Danes, lived in Milford-lane, Strand, from 1632 to 1639, which had then an unwelcome notoriety.—(Cunningham's *Handbook*). Baker was buried in the old church of St. Bride, Fleet-street, which was destroyed in the Great Fire of 1666.

various other works, a circumstance which should, perhaps, induce us to judge leniently of their short-comings. But Baker has been treated otherwise, probably through his own conceit or pretensions, in affirming that his *Chronicle* was collected and compiled "with so great care and diligence, that if all other of our Chronicles should be lost, this only would be sufficient to inform posterity of all passages worthy or memorable to be known." This is boastful overmuch. Yet, the *Chronicle* enjoyed great popularity for more than a century after its publication, among the squires and ancient gentlewomen of the school of Sir Roger de Coverley. The manner was new, and as the sarcastic author of the *Historical Library* remarked, "pleasing to the rabble," meaning by the term "rabble," all persons not eminently learned. Holinshed was too bulky, and Speed too dull a writer to be popular; while Sir Richard's residence in the Fleet was not very compatible with those numerous references to authorities and antiquarian researches which find favour in the eyes of learned men, but perplex and weary the general reader. Soon after the publication of the *Chronicle*, Thomas Blount, a barrister, printed his animadversions on it; which, however, did not impede its success. It was also ridiculed by Addison and Fielding, but it is by no means so flimsy a performance as the humour of our great essayist and novelist would have us believe.

Anthony à Wood styles Baker a noted writer; and Daines Barrington says, Baker is by no means so contemptible a writer as he is supposed to be: for more than a century his *Chronicle* was the text-book of English history to country gentlemen and their families, and has given more pleasure and perhaps diffused more knowledge than historical works of far higher pretensions.

Another critic writes: "Sir Richard Baker is, if you please, very stupid, very uncritical, quite unable to understand what he writes about; but he is in earnest from beginning to end. Sir Richard's folio is a prodigy of mere work. The whole thing is of course misconceived; there are plenty of particular blunders, the natural result of imperfect scholarship; but there is good honest work in abundance. The mass of information, seemingly honestly drawn from original sources, is really amazing. There is, to be sure, nothing worthy to be called criticism, and the whole goes on a theory that whatever a king did must, if possible, be shown to be right. Still, Sir Richard's comments are by no means void of occasional glimmerings of sound common sense. He tells his story simply and straightforwardly, without any attempt at either eloquence or jocularity: but, like many writers of his age, he is not wholly devoid of a certain vein of humour, conscious or unconscious, which is not inconsistent with earnestness and simplicity." — (*Saturday Review*.)

If Sir Richard Baker had been imprisoned in such a house as the British Museum instead of the Fleet, he would, doubtless, have produced a more correct book, with less pleasantry in it.

The first two editions extend only from the Romans to James I., but in 1660, it was re-published by Edward Phillips, the nephew of Milton, who continued it to the Coronation of Charles II., having the perusal of some of the papers of General Monk concerning the Restoration, which Phillips was censured for having misrepresented, though the account was really written by Sir Thomas Clarges. The best edition of Baker's *Chronicle* is that published in 1733, continued to the end of the reign of George I., though there are many curious papers in the former impressions which are omitted in this. We have already quoted some passages from this eccentric and much abused work.

DEFENCE OF LORD CHANCELLOR JEFFREYS.

It has been well said that the very atrocities of the brutal Jeffreys cannot overwhelm and silence the meed of approbation to which some parts of his judicial excellence are entitled. Of him as a statesman, or as a criminal judge, Lord Campbell details acts which show him in both capacities to deserve reprobation such as no language could adequately express. He cannot, like his predecessors, Lord Clarendon and Lord Nottingham, be accused of bigotry ; for all religious creeds as well as all political opinions seem to have been really indifferent to him, and in his choice of those which he professed he was guided only by his "desire to climb." Even the strong hatred against Dissenters which he affected when he had changed sides, he could (as in Rosewell's case), to please the Government, entirely lay aside or suspend. From his daring and resolute character he probably felt a genuine contempt for "a Trimmer;" and having no personal antipathy to an opponent who boldly went into extremes like himself, his bile was excited by watching a struggle between conscience and convenience. The revival of the Court of High Commission is the only great unconstitutional measure which he has the credit of having originated; but there were no measures, however illegal or pernicious, proposed by Charles or James, to the execution of which Jeffreys did not devotedly and recklessly abandon himself.

As a civil judge he was by no means without high qualifications, and in the absence of any motive to do wrong, he was willing to do right. He had a very quick perception, a vigorous and logical understanding, and an impressive eloquence.

When quite sober, he was particularly good as a *Nisi Prius* Judge. His summing up in what is called "the Lady Ivy's case," an ejectment between her and the Dean and Chapter of St. Paul's, to recover a large estate at Shadwell, is most masterly. The evidence was exceedingly complicated, and he gives a beautiful sketch of the whole, both documentary and parol ; and without taking the case from the jury, he makes some admirable observations on certain deeds produced by the Lady Ivy, which led to the conclusion that they were forged, and to a verdict for the Dean and Chapter.

Lord Campbell proceeds to say that Jeffreys must have been very poorly furnished for presiding in Chancery. Although he must often have betrayed his ignorance, yet with his characteristic boldness and energy, he contrived to get through the business without any signal disgrace ; and among all the invectives, satires, and lampoons by which his memory is blackened, Lord Campbell found little said against his decrees.

Lord Campbell discovered one benevolent opinion of this cruel Chancellor, and, strange to say, it is at variance with that of the humane magistrates who have adorned Westminster Hall in the nineteenth century. The Prisoners' Counsel Bill was condemned and opposed by almost all the judges in the reign of William IV., yet even Jeffreys was struck with the injustice and inequality of the law which, allowing the accused to defend himself by counsel, "for a two-penny trespass," refuses that aid "where life, estate, honour, and all are concerned;" and he lamented its existence while he declared himself bound to adhere to it. The venerable sages who apprehended such multiplied evils from altering the practice, must have been greatly relieved by finding that their objections have proved as unfounded as those which were urged against the abolition of *peine forte et dure;* and the alarming innovation so long resisted of allowing witnesses for the prisoner to be examined under the sanction of an oath.

There are two versions of the circumstances attending the capture of Jeffreys. That commonly received is, that attempting, after the abdication of King James, to make his escape in the disguise of a common seaman, he was captured in an obscure alehouse called the Red Cow, in Anchor and Hope Alley, near King Edward's Stairs, in Wapping; here he was found by a scrivener he had formerly insulted, looking out of a window in all the confidence of misplaced security. The other story is that Jeffreys lay concealed in his mansion at Leatherhead, in an underground vault, a few weeks after the Revolution of 1688,—when "being proscribed, and a reward set upon his head," he had ventured hither to see a daughter who was at the point of death, and whose funeral, as appears by the register at Leatherhead, was solemnized December 2nd, in the above year. The vault in which the ex-Chancellor took refuge, is well adapted for concealment, it being beneath one of the cellars, and covered over by a boarded flooring. It is traditionally asserted at Leatherhead, that Jeffreys was betrayed for the sake of the reward by his butler, who had accompanied him in his flight.

FATE OF SIR CLOUDESLEY SHOVEL.

In the Kimbolton Papers (*Court and Society from Elizabeth to Anne*), published in 1864, are two letters of Addison, then Secretary of State, which throw some light on the fate of Sir Cloudesley Shovel, and correct a common mistake. One letter contains an account of the loss of Sir Cloudesley Shovel's ship on the Scilly Islands, the other states how the Admiral's body was discovered. The popular story, according to the writer of the statement, is that the Cornish fishermen or wreckers, having found the Admiral's body, stripped it and burnt it on the sand, after taking from the finger a fine emerald ring. In reality, however, the tradition goes much further. It is said that Sir Cloudesley Shovel was thrown on shore alive, and was murdered for the sake of his ring.

The end of the story as reported in the Kimbolton Papers, is " that Mr. Paxton, purser of the *Arundel*, hearing of the circumstance, saw the ring, declared it to be the Admiral's property, and, disinterring the body, carried it to England (Portsmouth) in his own ship." Addison, in the following letter, puts the story right:—

" Mr. Addison to Mr. Cole.

" Cock Pit, Oct. 31, 1707.

" Sir,—Yesterday, we had news that the body of Sir Cloudesley Shovel was found on the coast of Cornwall. The fishermen who were searching among the wrecks took a tin box out of the pocket of one of the carcases that was floating, and found in it the commission of an admiral; upon which, examining the body more closely, they found it was poor Sir Cloudesley. You may guess the condition of his unhappy wife, who lost, in the same ship with her husband, her two only sons by Sir John Narborough. We begin to despair of the two other men-of-war, and fire-ship, that engaged among the same rocks, having yet received no news of them.—I am, Sir, your faithful humble servant,

" J. Addison."

BOTH SIDES OF THE QUESTION.

Swift received his deanery, which he ever held as a most inadequate reward, for his services to the Marlborough and Tory faction, in the course of 1713; but he had given his great offence to the Duchess nearly three years before, or immediately after his venal quarrels with the Whigs for their not giving him church-promotion so rapidly as he wished. In the *Examiner* of Nov. 23rd, 1710, he published a paper reflecting most severely on the Duke of Marlborough's insatiable avarice and enormous peculations. The Duke, he said, had had 540,000*l*. of the public money for doing work for which a warrior of ancient Rome (an odd parallel) would have received only 994*l*. 11*s*. 10*d*.; and at the end of his paper there was an innuendo that the Duchess, in the execution of her office as mistress of the robes during eight years, had purloined no less than 22,000*l*. a year. Here is the account itself from the *Examiner*, in a volume in reply to Sarah's, entitled *The Other Side of the Question*, and published in the same year:—

A Bill of Roman Gratitude.

Imprim.	£	*s.*	*d.*
For frankincense, and earthen pots to burn it in . . .	4	10	0
A bull for sacrifice	8	0	0
An embroidered garment	50	0	0
A crown of laurel	0	0	2
A statue	100	0	0
A trophy	80	0	0
1000 copper medals, value one halfpenny each . . .	2	1	8
A triumphal arch	500	0	0
A triumphal car, valued as a modern coach	100	0	0
Casual charges at the triumph	150	0	0

£994 11 10

A Bill of British Ingratitude.

Imprim.	£	*s.*	*d.*
Woodstock	40,000	0	0
Blenheim	200,000	0	0
Post-office grant	100,000	0	0
Mildenheim	30,000	0	0
Jewels, &c. , ...	60,000	0	0
Pall-Mall Grant, the Westminster rangership, &c..	10,000	0	0
Employments.	100,000	0	0
	£540,000	0	0

The anonymous author of *The Other Side of the Question* does not name Swift, but says this account was drawn up many years ago in the *Examiner*, for the use of the Marlborough family, "by one of the greatest wits that ever did honour to human nature."

We agree with Mr. Hannay (*Essays from the Quarterly Review*), that the above is one of the finest prose satires in the language; and the following on Marlborough, from one of the severest lampoons:—

> Behold his funeral appears,—
> Nor widows' sighs nor orphans' tears,
> Wont at such times the heart to pierce,
> Attend the progress of the hearse.
> But what of that? his friends may say,
> He had those honours in his day ;
> True to his profit and his pride,
> He made them weep before he died.

AVARICE OF MARLBOROUGH.

Spence has left the following sketch of the ruling passion of this great soldier. "Inconsistent as the Duke of Marlborough's character may appear, yet it may be accounted for, if we gauge his actions by his ruling passion, which was the love of money. He endeavoured, at the same time, to be well both at Hanover and St. Germain's: this conduct excited much surprise at the time, in those who were made acquainted with it, but the plain meaning of it was only this, that he wanted to secure the vast riches he had amassed together, whichever should succeed. He was calm in the heat of battle, and when he was so near being taken prisoner (in his first campaign) in Flanders, he was quite unmoved. It was true he was like to lose his life in the one, and his liberty in the other; but there was none of his money at stake in either. This mean passion of that great man operated very strongly in him in the very beginning of his life, and continued to the very end of it. One day, as he was looking over some papers in his scrutoire, with Lord Cadogan, he opened one of the little drawers, took out a green purse, and turned some broad pieces out of it. After viewing them for some time with a satisfaction that appeared very visible on his face, 'Cadogan,' said he, 'observe these pieces well,—they deserve to be observed. There are just forty of them; 'tis the very first sum I ever got in my life, and I have kept it always unbroken, from that time to this day.' This shows how very early and how strongly this passion must have been upon him, as another little affair which happened in his last decline at Bath, may serve (amongst many others) to show how miserably it continued to the end. He was playing there with Dean Jones at piquet, for sixpence a game. They played a good while, and the Duke left off when winner of one game. Some time after, he desired the Dean to pay him his sixpence; the Dean said he had no silver. The Duke asked him for it over and over, and at last desired that he would change a guinea to pay it him, because he would want it to pay the chair that carried him home. The Dean, after so much pressing, did at last get change, paid the Duke his sixpence, observed him a little after leave the room, and declared that (after all the bustle that had been made for this sixpence), the Duke actually walked home to save the little expense a chair would have put him to."

Marlborough has, however, been ably defended against such charges. Thus, it is maintained that the charge of Marlborough's taking money from the Duchess of Cleveland is almost certainly an impudent fable. It arose from an idle story that he once saved her reputation with Charles II. by a timely leap out of a window before the king surprised him. The tale rests on Lord Dartmouth's authority, and is supposed to be corroborated by the fact that Churchill, in 1674, bought an annuity from Lord Halifax ; but Burnet, whom Lord Halifax professes to elucidate, refers the incident to a time (1668) when Churchill was out of England, and winning his first laurels at Tangier. Moreover, much the same story of an escape from the king is told by Pepys, of Jermyn, with somewhat less romantic incidents ; and the fact that Churchill's favour with the Duchess dates between the times (1664–1666) when he was fourteen and sixteen years of age—a page whom the courtiers thought too listless ever to succeed in love—is a strong presumption that the lady, prodigal as she was of money, would find some more suitable present for a boy. A favourite page of the Duchess of York, brother to the Duke's mistress, son of a staunch courtier, and himself handsome and able, Churchill owed his fortune to more natural causes than the caprice of Charles II.'s discarded mistresses. The charge of parsimony was brought against him by men who meant to ruin his credit at any cost of slander, and who knew that the accusation was one which a man who has risen from the ranks can scarcely ever refute. Without any ancestral patrimony, Churchill was called upon to support the position of the first subject in England. It is probable that a certain love of order, such as Frederick II. and Wellington possessed, led him to regulate his expenses strictly ; but his avarice, if it ever existed, never hampered him when a great or necessary action was to be done. He gave 1000*l.* privately to an officer who wanted means to buy his promotion. He refused splendid appointments offered him in Holland, for fear of exciting jealousy. No charge was more virulently brought against him than that of embezzling the secret-service money ; yet if we look at his campaigns, it is clear that no general was ever better supplied with secret-service. The men who called him stingy could on occasion ridicule his extravagant pomp, his regal entry into London, and the great works at Blenheim. Those who accuse him of treachery never hint that he was bribed ; yet, Churchill had lived through the days when Algernon Sidney was on the roll of French pensioners. Perhaps the veneration felt for him by the passionate but high-minded Sarah Jennings in itself outweighs the attacks of Swift and Mrs. Manley, and is presumptive evidence, at least, that the great general was not a compound of little meannesses. On the other hand, his character has no stainless purity or heroic grandeur. He set himself early in life to succeed, and he had fallen on times when the path of promotion was slippery. By nature he was ever greater as a diplomatist than as a general ; in fact, his strategy has the fault of being too scientific and passionless ; it risked nothing ; but its successes, as the country felt, did not bring the troops nearer the gates of Paris. Marlborough was not needlessly immoral, but we suspect he was seldom moral from principle. He refused a bribe from Torcy, but he corresponded with James while he served William. Never General cared better for the health of his soldiers ; but no man was more prodigal of their blood if a costly and useless victory in Flanders would maintain his party's tenure of office in England. It is really no anomaly that the unscrupulous politician had all the better feelings of a man in his domestic relations. Lord Macaulay and Mr. Paget seem to us to err on the same principle. The first judges Churchill as a man by his conduct to James II. and William III. ; the second apologizes for his public treasons by a generous praise of his relations with his wife. It would be profaning the word to say that Marlborough represented a principle in his conduct to James II. and William III. ; but it was not so purely black and selfish as is commonly thought.—*National Review*, No. 25, pp. 93-95.

THE ECCENTRIC SARAH, DUCHESS OF MARLBOROUGH.

A few of the Duchess' eccentricities and extravagances have been put together somewhat in the humorous manner of our early story-books, as follows :—

This is the woman who wrote the characters of her contemporaries with a pen dipped in gall and wormwood. This is the Duchess who gave 10,000*l.* to Mr. Pitt for his noble defence of the constitution of his country ! This is the woman who said of King James II. that he had lost three kingdoms, for no other reason than that he might see his subjects dance attendance upon him in another ! This is the Duchess who, in her old age, used to feign asleep after dinner, and say bitter things at table pat and appropriate, but as if she was not aware of what was going on ! This is the lady who drew that beautiful distinction that it was wrong to wish Sir Robert Walpole dead, but only common justice to wish him well hanged. This is the Duchess who tumbled her thoughts out as they arose, and wrote like the wife of the great Duke of Marlborough. This is the lady who quarrelled with a wit upon paper (Sir John Vanbrugh), and actually got the better of him in the long run ; who shut out the architect of Blenheim from seeing his own edifice, and made him dangle his time away at an inn, while his friends were shown the house of the eccentric Sarah. This is the lady who laid out her money in land, in full expectation of a sponge being applied to the Government securities.

This is the Duchess who, ever proud and ever malignant, was persuaded to offer her favourite grand-daughter, Lady Diana Spencer, afterwards Duchess of Bedford, to the Prince of Wales, with a fortune of a hundred thousand pounds. He accepted the proposal, and the day was fixed for their being secretly married at the Duchess' Lodge, in the Great Park, at Windsor. Sir Robert Walpole got intelligence of the project, prevented it, and the secret was buried in silence.

This is the Duchess—

> The wisest fool much time has ever made,

who refused the proffered hand of the proud Duke of Somerset, for the sole and sufficient reason that no one should share her heart with the great Duke of Marlborough.

This is the woman who refused to lend to the Duchess of Buckingham the funereal car that carried her husband, because no one could deserve so great an honour. This is that "wicked woman of Marlborough," as Vanbrugh calls her, whose heart was made up, in the language of Swift, "of sordid avarice, disdainful pride, and ungovernable rage."—"A woman of little knowledge," as described by Burnet, "but of a clear apprehension and a true judgment." This is the woman who left 1000*l.* by will between two poets, to write the life of her illustrious husband—leaving it conditionally, however, "that no part of the said history may be in verse." This is the illustrious lady who superintended the building of Blenheim, examined contracts and tenders, talked with carpenters and masons, and thinking sevenpence-halfpenny a bushel for lime too much by a farthing, waged a war to the knife on so small a matter. This is the Duchess who felt in her old age, as many have since felt, the stern reality of Dryden's celebrated lines :—

> When I consider life, 'tis all a cheat,
> Yet, fool'd with hope, men favour the deceit—
> Trust on and think to-morrow will repay ;
> To-morrow's falser than the former day,
> Lies more, and when it says we shall be blest
> With some new joy, cuts off what we possest,
> Strange cozenage ! none would live past years again,
> Yet all hope pleasure in what still remain,
> And from the dregs of life think to receive
> What the fresh sprightly running could not give.
> I'm tir'd of waiting for this chemic gold,
> Which fools us young, and beggars us when old.

This is the celebrated Sarah, who, at the age of eighty-four, when she was told she must either submit to be blistered or to die, exclaimed in anger, and with a start in bed, "I won't be blistered, and I won't die!"

The Duchess died, notwithstanding what she said, at Marlborough House, in 1744.

WAS GEORGE II. AT THE BATTLE OF DETTINGEN ?

Strangely contradictory are the accounts of the share of George II. in this decisive battle between the British, Hanoverian, and Hessian army, commanded by King George in person, and the Earl of Stair, on one side; and the French army, under Marshal Noailles, and the Duke of Grammont, on the other. Walpole tells us that " the King was in all the heat of the fire, and safe." Frederick the Great, in his *Histoire de mon Temps*, gives the following account of the King in the field of Dettingen:—" The King was on horseback and rode forward to reconnoitre the enemy; his horse, frightened at the cannonading, ran away with his Majesty, and nearly carried him into the midst of the French lines; fortunately, one of his attendants succeeded in stopping him. George then abandoned his horse, and fought on foot at the head of his Hanoverian battalions. With his sword drawn, and his body placed in the attitude of a fencing master, who is about to make a lounge in carte, he continued to expose himself without flinching, to the fire of the enemy."—Lord Dover's *Notes to Walpole's Letters.*

Yet, elsewhere, Walpole has this precious piece of scandal about the matter: " Sir Watkin Williams, at the last Welsh races, convinced the whole principality (by reading a letter that affirmed it), that the King was not within two miles of the battle of Dettingen !"

THE DUKE OF NEWCASTLE'S VAGARIES.

There is scarcely any public man in our history of whose manners and conversation so many particulars have been preserved, as of the Duke of Newcastle, the well-known leader in the Pelham Administration under George II. Single stories may be unfounded or exaggerated. But all the stories about him, whether told by people who were perpetually seeing him in parliament, and attending his levées in Lincoln's Inn Fields, or by Grub-street writers who had never more than a glimpse of his star through the windows of his gilded coach, are of the same character. Horace Walpole and Smollett differed in their tastes and opinions as much as two human beings could differ. They kept quite different society. Walpole played at cards with countesses, and corresponded with ambassadors. Smollett passed his life surrounded by printers' devils and famished scribblers. Yet, Walpole's Duke and Smollett's Duke are as like as if they were both from one hand. Smollett's Newcastle runs out of his dressing-room, with his face covered with soap-suds, to embrace the Moorish envoy. Walpole's Newcastle pushes his way into the Duke of Grafton's sick-room to kiss the old nobleman's plasters. No man was so unmercifully satirized. But in truth he was himself a satire ready made. All that the heart of the satirist does for other men, nature had done for him. Whatever was absurd about him, stood out with grotesque prominence from the rest of the character. He was a living, moving, talking caricature. His gait was a shuffling trot; his utterance a rapid stutter; he was always in a hurry; he was never in time; he abounded in fulsome caresses and hysterical tears. His oratory resembled that of Justice Shallow. It was nonsense effervescent with animal spirits and impertinence. Of his ignorance many anecdotes remain, some well authenticated, some probably invented at coffee-houses, but all exquisitely characteristic:—"Oh —yes—yes—to be sure—Annapolis must be defended—troops must be sent to Annapolis—Pray where is Annapolis?"—"Cape Breton an island? wonderful!—show it me in the map. So it is, sure enough. My dear sir, you always bring us good news. I must go and tell the King that Great Britain is an island."

And this man was, during near thirty years, Secretary of State, and during near ten years, First Lord of the Treasury! His large fortune, his strong hereditary connexions, his great parliamentary interest, will not alone explain this extraordinary fact. His success is a signal instance of what may be effected by a man who devotes his whole heart and soul, without reserve, to one object. He was eaten up by ambition. He was greedy after power with a greediness all his own. He was jealous of all his colleagues, and even of his own brother. Under the disguise of levity he was false beyond all example of political falsehood. All the able men of his time ridiculed him as a dunce, a driveller, a child who never knew his own mind for an hour together; and he overreached them all round.—*Lord Macaulay, on Walpole's Letters.*

THE INSOLVENT THEODORE, EX-KING OF CORSICA.

This ill-fated gentleman, Theodore von Neuhoff, ex-king of Corsica, is chiefly remembered by his misfortunes in England, in the last century, and by his imprisonment here for debt; indeed, debt seems to have been his weak point throughout his chequered life. Theodore was the son of a Westphalian gentleman of good family, and was born at Metz, about 1696. He entered the French army, which he soon quitted, and rambled as an adventurer over the greater part of Europe. He was thrown into prison for debt at Leghorn. On emerging from this confinement, he joined the leaders of the Corsican insurgents, then striving to shake off the yoke of Genoa: for these services Neuhoff accepted the proffered sovereignty of the country, and in 1736, he was elected King by the general assembly. For some time he exercised all the arts of an independent sovereign, coining money, distributing patents of nobility, and instituting an order of knighthood. Failing in some military enterprises, his popularity soon diminished, when finding his position insecure, he made arrangements for the government in his absence, and quitted the island with the intention, as he asserted, of obtaining fresh succour. But he never resumed his sovereignty. After visiting Italy, France, and Holland, he was arrested for debt at Amsterdam. Some Jews and foreign merchants settled in that city, procured his release, and furnished him with the means to equip an armament for the recovery of his dominions.

With this he appeared off Corsica in 1738, but failed to land ; a similarly unsuccessful attempt was made in 1742.

Theodore now proceeded to England, and on his arrival in London, met with great kindness and sympathy as an exiled monarch. Horace Walpole, who had taken considerable interest in Theodore's former fortunes, received him kindly : he describes him as a comely, middle-sized man, very reverend, and affecting much dignity. On March 23rd, 1749, Walpole notes : " King Theodore [of Corsica] is here ; I am to drink coffee with him to-morrow at Lady Schaub's. I have curiosity to see him though I am not commonly fond of sights, but content myself with the oil-cloth picture of them that is hung out, and to which they seldom come up." What exquisite satire ! Additional mishaps, however, befel Theodore here, and he was sued for money which he had borrowed, and not being able to pay the debt he had to endure an imprisonment of some years' duration in the King's Bench Prison. Here, it is said, he used to affect a miserable display of regal state, sitting under a tattered canopy, and receiving visitors with great ceremony. Smollett has introduced a description of him in prison in his novel of *Ferdinand Count Fathom.* However, Walpole did not desert the ex-king. He wrote a paper in *The World* to promote a subscription for King Theodore in prison ; but he proved refractory and ungrateful. " His Majesty's character," says Walpole, " is so bad, that it only raised fifty pounds ; and though that was so much above his desert, it was so much below his expectation, that he sent a solicitor to threaten the printer with a prosecution for having taken so much liberty with his name—take notice, too, that he had accepted the money ! Dodsley (the publisher) laughed at the lawyer ; but that did not lessen the dirty knavery. It would, indeed (says Walpole), have made an excellent suit !—a printer prosecuted, suppose, for having solicited and obtained charity for a man in prison, and that man not mentioned by his right name, but by a mock title, and the man himself not a native of the country !—but I have done with countenancing kings !" However, the money proved of service, and enabled Theodore to obtain his release from prison under the Insolvent Debtors Act, having scheduled the kingdom of Corsica for the benefit of his creditors. The advertisement in the newspapers of the day announcing the opening of the subscription for the ex-sovereign had the prefix of "Date obolum Belisario," the words alleged to have been used by the general of Justinian, in his old age, to solicit alms.

Theodore did not long survive his liberation. As soon as he was set at liberty, he took a chair, and went to the Portuguese Minister, but did not find him at home ; not having sixpence to pay the chairmen, he prevailed on them to carry him to a tailor he knew in Soho, and who received him kindly ; but he fell sick the next day, and died in three more ; though, Walpole says, Theodore died " somewhere in the liberties of the Fleet prison." The friend who had given shelter to this unfortunate monarch, was himself so poor as to be unable to defray the cost of the ex-king's funeral. His remains were, therefore, about to be interred as a parish pauper, when one John Wright, an oilman in Compton Street, declared that *he for once would pay the funeral expenses of a king*, which he did, and the royal remains were laid in the churchyard of St. Anne's, Soho.

Walpole, although he had been disgusted with the kingly conduct, paid the last honours. He writes to Sir Horace Mann, Sept. 29th, 1757: "I am putting up a stone, in St. Anne's Churchyard, for your old friend, King Theodore: in short, his history is too remarkable to let perish. You will laugh to hear that when I sent the inscription to the vestry for the approbation of the minister and churchwardens, they demurred, and took some days to consider whether they wou'd suffer him to be called King of Corsica. Happily, they have acknowledged his title! Here is the inscription; over it is a crown exactly copied from his coin:—

> NEAR THIS PLACE IS INTERRED
> THEODORE, KING OF CORSICA,
> WHO DIED IN THIS PARISH, DECEMBER 11, 1756,
> IMMEDIATELY AFTER LEAVING
> THE KING'S BENCH PRISON,
> BY THE BENEFIT OF THE ACT OF INSOLVENCY;
> IN CONSEQUENCE OF WHICH
> HE REGISTERED THE KINGDOM OF CORSICA
> FOR THE USE OF HIS CREDITORS.

> The grave, great teacher, to a level brings
> Heroes and beggars, galley-slaves and kings.
> But Theodore this moral learned ere dead:
> Fate poured its lessons on his living head,
> Bestowed a kingdom, and denied him bread.

I think that at least it cannot be said of me, as it was of the Duke of Buckingham* entombing Dryden,

> And help'd to bury whom he help'd to starve.

I would have served him, if a king, even in a gaol, could he have been an honest man."

Theodore left a son, Colonel Frederick, who came to a sad end. The old man walked from the coffee-house at Story's Gate to the porch at Westminster Abbey, and there shot himself. He had long been familiar to the inhabitants of London, and was distinguished by his eccentricities and gentlemanlike bearing. He had fulfilled many employments, and witnessed many strange incidents. One strange passage in his life was his dining at Dolly's chop-house, with Count Poniatowski, when neither the son of the late King of Corsica, nor he who was afterwards King of Poland, had wherewith to settle the bill. Distress drove the Colonel to commit suicide, and his remains rest by those of his father, in St. Anne's Churchyard, Soho. The Colonel's daughter married a Mr. Clarke, of the Dartmouth Custom-house. Four children were the issue of this marriage. One of them, a daughter, was established in London, at the beginning of the present century, earning a modest liveli-

---

* This is a mistake. Pope's accusation is not against Sheffield, Duke of Buckingham, but against Montague, Earl of Halifax.

hood as an authoress and artist. The following is a copy of the card of this industrious lady :

Miss Clark,

Granddaughter of the late Colonel Frederick, Son of Theodore, King of Corsica,

PAINTS LIKENESSES IN MINIATURE, FROM TWO TO THREE GUINEAS, No. 116, NEW BOND STREET.

Hours of Attendance from Twelve in the Morning until Four.

Dr. Doran's volume, entitled *Monarchs retired from Business*, an amusing book, gossips further upon the insolvent ex-King.

GENERAL WOLFE, AND THE EXPEDITION TO QUEBEC.

When, in 1759, Pitt entrusted Wolfe with the expedition against Quebec, on the day preceding his embarkation, Pitt, desirous of giving his last verbal instructions, invited him to dinner at Hayes, Lord Temple being the only other guest. As the evening advanced, Wolfe, heated perhaps by his own aspiring thoughts, and the unwonted society of statesmen, broke forth in a strain of gasconade and bravado. He drew his sword and rapped the table with it ; he flourished it round the room, and he talked of the mighty things which that sword was to achieve. The two ministers sat aghast at an exhibition so unusual from any man of real sense and spirit. And when, at last, Wolfe had taken his leave, and his carriage was heard to roll from the door, Pitt seemed for the moment shaken in the right opinion which his deliberate judgment had formed of Wolfe : he lifted up his eyes and arms, and exclaimed to Lord Temple : · "Good God ! that I should have entrusted the fate of the country and of the administration to such hands !" This story was told by Lord Temple himself to the Right Hon. Thomas Grenville, the friend of Lord Mahon, who has inserted the anecdote in his *History of England*, vol. iv. Lord Temple also told Mr. Grenville, that on the evening in question, Wolfe had partaken most sparingly of wine, so that this ebullition could not have been the effect of any excess. The incident affords a striking proof how much a fault of manner may obscure and disparage high excellence of mind. Lord Mahon adds: "It confirms Wolfe's own avowal, that he was not seen to advantage in the common occurrences of life, and shows how shyness may, at intervals, rush, as it were, for refuge, into the opposite extreme ; but it should also lead us to view such defects of manner with indulgence, as proving that they may co-exist with the highest ability and the purest virtue."

The death of Wolfe was a kind of military martyrdom. He had failed in several attempts against the French power in Canada, dreaded a court martial, and resolved, by a bold and original stroke, to justify the confidence of Pitt, or die.

The want of a Life of Wolfe (says Mr. Robert Chambers)—a strange want, considering the glory which rests on the name—has caused some points regarding him to remain in doubt. It is doubtful, for example, if he was in service in the campaign of the Duke of Cumberland in the north of Scotland in 1746.

QUEEN CHARLOTTE AND ST. KATHARINE'S HOSPITAL.

On the east side of Regent's Park was rebuilt, in 1827, the Hospital of St. Katharine, on the demolition of the ancient hospital and church, by the Tower, for the site of St. Katharine's Docks. The foundation dates more than 700 years ago, in the reign of King Stephen, by Queen Matilda, confirmed by grants of succeeding sovereigns, and the revenues increased by Queen Eleanor and other royal donors. Provision was made for the master and priest; three brothers, priests; and three sisters; all under obligation of perpetual chastity, and to "serve and minister before God," and do works of charity. Masses were to be said daily in the chapel, one for the souls of all the kings and queens of England. Provision was to be made for twenty poor men and ten poor women, to be increased with the means of the hospital, the income of which was, in the reign of Henry VIII., 365*l.* a year. In 1866 the income exceeded 7000*l.* a year; to be increased to nearly 15,000*l.*, when the Tower house falls in, in the year 1900. The master receives nearly 1500*l.* a year, increased to 2000*l.* by the rent of his official residence which, as he is non-resident, he lets. Each brother, by the Chancery decree, was to receive 300*l.* a year, now, with the emoluments, 505*l.*; and each sister, 200*l.*, now 371*l.*; 20 bedesmen and 20 bedeswomen, 10*l.* each; and a school for 33 boys and 18 girls; besides various payments of officers and attendants. It is suggested by a Report made in 1866, that the revenue might be made more productive, the hospital be restored to the east of London, and a collegiate church be there established. The Lord Chancellor visits the hospital with his assessors, and with judicial powers, the foundation being exempt from any jurisdiction save that of the Sovereign in his Chancery. Four of such visitations have taken place in 600 years; the last in 1823, by Lord Lyndhurst. The hospital buildings in Regent's Park have cost, for upholding and repairing, 32,088*l.*, or little less than the original estimate for their re-construction. The officers of the institution are non-resident, and let their houses to augment their incomes!

The gift of the mastership of this hospital is described as the "prettiest bit of preferment" in the possession of a Queen Dowager, or the wife of a king of England. Soon after the period when Charlotte, Princess of Mecklenburgh-Strelitz became Queen Consort, she bestowed the appointment on Colonel Greene, as the reward for the exercise of his office of love's emissary, when he went from court to court in Germany in search of a Princess qualified to share the throne of Great Britain with George III. The gallant soldier happened to meet at the salutary springs of Pyrmont, with the Princess Dowager of Strelitz, and her two daughters. His report of the younger of the latter is stated to have been so favourable that it led to the offer of marriage subsequently made and promptly accepted.

We quote from the papers of Mrs. Stuart the following account of the negotiations for the hand of Queen Charlotte :—

"Her Majesty described her life at Mecklenburgh as one of extreme retirement. She dressed only *en robe de chambre*, except on Sundays, on which days she put on her best gown, and after service, which was very long, took an airing in a coach-and-six, attended by guards and all the State she could muster. She had not ' dined ' at table at the period I am speaking of. One morning her eldest brother, of whom she seems to have stood in great awe, came to her room in company with the Duchess, her mother. . . . . In a few minutes the folding doors flew open to the saloon, which she saw splendidly illuminated ; and then appeared a table, two cushions, and everything prepared for a wedding. Her brother then gave her his hand, and, leading her in, used his favourite expression,— ' *Allons, ne faites pas l'enfant, tu vas être Reine d'Angleterre.'* " Mr. Drummond then advanced. They knelt down. The ceremony, whatever it was, proceeded. She was laid on the sofa, upon which he laid his foot ; and they all embraced her, calling her ' La Reine.' "

HORNE TOOKE'S POLITICAL PREDICTION.

Horne was the son of a poulterer in Newport Market : when asked by some of his schoolfellows what his father was, he is said to have replied "a Turkey merchant." The somewhat turbulent tone of the politics of the son may have had something to do with the following circumstance. As Mr. Horne the father lived in Newport Street, he was a near neighbour to Frederick Prince of Wales, who then kept his court at Leicester House. Some of the officers of the household imagining that an outlet towards the Market would be extremely convenient to them and the inferior domestics, an adjoining wall was cut through, and a door placed in the opening, without any ceremony ; notwithstanding it was a palpable encroachment on, and violation of, the property of a private individual. In the midst of this operation, Mr. Horne remonstrated, as the brick partition actually appertained to him, and the intended thoroughfare would lead through, and consequently depreciate, the value of his premises. The representations of the dealer in geese and turkeys, although backed by law and reason, were disregarded by those who abused the authority of a prince. On this, Horne appealed from "the insolence of office" to the justice of his country ; and to the honour of our municipal jurisprudence, the event proved different from what it would have been, perhaps, in any other kingdom in Europe ; for a tradesman of Westminster triumphed over the heir apparent of the English crown, and orders were issued for the removal of the obnoxious door. It is not unreasonable to suppose that this successful start had its influence upon Tooke's aims in life.

Tooke was a man of remarkable sagacity, well acquainted with the state of England, and familiar with the course of public transactions in all times and nations. But, in his delight at the progress of the French Revolution, he boldly predicted that the same formidable process must be inevitably undergone by this country. On a man of more unprejudiced mind, the whole aspect of the empire must have irresistibly impressed the directly opposite conviction; but Horne Tooke wished, and therefore believed. He was perfectly certain that the overthrow of ranks, at least, must come within a short period : " I trust," said he, in the utmost sincerity of familiar intercourse, "we shall live to see the day when the distinctions of title will be abolished, and we may eat our mutton without being teased with such childish objects as ribbons, stars, and garters." He perpetually predicted the immediate downfall of the whole system of the country, and sneered habitually at the attempts to revive credit. On hearing of the bankruptcies frequent at that period, he could not dissemble his rebel gratification. "You are not going," he would say, "you are gone; it is not a slight hurt, but a mortal gangrene." Still, a very poor prophet he proved. He has been in his grave more than half a century, yet, how many of his predictions have come true !

What Tooke thought of the church may be seen in a letter of his to Wilkes, whose acquaintance he made at Paris in 1765, and to whom he thus wrote :—" You are now entering into correspondence with a parson, and I am greatly apprehensive lest that title should disgust; but give me leave to assure you, I am not ordained a hypocrite. It is true I have suffered the infectious hand of a bishop to be waved over me, whose imposition, like the sop given to Judas, is only a signal for the devil to enter. I hope I have escaped the contagion; and, if I have not, if you should at any time discover the black spot under the tongue, pray kindly assist me to conquer the prejudices of education and profession."

Tooke was, upon one occasion, memorably outwitted by Wilkes, who was then sheriff of London and Middlesex. Tooke had challenged Wilkes, who sent him the following cutting reply :—" Sir, I do not think it my business to cut the throat of every desperado that may be tired of his life; but as I am at present high sheriff of the City of London, it may happen that I shall shortly have an opportunity of attending you in my official capacity, in which case I will answer for it that *you shall have no ground* to complain of my endeavours to serve you."

Tooke's audacity was irrepressible. In 1777 he was carried to the King's Bench to receive sentence for publishing his advertisement for subscriptions for the Americans. Lord Mansfield ordered him to prison, he cried out, "What, before sentence?" Lord Mansfield was intimidated, and dismissed him. Some days after he was again brought into court, and the Attorney-General pleaded for his being set in the pillory, and even had the audacity to quote the Star Chamber, which he said had been laid aside for its rankness, implying, therefore, it was not totally without merit. Lord Mansfield was afraid, and would not venture the pillory, but sentenced Tooke to a fine and a year's imprisonment.

For many years Tooke was the terror of judges, ministers of state, and all constituted authorities. When put on trial for his life (for treason), "so far from being moved by his dangerous position, he was never in more buoyant spirits. His wit and humour had often before been exhibited in courts of justice; but never had they been so brilliant as on this occasion. Erskine had been at his request assigned to him as counsel; but he himself undertook some of the most important duties of his advocate, cross-examining the witnesses for the Crown, objecting to evidence, and even arguing points of law. If his life had really been in jeopardy, such a course would have been perilous and rash in the highest degree; but nobody in court, except, perhaps, the Attorney and Solicitor-General, thought there was the slightest chance of an adverse verdict. The prisoner led off the proceedings by a series of preliminary jokes, which were highly successful. When placed in the dock he cast a glance up at the ventilators of the hall, shivered, and expressed a wish that their lordships would be so good as to get the business over quickly as he was afraid of catching cold. When arraigned, and asked by the officer of the court, in the usual form, how he would be tried? he answered, 'I *would* be tried by God and my country—but——' and looked sarcastically round the court. Presently he made an application to be allowed a seat by his counsel; and entered upon an amusing altercation with the judge, as to whether his request should be granted as an indulgence or as a right. The result was that he consented to take his place by the side of Erskine as a matter of favour. In the midst of the merriment occasioned by these sallies, the Solicitor-General opened the case for the crown."—Massey's *History of England.*

LORD MAYOR BECKFORD'S MONUMENTAL SPEECH.

It will be remembered by any one familiar with the history of the Corporation of London, that Alderman Beckford, in his second mayoralty, in 1770, had the audacity to beard George III. as he sat upon his throne. The unconstitutional return at the Middlesex election of the candidate in the minority to be the sitting member, brought the Lord Mayor to the foot of the throne with a Remonstrance, to which the king replied :—" That he should have been wanting to the public, as well as to himself, if he had not expressed his dissatisfaction at the late Address."

Horace Walpole thus notes the affair:—"The City carried a new remonstrance,* garnished with my lord's own ingredients, but much less hot than the former. The Court, however, was put to some confusion by my Lord Mayor, who, contrary to all form and precedent, tacked a volunteer speech to the Remonstrance. It was wondrous loyal and respectful, but being an innovation, much discomposed the solemnity. It is always usual to furnish a copy of what

---

* The King is further known to have characterized this document as follows : "The remonstrance, according to the copy you have transmitted to me this day, has undoubtedly the marks of being the most violent, insolent, and licentious ever printed ; but when it is known how thin the meeting was that countenanced the proceeding, and their indifference to it, a dry answer, rather bordering on contempt than anger, may not be improper."

is said to the King, that he may be prepared with his answer. In this case, he was reduced to tuck up his train, jump from the throne, and take sanctuary in his closet, or answer extempore, which is not part of the royal trade; or sit silent and have nothing to reply. This last was the event, and a position awkward enough in conscience."—*Walpole to Sir Horace Mann,* May 24, 1770.

The citizens were so elated with Beckford's insulting conduct that they erected in the Guildhall, at some thousands' expense, a large monument, in which is a life-size statue of Beckford addressing the King in the speech which is sculptured in *red* letters upon the pedestal whereon Beckford stands.

Now, at the end of the Alderman's speech, in his copy of the City Addresses, Mr. Isaac Reed has inserted the following note:—" It is a curious fact, but a true one, that Beckford did not utter one syllable of this speech (on the monument). It was penned by John Horne Tooke, and by his art put on the records of the City, and on Beckford's statue; as he told me, Mr. Braithwaite, Mr. Sayers, &c., at the Athenian Club. *Isaac Reed.*" There can be little doubt, that the worthy commentator and his friends were imposed upon. In the *Chatham Correspondence,* vol. iii. p. 460, a letter from Sheriff Townsend to the Earl expressly states, that, with the exception of the words "and necessary" being left out before the word "revolution," the Lord Mayor's speech in the *Public Advertiser* of the preceding day, is verbatim the one delivered to the King.—(*Wright—Note to Walpole.*)

Gifford says (*Ben Jonson,* vi. 481) that Beckford never uttered before the King one syllable of the speech upon his monument— and Gifford's statement is fully confirmed both by Isaac Reed (as above) and by Maltby, the friend of Rogers and Horne Tooke. Beckford *made* a "Remonstrance Speech" to the King; but the speech on Beckford's monument is the after speech *written* for Beckford by Horne Tooke.—See Mitford's *Gray and Mason Correspondence,* pp. 438, 439. —*Cunningham's Note to Walpole,* v. 239.

THE BOSTON TEA-PARTY.

This was the name popularly given to the assemblage of citizens in Boston, Dec. 16, 1773, who met to carry out the non-importation resolves of the colony; and who, disguised as Indians, went on board three English ships which had just arrived in the harbour, and destroyed several hundred chests of tea. The British parliament retaliated by closing the port of Boston.—(*Wheeler's Dictionary.*)

In Walpole's *Last Journals,* Jan. 18, 1774, we read: "This week came accounts of very riotous proceedings at Boston, where the mob broke into the ships that had brought teas, and threw above 340 chests into the sea."

Upon this, Dr. Doran has an amusing note: " The Americans signalized the early occurrence of the outbreak by using very loyal tunes, to which, however, they adapted words which were accounted very undutiful *here*.   Thus, the air of 'Rule Britannia,' was chorused a hymn of liberty of many verses, from which I take one :

> Let us, your sons, by freedom warm'd,
> Your own example keep in view ;
> 'Gainst tyranny be ever arm'd,
> Though we our tyrant find in you.
> Rule Britannia ; Britannia rule the waves ;
> But never, never make your children slaves !

"Whitehead, the laureate, whose grand nonsense was pronounced 'insupportable' by Johnson, took occasion of a temporary 'lull' in the American excitement, a few months later than the period named in the text, to proclaim in a Birthday Ode the repentance of the colonists who incited to rebellion by putting new words to old tunes.   Thus sang the son of the wealthy Cambridge baker :

> The prodigal again returns,
> And on his parent's neck reclines,
> With honest shame his bosom burns,
> And in his eye affection shines :
> Shines through tears at once that prove
> Grief and joy and filial love.

"Before Whitehead could write another Birthday Ode to the King, the 'prodigal' had struck his 'parent' that blow at Lexington which seemed proof of anything but 'grief and joy and filial love.'   And then, as Bancroft remarks of the opening of the conflict : 'Kings sat still in awe, and nations turned to watch the issue.'

"It has been well said, 'The grain of corn which broke the camel's back, and in this instance caused the American War, was the imposition of the Tea-duty at Boston.' "

WILKES TRIUMPHANT !

In 1774, in the election of Lord Mayor, Wilkes entirely governed Bull, the actual Mayor, and made him decline the chair a second time. The Court on one side, and Alderman Townshend on the other, meant to gain or give the preference to any man over Wilkes.   They set up two insignificant Aldermen, Eisdale and Kennet, as competitors, not having been able to prevail upon Sawbridge to stand for it again.   Wilkes had regained him by promising to bring him into parliament for the City.   Wilkes and Bull had the majority of hands, and after a poll which was demanded for Eisdale and Kennet, Wilkes and Bull were returned to the Court of Aldermen, who at last did declare Wilkes Lord Mayor.   "Thus," says Walpole, "after so much persecution of the Court, after so many attempts on his life, after a long imprisonment in a gaol, after all his own crimes and indiscretions, did this extraordinary man, of more extraordinary fortune, attain the highest office in so grave and important a city as the capital of England, always reviving the more opposed and oppressed, and unable to shock fortune, or make her laugh at *him*, who laughed at every body and every thing.   [In the triumph of his heart Wilkes said, "if the King had sent me a pardon and a thousand pounds to Paris, I should have accepted them, but I am obliged to him for not having ruined me."—*Doran.*]

"The duration of Wilkes' career was the most wonderful part of his history. Masaniello, a fisher-boy, attained to supreme power of Naples, but perished in three days. Rienzi governed Rome, but lost it by his folly. Sacheverel balanced the glory of Marlborough in the height of his victories, but never was heard of more. Wilkes was seen through, detected, yet gained ground; and all the power of the crown, all the malice of the Scots, all the abilities of Lord Mansfield, all the violence of Alderman Townshend, all the want of policy and parts in the Opposition, all the treachery of his own friends, could not demolish him. He equally baffled the King and parson Horne, though both neglected no latitude to compass his ruin. It is in this his tenth year of his war on the Court that he gained so signal a victory!"

HOW THE AMERICAN WAR MIGHT HAVE BEEN PREVENTED.

We see from Lord North's letters to George III. in 1778, that he wished to retire from office, and that he urged the King to form an Administration of the Whigs combined under the presidency of Chatham. Had this been done it is not impossible that one of the darkest pages of our history might have taken a different colour. America, soothed by the return to power of her great advocate in the British Senate, might either have gone back to her allegiance or have separated from England without calling in our ancient foes to her support. The statesman of the Seven Years' War might have struck terror into the House of Bourbon; the combined fleets of France and Spain might not have appeared in the unguarded Channel, nor the name of Yorktown been inscribed on our annals; the Empire might have been spared dismemberment and years of disastrous war and misfortune. But George III. could not tolerate the Opposition; he hated Chatham with bitter hatred, and he refused peremptorily to form a Government that might have been the safeguard of England. In a letter to Lord North, the King does not object to see Lord Chatham in the Ministry; "but," he adds, I solemnly declare nothing shall bring me personally to treat with Lord Chatham. . . . . an opinion formed on an experience of a reign of now seventeen years, makes me resolved to run any personal risque rather than submit to Opposition. While I have no one object but to be of use to this country, it is impossible I can be deserted, and the road opened to a set of men who certainly would make me a slave for the remainder of my days."[*]

---

[*] The reign of George III. has been differently estimated during the last twenty years; and there is more rough-speaking of contemporaneous events than hitherto, as in the following instance: In the Court of Common Council, Sept. 17th, 1863, upon a motion to print all Addresses presented to the Throne from the Court, from 1778 to the present time, one of the Members opposed the resolution, observing that, "besides their literary defects, the papers in question were not creditable to them as statements of fact, seeing that one of them, for example, extolled the wisdom of George III., and another spoke of George IV.

GEORGE III. AND AMERICAN INDEPENDENCE.

In the *Men and Times of the American Revolution* we find this graphic picture of " How George the Third appeared when he declared the Independence of the United States":—

" After waiting nearly two hours, the approach of the King was announced by a tremendous roar of artillery. He entered by a small door on the left of the throne, and immediately seated himself upon the chair of state, in a graceful attitude, with his right foot resting upon a stool. He was clothed in royal robes. Apparently agitated, he drew from his pocket the scroll containing his speech. The Commons were summoned, and after the bustle of their entrance had subsided, he proceeded to read his speech. I was near the King, and watched with intense interest every tone of his voice, and every motion of his countenance. It was to me a moment of thrilling and dignified exultation. After some general and usual remarks, he continued :—' I lost no time in giving the necessary orders to prohibit the further prosecution of offensive war upon the continent of North America. Adopting, as my inclination will always lead me to do, with decision and effect whatever I collect to be the sense of my Parliament and my people, I have pointed all my views and measures, in Europe, as in North America, to an entire and cordial reconciliation with the colonies. Finding it indispensable to the attainment of the object, I did not hesitate to go to the full length of the powers vested in me, and offer to declare them.'—Here he paused, and was in evident agitation ; either embarrassed in reading his speech by the darkness of the room, or affected by a very *natural emotion.* In a moment he resumed :—' and offer to declare them *free and independent States.* In thus admitting their separation from the Crown of these Kingdoms, I have sacrificed every consideration of my own to the wishes and opinions of my people. I make it my humble and ardent prayer to Almighty God, that Great Britain may not feel the evils which might result from so great a dismemberment of the empire, and that America may be free from the calamities which have formerly proved, in the mother country, how essential monarchy is to the enjoyment of constitutional liberty. Religion, language, interests, and affections, may, and I hope will, yet prove a bond of permanent union between the two countries.' It is remarked that George III. is celebrated for reading his speeches in a distinct, free, and impressive manner. On this occasion he was evidently embarrassed ; he hesitated, choked, and executed the painful duties of the occasion with an ill grace, which does not belong to him."

---

as 'our most religious and gracious sovereign.'" What can exceed the savage spirit of Mr. Landor's epigram :—

> George the First was always reckoned
> Vile—but viler George the Second ;
> And what mortal ever heard
> Any good of George the Third ?
> When from earth the Fourth descended,
> Heaven be praised ! the Georges ended.

A PAGE OF POLITICAL HATE.

Horace Walpole writes of the stormy period of January, 1776: "I who had seen every injustice heaped on my father by Jacobitism and faction, and who now saw the ruin of the country procured by Jacobite principles, did wish to turn every art of party that was allowable on such guilty men. I had less delicacy than the Duke (of Richmond), and thought it meritorious to expose to clamour such Machiavels as Lord Mansfield, "qui sobrius ad evertendam Rempublicam accessit." Lord North was a pliant tool, without system or principle; Lord Germaine, of desperate ambition and character; Wedderburn a thorough knave; Lord Gower a villain, capable of any crime; Elliot, Jenkinson, Cornwall, mutes, that would have fixed the bowstring round the throat of the constitution. The subordinate crew to name is to stigmatize: they were Dr. Johnson, the pilloried Shebbeare; Sir John Dalrymple, and Macpherson! The pious though unconscientious Lord Dartmouth had been laid aside, after bequeathing to the Administration his hypocrite secretaries, Wesley and Madan; Lord Barrington remained to lie officially; Lord Weymouth has acceded with all his insensibility to honour, and by acceding had given new edge to Thurlow, who was fit to execute whatever was to be done. Almost every Scot was ready to put his sickle to the harvest, and every Jacobite country gentleman exulted in the prospect of reversing on the Whigs and Dissenters all their disappointments since the Revolution; and they saw a Prince of the House of Brunswick ready to atone for all the negative hurt his family had done to their ancestors, and for all the good his ancestors and the benefactor of his family—King William—had done to Great Britain. There was still another body ready to profit by the restoration of Stuart views—the bishops and clergy. How deeply and joyfully they waded into a civil war on the Constitution and on Dissenters, let their votes, addresses, and zeal for the war declare! This is a heavy picture; but if any of the individuals mentioned above, or any of the denominations of men, come out whiter in the eyes of impartial posterity, let this page be registered as a page of the blackest calumny!"—*Last Journals*, vol. ii.

LORD RODNEY IN DIFFICULTIES.

Admiral Lord Rodney, it is well known, from heavy losses at the gaming table, became so involved as to avoid the importunities of his creditors, to seek refuge in France. During his residence in Paris, he occasionally wanted even small sums to supply the necessities of his family; and it is a singular fact that he was indebted to the generosity of a French nobleman for the funds which enabled him to revisit England in 1778, and consequently to achieve his great victory over the French fleet under De Grasse, in 1782. He was very sanguine of the success he should obtain over the enemy; and while resident in Cleveland-row, St. James's, not only conceived, but delineated on paper the naval manœuvres of *breaking or intersecting the line*, to which he was mainly indebted for his brilliant victory over De Grasse. The French Government appear to have formed a high opinion of Rodney's professional talent, and from the persuasion, apparently, that his pecuniary difficulties rendered him open to temptation, went so far as to offer him, through the Duc de Biron, a post of high rank in the French navy. His reply was characteristic : " Monsieur le Duc, it is true that my distresses have driven me from my country, but no temptation can estrange me from her service; had this offer been voluntary on your part I should have considered it an insult, but I am glad that it proceeds from a source that can do no wrong." About the same time, when the Duc de Chartres informed him that he was likely to be appointed to the command of the French fleet, which was to be opposed to the squadron under Admiral Keppel, and inquired his opinion as to the probable result of an engagement between the two fleets ; " My opinion," he said, " is, that Keppel will carry your Highness home with him to teach you English."

On his return to England Rodney's embarrassments so disgusted him with life that, in a letter to a friend, he expressed a melancholy regret that, in his great action with De Grasse, a cannon ball had not struck off his head.

Lord Rodney directed in person every manœuvre, and preserved, during the twelve hours that the action lasted, the utmost presence of mind. He never quitted the quarter-deck for a minute, nor took any refreshment except the support he derived from a lemon, which he held constantly in his hand, and applied frequently to his lips. Burke said of this achievement, that " the great national benefit performed by the English admiral, obliterated his errors ; and, like the laurel-crown decreed by the Roman Senate to Julius Cæsar, covered, as well as concealed, his baldness."

CONFERRING THE GARTER.

Two of our Sovereigns appear to have shown ill manners and temper in conferring the insignia and decorations of this noble order. George II., who strongly disliked Lord Temple, "Squire Gawkey," as he was nicknamed, was compelled by political arrangements, very repugnant to his feelings, to invest that nobleman with the Order of the Garter, when the King took so little pains to conceal his aversion both to the individual and to the act, that, instead of placing the riband decorously over the shoulder of the new knight, his Majesty, averting his head, and muttering indistinctly some expressions of dissatisfaction, threw the riband across him, and turned his back at the same instant in the rudest manner. George III. exerted more restraint over his passions than did his grandfather, yet even he could be ill-tempered. When he invested the Marquis Camden with the Garter, he showed much ill-humour in his countenance and manner. However, as he knew the ceremony must be performed, Mr. Pitt having pertinaciously insisted upon it, the King took the riband in his hand, and turning to the Duke of Dorset, the assistant knight-companion, before the new knight approached, asked him if he knew Lord Camden's Christian name. The duke, after inquiring, informed him that it was John Jefferies. "What, what!" said the King, " John Jefferies! the first Knight of the Garter, I believe, that was ever called John Jefferies;" the King not considering his descent sufficiently illustrious.

In 1782, at the time of Lord North's resignation, there were on the King's table four Garters unappropriated, which the new ministers naturally considered as lawful plunder. One only fell to the share of the Sovereign, which he was allowed, though not without some difficulty, to confer on his third son, Prince William Henry, afterwards William IV. The Duke of Devonshire, as head of the Whig party, was invested with one blue riband, and the Duke of Richmond with another. Lord Shelburne took for himself, as was to be expected, the fourth Garter. At the investment never did three men receive the Order in so dissimilar and characteristic a manner. The Duke of Devonshire advanced up to the Sovereign, with his phlegmatic, cold, and awkward air, like a clown. Lord Shelburne came forward, bowing on all sides, and fawning like a courtier. The Duke of Richmond presented himself easy, unembarrassed, and with dignity, like a gentleman.

PITT, AS A WAR MINISTER.

Mr. Goldwin Smith, in his lecture upon the Heaven-born statesman, thus notices his deficiency as a War Minister. "He had not his father's eye for men. He was open to a worse censure than that of failing to distinguish merit. When he allowed himself to be made Minister by an unconstitutional use of the king's personal influence he had sold himself to the fiend, and the fiend did not fail to exact the bond. Twice Pitt had the criminal weakness to gratify the king's personal wishes by intrusting the safety of English armies and the honour of England to the incompetent hands of the young Duke of York. But could promotion by merit be expected at the hands of Governments whose essence was privilege? It was against promotion by merit that they were fighting. To accept it would have been to accept the Revolution. Pitt did not know why he had gone to war; therefore, when he found himself abandoned by most of his allies, the rest requiring subsidies to drag them into the field,—the cause of Europe, as it was called, renounced by Europe itself, everything going ill, and no prospect of amendment,--he did not know how or on what terms to make peace. This was called his firmness. At last, in 1801, peace, and an ignominious peace, was inevitable, and Pitt retired. But he came into power again to conduct a war, and this time a necessary war, for with the perfidy and rapine of Bonaparte no peace was possible. The struggle with him was a struggle for the independence of all nations against the armed and disciplined hordes of a conqueror as cruel and as barbarous as Attila. The lecturer looked with pride upon the fortitude and constancy which

England displayed in the contest with this universal tyrant. The position in which it left her at its close was fairly won, though she must now be content to retire from the temporary supremacy, and fall back into her place as one of the community of nations. But Pitt was still destined to fail as a War Minister. Trafalgar was soon cancelled by Austerlitz. ' How I leave my country !' were Pitt's last words, and, perhaps his truest epitaph. They well expressed the anguish of a patriot who had wrecked his country."

The reviewer in *The Times* observes : " No greater theoretical or practical financier than Pitt has yet appeared in England ; and, even as a War Minister, Pitt's powers have been too often undervalued by recent critics. The coalitions which he formed provided the only chance of destroying the power of Napoleon ; and it was not the fault of the English Minister that the French General and his soldiers were for a time invincible. It may be true that 'Trafalgar was cancelled by Austerlitz,' but in the course of twenty months between his return to power and his death, Pitt had relieved England from the immediate risk of invasion, and he had formed the combinations which compelled Napoleon to fight for his existence at Austerlitz, at Jena, at Eylau, and at Friedland. A statesman contending with a gigantic enemy can do no more than bring armies into the field, and Pitt accomplished his portion of the common task. The French understand better than Liberal English commentators on history the character and achievements of the minister, who seems to M. Thiers, as to M. Louis Blanc, to have been the deadliest enemy of the Revolution and the Empire. That he was able for so many years to wield the whole force of the nation, is a proof not only of the ascendancy of his eloquence and of his character, but also of the soundness of institutions, which were, undoubtedly, encumbered with many anomalies."

PITT AND THE PITTITES.

The memory of Pitt has been assailed, times innumerable, often justly, often unjustly ; but it has suffered much less from his assailants than from his eulogists. For during many years, his name was the rallying cry of a class of men with whom, at one of those terrible conjunctures which confound all ordinary distinctions, he was accidentally and temporarily connected ; but to whom on almost all great questions of principle he was diametrically opposed. The haters of Parliamentary Reform called themselves Pittites, not choosing to remember that Pitt made three motions for Parliamentary Reform, and that, though he thought that such a reform could not safely be made. While the passions excited by the French Revolution were raging, he never uttered a word indicating that he should not be prepared at a more convenient season to bring the question forward a fourth time. The toast of the Protestant Ascendancy was drank on Pitt's birthday by a set of Pittites who could not but be aware that Pitt had resigned his office because he could not carry Catholic Emancipation. The defenders of the Test Act called themselves Pittites, though they could not be ignorant that

Pitt had laid before George III. unanswerable reasons for abolishing the Test Act. The enemies of Free Trade called themselves Pittites, though Pitt was far more deeply imbued with the doctrines of Adam Smith, than either Fox or Grey. The very negro-drivers invoked the name of Pitt, whose eloquence was never more conspicuously displayed than when he spoke of the wrongs of the negro. This mythical Pitt who resembles the genuine Pitt as little as the Charlemagne of Ariosto resembles the Charlemagne of Eginhard, has had his day. History will vindicate the real man from calumny disguised under the semblance of adulation, and will exhibit him as what he was, a minister of great talents, honest intentions, and liberal opinions; pre-eminently qualified intellectually and morally, for the part of a Parliamentary leader, and capable of administering with prudence and moderation the government of a prosperous and tranquil country, but unequal to surprising and terrible emergencies, and liable in such emergencies to err grievously, both on the side of weakness and on the side of violence.—*Macaulay.*

Pitt died on the 25th of January, the 25th anniversary of the day on which he first took his seat in Parliament. He was in his 47th year, and had been, during nineteen years, First Lord of the Treasury, and undisputed chief of the Administration.

There was long a doubt as to the last words of Mr. Pitt. Earl Stanhope, in his *Life* of the great minister (1862), gave them from a manuscript left by his lordship's uncle, the Hon. James H. Stanhope, as "Oh my country! how I love my country!" But, upon re-examination of the MS., a somewhat obscure one, no doubt was left in Lord Stanhope's mind that the word "love" was a mistake for "leave." The expression, as in this manner finally authenticated, is in perfect and most sad conformity with the state of the national affairs at the time when Mr. Pitt was approaching his end. A new coalition, which England had, with great difficulty and vast expense, formed against Napoleon, had been dashed to pieces by the prostration of Austria; and Pitt must have had the idea in his mind that hardly now a stay remained.

WHAT DROVE GEORGE III. MAD.

How strange is it to find, upon a close examination of the biography of Mr. Pitt, that early in the present century, the *mention* of the measure which twenty-eight years later became the law of the land, had the effect of disturbing the reason of the sovereign: yet so it was. "Pitt had become in a manner pledged on the union of the Irish with the British Legislature, to provide for what has since been called the Emancipation of the Catholics. The probability is, that from the first he had underrated the King's repugnance to the measure; but it has been suggested that had there been no treachery in the camp, and had he been the first to broach the subject to George III., he might have had his own way, and carried the acquiescence of the king. As it was, Lord Loughborough had, contrary to all rule, made the King aware of Pitt's intentions, and had, for his own selfish purposes sought to strengthen his

Majesty in a most absurd view of his duty. So it happened that instead of Pitt breaking the subject to the King, the King, in a fit of impatience, breaks out upon Dundas. Referring to Lord Castlereagh, who had recently come from Dublin, he said, " What is it that this young lord has brought over which they are going to throw at my head ? . . . The most Jacobinical thing I ever heard of! I shall reckon any man my personal enemy who proposes any such measure." " Your Majesty," replied Dundas, " will find among those who are friendly to that measure some whom you never supposed to be your enemies." The time for action had evidently come : it was necessary for Pitt to break the silence ; he wrote to the King explaining his views, and pointing out that if they were not acceptable it would be necessary for him to resign. Pitt did resign ; his successor was appointed, but before the formal transfer of office cou'd take place, the King went mad, and it was this Catholic question that drove him mad. He recovered in a fortnight and told his physician to write to Pitt, " Tell him I am now quite well—quite recovered from my illness ; but what has *he* not to answer for who is the cause of my having been ill at all ?" Pitt was deeply touched, and at once conveyed an assurance to the King, through the same physician, that never again during the King's reign would he bring forward the Catholic question. Previous to that illness Pitt had two clear alternatives before him—" either I shall relieve the Catholics, or I shall resign,"— and he resigned accordingly. But after the illness all was changed. Any attempt to relieve the Catholics would incur the risk of the King's derangement. There was but a choice of evils, and it was natural that Pitt should regard it as the lesser evil to postpone indefinitely the settlement of the Catholic claims, which, nevertheless, he regarded as of the utmost importance.

During the latter part of the time, George III., notwithstanding the continuance of some delusions, was perfectly competent to understand the state of affairs, and there was every reason to suppose that he would become convalescent before his son could take his seat as Regent. For the remainder of his reign his Ministers and his subjects regarded his occasional insanity as one of the ordinary contingencies of the Constitution. Mr. Pitt, during his second Administration, sometimes obtained from the physicians a written certificate of the King's competence before he entered his presence for the transaction of business. Who would have supposed forty years ago that a day was coming when a Frenchman would unhesitatingly write the apology—we had almost said the panegyric—of William Pitt—" *ce* Pitt," as the members of the Jacobin Club used to call him ? And yet such is the case. By way of preface to a translation of Lord Stanhope's *Life* of Pitt, M. Guizot has given a very good estimate both of the political relation in which England stands to France, and also of the character of the great British statesman. He conclusively shows that Pitt was positively opposed to a war with France, and did all he could to prevent the inevitable catastrophe.

CHARACTER OF LORD NELSON.

The following character of our great naval hero, as sketched by Henry Edward 4th and last Lord Holland, the diplomatist, differs, in many respects, from the popular estimate of Nelson:—

" Of his person there are many representations, and will be nearly as many descriptions. It was insignificant, and announced none of the qualities of a commander; though his innumerable scars (for he had scarcely ever been in action without receiving a wound), the loss of an eye, and of an arm, and a weather-beaten countenance, marked the hard service he had seen, and gave him, at the age of forty-two, all the appearance of a veteran. His greatness (for who shall gainsay the greatness of the conqueror of Aboukir, Copenhagen, and Trafalgar ?) is a strong instance of the superiority of the heart over the head, and no slight proof that a warm imagination is a more necessary ingredient in the composition of an hero than a sound understanding. . . . It is perhaps no ill office to the memory of Nelson to correct any favourable opinion that may be entertained of his understanding; for what justification can be found for one period of his public life, if he was aware and capable of judging of the nature of the transactions in which he was engaged ? But his violation of good faith and justice at Naples, which, if he were considered as a man of sense, would tarnish all his glories, and hand him down to posterity as a perfidious politician, a bloody and relentless persecutor, is to be accounted for and can alone be palliated by the weakness of his understanding, by the ascendancy which an artful and worthless woman had obtained over a mind unversed in politics and ignorant of the world; and by the general violence with which the calamities and intolerance of the times had infected men less susceptible of delusion and bigotry than himself."

For some of the worst points in the disgraceful proceedings at Naples a partial apology is offered:—" That the base and wicked conduct of Lady Hamilton was known to him at the time to its full extent, is impossible. She received money from individuals to save the lives of themselves or their relations; and in the instance of a nephew of Duke Elzi, if not in more, she suffered the victims to perish without returning the bribe. That these transactions were subsequently known to Nelson I fear cannot be disputed; for he generously repaid such sums from the income of the Duchy of Bronte, and made all the reparation in his power to the injured, though he had not the resolution and virtue to expose, or to separate himself from, the person who committed the injustice. Such were the real stains in the character of Nelson; for his vanity, often ridiculous, was utterly unmixed with pride, arrogance, illnature, or jealousy. It was rather a diverting proof of his simplicity than a dangerous or offensive quality in his intercourse with others. He smiled with complacency when Lady Hamilton introduced him by the name of 'our saviour;' he would press her to sing the most fulsome couplets to his honour; and he acknowledged with the utmost *naïveté*, that his preference for her society to Lady Nelson's arose from the warm praises she bestowed upon him, after which the congratulations of his wife were, he said, cold, flat, and insipid. To his visitors he displayed, with the greatest complacency, his own portraits and busts laden with inscriptions, and decorated with laurels, &c."

FRENCH COLOURS TAKEN AT WATERLOO.

Untrustworthiness in an historian was, perhaps, never more directly proved than by a passage in the 20th volume of the *Histoire du Consulat et de l'Empire*, by M. Thiers, who writes, in page 208 :—

"Les Ecossais Gris enlèvent d'un côté le drapeau du 105ième (Division Alix), et de l'autre celui du 45ième (Division Marcoquet)."

M. Thiers thus admits the capture of two Eagles by the British dragoons. Page 209 states that—

"Un maréchal de logis des Lanciers, nommé Urban, se précipitant dans la mêlée, fait prisonnier le chef des Dragons, le brave Ponsonby. Les Ecossais s'efforçant de délivrer leur général, Urban le renverse, mort à ses pieds; puis, menacé par plusieurs dragons, il va droit à l'un d'eux qui tenait le drapeau du 45ième, le démonte d'un coup de lance, le tue d'un second coup, lui enlève le drapeau, se débarrasse en le tuant encore d'un autre Ecossais qui le serrait de près, et revient tout couvert de sang, porter à son colonel le trophée qu'il avait si glorieusement reconquis."

In page 252 M. Thiers reiterates his assertion as to the capture of this Eagle :—

"Chose remarquable, nous n'avions perdu qu'un drapeau, car le sous-officier de Lanciers Urban avait reconquis celui du 45ième, l'un des deux pris du corps d'Erlon."

In the teeth of these statements it is proved that in the Chapel of the Royal Hospital at Chelsea, among 13 Eagles captured from the French, are the above two which were taken at Waterloo, and are suspended from the walls right and left of the altar. The one on the left bears the following inscription :—"L'Empereur Napoléon au 45ième Régiment d'Infanterie de Ligne;" the other is inscribed, "L'Empereur Napoléon au 105ième Régiment d'Infanterie de Ligne." Both colours are emblazoned with the names of Marengo, Jena, Eylau, Friedland, Eckmuhl, and other victories.

In the *Times* next appeared the following evidence: "We are requested to state, by the best authority, that the Eagle of the 105th Regiment of the Line was taken from the French, at Waterloo, by the Royal Dragoons; that of the 45th by the Scots Greys."

To the *Kentish Gazette* of 1815 was communicated this evidence, written within ten days of the battle of Waterloo :—

"Canterbury, Friday, June 23rd, 1815.
(London, Thursday Night.)

" . . . . At three o'clock in the afternoon of Tuesday, the Hon. Major Percy, aide-de-camp to our illustrious hero, accompanied by

Captain White, of the navy, landed from a row-boat at Broadstairs, with the despatches of this important event, a copy of which is given in the preceding columns, and having also under their charge the eagles and standards of two French regiments of infantry, with which they immediately proceeded in a chaise and four to the metropolis. These emblems of victory belonged to the 45th and 104th Regiments, and were superbly gilt, and ornamented with broad gold fringe. That of the 45th was inscribed with the names of Jena, Austerlitz, Wagram, Eylau, Friedland, &c., being the battles in which this regiment, called the Invincible, had signalized itself. The other was a present from the Empress Louisa to the 104th. One was much defaced with blood and dirt, as if it had been struggled for, and the eagle was also broken off from the pole, as if from the cut of a sabre, but it was nevertheless preserved." [For 104th read 105th.]

Subjoined is an extract from a letter in the same year from Sergeant Ewart, of the Scots Greys, to his brother in Ayr, dated Rouen, 16th of August, 1815.—*Kentish Gazette*, October 2 :—

" . . . . Our brigade was ordered to advance to the support of our brave fellows, and which we certainly did in style. We charged through two of their columns, each about 5000. It was in the first charge I took the eagle from the enemy; he and I had a very hard contest for it. He thrust for my groin; I parried it off and cut him through the head; after which I was attacked by one of their Lancers, who threw his lance at me, but missed the mark by my throwing it off with my sword by my right side; then I cut him from the chin upwards, which cut went through his teeth. Next I was attacked by a foot soldier, who after firing at me charged me with his bayonet, but he very soon lost the combat, for I parried it and cut him down through the head; so that finished the contest for the eagle. After which I presumed to follow my comrades, eagle and all, but was stopped by the General, saying to me,—' You brave fellow, take that to the rear. You have done enough till you get quit of it;' which I was obliged to do, but with great reluctance. I retired to a height and stood there for upwards of an hour, which gave me a general view of the field, but I cannot express the sight I beheld—the bodies of my brave comrades were lying so thick upon the field that it was scarcely possible to pass, and horses innumerable. I took the eagle into Brussels amid the acclamations of the thousands of spectators that saw it."

The etymology and grammar of the above are exactly the same as in the original.

One of the very few remaining men of the Scots Greys who were at Waterloo, wrote, in 1862, as follows:—

" I, Peter Swan, late Sergeant of the Scots Greys, do hereby declare, on the honour of a soldier, that I was present at the battle of Waterloo when the standard of the 45th French Regiment was taken by my corps, and I declare the following to be true:—

" I belonged to the centre squadron and charged with the corps. The flag in question, and the largest of the two hanging in Chelsea Hospital, was taken in the first instance, in the first charge, by a trumpeter named Hutchinson, who, with his horse, was immediately killed; whereupon Ewart, then a corporal, seized the colour, and having fought hard for it, kept it. I did not see him take the standard, nor fight for it (and he had tough work to keep it), as I had enough to do to mind myself, but on coming out of action after the first charge, Captain Cheency, the senior officer living of the Scots Greys, ordered Captain Fenton, of my troop, to take four good men and true with him and carry the standard to Brussels, which I saw them do at about twelve or one o'clock in the day, and the standard was never again in the hands of the French.

> "Peter Swan, D Troop, Scots Greys.

"Weston-common, near Southampton, Aug. 29th."

A correspondent of the *Times*, who served as a subaltern in the Scots Greys at the battle of Waterloo, during the whole of the day, asserts, that the standard of the 45th French Regiment was taken by Sergeant Ewart; that it never left his hands until he deposited it at Brussels on the afternoon of the same day; and that no standard was picked up by the Scots Greys from the ground after the French retreat, nor does the writer believe it possible that they would have deserted their standard in such a manner.

Mr. Gutteridge, of Brighton, who was in Brussels during the battle, on the afternoon of the 18th of June, saw a large number of prisoners (3000 or 4000) being escorted in by the Scots Greys and 5th Dragoon Guards; the writer then saw the two colours of the 45th and 105th Regiments, and was allowed to take hold of them by the corners; and he recollects distinctly reading the names of the battles they had been engaged in inscribed on them. They were—Austerlitz, Friedland, Jena, Marengo, &c.

Here is another instance of the mendacity of the same historian; describing, be it remembered, an event of his own time—the Duke of Wellington's presence at Quatre Bras—M. Thiers states:—"He (Marshal Ney) thought . . . . that the advance guard of Lord Wellington, which he saw before him, would suddenly fold up like a curtain, and discover soon the English army itself. . . . . He paused before the open route of Quatre Bras—that is to say, before the fortune of France, which was there, and which, by extending his hand, he might infallibly have seized! What had he at this moment before him! Exactly what he saw, and nothing more. In effect, the Duke of Wellington remaining at Brussels, and only having received vague news on that morning, had not yet ordered anything."

In contradiction of the above, Major-General Fitzmaurice (late of the Rifle Brigade), writes to the *Times*, December 29, 1863:—

"I send you a short narrative of what I saw and heard on the 16th of June (the day in question), and hope that you will insert it in your columns. Having the honour of commanding in the absence of my captain, Brevet-Major Leach (detained on other business at Brussels), the 1st company of the 1st battalion of the old 95th, I descried at about 2 P.M., from the point where the four roads meet at Quatre Bras, the

Duke of Wellington between us and the French returning from reconnoitering their advance. Shortly after he rode up to me, calling out ' Where is Barnard?' (the late Sir Andrew). I instantly passed the word to the rear, and on Sir Andrew Barnard galloping up, the Duke said, pointing to a detached wood on our left, ' Barnard, these fellows are coming on, you must stop them by throwing yourself into that wood.' Sir Andrew then gave me the order to do this, 'and amuse them,' until he should come up with the rest of the battalion, and as I moved rapidly off, the Duke called out to me to go round a knoll, by which I should be obscured from the enemy.

"This incident proves not only that the Duke was present at an early hour at Quatre Bras, but also that, with the fate of Europe depending upon him, he could with his usual coolness give orders for the safe advance of a company of skirmishers."

GEORGE IV. AND HIS QUEEN.

Immediately after the death of George III., Queen Caroline, although with more than suspicion hanging over her head, hastened, to England to claim her right to the throne of a man who could hardly be considered her husband. His estrangement from her, the aversion he had manifested from the first moment of their ill-assorted marriage, was the only excuse the unfortunate woman could plead for her errors. The announcement of her journey to England and the news of her demands for a regal reception caused a great sensation. " Great bets," says Lord Eldon, " are laid about it. Some people have taken 50 guineas, undertaking in lieu of them to pay a guinea a day till she comes." 50,000*l.* a year were offered if she would consent to play the Queen of England at some continental court. She in her turn demanded a palace in London, a frigate, and the restoration of her name to the church service. Nothing short of the prayers of the faithful would satisfy her craving for worldly distinction. Mr. Wilberforce, with characteristic indulgence, admired her for her spirit, though he feared she had been " very profligate." Her arrival in London was the signal for a popular ovation, " more out of hatred to the king than out of regard for her." For many weeks the stout lady in the hat and feathers was the favourite of the populace, and Alderman Wood's house, No. 77, South Audley-street, where she had taken up her quarters, was at all hours of the day surrounded by a mob of noisy king-haters. Mr. Wilberforce, in a letter to Hannah More, recounts their proceedings: " A most shabby assemblage of quite the lowest of the people, who every now and then kept calling out 'Queen! Queen!' and several times, once in about a quarter of an hour, she came out of one window of a balcony, and Alderman Wood at the other." At which the crowd cheered prodigiously. When her trial was decided upon, this misguided woman, determined to brazen it out at all hazards, threatened to come daily to Westminster Hall in "a coach and six in *high style*," and she also insisted on being present at the coronation. "She has written to the king," says Mr. Th. Grenville, " when and in

what dress she should appear at the coronation. I presume the answer
will be: in a white sheet, in the middle aisle of the Abbey."

The strictest orders were given for her exclusion, but still she came,
and among the extraordinary and disgraceful scenes of the time is that
of a Queen of England "trying every door of the Abbey and the Hall."
She at length withdrew.

"It is worthy of remark that no diary or journal published since
1821 throws any new light upon the question of the guilt or innocence
of the Queen: but it is significant that Lord Grenville, who had excul-
pated her in 1806 upon the occasion of the *Delicate Investigation*, seems
to have had no doubt as to her misconduct in 1821, and both voted
and spoke against her on the second reading of the Bill. This is not the
place to discuss a nasty personal subject, with regard to which, we suppose, most historians will not differ; but whatever may have been the
sins of Caroline of Brunswick, the behaviour of George IV. towards
her had been of such a kind that, in our judgment, political considerations alone can account for the support which the majority of the
House of Lords afforded him at the trial. In fact, it is evident from
many sources, that the real issue in the case was lost sight of by all parties; and, if it may be laid to the charge of the people that they backed
the Queen solely in the interest of revolution, it is equally certain that
the mass of the aristocracy who sided with the King, only did so because
they thought that the constitution was in danger."—*Saturday Review.*

SIR ROBERT WILSON AS A POLITICIAN.

Although Wilson hated Buonaparte as an oppressor generally, and as
the treacherous assassin of the Duke d'Enghien in particular, he disapproved of his forcible dethronement. He saw that it would lead to the
extinction of Poland and Italy, the restoration of a cruel Papal domina-
tion, and to increase of power for evil on the part of Austria. Of the
ultimate downfall of Napoleon, he was sure; but he thought its earlier
advent dearly purchased by a restoration of the old feudal tyrannies.
His views on a particular part of this question, which still vexes mankind,
will be read with interest:—

"I much fear that the re-establishment of the Pope will have more fatal power
to depress the liberties of Italy than all the efforts of enlightened patriots can
counteract. I have expressed to Lord William Bentinck my fears on that
subject, as he is one of His Holiness's great allies. 'My friends,' I wrote,
'are encroaching by sap, but I much fear that *your friend*, the Pope, will use
all the power of St. Peter's to enforce the maxim of the Church—'Divide, and
Govern.' It is on that point that you and I differ most. I regard the Papal
throne as incompatible with Italian nationalization and freedom. Beware how
you extend its influence and extol its benefits to mankind. You never can hope
to make that government philosophical or flexible to the times. Monarchs are
sometimes young and generous, or old and timid, but the veterans selected for
the papal chair are champions of the triple crown, whom philanthropy cannot
persuade and whom menaces cannot daunt."

Paris was captured; the Emperor was sent to Elba; peace was concluded; but, says Wilson, now a prophet indeed,—" I shall be much surprised if the cannon does not rattle through Europe again before there is an anniversary of the Peace." He wrote this in June, 1814, and in June of the following year, Waterloo was fought and gained, and Paris again occupied by a foreign army. This catastrophe might have been avoided, had Napoleon been content to live as Talley-rand had counselled, not as an Emperor of the French, dependent on the terrors of Europe and the feeling of his army, but as a wise and liberal King of France. He chose, however, a course of appalling lying; while feigning a desire to be at peace with all men, he was preparing to wage war even with those with whom he affected to be most strongly moved to cultivate friendship. Such a course has its surprises and its triumphs; but it has its costs also, and, as Talleyrand is recorded to have said, it may give transitory glory to an individual, but it must end in the ruin of a dynasty,—especially of a dynasty of whom it has already been noted, that they have shed more French blood for the aggrandize-ment of their own family than all the other sovereigns of France united. —*Athenæum* Review of *the Life of Sir Robert Wilson.*

VISCOUNT MELBOURNE, THE MINISTER.

When Lord Melbourne declared himself quite satisfied with the Church as it is, but if the public had any desire to alter it, they might do as they pleased, it drew upon him this reproval from Sydney Smith, of his habitual carelessness and contempt of duty:—" If the truth must be told, our Viscount is something of an impostor. Everything about him seems to betoken careless denotation: any one would suppose from his manner that he was playing at chuck-farthing with human happiness; that he was always on the heels of pastime; that he would giggle away the great Charter, and decide, by the method of tee-totum, whether my Lords the Bishops should or should not retain their seats in the House of Lords. All this is the mere vanity of surprising and making us believe that *he can play with kingdoms as other men with ninepins.* Instead of this lofty nebulo, this miracle of moral and intel-lectual felicities, he is nothing more than a sensible, honest man, who means to do his duty to the Sovereign and to the country; instead of being the ignorant man he pretends to be, before he meets the deputa-tion of tallow-chandlers in the morning, he sits up half the night, talking with Thomas Young (his private secretary) about melting and skim-ming; and then, though he has acquired knowledge enough to work off a whole vat of prime Leicester tallow, he pretends next morning not to know the difference between a dip and a mould. In the same way, when he has been employed in reading Acts of Parliament, he would persuade us that he has been reading *Cleghorn on the Beatitudes,* or *Bickler on the Nine Difficult Points.* Neither can I allow this Minister (however he may be irritated by the denial) the extreme merit of indif-ference to the consequence of his measures. I believe him to be con-scientiously alive to the good or evil that he is doing, and that his caution has more than once arrested the gigantic projects of the Lycurgus of the Lower House. I am sorry to hurt any man's feelings, and to brush away the magnificent fabric of levity and gaiety he has reared; but I accuse our minister of honesty and diligence: I deny that he is careless or rash; he is nothing more than a man of good understanding and good principle, disguised in the eternal and somewhat wearisome affectation of a political roué."

Such affectation is not uncommon. We remember to have called upon a barrister in chambers, with the view of refreshing his memory with the points of an arbitration case, upon which he was to sum up next morning. He appeared listless and indifferent, and we left him with the impression that he knew little of the matter; yet, next morning, he most lucidly stated the case without missing a material point, and the award was given in his client's favour. He is now one of the most independent Judges of the land.

ANCESTRY OF VISCOUNT PALMERSTON.

It has been the fortune of the Temples to find themselves associated with one of the prettiest legends of the Middle Ages, which has formed the subject of one of the prettiest poems of our own time. They have been given out as coming from the stout old Earl Leofric, of the Confessor's time, and his Lady Godgifa or Godiva, who saved Coventry from a harsh impost by riding through the market-place clad only in her beautiful long hair. Leofric (who died A.D. 1057) and his spouse are, of course, as really historical personages as the Confessor and Edith. And though the Godiva legend does not occur in the Saxon Chronicle, in William of Malmesbury, or in Florence of Worcester, it is found in Brompton, who flourished in 1193, less than a century and a half after the date of its heroine. Nor have we a right to doubt the truth of any story simply because there is a noble and daring poetry about it. But as regards the descent of the Temples from Leofric and Godiva, that is a comparatively modern statement. Dugdale knew nothing of it, though he gives a full account of the earl's real successors and family in his *Baronage*, and much information about him, his wife, and their pious and generous doings, in his *Warwickshire*. An earlier writer, and more important for this special question than even Dugdale—a writer whose *Leicestershire* is said to have suggested Dugdale's *Warwickshire* —knew no more of the fact than he. We speak of William Burton, the elder brother of the author of the *Anatomy of Melancholy*, to whose curious mind his own bore a strong family resemblance. Burton was a Leicestershire squire himself, and in speaking of the lands of Temple, in Sparkenhoe Hundred, near Bosworth, from which the whole family of Temple derived its name, this is what he tells us:—"This land was granted by one of the old earls of Leicester to the Knights Templars. This land was afterwards granted by the Templars to a family of the place called Temple, being of great account in these parts. (Burton's *Leicestershire*, p. 264.) Burton, then, knew nothing of the Saxon origin of the family; and it is certain that in the famous Sir William

Temple's time they looked upon themselves as having "come in with the Conquest." It is often loosely assumed that a family must be either Norman or Saxon, though Burgundians and Flemings, Angevins and Poitevins, are found among the settlers in England in the stormy and adventurous ages during which the foundations of its modern life were laid. To which of the various races struggling for place and power the founder of the Temples belonged cannot now be known. The earliest names in the pedigree, Robert, William, and Henry, are those of Norman dukes and sovereigns—an indication which has sometimes been allowed to have suggestive value in such cases. At all events, we are safe in assuming that the man to whom the Templars gave land would have the qualities which the Order of the Temple held in honour, and that he acquired his estate, as his descendant acquired his premiership, by being superior to other rivals in the battle of life. Dismissing, then, the descent from Leofric as fabulous and modern, and trusting to old writers and official pedigrees, we shall be content to derive the Temples from Robertus Temple de Temple Hall, living in the reign of Henry III.— *Cornhill Magazine.*

CHARACTERISTICS OF COBBETT.

We do not remember to have seen any better estimate of the characteristics of this "contentious man" than that given by Sir Henry Bulwer, in his *Historical Characters*, although we hardly consider Cobbett to have attained this rank. Speaking of the general regret at Cobbett's death, Sir H. Bulwer remarks, "It extended to all persons. Whatever a man's talents, whatever a man's opinions, he sought the *Register* on the day of its appearance with eagerness, and read it with amusement, partly, perhaps, if De Rochefoucault is right, because whatever his party, he was sure to see his friends abused. But partly, also, because he was certain to find, amidst a great many fictions and abundance of impudence, some felicitous nickname, some excellent piece of practical-looking argument, some capital expressions, and very often some marvellously fine writing, all the finer for being carelessly fine, and exhibiting the figure or sentiment it set forth, in the simplest as well as the most striking dress. Cobbett, himself, indeed, said that 'his popularity was owing to his giving truth in clear language;' and his language always did leave his meaning as visible as the most limpid stream leaves its bed. But as to its displaying truth, that is a different matter, and it would be utterly impossible unless truth has at least as many heads as the Hydra of fable, in which case our author may claim the merit of having portrayed them all.

"This, however, is to be remarked, he rarely abused that which was falling or fallen, but generally that which was rising or uppermost. He disinterred Paine when his memory was interred, and attacked him as an impostor amongst those who hailed him as a prophet. In the heat of the contest and cry against the Catholics—whom, when Mr. Pitt was for emancipating, he was for grinding into the dust—he calls the Reformation a devastation, and pronounces the Protestant religion to have been established by gibbets, racks, and ripping knives. When all London was yet rejoicing in Wellington hats and Wellington boots, he expects that the celebrated victory of Waterloo had caused to England more real shame, more real and substantial disgrace, more debt, more distress among the middle class, and more misery amongst the working class, more injuries of all kinds, than the kingdom could ever have experienced by a hundred defeats, whether by sea or by land." He had a sort of itch for bespattering with mud everything that was popular, and gilding everything that was odious. Mary Tudor was with him "Merciful Queen Mary;" Elizabeth, "Bloody Queen Bess;" our Navy, "the swaggering Navy;" Napoleon, "a French coxcomb;" Brougham, "a talking lawyer;" Canning, "a brazen defender of corruptions."

.   .   .   .

As for absurdity, nothing was too absurd for him coolly and deliberately to assert : "The English Government most anxiously wished for Napoleon's return to France." "There would have been no National Debt and no paupers, if there had been no Reformation." "The population of England had not increased one single soul since he was born." Neither did his coarseness know any bounds. He called a newspaper, "a cut and thrust weapon," to be used without mercy or delicacy, and never thought of anything but how he could strike the hardest. "There's a fine congress-man for you ! If any d——d rascally rotten borough in the universe ever made such a choice as this (a Mr. Blair MacClenashan) you'll be bound to cut my throat, and suffer the *sans culottes* sovereigns of Philadelphia—the hob-snob snigger-snee-ers of Germans, to wit— to kick me about in my blood till my corpse is as ugly and disgusting as their living carcases are." " Bark away, hell-hounds, till you are suffocated in your own foam." " This hatter turned painter, whose heart is as black and as foul as the liquid in which he dabbles."

His talent for fastening his claws into any thing or any one, by a word or an expression, and holding them down for scorn, or up to horror, was unrivalled. "Prosperity Robinson," "Æolus Canning," "The Bloody *Times*," "The pink-nosed *Liverpool*," "The unbaptized, buttonless blackguards" (in which way he designated the disciples of Penn),—were expressions with which he attached ridicule where he could not fix reproach ; and it is said that nothing was more teasing to Lord Erskine than being constantly addressed by Cobbett by his second title of " Baron Clackmannan."

The late Lady Holland once asked Sir Henry Bulwer if he did not think she sometimes said ill-natured things ; and on his acquiescing, she rejoined : "I don't mean to burn any one, but merely to poke the fire." Cobbett liked to poke the fire, to make a blaze; but in general, not always—he thought more of sport than of mischief.

It is curious to observe how frequently Fox alludes to the early writings of Cobbett, bearing unconscious testimony to the influence, temporary but decisive, exerted by the *Register* over the opinions even of the leading statesmen of the time.

French History.

THE CHRONICLES OF FROISSART.

HE Rev. James White, in his *Eighteen Christian Centuries*, gives the following sparkling picture of the Herodotus of the Middle Ages, as Froissart is happily styled : "More important than the poems of Dante and Chaucer, or the prose of Boccaccio, was the introduction of the new literature represented by Froissart. Hitherto chronicles had for the most part consisted of the record of such wandering rumours as reached a monastery, or were gathered in the religious pilgrimages of holy men. But at this time there came into notice the most inquiring, enterprising, picturesque and entertaining chronicler that had ever appeared since Herodotus read the result of his personal travels and sagacious inquiries to the assembled multitudes of Greece. John Froissart, called by the courtesy of the time Sir John, in honour of his being priest and chaplain, devoted a long life to the collection of the fullest and most trustworthy accounts of all the events and personages characteristic of his time. From 1326, when his labours commenced, to 1400, when his active pen stood still, nothing happened in any part of Europe that the Paul Pry of the period did not rush off to verify on the spot. If he heard of an assemblage of knights going on at the extremities of France, or in the centre of Germany ; of a tournament at Bordeaux, a court gala in Scotland, or a marriage festival at Milan, his travels began—whether in the humble guise of a solitary horseman, with his portmanteau behind his saddle, and a single greyhound at his heels, as he jogged wearily across the Border, till he finally arrived in Edinburgh ; or in his grander style of equipment, gallant steed, with hackney led beside him, and four dogs of high race, gambolling round his horse, as he made his dignified journey from Ferrara to Rome. Wherever life was to be seen and painted, the indefatigable Froissart was to be found. Whatever he had gathered up on former expeditions, whatever he learned in his present tour, down it went in his own exquisite language, with his own poetical impression of the pomps and pageantries he beheld; and when at the end of his journey he reached the court of prince or potentate, no higher treat could be offered to the 'noble lords and ladies bright' than to form a glittering circle round the enchanting chronicler, and listen to what he had written. From palace to palace, from castle to castle, the unwearied ' picker-up of unconsidered trifles ' (which, however, were neither trifles nor unconsidered, when their true value became known), pursued his happy way, certain of a friendly reception when he arrived, and certain of not losing his time by negligence or blindness on the road. If he overtakes a stately cavalier, attended by squires and men-at-arms, he enters into conversation, drawing out the experiences of the venerable warrior by relating to him all he knew of things and persons in which he took an interest. And when they put up at some hostelry on the road, and while the gallant knight was sound asleep on his straw-stuffed couch, and his followers were wallowing amid the rushes on the parlour floor, Froissart was busy with pen and note-book, scoring down all the old gentleman had told him, all the fights he had been present at, and the secret history (if any) of the councils of priests and kings. In this way knights in distant parts of the world became known to each other. The same voice which described to Douglas at Dalkeith the exploits of the Prince of Wales, sounded the praises of Douglas in the ears of the Black Prince at Bordeaux."

VANITY OF THE FRENCH.

The French, notwithstanding their many admirable qualities, have always been more remarkable for personal vanity than the English; a peculiarity partly referrible to those chivalric traditions which, even their occasional republics have been unable to destroy, and which makes them attach undue importance to external distinctions—that is, not only dress and manners, but also medals, ribbons, stars, crosses, and the like, which we, a prouder people, have never held in such high estimation. The other circumstance is that duelling has, from the beginning, been more popular in France than in England; and as this is a custom which we owe to chivalry, the difference in this respect between the two countries supplies another link in that long chain of evidence by which we must estimate their national tendencies.

The above is not a mere popular opinion, but rests upon a large amount of evidence, supplied by competent and impartial observers. Addison, a lenient as well as an able judge, and who had lived much among the French, calls them "the vainest nation in the world." Napoleon says: "Vanity is the ruling principle of the French." Dumont and Ségur declare it to be the dominant trait of the French character. It is moreover stated that phrenological observations prove that the French are vainer than the English.—Buckle's *Hist. Civilization*, vol. i. p. 583.

AUDACITY OF DU HAILLAN, THE FRENCH
HISTORIAN.

Till the end of the sixteenth century, France, though fertile in annalists and chroniclers, had not produced a single historian, because she had not produced a single man who presumed to doubt what was generally believed. In 1576, Du Haillan published his *History of the Kings of France*, in the dedication of which to the King (Henry III.) he says: "I am, Sire, the first of all the French who have written the history of France, and, in a polite language, shown the dignity and grandeur of our kings, for before there was nothing but the old rubbish of the chroniclers which spoke of them." He adds, in the preface: " Only, I will say, without presumption or boasting, that I have done a thing which had not been done before, or seen by any of our nation, and have given to the history of France a dress it never appeared in before." Du·Haillan's work was very successful ; he was looked upon as one of the glories of the French nation, and was rewarded by the king conferring on him the office of Secretary of Finance. But he had taken as the basis of his famous history a gossiping compilation, by an Italian named Paulus Æmilius, on the " Actions of the French," to whose idle stories he added some of his own invention. Thus, he opens his history with a long account of a council, which was held, he says, by the celebrated Pharamond. But it is doubtful if any such person as Pharamond ever existed ; and it is certain that if he did exist at all, all the materials had long perished from which an opinion could be formed respecting him. But Du Haillan, regardless of these little difficulties, gives us the fullest information touching the great chieftain ; and, as if determined to tax to the utmost the credulity of his readers, mentions, as members of the council of Pharamond, two persons, Charamond and Quadrek, whose very names are invented by the historian.

HOW FRENCH HISTORY IS WRITTEN.

Comparatively few persons in England have read the once famous book on the origin of the French, published in 1676, by Audigier. In this great history, we are told, that 3464 years after the creation of the world, and 590 years before the birth of Christ, was the exact period at which Sigovese, nephew to the King of the Celts, was first sent into Germany. Those who accompanied him were necessarily travellers ; and as, in the German language, *wandeln* means *to go*, we have here the origin of the Vandals. But the antiquity of the Vandals is far surpassed by that of the French. Jupiter, Pluto, and Neptune, who are sometimes supposed to be gods, were in reality Kings of Gaul. And if we look a little further back, it becomes certain that Gallus, the founder of Gaul, was no other than Noah himself ; for in those days the same man had frequently two names. As to the subsequent history of the French, it was fully equal to the dignity of their origin. Alexander the Great, even in all the pride of his victories, never dared to attack the Scythians, who were a colony sent from France. It is from these great occupiers of France that there have proceeded all the gods of Europe, all the fine arts, and all the sciences. The English themselves are merely a colony of the French, as must be evident to whoever considers the similarity of the words Angles and Anjou ; and to this fortunate descent the natives of the British Islands are indebted for such bravery and politeness as they still possess.

Several other points are cleared up by this great critic with equal facility. The Salian Franks were so called from the rapidity of their flight ; the Bretons were evidently Saxons ; and even the Scotch, about whose independence so much has been said, were vassals to the Kings of France—Buckle's *Hist. Civilization*, vol. i. p. 720.

WAS JOAN OF ARC BURNT AS A WITCH?

On the morning of the 30th of May, 1431, Jeanne the Maiden, or Joan of Arc, was burned as a witch and heretic in the old market at Rouen, where a memorial to her has since been erected. Such is the narrative of one of the most remarkable revolutions in history. A country girl overthrew the power of England. However easy it may be to suppose that a heated and enthusiastic imagination produced her own visions, it is a much easier problem to account for the credit they obtained, and for the success that attended her. It is certain that the appearance of Joan of Arc turned the tide of war; a superstitious awe enfeebled the sinews of the English, who conceived her to be a female magician. "As man always make sure of Providence for an ally, whatever untoward fortune appeared to result from preternatural causes, was at once ascribed to infernal enemies; and such bigotry may be pleaded as an excuse, though a very miserable one, for the detestable murder of this heroine." (*Hallam.*) Historians, one copying the words of another, assert that Joan was burned at Rouen in 1431; while documentary evidence of the most authentic character, completely negativing the story of her being burned, shows she was alive and happily married several years after the period alleged to be that of her execution. Many of these documents are in the registry of the city of Mentz, and prove that Joan came thither in 1436, when the magistrates, to make sure that she was not an impostor, sent for her brothers, Pierre and Jean, who at once recognised her. The documents at Mentz are detailed by M. Delepierre, in his *Historical Difficulties and Contested Events*, published in April, 1868, pp. 105–115. Several entries in the city records enumerate the presents, with the names of the donors, that were given to Joan on her marriage with the Chevalier d'Armoise; and even their marriage contract has been discovered. In the archives of the city of Orleans, in the treasurer's accounts for 1435, is an entry of payments to messengers, who had brought letters from Jeanne la Pucelle. Under date 1436, is an entry of twelve livres paid to Jean de Lys, brother of Jeanne la Pucelle, that he might go and see her. The King of France ennobled Joan's family, giving them the appellation of de Lys, derived from the *fleur de lys*, on account of her services to the State; and the entry in the Orleans records corresponds with and corroborates the one in the registry of Mentz, which states that the magistrates of the latter city sent for her brothers to identify her. These totally independent sources of evidence confirm each other in a still more remarkable manner. Thus, in the Orleans treasurer's accounts are the expenses for wine, banquets, and public rejoicings, in 1439, when Robert d'Armoise and Jeanne, his wife, visited that city; also a memorandum of 210 livres paid to Jeanne d'Armoise, for the services rendered by her during the siege of the said city of Orleans.

It has been urged, however, that Dame d'Armoise was an impostor; but if she were, why did the brothers of the real Joan recognise and identify her? Admitting that they did, for the purpose of profiting by the fraud, how could the citizens of Orleans, who knew her so well, and who fought side-by-side with her, during the memorable siege, allow themselves to be so grossly deceived? Immediately after the burning there was a common rumour that Joan was not dead, and that another victim had been substituted for her. In the *Histore de Lorraine*, by Dom Calmet, we read that the Maid of Orleans escaped in the crowd, and no one knew what became of her. Some supposed her to have been captured and carried to Rouen, and burnt; others affirm that the army was aware of her death. The chronicle of Mentz relates her death at the stake, with this addition: "it was so asserted, but since that time a contrary opinion has been held." M. Delepierre quotes from Pasquier, that "the inexplicable delay, between the condemnation and execution, and still more the extraordinary precautions that were taken to hide the victim from the eyes of the public, are very remarkable. When she was led to the stake a large mitre was placed on her head, which concealed the greater part of her face, and a huge frame covered with insulting phrases, was carried before her, and completely concealed her person."

In fine, the French antiquaries best qualified to form a correct opinion on the subject, believe that Joan was not burned but kept in prison until after the death of the Duke of Bedford, Regent of France, in 1435, when Joan was liberated; this being the year before she married Robert d'Armoise.

D'Israeli tells us he has read somewhere that a bundle of fagots was substituted for Joan, at the burning at Rouen, though none of our historians notice this anecdote. "Whether she deserved to have been distinguished by the appellation of the *Maid of Orleans*, we have great reason to suspect; and some in her day, from her fondness for man's apparel, even doubted her *sex*."

It would almost justify the popular belief in the celestial mission of Joan of Arc, that her fame survived the ribaldry of Voltaire in the memory of the French people. The most enthusiastic admirers of the "Patriarch of Ferney," however lax in precept or practice, cannot but reprobate the gross buffoonery of his *Pucelle d'Orleans*, which the Shakspeare forger, W. H. Ireland, translated in 1823. Yet the memory of the poor peasant girl of Domremy is still cherished—of the enthusiast, who at twelve years old had already begun to invest with visible forms the creations of her own fancy; who turned her enthusiasm to the deliverance of her country from its oppressors, and who believed that she was "the Maid" who, according to the traditionary prophecy, was to issue from the forest of oaks adjoining her native village, and become the saviour of France.

The city of Orleans still celebrates the anniversary of its deliverance by Joan of Arc. Of the 435th celebration we read: "On the eve of the festival the municipal body of Orleans (whose predecessors, in 1429, had done good service that Sunday morning when Suffolk, disconcerted by repeated losses, resolved to raise the siege) marched to the stately cathedral to deposit the banner of the Maid, which is preserved in the Town-house. The whole body of the clergy attended the ceremony, while hymns were chanted by hundreds of voices. The banner was blessed and received by the bishop, and the church, covered with flags and displaying the arms of the towns which assisted Orleans during its struggle against the English and the Burgundians, was magnificently illuminated. On the following day the Prefect of the department, the magistracy, the clergy of the city and of the adjoining towns and villages, the troops of the garrison, the municipal councils of the neighbouring communes, the medallists of St. Helena, the corporations of the working classes, assembled in the cathedral to hear the panegyric on Joan of Arc delivered by the Abbé Bougaud. The procession, in going to and returning from the church, traversed the streets of the city, which tradition says Joan rode through in full armour, bearing her sacred banner, the day she convoyed a supply of provisions from Blois to the famished defenders of Orleans, and visited the ruins of the fort of the Tourelles, where she was wounded by an English arrow.

"On the eve of the fête, M. E. Morin delivered at the Literary Hall, and before a numerous audience, a panegyric on the deliverer of Orleans. He described with most interesting detail the visit of Joan to the Court of Chinon, the taking of Orleans, and the expeditions to Paris and Compiègne. He alluded, too, to the retribution which fell upon the judges and persecutors of the Maid, and in conclusion invited France and England to 'a fraternal rivalry of peace,' and expressed a hope that both countries would before long join in raising a monument of expiation to the memory of the Maid of Orleans."

TRAGIC TALES OF CHARLES VI. OF FRANCE.

M. A. Jal, in his *Dictionnaire Critique*, devotes a curious article to Charles VI. of France, about whom the most absurd stories have been told, not only by modern historians, but by the annalists who flourished during the fifteenth century. "C'estoit grande pitié," says Juvénal des Ursins, "de la maladie du Roy, laquelle luy tenoit longuement. Et quand il mangeoit, c'estoit bien gloutement et louvissement (*after the fashion of wolves*); et ne le pouvoit on faire despouiller, et estoit tout plein de pouz, vermine et ordure" . . . . &c. Of course, on the authority of so grave an historian as Juvénal des Ursins, the tragic tale soon spread. It is so exciting! so effective! Charles VI. victim of Isabel of Bavaria and of the Duke d'Orleans, her paramour! See the country a prey to English invasion, misery everywhere, and whilst a few unprincipled courtiers are forgetting the ruin of France in the midst of noisy pleasures, behold the wretched King, forgotten in his apartments, starving, eaten up by vermin, and totally bereft of his senses! The theme is a splendid one for a tragedy or a picture, and some persons still remember Talma when he appeared on the stage, saying in a hollow voice—"Du pain! du pain! je n'en ai pas!" Now, what are the *facts* of history? Between the different fits which impaired so lamentably the monarch's health and strength, Juvénal des Ursins himself numbers *eleven* lucid intervals. Now, during these intervals, which were of unequal length, Charles VI. received the members of his council and the principal State officers. Is it to be supposed that he held these audiences otherwise than dressed and attired as became a sovereign? Surely it was the interest of every one that he should be clean, to say the least. And as no one knew when these moments of lucidity would occur, when the light of reason would assume its position in the King's brain, was there no danger on the part of Charles' officers to run the chance of his suddenly waking up, finding himself destitute of even ordinary care, and therefore chastising heavily those who thus neglected him? In point of fact, M. Jal has been able to discover and to study in the Imperial Record Office of France documents proving beyond a doubt that from 1392, when the King first felt the attack of his malady, to the last days of his life, he was abundantly provided with everything he needed. We are thus led to the conclusion that the whole story of the destitution, dirt, and loneliness from which he is reported to have suffered was a gross fabrication, invented by the personal enemies of Isabel of Bavaria. This wicked Queen's conduct was in many respects as bad as it could be, but that is not a reason why she should be calumniated.

LOUIS XI.

Comines, the contemporary and confidant of Louis XI., gives the best account of this ill-fated Sovereign. He exhibited early a duplicity of disposition, for which his father mistrusted him. He revolted against his father in 1456, and being defeated had taken refuge at the court of Philip, Duke of Burgundy, who protected him, and maintained him for six years, until his father's death. Louis, when king, became the bitterest enemy of Charles, the son of Philip. When Charles made Louis XI. prisoner, in 1468, Comines conciliated the two princes, and brought about a treaty of peace between them: this timely service was not forgotten by Louis, into whose service passed Comines as chamberlain and seneschal of Poitou, the reasons for which step by Comines have remained a secret.

Louis aimed at being an absolute Sovereign, and set himself to crush the feudal nobility, and raise the cities, so as to balance their power. His measures were often dreadfully cruel. At Loches he had a dungeon, where offenders were imprisoned, and often cruelly tormented, by being put into iron cages, where they had not room to stand upright, or to lie at full length. The most horrible of all Louis's cruelties was exercised on Henri and François, the two young sons of the Duke de Nemours, who, after their father had been executed, were shut up in these cramping cages, and condemned to lose a tooth every day, which Louis desired should be brought to him. Henri, who was only ten years old, entreated the jailor to draw two of his teeth, and spare his little brother, which was done until death put an end to Henri's sufferings. Little François was then released from his cage and confined in a room; he lived to be released and restored to his dukedom, but his limbs had become strangely deformed by his confinement.

King Louis, in the meantime, lived in terror and dread, in his strongly fortified castle of Plessis le Tours, apart from his brave barons, with no better companions than Olivier, the barber, and Tristan, the hangman. Other kings showed themselves in their towns, held banquets openly, and rode forth among their knights; but Louis XI. shut himself up in the gloomy double-walled Plessis, watched day and night by the Scottish archers. From this den Louis greatly extended his power; for Comines, who gives a faithful picture of the King, greatly extols him for his political art. Yet he had a great dread of death, which, in his declining health, he strove to conceal from others. Thus he made schemes for wars, and imported animals for the chase, that he might be supposed in full health. He superstitiously surrounded himself with relics from churches, and the sacred oil of Rheims, *as charms against death;* and hermits were sought out from their cells, as if they could prolong his life. Amidst these delusions he died, August 30, 1485, leaving behind him one of the most detested names in history. He was the first who assumed the title of "Most Christian King," which was given him by the Pope in 1469.

REAL CHARACTER OF LOUIS XIV.

We find the following masterly "reckoning up" (to use a vulgar, but not inexpressive, term) of this Ninepin of French History, in *The Edinburgh Review,* 1832:—

"Concerning Louis the Fourteenth himself, the world seems, at last, to have formed a correct judgment. He was not a great general; he was not a great statesman; but he was, in one sense of the word, a great king. Never was there so consummate a master of what our James the First would have called king-craft—of all those arts which most advantageously display the merits of a prince, and most completely hide his defects. Though his internal administration was bad; though the military triumphs which gave splendour to the early part of his reign were not achieved by himself; though his later years were crowded by defeats and humiliations; though he was so ignorant that he scarcely understood the Latin of his mass-book; though he fell under the control of a cunning Jesuit, and of a more cunning old woman; he succeeded in passing himself off on his people as a being above humanity. And this is the more extraordinary because he did not seclude himself from the public gaze like those Oriental despots, whose faces are never seen, and whose very names it is a crime to pronounce lightly.

"It has been said that no man is a hero to his valet; and all the world saw as much of Louis XIV. as his valet could see. Five hundred people assembled to see him shave and put on his breeches in the morning. He then kneeled down at the side of his bed, and said his prayer, while the whole assembly awaited the end in solemn silence—the ecclesiastics on their knees, and the laymen with their hats before their faces. He walked about his gardens with a train of two hundred courtiers at his heels. All

Versailles* came to see him dine and sup. He was put to bed at night in the midst of a crowd as great as that which had met to see him rise in the morning. He took his very emetics in State, and vomited majestically in the presence of all the *grandes* and *petites entrées*. Yet, though he constantly exposed himself to the public gaze, in situations in which it is scarcely possible for any man to preserve much personal dignity, he to the last impressed those who surrounded him with the deepest awe and reverence. The illusions which he produced on his worshippers can be compared only to those illusions to which lovers are proverbially subject during the season of courtship. It was an illusion which affected even the senses. The contemporaries of Louis thought him tall. Voltaire, who might have seen him, and who had lived with some of the most distinguished members of his court, speaks repeatedly of his majestic stature. Yet, it is as certain as any fact can be, that he was rather below than above the middle size. He had, it seems, a way of holding himself, a way of walking, a way of swelling his chest and rearing his head, which deceived the eyes of the multitude. Eighty years after his death, the royal cemetery was violated by the Revolutionists; his coffin was opened, his body was dragged out; and it appeared that the prince, whose majestic figure had been so long and so loudly extolled, was in truth a little man.

His person and his government have had the same fate. He had the art of making both appear grand and august, in spite of the clearest evidence that both were below the ordinary standard. Death and time have exposed both the deceptions. The body of the great king has been measured more justly than it was measured by the courtiers, who were afraid to look above his shoe-tie. His public character has been scrutinized by men free from the hopes and fears of Boileau and Molière. In the grave the most majestic of princes is only five feet eight. In history, the hero and the politician dwindles into a vain and feeble tyrant—the slave of priests and women; little in war, little in government, little in everything but the art of simulating greatness.

He left to his infant successor a famished and miserable people, a beaten and humbled army, provinces turned into deserts by misgovernment and persecution; factions dividing the court; a schism rising in the church; an immense debt; an empty treasury; immeasurable palaces; an innumerable household; inestimable jewels and furniture. All the sap and nutriment of the State seemed to have been drawn to feed one bloated and unwholesome excrescence. The nation was withered. The court was morbidly flourishing. Yet it does not appear that the associations which attached the people to the monarchy had lost

---

* It was long a common opinion that Louis XIV. burnt all the bills relating to the building of the palace of Versailles—like a citizen after an expensive excursion. It has, however, been ascertained that the money expended on Versailles from 1664 to 1690, was 81,151,414 francs, or about 6,300,000*l.* at the present day. Amongst the items we find that the machine of Marly cost, without the pipes or aqueducts, nearly 280,000*l.* For plate, pictures, medals, &c., not comprised in the above, upwards of 500,000*l.*

strength during his reign. He had neglected or sacrificed their dearest interests; but he had struck their imaginations. The very things which ought to have made him most unpopular—the prodigies of luxury and magnificence with which his person was surrounded; while beyond the enclosures of his parks, nothing was to be seen but starvation and despair —seemed to increase the respectful attachment which his subjects felt for him."

Here are two other estimates of the *Grand Monarque.* A writer in the *Saturday Review,* says :—

" After divesting the character of Louis XIV. of the exaggerated praise bestowed on him by flattery or national vanity, after animadverting upon his numerous faults, and even crimes, it must be fairly acknowledged that he was a remarkable prince, and had many valuable qualities. He was active, intelligent, and regular in business; quick in discovering the abilities of others, an able administrator himself, endowed with a constant equanimity in adversity as well as prosperity, and a perfect self-command; a kind master, he was not prone to change his servants capriciously, was not harsh in rebuking them, and was ever ready to encourage merit, and praise and reward zeal for his service. Hence he had many faithful and devoted servants. His manner was noble, and his appearance imposing; he acted the king, but he acted it admirably, at least to the then taste of the people; he had a lively sense of decorum and outward propriety, which never forsook him. What he knew he learnt by himself: his natural gifts and the experience of his youth, passed among civil wars, made up for his want of learning and of study. If he carried his notions of absolutism to an extreme, he was evidently persuaded of his supposed right, and acted as much from a sense of duty as from inclination. In his reign of seventy-two years he reared the fabric of the absolute monarchy in France, which continued for seventy-two years more after his death; and when it was shaken to pieces in the storm of the Revolution, still the ruling principles of his administration, uniformity and centralization, survived the wreck, and France is still governed by them. "

Mr. Buckle, on the other hand, contends, with some ingenuity, that "the reputation of Louis XIV. originated in the gratitude of men of letters; but it is now supported by a popular notion that the celebrated literature of his age is mainly to be ascribed to his fostering care. If, however, we examine this opinion, we shall find that like many of the traditions of which history is full, it is entirely devoid of truth; and that the literary splendour of his reign was not the result of his efforts, but was the work of that great generation which preceded him, and that the intellect of France, so far from being benefited by his munificence, was hampered by his protection."

THE ANCIEN REGIME.

The Rev. Charles Kingsley defines the *Ancien Régime* as it existed on the Continent before the French Revolution, to signify a " caste " of society distinguished from "class" and different from aristocracy. The members of this caste, presuming on a supposed superiority over the other portions of the community, whom they affected to control, refused to intermarry with any one not belonging to their own privileged set. The *ancien régime* took its rise after the Thirty Years' War, and flourished during the seventeenth and eighteenth centuries; and Mr. Kingsley attributes its origin to the reactionary conservative feeling which followed that devastating war, when the people, disgusted with constant turmoil, sought anxiously for rest, and were inclined to reverence the forms and practices of a bygone age when those forms and ceremonies were associated with honourable acts and useful works. It was an attempt to restore chivalry without the spirit that gave it vitality, or the benefits it conferred. It is like mounting the empty suits of armour in the Tower on wooden horses and endeavouring to make them pass with the multitude for living knights on their chargers, ready to redress the wrongs of mankind. He attributes the immediate origin of the *ancien régime* to Louis XIV., who invited the principal nobles of France to Paris, where they passed their time in frivolity and idleness. He condemns in no measured terms the institution of this caste, founded on pride and idleness; those who were included in it having neglected all the duties belonging to them as nobles and landed proprietors, endeavouring to grind down and keep under the people whom they were bound to help and succour. In England there never was an *ancien régime*. The natural freedom of the people resisted it, and the love of liberty inherent in them was transplanted to America, whence it was reflected back to France, and bore its fruits in the French Revolution, by which the *ancien régime* of that country was destroyed.

The wickedness and pride of the French *noblesse* are well known; but the following reason why they were so hated has not been sufficiently noticed. Mr. Kingsley says:—" Why so cruel? Because, with many of these men, I more than suspect there were wrongs to be avenged deeper than any wrongs done to the sixth sense of vanity, wrongs common to them, and to a great portion of the respectable middle class, and much of the lower class; but wrongs to which they and their families, being most in contact with the *noblesse*, would be especially exposed—namely, wrongs to women. Every one who knows the literature of that time must know what I mean."

Mr. Kingsley does not fail to enforce that the duty of governing bodies of men is to endeavour to raise those below them to their own level, for if they did not he said they might be sure that in the course of time they would be dragged down to the lower level of the populace.

CHARACTER OF CARDINAL RICHELIEU.

M. Van Praet, one of the new Belgian school of historians, presents us with this masterly portrait of Richelieu, in one of his essays, edited by Sir Edmund Head. "The life of Richelieu; the reserve which he maintained before he acquired the height of power; his guarded beha-

viour towards those who had it in their power to injure him without
his being able to retaliate; his rigour towards such of his personal
enemies as he was able to reach; his care not to create new adversaries; his large views and his minute precautions; his natural severity;
his insensibility, which was more evident when he was menaced, ill,
or unfortunate; his anxiety the day after he had shed the blood of an
adversary; the care he took of his dignity at such times when his conduct might compromise him; the precision which he brought to bear
on the execution of an idea which was bold or somewhat immoral,—
everything in his career proves the firmness, exactness, and courage of
his mind, and the lukewarm character of his feelings. His jealousies
were never vulgar or blind; he was not afraid of employing and favouring men of position, reserving to himself the right of crushing them if
they were rebellious or unfaithful. He removed or sacrificed those
who might have ruined his credit or menaced his life; not those who
could serve him with distinction and even with glory. What is so
remarkable in him is the power and resolution of a great intellect,
plunging at once calmly and fearlessly into the vast and complicated
future of a bold policy; while he saw, with a glance as comprehensive
as it was just, the distance of the goal and the obstacles on the road.
As soon as he had become powerful, he revealed his designs; he nego-
tiated with the United Provinces, and manifested his true sentiments
with regard to Spain. What distinguished his genius was that his
audacity was tempered by rule, and by reflection; the energy of this
enterprising spirit, and the activity of this suffering body, were governed
by cool calculation and by reason. The union of qualities which he
possessed—his mind at once indomitable and prudent, bold and watchful
—justly places him very high in the admiration of the world, as one
among the men who have exercised most influence on the destinies of a
great country."

KEEPING PIGEONS IN FRANCE.

Before the Revolution, to avoid the least chance of confusion between
the aristocracy and the people, great vigilance was displayed in the most
trifling matters, and care was taken to prevent any similarity, even in
the amusements of the two classes. To such a pitch was this brought
that in many parts of France the right of having an aviary or a dove-
cote, depended entirely on a man's rank, and no Frenchman, whatever
his wealth might be, could keep pigeons unless he were a noble; it
being considered that these recreations were too elevated for persons of
plebeian origin.

M. Tocqueville, (*L'Ancien Régime*, p. 448), mentions, among other
regulations still in force in the eighteenth century, that in Dauphiny,
Brittany, and Normandy, plebeians were not allowed to have dovecotes
or aviaries, and that only the nobles had the privilege of keeping
pigeons.

THE STORY OF THE "VENGEUR DU PEUPLE."

Amid all the sanguinary horrors of the great French Revolution stands forth that famous engagement between English men-of-war and the ships of the Republic, fought on " the glorious first of June," 1794; when, in the universal crash of defeat and scudding wrecks, the *Vengeur*, being summoned to strike, still held on the fight; and though maimed hopelessly right and left, stem and stern, and sinking to the bottom steadily, fought the battle to the last. The lower-deck guns were kept firing, until the water rushing in, effectually stopped the labours of the gallant sailors. Driven to the upper deck, they worked the guns there with equal fierceness, until similarly interrupted. Finally, with colours flying, with deck crowded with frantic *sans-culottes* sailors, tossing their arms in defiance, shrieking one vociferous chorus of " Vive la République," down sinks the *Vengeur*, and is never seen more. Here was a subject for painter, for poet, or story-teller !

But this, it would appear, is the cruel practical version of the whole affair. Lord Howe had come up with Villaret Joyeuse, off Brest, and a tremendous sea-fight had taken place, with the usual issue six French ships taken, and a seventh, the *Vengeur*, gone to the bottom. This was the news brought to London, and proclaimed at the opera-house to the music of God save the King. To the French capital, then, in utter chaos, news of a victory must be announced, for anything like a defeat would be guillotining matter for those who announced it. Gradually, however, the truth comes out ; that ruinous business of six vessels absent and a *Vengeur* sunk, sounds queerly as a victory. Something must be done, and that speedily, and the ingenious forthwith manufacture the splendid transparency of the sinking *Vengeur*, and the " all hands" shouting " Vive la République" as they go down.

Curious to say, perfidious Albion at once accepted the transparency, and admired it more than any others ; until, unluckily, the story being resuscitated in 1862—sixty-eight years after the fight—an English naval man, actually in the fight, and not a cable's length from the sinking vessel, comes forward, and slits the mendacious wind-bag open. It was, he says, at the end of the fight, the poor *Vengeur* was in a helpless condition, and settling down fast. There were no colours flying, and there were plenty of *sans-culottes*, frantic indeed, and shouting, not defiance, but in despair. The boats of perfidious Albion were hard at work, almost swamped, bringing them off. A hundred of these " defiant *Vengeurs*" were dragged on board the *Culloden* ; more in that ship, more in this ; and above all, the Captain, Renaudin, at lunch in the conqueror's cabin ! " Never, in fact," says that officer, " were men more anxious to be saved." Here, indeed, is a collapse !— (Abridged from *All the Year Round*, with additions.)

M. Jal, in his *Dictionnaire Critique*, places the whole facts of the *Vengeur* episode in their true light, and shows that the *sans-culotte* enthusiasm has mis-stated, in the grossest manner, the various circumstances of the naval engagement. He who would represent the last moments of the *Vengeur du Peuple* with a due regard to historic truth, must paint the poor ship sinking without a mast, *without a flag,* and without officers, for they had all been taken prisoners.   On the deck is a group of men, some in despair, others calm and gloomy, a few accomplishing that sacrifice amidst the cries of Vive la République.   Further on, the boats of the *Culloden* and of the *Alfred* should be introduced, full of sailors who have been rescued from death, and who are awaiting their unfortunate comrades.   In everything that has been painted and written in France on the subject, there is much to be altered.   Renaudin, captain of the French ship, saved with several of his crew, was sent to Tavistock and remained a prisoner only for a very short time.   M. Jal gives us the letter which Captain Oakes, of the Royal Navy, wrote to the French officer for the purpose of informing him that he was set free.   It is, and our author acknowledges it himself, a model of courtesy and kindness.   Renaudin, we are sorry to say, behaved in a totally different manner ; we presume that he considered it the duty of a true republican to be wanting in common civility ; he thoroughly succeeded; and his answer to Captain Oakes, likewise transcribed by M. Jal, is very curious, examined from that point of view.

THE FRENCH REVOLUTION.

The following account of the victims of the first French Revolution is from the statement of the Republican Prudhomme :

Nobles	1,278
Noble women	750
Wives of labourers and of artisans	1,467
Religieuses	350
Priests	1,135
Common persons (not noble)	13,623
Guillotined by sentence of the Revolutionary Tribunal	**18,603**
Women died of premature childbirth	3,400
In childbirth from grief	348
Women killed in La Vendée	15,000
Children killed in La Vendée	22,000
Men killed in La Vendée	900,000
Victims under Carrier at Nantes	32,000

Of whom were—Children shot . . 500
Children drowned . 1500
Women shot . . 264
Women drowned . 500
Priests shot . . . 300
Priests drowned . 460
Nobles drowned . 1400
Artisans drowned . 3500

Victims at Lyons	31,000
Total	1,022,351

It is in an especial manner remarkable in this dismal catalogue, how large a proportion of the victims of the Revolution were persons in the middling and lower ranks of life. The priests and nobles guillotined are only 2413, while the persons of plebeian origin exceed 13,000! The nobles and priests put to death at Nantes were only 2160, while the infants drowned and shot were 2000, the women 7641, and the artisans 5300! So rapidly in revolutionary convulsions does the career of cruelty reach the lower orders, and so wide-spread is the carnage dealt out to them, compared with that which they have sought to inflict on their superiors.—Sir Archibald Alison's *History of Europe.*

EXECUTION OF CHARLOTTE CORDAY.

In this terrific episode of the French Revolution, one of the executioner's assistants having, as he held up the head of Charlotte Corday, smote it with his hand on the cheek, and of that cheek having blushed with indignation, a theory has been advanced that sensibility does not immediately die with the body, when violent death kills the latter by decapitation. The German anatomist, Sömmering, appeals to the above incident as a "well-known fact," witnessed by many people, in proof of the theory of sensation after death by beheading. Dr. Sue indorses the theory, the more readily, as he says, the cheek of an ordinary corpse will not redden by being struck; and that, when the head of Charlotte Corday was held up, it was only smitten on *one* cheek, and that *both* cheeks blushed with shame, a perfect proof, says Dr. Sue, that "after decollation there is undoubtedly in the brain some remains of judgment, and in the nerves remains of sensibility." An equally illustrious man, Cabanis, declared that he did not believe a word of the theory of his celebrated colleagues. Cabanis, in a learned dissertation on the subject, further stated, that a medical man of ability, a friend of his, followed Charlotte Corday from the prison to the scaffold; that he never lost sight of her for a moment; that she turned slightly pale on ascending, but that her face soon shone more beautiful than ever; and that as for the reputed blush mantling her dead cheek when the hangman struck them, he saw nothing whatever of the sort. Dr. Leveillé also discredits the story; but he is not prepared, he says, to assert that the recently dead cheek, still warm, might not have reddened when struck. A blow, he thinks, might arrest the downward flow of remains of blood in the small vessels, and thus produce a momentary redness; but as for judgment or sensibility being there, or both cheeks blushing when only one is struck, he wisely rejects all such conclusions as sheer nonsense. Between these statements it is easy to choose.

EXECUTION OF LOUIS XVI.

Every schoolgirl knows the story of pure, good, soft-hearted, stupid Louis, who could not read the signs of the times, and whom we actually lose temper with for his obtuseness. But we are agreed how nobly he played his part at the end, and how a courageous Irish clergyman, of the Edgeworth family, was found to stand by him on the scaffold. Happily, there is no false colouring so far. We know all the incidents of that terrible scene, the rolling of the drums when he would speak his indignant protest against his hands being tied like a common malefactor's, and his ready consent to a whisper from the priest. So far, all true. But, alas! that we must sponge out that grand apostrophe which is, indeed, the culmination of the whole. " Fils de Saint Louis, montez au ciel!" It is like tearing up a tree by the roots. It grieves one to the soul to have to give up that darling bit of sentiment. The whole scene, otherwise pathetic, somehow seems to halt, and become tame, after that excision. Yet, it could not stay, except out of mere compliment to the poor King, for the words were never spoken. Who, indeed, was to pick them up? Not the poor King, certainly. Not the crowd, for the drums were beating furiously. Sanson (the executioner) and his brethren were not likely to treasure up a bit of sentiment. Clearly then, it rests with the Abbé Edgeworth himself, who, when pressed on the subject, had no recollection of having made such an apostrophe. The moment was one of agitation. He does not know or recollect any words of the kind, and might have spoken twenty other such speeches. This is unsatisfactory. . . . . When the Restoration came, almost every one had in their mouth the happy *mot* of the King, so full of tact and wit. "There is nothing changed in France, only one Frenchman more." But every one did not know that the French ex-bishops had been asking perseveringly, " Had he said anything?" and finally, in despair at anything neat or appropriate from such a quarter, had sent forth their pleasant guess. Thus is history written.—*All the Year Round.*

EXECUTION OF THE DUC D'ENGHIEN.

Many details attending this transaction are still in dispute; but the broad outline of it is as follows:—The pure Republicans (as they were then called) had, on the one hand, at this period, become desperate; on the other hand, the latitude that had for a time been allowed to the Royalists, had given that party courage. The renewal of an European war increased this courage. The power and prestige of the marvellous person at the head of the consular government had made both parties consider that nothing was possible to them so long as he lived.

A variety of attempts had consequently been made against his life. The popular belief, that of Bonaparte himself, was that these attempts proceeded mainly, from the emigrés, aided by the money of England. Georges Cadoudal, the daring leader of the Chouans, who had already been implicated in plots of this kind, was known to be in Paris and engaged in some new enterprise, with which Pichegru certainly, Moreau apparently, was connected. But in the reports of the police it was also stated that the conspirators awaited the arrival at Paris of a prince of the house of Bourbon.

The Duc d'Enghien, then residing at Ettenheim, in the Duchy of

Baden, seemed the most likely of the Bourbon princes to be the one alluded to; and spies were sent to watch his movements. The reports of such agents are rarely correct in the really important particulars. But they were particularly unfortunate in this instance; for they mistook, owing to the German pronunciation, a Marquis de Thumery, staying with the Bourbon Prince, for Dumouriez, and the presence of that general on the Rhenan frontier, and with a Condé, strongly corroborated all other suspicions.

A council was summoned, composed of the three consuls—Bonaparte, Cambacères, Lebrun—the minister of justice and police, Régnier—and Talleyrand, minister of foreign affairs.

At this council (March 10th, 1804) it was discussed whether it would not be advisable to seize the Duc d'Enghien, though out of France, and bring him to Paris; and the result was the immediate expedition of a small force, under Colonel Caulaincourt, which seized the Prince on the Baden Territory (March 15th); M. de Talleyrand, in a letter to the Grand Duke, explaining and justifying the outrage. Having been kept two days at Strasburg, the royal victim was sent from that city on the 18th, in a post-chariot, arrived on the 20th at the gates of Paris, at eleven in the morning; was kept there till four in the afternoon; was then conducted by the boulevards to Vincennes, which he reached at nine o'clock in the evening; and was shot at six o'clock on the following morning, having been condemned by a military commission composed of a general of brigade (General Hallin), six colonels, and two captains, according to a decree of the Governor of Paris (Murat) of that day (March 20th); which decree (dictated by Napoleon) ordered the unfortunate captive to be tried on the charge of having borne arms against the Republic, of having been and being in the pay of England, and of having been engaged in plots, conducted by the English in and out of France, against the French government. The concluding order was that, if found guilty, he should be at once executed.

The whole of this proceeding is atrocious. A prince of the dethroned family is arrested in a neutral State, without a shadow of legality; he is brought to Paris, and tried for his life on accusations which, considering his birth and position, no generous enemy could have considered crimes; he is found guilty without a witness being called, without a proof of the charges against him being adduced, and without a person to defend him being allowed.

The trial takes place at midnight, in a dungeon; and the prisoner is shot, before the break of day, in a ditch!

It is natural enough that all persons connected with such a transaction should have endeavoured to escape from its ignominy. General Hallin has charged Savary (afterwards Duc de Rovigo) who, as commander of the Gendarmerie, was present at the execution, with having hurried the trial, and prevented an appeal to Napoleon, which the condemned prince demanded. The Duc de Rovigo denies with much plausibility these particulars, and indeed, all concern in the affair beyond his mere presence, and the strict fulfilment of the orders he had received; and accuses M. de Talleyrand, against whom, it must be observed, he had a

special grudge, with having led to the prince's seizure by a report
read at the council on the 10th March; with having intercepted a letter
written to the first consul by the illustrious captive at Strasburg, and
with having hastened and provoked the execution, of which he offers no
other proof than that he met Talleyrand, at five o'clock, coming out of
Murat's (who was then Governor of Paris), and who had just given
orders for the formation of the military commission.

As to the supposed letter written by the Duc d'Enghien, the persons
about the Duc declared that he never wrote a letter at Strasburg. As
Murat himself blamed the execution, and did what he could to avert it,
there is some probability that, if M. de Talleyrand sought Murat, it was
with the view of seeing what could be done to save the prince, and not
with the view of destroying him.   On the other hand, Bourrienne, who
had opportunities of knowing the truth, asserts that M. de Talleyrand,
so far from favouring this murder, warned the Duc d'Enghien, through
the Princess de Rohan, of the danger in which he stood.

The Duc Dalberg, minister of Baden at Paris in 1804, also speaks of
M. de Talleyrand as opposed to all that was done in this affair.

Louis XVIII., to whom M. de Talleyrand wrote when the Duc de
Rovigo's statement appeared, ordered that personage to appear no more
at his court. Fouché declared the act to be entirely that of the first
consul; and lastly, Napoleon himself always maintained that the act was
his own, and justified it.

Sir Henry Bulwer, after weighing all the evidence before him, is persuaded that the first consul had determined either to put the prince in
his power to death, or to humiliate him by a pardon granted at his
request; and it seems not improbable that he hesitated, though rather
disposed, perhaps, to punish than to spare, till all was over.

As to Talleyrand taking an active part in this tragedy, such conduct
would be in direct opposition to his whole character, and is unsupported by any trustworthy testimony. To have lent himself, even in
appearance, to so dark a deed, and to have remained an instrument in
Napoleon's hands after its committal, evinces a far stronger sense of the
benefits attached to office, than of the obloquy attached to injustice.
This, it is said, he did not deny; and when a friend advised him to resign, is reported to have replied, "if Bonaparte has been guilty, as you
say, of a crime, that is no reason why I should be guilty of a folly."

The execution of the Duc d'Enghien took place on the 20th March.
On the 7th of April, Pichegru, who had been arrested, was found
strangled in his room, as some thought, by the police—as the government declared, by his own hands; Georges Cadoudal, who had also
been captured, suffered on the scaffold; and Moreau, after being brought
before a tribunal which condemned him to two years' imprisonment, had
this absurd sentence commuted into exile. Bonaparte, having thus struck
terror into the partisans of the ancient dynasty, and having rid himself
of his most powerful military rival, placed on his head, amidst the servile
approbation of the legislature, and the apparent acquiescence of the
nation, a crown which was solemnly consecrated by Pius VII. (2nd
December, 1804.)—Abridged from Sir H. Bulwer's *Historical Characters,*
vol. i. pp. 219-229.

NAPOLEON'S STAR OF DESTINY.

Dr. Sigmond, in his remarks on Hallucination, says " There is scarcely a man of eminence who has written his biography, or laid open the secrets of his inmost soul, but has acknowledged some preternatural event in his life: the most sceptical have felt, at some period or other, a mental emotion, either a fantasia or a hallucination."

This hallucination, however improbable, may be mistaken for a reality, without the reason of the individual being affected by it. Many great men have believed in the existence of their *Star*, or their guardian spirit, and hence they have not been unprepared to witness miraculous apparitions.

Dr. De Boismont, in his *Treatise on Hallucination* (translated by R. T. Hulme), considers the distinctive character of such hallucinations as the above to be that they do not prejudice the conduct, and the individual may maintain in the world a high reputation for virtue, ability, and wisdom ; often, indeed, we believe, they have served as an additional stimulus to the individual in carrying out the projects he had previously conceived.

Many instances of this kind have occurred, the truth of which is guaranteed by the high position of the persons themselves, and by the undoubted veracity of those who were present. On the 4th of April, 1846, M. Passy related, at the meeting of the Académie des Sciences Morales et Politiques, the following anecdote which he had from General Rapp. It appears that in 1806, the General, on his return from the Siege of Dantzic, having occasion to speak to the Emperor Napoleon, entered his cabinet without being announced. He found him in such profound meditation that his entrance was not noticed. The General seeing that he did not move, was afraid he might be indisposed, and purposely made a noise. Napoleon immediately turned round, and seizing Rapp by the arm, pointed to the heavens, saying, " Do you see that ?" The General made no reply ; being interrogated a second time, he answered that he perceived nothing. " What !" responded the Emperor, " you did not discover it ? It is my star, it is immediately in front of you, most brilliant ;" and, becoming gradually more excited, he exclaimed, " It has never abandoned me, I behold it on all great occasions ; it commands me to advance, and to me is a sure sign of success."

Napoleon himself had, indeed, nearly fallen a victim to a hallucination of this kind. The young German who intended to assassinate Napoleon at Schönbrunn, also had visions. He saw the guardian genius of Germany, who commanded him to deliver his country

———◆———

LOUIS XIV. AND NAPOLEON I.—A PARALLEL.

The foreign wars of Louis XIV. proceeded in great measure from the same ruling principles or prejudices of his mind. He disliked the Dutch, whom he considered as mercantile plebeians, heretics, and republicans,

" a body formed of too many heads, which cannot be warmed by the fire of noble passions" (*Instructions pour le Dauphin*, vol. ii. p. 201); and he carried his antipathy to the grave, without having succeeded in subjecting that small nation, whose wealth excited enemies against him everywhere. It is impossible not to be struck with the similarity of prejudices in two men, however dissimilar in some respects, Napoleon I. and Louis XIV. The hatred of Napoleon against England, which he designated as a nation of shopkeepers, was like that of Louis against the Dutch, and it produced similar results to his empire. The same determination of establishing uniformity in everything; the same mania for a unity and singleness of power, which both mistook for strength ; the same ambition of making France the ruling nation of Europe under an absolute ruler, were alike the dominant principles, or rather passions, of the "legitimate and Most Christian king," and of the plebeian "child and champion of the Revolution." Several of the plans and schemes of Louis XIV., relative to foreign conquests, were found in the archives, and were revived and acted upon by Bonaparte.

SHORTSIGHTEDNESS OF NAPOLEON I.

Although the 19th volume of the *Correspondence of Napoleon I.* (May to October, 1809) is less interesting to the general reader than many volumes which preceded it, to those who take pleasure in dwelling on a turning-point in a crisis of history, or who see in history a drama full of lessons taming to the pride of man, this volume will be of very great interest. Reflecting as it does the will and thought of the personage who, in 1809, was almost the arbiter of the Continent, it suggests how different might have been the destinies of Europe for many years had Napoleon, instead of devoting his strength to a scheme of Austrian conquest and alliance, concentrated his enormous forces against the enemy in the Peninsula who was to lead to his final overthrow. And showing, as it does, that he never dreamt of a policy which now appears obvious, that the fate of his dynasty and of his Empire seemed to him to depend on the struggle in Germany, and that he considered the war in Spain as a secondary and inferior operation, it forms a very significant example of the incapacity of the finest intellect to interpret events and scan the future. This volume also, especially in the correspondence relating to the Peninsula and Walcheren, illustrates forcibly the inherent weakness of Napoleon's despotism in many respects; how even in war it led repeatedly to mistakes, false calculations, and failure; how at any emergency that required efforts to be made spontaneously and with vigour, it could not rely on its docile instruments; how jealous it proved of all national forces except those habituated to servitude.

Napoleon's Peninsular letters, in fact, show that he did not even yet appreciate the real character and danger of the contest; and they form a most remarkable commentary on the inevitable failure of strategy from a distance, and on the vices of the military system of the Empire. How little he conceived the ultimate issue to be even within the range of possibility may be gathered from the following passage in a report, a striking example of the irony of fate:—

"In considering the state of your Majesty's armies and the issue of English expeditions I can only rejoice to behold England making efforts disproportionate to her population, and to the requirements of her fleet. *She wishes to struggle on land to the death with France; she will reap nothing but confusion and disgrace, and the French people will owe to your Majesty the glory and the inexpressible advantage of a peace extorted without risk on the sea from an enemy who believed that his insular situation protected him from our armies. Every serious enterprise of the English on the Continent is the forerunner of a general pacification . . . . Engaged in the struggle in Spain and Portugal, from which they cannot retreat with credit, the Peninsula will be the grave of their bravest men, and this loss will at last induce the people of England to desire peace and to detest those cruel statesmen who, through ambition and extravagant animosity, have made a proclamation of perpetual war, and have devoted this generation to strife and to tears.*"

The victory of Wagram was the reward of Napoleon's ability and great exertions. It was not, however, as is well known, a triumph like Austerlitz, Jena, or Friedland; and had the corps of the Archduke John been on the field at the decisive moment, it certainly would have ended differently. This battle, while it displayed once more the strategic art of the French Emperor, revealed also the comparative decline of the military forces of the Empire; the French conscripts and German auxiliaries were very different from the veteran bands that had gathered round the eagles at Boulogne; and, notwithstanding the lies of the bulletin, few guns and hardly a prisoner were taken. For a time, however, it produced the results which Napoleon had anticipated in his calculations; reluctant Germany acquiesced in the issue; and Austria once more submitted to the conqueror. At this juncture, the abdication of the Emperor of Austria was a project seriously in contemplation in preference to the dynastic alliance, which was one of the causes of Napoleon's ruin; had the first alternative been adopted, the course of history might have run differently during many years of the present century.—*Times* journal.

CHARACTER OF NAPOLEON I.

In the *Edinburgh Review* we find the following fair and able appreciation of the character of Napoleon:

"Sound philosophy and a sound morality equally forbid his being placed amongst the most illustrious characters 'whose names adorn the age in which they flourished, and exalt the dignity of human nature.' His principal characteristic was an insatiable and selfish ambition, to the gratification of which he sacrificed, without scruple or remorse, the interests and the happiness of all mankind. The good which he did bears no proportion to the misery of which he was, directly or indirectly, the cause: havoc, desolation, and death marked his terrible career, and in the prosecution of his designs and objects he trampled upon every principle of justice and humanity. He had no sympathy with his fellow-creatures, and regarded them with such profound contempt that he was indifferent to human suffering, and reckless of human life. It was not from any pleasure in shedding blood, but in order to strike terror into the Royalists, that he caused the Duc d'Enghien to be kidnapped and put to death. When the deed was done, he recoiled from the odium to which he saw that it would expose him, endeavoured to shift it on his instrument, and to cast the blame upon his precipitate zeal, imitating the behaviour of Queen Elizabeth in respect to the execution of the Scottish queen. Although he became a mighty monarch, he never was actuated by the feelings and sentiments of a *gentleman*, and he had a total and habitual disregard for truth. His testamentary approval of the attempt to assassinate the Duke of Wellington is alone sufficient to deprive him of all claim to the praise of magnanimity. Really great men, who have been enemies, have always esteemed and honoured each other, and it was reserved to Napoleon to reveal to the world the vindictive spite which rankled in his mind to the last against his great conqueror, by the bequest of a sum of money to his assassin. To a character tarnished with such defects, stained by so many crimes, and not elevated by any moral dignity, a career crowned by complete and enduring success must be considered an indispensable condition of the highest order of greatness; and not only was this wanting to Napoleon, but his decline was even more rapid than his rise."

M. Thiers concludes his *History of the Consulate and the Empire* with this emphatic estimate of the genius of his hero:

" Assuredly we are not of those who reproach Napoleon with having on the 18th Brumaire rescued France from the hands of the Directory, in which she would, perhaps, have perished. But because it may have been necessary to tear her from those feeble and corrupt hands, there was no reason to deliver her up body and soul to the powerful but rash hands of the conqueror of Rivoli and Marengo. Doubtless if ever a nation had an excuse for surrendering itself to a man, it was France, when in 1800 she took Napoleon for her chief. It was no false anarchy that terrified the nation into chains. Alas, no! Thousands of innocent victims had perished on the scaffold, in the prisons of the Abbaye, or in the waters of the Loire. The horrors of barbarous times had all at once reappeared in the midst of a terrified civilization. And even when these horrors passed away, the French Revolution still oscillated between the headsman from whom it was snatched, and the foolish emigrants who desired to make it go back through blood to an impossible past, while over this chaos the menacing sword of the foreigner was visible. At this moment there returned from the East a young hero, full of genius, who was everywhere the conqueror of nature and of men, wise, moderate, religious, and who seemed born to enchain the world. Never, surely, were people more excusable in giving themselves up to one man, for never was terror less simulated than that which they fled from, and never was genius more real than that in which they sought a refuge. And yet, after some years, this wise man became mad, mad with other folly than that of '93, though not less disastrous; immolated a million of men on fields of battle; drew Europe upon France, which he left vanquished, drowned in her own blood, despoiled of the fruit of 20 years' victories, desolate, and having nothing to invigorate her but the germ of modern civilization within her. Who, then, could have foreseen that the wise man of 1800 would be the madman of 1812 and 1813? Yes, it might have been foreseen, had people called to mind that great power bears within itself an incurable folly—the temptation of doing everything when one can do everything, even the evil after the good. Thus in this great career, where military men, administrators, and politicians may find so much to learn, let citizens also learn this one thing—never to deliver up their country to one man, be he who he may, or be the circumstances what they may. In closing this long history of our triumphs and our reverses, it is the last cry which escapes from my heart—a sincere cry which I desire to see penetrate the heart of all Frenchmen, and show them that liberty should never be alienated, and that to escape being alienated it should never be abused."

In the *Times* journal we find these retributive remarks:—

"It seems absurd in the present day to deny that it was the boundless and selfish ambition of Napoleon which led to the two invasions of France, or to affirm that his fall was brought about by the coalition of hostile parties. Napoleon declared that France desired another Government; and the men whom his insatiable and selfish ambition had forced to become his adversaries were the men of his own choice, and assuredly were neither Republicans nor Legitimists. The decree deposing him was drawn up by his own senators, and their proclamation of the 2nd of April, 1814, was as follows:—

'Frenchmen! On emerging from civil dissensions you chose for your chief a man who appeared on the theatre of the world with an air of grandeur. You reposed in him all your hopes; those hopes which have been deceived; on the ruins of anarchy he has founded only despotism. He was bound in gratitude to, at least, become a Frenchman with you; he has not done so. He has never ceased to undertake, without aim or motive, unjust wars, like an adventurer impelled by thirst for glory. In a few years he has destroyed at once your wealth and your population. Every family is in mourning, but he is regardless of our calamities. Possibly he still dreams of his gigantic designs, even after unheard-of reverses have punished in so signal a manner his pride and his abuse of victory. He has shown himself not even capable of reigning for the interests of his despotism. He has destroyed all that he wished to create. He has believed in no other power but that of force. Force now overwhelms him,—the just retribution of mad ambition.'"

Napoleon delighted in mortifying flatterers. After his return from Austerlitz, Denon presented him with silver medals, illustrative of his victories. The first represented a French eagle tearing an English leopard. "What's this?" asked Napoleon. Denon explained. "Thou rascally flatterer, you say that the French eagle crushes the English leopard; yet I cannot put a fishing-boat to sea that is not taken. I tell you it is the leopard that strangles the eagle. Melt down the medal and

never bring me such another." He found similar fault with the medal
of Austerlitz. "Put Battle of Austerlitz on one side, with the date;
the French, Prussian, and Austrian eagles on the other, without distinction—posterity will distinguish the vanquisher."

TERRITORY AND MONEY-COST OF NAPOLEON'S WARS.

By the treaty of Chaumont, France was to be reduced to its anci·nt
limits; Germany formed into a federative union; Holland, Switzerland,
and the lesser States of Italy, were to be independent; Spain and Portugal were to have their ancient sovereigns; and the restoration of the
Bourbons left to the French people. If Napoleon refused these terms,
the four Powers bound themselves to maintain against him each an army
of 150,000; Great Britain paying, in addition, an annual subsidy of
5,000,000*l.*, besides 20*l.* for each foot, and 30*l.* for each horse-soldier
short of her contingent.

By the treaty of Paris, or rather Fontainebleau, Napoleon renounced
for himself and his descendants the empire of France and the kingdom
of Italy, but retained the title of emperor with the island of Elba, and
an income of 2,500,000£. (or 104,166*l.* 3*s.* 4*d.*) from the revenues of
the ceded countries, and 2,000,000£. from that of France, besides
an annuity of 1,000,000 francs for Josephine. Four hundred soldiers
were given to him as a body-guard, and the Duchies of Parma and
Placentia were settled on Maria Louisa and her son.

By the treaty of Paris (1815), France lost the fortresses of Landau,
Sarre Louis, Philippeville, and Marienburg, with their adjacent territory;
Huningen was demolished; all the frontier fortresses were to be held
for five years, by an allied army of 150,000 men, under Wellington;
28,000,000*l.* were to be paid for the expenses of the war, besides
29,500,000*l.* as indemnities for the spoliations inflicted on the different
States during the Revolution, and 4,000,000*l.* to the minor States. So
that the total sum France had to pay, besides maintaining the Army of
Occupation, was 61,500,000*l.*—From *Dates, Battles, and Events,* by
Lord Eustace Cecil, 1857.

THE FRENCH INVASION OF RUSSIA.

In this vast project and the preparations for it, the character of its
originator, Napoleon I., stands clearly revealed. In the selection of the
point of attack, in the measures taken to assure success, in the organiz-
ing his immense forces, in the dexterity with which his plans were concealed, we see the master of the art of war, the consummate strategist,
the indefatigable administrator. But if we consider the design itself
with reference to the state of Europe, to the true policy for the French
Empire, and to the real resources of the French armies, it appears
simply a splendid chimera, and its author a visionary carried away by
the lust of conquest and unbridled ambition. Granting that Napoleon
was stronger than the Czar, what chance had he of subjugating Russia?

Was he not certain to throw that Power once more into the arms of England? Was he not for a chance incurring a peril of an evident and most terrible kind—the uprising of Europe against his despotism? How insensate, too, the project appears when we remember that, at this very juncture, Spain continued defiant and unsubdued, that an English General had established his hold over part of the Peninsula, that the pride and flower of the Imperial armies was being destroyed in this internecine contest! The scheme of invading Russia, in fact, was what M. Thiers describes it, "mere folly;" it was one of those extravagant conceptions, like that of attacking England in the East, or of setting up a universal Monarchy, which often overcame Napoleon's judgment. And its unreasonableness becomes even more apparent when we examine the nature and composition of the forces arrayed for this wonderful attempt. In this respect Napoleon's *Correspondence* contains a number of interesting details, and throws a good deal of new light on the subject. The best and most faithful soldiers of France were engaged in 1811-12 in the struggle beyond the Pyrenees, consumed in skirmishes with the guerillas, misdirected by generals at feud with each other, or baffled by the unconquerable warriors whom Wellington was conducting to victory. The gigantic hosts that were to enter Russia were made up, to a considerable extent, of allies or subjects beyond old France, of the contingents of the Confederation of the Rhine, of Italians, Spaniards, and Portuguese, of the reluctant conscripts of Belgium and Holland, of the half savage mercenaries of the Illyrian provinces. Was this vast congeries of motley races, indifferent, ill-trained, or hostile, an army fitted to carry the fortunes of the Empire across resentful Germany, to affront the perils of a Russian campaign, to bear with devotion extraordinary hardships? The failure of Napoleon's manœuvres at the very outset of the war, the comparative slowness of his advance, and the frightful horrors of the retreat from Moscow, caused not only by the severity of the cold, but by reckless indiscipline and despair, are the answers of history to this question.—*Times* journal.

SUCCESS OF TALLEYRAND.

Not long before the death of Talleyrand, an able English writer, speaking of his brilliant apophthegms, said: "What are they all to the practical skill with which this extraordinary man has contrived to baffle all the calamities of thirty years, full of the ruin of all power, ability, courage, and fortune? Here is the survivor of the age of the Bastile, the age of the guillotine, the age of the prison-ship, the age of the sword. After baffling the Republic, the Democracy, the Despotism, and the Restoration, he figures in his eightieth year as the Ambassador to England, the Minister of France, and retires from both offices only to be chief counsellor, almost the coadjutor of the king. That where the ferocity of Robespierre fell, where the sagacity of Napoleon fell, where the experience of the Bourbons fell, this one old man, a priest in a land of daring spirits, where conspiracy first and soldiership after, were the great

means of power, should survive all, succeed in everything, and retain h
rank and influence through all changes, is unquestionably among th
most extraordinary instances of conduct exhibited in the world."

SUCCESSION TO THE THRONE OF FRANCE.

Not a little remarkable is it to observe, that from the accession c
Louis XIV. to the present time not a single king or governor of Franc
—though none of them, with the exception of Louis XVIII., have bee
childless—has been succeeded at his demise by his son. Louis XIV
survived his son, his grandson, and several of his great-grandchildren
and was succeeded at last by one of the younger children of his grand
son, the Duke of Burgundy. Louis XV. survived his son, and wa
succeeded by his grandson. Louis XVI. left a son behind him; bu
that son perished in the filthy dungeon to which the cruelties of th
terrorists had confined him. The King of Rome, to whom Napoleon
fondly hoped to bequeath the boundless empire he had won, died
colonel in the Austrian service. Louis XVIII. was, as we have said
childless. The Duke de Berri fell by the hand of an assassin in th
lifetime of Charles X.; and his son, the Duke de Bordeaux, is an exil
from the land which his ancestors regarded as their own estate. Th
eldest son of Louis Philippe perished by an untimely accident; and hi
grandson and heir does not sit upon the throne of his grandfather. Thus
then, it appears that for upwards of two hundred years, in no one of th
dynasties to which France has been subjected has the son succeeded t
the throne of the father.—*Times* journal, 1856.

HISTORICAL LORE IN THE FRENCH SENATE.

Baron Dupin, in a speech in the French Senate, is reported to have
made the following astounding statement :—

" La France occupe, depuis quatorze siècles, le premier rang parmi le
nations Chrétiennes. Clovis, quand il eut été baptisé par l'influence de
la Reine Clotilde, passa en Italie, pour forcer les Lombards à respecte
le Saint Père; il mérita ainsi le nom de fils aîné de l'Eglise."

Can it be believed that this strange reading of national history caused
no remark in the French Senate,—that none of the " fathers of the
country" remembered what must be familiar to every schoolboy in
France—viz., that Clovis, who was baptized at Reims, and who may
well, for aught we know, have done so to please his wife Clotilde, never
" went into Italy," where in his time the Lombards or Longobards had
never been heard of, and where they could, therefore, never have been
wanting in respect to the Holy Father? What would the House of
Lords say if told by one of their number that King Alfred spared the
lives of the citizens of Calais, or that King Arthur was at the siege of
Acre in Palestine? Yet the blunder would scarcely be more unaccount-
able.—*Letter to the Times.*

THE REIGN OF LOUIS XVIII.

M. Ponjoulet, in his *History of France* from 1814 to the present day, gives the following thoughtful and spirited portrait of this sovereign :—

" Historians hostile to the House of Bourbon have not spared Louis XVIII., and they have assigned to him as his sole merit the pride of being King of France. But to the reign of Louis XVIII. attaches an importance and a lustre peculiar to itself. This Prince was the man of his time and of the circumstances reserved for his destiny. An Emperor who was always on horseback had fatigued the world. France, from her immense desire for repose, was not displeased at having a King quietly seated in his arm-chair, but whose fathers had known what battles were. The nation was vexed and wearied out by a restless and terrible will ; and a sovereign whom his infirmities unfitted for a life of activity was, as it were, naturally sent to establish among us a constitutional system of government. Amid the disasters which an ambition that had grown to insanity brought upon us, we wanted a King, the most ancient of kings, who could speak from the height on which the grandeur of twelve centuries placed him ; a King whose misfortunes invested with interest ; whose soul was thoroughly French; whose moderation inclined him to political compromises; and whose clear perception enabled him at his mature age to judge of men and things. Such a King was found in Louis XVIII. Never was any prince's position more difficult than his ; he had so many knots of policy to unloose that he left each for its own hour, and acted with hesitation. Called to bear the sceptre at a late period of life, he had, nevertheless, during his long experience, acquired a considerable knowledge of mankind. His will was persistent even when he appeared to yield. Nothing troubled him: his soul was firm, and his intellect keen ; but why should we not admit that he was crafty ? Politics are so intricate that a little subtlety is pardonable in a constitutional Sovereign. Sly, but not malignant, he satisfied or revenged himself with quotations from Horace. Ever master of himself, he was ever courteous ; and politeness presupposes a certain kindness of disposition and a command of one's self. Had Louis XVIII. been hasty or passionate he could not have performed the task which Providence marked out for him. The eighteenth century had left its marks in his thoughts ; but if at times the man was frivolous, the King was never so.

" During the ten years of his reign he practised in all sincerity the representative *régime*, and it is to the constitutional predominance of this or that political system that should be assigned the successive changes in the conduct of Louis XVIII.'s Government. He delivered us promptly from the foreign armies which, it was pretended, he needed to prop up his throne. He paid our ransom, and debts which were none of his incurring ; he gave us liberty, re-established our credit, led us once more to glory, and imparted to our country an immense movement of confidence. Conspiracy was ever busy during his reign, and, in spite of the assaults on his crown, if he only consulted his heart, not a drop of blood would have been shed. Napoleon had exhibited the terror of the sword; Louis XVIII. displayed the power of the sceptre, and that power was for us liberal and conservative. After so many terrible shocks, after the excesses of brute force, people had lost all notion of the majesty of right. They saw it appear in its calmer grandeur. Louis XVIII. showed it living and invincible. The axe might cut it down, but intimidation would not make it bend. On the 24th of October, 1824, were celebrated, in presence of a vast concourse of people, and pursuant to the ceremonial of the ancient monarchy, the obsequies of the King. The coffin reposed for a month in the Church of St. Denis, was lowered by twelve of the Body Guard into those vaults from which the remains of his ancestors had been torn thirty years before. The Grand Master of the Royal Household reversed his staff of command, and cried, 'the King is dead!' and the King-at-Arms having answered, 'Long live the King!' the cry was repeated by all present to the sound of trumpets and drums, and, amid military music, Louis XVIII. went to his sleep where his fathers had slept; and Charles X., whose accession was proclaimed by the cannon outside the church, was fated not to attend the rendezvous to which his brother summoned him. The vaults of St. Denis await in vain his royal remains, as the palaces also await in vain the return of their ancient inmates."

THE ORLEANS FAMILY.

Immediately after the death of Queen Marie Amelie, appeared in print this semi-official notification from the friends of the Orleans family, of their correction of two opinions which are founded in error. "In the first place, the Queen has been generally represented as separated in politics from the King, and as confining herself, consequently, to her duties as wife and mother. The Queen may have regretted that the Revolution of 1830 called her husband from the happiness of private life to impose upon him the trials and dangers of government; but she sympathized with her whole heart with all the acts of a reign which for eighteen years gave order and liberty to France. She was proud of the King, she was proud of his government, and in her exile she loved to recal all that he had done for France. In the second place, during the events of 1848 an entirely romantic rôle has been attributed to the Queen, in order to contrast her courage with the pretended weakness of the King. With this intention a scene is related which never existed except in the poetic imagination of M. de Lamartine and the diplomatic imagination of Lord Normanby. The personal courage of the King does not admit of a doubt; he gave too many proofs of it, from Jemappes to the last of the too numerous attempts at assassination of which he was the object. One may approve or blame his political conduct in 1848, but it is impossible to doubt that it was dictated purely by political scruples. The time had not yet come when it would seem only natural to establish one's supremacy by striking terror into the people of Paris. Is it not to be regretted that in these tributes of respect and admiration to the dead Queen, so many writers should have carelessly repeated what would have most surprised and troubled her had it been said during her life? Such mistakes are common in our daily literature, but it is, perhaps, wise to correct them when it regards a family whose honour is dear to the French nation. The time will come when the humane and conscientious scruples of King Louis Philippe, in 1848, will constitute one of the strongest titles of his family in the eyes of his countrymen."

THE GREAT POLITICAL MONTH OF JULY.

A writer in the *Siècle*, in 1866, recommended the learned Academics of the French Institute to offer a prize for an Essay which shall best explain why revolutions, battles, and the great political events which influence the destinies of nations, generally take place in the month of July, as also the relations that exist between the temperature of the atmosphere and the revolutionary and combative temperament of men. Those learned bodies often propose questions of little or no practical advantage; and why, he asks, should they not invite investigation on a subject of such vital importance to mankind? The fact of the month of July having this peculiarity is unquestionable. The States-General, convoked by Louis XVI., in 1789, met on the 5th of May, the day when Mirabeau addressed his memorable defiance to the Marquis de Dreux-Brezé, who was sent to expel the representatives from their Hall, but two months elapsed before the first great act of the Revolution was performed. The people had their eyes long turned to the Bastile, but they waited for the burning rays of July to attack and take it. Forty years passed away, during which the greatest events of which history makes mention, took place throughout Europe,—the wars of the Republic, the Reign of Terror, the Consulate, the Empire, the Invasion, the Restoration. The rights which the people had gained at so much cost were menaced by Charles X. Had he tried his *coup d'état* against the press a month sooner or a month later it might have succeeded like that of the 18th Brumaire. But the revolutionary sun of July darted its fiery beams on the streets and squares of Paris, and in three days the Government, with an army at its back, was overthrown for ever. Great heat and great cold seem to produce similar effects on the human temperament. Revolution of July, or Revolution of February, it is all one from his point of view; the same effect is produced by the same cause. It was during the heat of summer that the independence of Italy was won. It was in July that the structure raised on the Treaties of 1815 fell in the dust; that Austria was vanquished at Königgrätz and Sadowa, excluded from the Germanic Confederation, and Venetia given over to France to be transferred to Italy; and, observes the writer, " it was while Austria was humbled, and the reactionists of Europe lost all the ground which they held since 1815, that the electors of a French college signified their decision to one of the most illustrious champions of the Catholic and feudal reaction. The defeat of M. de Falloux in the department of the Maine-et-Loire is the defeat of Austria seen from the large end of the telescope!" It is not for the idle pleasure of pointing out the singularity of the month of July that M. Louis Jourdan notices these events. He professes ultra-Liberalism, and if he rejoices in the victories of Prussia it is only because they complete Italian independence and humble Catholic Austria. He continues:—

"Yes, the defeat of Austria is one of the most remarkable victories won by the Revolution. Vienna was the head-quarters of the reaction; a sort of chapel of ease to Rome; the centre of all counter-revolutionary intrigues. Had Austria been victorious, the labours of our fathers would have to be begun again; the people would again have been bowed to the yoke; Venetia would have remained an Austrian province. All the blood shed in Italy during the glorious campaign of 1859 would have been shed in vain. The reaction was re-appearing to dictate its conditions; but Austria is now prostrate, and since the month of July last our principles have again made way."

M. Jourdan does not elucidate the point he set out with,—why all these great events take place in the month of July.

DEFEAT OF THE IMPERIAL GUARD AT WATERLOO.

The Rev. William Leeke, who formerly, as an ensign of the 52nd, carried the colours of that distinguished corps at Waterloo, has published a History of his old regiment, in which he claims for it the credit of having defeated the Imperial Guard at Waterloo, a feat hitherto attributed to the Guards. Mr. Leeke makes out a strong case in favour of the 52nd, and corroborates it by the following anecdote:—

"Shortly after the 52nd reached Paris and were encamped in the Champs Elysées, Sir John Colborne gave us the following account of what Sir John Byng had said, on meeting him a day or two before. He said:—'How do your fellows like our getting the credit of doing what you did at Waterloo? I could not advance when you did, because all our ammunition was gone.' Some little time afterwards, when Sir John Colborne met Byng, and tried to lead him to speak on the subject again, he found him quite disinclined to do so. Many years afterwards, I think it was in 1850, when I was dining with Lord Seaton in town, one of his sons requested me to try and draw his father out to talk about Waterloo, saying that he often told them about his other battles, but they could not get him to speak much about that. I took an opportunity of asking him if he recollected much about Waterloo, and I suppose I particularized the charge of the 52nd, on the Imperial Guard, for I remember he said, 'Did you ever hear what Sir John Byng said to me at Paris?' I replied that I had a very distinct recollection of it, but that I should be very much obliged to him if he would repeat to me what Sir John Byng had said, in order that I might see if my recollection of it exactly tallied with his. Lord Seaton then gave me the account of what passed on the two occasions of his meeting Byng, just as I have related it above, and exactly as I remember to have heard it from him 35 years before in the camp at Paris."

Historico-Political Information.

THE NATIONAL DEBT.[*]

GRAVE apprehensions were expressed, just after the great Revolution in 1688, at the magnitude of our Debt. One writer declared, six years after this great event happened, "that not one man in a hundred would have contributed to it, if they could have foreseen how it would have helped to the utter beggaring of ourselves by the decay of traffic and unsupportable taxes."

Lord Lyttelton, who, as an historian, ought to have been better instructed, writing in 1739, said, "that our credit was sunk at home and abroad, the people dispirited and discontented, because we owed almost forty millions."

Again, Lord Bolingbroke, a statesman singularly well acquainted with the affairs of Europe, and a philosopher not accustomed to indulge in restricted ideas, says in his *Reflections on the State of the Nation, principally with regard to her Taxes and her Debts, their causes and their consequences*, "Our Parliamentary aids from the year 1740 exclusively to the year 1748, amount to 55,522,159l. 16s. 3d., and the new Debt we have contracted to more than thirty millions, a sum that will appear incredible to future generations."

Hannay, another writer, speaking on the same subject in 1756, says, "It has been a general notion amongst political arithmeticians that we may increase our Debt to one hundred millions; but they acknowledged that it must then cease by the debtor becoming bankrupt. But it is very difficult to comprehend, if we do not stop at seventy-five millions, where we shall stop."

Hume, Adam Smith, Dr. Price, Lord Kaimes, and many other writers during the last century, asserted we had actually reached the goal of national ruin. Yet, judging from all that has passed in fiscal administration during the present century, and drawing information from whatever quarter we may, there is no reason for crediting the statement made a few years before the revolution, that "a kind of common consumption hath crowded upon us;" still less is there any reason for fearing either a diminution of the national wealth or that the increasing power and progress of the country will decline. In the words of Dryden:

> We know those blessings which we must possess,
> And judge of future by past happiness.

"ALL MEN HAVE THEIR PRICE."

During the administration of Sir Robert Walpole, he wanted to carry a question in the House of Commons, to which he knew there would

---

[*] The Rev. C. H. Hartshorne : *Journal of the British Archæological Association*, 1865.

be great opposition, and which was disliked by some of his own dependents. As he was passing through the Court of Requests (in the old palace at Westminster), he met a member of the Opposition, whose avarice he imagined would not reject a large bribe. He took him aside, and said, "Such a question comes on this day; give me your vote, and here is a bank-bill of 2000*l*.," which he put into his hands. The member made him this answer: "Sir Robert, you have lately served some of my particular friends; and when my wife was last at court, the King was very gracious to her, which must have happened at your instance. I should, therefore, think myself very ungrateful (*putting the bank-bill into his pocket*) if I were to refuse the favour you are now pleased to ask me."

Sir Robert was called the Grand Corrupter in the libels of his time: he is said to have thought all mankind rogues, and to have remarked that every one had his price. Pope refers to this:

> Would he oblige me, let me only find
> He does not think me what he thinks mankind.

Or as he at first printed it:

> He thinks one poet of no venal kind.

That Walpole said something very much like the saying attributed to him is what even his son does not deny; but there is reason to believe that he said it with a qualification—" all *those* men have their price," not " all men have their price."

The saying as recorded by Richardson, the painter, who had ample means of being well-informed, was in these words: "There was not one, how patriot soever he might seem, of whom he did not know the price." (*Richardsoniana*, 8vo, 1776, p. 178.) Dr. King, whose means of information were as good as Richardson's, records a remark made during a debate in Parliament by Walpole to Mr. W. Leveson, the brother of the Jacobite Lord Gower. " You see," said Sir Robert, "with what zeal and vehemence these gentlemen oppose; and yet I know the price of every man in this house except three, and your brother is one of them." Dr. King adds, that Sir Robert lived long enough to know that my Lord Gower had his price as well as the rest. (King's *Anecdotes*, p. 44.) His son modifies the saying: " Some are corrupt," Sir Robert Walpole said; " but I will tell you of one who is not; Shippen is not." (*Walpoliana*, i. 38.) And Sir Robert said, that " it was fortunate so few men could be prime ministers, as it was best that few should thoroughly know the shocking wickedness of mankind. I never heard him say that all men had their prices; and I believe no such expression ever came from his mouth."

Lord Brougham, also, doubts whether the above words were ever used by Walpole; or, if used, whether they are properly interpreted. " His famous saying that ' all men have their price,'" said Lord Brougham, " can prove nothing unless ' price' be defined; and if a large and liberal sense is given to the word, the proposition more resembles a truism than a sneer, or an ebullition of official philanthropy. But it has been positively affirmed that the remark was never made; for it is said that an important word is omitted, which wholly changes the sense; and that Walpole only said, in reference to certain actions of profligate adversaries, and their adherents resembling themselves, " All *these* men have their price." (Coxe's *Life of Walpole*, vol. i. p. 757.) His general tone of sarcasm, when speaking of patriotism and political gratitude, and others of the more fleeting virtues, is well-known. " Patriots," he said, " are easily raised; I have myself made many a one. 'Tis but to refuse an unreasonable demand, and up springs a patriot!" So, the gratitude of political men he defined to be "a lively sense of favours to come."—*A Century of Anecdote*, vol. i.

BRIBING MEMBERS OF PARLIAMENT.

About the year 1767 one Roberts, who had been Secretary to the Treasury, and Mr. Pelham, divulged some strange details of the mode in which the House of Commons was managed in his time, when a number of members received from him, at the end of every session, a stipend in bank notes, the sums varying from 500*l.* to 800*l.* per annum. Roberts, on the day of the Prorogation, took his stand in the Court of Requests, and as the gentlemen passed, in going to or returning from the House, Roberts conveyed the money in a squeeze of the hand. The names of the recipients were entered in a book, which was preserved with the deepest secrecy, it being never inspected by any one except the King and Mr. Pelham. On the decease of that minister, in 1754, his brother, the Duke of Newcastle, and others of the succeeding Cabinet, were anxious to obtain information of the private state of the House, and besought Roberts to give up the book containing the names of the bribed. This Roberts refused to do, except by the King's command, and to his majesty in person. Of this refusal the ministers acquainted the King, who sent for Roberts to St. James's, where he was introduced into the closet, more than one of the ministers being present. George II. ordered him to return him the book in question, which injunction was complied with. At the same time, taking the poker in his hand, the King put it into the fire, made it red hot, and thrust the book into the flames, where it was immediately burnt. He considered it too confidential a register to be transferred to the new ministers, and as having become extinct with the administration of Mr. Pelham.

Another official person, who had been private secretary to the Earl of Bute, and seventeen years Treasurer of the Ordnance, testified to the Peace of 1763 having been carried by money: he secured above 120 votes, with 80,000*l.* set apart for the purpose, forty members receiving 1000*l.* and 500*l.* each.—*A Century of Anecdote*, vol. i.

SUPPOSED PREROGATIVE OF THE CROWN IN MATTERS OF PEACE, WAR, AND ALLIANCES.

It is a generally-accepted doctrine that all that relates to Peace, War, or Alliances, falls peculiarly within the prerogative of the Crown; and that Parliament, the Grand Council of the Nation, has no right to interpose its authority, or even its advice, in such a manner as to restrain, even in semblance, the free action of the Sovereign. In pursuance of this theory, if a member of Parliament, as has occurred occasionally within our time, should venture to ask a question of the minister as to the provisions of a Treaty of Peace, or of Commerce, whilst in course of negotiation, he is very curtly put down with a reply to the effect that, according to "the spirit and practice of the Constitution," to use Lord Palmerston's words in reference to the treaty on the Danish question, the contents of a treaty cannot be in any way discussed or referred to until after its ratification by the Sovereign. In the course of a series of articles entitled "Notes on Diplomacy and Diplomatic History," by Mr. Henry Ottley, published in *Fraser's Magazine* (Aug.—Dec. 1864), this position is stoutly resisted, abundance of authority being cited to the contrary. This writer affirms that the venerable Gothic institutions of the Middle Ages were imbued with the principles of freedom, and carried checks upon the royal authority to a degree hardly conceivable by those who view the recent history of European States. It was not until towards the 15th century, when the potentates became almost despotic, that this principle was suppressed, and the prerogative of the Crown raised in its place. In Germany the Emperor was subordinated to the Diet in all that related to war and alliances. In Hungary, Bohemia, Sweden, Denmark, Poland, also. By the capitulation of Matthias with the Hungarian States, so late as 1615, it was stipulated that there should be no measures of peace or war without the consent of the Diet, and this was ratified by Ferdinand and his successors. In the various kingdoms of the Spanish peninsula the monarch was elected with restricted powers, particularly in matters of peace and war, until a comparatively modern period, the times indeed of the Hapsburgs and the Bourbons. In France from the earliest times the same principle prevailed. Charles the Bald, the first of a long line of Princes, promised his nobles not to undertake any matters of State policy without their concurrence, and during many reigns this principle was insisted upon, and strictly adhered to. It was under Charles VII., and Louis XI., that arbitrary rule in these matters began to be introduced. But Philip de Comines, in his Memoirs, denounced the innovation. "It may be objected," he said, "that in some cases there may not be time to assemble them (the representatives of the people), and that war will bear no delay; but I reply that such haste ought not to be made, and there will be time enough; and I tell you that princes are more powerful and more dreaded by their enemies when they undertake anything with the consent of their subjects."

Mr. Ottley goes on to remark that in England these rights and constitutional liberties, derived from a common source with those of Europe generally, survived long after despotism had asserted its domain in continental states, and were asserted with boldness, dignity, and authority until within the present century. Citing the Rolls of Parliament as his authority, he maintains and shows that from the time of William the Conqueror down to that of George III., there was, with perhaps a single exception, afterwards referred to, "no measure of war or peace undertaken without the previous advice and consent of Parliament." Amongst numerous cases cited it may be satisfactory to reproduce the following. Edward III. called together no less than sixteen parliaments to advise with them in matters of war, peace, and alliances. In the fifth year of his reign he called a Parliament to consult upon the then state of his differences with the King of France, asking their advice whether he should refer them to arbitration, or treat amicably with him, or proceed to open war. "The prelates, earls, barons, and other great men, thereupon advised in favour of a treaty; and the King in Parliament, and with its consent, named the commissioners for this treaty, and part of their powers and business was then prescribed to them." Nor were these submissions to Parliamentary authority mere matters of form. In the thirty-sixth year of the same monarch, an offer of peace from Robert Bruce of Scotland having been referred to the Lords, they unanimously answered that "they could not assent to it, as prejudicial to the King's Crown."

In the seventh year of the reign of Richard II. a very curious case occurs, in which the reason is fairly stated why the people ought to be consulted, not only before making war, but in making peace also. The making of a treaty with France was then under consideration, but the Chancellor, Michael de la Pole, told both Houses "that the King, out of tender love to his people, and in consideration of the great expenses they had been at during the war, would not finally conclude the peace without their assent and knowledge;" and then went on to say, "though he might do it, because (as it was conceived) France was the King's own proper inheritance, and not belonging to the Crown of England." The exception suggested rather than asserted in the latter passage is very significant, as proving the existence of a rule, and its unquestioned authority. The Chancellor, in fact, concluded by declaring "that the King desired and earnestly charged them carefully to examine and consider the said articles in relation to this treaty, and advise what was best to be done for the kingdom's honour and advantage." It was under the Stuarts that the infraction of this ancient constitutional principle was attempted, and "prerogative" asserted in matters of war, peace, and State policy; and these pretensions led to contests which ended in the extermination of the dynasty. William III. and Queen Anne, throughout the long foreign wars in which the country was then engaged, constantly and as a matter of admitted duty and acknowledged caution, applied to the authority and advice of Parliament on all projects of peace and war. During the long negotiations which led to the Treaty of Utrecht, Parliament was frequently applied to in this way. On the 11th June,

1712, for instance, the Queen came down to the House of Peers, and stated to both Houses, in a long speech, "the terms on which peace might be made," for, as was stated at the time, "such was the caution of the Lord Treasurer, that he was determined to conclude nothing without the previous sanction of Parliament."

On the accession of the House of Hanover, the wholesome and constitutional principle of Parliamentary control in State affairs first began to be seriously invaded; but the resistance offered to the encroachments of prerogative was uncompromising in character, and affords many noble passages in Parliamentary history, and was in the main successful. The only notable infraction of the Parliamentary authority was in the case of the war with Sweden, under George I., accompanied by the nefarious purchase of Bremen and Verden, as additions to the Hanoverian possessions of the King. But on this and other occasions Parliament manfully asserted its powers, which George II. and George III. had to yield, insomuch that not a single treaty of peace was agreed to in either reign without being submitted for the approval of Parliament, down to and including that of Amiens in 1802, which was discussed and considerably modified in its preliminaries. The war with the French Republic and Empire was indeed the first commencement of the almost independent Government action which has prevailed since; and the Treaty of Vienna—unpropitious example!—was the first solemn act of the sort engaged in by the monarch of this country without the advice and authority of Parliament. Nor did the proceeding pass unnoticed : on the contrary, it formed the subject of severe comment and repudiation, which are recorded in the Parliamentary reports of the day.

————

MARITIME SUPREMACY OF ENGLAND.

Mr. Froude in the latest volume of his *History of England* has dedicated an entire chapter to the development of a proposition which will probably take the present generation by surprise. He tells us, and tells us truly, that the Maritime Supremacy of England originated in successful piracy. That the practice was justified or disguised by many persuasions peculiar to the times is not to be denied; but, except for the consideration due to these views, it would be difficult to describe the system by any other name than that applied to the deeds of the most desperate rovers. The age, too, in which these customs prevailed was not a remote age, like that of the Sea Kings of the North. It was the age of Queen Elizabeth and Shakspeare; and yet in those days the gentlemen of our maritime counties, men of good lineage and respectable education, thought it no shame to fit out ships for the express purpose of robbing other ships. Strange to say, there was a religious impulse in the matter. The common prey of these adventurers was the Spaniard, and the Spaniard was an object of abhorrence and dread as the champion of Papal fanaticism. So the Protestant gentlemen of England made war upon the great adversary, and plundered his treasure ships with the comfortable conviction that they were making righteous as well as handsome profits, until in the end their adventures produced that intrepid and skilful race of seamen who afterwards defeated the Armada, and founded the maritime power of Britain.

Mr. Froude thereon proceeds to remarks: "the ancient Greeks, says Thucydides, even those not lowest in rank among them, when they first crossed the seas, betook themselves to piracy. Falling on unprotected towns or villages they plundered them at their pleasure, and from this resource they derived their chief means of maintenance. The employment carried no disgrace with it, but rather glory and honour ; and in the tales of our poets, when mariners touch anywhere, the common question is whether they are pirates—neither those who are thus addressed being ashamed of their calling, nor those who inquire meaning it as a reproach.

" In the dissolution of the ancient order of Europe, and the spiritual anarchy which had reduced religion to a quarrel of opinions, the primitive tendencies of human nature for a time asserted themselves, and the English gentlemen of the 16th century passed into a condition which, with many differences, yet had many analogies with that of the Grecian chiefs. With the restlessness of new thoughts, new hopes and prospects, with a constitutional enjoyment of enterprise and adventure, with a legitimate hatred of oppression, and a determination to revenge their countrymen, who from day to day were tortured and murdered by the Inquisition, most of all, perhaps, with a sense that it was the mission of a Protestant Englishman to spoil the Amalekites—in other words, the gold ships from Panama, or the richly-laden Flemish traders—the merchants at the seaports, the gentlemen whose estates touched upon the creeks and rivers, and to whom the sea from childhood had been a natural home, fitted out their vessels under the name of traders, and sent them out armed to the teeth with vague commissions to take their chance of what the gods might send."

Our Supremacy of the Sea may be said to date from the reign of Henry VIII. In the summer of 1512, England fleshed its sword in a Continental war. But her first efforts were disastrous. A mutiny broke out at St. Sebastian, and the English army resolved to return home, in direct violation of the King's commands. Henry wrote to Ferdinand, with whom they had been sent to co-operate, to stop them at all hazards, and cut every man's throat who refused obedience. But the order came too late, and England incurred no insignificant disgrace. War was not the wish of Fox or Wolsey, but Wolsey was forced into it by this disaster until he became the very soul of the war. His vast influence with the King dates from this event. England was for the moment destitute of military organization, but Wolsey, by his penetrative spirit, recovered it at a bound. In his preparations he displayed an amount of forethought, energy, patience, and administrative genius not to be found in any other man of that age. Thus the expedition under Sir Edward Howard, which in April, 1513, attacked the French galleys at Brest, and where Sir Edward fell a sacrifice to his impetuous valour, was signally victorious, and retrieved the honour of the English name. It fastened on the imagination of both nations. From this man's example his countrymen jumped to the conviction that nothing was too arduous, and no odds on the side of an enemy justified retreat. From this man's daring the world took the measure of English courage generally, and the French dared no longer dispute the possession of the narrow seas.—*Times* journal.

PROPHECIES AND GUESSES.

Among predictive marvels is the remarkable guess of M. Lumm, chaplain of the Edinburgh gaol at the beginning of the present century. He had a habit of prophesying; he predicted, for example, *it is said*, in 1804, that the Bourbons, then in Scotland, would be expelled France for ever in 1830, but of this there is no other evidence. It is quite certain, however, that the following was in type in 1842 : " In 1848 there would be a terrible convulsion, and there would be no peace till 1863." " In 1868, there would be a restoration of peace to the Church, and all the true churches would be united. The Jews are to be restored to their own land, and to be a political power there, as in the days of Solomon. Russia is to be the instrument of restoring them."

A prophecy of trouble is always safe, but the guess at the year involves a really notable coincidence. But which is the more probable, that an old gentleman always maundering about events to come, made in his lifetime one or two good guesses, or that the laws of nature were suspended in order that he should be an oracle in his own parlour?

Fleming's prophecies are more curious, and are believed even by educated men. This man, who wrote on the Apocalypse in 1701, undoubtedly did predict the fall of the French Monarchy " before 1794;" and he added a computation which, when corrected by the true length of the year, really brings him within a few days of the execution of Louis XVI. Fleming believed also that the Fifth Vial, which began in 1793, would end in 1848 ; and the period did, undoubtedly, embrace a cycle of some sort, the battle, as it were, between the French people and the Capetian family occupying the whole time. But these are the only accurate "Prophecies of Fleming." The Rev. G. S. Faber, in 1818, only three years after Waterloo, predicted the revival of the French Empire as absolutely essential to the fulfilment of prophecy, though he declined to pledge himself to the date. The simple fact is, that there exist hundreds of interpretations of the Revelations, and as all are constrained by the figures there given to keep within the nineteenth century, there must be several which light upon the year 1848. These alone are remembered, and Fleming, as the oldest among them, is regarded almost as a prophet. He was, in fact, a guesser, who guessed by rule, *i. e.*, by what he believed the mystic numbers in the Apocalypse to mean : and like all guessers by rule, he was once or twice right.—*Spectator* newspaper, 1862.

CHARACTER OF A TRIMMER.

To George Savile, Marquis of Halifax, was this term first applied. Being hereditarily attached to the Stuarts, ambitious, and endowed with brilliant talents, he played an active and successful part in the intriguing reigns of Charles II. and James II. It is hard to state shortly his political history or principles, except by saying that he was the chief of the body to which the expressive name of Trimmers was given. So far, however, as he was attached to any principle, it seems to have been the cause of civil liberty as then understood. He opposed the Non-resisting Test Bill in 1675, as well as, both in those times and after the accession of James, the relaxation of the tests against the Papists. He opposed the scheme for excluding the Duke of York from the succession, preferring to limit his authority when the crown should devolve on him. He declined to take part in bringing over the Prince of Orange; but was president of the convention parliament, and strongly supported the motion for declaring the throne vacant. On the accession of William and Mary, he was made privy seal; but he soon retired from the administration, upon inquiry being proposed to be made as to the authors of the prosecutions of Lord Russell, Sidney, &c., in which he, as a member of the then existing government, had concurred; and he continued in opposition thenceforward till his death.

"He was," says Burnet, "a man of great and ready wit, full of life, and very pleasant, much turned to satire . . . . He was punctual in his payments, and just in all private dealings, but with relation to the public he went backward and forward, and changed sides so often that in the conclusion no side trusted him; he seemed full of commonwealth notions, yet he went into the worst part of King Charles's reign. The liveliness of his imagination was always too hard for his judgment. His severe jest was preferred by him to all arguments whatever; and he was endless in council, for when, after much discourse, a point was settled, if he could find a new jest whereby he could make that which was digested by himself seem ridiculous, he could not hold, but would study to raise the credit of his wit, though it made others call his judgment into question," &c. His works are lively and elegant; one is the "Character of a Trimmer."

POTWALLOPERS.

In the *Gentleman's Magazine*, June, 1852, p. 387, Mr. J. Gough Nichols notices at least three distinct meanings of the verb *to wallop*: first, to *gallop*; secondly, to *drub*; thirdly, to *boil*. This last meaning has been generally received and recognised in explanation of the familiar term *potwallopers*. To *boil* is in Sa. *wealan*, and in Ger. *wallen*; to *boil up*, Ger. *aufwallen*, Old Du. *opwallen*. We here, it has been supposed, transfer the particle from the beginning of the word to the end, as we do in many other instances; so that *opwallen* becomes *wallenop* (to boil up) or wallop. Mr. Nichols is disposed to question this derivation; giving it at the same time as his opinion that the original term was not *potwalloper*, but *potwaller*, or *potwealer*, which, however, comes to the same thing. Yet, on behalf of the word *potwalloper*, we may urge an independent plea. Potwallopers were not only those recognised constituents who had in some places acquired the right of suffrage by keeping house, and boiling a pot, *i. e.*, maintaining themselves without charitable or parochial aid. The term also included "every poor wretch" who belonged to the parish, and was "*caused* to boil a pot" in order to qualify him as a voter; and this was sometimes done by erecting a thing like a chimney in a field or in the street, where they kindled a fire, on which they boiled a pot! This, it is clear, was something like manufacturing fictitious votes, and voting in a fictitious character. Now, in old German law-Latin, walapaus (*walapa*, walpor, ewalaput) was a *counterfeit;* strictly speaking, one who for fraudulent purposes *assumed a disguise.* The *potwalloper* then, may have been originally the *potwalapa* (pot counterfeit); and *potwalapa* may have gradually passed into our vernacular *potwalloper* (pot boiler).

ANACHARSIS CLOOTZ.

This name was assumed by Baron Jean Baptiste Clootz, who was born at Cleeves in 1755. He conceived the idea of reforming the human race, and travelled through England, Germany, Italy, &c., denouncing all kings, princes, and rulers, and even the Deity himself. He called himself Anacharsis, in allusion to the Scythian philosopher of this name, who flourished about six centuries before the Christian era, and who travelled to Greece and other countries for the purpose of gaining knowledge, in order to improve the people of his own country (Wheeler's *Dictionary*). Among his classic freaks, Anacharsis Clootz got up at Paris, in 1793, a sort of national pageant or procession, in which England was personified by Captain Skinner, as a man of elegant manners.

MRS. PARTINGTON AND HER MOP.

This "labour in vain" will be found illustrated in the following passage from the Rev. Sydney Smith's speech at Taunton on the rejection of the Reform Bill, October, 1831:

"The attempt of the Lords to stop the progress of reform reminds me very forcibly of the great storm off Sidmouth, and the conduct of the excellent Mrs. Partington on that occasion. In the winter of 1824, there set in a great flood upon that town; the tide rose to an incredible height, the waves rushed in upon the houses, and everything was threatened with destruction. In the midst of this sublime and terrible storm, Dame Partington, who lived upon the beach, was seen at the door of her house with mop and pattens, trundling her mop, squeezing out the sea-water, and vigorously pushing away the Atlantic Ocean. The Atlantic was roused; Mrs. Partington's spirit was up; but I need not tell you that the contest was unequal. The Atlantic beat Mrs. Partington. She was excellent at a slop or a puddle, but she should not have meddled with a tempest."

The Americans, however, lay claim to the first use of the Partington and Mop image; she has latterly become a very popular personage in the States, and the American humorist, B. P. Shillabeer, has collected and recorded the old lady's laughable sayings.

KING BOMBA.

This was the *sobriquet* given to Ferdinand II., King of the Two Sicilies. *Bomba* is the name of a children's game in Italy, resembling our "prisoners' base," and as Ferdinand was fond of childish amusements, playing at soldiers, &c., the nickname is traced to this pastime. But, a more reasonable cause is the charge against Ferdinand of his having called upon his soldiers to "bombard" his people during one of their insurrections. This is denied; but the book, *Naples and King Ferdinand*, repeats the charge, adding that the King kept crying out, "Down with them! down with them!" though it is added, in a note, that the particular expression was "Bombardare;" "hence," says the author, "arose his well-known sobriquet of *Bomba*."—(*Leigh Hunt*.) The *Dublin Evening Gazette* controverts this interpretation, saying that in Italy, "when you tell a man a thing which he knows to be false, or when he wishes to convey to you the idea of the utter worthlessness of any thing or person, he puffs out his cheek like a bagpiper's in full blow, smites it with his forefinger, and allows the pent breath to explode, with the exclamation, '*Bomba !*' I have witnessed the gesture and heard the sound. Hence, after 1849, when royal oaths in the name of the Most Holy Trinity were found to be as worthless as a beggar's in the name of Bacchus, or the Madonna, when Ferdinand was perceived to be a worthless liar, his quickwitted people whispered his name. He was called King Bomba, King Puffcheek, King Liar, King Knave. The name and his character were then so much in harmony, that it spread widely. Longfellow sings:

> After Palermo's fatal siege,
> Across the western seas he fled,
> In good King Bomba's happy reign.

—Wheeler's *Dictionary of the Noted Names of Fiction*, 1866.

SIGNING THE TREATY OF UTRECHT.

The treaties were signed between England and France at two o'clock in the afternoon; the Ministers of the Duke of Savoy, and the King of Prussia, in the course of the same evening, set their hands and seals to the parchment; and the Dutch characteristically came in last, signing at midnight. Prior had had the distinction of bringing over the treaty of Ryswick to England. The honour of bringing over the Treaty of Utrecht was reserved to Bolingbroke's young brother George, who arrived in London with the precious document about two o'clock in the afternoon of Good Friday, the 3rd of April. The Secretary welcomed his brother with open arms, as, covered with dust, he alighted from his post-chaise at Whitehall. All Bolingbroke's cares seemed at an end. He could scarcely believe in the reality of the great treaty that he so eagerly glanced over. The words which came from the mouth of Elizabeth when the news came to Hatfield that her sister Mary was dead, and that she, the persecuted princess, was now the Queen of England, came to Bolingbroke's mind: "It is the Lord's work, and it is marvellous in our eyes."—Macknight's *Life of Lord Bolingbroke.*

Peace with France might have been concluded with Great Britain on infinitely better terms two years before the Treaty of Utrecht; but the negotiations were broken off principally on account of an *assiento* made with the French Guinea Company, who were to furnish to the English 4800 negroes annually: this Great Britain most pertinaciously insisted on, and Louis XIV. most reluctantly conceded, although he gained political objects of great magnitude. Several bloody battles, and still more bloody sieges, took place, and much treasure was expended; but the English nation persisted in engrossing this now reprobated privilege, which, although nominally limited to 4800 negroes, furnished a pretext for smuggling in three times that number. On such matters national feelings seem periodically subject to hot and cold fits.—*Notes to assist the Memory. Second Edition,* 1827.

HOW THE HABEAS CORPUS ACT WAS OBTAINED.

Bishop Burnet relates a circumstance respecting the Habeas Corpus Act which is more curious than creditable; and though we cannot be induced to suppose that this important statute was obtained by a jest and a fraud, yet the story proves that a very formidable opposition was made to it at the time. "It was carried" (says he) "by an odd artifice in the House of Lords. Lord Grey and Lord Norris were named to be the tellers; Lord Norris, being a man subject to vapours, was not at all times attentive to what he was doing, so a very fat lord coming in, Lord Grey counted him for ten, as a jest at first, but seeing that Lord Norris had not observed it, he went on with his misreckoning of ten: so it was reported to the House, and declared, that they who were for the Bill were the majority, though it indeed went on the other side; and by this means the Bill passed."—*Hist. Car. II.* 485; Christian's *Blackstone.* See, also, ante, p. 66.

SMALL MAJORITIES.

Some of the most eventful changes in our constitution have been carried by feeble majorities. The great points of the national religion, under Elizabeth, were carried by six votes. The great question on the danger of Popery, in Queen Anne's reign, was decided by a majority of 256 to 208. The Hanover succession was carried by a single vote!

The Remonstrance, in Charles I.'s time, by eleven. The Union with Scotland and Ireland by very small majorities. The Reform in Parliament in 1831, by one!—Duncan's *Essays.*[*]

FREE-SPEAKING.

Archbishop Whately, in his very able Lecture on Egypt, referring to the writers on Public Affairs at home, reprehends "the practice of exaggeration, with keen delight, every evil that they can find, inventing such as do not exist, and keeping out of sight what is good. An Eastern despot, reading the productions of one of these writers, would say that, with all our precautions, we are the worst governed people on earth ; and that our law courts and public offices are merely a complicated machinery for oppressing the mass of the people ; that our Houses of Lords and Commons are utterly mismanaged, our public men striving to repress merit, and that our best plan would be to sweep away all those, as, with less trouble, matters might go on better, and could not go on worse. Charges of this nature cannot be brought publicly forward in the Turkish Empire. In Cairo, a man was beheaded because he made too free a use of his tongue. He was told not to be speaking of the insurrection in Syria, and had dared to be chatting of the news; and there are other countries also, where because such charges are true, it would not be safe to circulate them. But these writers do not mean half what they set forth. They heighten their descriptions to display their eloquence; but the tendency of such publications is always towards revolution, and the practical effect on the minds of the people is to render them incredulous. They understand that these overwrought representations are for effect, and they go about their business with an impression that the whole is unreal. If one of these writers were visited himself with a horrible dream that he was a peasant under an Oriental despot, that he was taxed at the will of the Sovereign, and had to pay the assessment in produce valued at half the market-price, that he was compelled to work and receive four-fifths of his low wages in food, consisting of hard, sour biscuit—let him then dream that he had spoken against the Ministry, and that he finds himself bastinadoed till he confesses that he brought false charges; that his grown-up son had been dragged off for a soldier, and himself deprived of his only support, and he would be inclined to doubt whether ours is the worst system of government."

" CAUCUS."

The term *Caucus* is applied to all party meetings held in secret in the United States. It is a corruption of the word *caulkers;* the disguised patriots of Massachusetts, in 1776, having been so called because they met in the ship-yards. The phrase in question has been applied to the political meetings held at the private residences of statesmen ; which is conceived to be a singular perversion of its use and meaning. Such

---

[*] See "Great Events from Little Causes," ante, p. 66.

gatherings, or receptions, are neither cabals nor secret conclaves; on the contrary, the reporters of several newspapers, without regard to their political aims, are admitted; and the whole proceedings are as freely made known to the outside public as the debates in Parliament. *Caucus* is by no means a pretty, much less a desirable word, to be added to our national vocabulary; but, if it be adopted at all, let us at least make a *right* use of it.—*Notes and Queries.*

THE CAVE ADULLAM.

This opprobrious appellation, which has been applied to the political malcontent in our times, is of Scriptural origin. The *Cave Adullam* is first mentioned in 1 Samuel xxii. 1, 2. David, when he was fleeing from Saul, went over to Gath, in Philistia; but finding that he was not safe there, he fled to the Cave Adullam. And it is recorded, that there, *" every one that was in distress,* and every one that was in debt, and *every one that was discontented,* gathered themselves unto him, and he became captain over them." The point, the appropriateness, and the sting of the analogy between the old Adullamites and the new, lies in the words in Italics.

In David's company there were, one can imagine, many young men who felt that they had been neglected in the Court of Saul; and in our time, 1866, it was said, or shrewdly thought, that there were many persons who were distressed and discontented, because when Earl Russell formed his Government, they were neglected and passed by. But perhaps there is a more subtle analogy. David and his friends were outcasts, and two courses were before them. They could go over to the Philistines, but this course was repugnant to them, and so they determined to have an independent party. And, as with the old, so with the new Adullamites. They, too, might go over to the Philistines, but were not prepared for so extreme a policy; and they, too, determined to set up for themselves.

Mr. Bright, in the House of Commons, applied Adullamites to the above party; but, according to a statement in a work entitled *Six Months in the White House with Abraham Lincoln,* by Mr. Carpenter, an artist, who remained in the White House while painting an historical picture of the President reading his Proclamation of Emancipation to his Cabinet, it would seem that Mr. Bright's "Adullam" illustration was originally used by Mr. Lincoln. When the dissatisfied anti-slavery men nominated Mr. Fremont for the Presidency, and a number of others who had personal reasons for opposing the re-nomination of Mr. Lincoln, the late President, in the course of a conversation with Colonel Deming, turned over the leaves of a Bible, which had just been given him by the negroes of Baltimore, and read, in his peculiar, slow, waggish tone, " And every one that was in distress, and every one that was in debt, and every one that was discontented, gathered themselves unto him; and he became a captain over them; and there were with him about four hundred men."

FOLLOWING AND LEADING.

Mr. Buckle, in his thoughtful *History of Civilization*, remarks: " In the present state of knowledge, Politics, so far from being a science, is one of the most backward of all the arts ; and the only safe course for the legislator is to look upon his craft as consisting in the adaptation of temporary contrivances to temporary emergencies. His business is to follow the age, and not at all to attempt to lead it. He should be satisfied with studying what is passing around him, and should modify his schemes, not according to the notions he has inherited from his fathers, but according to the actual exigencies of his own time. For he may rely upon it that the movements of society have now become so rapid that the wants of one generation are no measure of the wants of another ; and that men, urged by a sense of their own progress, are growing weary of idle talk about the wisdom of their ancestors, and are fast discarding those trite and sleepy maxims which have hitherto imposed upon them, but by which they will not consent to be much longer troubled."

LEGITIMACY AND GOVERNMENT.

It is an unguarded idea of some public writers that " the Sovereign holds her crown not by hereditary descent, but by the will of the nation." This doctrine is too frequently stated in and out of Parliament; and without qualification or explanation it would be apt to breed mischief in the minds of an ignorant and excited multitude, if the instinctive feelings of common sense did not invariably correct the popular errors of theorists.

"They who have studied the Constitution attentively hold that her Majesty reigns by hereditary right, though her predecessor in 1688 received the Crown at the hands of a free nation. To refer to the right of election, which can be exercised only during a revolution, and to be silent on hereditary right, is to lower the Regal dignity to the precarious office of the judges when they held their patents *durante bene placito*. Suppose a nation so divided that one casting vote would carry a plebiscite, changing the form of government, or the dynasty, and there would be a practical illustration of a principle—if principle at all—which, when taken as a broad palpable fact, is undeniable in the founder of a dynasty, but when erected into a legal theory, it becomes neither more nor less than a permanent code of revolution. Hence the successor of that founder, if his power be not supported by military despotism, is invariably a staunch advocate of his indefeasible hereditary right, though originally derived from the consent of the nation."—*Saturday Review*.

" MEASURES, NOT MEN."

Canning denounced what he calls the idle cant of " Measures, not men ;" the belief that " it is the harness, not the horses, which draw the chariot along;" and he affirmed, that to contend with Bonaparte, one great commanding spirit was worth all our preparations. Upon this Sir H. Bulwer says:—" Mr. Canning was right. No cant betrays more ignorance than that which affects to undervalue the qualities of public men in the march of public affairs. However circumstances may contribute to make individuals, individuals have as great a share in making circumstances. Had Queen Elizabeth been a weak and timid woman, we might now be speaking Spanish, and have our fates dependent on the struggle between Prim and Narvaez. Had James II. been a wise and prudent man, instead of the present cry against Irish Catholics, our saints of the day would have been spreading charges against the violence and perfidy of some Puritan Protestant; some English, or perhaps Scotch, O'Connell. Strip Mirabeau of his eloquence, endow Louis XVI. with the courage and the genius of Henry IV., and the history of the last eighty years might be obliterated."

A SUFFERER BY REVOLUTIONS.

A great sufferer by revolutions was King Louis of Bavaria, who abdicated after an insurrection in 1848, and died in 1868. He had seen his family extensively affected by the dynastic changes which had taken place since 1859. His second son is Otho, the ex-King of Greece, born on the 1st of June, 1815; his third, Luitpold, is married to the daughter of the Grand Duke of Tuscany; one of his daughters to the Duke of Modena; and one of his grandsons, or his youngest son Adalbert, was to have succeeded Otho on the throne of Greece. Lastly, the Queen of Naples and her sister, the Countess de Trani, belong to a collateral branch of the Royal family, that of Maximilian, Duke of Bavaria. The House of Wittelsbach has therefore suffered most materially from the revolutions of Germany, Italy, and Greece, and its members might give a second representation of the famous dinner at Venice mentioned in Voltaire's *Candide.*—*Le Temps.*

ORIGIN OF CROSS-READINGS IN NEWSPAPERS.

These amusing trifles are about a century old. Walpole writes, at the close of 1766, to George Montagu: " *Apropos*, have you seen that delightful paper composed out of scraps in the newspaper? I laughed till I cried, and literally burst out so loud that I thought Favre, who was waiting in the next room, would conclude I was in a fit. It is the newest piece of humour, except the *Bath Guide*, that I have seen of many years." It was entitled Cross Readings, or " A New Method of reading the Newspapers," by Caleb Whitefoord, " Papyrius Cursor," a signature which Dr. Johnson thought singularly happy, as the real name of an ancient Roman.

Walpole refers to it in 1789, as follows: " Mr. Fox, I am told, is better, but I have seen nobody that is particularly informed, though my house is well situated as a coffee-house, and I very seldom stir from the bar in the morning. I have no intelligence but from those who accidentally drop in, consequently my Gazette is commonly striped of two colours, as opposite as black and white, and, if repeated, would sound like the *cross readings* from newspapers. Truth is said to lie at the bottom of a well, to which I am sure at present there are two buckets, which clash so much that each brings up as much mud as pure grain. If I do not sift them, at least I do not retail one for the other."

Walpole has here misquoted. Cleanthes, the stoic, said that "truth was hid in a *pit.*" "Yes," was the reply, "but you Greek philosophers were the first that put her there, and then claimed so much merit to yourselves in drawing her out."

POLITICAL NICKNAMES.

Political nicknames were the light artillery of Cobbett, in his *Register*, perhaps never more felicitously applied than by this sarcastic politician, in the memorable instance, when, in 1825, the Right Hon. F. J. Robinson, as Chancellor of the Exchequer, boasted in Parliament of an expanded circulation exceeding by nearly 50 per cent. the amount in 1823. This was the era of "Prosperity Robinson" (afterwards first Earl of Ripon), who boasted of "dispensing the blessings of civilization from the portals of ancient monarchy." In the King's Speech of 1825, his Majesty said: "There never was a period in the history of the country when all the great interests of society were at the same time in so thriving a condition." But the sunshine was succeeded by the murkiest of gloom—"the Panic of 1825," when one-eighth of the country banks were ruined, and six of the London banks stopped payment; and the two years' increase in the circulating medium was annihilated in a few weeks. In contradistinction to Prosperity Robinson, Joseph Hume was called "Adversity Hume," owing to his constant presages of ruin and disaster to befal the people of Great Britain. Cobbett used to address Daniel O'Connell as *Big O.*

When, in 1821, Alderman Wood was reproached with having ill advised Queen Caroline, he diffidently admitted that his conduct might not be "*Absolute Wisdom*," by which distinction, for a considerable time, he was jocularly known.

Finality John was the somewhat too familiar *sobriquet* applied to Lord John Russell, who involuntarily proved the true prophet of the fate of his own measure: he it was who declared the *finality* of the Reform Bill; and when, in 1861, his lordship proposed to amend the law, the country took Lord John at his word, and by their indifference, pronounced the Reform Act to be final. Sydney Smith oddly said, that when Lord John visited the West of England after one of his political defeats on the Reform Bill, the country-people thought him of very small stature, which Sydney humorously attributed to these mortifications.

In December, 1834, a small party in the House of Commons was nicknamed by O'Connell as the *Derby Dilly*, " carrying six insides," the leader of whom was Lord Stanley, now Earl of Derby.

Lady Hester Stanhope tells us that Lord Chatham's first coachman being taken ill, the postillion was sent into the town for the family doctor; but he being from home the messenger brought with him Mr. Addington, who, by consent of Lord Chatham, attended the coachman. His lordship was so pleased with Mr. A. that he took him as apothecary for the servants, then for himself; and finding he spoke good sense on medicine, then on politics, he at last made him his physician. Dr. Addington, after practising in London for some time with distinction, retired to Reading, and there married; and in 1757, was born their eldest son, Henry Addington, afterwards Viscount Sidmouth. Hence his lordship's political *sobriquet* of " the Doctor ;" and in George Cruikshank's clever woodcut caricatures of the unpopular minister, made familiar to thousands of readers, illustrating the political squibs of William Hone, " the Doctor" invariably carries his professional insignia of the clyster bag and pipe. Little, it has been observed, did Walpole or anybody else foresee that the son of the empiric (Dr. Addington) should, within a few years after Walpole's death, be Prime Minister of England, and that his cant appellation (from his father's profession) would be that of " the Doctor !"

WASTE OF LIFE.

How cheaply life was held in former ages is shown in the records of the Lancaster and York feuds—a thorough family quarrel in its bitterness, its endurance, and its recklessness—in which relatives were killed by relatives after every battle. No regard was had to kinsmanship when the next-of-kin stood a captive adversary before the victor in the fight : the conquering Prince sent his chained cousins to the block, by dozens. The Plantagenets had no scruples about murdering their nearest connexions when these lay in their way and impeded their advance.

With later times came improved ideas. Henry VII. felt himself bound to find a reason for the killing of young Warwick, whose claims to the crown excited in him fear and disgust; but when Lady Arabella Stuart was in the hands of James, who had similar fears and feelings with regard to that descendant of the daughter of Henry VII., he only locked her up. But he did not escape imputation of poisoning her when she died : so recent were the times, or so fresh the memory of them, when such deeds were done on heirs presumptive. So, at a later period, James II. killed his nephew, Monmouth, after admitting him to an audience, which was tantamount to pardon, for the King's shadow casts grace where it falls; but the law, at all events, justified James. * * *

There are examples abroad where reigning sovereigns have killed their own sons. The Czar Peter would stand very uneasily at the Old Bailey if he could be tried there with respect to that little affair of his boy Alexis. Others, again, have for the mere luxury of the thing seized an unsuspecting prince, accused him of being a pretender, and murdered him right out, as Napoleon I. did in the person of the Duc d'Enghien, for whose bloody disposing-of he found so ready a Tyrrell, a Deighton, and a Forrest. Yet observe how ideas changed within a few years. The nephew of the same Napoleon invaded the kingdom of Louis-Philippe twice. The old king pardoned the first attempt, and placed the offender under mild restraint for the second; and by giving him life, afforded him his last and successfully-used opportunity to mount the throne and confiscate his predecessor's family property. It was to obviate such possible consequences that kings of old followed more rigorous courses, and found ready absolution if they only accomplished the course thoroughly.—Abridged from the *Athenæum.*

THE MONEY-COST OF WAR.

The standing armies of Europe amount to about six millions of men. What is it that this simple statement really means? Setting aside the agonies of maiming and of death, the tears of forlorn women, the desolation of households, and the hideous passions which wake up upon the battle-field, what is the actual material loss to humanity which is involved in the fact that six millions of men devote their lives to the business of war? It means that something very like the whole adult male population of Great Britain are withdrawn from the production of the materials of comfort and enjoyment, and make it the work of their lives not merely to cease from the production of what is essential to the well-being of their fellow-creatures, but to train themselves to inflict the utmost possible destruction of everything that may stand in the way of conquest.

At a moderate calculation, it may be said that war costs Europe about 500 millions sterling every year, by the mere withdrawing of heads and hands from the daily work by which the necessities and comforts of life are supplied. That is to say, a sum much exceeding half the national debt of Great Britain is annually thrown away in the form of the food, clothes, habitations, and luxuries which would otherwise have been created for the benefit of the world. The income tax for Great Britain and Ireland in the year 1865 produced about eight millions sterling. By more than sixty times that amount was Europe impoverished during the same year in order that a countless multitude of men might do nothing but prepare for the cutting each other's throats with the utmost practicable rapidity and on the largest possible scale. Further still, there is not only the loss which is the consequence of enforced idleness, but there is the actual annual expenditure upon each army and navy to be taken into account. Our own army and navy cost us about twenty-five millions sterling every year, exclusive of additional expenditure on such occasional trifles as the fortifications of Portsmouth and the Ise of Wight.

The destruction of the produce of human labour in the conflicts of actual war is tremendous. What are Virginia and South Carolina at this hour? What was England after the Wars of the Roses? What was half Europe at the end of the wars that were finally terminated at Waterloo? "Man marks the earth with ruin," sang Lord Byron, and he said few things so simply true and terrible. So that it is only with a very large qualification that it can be urged that our annual expenditure of twenty-five millions for fighting purposes is not a positive pauperizing of the nation to that same amount.

It is well now and then to remind ourselves that Europe annually throws away the power of producing as much as would support fifteen millions of families in the condition of the well-paid portion of the English peasantry. That wars will ever be brought to an end by such calculations can be expected by none but the blindest devotees to the pounds, shillings, and pence theory of human nature. It is, however, desirable every now and then to look over the balance-sheet of profit and loss, and see what we are doing with our money. Twenty-five millions spent yearly upon our army and navy means 20s. a week for about 500,000 families. Yet we dare not dismiss our soldiers and sailors to peaceful toils, because Europe has six millions of men under arms.—Abridged from the *Pall-mall Gazette.*

ABSOLUTE MONARCHY OF DENMARK.

Lord Molesworth, who resided, in 1660, as envoy of the King of England at the Court of Copenhagen, relates that in the above year the three States of Denmark, that is the Nobility, Clergy, and Commonalty being assembled in order to pay and disband the troops which had been employed against Sweden, the Nobility endeavoured to lay the whole burden on the Commons; while the latter, who had defended their country, their prince, and the nobility themselves, with the utmost bravery, insisted that the nobles, who enjoyed all the lands, should pay their share of the taxes, since they suffered less in the common calamity, and had done less to prevent its progress.

The Commons were then officially informed that they were slaves to the nobility, but the word *slaves* not being relished by the clergy and burghers, they, on consultation, determined, as the most effectual way to bring the nobility to their senses, and to remedy the disorders of the state, "to add to the power of the King, and render his crown hereditary." The nobles were in a general state of consternation at the suddenness of this proposal, but the two other states—the clergy and commons—were not to be wrought upon by smooth speeches, explanations, and appeals for time and delay. The bishop made a long speech in praise of his Majesty, and concluded with offering him an *hereditary* and absolute dominion. The King returned them his thanks; but observed that the concurrence of the nobles was necessary. The nobles, "filled with the apprehensions of being all massacred," were now in a great hurry to confirm the decision of the two other states; but the King would not allow of such cowardly precipitation, and consequently, with all the formalities, on the 27th of October, 1660, "the homage of all the senators, nobility, clergy, and commons was received by the King; this was "performed on their knees, each taking an oath faithfully to promote his Majesty's interests in all things, and to serve him faithfully, as became hereditary subjects." One Gersdorff, a principal senator, expressed a wish that his Majesty's successors might "follow the example his Majesty would undoubtedly set them, and make use of that unlimited power for the good, and not the prejudice of his subjects." "The nobles," continues Molesworth, "were called over by name, and ordered to subscribe the oath they had taken, which they all did. Thus, in four days' time, the Kingdom of Denmark was changed from a state, but little different from that of aristocracy, to that of an unlimited monarchy, and the kettle-drums and trumpets which are ranged before the palace, proclaim aloud the very minute when the King sits down to table.'

" What is most admirable with respect to Denmark are its laws, which are founded on equity, and are remarkable for their justice, perspicuity, and brevity. These are contained in *one quarto volume*, wrote in the language of the country, with such plainness that every man who can read is capable of understanding his own case, and pleading it too, if he pleases, without the assistance of either an attorney or of counsel."
—T. J. Buckton, *Notes and Queries*, 3rd S., No. 114.

INVASION PANICS OF 1847-8 AND 1851.

The first of these Panics originated in the publication of a letter addressed to Sir John Burgoyne, Inspector-General of Fortifications, by the Duke of Wellington, who exposed the defenceless state of the country, which thus produced a great sensation, and no doubt enabled the Executive to stay the progress of dangerous retrenchments in the naval and military services, and eventually to obtain power to raise a new Militia.

Upon this famous letter Mr. Cobden, in a pamphlet published by him in 1862, states the public had never been fully informed of the circumstances which led to its publication, and which he thus proceeds to narrate:

" In a pamphlet which appeared in France, just previous to the opening of the session of 1848, written by M. Chevalier, who had already devoted his accomplished pen to the cause of the Anglo-French alliance, the Duke's letter had been treated in the character of an answer to Prince Joinville's publication. This drew from Lord John Russell an explanation in the House, on the authority of the Duke himself, in which he said that, ' nothing could have given greater pain,' to the writer, ' than the publication of sentiments which he had expressed confidentially to a brother officer.' It was stated by Lord Palmerston, at a subsequent date, that the letter was written 'in consequence of an able memorandum drawn up by Sir John Burgoyne.' Whoever gave it to the world must have assumed that it would possess an authority above criticism ; otherwise, it contains passages which would have induced a friend to withhold it from publication. The concluding sentence, where, in speaking of himself, he says, 'I am bordering upon seventy-seven years of age, passed in honour,' affords sufficient proof that it was not intended for the public eye. The entire production, indeed, gives painful evidence of enfeebled powers. One extract will be sufficient ; the italics are not in the original : 'I am accustomed to the consideration of these questions, and have examined and reconnoitred, over and over again, the whole coast from the North Foreland, by Dover, Folkestone, Beachy Head, Brighton, Arundel, to Selsey Bill, near Portsmouth ; and I say that, excepting immediately under the fire of Dover Castle, *there is not a spot on the coast on which infantry might not be thrown on shore at any time of tide, with any wind, and in any weather,* and from which such body of infantry so thrown on shore would not find within a distance of five miles a road into the interior of the country, *through the cliffs,* practicable for the march of a body of troops.' Now, any person who has been in the habit of visiting Eastbourne and Hastings, knows that for half the year no prudent mariner brings his vessel within several miles of that coast, and that there is a considerable extent of shore where a landing is at all times impracticable. It may be safely affirmed, that if any one but the Duke of Wellington had stated that there was any shore in the world, on which a body of troops could be landed 'at any time of the tide, with any wind, and in any weather,' the statement would have been deemed undeserving of notice. The assertion, however, passed unchallenged at the time, and the entire letter was quoted as an unanswerable proof that the country was in danger. To have ventured on criticism or doubt would have only invited the accusation of want of patriotism."

The Panic of 1851 led to the introduction of a Militia Bill, under the administration of Lord Derby, although the bill was in substance the measure of Lord Palmerston, who advocated it much more boldly than the Government. Mr. Cobden, however, says of it :—" Falling back on his own idea of steam navigation having given an advantage to our neighbour, or, to use his favourite phrase, having 'thrown a bridge across the Channel,' Lord Palmerston now insisted on the practicability of 50,000 or 60,000 men being transported, without notice, from Cherbourg to our shores in a single night. Such a declaration had not been before heard from one holding high rank in that House. It overleapt all reliance on our diplomacy or our fleets ; and, strange enough in one who had offered such eager congratulations to the author of the *coup-d'état,* the assumption of such a danger as this implied that our neighbour was little better than a buccaneer. But this hypothesis of sudden invasion is absolutely indispensable for affording the alarmists any standing ground whatever. Take away the liability to surprise, by admitting the necessity of a previous ground of quarrel, and the delays of a diplomatic correspondence, and you have time to collect your fleet and drill an army."

Indeed, Lord Palmerston went so far as to say: "The very ship despatched to convey to this country intelligence of the threatened armament would probably not reach our shores much sooner than the hostile expedition."

Mr. Cobden, on the other hand, maintained that time could be insured to drill an army to receive the invaders; and quoted a corroborative remark from Lord Hardinge. "Give me," said the Commander-in-Chief before the Sebastopol Committee, "a good stout man; and let us have him for sixty days to train him, and he will be as good a soldier as you can have."

SEEKING A PLACE.

Grund, in his sketches of *American Aristocracy*, relates: One morning, scarcely a fortnight after General Jackson's arrival at the White House, a shabby-genteel looking man presented himself at his parlour, and after the usual salutation of shaking hands, expressed his joy at seeing the venerable old gentleman at last hold the situation of Chief Magistrate of the country, to which his bravery, his talents, and his unimpeachable rectitude fully entitled him. "We have had a hard time of it," said he, "in our little place; but our exertions were unremitting; I myself went round to stimulate my neighbours, and at last the victory was ours. We beat them by a majority of ten votes, and I now behold the result of this glorious triumph." The General thanked him in terms of studied politeness, assuring him that he would resign his office in an instant if he did not think his election gave satisfaction to a vast majority of the people; and at least regretted that his admirer's zeal for the public weal should have been so severely taxed on his account. "Oh! no matter for that, sir," said he, "I did it with pleasure, I did it for myself and for my country" (the General bowed); "and I now come to congratulate you on your success" (the General bowed again). "I thought, sir," continued he, "that as you are now President of the United States, I might be useful to you in some official capacity." (The General looked somewhat embarrassed). "Pray, sir, have you already made choice of your cabinet ministers?" "I have," was the reply of the General. "Well, no matter for that, I shall be satisfied with an embassy to Europe."—"I am sorry to say there is no vacancy."—"Then you will, perhaps, require a head clerk in the department of state?"—"These are generally appointed by the respective secretaries."—"I am very sorry for that: then I must be satisfied with some inferior appointment."—"I never interfere with these, you must address yourself to the heads of departments."—"But, could I not be the postmaster in Washington? Only think, General, how I worked for you!"—"I am much obliged to you for the good opinion you entertain of me, and for your kind offices at the last election; but the postmaster for the city of Washington is already appointed."—"Well, I don't particularly care for that; I should be satisfied with being his clerk."—"This is a subject you must mention to the postmaster."—"Why, then, General," exclaimed the disappointed candidate for offices, "*haven't you got an old black coat?*" You may well imagine that the General gave him one.

THE MODERN GREEKS.

Public opinion in England has altered its estimate of the Greek people several times during the last sixty years. In the early part of the century we were too busily engaged in wrestling with Bonaparte to inquire whether the Moslem was justified in enslaving the Christian. The only question we asked was, "Are you for the French, or for us?" When the Turks sided against the French we supported them; when they sided with the French, we attacked them. In those days Englishmen visited Greece in two characters only. They went either as traders or antiquaries. As traders they merely touched at the maritime towns, and limited their inquiries to the state of the currant crop; as antiquaries, they went about measuring temples and theatres, and, as has been justly observed, "pronounced the people vile and base if every unfortunate peasant and every ignorant priest did not exhibit the valour of a Brasidas and the wisdom of a Solon." In fact, the sympathies of these enthusiasts too often stopped short at the date of the battle of Chæronea; they regarded the subsequent twenty centuries as an uninteresting record of Macedonian, Roman, Byzantine, Venetian, and Ottoman subjugation. But a change was at hand. The Greeks had always fretted under their slavery, had always cherished the intention of recovering their ancient independence, and the time had arrived for striking a decisive blow. For more than a century the political power of the Turks had been gradually waning, and, in addition to this, while the Greeks had advanced together with the rest of Europe in commercial enterprise and general cultivation, their masters remained immersed in their original barbarism.

In 1821, the Greek Revolution began, and immediately all the ardent youth of England became philo-Hellenes. Hundreds of men and women are yet among us who can remember how their hearts vibrated with triumphant joy or indignant sorrow as successive items of news arrived from the seat of revolt. Nor were their sympathies confined to words only. Money was liberally subscribed, and numerous volunteers flocked to the scene of action, who atoned by their enthusiasm for their lack of military skill. The most famous poet of the day was numbered among the crusading band, but, though death speedily put an end to his new career, he did not die until his preconceived ideas of Hellenic patriotism had received a rude disenchantment. "Of the Greeks," he wrote mournfully, "I can't say much good hitherto, and I do not like to speak ill of them, though they do of one another." The truth was that the crusaders had pitched their expectations too high. They fancied that a people who had been enslaved for 2000 years would suddenly display the military skill of Miltiades and the virtue of Aristides. In place of this they found that the insurgent chiefs were principally occupied in schemes of personal aggrandizement, and that patriotism of an enlarged type was almost unknown to them. Petro Bey plainly told Lord Byron that the true way to save Greece was to lend him (the Bey) a thousand pounds. Moreover, the war was conducted on both sides with the utmost savagery. While the Turks massacred their thousands in Cyprus and Chios, the Greeks retaliated at the capture of Athens by butchering every Moslem woman and child who was not rescued by French intervention.

But, besides these grander crimes, the Greeks were found to be financially dishonest. They borrowed money from the confiding English, squandered and jobbed it away, and paid neither principal nor interest. They set up Capo d'Istrias, one of their purest patriots, as President, and presently assassinated him. At last they obtained a young German Prince—Otho of Bavaria—and made him King in 1833. For some time after this we troubled ourselves but little about the Greeks until 1850, when Admiral Parker blockaded the Piræus, ostensibly to enforce the claims of the redoubtable Don Pacifico, but in reality to check the intrigues of Russia. The Crimean War followed, during which Greek sympathies were naturally still more strongly enlisted in favour of their co-religionists. At last came another revolution. The Greeks grew weary of their Bavarian ruler, and bade him depart. Compared with the first revolution, however, the second was as the report of a popgun to the thunder of a 68-pounder. It might almost be said to have been made in rose-water, and, as such, was an encouraging proof of the calming effect of thirty years' independence. There were no terrible wrongs to redress, no irreconcilable foes to exterminate; there was simply a good deal of discontent, more or less well-founded, and the Greek nation determined to solve the difficulty by sending poor Otho back to Bavaria.

We believe that at the present time the Greeks are more justly estimated than at any former period. We no longer regard them as a race of resuscitated demigods, nor as a set of venal brigands and pirates. We no longer regard them as unadulterated descendants of the old Hellenic stock, nor as a tribe of ethnological impostors, masquerading under classical names. We think that, like the Greeks of old, they have their virtues and their failings; and that, though undoubtedly commingled with other races, the genuine Greek type still remains predominant, just as an Englishman is still an Englishman, though Celtic and Norman blood flow in his veins with the original Anglo-Saxon.—*Times* journal.

To this unsparing *exposé* we may add Byron's memorable lines on the decadence of this famous nation of antiquity :—

> 'Twere long to tell, and sad to trace,
> Each step from splendour to disgrace.

" SIGHTS THAT I HAVE SEEN."

The Rev. Mr. Dutens, in 1811, published a work with the above title, whence the following are extracts :

" I have seen a King imprisoned by his son ;* five Emperors mas-

---

* Victor, King of Sardinia. in 1782.

sacred ;* five Kings assassinated ;† six Kings deposed ;‡ five Republics annihilated ;§ a great kingdom effaced from the map of Europe.| I have seen England lose in eight years half North America, after possessing it for more than a century. I have seen her (verifying the sentiment of an ancient, that the empire of the sea gives that of the land) take the Cape of Good Hope and the island of Ceylon from the Dutch ; Malta, Egypt, and several colonies, from the French. I have seen her dictate the law to the King of Denmark at Copenhagen, and carry her victorious arms into the most remote parts of the world. I have seen this same England, in 1780, resist the combined efforts of Europe, of America, and of the Northern powers, who formed an armed neutrality against her maritime dominions; I have seen her, in the revolutionary war, often destitute of allies and alone, opposing the enormous power of France, of Italy, of Denmark, and of Russia.¶ I have seen the son of an English gentleman go out to India, as writer to a mercantile company (but quitting this service when very young to embrace the military life), afterwards rising to the head of the army, dethrone a powerful Prince in the East, place another on his throne, conquer a part of Hindostan, and raise the British dominions in that quarter to the preeminence it now enjoys.**

" I have seen what has no example in history, a little Corsican gentleman conquer Italy; force the Emperor of Germany to make a disgraceful peace ;†† take Malta in two days; Egypt in a month; return from thence, and place himself on the throne of the Bourbons, and all in less than four years (from May, 1796, to November, 1799).

" I have seen him transport his army and artillery in the midst of winter over the most difficult pass of the Alps, and in a single battle ‡‡ decide at once the fate of Germany and of Italy. I have seen the same Corsican gentleman order the Pope to Paris, in 1804, to crown him Emperor of the French, and afterwards depose this same Pope, and deprive him of the temporal possessions which his ancestors had enjoyed for more than 1000 years.§§

" I have seen him declare himself King of Italy. I have seen him braving a formidable league which was directed against him, march to

---

* Peter III., John VI., Paul I., Emperors of Russia ; Selim III. in July, 1803, and Mustapha IV., Nov. 17, 1808, Emperors of Constantinople.

† Joseph, King of Portugal ; Louis XV., Louis XVI., and Louis XVII., Kings of France ; Gustavus III., King of Sweden, in 1792.

‡ Stanislaus Poniatowski, King of Poland. The King of Sardinia, December 10, 1798. Ferdinand IV., King of Naples ; Charles IV. ; Ferdinand VII., King of Spain, May, 1808 ; and Gustavus IV.

§ Holland, Sweden, Venice, Genoa, and Lucca.

| The kingdom of Poland.

¶ After the treaty of Luneville.

** Lord Clive, from 1747 to 1767.

†† The peace of Campo Formio, on the 17th of October, 1797 : preliminaries were signed April 17, 1797, at Leoben.

‡‡ At Marengo, on the 14th of June, 1800, after having passed the Great St. Bernard.

§§ In December, 1809.

Vienna, and even into Hungary, in six weeks; give the law three times to the Emperor of Germany,* compel him to abdicate the Imperial crown of the Cæsars, deprive him of a part of his dominions; force the Emperor of Russia twice to retire,† and soon after oblige him to march to his assistance against the Emperor of Austria.

"I have seen him destroy the power of the King of Prussia in fifteen days, and strike all Europe with dismay: I have seen him dethrone five Kings,‡ and create eight others;§ annex Holland to France,‖ dictate to Spain as if it were one of his provinces, employ her forces as his own, and at last take possession of the whole kingdom. In short, I have seen him extend his dominion farther than that of Charlemagne, and find nothing could resist his ambition but the King of Great Britain; sometimes alone against the whole host of European power, and sometimes with the troops of the Continent in his pay."

Had Mr. Dutens lived but a few years longer, how greatly might he have increased this long list! He would have seen Great Britain, aided only by raw troops, drive the veterans of France before her armies, through the Peninsula, freeing Portugal and Spain, and carrying her victorious arms even into France itself.

MORGANATIC MARRIAGES.

Dr W. Bell has communicated to *Notes and Queries*, 3rd S., No. 116, a paper, wherein he says: "For *Morganatic*, the best, in fact, the only solution is found in the derivation of the word. When in the arid deserts of Arabia the parched traveller is mocked by the optical delusions of running streams and green meadows; these the Italians call *Fata Morgana*, the delusions of the Morgana. Something thus delusive is a Morganatic marriage. For though it involves no immorality, and has always the full sanction of the Church, it is, as regards the wife and children, an illusion and a make-believe. They do not enjoy the rights of the husband, if a sovereign prince, nor take his title; and it is only among sovereign princes that the practice obtains. The children have only the rights of the mother, unless she is *ebenbürtig*, or, as is expressed in the closing act of the Treaty of Vienna, 1815, *d'une naissance égale avec les princes souverains*, or those in succession to become so.

"It was, therefore, a prudent arrangement for princes who preferred the claims of natural affection to those of ambition, to form a Mor-

---

* By the treaties of Campio Formio, 1797; of Luneville, 9th of February, 1801; and of Vienna, 14th of October, 1809.

† At Austerlitz, the 2nd of December, 1805, and by the peace of Tilsit, the 8th of July, 1807.

‡ The Kings of France, of Naples, and Sardinia, and two Kings of Spain, Charles IV. and Ferdinand VII.

§ The Kings of Etruria, of Italy, of Naples, of Holland, of Bavaria, of Wurtemberg, of Saxony, and of Westphalia.

‖ The 15th of December, 1809, the day of the most ceremonious and extraordinary divorce which is mentioned in history.

ganatic marriage, which would reconcile the duties of their station with their social wishes. In this manner, after the death of his first wife, the Princess of Mecklenburg-Strelitz, Frederic William III., father of the present and previous King of Prussia, was enabled to follow the dictates of his affection for the Countess of Liegnitz, who was received by all his family as a true wife, and still continues to enjoy their respect. In a similar manner, the last King of Denmark associated to himself and ennobled the Countess Danner. Nor would, in our country, the union of the late Duke of Sussex with the Duchess of Inverness be dissimilar. The social position of all three families was affected in no disreputable manner by such a connexion, but they could not attain the full rights of marriage or the civil state of their husbands, because they were not *ebenbürtig* or *de naissance égale.*

" In the Golden Bull of the Empire promulgated in the fourteenth century, legitimacy is expressly demanded as an imperative condition to any sovereignty ; and it is of no consequence how long or how distant that stain may have blemished a family. Our ducal houses of Grafton and St. Albans have every right of their high rank, but in their royal quarterings the bar sinister is indelible."

CHARACTER OF THE NABOB.

The Nabob, from *naib*, in the popular language of India, is defined by Sir Thomas Herbert, in his Travels, published in 1634, as " a nobleman in the language of the Mogul's kingdom, which hath mixed up with much of the Persian." The term, applied to a man grown rich in India and returning to England, became familiar enough, and was frequently a character upon our stage. Dr. Knox, in his *Spirit of Despotism*, thus portrays the class of men to which the Nabob belonged. Speaking of the ideas imbibed in youth, in the East Indies, as unfavourable to liberty, our essayist remarks :—" Enriched at an early age, the adventurer returns to England. His property admits him to the higher circles of fashionable life. He aims at rivalling or excelling all the old nobility in the splendour of his mansions, the finery of his carriages, the number of his liveried train, the profusion of his table, in every unmanly indulgence which an empty vanity can covet, and a full purse procure. Such a man, when he looks from the window of his superb mansion and sees the people pass, cannot endure the idea that they are of as much consequence as himself in the eye of the law ; and that he dares not insult or oppress the unfortunate being who rakes his kennel, or sweeps his chimney."

We find a satirical portrait of the *Nabob* in the *New Monthly Magazine* of thirty years since. The writer is describing the clubmen of the Oriental, in Hanover-square. " From the outside the club-house looks like a prison ; enter it—it looks like an hospital, in which a smell of curry-powder pervades the 'wards,' wards filled with venerable patients, dressed in nankeen shorts, yellow stockings and gaiters, and faces to match. *There* may still be seen pigtails in all their pristine perfection. It is the region of calico shirts, returned writers, and guinea-pigs grown into bores. Such is the *Nabobbery* into which Harley-street, Wimpole-street, and Gloucester-place, daily empty their precious stores of bilious humanity."

Macaulay, in his masterly paper on the great Lord Clive, portrays the Nabob of a century since, in his fearful picture of the singular atrocity of "the Black Hole," when the answer to the poor captives, who strove to bribe their gaolers, was, that nothing could be done without the Nabob's orders; that the Nabob was asleep, and that he would be angry if anybody woke him. Nor did the horrors of that night awake either pity or remorse in the bosom of the savage Nabob. The Nabobs were native princes, though in the conquest of India they stood to the British authorities in the same relation in which the last drivelling Chilperics and Childerics of the Merovingian line stood to their able and vigorous Mayors of the Palace, to Charles Martel and to Pepin. Then the great events which had taken place in India, had called into existence a new class of Englishmen, to whom their countrymen gave the name of Nabobs. These persons, whom Knox has so well characterized, soon became a most unpopular class of men. "That they had sprung from obscurity," says Macaulay; "that they had acquired great wealth; that they exhibited it insolently; that they spent it extravagantly; that they raised the price of everything in the neighbourhood, from fresh eggs to rotten boroughs; that their liveries outshone those of dukes; that their coaches were finer than that of the Lord Mayor; that the examples of their large and ill-governed households corrupted half the servants in the country; that some of them, with all their magnificence, could not catch the tone of good society; but, in spite of the studs, the crowd of menials, of the plate and the Dresden china, of the venison and Burgundy, were still low men. These things excited—both in the class from which they had sprung, and the class into which they attempted to force themselves—the bitter aversion which is the effect of mingled envy and contempt. But when it was also rumoured that the fortune which had enabled its possessor to eclipse the Lord-Lieutenant on the race-ground, or to carry the county against the head of a house as old as Domesday Book, had been accumulated by violating public faith; by deposing legitimate princes; by reducing whole provinces to beggary, all the higher and better, as well as all the low and evil parts of human nature, were stirred against the wretch who had obtained by guilt and dishonour the riches which he now lavished with arrogant and inelegant profusion. The unfortunate Nabob seemed to be made up of those foibles against which comedy has pointed the most merciless ridicule; and of those crimes which have thrown the deepest gloom over tragedy, of Turcaret and Nero, of Monsieur Jourdain and Richard the Third. A tempest of execration and derision, such as can be compared only to that outbreak of public feeling against the Puritans, which took place at the time of the Restoration, burst on the servants of the Company. The humane man was horror-struck at the way in which they had got their money; the thrifty man at the way in which they spent it. The Dilettante sneered at their want of taste; the Maccaroni blackballed them as

T 2

vulgar fellows. Writers, the most unlike in sentiment and style, Methodists and libertines, philosophers and buffoons, were for once on the same side. It is hardly too much to say that, during a space of about thirty years, the whole lighter literature of England was coloured by the feelings which we have described. Foote brought on the stage an Anglo-Indian chief, dissolute, ungenerous, and tyrannical, ashamed of the humble friends of his youth, hating the aristocracy, yet childishly eager to be numbered among them; squandering his wealth on panders and flatterers, tricking out his chairmen with the most costly hothouse flowers, and astounding the ignorant with jargon about rupees, lacs, and jaghires. Mackenzie, with more delicate humour, depicted a plain country family raised by the Indian acquisitions of one its members to sudden opulence, and exciting derision by an awkward mimicry of the manners of the great. Cowper, in that lofty expostulation which glows with the very spirit of the Hebrew poets, places the oppression of India foremost in the list of those national crimes for which God had punished England with years of disastrous war, with discomfiture in her own seas, and with the loss of her transatlantic empire. If any of our readers will take the trouble to search in the dusty recesses of circulating libraries, for some novel published sixty years ago, the chance is that the villain or sub-villain of the story will prove to be a savage old Nabob, with an immense fortune, a tawny complexion, a bad liver, and a worse heart." This is Macaulay Severus.

MEMORY OF DANIEL O'CONNELL.

A tourist, who visited O'Connell's residence, in Ireland, not long after the Liberator had been gathered to his fathers, gives the following touching picture of the place:—" The wild ruin of the house where Daniel was born stands in an admirable situation for smuggling, and so does the abbey; and the legend runs that the facility was abundantly used. Smuggling is quite over now, as the coast-guard tell with a sigh. And agitation is over too. So the one house stands a ruin, and the other is rotting away in damp and neglect. It is inhabited; it is even filled with company at times; but not the less forlorn in its appearance, when seen from a nearer point than the mountain roads, choked by its own woods, which grow almost up to the windows, stained with damp, out of joint, unrepaired, unrenewed: it is a truly melancholy spectacle. Melancholy to all eyes, it is most so to the minds of those who can go beyond a quarter of a century and hear again the shouts which hailed the advent of the Liberator, and see again the reverent enthusiasm which watched him from afar, when he rested at Derrynane from his toils, and went to hunt among the hills, or cruise about his bay. Now, there is his empty yacht in the sound, and his chair in the chapel covered with black cloth. All else that he enjoyed there, in his vast wealth of money, fame, and popular love, seems to be dropping away to destruction. It is said that his name is scarcely ever mentioned in Ireland now. When the news of his death arrived, there was grief for three or four days, and then he seemed to be forgotten."

Ecclesiastical History.

SPURIOUS CHARTERS.

CHARTERS require to be examined and investigated with much care. If authentic, they are the best possible guides to history; if spurious, the most mischievous deluders. Worldly interest often tempted the monks to commit forgery, though their falsifications were chiefly defensive. Lands which unquestionably belonged to the Church were frequently held merely by prescriptive possession, unaccompanied by deeds and charters. The right was lawful, but there were no means of proving the right. And when the monastery was troubled and impleaded by the Norman Justitiar, or the *Soke* invaded by the Norman Baron, the Abbot and his brethren would have recourse to the pious fraud of inventing a charter for the purpose of protecting property which, however lawfully acquired and honestly enjoyed, was likely to be wrested from them by the captious niceties of the Norman jurisprudence or the greedy tyranny of the Norman sword. These counterfeits are sometimes detected by the pains which were taken to give them currency. It is familiarly known that the Anglo-Saxons confirmed their deeds by subscribing the sign of the cross, and that the charters themselves are fairly but plainly engrossed upon parchment. But instead of imitating these unostentatious instruments, the elaborate forgers often endeavoured to obtain respect for their fabrications by investing them with as much splendour as possible ; and those grand crosses of gold, vermilion, and azure, which dazzled the eyes and deceived the judgment of the court when produced before a bench of simple and unsuspecting lawyers, now reveal the secret fraud to the lynx-eyed antiquary. According to Ingulphus these modes of adornment prevailed long before the reign of the Confessor. The foundation charter of Croyland, purporting to have been granted by Ethelbald, is richly adorned, from whence it obtained the name of the "Golden Charter," and the ancient chirographs, gay with paintings and illuminations, and the charters of the Mercian kings covered with embellishments, are enumerated by him amongst the treasures which were consumed when the monastery was destroyed by fire in the year 1091.[*] But we can state, upon the information of the most competent living authority, that there is no charter of this descrip-

---

[*] The Croyland charter, in Saxon characters, in the possession of Robert Hunter, Esq., lord of the place, was shown to the Society of Antiquaries, as appears by their minutes, by Mr. Lethellier, in 1734.—(Gough's *Croyland*, Pref. viii.) In the opinion of Humphry Wanley, "it was not much older, if anything at all, than Henry II.'s time." The fac-simile given by Hickes (*Dissertatio Epistolaris*, tab. D) does not leave the slightest doubt of the imposture.

tion which is not manifestly spurious. The "Golden Charter" bears the impress of falsity; and unless it be supposed that all the genuine illuminated charters in England perished by sympathy when those at Croyland felt the flame, we must infer that the writer of the history of Ingulphus erred either through ignorance or design.—*Quarterly Review.*

THE INQUISITION.

Endless was the catalogue of most pious men and eminent scholars who underwent purification as it was termed, in this den of superstition and tyranny. The culprit was not permitted to speak with his attorney except in the presence of the inquisitor, and a notary who took notes and certified what passed; and so far from the names of the informer or of the witnesses being supplied, everything that could facilitate the explanation of them was expunged from the declarations; and the prisoners, one and all, in their dungeons, might truly exclaim with Fray Luis de Leon, "I feel the pain, but see not the hand which inflicts it." Even in the early days of the Inquisition, torture was carried to such an extent, that Sixtus IV., in a brief published Jan. 29, 1482, could not refrain from deploring the well-known truth, in lamentations which were re-echoed from all parts of Christendom. The formula of the sentence of torture began thus, *Christo nomine invocato;* and it was therein expressed that the torture should endure as long as it pleased the Inquisitors; a protest was also added, that if during the torture the culprit should die, or be maimed, or if effusion of blood, or mutilation of limb should ensue, the fault should be chargeable to the culprit, and not to the Inquisitors. The culprit was bound by an oath of secrecy, strengthened by fearful penalties, not to divulge anything that he had seen, known, or heard in the dismal precincts of that unholy tribunal— a secrecy illegal and tyrannical, but which constituted the soul of that monstrous association, and by which its judges were sheltered against all responsibility.

In *Don Quixote* are various passages which are levelled at the abominable tyranny of the Inquisition, the absurd doctrines of flagellation, and the vices and frauds of Papal Rome. The disenchantment of Dulcinea by the whipping of Sancho, has an evident reference to what was then a great source of wealth to the clergy, who exacted large sums from the opulent, under the pretence of self-inflicted flagellations, to compensate for the sins of those who could afford to pay for the compromise. There were, however, some who inflicted this penance on themselves with real severity. The great Lope de Vega, then Secretary of the Inquisition, is said to have died of the effects of the self-applied discipline. Sancho, at first, objects to it; he does not see what his penance and sufferings can have to do with the sins and transgressions of others. But as soon as he is to be paid for every lash, he undergoes the penance like a true friar, taking care so to manage it, as he intimates the priests did their flagellations, as not to feel any pain from it.

What shall we say of the Quixotism of Cervantes in thus boldly attacking this abuse, amidst a credulous laity attached to it, and a knavish clergy interested in the continuance of the imposition? The adventure of the *speaking head,* which Cervantes tells us " was broken in pieces by order of those watchful sentinels of our faith, the gentlemen of the Inquisition," and that of the *prophesying ape,* as to whom Don Quixote expresses his surprise that he has not been accused before the Inquisition, *and examined by torture,* till he confessed by what or whom he divines —are both levelled at the Inquisition. In that of the restoration of Altisidora to life, Sancho Panza was dressed in the ridiculous suit which was worn at the stake by the victims of the Inquisition, as Cervantes himself tells us. Even if he had not risked the observation, the allusion would have been obvious, in comparing the account of Sancho's dress, with the following account of the execution of the Bohemian martyr, John Huss, who was burnt alive in 1415, for holding that in the eucharist, the wine as well as the bread ought to be administered to the laity,—"They put a paper coronet on his head, on which they painted three devils, with this inscription, an *arch heretic ;*" and said, " we devote thy soul to the infernal devils." When the painted paper was put on his head, one of the bishops said, " now we commit thy soul to the devil." At the stake the paper crown falling off his head, the soldiers put it on again, saying, " that it must be burnt with the devils whom he served." The devoting of the soul of their victim to the infernal devils was *pro salute animæ.* On these painted flames and painted devils, however, Sancho sarcastically observes, " Well enough yet ! these do not burn me, nor do these carry me away." Sancho's account of his own orthodoxy is very Catholic:—I " believe in all that our Holy Church prescribes ; and I mortally hate all Jews and heretics." What, however, this original and inimitable author might have done, and how far, in his display of the corruptions of Papal Rome, he would have surpassed all that Lucian has said on the follies and absurdities of polytheism, may be conjectured from an anecdote in the *Segrasiana:* upon the French ambassador complimenting Cervantes on the wit and humour of Don Quixote, he replied, " I would have made it much more diverting if I had not been afraid of the Inquisition."

FIGHTING ABBOTS AND PRELATES OF THE MIDDLE AGES.

In the lively pages of Froissart we find some brilliant episodes of the military Abbots and Prelates of the Middle Ages. We have all heard of Odo, Bishop of Bayeux, who, at the battle of Hastings,

Un baston teneit en son poing.

Philip de Dreux, Bishop of Beauvais, beat down with a mace, at the battle of Bouvines, Longsword, Earl of Salisbury. This was the same bishop whose bloody hauberk King Richard I. sent to the Pope with the message, " This have we found. Know now whether it be thy son's coat or no !" The Archbishop of Sens was killed at Agincourt. An

Abbot who defended the town of Hainecourt in 1339, seems to have had the spirit and strength of Friar Tuck. He was a very bold and valiant man in arms, says Froissart, and was seen in the front rank dealing and receiving blows. In an encounter at the barriers of the town, my lord Abbot seized the spear of Messire Henri de Flandre, and drew it through the clefts of the palisade. Then he got hold of the knight's arm, and drew it through as far as the shoulder, and would have drawn him in altogether if the opening had been wide enough. "I assure you," says Froissart, "that the said Messire Henri was not at his ease while the Abbot thus held him, for the Abbot was strong and fierce, and pulled at him without sparing him. On the other hand, the knights pulled against him to rescue Messire Henri; and this wrestling and pulling continued a long time, so that Messire Henri was much hurt." At last he was rescued, but the Abbot kept his spear. The same author speaks of great feats of arms performed by a churchman who wielded a two-handed sword. The clergy imitated or even excelled the laity, not only in strength and skill in arms, but also in appetite for blood and plunder. Henry Spenser, Bishop of Norwich, *militiæ quam theologiæ peritior*, raised an army, with the sanction of King Richard II., to fight for Pope Urban against the rival Pope Clement. The popularity of the Bishop and the holiness of the cause enabled him to collect an army rapidly. They sailed from Sandwich to Calais, where they were to wait for Sir William Beauchamp, whom the King had appointed to command. But the Bishop soon grew tired of inactivity. He was determined to fight some one; and as it was not convenient to attack France with his small force, he announced his intention of leading it against Flanders, although the Count of Flanders was Urbanist like himself, and he was engaged to make war on Clementines only. But the Bishop was not to be disappointed. His army marched into Gravelines, where they attacked and pillaged a church, and killed a great many men, women, and children, who had taken refuge there. They became masters of the town, where they found themselves in very pleasant quarters. The Bishop next led them against Dunkirk. An officer remonstrated, urging that the people of Dunkirk were Urbanists. "How do we know that?" asked the Bishop. The officer begged that a herald might be sent to inquire. A herald was sent, but he was killed by the country people in ignorance. The Bishop was delighted. Here was a good *casus belli*. He attacked Dunkirk, and carried it with great slaughter of the Dunkirkers. Afterwards he made himself master of all the coast from Gravelines to Sluys, and laid siege to Ypres. The King of France now assembled a great army, which caused the Bishop to raise the siege and retire to Calais, whence he returned to England. He was fined and disgraced for having so badly expended the Pope's money.—*Saturday Review*, 1868.

ASSASSINATION OF THOMAS A'BECKET.

In the *Quarterly Review*, No. 186, the circumstances attending the murder of this bold priest have been carefully collated, and present some new researches. Contrary to the received notion, Becket was not killed in front of the altar of Canterbury Cathedral; he was slain in the choir confronting his pursuers, when they succeeded in arresting his flight upwards to the sacrosanct chapel of St. Blaise, in the roof of the cathedral. The assassins had challenged him, on the part of Henry, in the course of the afternoon, and a long-continued angry altercation had passed between them in the presence of the monks, who surrounded their archbishop, in his private chamber. When the murderers left to get their arms, the monks hurried Becket by the cloisters into the church, in the vain hope of sanctuary. When Tracy, one of the assassins, attacked Becket, the latter grappled with and flung him on the floor of the choir. Fitzurse then struck at the archbishop with his sword, but only wounded him slightly in the head; breaking, however, the arm of Grim, a German monk, which was raised to ward off the blow. Another sword-cut prostrated Becket, and then, as he lay, Tracy smote him with such force that he cut off the crown of his head, cleaving through brain and bone, and breaking his sword on the stone pavement. So ended the career of the archbishop.

The Dean of Chichester (Dr. Hook) gives this picturesque description of this terrific scene, founded on a close study of authorities:

" His friends had more fear for Becket than Becket for himself. The gates were closed and barred, but presently sounds were heard of those without, striving to break in. The lawless Robert de Broc was hewing at the door with an axe. All around Becket was the confusion of terror: he only was calm. Again spoke John of Salisbury with his cold prudence—'Thou wilt never take counsel: they seek thy life.'— 'I am prepared to die.'—'We who are sinners are not so weary of life.'—'God's will be done.' The sounds without grew wilder. All around him entreated Becket to seek sanctuary in the church. He refused, whether from religious reluctance that the holy place should be stained with his blood, or from the nobler motive of sparing his assassins this deep aggravation of their crime. They urged that the bell was already tolling for vespers. He seemed to give a reluctant consent; but he would not move without the dignity of his crosier carried before him. With gentle compulsion they half drew, half carried him through a private chamber, they in all the hasty agony of terror, he striving to waintain his solemn state, into the church. The din of the armed men was ringing in the cloister. The affrighted monks broke off the service; some hastened to close the doors; Becket commanded them to desist— ' No one should be debarred from entering the house of God.' John of Salisbury and the rest fled and hid themselves behind the altars and in other dark places. The Archbishop might have escaped into the dark and intricate crypt, or into a chapel in the roof. There remained only the Canon Robert (of Merton), Fitz-Stephen, and the faithful Edward Grim. Becket stood between the altar of St. Benedict and that of the Virgin. It was thought that Becket contemplated taking his seat on his archiepiscopal throne near the high altar.

" Through the open door of the cloister came rushing in the four, fully armed, some with axes in their hands, with two or three wild followers, through the dim and bewildering twilight. The knights shouted aloud, 'Where is the traitor?' No answer came back. 'Where is the Archbishop?'—'Behold me, no traitor, but a priest of God!' Another fierce and rapid altercation followed: they demanded the absolution of the bishops, his own surrender to the King's justice. They strove to seize him and to drag him forth from the church (even they had awe of the holy place), either to kill him without, or carry him in bonds to the King. He clung to the pillar. In the struggle he grappled with De Tracy, and with desperate strength dashed him on the pavement. His passion rose; he called Fitzurse by a foul name, a pander. These were almost his last words (how unlike those of Stephen and the greater than Stephen!) He taunted Fitzurse with his fealty sworn to himself. 'I owe no fealty but to my King!' returned the maddened soldier, and struck the first blow. Edward Grim interposed his arm, which was almost severed off. The sword struck Becket, but slightly, on the head. Becket received it in an attitude of prayer—'Lord, receive my spirit,' with an ejaculation to the saints of the church. Blow followed blow (Tracy seems to have dealt the first mortal wound), till all, unless perhaps De Morville, had wreaked their vengeance. The last, that of Richard de Brito, smote off a piece of his skull. Hugh of Horsea, their follower, a renegade priest surnamed Mauclerk, set his heel upon his neck, and crushed out the blood and brains. 'Away!' said the brutal ruffian, 'it is time that we were gone.' They rushed out to plunder the archiepiscopal palace.

"The mangled body was left on the pavement; and when his affrighted followers ventured to approach to perform the last offices, an incident occurred which, however incongruous, is too characteristic to be suppressed. Amid their adoring awe at his courage and constancy, their profound sorrow for his loss, they broke out into a rapture of wonder and delight on discovering not merely that his whole body was swathed in the coarsest sackcloth, but that his lower garments were swarming with vermin. From that moment miracles began. Even the populace had before been divided; voices had been heard among the crowd denying him to be a martyr; he was but the victim of his own obstinacy. The Archbishop of York even after this dared to preach that it was a judgment of God against Becket—that 'he perished, like Pharaoh, in his pride.' But the torrent swept away at once all this resistance. The Government inhibited the miracles, but faith in miracles scorns obedience to human laws. The Passion of the Martyr Thomas was saddened and glorified every day with new incidents of its atrocity, of his holy firmness, of wonders wrought by his remains."*

South Malling, an archiepiscopal manor of Canterbury, was, as late as the fourteenth century, invested with supernatural terrors from the popular tradition connected with the assassins of à Becket, so well told by Dr. Stanley, in his *Memorials of Canterbury*: "They rode to Saltwood the night of the deed; the next day (forty miles by the coast) to South Malling. On entering the house they threw off their arms

---

and trappings on the dining-table, which stood in the hall, and after supper gathered round the blazing hearth. Suddenly, the table started back, and threw its burden to the ground. The attendants, roused by the crash, rushed in with lights, and replaced the arms. But soon a second and still louder crash was heard, and the various articles were thrown still further off. Soldiers, and servants with torches scrambled in vain under the solid table to find the cause of its convulsions, till one of the conscience-stricken knights suggested that it was indignantly refusing to bear the sacrilegious burden of their arms—the earliest and most memorable instance," adds Dr. Stanley, sarcastically, " of a rapping, leaping, and turning table."

The well-known legend has it that evil befel the murderers by sea and land, and that no one of them ever after throve or prospered, and such was, indeed, the popular belief for nearly seven centuries. But the facts are totally different. Moreville, who kept back the crowd at the door of the choir, while the associate assassins were doing the king's will on Becket, lived and died Chief Justice in Eyre, north of Trent— that is to say, one of the principal judges of England. Tracy was created Grand Justiciary of Normandy, by Henry, within four years of the assassination. Fitzurse went to Ireland and founded the Celto-Norman sept, known as the Macmahons of the county of Wexford ; and Bret, the fourth murderer, died in his bed in due course, after spending a long life in the enjoyment of his estates, in Devonshire, thus negativing the historical justice. The notorious atrocity of the crime is thought to have given rise to the exclamation, still to be occasionally heard in expression of surprise and inquiry, " What have I done ; have I murdered an archbishop ?"

A curious legendary tale is related of the marriage of à Becket's parents. It is said that Gilbert, his father, had, in his youth, followed the Crusaders to Palestine, and while in the East had been taken prisoner by a Saracen, or Moor, of high rank. Confined by the latter within his own castle, the young Englishman's personal attractions and miserable condition alike melted the heart of the captor's daughter, a fair Mohammedan, who enabled him to escape from prison, and regain his native country ; the Moor's daughter obtaining a promise from Gilbert, that as soon as he had settled quietly in his own land, he would send for and marry his protectress. Years passed on, but Gilbert did not keep his promise, when the love-lorn maiden proceeded to England, and though knowing nothing of the English language beyond the Christian name of her lover, and his place of residence, Cheapside, in London,* she continued to search him out, and found him ready to fulfil his former promise, by making her his wife. Previous to her marriage, she professed her conversion to Christianity, and was baptized with great solemnity, in S. Paul's Cathedral, no less than six bishops assisting at the ceremony. The only child of this union was the celebrated Thomas à Becket.

---

* According to the *Annals of Dunstable*, in the year 1132, *all* London was burnt, through a fire which began in the house of Gilbert Becket, father of the Archbishop.

This singular story has found credence in recent times, with Dr. Giles, M. Thierry, Mr. Froude, and M. Michelet; but by an accredited biographer of Becket, Canon Robertson, it is rejected as a legendary story, wholly unsupported by the evidence of those chroniclers who were Becket's contemporaries. It gave rise, both in England and Scotland, to more than one ballad, with various embellishments.

The views of the character of Thomas à Becket have changed with the times. From the period of his death to the Reformation his shrine in Canterbury Cathedral continued to be visited by crowds of pilgrims, whose offerings proved a valuable source of revenue. At the Reformation, the shrine was dismantled and plundered, and the name of the saint himself excluded from the calendar in the reformed liturgy. An entire revulsion of feeling now took place regarding him, and from the rank of a holy man and a martyr he descended, in general estimation, to the level of a presumptuous priest, and audacious rebel. This view of his character prevailed generally up to the present day, when a second revolution in public opinion took place; and à Becket has found several able eulogists, not only as an ecclesiastic, but in reference to principles of a different nature: motives of patriotism and resistance to feudal tyranny. These last mentioned views are advocated by M. Thierry and Mr. Froude, the former of whom regards à Becket in the same aspect that he does Robin Hood, as the vindicator of Saxon rights and liberties against Norman oppression; the latter sees in him a bulwark to the people against monarchical and baronial outrages, such as the power of the church often was in mediæval times. M. Thierry's view seems to be entirely fanciful; and neither in this light, nor in the view taken by Mr. Froude, is it possible to attribute to à Becket the character of a hero or a martyr; though as the former he must ever appear to parties who consider it impossible to exalt too highly the power of the church.

Archbishop Manning has declared that "St. Thomas died in defence of the law of England. As an Englishman he stood up for the law of the land against the most atrocious, corrupt, and oppressive exercise of royal prerogative by one whom no English historian would venture to defend. The first article of Magna Charta is 'The Church shall enjoy its liberty.' That embodies and expresses the very cause for which St. Thomas laid down his life. That St. Thomas resisted the excess of royal power, interfering with the freedom of religion and conscience. Take one great example: the King claimed that no one should be put out of the church, by spiritual authority, without his leave. Another point was that in the election of bishops the persons should be chosen by his recommendation. The truth is that we have come to a time when the people of England and of Scotland have literally vindicated for themselves the very principle of spiritual liberty for which St. Thomas suffered."

Nevertheless, the evidence upon this controverted event lies far and wide, and it has been inquired by an *exigeant* critic, athirst for the whole truth, "When, we ask, for the ten thousandth time, are we to have a decent edition of all that appertains to Saint Thomas of Canterbury "

HOSTILITY TO HOBBES.

The most dangerous opponent of the clergy in the seventeenth century, was certainly Thomas Hobbes, the subtlest dialectician of his time; a writer, too, of singular clearness, and among British mathematicians inferior only to Berkeley. This profound thinker published several speculations very unfavourable to the church, and directly opposed to principles which are essential to ecclesiastical authority. As a natural consequence he was hated by the clergy; his doctrines were declared to be highly pernicious; and he was accused of wishing to subvert the national religion, and corrupt the national morals. So far did this proceed, that, during his life, and for several years after his death, every man who ventured to think for himself, was stigmatized as a Hobbist, or, as it was sometimes called, a Hobbian: this was a common expression for whoever attacked established opinions, late in the seventeenth and early in the eighteenth century. Such marked hostility on the part of the clergy was a sufficient recommendation to the favour of Charles II. The King, even before his accession, had imbibed many of his principles; and after the Restoration he treated the author with what was deemed a scandalous respect. He protected him from his enemies: he somewhat ostentatiously hung up his portrait in his own private room at Whitehall; and he even conferred a pension on this, the most formidable opponent who had yet appeared against the spiritual hierarchy.—Buckle's *Hist. Civilization*, vol. i. pp. 356-357.

In 1838, when the life of Hobbes appeared in the *Penny Cyclopædia*, it was strongly objected to as unsuited by its partisan feeling for that work; at its close the writer remarks: " so deep and enduring is the impression made upon the public mind, that 'Hobbes, the atheist,' or 'Hobbes, the apologist of tyranny,' is still regarded with pious or with republican horror by all but the extremely few, who have ventured to examine his writings." (Austin's *Province of Jurisprudence determined*, p. 299, note.) The last published edition of the Works of Hobbes is that edited and printed by the late Sir William Molesworth, at great cost, in fourteen 8vo volumes.

----◆----

WHO WERE THE PURITANS ?

Dr. Vaughan, in his *Revolutions in English History*, gives an estimate of the Puritans, which his critic, in the *Saturday Review*, considers striking, and in a measure, new. Dr. Vaughan may have had very natural prepossessions in favour of the Puritans, but he judges them with candour, and, as we think, with considerable insight into their real character and position. Puritanism is apt to be misjudged in these days because it has become identified, to many minds, with some of its fruits of very mixed value which have endured to the present day; and as we have had to resist the attacks of a blind and domineering bigotry, we are apt to look with disfavour on the primary authors of what we have had cause to dislike in our own times. But it should be remembered, as

Dr. Vaughan shows at some length, that the Puritans, in the first period at least of the parliamentary struggle, were only men who were strongly inclined to the Reformed religion, and who had a peculiar theory about the Bible. They were not separated by any social barrier like that which, since the Restoration, has divided the Nonconformists from the members of the Church of England. They were not out of the Church of England at all. One squire was a Puritan, and the next squire was not. The rector of one parish was a Puritan, and the rector of the next parish was an Arminian or a follower of Laud. Puritanism did not disconnect itself from any form or part of a liberal education. It was a way of thinking on a particular subject, and that was all, just as, fifteen years ago, before every one was converted in England to Free Trade, one earl might be a Protectionist and another a Free Trader; but both might buy horses and pictures, and make Latin quotations, and go to county balls, and be in all respects the same sort of men, except for this one difference of opinion. The theories of the Puritans on religion also led them to entertain views on politics hostile to the excessive power of any temporal authority; and thus they came to be marked off into a political party, and, as a political party, embarked on that course which led to the death of Charles and the restoration of his son. Originally, however, they were ordinary Englishmen, of all tastes, habits, and positions, though with a peculiar set of views about religion. There is much instruction in this way of regarding them, short as is the period to which it can historically be applied. At any rate it is worth noticing that, after holding a different position for the century and a half after the Restoration, they, or the inheritors of their peculiar opinions, have again returned to the position held by the Puritans in the early part of Charles I.'s reign, and now it can no longer be said that the holders of different theological opinions are divided by lines of social demarcation.

THE STORY OF JOHN OF LEYDEN.

The revolt of the fanatic Anabaptists in Münster (Westphalia) is a strange admixture of the ludicrous with the terrors of the Reformation, the interest of which has been resuscitated by the popularity of Meyerbeer's grand opera of "Le Prophète." The story, briefly told, is this: In 1530 John Matthias of Haarlem, and John Boccold (John of Leyden) at the head of their followers, among the most conspicuous of whom were Knipperdoling and Bernard Rothman, a celebrated preacher, succeeded in making themselves masters of the city of Münster, which was soon besieged by its bishop, Count Waldeck. Matthias, a baker, appeared next day, armed with a spear, and, crying out that God had commanded him to beat off the enemy, again sallied forth at the head of only thirty of his followers, and, with them, was speedily despatched. John of Leyden, a tailor, now came to the rescue, declaring that the *fate* of Matthias had been revealed to him in a vision long before.

Leyden made no rash sallies upon the opposing army, but contented himself by defending the city from assault. Having, by prophecies and preaching, prepared the minds of the people for some extraordinary event, he went naked through the streets proclaiming that the kingdom of Sion was at hand, that whatever was highest upon earth should be debased, and what was lowest should be exalted. He then ordered most of the churches to be pulled down and the senators to be degraded, at the same time appointing Knipperdoling, who had joined the Anabaptists with Rothman, to exercise the office of common hangman. A new prophet arising called the mob into the market place, and informed them that by command of Heaven John of Leyden was to be made King of the World, and that he should slay all the kings and princes upon earth. This prophet had no sooner ended his speech than Boccold fell upon his knees, and, raising, his hands to heaven, declared that all this had been revealed to him many days since. Thereupon he assumed all the state of majesty, abrogated the authority of the twelve judges, and ordained an order of nobility to wait upon him. He had a throne, covered with cloth of gold, erected in the market place, and there he sat in the administration of justice: having decreed that polygamy was lawful, he took to himself three wives, and shortly after added eleven more. His example was speedily followed by the rest of the Anabaptists; and, when some of the citizens attempted to resist the innovation, fifty of them were killed upon the spot, and others were bound to trees and shot, or put to death in a manner less merciful.

But retribution was at hand. The bishop's hands having been strengthened by a fresh supply of men, the city was closely invested. Provisions within began to fail. Fearful of a famine, the people talked of laying hands on the tailor-king and surrendering him to the besiegers. One of the monarch's wives, pitying the sufferings of the inhabitants, ventured to say that she did not see how it could be the will of God that poor people should daily perish for lack of food. Boccold had the unfortunate woman taken to the market-place, and there, in the presence of his other wives, he struck her head off. Still the famine increased. Many died every day, and others stole away to the besieging army. The general commanding the beleaguering forces determined to assault the place. The Anabaptists, by this time awake to their peril, rushed to the spot, and opposed the entrance of any more of the besiegers, but were at length overwhelmed. Rothman, dreading to fall alive into the enemy's hands, threw himself upon them and was cut to pieces. The king, Knipperdoling, and Krechting were made prisoners.

After the capture of the place, the king and his chief followers were led about from city to city, exposed to the contempt and mockery of the people, for above six months. They were at last carried back to Münster, and on the 25th of January, 1536, John of Leyden, Knipperdoling, and Krechting, were brought out for execution. John of Leyden was the first who suffered. Placed on a scaffold, and tied to a stake, he was subjected to the most cruel tortures for above an hour, and was then killed by being run through the breast. His two companions were tortured and executed in the same manner, and the three bodies were afterwards hung out in iron cages from the lofty tower of Lamberti Church, where the cages remain to this day.

In the Rathhaus, too, are shown John of Leyden's hand, which wa cut off before his execution; his carved bedstead, and his wife's shoes and in the market place a handsome house, ornamented with curiou carvings, is still exhibited as that in which he lived during the " fitfu fever " of his sway as " King of the World."

EXHUMATION OF BODIES.—WORTH OF RELICS.

There is always something that provokes curiosity when we hear the great of former times being taken up from the grave, especially when artificial means have been used to arrest the progress of decay, and the form and features of persons of whom we have heard so much are re vealed for a few minutes to men of a modern generation. In 1774 the tomb of Edward I. was opened in presence of the Dean of Westminster and two Prebendaries. The body was found in a state of complete preservation, having on two robes, one of gold and silver tissue, the other of crimson velvet. In 1834 the tomb of Henry IV. was opened. The countenance was found to be unchanged except in colour; but, after a few minutes' exposure to the air, côllapsed. The coffin of Charles I was opened in 1813 in presence of the Prince Regent; and the skull o Pope was disturbed accidentally some years ago, when a grave wa being dug in Twickenham churchyard, but it was at once reverently re placed. There is also a disgusting story of a Mr. Thompson, of Wor cester, who baited his angling-hook with part of the corrupted form o King John, and carried the fish he caught with it in triumph through the streets!

In 1867, at the chapel of the Sorbonne, an edifice of considerable pre tension, in Paris, an actual translation was celebrated. The remains o Cardinal Richelieu were restored to the splendid mausoleum in which they were laid two centuries ago, but from which they were ruthlessly torn, to be insulted in the streets, in the great Revolution. In every outward circumstance, and in the personages taking part in the cere mony, France did her duty to one ot her greatest men. There was profusion of crimson velvet, and there were present, we are told, " the representatives of the great bodies ot the State, high functionaries, Minis ters, members of the learned corporations, deputies from the French Academy, which was founded by the great Cardinal-Minister, among whom were Berryer, Cousin, Nisard, and others, and many members o the University." The remains consisted of a piece of the skull, which some good man had rescued from the rabble in 1793, and had cut in two in order to prevent an identification that would have cost his own head.

Innumerable relics, that had at least the sanction of an unknown an tiquity, have perished ignominiously, to have their places filled after wards by the grossest imposture. The question that most forces itself on us is not whether any of "the relics" are genuine, but whether it i not a simple imprudence to do much for their preservation, even if they are. The remains of the Conqueror have been twice outraged, and whatever the Archbishop of Paris may expect, this poor bit of skull, which might have been laid quietly in its old place, is put a little in danger's way by this imposing act of restitution. Meanwhile, and on the most favourable supposition, what is it that the Sorbonne has to show its visitors? It is the fragment of a skull that has been dragged from the grave, carried about the streets by a mad rabble, and rescued only to be sawn in two by the frightened preserver. After a time, when the first superficial excitement of curiosity has passed away, the disagreeable part of the impression survives, and is always aggravated by any circumstances that bear a ludicrous character. Beware of hoarding relics, whether public or private, we say to all our readers. Beware of making a relic, of investing a senseless thing with a sentimental value, and enthroning it in some place from which it cannot easily or decently be moved. It is but a sort of small idolatry. Thanks to time, accident, bad memory, death, fire, war, and occasionally Huguenots or Jacobins, there is sometimes a very clean sweep of them. But they sometimes accumulate till they bury the victim or the victims of the delusion of idle sentiment varied with mischievous imposture.—(*Times* journal.)

The three great founders and expositors of Methodism have now, we learn, been formally canonized, and their relics are being exhibited to the admiring faithful. The Rev. Samuel Dunn, happy in the possession of these memorials of departed worth, is displaying them to pious congregations, and the Wesleyan mind is spoken of as being appropriately edified. A piece of John Wesley's preaching-gown, two neckcloths formerly worn by his brother Charles, and the spectacles, comb, and pocket-book of Dr. Adam Clarke, convince the most sceptical that it is not at Rome or Moscow alone that the relics of the saints are held in veneration and the saints themselves duly worshipped. If we remember aright, it is not very long ago that some admirer of John Wesley had in his possession a wig, or a portion of a wig, that had been worn by that remarkable person; and there was some controversy as to the genuineness of the wig itself, or as to the amount of veneration which it was supposed to excite. At any rate, it is clear all that is now necessary is to prove the pedigree of the interesting relics themselves. For, after all, it is just as easy to manufacture sacred gowns, combs, and neckties, as those curious little bits of bone which are to be had in Rome, all duly authenticated by official signatures and seals. When the pedigree is established, and the cavils of the incredulous utterly destroyed, the next thing will be to dedicate some chapels to the honour of the saints whose remains are thus devoutly preserved; and it might even be desirable to set apart certain days in the year for their especial remembrance. —Abridged from the *Pall Mall Gazette.*

CREDULITY OF GREAT MINDS.

Sir Richard Baker, having described the imposture of Elizabeth Barton, "the Holy Maid of Kent," her counterfeit trances and predictions, says: "Here we may see how credulous ofttimes great scholars are in believing impostures, when Warham, Archbishop of Canterbury, and Fisher, Bishop of Rochester, were thought to give credit to this counterfeit; so that we need not wonder at St. Austin, who, though he gave credit to many lying miracles, yet they were such as had more probability in them than this, which consisted in nothing but making faces, as, upon examination of the Maid and her abettors, was confessed; and, thereupon, she and most of them were condemned, drawn to Tyburn, and there hanged."

TRANSMIGRATION OF SOULS.

In Egypt, as we learn from Herodotus, the priesthood taught the doctrine of the passage of the soul, after quitting the body, through a succession of forms of beasts, fishes, and birds; until, after a cycle of 3000 years, it entered anew into humanity in the body of a new-born child. This notion of the entrance of the soul into a new body shows that the object of embalming their dead has been misconstrued. It was not with the view of the soul re-entering its ancient receptacle that the remains of the dead were kept so long from decay, but with the aim of delaying as long as possible the transmigration to lower forms, which was held only to commence with the dissolution of the corpse. Servius, in his commentary on the Æneid, contrasts this tenet with the practice of the Romans in burning their dead, in order to accelerate as much as possible the freedom of the soul from the body, and its return to "generality," its proper nature. * The teachings of Pythagoras and Plato upon the subject of the transmigration and re-incarnation of souls need hardly to be particularized.* Neither need it be pointed out how deeply a belief of this kind entered into the popular religion of Greece, through the mythical elevation of the heroes among the ranks of the divinities; or how the subtle mysticism of Plotinus handed over to the theosophy of the new world a germ from the ancient stock, in the idea of a series of purgatorial states in harmony with the moral and spiritual antecedents of the soul—κατὰ ἀμοιβὰς βίων. The dogma of pre-existence was prominently upheld by the Druids. That souls were thought by them to pass on after death to other bodies, Cæsar expressly tells us; and Lucan, whose mind was steeped in the ancient Gallic ideas, sees in death but the intermediate stage of existence.

M. Pezzani, a French barrister, believes that he has succeeded in raising the doctrine of the transmigration of souls from the level of a low and dreary superstition to that of a truth of philosophy and an article of religious faith; compiled, he is careful to inform us, in the main, from a

---

* With Pythagoras the transmigration of souls was a mere physical event, wholly independent of all moral considerations. In proof of the reality of the transmigration, Pythagoras pretended that he distinctly remembered the different bodies which his soul had inhabited. He recollected being first Œthalides, and then Euphorbus the son of Panthous. To prove this false assertion, he went to Argos, and in the temple of Juno pointed out the shield with which he had fought in the Trojan war, hanging amidst many others of the same form. He next became Hermotimus, a fisherman; and, last of all, Pythagoras.

series of successive essays of his, not less than fifteen in number, extending over a period of nearly thirty years. Time and reflection, the progress of science and philosophy, and the more critical knowledge of the past having in no instance shaken or even seriously modified his original convictions.—*Saturday Review*, 1865.

WHO WAS APOLLONIUS OF TYANA?

The Pagan Christ of the third century, who, two centuries later, was set up by Julia Domna, the wife of Septimius Severus, as a rival to the Christ of the Gospel.

Apollonius was born at Tyana, a Greek city in Cappadocia, about the commencement of the Christian era. At an early age he became imbued with the doctrines of the Pythagorean sect, and visited several of the principal cities of Asia Minor. He is next reported to have travelled to Babylon, and to have conversed with the Magians. He then proceeded to India, accompanied by his faithful disciple Damis. Philostratus reports, on his return westwards the fame of his wisdom was very widely spread. At Smyrna, he allayed the factious quarrels of the citizens, and restored tranquillity. At Ephesus he predicted a pestilence, which he is said to have made to cease by destroying an evil spirit who appeared in the form of a beggar. At Pergamus he was not less successful, and performed many marvellous cures. At Troy he had an interview and a long conversation with the ghost of Achilles, and after wandering in Greece arrived finally at Rome. By his predictions he awakened the fears, but by his miraculous powers escaped the vengeance of Nero. However, as the tyrant had decreed the banishment of all philosophers from Rome, he thought it more prudent to depart, and continued his travels in Spain, Africa, and Egypt. Wherever he went he attracted disciples, and by his teaching endeavoured to reform the people that he came among. At length he was accused, in the reign of Domitian, of practising magic arts, and was imprisoned, but, as it is stated, escaped miraculously. Shortly afterwards he is said to have died, but to have appeared after death to a young man at Tyana who had ventured to disbelieve in the doctrine of the immortality of the soul.

In 1862, M. Chassang published a new translation of the Life of Apollonius, originally written in Greek by Philostratus. In the seventeenth century anti-Christian controversialists found in his life a whole armoury of weapons. But by this time his divinity has vanished, his philosophy has been exploded, and we can only find in Apollonius a worker of wonders. At one time regarded as the successor of Pythagoras and the rival of our Saviour, he now appears to us merely in the light of a predecessor of Swedenborg. M. l'Abbé Freppel discovers in Apollonius a kind of philosophical Don Quixote, who goes through the world in search of adventure and combats, and who had in Damis his Sancho Panza.

The conclusion at which M. Chassang arrives is, that, so far as Philostratus goes, we can only look upon Apollonius as a magician or thaumaturge.   He seems to regard his biography as an idealized portrait of one of the last representatives of the wisdom of antiquity.   M. Chassang thinks that the superficial, confused, and incomplete account supplied by Philostratus fails to establish the philosophical position of Apollonius. Ritter, on the other hand, judging from the state of philosophical opinion at the time, and arguing from what slight traces can be detected, believes Apollonius to have been a neo-Pythagorean strongly imbued with the learning and the superstitions of the East.—*Saturday Review.*

WHAT IS PANTHEISM ?

This momentous inquiry has been answered by the Rev. John Hunt, in his *Essay on Pantheism*, published in 1866.   This treatise is valuable as an introduction to the study of his great subject : it has been described as introductory to the final chapter, " What is Pantheism ?"—Brahmanism and Buddhism, the Persian, Egyptian, and Greek religions, Greek philosophy, the philosophy of the Jews, the Church, the Gnostics, Manichæism, Scholasticism, the Italian revival, the German, French, and English mystics, Sufism, Des Cartes, Spinoza, Malebranche, Leibnitz, the German transcendental philosophers, and the Pantheism of the poets, all come under review before the author arrives at his proper theme.

Excluding *material Pantheism*, or, in other words, Atheism, from the view (says a critic in the *Athenæum*), the author treats of *spiritual Pantheism*, which, as he rightly supposes, enters into all religions and philosophies worthy of the name.   There is a sense in which the most religious men and the profoundest metaphysicians are Pantheists,—in which both St. John and St. Paul have been called so.   Mr. Hunt's mind sympathizes with this.   He feels that the more it is studied the more it brings a man into that close union with the Infinite which the human soul longs for in its highest moods.   But he is aware that the word has been employed as a symbol of the grossest heresy and impiety, —that it has been fastened upon others by their opponents as a sign of opprobrium,—and that the odour of it has been thoroughly bad among the ignorant or bigoted.   Indeed, men of opposite opinions and feelings have been termed Pantheists—the devout Bunsen and the strong-minded Carlyle, the poet Wordsworth no less than Shelley.   In the interests of charity as well as of truth it is a duty to ascribe only spiritual Pantheism to men like Spinoza and Malebranche, unless their own writings show clearly that they meant otherwise.

" Pantheism," says Mr. Hunt, " is, on all hands, acknowledged to be the theology of reason—of reason it may be in its impotence, but still of such reason as man is gifted with in this present life.   It is the philosophy of religion—the philosophy of all religions.   It is the goal of Rationalism, of Protestantism, and of Catholicism, for it is the goal of thought.   There is no resting-place but by ceasing to think or reason on God and things divine.   Individuals may stop at the symbol, churches and sects may strive to make resting-places on the way by appealing to the authority of a church, to the letter of the Sacred Writings, or by trying to fix the 'limits' of religious thought, when God Himself has not fixed them. But the reason of man in its inevitable development and its divine love of freedom will break all such bonds and cast away all such cords. They are but the inventions of men, and the human soul in its progess onwards will hold them in derision. It knows that God is Infinite, and only as the Infinite will it acknowledge Him to be God. But what is Pantheism? Substantially and primarily, Pantheism is the effort of man to know God as Being, infinite and absolute. It is ontological Theism—another, a necessary and an implied form of rational Theism. The argument from teleology proves a God at work; the argument from ontology proves a God infinite. We cannot take the one without the other, whatever may be our difficulties in reconciling the conclusions to which each leads us. The difficulties arise from the vastness of the subject; and, though we cannot see further than we do see, that is no reason for shutting our eyes to what is manifest."

WHAT IS MUSCULAR CHRISTIANITY?

Some clever wag or wags, after the study of Professor Kingsley's novels and essays, and possibly of his sermons also, gathered from them a presentment of Mr. Kingsley's ideal hero and saint, and named him "Muscular Christian." Mr. Brown closes his lecture on "Wesley's Theology," with a demand for a "Christianity muscular,—morally muscular, gigantic in its moral strength." He tells us that he does not desire to have it "in Kingsley's puerile sense," but in some Wesleyan Methodist sense. He here only expresses the general opinion of the reading world that Mr. Kingsley *is* responsible, in some degree or other, for this singular new term. It is, at least, a witty description (with some dash of parody) of his heroes.

Mr. Kingsley confesses that he had this term in mind when he chose David as the subject of his four sermons before the University of Cambridge. "We have heard much of late," he says in the beginning of his first sermon, "about muscular Christianity. A clever expression, spoken in jest by I know not whom, has been bandied about the world, and supposed by many to represent some new ideal of the Christian character. For myself I do not understand what it means. It may mean one of two things. If it mean the first, it is a term somewhat unnecessary, if not somewhat irreverent. If it means the second, it means something untrue and immoral." The first meaning may be "a healthful and manly Christianity, one which does not exalt the feminine virtues to the exclusion of the masculine." This is the good meaning. The other is expressed thus by Mr. Kingsley. "There are those who say, and there have been of late those who have written books to show, that provided a young man is sufficiently frank, brave, and gallant, he is more or less absolved from the common duties of morality and self-restraint." This is, of course, the evil meaning.—Review in the *Churchman*, 1865.

PROPHECY-RIDDEN PRINCES.

In Pagan times, it has been asserted that popular superstitions blended themselves with the highest political functions, gave a sanction to national counsels, and oftentimes gave the starting-point to the very primary movements of the State. Prophecies, omens, miracles, all worked concurrently with senates or princes. " Whereas, in our days," says Charles Lamb, " the witch who takes her pleasure with the Moor, and summons Beelzebub to her sabbaths, nevertheless trembles before the beadle, and hides herself from the overseer." Now, as to the witch, even the horrid Canidia of Horace, or the more dreadful Erichtho of Lucan, seems hardly to have been much respected in any era. But for the other mode of the supernatural, they have entered into more frequent combinations with state functions and state movements in our modern ages than in the classical age of Paganism. Look at prophecies, for example: the Romans had a few obscure oracles afloat, and they had the Sibylline books under the state seal. These books, in fact, had been kept so long, that, like port wine superannuated, they had lost their flavour and body. On the other hand, look at France. Henry, the historian, speaking of the fifteenth century, describes it as a national infirmity of the English to be prophecy-ridden. Perhaps there never was any foundation for this as an exclusive remark, but assuredly not in the next century. There had been with us British, from the twelfth century, Thomas of Ercildoune in the north, and many monkish local prophets for every part of the island; but latterly England had no terrific prophet, unless indeed Nixon of the Vale Royal in Cheshire, who uttered his dark oracles sometimes with a merely Cestrian, sometimes with a national reference. Whereas, in France, throughout the sixteenth century, every principal event was foretold successively, with an accuracy that still shocks and confounds us. Francis I., who opens the century (and by many is held to open the book of *modern* history, as distinguished from the middle or *feudal* history), had the battle of Pavia foreshown to him, not by name, but in its results—by his own Spanish captivity—by the exchange for his own children upon a frontier river of Spain—finally, by his own disgraceful death, through an infamous disease conveyed to him under a deadly circuit of revenge. This king's son, Henry II., read some years *before* the event a description of that tournament, on the marriage of the Scottish Queen with his eldest son, Francis II., which proved fatal to himself, through the awkwardness of the Comte de Montgomery and his own obstinacy. After this, and we believe a little after the brief reign of Francis II. arose Nostradamus, the great prophet of the age. All the children of Henry II. and of Catharine de Medici, one after the other, died in circumstances of suffering and horror, and Nostradamus pursued the whole with ominous allusions. Charles IX., though the authorizer of the Bartholomew massacre, was the least guilty of his party, and the only one who manifested a dreadful remorse. Henry III., the last of the brothers, died, as the reader will remember, by assassination. And all these tragic successions of events are still to be read more or less dimly prefigured in verses of which we will not here discuss the dates. Suffice it, that many authentic historians attest the good faith of the prophets; and finally, with respect to the first of the Bourbon dynasty, Henry IV., who succeeded upon the assassination of his brother-in-law, we have the peremptory assurance of Sully and other Protestants, countersigned by writers both historical and controversial, that not only was he prepared, by many warnings, for his own tragical death—not only was the day, the hour, prefixed—not only was an almanack sent to him, in which the bloody summer's day of 1610 was pointed out to his attention in bloody colours; but the mere record of the king's last afternoon shows beyond a doubt the extent and the punctual limitation of his anxieties. In fact, it is to this attitude of listening expectation in the king, and breathless waiting for the blow, that Schiller alludes in that fine speech of Wallenstein to his sister, where he notices the funeral knells that sounded continually in Henry's ears, and, above all, his prophetic instinct, that caught the sound from a far distance of his murderer's motions, and could distinguish, amidst all the tumult of a mighty capital, his stealthy steps.—*Blackwood's Magazine.*

THE REFORMATION—LUTHER AND TRANSUBSTANTIATION.

In the progress of the Reformation Luther himself, but for one doctrine, which had become the very life and soul of the man, would have been persuaded or alarmed into an accommodation with the Church of Rome. There was one period in the negotiations between the two parties, when, by mutual concessions, a compromise appeared possible, if Luther could but have relinquished his doctrine of "justification by faith alone." Writing of the great German reformer, Mr. White says in *Eighteen Christian Centuries:*—" Hungering after better things than the works of the law—abstinence, prayers, repetitions, scourgings, and all the wearisome routine of mechanical devotion—he dashed boldly *into the other extreme,* and preached free grace—grace without merit, the great doctrine which is called, theologicaliy, 'justification by faith alone.'" This *other extreme* was the sheet-anchor of the Reformation. And it is curious to notice that a doctrine on which Protestants are now divided, was precisely the doctrine which irrevocably separated the Reformed Churches, in the first instance, from the great Catholic hierarchy. So far as the Reformation depended upon Luther and his faithful disciples, it was the only vital point on which no compromise was possible. The doctrine of *transubstantiation,* which to the Protestants of a later period seemed the most astounding error of the ancient Church, was maintained to the last by Luther. Some slight modification he may have made, which is indicated in controversial language by the substitution of the term *consubstantiation;* but if Luther could have kept his disciples upon that line at which he himself rested, there would have been no incurable schism on this head. D'Aubigné gives us a most spirited and graphic account of the conference held upon this subject before the Landgrave at Marburg, between the Swiss reformer Zuinglius and Martin Luther. Luther was supported by Melancthon, Zuinglius by Œcolampadius. The Landgrave sat behind a table; "Luther, taking a piece of chalk, bent over the velvet cloth which covered it, and steadily wrote four words in large characters. All eyes followed the movement of his hand, and soon they read, *Hoc est Corpus Meum.* Luther wished to have this declaration continually before him, that it might strengthen his own faith, and be a sign to his adversaries." And no Catholic could have adhered more pertinaciously to the literal meaning of his text. "I differ, and shall always differ," he exclaimed. "Christ hath said, *This is my body.* Let them show me that a body is not a body. I reject reason, common sense, carnal arguments, and mathematical proofs. We have the word of God. *This is my body,*" he repeated, pointing with his finger to the words he had written; "the devil himself shall not drive me from that. To seek to understand it is to fall away from the faith." Zuinglius objected that Christ's body had ascended into heaven; and if in Heaven, it is not in the bread. Luther replied, "I repeat that I have nothing to do with mathematical proofs. I will not, when Christ's body is in question, hear speak of a particular place. I absolutely will not. Christ's body is in the sacrament, but it is not there as in a place." Then, no longer content with pointing his finger at the text he had written, he seized the velvet cover, tore it off the table, and held it up to the eyes of Zuinglius and Œcolampadius. "See! see!" he said, "this is our text; you have not yet driven us from it, and we care for no other proof."

Happily it is not one mind, however energetic, that can arrest or determine a movement like that of the Reformation. It ran its destined course. And now, looking round upon the nations of Europe, we may assuredly congratulate those countries in which, owing to favourable circumstances, the doctrines of the Reformed Church were able freely to develope themselves. There is no room for doubt or cavil on this head. It is not a question of subtle or disputable tenets. There is this broad matter-of-fact distinction between Protestantism and Catholicism, —the one is the religion of the book, the other of the Priest. In the one, every peasant consults his Bible as his sacred oracle; in the other, the Priest is his sacred oracle.—*Blackwood's Magazine.*

FABLES ABOUT LUTHER.

Dr. Forbes Winslow having indulged in some theories on the subject of Luther's supposed vision of spirits, as when he is said to have thrown the inkstand at the devil in the Wartburg, he has been replied to by Mr. C. H. Collette, as follows: "I am sure if Luther were alive he would be much obliged to Dr. Forbes Winslow for his elaborate 'psychological' disquisition on his case; but he would have, as I now propose to do, pointed out a much more simple solution of the difficulty. The fact is, Luther not only never had the privilege of an interview with his Satanic Majesty, but he never said that he had. The story is one of the many hoaxes got up to bring ridicule not only on the 'great reformer' himself, but on the great work in which he was privileged to be a conspicuous and efficient actor. The alleged interview with the devil is one of the numerous perversions of Luther's writings after he was dead. The portion of Luther's writings (see vol. vii. p. 228, edit. Wittemb. 1557) upon which the traditionary tale of his interview with the devil is built, has been long since most completely exposed. The matter was decisively set at rest by Seckendorf, a Lutheran writer, who proved that one Justus Jonas, formerly a colleague in divinity of Luther, translated this piece of Luther's writings from the German into Latin, but garbled the text in many places, and left out these words, ' Meo corde; multas enim noctes mihi acerbas et molestas fecit,' which ought immediately to follow the first sentence, ' Satan mecum cæpit ejusmodi disputationem ;' so that the passage would run thus, ' Satan began with me, *in my heart*, the following disputation.' (See Seckendorf's *Commentarius de Lutheranismo*, etc., lib. i. sec. cii. Lips. 1694)."

PORTRAIT OF MOHAMMED.

Dr. Arnold has drawn the following very interesting description of Mohammed's personal appearance and habits:

Mohammed is said to have been of middle stature; to have had a large head, strong beard, round face, and reddish-brown cheeks. His biographers state that his forehead was high, his mouth wide, his nose long and somewhat of an aquiline shape; that he had large black eyes; that a vein which extended from his forehead to his eyebrows enlarged when excited by anger; that his splendidly white teeth stood far apart; and upon his lower lip was a small mole. His hair hanging over his shoulders retained its dark colour to the day of his death : he sometimes dyed it brown, but more frequently applied to it odoriferous oils. It was only at his last pilgrimage that he had his head shaven. He trimmed his moustache and his finger-nails every Friday before prayer. His neck, it is said, " rose like a silver bar upon his broad chest." Between his shoulders he had a large mole, which was looked upon as the prophetic seal. A physician once wishing to remove it, Mohammed objected, saying, " He who made it shall also heal it." His hands and feet were very large, yet his step was so light as " to leave no mark on the sand." Mohammed spoke but little, yet occasionally permitted himself a joke. A woman once came to him, saying, " My husband is ill, and begs thee to visit him ;" upon which he inquired, " Has not thy husband something white in his eye?" She returned in order to examine it. On her husband asking what she was doing, she replied: " I must see whether you have anything white in your eye, for the Apostle of God asked the question." Her husband at once recognising the joke, convinced her that this was common to all eyes. On one occasion, when an old woman conjured him to pray for her that she might enter paradise, he replied: " No *old* woman dares enter paradise !" As she began to weep, he reminded her of the verse in the Koran which declares that perpetual youth will be restored to women. The Arab prophet was compassionate towards animals, and would wipe down his horse when it perspired with his sleeve; but this was nothing extraordinary among his countrymen. His cat was lifted up to share his own dish; and a white cock which he had he called his friend, considering him a protection against devils, genii, witchcraft, and the evil eye!

ORIGIN OF KISSING THE POPE'S TOE, AND OF THE LATERAN.

Some questions had been raised as to the propriety of Kissing the Pope's toe, and even theologians had their doubts touching so singular a ceremony. But this difficulty has been set at rest by Matthew of Westminster, who explains the true origin of this custom. He says that formerly it was usual to kiss the hand of his holiness; but that towards the end of the eighth century, a certain lewd woman, in making an offering to the Pope, not only kissed his hand but also pressed it. The Pope—his name was Leo,—seeing the danger, cut off his hand, and thus escaped the contamination to which he had been exposed. Since that time, the precaution has been taken of kissing the Pope's toe, instead of his hand; and lest any one should doubt the accuracy of this account, the historian assures us that the hand, which had been cut off five or six hundred years before, still existed in Rome, and was indeed a standing miracle, since it was preserved in the Lateran in its original state, free from corruption.

And as some readers might wish to be informed respecting the Lateran itself, where the hand was kept, this also is considered by the historian, in another part of his great work, where he traces it back to the Emperor Nero. For it is said that this wicked persecutor of the faith, on one occasion, vomited a frog covered with blood, which he believed to be his own progeny, and, therefore, caused to be shut up in a vault, where it remained hidden for some time. Now, in the Latin language, *latente* means hidden, and *rana* means a frog; so that, by putting these two words together, we have the origin of the Lateran, which, in fact, was built where the frog was found.—Buckle's *Hist. Civilization,* vol. ii. p. 291.

THE HISTORIC CHURCH OF ENGLAND.

Certain Episcopal writers are prone to boast of their Churchmanship by hurling anathemas against sects. The historic Church of England, it is maintained, is not of this type. The late accomplished author of the *Christian Year* admits, in his edition of Hooker's works, that "numbers have been admitted to the ministry of the Church of England with no better than Presbyterial ordination;" and that "neither Hooker, nor Jewel, nor Whitgift ventured to urge the exclusive claims of episcopacy."

Hooker writes:—" There may sometimes be very just and sufficient reason to allow ordination made without a bishop. Therefore, we are not simply without exception to urge a lineal descent of power from the Apostles by continual succession of Bishops in every effectual ordination."

" Let the Bishops bear in mind that it is more by the force of custom than by any true and heavenly law that the Lord hath appointed Presbyters to be under Bishops." " There may be just and sufficient reason to allow ordination without a Bishop."

Warburton writes:—" The great Hooker was not only against, but laid down principles that have entirely subverted, all pretences to a Divine unalterable right in any Church government whatever."

Bishop Cosens says:—" Are all the Churches of Denmark, Germany, France, and Scotland, in all points, either of substance or circumstance, disciplinated alike? They neither are nor can be, nor yet need be, since it cannot be proved that any set and exact particular form is recommended to us by the Word of God."

Francis Mason, an enthusiastic and able Anglican champion, writes: —" Seeing a Presbyter is equal to a Bishop in the power of order, he hath equally intrinsic power to give orders."

Whitgift.—" I deny that the Scripture hath set down any one certain form and kind of government in the Church."

Stillingfleet.—" The ground for settling episcopal government in this nation was not any pretence of Divine right, but the conveniency of that form to the state and condition of this Church at the time of the Reformation."

Bishop Hall.—" There is no difference in any essential matter between the Church of England and her sisters of the Reformation."

Archbishop Bramhall.—" Because I esteem the other Reformed Churches as not completely formed, do I esteem them aliens and strangers and schismatics? No such thing."

Archbishop Usher.—" I do profess that with like affection I would receive the blessed Sacrament at the hands of the Dutch and French ministers."

Archbishop Wake.—" I should be unwilling to affirm that where the ministry is not episcopal there is no Church, nor any true administration of the Sacraments."

Bishop Tomline.—" There is no precept in the New Testament which commands that every Church shall be governed by Bishops."

Bishop Jewel.—" By the Scriptures a Bishop and a Priest are all one. Verily, Chrysostom saith, " Inter episcopum et presbyterum interest ferme nihil.' Augustine saith, ' Quid est episcopus nisi primus presbyter.' "

Dean Sherlock.—" A Church may be a truly Catholic Church, and such as we may and ought to communicate with, without Bishops."

Dr. Claget.—" The Church of England does not unchurch those parts of Christendom that hold the unity of the faith. Hence the folly of the conceit that there must be one Church, which is the only Church, to the exclusion of all the rest."

A far greater number of authorities could be added ; but the above must satisfy the impartial reader that the great luminaries of the Church of England had no sympathy with arrogant and intolerant pretensions of Episcopacy.—Communication to the *Times.*

BURNING OF VEDAS WIDOWS.

The burning of these poor women appears to have been in violation of authority—in plain words, to have been a *mistake.* Professor Wilson, in a lecture on the Vedas, notices some remarkable passages in the Rigveda upon this subject; and, among the rest, the hymn cited as authority for the burning of widows. The opinions which he had then formed upon a cursory view of the subject, have been fully confirmed by an examination of the various passages on the subject, and his conclusions are, that the text usually cited as authority for the burning of widows enjoins the very contrary, and directs them to remain in the world ; and that although the expressions relating to the disposal of the dead are somewhat equivocal, yet it seems probable that the corpse was burned, although the ashes and bones were afterwards buried. After giving a translation of the hymn in which the practice is said to be enjoined, he proceeds to show the origin of the error, or wilful misapprehension, which arose from reading the word *agneh,* instead of the real word *agre,* thereby changing the sentence,—"let them go up into the dwelling first," into "let them go up into the place of the fire." The reading *agre* is confirmed by the commentator; and the translation made by Professor Wilson agrees, in all essential respects, with another made by Dr. Max Müller. Aswalayana, the author of the *Grihya Sutras,* a work little inferior in authority to the Vedas, furnishes further proof of what is meant, as he defines the person who is to lead the widow away after the performance of the funeral rites. As regards the disposal of the dead, the phraseology is more in favour of burying than burning ; but it is possible that the burying may refer to the ashes and bones after burning,—a practice analogous to that of other ancient nations, and which may account for the stone coffins found in many parts of India having cinders or burnt human remains within them. The funeral ceremonies, as prescribed by the *Grihya Sutras,* differ in many respects from those now observed. A law permitting the remarriage of Hindoo widows has, however, been passed, and carried into effect in Bengal. Anybody may marry a widow without fear of consequences. This result is admitted by the most bigoted opponents of the reform, so there is an end of one of the oldest social evils that ever afflicted a community.

Retributive Justice.

I T has been often remarked that a kind of poetical justice has been manifested in the *Nemesis* which has overtaken those persons who have devised modes of punishment, torture, or death for their fellow-creatures. The Scriptures assure us that "an eye for an eye, and a tooth for a tooth," will be exacted; "that all they who take the sword shall perish with the sword;" and that "whatsoever a man soweth, that shall he also reap;" they afford us, moreover, an illustration in the case of "the wicked Haman," who expiated his enmity to the Jewish people on the "gallows, fifty cubits high, which he had made for Mordecai."

In profane history, will at once suggest itself the Brazen Bull, which Phalaris, the despot of Agrigentum, had constructed for roasting alive his own subjects. This piece of mechanism was hollow, to contain one or more victims enclosed in it, to perish in tortures when the metal was heated: the cries of these suffering prisoners passing for the roarings of the animal. The artist who constructed the Bull was named Perillus, and is said to have been the first person burnt in the bull by order of the despot. The reality of this ingenious torture appears to be better authenticated than the nature of the story would lead us to presume; for it is not only noticed by Pindar, but even the actual instrument—the Brazen Bull itself—which had been taken away from Agrigentum as a trophy by the Carthaginians, was returned by the Romans, on the subjugation of Carthage, to its original place of deposit.

Ludovico Sforza, Duke of Milan, it is asserted, was crushed to death in a metallic collapsible prison of his own invention; and a tale founded upon it entitled "the Iron Shroud," will be found in *Blackwood's Magazine*, vol. xxviii. History tells us that Ludovico died imprisoned in the castle of Loches, in France: the "collapsible prison" is an embellishment.

A fatality seems to have pursued the men by whom the Bastile was raised. It was founded by Stephen Marcel, Provost of the Merchants: in attempting to save himself by flight, he was struck on the head by an axe, by De Charny, and he fell at the foot of the Bastile, which he himself had built. Hugues Aubriot, who added to the Bastile, for his vigilance as Provost of Paris, was imprisoned therein before he was consigned to the *oubliettes*.

The Bishop of Verdun was the inventor of the iron cages in the time of Louis XI. of France, and he himself became the very first tenant, being shut up in his own invention for eleven years.

The poisoner Sainte-Croix, as is well known, having inadvertently let fall the precautionary glass mask which he was in the habit of wearing, lost his life through the noxious fumes of the destructive preparation he was compounding; and in his sudden fate was involved that of the participator in his crimes, his pupil and mistress, De Brinvilliers.

Another instance of death by poison is that of the infamous monster Pope Alexander VI. He once meditated taking off one of the richest of the cardinals by poison; his intended victim, however, contrived, by means of presents, promises, and prayers, to gain over the head cook, and the dish which had been prepared for the cardinal was placed before the pope. He died of the poison he had prepared for another."—Ranke, *History of the Popes*, vol. i. p. 52.

This was a case of the—

> Bloody instructions, which, being taught, return
> To plague the inventor : thus even-handed Justice
> Commends the ingredients of our poisoned chalice
> To our own lips.
>
> *Macbeth*, act i. sc. 7.

Voltaire throws discredit upon this legend, of which he gives a somewhat different version, *Essai sur les Mœurs*, chap. cxi.

Our own history affords the next example of retributive death. Richard Cœur de Lion died of a wound received from a crossbow, while besieging a small castle in France. He met his death by a weapon introduced into warfare by himself, much to the displeasure of the warriors of his time, who said that "heretofore brave men fought hand to hand, but now the bravest and noblest might be brought down by a cowardly knave lurking behind a tree."

Hopkins, the witchfinder,—

> Who after prov'd himself a witch,
> And made a rod for his own breech,—

went on searching and swimming the poor creatures till some gentleman, out of indignation at the barbarity, took him and tied his own thumbs and toes, as he used to tie others, and when he was put into the water, he himself swam as they did. This cleared the country of him, and it was a great deal of pity that they did not think of the experiment sooner.

Deacon Brodie was executed in 1788 at Edinburgh, for robbery of the Excise Office; the machine by which the law was carried into effect was the invention or improvement of the patient himself; thus, to the fact that Deacon Brodie suffered by his own improved drop, common fame has added the embellishment that he was the first to prove its efficiency. However this latter point may be, in its efficiency he seems to have taken a most paternal interest. He found the rope too short, descended till it was made longer, ascended again, and found it still too short; when he once more stepped lightly down, and waited till it was made somewhat longer. Being at length satisfied, he reascended, helped the executioner to adjust the rope, shook hands with a bystander, whom he desired to acquaint his friends that he died like a man, and went carelessly out of the world, with his hand slung in the breast of his vest.

Towards the latter end of the sixteenth century, an attempt was made by the Regent, James Earl of Morton, to introduce into Scotland the *Mannaja, Mannaye*, or Halifax Gibbet, as an instrument of judicial execution; it was by this that he lost his own head. Sir Walter Scott informs us that it was remarked with interest by the common people, that he suffered decapitation by a rude guillotine of the period which he himself, during his administration, had introduced into Scotland from Halifax; it was called the "Maiden." (*History of Scotland*, vol. ii. p. 168.) Hone gives the favourite "embellishment" added by popular tradition, that the Regent was the first and last person who suffered by it in Scotland.

So also in an epigram preserved in Kelly's *Collection of Proverbs:*

He that invented the *Maiden* first *hanselled* it.

Such, however, is not the fact, for an excerpt from the books of the Treasurer of the City of Edinburgh, "To Andro Gotterson, smith, for grynding of the *Madin*, v. sh.," is of earlier date than the execution of Morton; and a subsequent entry of five shillings to the same individual, "for grynding of the *Widow*," testifies to the frequency of its use, and the appropriate change of name, after the first spouse of the Maiden had perished in her fatal embrace. It seems too, as is gathered from the same paper, to have been the custom to give, when possible, a retributive significance to the mode of its working: "By a quaint regulation, highly characteristic of our ancestors, when a cow or horse was the piece of property stolen, the animal was caused, by means of a rope, to pull the trigger, and thus become the proximate executioner of justice upon the offender."

The Earl of Argyle, the last who suffered by this instrument, declared, as he pressed his lips upon the block, that it was "the sweetest maiden he had ever kissed."

There are two obstinate errors in the common history of the Guillotine, employed to this day in public executions in France. It is said to have been invented by Dr. Guillotin, who is stated to have been one of the very first that suffered death by its stroke; but upon reference to the biography of Dr. Guillotin we find that, during the French Revolution, he merely pointed out the adoption of this machine, which had been long known as proper for the infliction of death without giving any pain to the sufferer; and for that reason it was chosen as a kind of compromise among the first French revolutionists, many of whom wanted to abolish the punishment of death altogether. Unfortunately for Guillotin, some wags gave his name to the machine of which he was not the inventor, and which he had only brought into notice. It is true that Guillotin was imprisoned, and nearly fell a victim to the carnage of the Revolution; but he escaped, and after the termination of his political career resumed the functions of a physician, and became one of the founders of the Academy of Medicine at Paris. He died May 26, 1814, aged seventy-six, after enjoying up to his last moments the esteem of all who knew him. It is said that the *slanting* descent of the hatchet of the guillotin, which renders instant decapitation more certain, and consequently less painful, was an improvement suggested by Louis XVI. himself, who had a great taste for mechanics.

In no period, perhaps, is retributive fate more clearly to be discerned, than in the end which awaited the sanguinary leaders of the Revolution.

That of Danton may be cited, who, condemned by a decree of the irresponsible Extraordinary Tribunal, of which he was the originator, exclaimed on the platform: " This time twelve months I proposed that infamous tribunal by which we die, and for which I beg pardon of God and man."

It may be added, that it is not alone upon those who compass by active means the injury or destruction of their fellow men, that the sword of retributive justice has been supposed to fall. The Eastern saying quoted by Damas to the discomfited Beauseant, may be cited as exhibiting the belief that the imprecations of those who call down the anger of heaven upon others, will, like " bread cast upon the waters, return after many days" to the utterers themselves:

> Curse away !
> And let me tell thee, Beauseant, a wise proverb
> The Arabs have—"Curses are like young chickens,
> And still come home to roost."—Bulwer, *Lady of Lyons.*

> 'Tis sport to have the engineer
> Hoist with his own petar.—*Hamlet.*

One more proof in conclusion, that, sooner or later—

> Measure for measure must be answered.—*Henry VI.*

" Who is there that sadly, yet calmly, reflects upon the fate of the First Napoleon—the protracted eating away of the heart, which forced quiescence became in one whose life was energetic action, the miserable confinement of ' that spirit poured so wildly forth ' within the narrow precincts of Longwood—and does not recognise the awful significance of the Scriptural warning, 'with what measure ye mete, it shall be measured to you again,' in the analogy of this miserable termination of the tyrant's career with that of his victim—that ' most unhappy man of men,' as Wordsworth apostrophises him in his fine sonnet — that brightest of occidental heroes, Toussaint l'Ouverture ?"

Some of these instances have been selected and abridged from *Notes and Queries,* the contributor of which (W. Bates) terms the incidents a few of the more definite and striking instances which, whether actual or mythic, may serve sufficiently to point the moral of the poet:

> To wrongdoers the revolution of time
> Brings retribution.
> *Twelfth Night.*

Or to illustrate the more emphatic Scriptural warning :

> Whoso diggeth a pit shall fall therein : and he that rolleth a stone, it will return upon him.—Prov. xxvi. 27.

Science applied to the Arts.

PRÆHISTORIC ARCHÆOLOGY.

PRÆHISTORIC Archæology is the history of men and things that have no history. All over this country and other countries of Western Europe—perhaps, indeed, all over the world—are scattered vestiges and relics of unknown races and times—of races which existed in times before history commenced. These relics are of various kinds; some so common and conspicuous as to be familiar objects, like Stonehenge and similar monuments on a smaller scale; some rarer, like the subterranean habitations in the Orkneys, and the "Picts' houses" in various parts of Scotland; some doubtful and mysterious, like the instruments fashioned by human hands, and yet discovered in connexion with remains thought to be older than man. It is certain, however, that in ages more or less remote there did exist people of whom, except in the discoveries thus brought to light, we have no record. If we wish to know anything of their history, we must unravel or compose it from what we can find in these relics, and that is the task which Præhistoric Archæologists have proposed to themselves.

Though the races in question are all præhistoric, they are not all extinct. In a certain sense many a living people may be regarded as præhistoric down to a certain period of its annals—that is to say, its origin and early progress are lost in the night of antiquity, or commemorated only in extravagant fables. The Hindoos themselves, for instance, are præhistoric. That they were invaders of India, like the Mahommedan conquerers after them, and that they dispossessed a more ancient, if not an indigenous population, is well known; but when their migration occurred, or how long they had been settled in India when they were invaded in turn, nobody can even conjecture. They claim for themselves an incredible antiquity; but of authentic history they have so little as to be without any record or even distinct tradition of an event so comparatively recent as the invasion of Alexander the Great. But here comes the remarkable part of the story. Old as the Hindoos may be, those older races which they dislodged still survive, and in very great numbers. A people completely distinct from the Hindoos in physical form, manners, and customs may be found in India at the present day. They exist in scattered tribes under various denominations, but a late census showed that in North-Western and Central India alone they numbered between eight and nine millions. Here, then, is a race, largely represented, which is certainly older than another race old enough to be præhistoric.

Of all the monuments of præhistoric man, none, as we have said, are more conspicuous than the megalithic fabrics usually described as

Druidical circles. They exist in many parts of these islands, and are very commonly known and talked about. Now, who raised these monuments? Who set up these stones in these places? The work is usually ascribed to the Celtic races; but there were certainly races earlier than the Celts in these parts, and Stonehenge may possibly be even older than we imagine. But, however this may be, Dr. Hooker stated at the Meeting of the British Association, in August, 1868,[*] on the authority of his own personal knowledge and observation, that a race practising these very customs survives to this very day. In a certain district of Eastern Bengal a people may be found who in this our own age still raise monuments of this identical character. Dr. Hooker has lived with these people. He has seen with his own eyes "cromlechs" and "dolmens" not six months old. He was told how the stones were cut from the rock, how they were moved from place to place, why they were set up, and what the erection signified; so that any enterprising traveller may go and see "Druids" actually at work in our own generation upon precisely such monuments as in this country are altogether and hopelessly præhistoric. Of course the suggestion is that these living specimens of a race lost in antiquity may give us, or be insensibly made to yield, some information which may stand in the light of history. They actually call a stone, Dr. Hooker tells us, by the same name as is given to it in the Celtic idioms of Wales and Brittany, though of their language generally little is yet known. Such is the curious prospect now opened to us. Races præhistoric in these islands are not præhistoric in other parts of the world. There are countries in which tombs and places of worship are still built after the fashion of Stonehenge. Perhaps there are tribes still using exactly such knives and arrow-heads as are found in the "drift." At any rate, the idea of attacking the subject from this end is singularly practical, and the result, perhaps, may give an unexpected character of exactness to this last-born of sciences.—*Times* journal.

MAN UPON THE EARTH.

In October, 1860, there appeared in *Blackwood's Magazine*, a searching examination of this great question, entitled, "The Reputed Traces of Primæval Man," in which, having discussed the leading topics, the writer thus recapitulates his conclusions:—

---

[*] During this Meeting, at Norwich, assembled the International Congress of Præhistoric Archæology, which originated at Spezzia in 1865. The subjects discussed by the *savans* included—1, the earliest traces of the existence of man; 2, researches in caverns inhabited at a remote period by man; 3, the structural character of primeval man; 4, the character of the Fauna associated with him; 5, megalithic monuments; 6, stone and bronze antiquities, their character and use; 7, earliest use of iron in Britain; 8, early habitations; 9, intrenchments and implements of war; 10, early methods of interment: 11, existing customs and implements, as illustrations of præhistoric times; 12, indications of continuous progress in arts and civilization during successive præhistoric periods.

1. To the question, Are the so-called flint implements of human workmanship or the results of physical agencies? My reply is, They bear unmistakeably the indications of having been shaped by the skill of man.

2. To the inquiry, Does the mere association in the same deposit of the flint-implements and the bones of extinct quadrupeds prove that the artificers of the flint-tools and the animals coexisted in time? I answer, That mere juxtaposition of itself is no evidence of contemporaneity, and that upon the testimony of the fossil bones the age of the human relics is *not proven*.

3. To the query, What is the antiquity of the Mammalian bones with which the flint-implements are associated? My answer is, That, apart from their mixture with the recently-discovered vestiges of an early race of men, these fossils exhibit no independent marks by which we can relate them to human time at all. The age of the Diluvium which embeds the remains of the extinct mammalian animals must now be viewed as doubly uncertain—doubtful from the uncertainty of its coincidence with the age of the flint-implements—and again doubtful, if even this coincidence were established, from the absence of any link of connexion between those earliest traces of man and his historic ages.

Upon the special question involved in this general query, What time must it have required for the physical geography adapted to the Pachyderms of the antediluvian period to have altered into that now prevailing, suited to wholly different races? the geological world is divided between two schools of interpretation—the Tranquillists, who recognise chiefly Nature's gentler forces and slower mutations, and the Paroxysmists, who appeal to her violent subterranean energies and her more active surface-changes.

4. To the last interrogation, How far are we entitled to impute a high antiquity to these earliest physical records of mankind from the nature of the containing and overlying sedimentary deposits? My response again is, That as the two schools of geologists now named differ widely in their translation into geologic time of all phenomena of the kind here described, this question, like the preceding, does not admit, in the present state of the science, of a specific or quantitative answer.

In conclusion, then, of the whole inquiry, condensing into one expression my answer to the general question, Whether a remote præhistoric antiquity for the human race has been established from the recent discovery of specimens of man's handiwork in the so-called Diluvium, I maintain it is not proven, by no means asserting that it can be *disproved*, but insisting simply that it remains—*Not Proven.*

GEOLOGY AND HISTORY.

Professor von Cotta has published an interesting work, in which he specially devotes himself to the condition of the Earth and of Man during the times that have preceded history. He does not pretend, however, to mark the precise period at which man first appeared on the earth. The relative position of rocks are to the geologist what ancient monuments are to the historian; but in the case of both, the earlier periods are involved in obscurity. History, however, can measure time by years; geology can only assign an earlier or a later place in a series. One stratum may be certainly older than another, but how long a period was required for the formation of either it may be impossible to determine; and if it were even possible to ascertain this, there are breaks in the series which cannot be measured. It may, however, be found, as has been suggested, that climatal conditions of the earth's surface, and the formation of sedimentary deposits, are related to periodical changes in the excentricity of the earth's orbit, in connexion with the precession of the equinoxes.

Admiral Fitzroy adduces the following striking facts strongly bearing on the great geological inquiry of " Flint Tools," and " Implements in the Drift."

In 1830 four of the aborigines of Tierra del Fuego were brought to England; they acquired enough of our language to talk about common things. From their information and our own sight are the following facts:—The natives of Tierra del Fuego use stone tools, flint knives, arrow and spear heads of flint or volcanic glass, for cutting bark for canoes, flesh, blubber, sinews, and spears, knocking shell-fish off rocks, breaking large shells, killing guanacoes (in time of deep snow), and for weapons. In every sheltered cove where wigwams are placed, heaps of refuse—shells and stones, offal and bones—are invariably found. Often they appear very old, being covered deeply with wind-driven sand, or water-washed soil, on which there is a growth of vegetation. These are like the "kitchen middens" of the so-called "Stone Age" in Scandinavia.

No human bones would be found in them (unless dogs had dragged some there), because the dead bodies are sunk in deep water with large stones, or burnt. These heaps are from six to ten feet high, and from ten or twenty to more than fifty yards in length. All savages in the present day use stone tools, not only in Tierra del Fuego, but in Australia, Polynesia, Northernmost America, and Arctic Asia. In any former ages of the world, wherever savages spread, as radiating from some centre, similar habits and means of existence must have been prevalent; therefore casual discovery of such traces of human migration, buried in or under masses of water-moved detritus, may seem scarcely sufficient to define a so-called "Stone Age."

WHO ARE THE IMPROVERS OF MANKIND?

It is strange to find one of the silken barons of civilization and refinement writing as follows:—The polite Earl of Chesterfield says, "I am provoked at the contempt which most historians show for humanity in general; one would think by them that the whole human species consisted but of about a hundred and fifty people, called and dignified (commonly very undeservedly too) by the titles of emperors, kings, popes, generals, and ministers."

Sir Humphry Davy has written thus plainly in the same vein: "In the common history of the world, as compiled by authors in general, almost all the great changes of nations are confounded with changes in their dynasties; and events are usually referred either to sovereigns, chiefs, heroes, or their armies, which do, in fact, originate entirely from different causes, either of an intellectual or moral nature. Governments depend far more than is generally supposed upon the opinion of the people and the spirit of the age and nation. It sometimes happens that a gigantic mind possesses supreme power, and rises superior to the age in which he is born: such was Alfred in England, and Peter in Russia. Such instances are, however, very rare; and in general it is neither amongst sovereigns nor the higher classes of society that the great improvers and benefactors of mankind are to be found."—*Consolations in Travel*, pp. 34, 35.

SCIENCE AND SUPERSTITION.

The Rev. Charles Kingsley has well observed that, as Superstition has its root in fear, the child of ignorance, so Science is the child of courage. The brave man faces nature boldly, and, like Rarey the horse-tamer, tries to find out "what she is thinking of." But only a few men of courage, in few countries and at rare intervals, have dared to do so, and then in opposition to public opinion. The Biblical writings testify to this having occurred among the Jews; some of them did not blindly fear or worship nature, but viewed her lovingly and reverently; while the Chaldeans, who made great discoveries in astronomy, sank eventually into astrology and planet-worship. Among the Greeks the fate of Socrates is an evidence of the popular dread of science; and among the Romans, in the days of the Antonines, it sank under the mud-waves of neo-Platonism. To the northern nations, under the guidance of Divine Providence, was reserved the honour of the true cultivation of physical science. In spite of the opposition of their contemporaries, those brave spirits, Gerbert, Roger Bacon, Albertus Magnus, Galileo, and others, boldly investigated nature. In the seventeenth century much was effected for the emancipation of the human intellect by the Royal Society and by other philosophers, and in the eighteenth more real progress was made in the accurate knowledge of nature than in all the fifteen preceding centuries. This result Mr. Kingsley considers to be greatly due to the influence of the study of the Bible, delivering the mind from the slavery of superstition. Scientific method he asserts to be simply the exercise of common sense, the ordinary use of our inductive and deductive faculties, especially in the study of botany, zoology, and geology: and he refers to the writings of Thomas Carlyle as products of a mind fraught with the reverent spirit of science and intellectual truth. Science and superstition, Mr. Kingsley says, are internecine enemies; and there always has been fierce opposition to science on the part of those interested in the fears of mankind. But science also suffers much from the injurious patronage of those who would at the same time check her progress and restrain her utterances. Yet her votaries will still go on keeping their rank in the warfare against ignorance, fear, and cruelty, although they receive but very little of their due recompense for the inconceivable benefits their labours have conferred upon the human race, among which are the immense increase of material wealth by creating new and lucrative employment for our redundant population ; numerous remedies for disease and pain ; humane and rational treatment of the insane ; more enlightened mental and physical education ; increase of life by the study of the laws of health ; and the saving of life and prevention of crime by overcoming the inhuman witch mania. From what has been done, how much may be looked for hereafter ! Mr. Kingsley concludes with part of the description of wisdom from the eighth chapter of the Book of Proverbs.

WHO DISCOVERED THE COMPOSITION OF WATER?

Watt, the Scotchman, and Cavendish, the Englishman, neither of whom seems to have been aware of what the other was doing. Mr. Muirhead, in his *Life of Watt*, seems to have put the priority of Watt beyond further doubt ; though he is somewhat hard upon Cavendish, who, there can be little question, made the discovery himself. Mr. Buckle, in a note upon this passage, says :

That there was no plagiarism on the part of Watt, we know from positive evidence ; that there was none on the part of Cavendish, may be fairly presumed, both from the character of the man, and also from the fact that in the then state of chemical knowledge the discovery was imminent, and could not long have been delayed. It was antecedently probable that the composition of water should be ascertained by different persons at the same time, as we have seen in many other discoveries which have been simultaneously made, when the human mind, in that particular department of inquiry, had reached a certain point. We are too apt to suspect philosophers of stealing from each other what their own abilities are sufficient to work out for themselves. It is, however, certain that Watt thought himself ill-treated by Cavendish.

Between the two (continues Mr. Buckle), there was this difference. Watt, for several years previously, had been speculating on the subject of water in connexion with air ; and having, by Black's law of latent heat, associated them together, he was prepared to believe that one is convertible into the other. The idea of an intimate analogy between the two bodies having once entered his mind, gradually ripened ; and when he at last completed the discovery, it was merely by reckoning from data which others possessed besides himself. Instead of bringing to light new facts, he drew new conclusions from former ideas. Cavendish, on the other hand, obtained his results from the method natural to an Englishman. He did not venture to draw a fresh inference until he had first ascertained some fresh facts. Indeed, his discovery was so completely an induction from his own experiments, that he omitted to take into consideration the theory of latent heat, from which Watt had reasoned, and where that eminent Scotchman had found the premises of his argument. Both of these great inquirers arrived at truth, but each accomplished his journey by a different path. And this antithesis is accurately expressed by one of the most celebrated of living chemists (Liebig), who, in his remarks on the composition of water, truly says, that while Cavendish established the facts, Watt established the idea.

It is important to quote the remarkable passage, which is quite decisive as to the real history of Watt's discovery, in his *Correspondence*, pp. 84, 85. On the 26th of November, 1783, he writes: "For many years I have entertained an opinion that air was a modification of water, which was originally founded on the facts, that in most cases where air was actually made, which should be distinguished from those wherein it is only extricated from substances containing it in their pores, or otherwise emitted to them in the state of air, the substances were such as were known to contain water as one of their constituent parts; yet no water was obtained in the process, except what was known to be only loosely connected with them, such as the water of the crystallization of salts. *This opinion arose from a discovery that the latent heat contained in steam diminished in proportion as the sensible heat of the water from which it was produced increased*; or, in other words, that the latent heat of steam was less when it was produced under a greater pressure, or in a more dense state, and greater when it was produced under a less pressure, or in a less dense state; which led me to conclude that when a very great degree of heat was necessary for the production of the steam, the latent heat would be wholly changed into sensible heat; and that in such cases the steam itself might suffer some remarkable change. I now abandon this opinion in so far as relates to the change of water into air, as I think that may be accounted for on better principles."

WHO INVENTED THE STEAM-ENGINE?

In 1543, experiments were made by the Spaniard Don Blasco de Garay, a sea-captain, to propel vessels by a contrivance which has been loosely assimilated to a steam-engine. In going over the ground of history, practised writers are continually stumbling. Thus, a popular journalist, referring to the above experiment, said: "Three centuries ago, Blasco de Garay attempted to propel a boat by steam in the harbour of Barcelona." To this positive assertion it was replied, "The evidence cited by the Spaniards, often repeated, is a letter from Blasco himself. By permission of the Queen of Spain, but after much hindrance, the person who questioned the statement, was enabled to inspect this letter, which is preserved with the archives at Simancas, near Valladolid, and there is not one word about *steam* in the document. Blasco describes minutely a vessel propelled by paddles worked by 200 men. It is true that the two letters at Simancas do not mention *steam*, as pointed out by Mr. Macgregor to the Society of Arts, in 1858; but the account of the experiment as mentioned by Navarrete, leaves no doubt. We have not space for the entire details. Blasco de Garay is described to have presented to the Emperor Charles V. *an engine* which he had invented to propel large vessels without sails or oars. "The inventor did not publish a description of his engine; but the spectators saw that it consisted principally of an apparatus for boiling a great quantity of water; in certain wheels, which served as oars; and a machine that communicated to them the *steam* produced by the boiling water." Then we have the treasurer, Ravago's, objection, that "the boiler continually exposed the vessel to an explosion." The account concludes thus: "These facts are extracted from the original register in the archives at Simancas, among the papers of Catalonia, the register of the War Office of the year 1543." The "cauldron of boiling water" is also mentioned in the account from Navarrete, under "Barcelona," *Penny Cyclopædia*, vol. iv. p. 438. Mr. Macgregor impugns Navarrete's report; and, as the result of his inquiries in Spain, he attests that not only are the letters at Simancas without mention of the "steam," but it is not known there or at Barcelona, by the public officers. Supposing the evidence to be strictly correct, it bears only conjectural proof of the use of *steam*, though a boiler was used. Garay took away the machinery. It has been suggested that the moving power was obtained by an apparatus resembling the primitive steam-engine of Hero. Yet Dr. Delepierre records this experiment as complete, in these words: "On the 17th of April, 1543, the Spaniard Don Blasco de Garay launched a steam-vessel at Barcelona, in the presence of the Emperor Charles V."[*]

Garay was rewarded, and the usefulness of the contrivance in towing ships out of port was admitted. The vessel was found to progress at the rate of a league an hour, or, according to Ravago, the treasurer, who was one of the commissioners (but unfriendly to the design), at the rate of three leagues in two hours; but it *did* progress, and was found to be easily under command, and turned with facility to any point where it was directed. Favourable reports were made to the Emperor, and his son Philip; but the design was not carried to any practical extent. The next claim to the invention was that made by Arago for Salomon De Caus, as described in his work, published at Frankfort in 1615, and reprinted at Paris in 1624. De Caus was at one time in the service of Louis XIII., and afterwards in that of the Elector Palatine, who married the daughter of our James I. During the latter period he visited this country, and was employed by Henry, Prince of Wales, in ornamenting the Gardens of Richmond Palace. The passage referred to by Arago is much as follows:—Let there be attached to a ball of copper a tube and stopcock, and also another tube; these tubes should reach almost to the bottom of the copper ball, and be well soldered in every part. The copper ball should then be filled with water through the tube, and the stopcock be shut, when, if the ball is placed on a fire, the heat acting upon it will cause the water to rise in the other tube. De Caus ascribed the force entirely to the air, and not to the *steam*, which he does not mention, though the pressure may have caused the ball to burst with a noise like a petard. Notwithstanding the advocacy of M. Arago,

---

[*] *Historical Difficulties and Contested Events*, 1868, p. 146.

De Caus is not entitled to any share in the invention of the steam-engine.

We now come to the Marquis of Worcester's "fire-engine, or water commanding engine, or an elementary steam-engine, a modern name applied to an old invention, previously known, and afterwards known as an atmospheric engine," described in a MS. of 1655, and in Lord Worcester's *Century of Inventions*, 1663. Next, a pretended claim was set up by the French, asserting that Lord Worcester took the idea of his steam-engine from De Caus, and in proof of this assertion there appeared, six years after Arago's claims, a letter in the *Musée des Familles*, purporting to have been written by Marion Delorme, on the 3rd of February, 1641, to her lover Cinq Mars. In this letter the writer says: " Pursuant to the wishes you have expressed, I am doing the honours to your English 'ord, the Marquis of Worcester, and I am taking him, or rather, he is taking me, from sight to sight. . . . . For example, we paid a visit to Bicêtre, where he thinks he has discovered in a maniac a man of genius. . . . . As we were crossing the court-yard of the asylum, I more dead than alive from fright, a hideous face appeared behind the large grating, and began to cry out in a crazy voice : ' I am not mad, I have made a great discovery that will enrich any country that will carry it out.' ' What is this discovery ?' said I to the person who was showing us over the asylum. ' Ah !' said he, shrugging his shoulders, 'it is something very simple, but you would never guess it. It is the employment of the steam of boiling water.' At this I burst out laughing. 'This man,' resumed the warder, ' is called Salomon De Caus. He came from Normandy four years ago to present a memoir to the king upon the marvellous effects that might be produced from this invention. To listen to him, you might make use of steam to move a theatre, to propel carriages, and in fact to perform endless miracles. The cardinal dismissed this fool without giving him a hearing.

"Salomon De Caus, not at all discouraged, took upon himself to follow my lord cardinal everywhere, who, tired of finding him incessantly at his heels, and importuned by his follies, ordered him to Bicêtre, where he has been confined three years and a half, and where, as you have just heard, he cries out to every visitor that he is not mad, and that he has made a wonderful discovery. He has even written a book on the subject, which is in my possession.

"My Lord of Worcester, who all this time appeared to be in deep thought, asked to see the book, and after having read a few pages, said, ' this man is not mad, and in my country, instead of being shut up in a lunatic asylum, he would be laden with wealth. Take me to him, I wish to question him. He was conducted to his cell, but came back looking grave and sad. ' Now he is quite mad,' said he; 'it is you who have made him so; misfortune and confinement have completely destroyed his reason ; but when you put him into that cell, you enclosed in it the greatest genius of your epoch.' Thereupon we took our leave, and since then he speaks of no one but Salomon De Caus."

This story was copied into standard works, and represented in engravings; but the letter proved to be a hoax; and it was shown that not only had De Caus never been confined in a lunatic asylum, but that he had held the appointment of engineer and architect to Louis XIII. up to the time of his death, in 1630; whereas Marion Delorme is stated to have visited Bicêtre in 1641. Dr. Delepierre has traced the hoax to one Berthoud, who confessed having written the letter signed by Marion Delorme, to suit an engraving which had been designed by Gavarni for another tale in the *Musée des Familles*, the subject being a madman looking through the bars of his cell. Berthoud's confession was, however, disbelieved, and a Paris journal declared the Delorme letter was to be seen in a library in Normandy; this was denied by Berthoud, who offered a million of francs to any one who would produce the letter. In a manuscript note in a volume in the castle of Heidelberg, the pretended letter of Delorme is stated to have been extracted from the *Gazette de France*, 3td March, 1834; and at a banquet given at Limoges, so recently as 1865, M. le Vicomte de la Guéronnière, in a speech repeated the anecdote of De Caus and Bicêtre, which was reported in the *Moniteur*. The Rev. Sydney Smith believed the above letter to be authentic; and Arago, who was rich in inventive faculty, and of very ardent temperament, was imposed upon by the above romantic fiction, conclusively proved by M. Figuier to be a forgery.

In reference to the invention of Lord Worcester, Dr. Lardner observes, that on comparing it with the contrivance previously suggested by De Caus, it will be observed that even if he (De Caus) knew the physical agent by which the water was driven upwards in the apparatus described by him, still it was only a method of causing a vessel of boiling water to empty itself, and before a repetition of the process could be made, the vessel should be refilled, and again boiled. In the contrivance of Lord Worcester, on the other hand, the agency of the steam was employed in the same manner as it is in the engines of the present day, being generated in one vessel and used for mechanical purposes in another. Nor must this distinction be regarded as trifling or insignificant, because on it depends the whole practicability of using steam as a mechanical agent. Had its action been confined to the vessel in which it was produced, it never could have been employed for any useful purpose."
—See *History of Wonderful Inventions*, 1868.

THE OLD PHILOSOPHERS.

Horace Walpole, who possessed great knowledge of life, though himself disfigured by arrogant conceits, has left this satirical view of the wisdom of the ancient philosophers:

"I thought that philosophers were virtuous, upright men, who loved wisdom, and were above the little passions and foibles of humanity. I thought they assumed that proud title as an earnest to the world that they intended to be somethig more than mortal; that they engaged themselves to be patterns of excellence, and would utter no opinion, would pronounce no decision, but what they believed the quintessence of truth; that they always acted without prejudice and respect of persons.

Indeed, we know that the ancient philosophers were a ridiculous composition of arrogance, disputation, and contradictions! that some of them acted against all ideas of decency; that others affected to doubt of their own senses; that some, for venting unintelligible ncnsense, pretended to think themselves superior to kings; that they gave themselves airs of accounting for all that we do and do not see—and yet that no two of them agreed in a single hypothesis; that one thought fire, another water, the origin of all things; and that some were even so absurd and impious as to displace God, and enthrone matter in his place. I do not mean to disparage such wise men, for we are really obliged to them: they anticipated and helped us off with an exceeding deal of nonsense, through which we might possibly have passed if they had not prevented us."

SIR ISAAC NEWTON'S APPLE-TREE, ETC.

About the life of Newton what a number of misstatements and fallacies cling to this day, notwithstanding the vigilance of his biographers. Some of these are but idle tales of wonder; others are prompted by baser motives. The tree which, by the falling of its fruit, suggested to Newton the idea of Gravity, is of paramount interest. It appears that, in the autumn of 1665, Newton left his college at Cambridge for his paternal home at Woolsthorpe. "When sitting alone in the garden," says Sir David Brewster, "and speculating on the power of Gravity, it occurred to him, that as the same power by which the apple fell to the ground was not sensibly diminished at the greatest distance from the centre of the earth to which we can reach, neither at the summits of the loftiest spires, nor on the tops of the highest mountains, it might extend to the moon and retain her in her orbit, in the same manner as it bends into a curve a stone or a cannon-ball when projected in a straight line from the surface of the earth." (*Life of Newton,* vol. i. p. 26.) Sir David Brewster notes, that neither Pemberton nor Whiston, who received from Newton himself his first ideas of gravity, records this story of the falling apple. It was mentioned, however, to Voltaire by Catherine Barton, Newton's niece; and to Mr. Green by Sir Martin Folkes, President of the Royal Society. Sir David Brewster saw the reputed apple-tree in 1814, and brought away a portion of one of its roots.

Professor de Morgan, however, *questions whether the fruit was an apple,* and maintains that the anecdote rests upon very slight authority. The story of the dog Diamond, who threw down a lighted candle, which consumed some papers, the almost finished labour of some years, is given by M. Biot as a true story; and he characterizes the accident as having deprived the sciences for ever of the fruit of so much of Newton's labours. Dr. Newton remarks, that Sir Isaac never had any communion with dogs or cats; and Sir David Brewster adds, that the view which M. Biot has taken of the idle story of the dog Diamond, charged with fire-raising among Newton's manuscripts, and of the influence of this accident upon the mind of their author, is utterly incomprehensible. The fiction, however, was turned to account in giving colour to M. Biot's misrepresentation.

Whatever may have been the misstatements respecting Newton, they are exceeded in enormity by the attempt made in 1867, by M. Chasles, the French mathematician, on the authority of a series of documents purporting to be letters written by Newton and some of his most famous contemporaries ; and including in particular a correspondence which is supposed to have passed between him and Pascal, the celebrated French mathematician and divine. Their effect is to show that Newton was indebted to that illustrious man, and other French philosophers, for many of the ideas on which his fame depends. It is not denied, as we understand, that Newton was the first to publish, as well as to develope, that marvellous induction which is the foundation of half our knowledge about the universe. What is asserted is that he was led to it under the inspiration of Pascal, whose mathematical genius, as is well known, was equal to his theological learning. It is this assertion which crumbles to pieces on the first touch of the facts adduced. No explanation was given by M. Chasles, of the source whence the papers were derived. They were compared with Newton's letters in the possession of the Royal Society, at Burlington House, and their falsity was conclusive. Next, in a volume of extracts, compiled by a certain Pierre Desmaiseaux, three out of the five alleged specimens of Newton's handwriting were *verbatim* copies of isolated passages occurring in the French translation of three letters originally written by Newton in English. In other words, Newton, who could not even read French without a dictionary, had been made by the fabricator to repeat in French to one correspondent, word for word, the identical expressions which he really used elsewhere in writing to another correspondent in English.

In the autumn of 1867, Sir David Brewster read to the British Association the following observations, tending to show that this was a gigantic fraud—the greatest ever attempted in the world as connected with science and literature. " 1. The correspondence was founded on the assumption that Newton was a precocious genius, having written on the infinitesimal calculus, &c., at the age of eleven, whereas he was then at school, and knew nothing of mathematics, occupying himself only with water-wheels and other boyish amusements. 2. There is no evidence that Pascal and Newton had any correspondence. Having examined the whole of Newton's papers in the possession of the Earl of Portsmouth, he never found any letter or paper in which Pascal was mentioned. 3. The letters from Hannah Ayscough, Newton's mother, bear his signature, although she was a married woman, and could have signed Hannah Smith. 4. The letters of Pascal have been found by M. Fauquere to be another hand, and the signature not that of Pascal. 5. The letters of Newton are not in his hand, and some of them bear a signature which he never used. One of them is signed ' Newton,' as if he had been a member of the Peerage, and many of them ' J. Newton,' a sign which he never used. 6. An experiment with coffee is mentioned in one of the letters of Pascal, whereas coffee was at that time unknown in France. 7. All Newton's letters are in French, a language in which he never wrote. All his letters to the celebrated French mathematician, Vangnon, are in Latin, and Newton himself has stated that he could not read French without a dictionary. 8. The style and sentiments in Newton's letters are such as he never could have used. He expresses 'eternal' gratitude to Pascal, a word which no Englishman ever uses. 9. According to the correspondence, M. Desmaiseaux got access to Newton's papers after his death, and carried off a great many papers. Now, it is certain that Mr. Conduitt, Newton's nephew, arranged and examined all Newton's papers, in order to obtain materials for a life of him, and having failed to find a competent person to write, he undertook it himself, and obtained by persons then alive all the information that existed respecting Newton's early life and studies. There could be no doubt, therefore, that the letters of Newton and Pascal were forgeries calculated and intended to transfer to Pascal the glory of the discovery of the law of gravitation which was due to Newton."

One hundred and thirty years had elapsed since the death of the great Newton, when (in 1858) the men of Lincolnshire raised in Grantham, the birthplace of their illustrious townsman, a statue to his memory. We grow impatient to place the effigies of a great soldier upon some lofty column, or of a showy political leader upon some ornate pedestal; but we suffer generation after generation to pass away ere we mark the place which gave birth to our most profound interpreter of the book of nature. "Happy," says an eloquent contemporary, "not only in his surpassing genius, but in the time of his birth, he conquered a universe where others may be justly proud to win a province. For all time he must in some sense remain thus alone. An equal or even a brighter genius, should such arise in the course of time, can never cast his greatness into shade; for never again can so sublime a problem be presented to the intellect of man as the great secret of the material universe which Newton was born to solve." Frankly as the pre-eminence of the English discoverer was admitted by men like La Grange, who followed in his track, there is a tinge of noble envy in the saying which Lord Brougham quotes from the French philosopher. "Newton," said La Grange, "was not only the greatest but the most fortunate genius that ever existed; because there can only once be found a system of the universe to be established." His good fortune, indeed, secures him from all future rivalry to the end of time, as amply as his matchless insight gave him the supremacy over all the explorers of nature who had lived before him.

Halley writes of Newton's *Principia*: "It may be justly said that so many and so valuable philosophical truths as are herein discovered and put past dispute, were never yet owing to the capacity and industry of any one man." "The importance and generality of the discoveries," says Laplace, "and the immense number of original and profound views, which have been the germ of the most brilliant theories of the philosophers of this (18th) century, and all presented with much elegance, will insure to the work on the *Mathematical Principles of Natural Philosophy* a pre-eminence above all the other productions of human genius."

WHAT THE ENGLISH OWE TO NATURALIZED
FOREIGNERS.

The industry of England owes much to the foreigners who have from time to time become settled and naturalized amongst us. We are indebted to German miners, introduced into England by the wisdom of Elizabeth, for the early development of our mineral resources. The Dutch were our principal instructors in civil and mechanical engineering ; draining extensive marsh and fen lands along the east coast in the reign of James I., and erecting for us pumping-engines and mill-machinery of various kinds. Many of the Flemings, driven from their own country by the Duke of Alva, sought and found an asylum in England, bringing with them their skill in dyeing, cloth-working, and horticulture; while the thousands who flocked into the kingdom on the revocation of the Edict of Nantes by Louis XIV., introduced the arts of manufacturing in glass, silk, velvet, lace, and cambric, which have since become established branches of industry. The religious persecutions in Belgium and France not only banished from those countries free Protestant thought, but at the same time expelled the best industrial skill, and England eventually obtained the benefit of both.

Our mechanical proficiency, however, has been a comparatively recent growth. Like many others of our national qualities, it has come out suddenly and unexpectedly. The invention of the steam-engine, towards the end of last century, had the effect of giving an extraordinary impetus to improvement, particularly in various branches of iron manufacture; and we began to export machines, engines, and ironwork to France, Germany, and the Low Countries, whence we had before imported them. Although this great invention was perfected by Watt, much of the preliminary investigation in connexion with the subject had been conducted by eminent French refugees: as by Desaguliers, the author of the well-known *Course of Experimental Philosophy*, and by Denis Papin, for some time Curator of the Royal Society, whose many ingenious applications of steam-power prove him to have been a person of great and original ability. But the most remarkable of these early inventors was unquestionably Thomas Savery—also said to have been a French refugee, though very little is known of him personally—who is entitled to the distinguished merit of having invented and constructed the first working steam-engine All these men paved the way for Watt, who placed the copestone on the work of which the distinguished Frenchmen had in a great measure laid the foundations.

Many other men of eminence, descendants of the refugees, might be named, who have from time to time added greatly to our scientific and productive resources. Amongst names which incidentally occur to us are those of Dollond the optician, and Fourdrinier, the inventor of the paper-making machine. Passing over these, many were the emigrés who flocked over to England at the outbreak of the great French Revolution of 1789, and who maintained themselves by teaching the practice of art, and by other industrial pursuits. Of these, perhaps the most distinguished was Marc Isambard Brunel, who for the greater part of his life followed the profession of an engineer, leaving behind him a son as illustrious as himself,—Isambard Kingdom Brunel, the engineer of the Great Western and other railways, the designer of the *Great Eastern* steamship, and the architect of many important public works.— Abridged from the *Quarterly Review*, No. 223.

THE ALPHONSINE TABLES.

A splendid folio edition of the Astronomical books of King Alphonso X. of Castile, has been printed at Madrid by order of the Queen of Spain from the manuscript in the University of Alcala. The work is written in Spanish, being almost the first book of Western science written in a modern language, a great step towards the diffusion of knowledge in the thirteenth century. The introduction is the catalogue of the fixed stars, celebrated as the Alphonsine Tables. They are described as containing, besides the methods and tables, some eloquent and poetical explanations, and some short hints about astrology. The following passage will show how King Alphonso treated certain astronomical questions :

Of Ursa Minor he says, " Some astronomers have taken it for a wain with its pole : others say it has the form of an animal, which might as well be a lion, a wolf, or a dog, as a male or female bear. Here, then, are heavenly animals inhabiting that part of the sky where this constellation is to be found, and recognised by ancient astronomers, because they saw four stars forming a square and three in a right line. They must have been endowed with a better eyesight than ours, and the sky must have been very clear. Since they say it is a she-bear, let it be one; they were very lucky in being able to distinguish it."

This reads like comic astronomy. If it be a fair specimen, the old astronomers did not err much in their estimate of the Alphonsine Tables. Regiomontanus says, " Beware lest you trust too much to blind calculation and Alphonsine dreams ;" and Tycho Brahe reports that the 400,000 ducats expended upon the Tables would have been better laid out in actual observation of the heavens. In justice to Alphonso, however, we should add that the King had little or nothing to do with the construction of the Tables which bear his name.

GREEK ART.

Mr. Falkener, in his ingenious work *Dædalus*, has the following wholesome Advice to the Critic:—" Of one thing we cannot be too careful, lest we fall into a pedantry of art which leads us to praise Greek art merely because it is Greek, and to despise modern art because it is not Greek. One reason will suffice to show this, though many others might be adduced—the injustice which is done to the modern artist. The ignorant critic may praise the antique, because he knows it to be safe, but let him pause before he proceeds to condemn a work which has entailed labour, thinking, and expense, united with a long study of the antique, and a constant analysis of modern wants. Let him reflect that he is seeking to gain a transient reputation from his pen, at the permanent loss of reputation to the artist ; that possibly his criticism may be false, and therefore, as the artist has no opportunity of being heard in defence, he is taking upon himself the part of a calumniator rather than that of a critic. Let him consider that he will more surely found a reputation, and gain respect, by making himself sufficiently acquainted with the art to be able to appreciate excellences ; and let the man of fortune consider that while possession of the antique may constitute, or be supposed to do so, the title for taste, the patronage of living artists will prove that he is imbued with a love of art, and wishes to improve it."

INVENTION OF THE LOCOMOTIVE.

The commonly received notion, for a length of time, was that George Stephenson was the inventor of the Locomotive for Railways. This is an error, as is also the belief that Stephenson first applied steam-power to Locomotive engines on railways. A critic in the *Athenæum* thus explains away both these errors : " Trevithick, in 1804, built a locomotive which drew along the Merthyr Tydvil (South Wales) Railway a train of wagons loaded with ten tons of bar-iron, at the rate of five miles an hour ; and when George Stephenson built his first locomotive at Killingworth, he merely adopted the principles of a successful steam-locomotive which had been running for about two years on a railway within a few miles of his door. At this date, persons who presume to write about George Stephenson ought to know that so far as the Locomotive is concerned he was merely a copyist of a near neighbour's work, and has not the faintest shadow of a claim to be regarded as an inventor, or even an improver."

The marble statue of Stephenson, at the Euston Terminus of the London and North-western Railway would, therefore, seem better to commemorate his engineering connexion with that line than his claims to be inventor of the Locomotive.

ENGINEERING MISCALCULATION.

Mr. Robert Stephenson, it will be recollected, stated that either iron or ice will bear a weight passing over it at a great velocity, which it could not bear if it went slower ; and that "when it goes quick, the weight in a manner ceases." To this a Correspondent of the *Athenæum*, No. 1635, replies : " The very reverse of this is the truth, as was clearly established by the 'Iron Commission,' which was appointed a few years since, to inquire into the causes of the breaking down of the iron bridge over the Dee. And the principle so established is now universally acted upon throughout our railways ; the speed of the trains, upon approaching bridges of any considerable length, whether of iron or wood, is usually slackened to 8, 6, or even 4 miles an hour, according to circumstances; and the same rule—viz., of going slow, and not of going quick, is always observed in passing over an unsound part of an embankment. I was myself present at some very interesting experiments made by this Commission at the iron bridge of the South-eastern Railway near Epsom, in the presence of Lord Wrottesley, Sir W. Cubitt, the Astronomer Royal, and several others. Prof. Willis had contrived a very ingenious apparatus, which, fixed to the centre of one of the iron girders, measured and registered the deflection of the bridge at the passing over of any weight. An engine with a heavily-laden tender was then passed over the bridge at speeds varying from 10 to 60 miles an hour, and it was found that the greater the speed the greater was the deflection of the girder."

THE "GREAT EASTERN" STEAM-SHIP AND THE ARK.

While the *Great Eastern* was building, there appeared a pamphlet, in which this gigantic steam-ship was stated to be *larger than the Ark*, by persons to whom it did not occur that such an assertion could easily be tested. It has, however, been proved, beyond dispute, that so far from being larger, this monster ship is not so large by several hundred thousand cubic feet. The *Great Eastern*, then, is, in its longest part, 692 feet; in the broadest, 83 feet, and 60 feet deep. "In order to be certain of measuring the ship correctly," says the Correspondent by whom the calculation was made, "I planed up a rectangular prism of dry mahogany, corresponding to the above dimensions, to a scale of the 64th part of an inch to a foot. This piece of wood contained 13·1295 cubic inches, and it weighed sixty-four pennyweights. I then formed it to the model of the hull of the ship, and weighed it again, and it weighed forty-four pennyweights; it now became an easy arithmetical process to find this model contained only 9·0265 cubic inches; this number multiplied into the cube of 64, gives 2366242·816 cubic feet for the content of the whole ship. According to the best commentators a cubit equals 21·888 inches, or 1·824 foot: and we read in Genesis, 'Thou shalt make the ark 300 cubits long [or 547·2 feet], 50 cubits broad [or 91·2 feet], 30 cubits deep [or 54·72 feet].' These numbers multiplied into each other give nearly 2,730,782 cubic feet for the content of the whole ark, which it will be seen is 364539·184 cubic feet more than the *Great Eastern*. The writers of the pamphlet above alluded to say this ship is six times the size of the *Duke of Wellington* line-of-battle ship, therefore,—

$$2366242·816 + \frac{2366242·816}{6} = 2760616·6186$$

cubic feet for both these vessels. It will be seen by an inspection of these figures that the ark is within 29,835 feet of being as large as both these large ships put together."

Y

Two points in this letter will be considered open to question. 1. He treats the ark as a *parallelogram*. 2. The cubit is ordinarily considered to be about 18 English inches.

HISTORY OF MANNERS.

We should not venture to call our levées and drawing-rooms the remnants of barbarism and savagery. Yet they must clearly be traced back to the Middle Ages, when homage was done by each subject by putting his hands joined between the hands of the King. This, again, was originally a mere symbol, an imitation of the act by which a vanquished enemy surrendered himself to his despoiler. We know from the sculptures of Nineveh and from other sources that it was the custom of the conqueror to put his foot on the neck of his enemy. This, too, has been abbreviated; and as in Europe gentlemen now only kiss the King's hand, we find that in the Tonga Islands, when a subject approaches to do homage, the chief has to hold up his foot behind, as a horse does, and the subject touches the sole with his fingers, thus placing himself, as it were, under the sole of his lord's foot. Every one seems to have the right of doing reverence in this way when he pleases; and chiefs get so tired of holding up their feet to be touched that they make their escape at the very sight of a loyal subject.

Who has not wondered sometimes at the fumbling efforts of gentlemen in removing their gloves before shaking hands with a lady, the only object being, it would seem, to substitute a warm hand for a cool glove? Yet in the ages of chivalry there was a good reason for it. A knight's glove was a steel gauntlet, and a squeeze with that would have been painful.

Another extraordinary feature in the history of manners is the utter disability of people to judge of the manners of other nations, or of former ages, with anything like fairness or common sense. An English lady travelling in the East turns away her face with disgust when she sees Oriental women passing by with bare feet and bare legs; while the Eastern ladies are horrified at the idea of women in Europe walking about barefaced. Admirers of Goethe may get over the idea that this great poet certainly ate fish with a knife; but when we are told that Beatrice never used a fork, and that Dante never changed his linen for weeks, some of our illusions are rudely disturbed. We mourn in black, and think that nothing can be more natural; the aborigines of Australia mourn in white, and their clothing being of the scantiest, they plaster their foreheads, the tips of their noses, and the lower part of the orbits of their eyes with pipe clay. As long as the people of Europe represented the Devil in human form they represented him in black. In Africa the natives of the Guinea coast paint him in the whitest colours. To Northern nations Hell was a cold place, a dreary region of snow and frost; to Eastern nations, and those who derive their notions from the East, the place of torment was ablaze with fire and flame. Who shall tell which is right?—*Times* journal.

ASSYRIAN ART.

Was the art of the Assyrians really of home growth, or imported from the Egyptians, either directly or by way of Phenicia? The latter view has been sometimes taken; but the most cursory study of the Assyrian remains, in chronological order, is sufficient to d sprove the theory, since it will at once show that the earliest specimens of Assyrian art are the most un-Egyptian in character. No doubt there are certain analogies even here, as the preference for the profile, the stiffness and formality, the ignorance or disregard of perspective, and the like; but the analogies are such as would be tolerably sure to occur in the early efforts of any two races not very dissimilar to one another, while the *little* resemblances, which alone prove connection, are entirely wanting. These do not appear until we come to monuments which belong to the time of Sargon, when direct connection between Egypt and Assyria seems to have begun, and Egyptian captives are known to have been transported into Mesopotamia in large numbers.—Rawlinson's *Ancient Monarchies.*

FASHIONS IN DRESS.—MALE AND FEMALE.

The following is from a popular paper on the art of Dress, reprinted from the *Quarterly Review,* in 1852:—

"A certain old father, soured by the circumstances of his lot, relieved some of his spleen by defining woman as ζῶον φιλοκοσμον—*Anglice,* an animal that delights in finery; and this saying, naturally so acceptable to disappointed gentlemen of all orders, continued an authority even to the time of the amiable *Spectator,* who was not ashamed to quote it. We had nevertheless, long ago, serious doubts on the venerable *dictum;* and it now appears, from Mr. Planché's *History of Costume* and other meritorious works now before us, that we cannot point to one single excess or caprice of dress which has appeared on the beautiful person of woman, that has not had its counterpart, as bad, or worse, upon the ugly body of man. We have had the same effeminate stuffs—the same fine laces—the same rich furs—the same costly jewels. We have had as much gold and embroidery, and more tinsel and trumpery. We have worn long hair, and large sleeves, and tight waists, and full petti-coats. We have sported stays and stomachers, muffs, ear-rings, and love-locks. We have rouged and patched, and padded and laced. Where they have indulged a little extravagance in one part, we have broken out ten times worse in another. If they have had head-dresses like the moon's crescent, we have had shoes like a ram's horn. If they have lined their petticoats with whalebone, we have stuffed our trunk-hose with bran. If they have wreathed lace ruffs round their lovely throats, we have buttoned them about our clumsy legs. If they carried a little mirror openly in their fans, we have concealed one slily in our pockets. In short, wherever we look into the history of mankind, whether through the annals of courtiers, the evidence of painters, or, as now, through the condescending researches of a Lady of Rank, we find two animals equally fond of dress, but only one worth bestowing it on, which the Greek father doubtless knew as well as we."

HOUBRAKEN'S HEADS.

Jacob Houbraken, the eminent Dutch engraver, who chiefly excelled in portraits, in which he was principally employed, is more noted for the boldness of his stroke, brilliancy of colour, and correct drawing, than for reliable accuracy. Lord Orford tells us, that Houbraken "was ignorant of our history, uninquisitive into the authenticity of the drawings which were transmitted to him, and engraved whatever was sent." Two instances are adduced, namely, Carr, Earl of Somerset, and Secretary Thurloe, as not only spurious, but not having the least resemblance to the persons whom they pretend to represent. An anonymous but evidently well informed writer in the *Gentleman's Magazine,* further states that "Thurloe's, and about *thirty* of the others, are copied from heads painted for no one knows whom."

STORY OF AN ARUNDEL MARBLE.

Early in 1868 there was exhibited to the British Archæological Association a marble head, which, through the assistance of coins and medals, had been identified as the head of the Empress Magnia Urbica, one of the *nine wives* of the cruel and profligate Marcus Aurelius Carinus, who was proclaimed Cæsar in the year 282; on the mysterious death of his father in 283, he became joint emperor with his brother Numerianus, and, after a brief reign, was assassinated in the moment of victory, at Margum, in Mœsia, A.D. 285; his rival, Diocletian, thus becoming sole master of the Roman Empire.

The bust of Magnia Urbica, of the saccharine marble of Massa Carrara, is radiant with natural loveliness of feature and expression, "in pride of youth, in beauty's bloom," when innocence and affection had full possession of her heart and mind. It bears all the peculiarities of busts of the third century of our era—marked attention to the details of features, the chiselling out of the eyeballs and pupils, and careful delineation of the nostrils, ears, and hair. The statement respecting this remnant of antiquity is, that it was once in the collection of Thomas, Earl of Arundel, and that when this nobleman's mansion in the Strand was pulled down in 1678, this, with other mutilated pieces of sculpture, was obtained by Boyder Cuper, who had been gardener in Lord Arundel's family, and who employed these ancient relics in ornamenting a place of public amusement he had opened on the Surrey side of the Thames, just opposite Somerset House. Aubrey, speaking of Cuper's garden, says that "the convenience of its arbours, walks, and several remains of Greek and Roman antiquities, have made this place much frequented." The establishment, however, became disreputable, and was closed in the year 1753, whilst under the management of Widow Evans; but one who knew well the locality before the Waterloo Road was formed through the centre of the grounds, told the writer he distinctly remembered pieces of antique sculpture lying about unheeded on banks, and in hollows of the grounds, though the bulk of "the Arundel Marbles" had gradually been dispersed to enrich the rockwork of suburban gardens. Thus, our marble effigy of the august Magnia Urbica, which once probably adorned the stately palace of a proud Cæsar, in lovely Italy, after resting for awhile in the princely dwelling of an English nobleman, at length became the property of the keeper of a public garden in swampy Lambeth, and helped to decorate a rendezvous of vice and infamy.

VAST BUILDINGS ERECTED BY SLAVERY.

In Mexico and Peru, the lower classes being at the disposal of the upper, there followed that frivolous waste of labour which we observe in Egypt, and evidence of which may be seen in the remains of those temples and palaces that are still to be found in several parts of Asia. Both Mexicans and Peruvians erected immense buildings, which were as useless as those of Egypt, and which no country could produce, unless the labour of the people were ill-paid and ill-directed.* The Mexicans appear to have been even more wantonly prodigal than the Peruvians: one of their immense pyramids, Cholula, had a base twice as broad as the largest Egyptian pyramid. The cost of these monuments of vanity is unknown; but it must have been enormous; since the Americans, being ignorant of the use of iron, were unable to employ a resource by which, in the construction of large works, labour is greatly abridged. Some particulars, however, have been preserved, from which an idea may be formed on this subject. To take, for instance, the palaces of their kings: we find that in Peru, the erection of the royal residence occupied during fifty years 20,000 men: striking facts, which, if all other testimonies had perished, would enable us to appreciate the condition of countries in which, for such insignificant purposes, such vast power was expended.—Buckle's *History of Civilization*, vol. i.

THE ROUND TOWERS OF IRELAND.

The learned Dr. Petrie, who died in 1867, by his researches into the history of the Round Towers of Ireland—an inquiry more thoroughly vexed than almost any modern one of the sort—is considered to have

---

* Prescott notes: "The Tezcucan monarchy, like those of Asia and ancient Egypt, had the control of immense masses of men, and would sometimes turn the whole population of a conquered city, including the women, into the public works. The most gigantic monuments of architecture which the world has witnessed would never have been reared by the hands of freemen!"

set the question at rest. He has shown that they are, undoubtedly, Christian buildings intended as *Bell-houses*, which their name in Irish signifies; and further, probably, for the safe keeping of the sacred vessels, &c., in time of war or tumult. In 1832, for his *Essay on the History of the Round Towers*, Dr. Petrie received the prize offered by the Irish Society, in all 900*l.*, on account of the work; besides which, other rewards were bestowed upon him, including a pension of 300*l.* per annum. Yet a critic in the *Athenæum* demurs to Dr. Petrie's settlements, and maintains that, although Dr. Petrie's researches have been of great service, the conclusion at which he arrived obtained slight acceptation among the really learned, and may be said to have rather added fuel to the disputes than assuaged their intensity; those disputes remain at present in abeyance for lack of material rather than energy on the part of those who have interested themselves in the matter. Dr. Petrie attributed to the Round Towers a Christian origin, in which he was probably correct, although it can hardly be doubted that he set too far back in time the date of their erection. These structures have been the causes of no less wit than controversy; the best thing said about them is that they were built on purpose to puzzle the moderns. Beyond all possibility of doubt, they were not built solely, if at all, for the purposes ascribed to them by Dr. Petrie. Had they been castles of the ancient Irish, their form would alone suffice to justify all that has been alleged about the national blunderings; that they were not belfries cannot be considered settled by the fact that belfries were in some cases built beside them. Some have claimed for them an origin coeval with that of the Pyramids; others have found in the *fanaux de cimetière* of France similar and allied structures of the twelfth and thirteenth centuries.

Among the many contributions to the controversy, is a *Discourse of the Round Towers*, by John Flanagan, published 1843; it is a small quarto of 24 pages, beautifully printed. The author boldly says that "there are no Round Towers in Ireland," p. 8; however, it seems doubtful whether this work is genuine; so much having been written in jest as well as earnest upon the Towers.

FALLACIES OF STATISTICS.

Archbishop Whately acutely remarks upon the overrated importance of Statistics: Increase of a thing is often confounded with our increased knowledge of it. When crimes or accidents are recorded in newspapers more than formerly, some people fancy that they happen more than formerly. But crimes, especially (be it observed) such as are most remote from the experience of each individual, and therefore strike him as something strange, always furnish interesting articles of intelligence. I have no doubt that a single murder in Great Britain has often furnished matter for discourse to more than twenty times as many persons as any twenty such murders would in Turkey. Some foreign traveller in England is said to have remarked on the perceptible diminution in the number of crimes committed during the sitting of Parliament as a proof of our high reverence for that assembly; the fact being, as we all know, that the space occupied in the newspapers by the debates causes the records of many crimes to be omitted. Men are liable to form an over-estimate of the purity of morals in the country as compared with a town, or in a barren and thinly-peopled as compared with a fertile and populous district. On a given area, it must always be expected that the absolute amount of vice will be greater in a town than in the country, so also will be that of virtue; but the proportion of the two must be computed on quite different principles. A physician of great skill and in high repute probably loses many more patients than an ordinary practitioner; but this proves nothing till we have ascertained the comparative numbers of their patients. Mistakes such as this (which are very frequent) remind one of the well-known riddle, " What is the reason that white sheep eat more than black ones?"

In 1867 Mr. Saville Lumley, in his report on the Russian Tea Trade, set down the number of tea consumers in Russia at 60,000,000, out of a population of 75,000,000; to which a Correspondent of the *Times* replied that, "probably, Mr. Lumley established this proportion from what he saw of the St. Petersburghers and Muscovites, inveterate tea-drinkers; this proportion, however, will not stand good for the whole country. I generally reside in Russia, and fully half my time is occupied in travelling through the wealthiest as well as the poorest governments of the empire; and many are the times that I have had to hunt through half a dozen villages before I could find a Samovar, the indispensable adjunct to tea drinking in Russia. No children, and comparatively few women in Russia drink tea; while, say 30 per cent of the male peasantry are non-habitual drinkers, either because they cannot afford the luxury, or have not the opportunities which others possess, of laying themselves in soak. Deducting, therefore, 25 millions for children and women, and ten millions for the non-habitual male drinkers, there remain 40 millions of regular tea drinkers; this I think far nearer the mark than Mr. Lumley's proportion. By far a larger quantity of hot water is consumed in Russia over the 30 millions of pounds of tea, than in England over the 200 millions pounds." These facts are interesting, in addition to their showing the fallacy of evidence taken from one portion of a country being taken as proof of the general custom of the whole people.

THE LAST HALF CENTURY OF INVENTIONS.

It is in the three momentous matters of Light, Locomotion, and Communication, that the progress effected in this generation contrasts most surprisingly with the aggregate of the progress effected in all previous generations put together since the earliest dawn of authentic history. The lamps and torches which illuminated Belshazzar's feast were probably just as brilliant, and framed out of nearly the same materials, as those which shone upon the splendid fêtes of Versailles, when Marie Antoinette presided over them, or those of the Tuileries during the Imperial magnificence of the First Napoleon. Pine-wood, oil, and perhaps wax, lighted the banquet halls of the wealthiest nobles alike in the eighteenth century before Christ and in the eighteenth century after Christ. There was little difference, except in finish of workmanship and elegance of design—little, if any, advance, we mean, in the illuminating power, or in the source whence that power was drawn—between the lamps used in the days of the Pyramids, the days of the Coliseum, and the days of Kensington Palace. Fifty years ago, that is, we burnt the same articles and got about the same amount of light from them, as we did 5000 years ago. Now we use gas, of which each burner is equal to fifteen or twenty candles; and when we wish for more can have recourse to the electric light or analogous inventions, which are fifty-fold more brilliant and far-reaching than even the best gas. The streets of cities, which from the days of Pharaoh to those of Voltaire, were dim and gloomy, even where not wholly unlighted, now blaze everywhere (except in London) with something of the brilliancy of moonlight. In a word, all the advance that has been made in these respects has been made since many of us were children. We remember light as it was in the days of Solomon; we see it as Drummond and Faraday have made it.

The same thing may be said of locomotion. Nimrod and Noah travelled just in the same way, and just at the same rate, as Thomas Assheton Smith and Mr. Coke of Norfolk. The chariots of the Olympic games went just as fast as the chariots that conveyed our nobles to the Derby, "in our hot youth, when George the Third was king." When Abraham wanted to send a message to Lot, he despatched a man on horseback who galloped twelve miles an hour. When our fathers wanted to send a message to their nephews they could do no better and go no quicker. When we were young, if we wished to travel from London to Edinburgh we thought ourselves lucky if we could average eight miles an hour— just as Robert Bruce might have done. Now, in our old age, we feel ourselves aggrieved if we do not average forty miles. Everything that has been done in this line since the world began—everything, perhaps, that the capacities of matter and the conditions of the human frame will ever allow to be done—has been done since we were boys. The same at sea. Probably when the wind was favourable, Ulysses, who was a bold and skilful navigator, sailed as fast as a Dutch merchantman of the year 1800, nearly as fast at times as an American yacht or clipper of our fathers' day. Now we steam twelve and fifteen miles an hour with wonderful regularity, whether wind and tide be favourable or not; nor is it likely we shall ever be able to go much faster. But the progress in the means of communication is the most remarkable of all. In this respect Mr. Pitt was no better off than Pericles or Agamemnon. If Ruth had wished to write to Naomi, or David to send a word of love to Jonathan when he was a hundred miles away, they could not possibly have done it under twelve hours. Nor could we to our friends thirty years ago. In 1867 the humblest citizen of Great Britain can send such a message, not 100 miles, but 1000 in twelve minutes.—From the *Spectator* newspaper.

Books, Phrases, etc.

FALSE ESTIMATES OF POPULAR BOOKS.

PEPYS' Mistakes.—Samuel Pepys, the diarist, has some pretension to notice as a man of letters,—having written a romance, and, at least, two songs. The former he prudently burned, though not without some regret, doubting he could not do it so well over again if he should try. He does not appear to have got beyond the false taste of his times, as he extols *Volpone* and *The Silent Woman*, as the best plays he ever saw ; and accounts the *Midsummer Night's Dream* the most insipid and ridiculous. *Othello* he sets down as "a mean thing;" *Henry VIII.*, although much cried up, did not please him, even though he went with purpose to be pleased; it was, in his opinion, "a simple thing, made of patches ;" "and, besides the show and processions in it, there was nothing well done." But the most diverting circumstance is the series of unsuccessful efforts which Pepys made to relish the celebrated *Hudibras* of Butler, then enjoying all the blaze of novel popularity. Possibly some remaining predilection for the opinions which are ridiculed in that witty satire prevented his falling in with the universal fashion of admiring it. The first part of *Hudibras* cost him two shillings and sixpence, but he found it so silly an abuse of a Presbyterian knight going to the wars, that he became ashamed of it, and prudently sold it for eighteenpence. Wise by experience, he did not buy the second part, but only borrowed it to read.

Popularity of Milton.—Waller, upon the coming out of the *Paradise Lost*, wrote to the Duke of Buckingham, amongst other pretty things, as follows : "Milton, the old blind schoolmaster, has lately written a poem on the Fall of Man—*remarkable for nothing but its extreme length !*" Our divine poet asked a fit audience, although it should be but few. His prayer was heard : a fit audience for the *Paradise Lost* has ever been, and at this moment must be, a small one, and we cannot affect to believe that it is destined to be much increased by what is called the March of Intellect. —*Quarterly Review*, 1824.

Gil Blas and Télémaque.—Professor Kingsley, in some ingenious remarks on the literature of the *ancien régime*, has chosen *Gil Blas* and *Télémaque* as specimens of its worst and best spirit. We quote what he says of *Gil Blas* :—"It is the *ancien régime* itself. It sets forth to the men thereof themselves, without veil or cowardly reticence of any kind; and inasmuch as every man loves himself, the *ancien régime* loved *Gil Blas*, and said, 'The problem of humanity is solved at last.' But, ye long-suffering powers of Heaven, what a solution ! It is beside the matter to call the book ungodly, immoral, base. Le Sage would have answered, ' Of course it is, for so is the world of which it is a picture.' No ; the most notable thing about the book is its intense stupidity, its barrenness, dreariness, ignorance of the human heart, want of any human interest. If it be an epic, the actors in it are not men or women, but ferrets—with here and there, of course, a stray rabbit on whose brains they may feed. It is the inhuman mirror of an inhuman age, in which the healthy human heart can find no more interest than in a pathological museum."

This is Mr. Kingsley's view of *Télémaque* :—" The king with Fénélon is always to be the father of his people, which is tantamount to saying that the people are to be always children, and in a condition of tutelage, voluntary if possible, but if not, of tutelage sti L Of self-government, and education of human beings into free manhood by the exercise of self-government, free will, free thought—of this Fénélon had surely not a glimpse. . . . . There is a defect in *Télémaque* which is perhaps deeper still. No woman in it exercises an influence over man except for evil."

Tristram Shandy.—Horace Walpole,[*] in his *Letters*, vol. iii. p. 298, writes: " At present nothing is talked of, nothing admired, but what I cannot help calling a very insipid and tedious performance: it is a kind of novel, called *The Life and Opinions of Tristram Shandy*, the greatest humour of which consists in the whole narration always going backwards. I can conceive a man saying that it would be droll to write a book in that manner, but have no notion of his persevering in executing it. It makes one smile two or three times in the beginning, but in recompense makes one yawn for two hours. The characters are tolerably kept up, but the humour is for ever attempted and missed. The best thing in it is a sermon, oddly coupled with a good deal of bawdy, and both the composition of a clergyman. The man's head, indeed, was a little turned before, and he is now topsy-turvy with his success and fame. Dodsley has given him 650*l.* for the second edition, and two more volumes (which I suppose will reach backwards to his great-great-grandfather) ; Lord Fauconberg a donative of 160*l.* a year ; and Bishop Warburton gave him a purse of gold, and his compliment (which happened to be a contradiction), 'that it was quite an original composition, and in the true Cervantic vein;' the only copy that ever was an original, except in painting, where they all pretend to be so. Warburton, however, not content with this, recommended the book to the bench of bishops, and told them Mr. Sterne, the author, was the English Rabelais. They had never heard of such a writer."

Bunyan's Pilgrim's Progress has attained the greatest notoriety of all his works. "If," says the Editor of the *Penny Cyclopædia*, "a judgment

---

[*] Lord Macaulay has left this very *trenchant* estimate of Walpole : Horace Walpole was "the most eccentric, the most artificial, the most fastidious, the most suspicious of men. His mind was a bundle of inconsistent whims and affectations. In everything in which he busied himself, in the fine arts, in literature, in public affairs, he was drawn by some strange attraction, from the great to the little, and from the useful to the odd. . . . . There is scarcely a writer in whose works it would be possible to find so many contradictory judgments, so many sentences of extravagant nonsense."

is to be formed of the merits of a book by the number of times it has been reprinted, and the many languages into which it has been translated, no production in English literature is superior to this coarse allegory, (*Pilgrim's Progress.*) On a composition which has been extolled by Dr. Johnson, and which in our times has received a very high critical opinion in its favour, it is hazardous to venture a disapproval; and we, perhaps, speak the opinion of a small minority when we confess that, to us, it appears to be *mean, jejune, and wearisome.*"

Shakspeare and his Commentators. — In the *Diversions of Purley*, Tooke says: "The ignorance and presumption of his commentators have shamefully disfigured Shakspeare's text. The first folio, notwithstanding some few palpable misprints, requires none of their alterations. Had they understood English as well as he did, they would not have quarrelled with his language." And again, "Rack is a very common word, most happily used, and ought not to be displaced because the commentators knew not its meaning. If such a rule were adopted, the commentators themselves would, most of them, become speechless." Yet, he departs from the folio to read "one dowle that's in my *plume*," for the folio *plumbe*, in the *Tempest*; and in *Antony and Cleopatra*, his commentary alters the rack *dislimes* into *dislimbs*. Matthias's attack on the commentators, in his *Pursuits of Literature*, was once very popular. It is alluded to even by Schlegel.

Baron Munchausen. — It is generally believed that Munchausen is only a *nom-de-guerre*. Such, however, is not the fact. Baron Munch-Hausen was a Hanoverian nobleman, and so late as forty-five years ago, he was alive and *lying*. It is true that the travels published as his, though not by him, were intended as a satire or parody on the travels of the famous Baron de Tott; but Munch-Hausen was really in the habit of relating the adventures now sanctioned by the authority of his mendacious name, as having positively occurred to him; and he is supposed to have, at length, believed what he related. There was nothing of the *fanfaron* or braggart in his manner; on the contrary, he was distinguished by the peculiar modesty of his manner and demeanour.—*New Monthly Magazine.*

Chesterfield's Letters have been much abused, but have found defenders. Some other wit has not unhappily called them the *Scoundrel's Primer.* When they were published, Dr. Johnson said they inculcated the morals of a strumpet and the manners of a dancing-master. —"After all," says Mr. Malone, "these ' Letters' have been, I think, unreasonably decried; for supposing a young man to be properly guarded against the base principles of dissimulation, &c., which they enforce, he may derive much advantage from the many minute directions which they contain, that other instructors, and even parents, don't think it worth while to mention. In this, and almost everything else, the world generally seizes on two or three obviously ridiculous circumstances, talks a great deal about them, and passes over all the valuable parts that may still be found in the work, or in the character they are criticizing. I have heard persons laugh at the noble writer's laying weight upon such trifling matters as paring nails, or opening a dirty pocket handkerchief in company. Yet, trifling as these instructions are, I have observed these very people greatly negligent in those very particulars. Lord Chesterfield, however, by his perpetual attention to propriety, decorum, *bienséance*, &c., had so *veneered* his manners, that though he lived on good terms with all the world, he had not a single friend."

Worthless and Despised Books.—In a paper in the *Edinburgh Review* on the "Library of the British Museum," we read:—"Setting aside the unforeseen value which events may give to intrinsically worthless books, and the fact that posterity is not always of our way of thinking as to the merits of others, it is not to be forgotten that our very contempt tends to endow a book with an ultimate bibliographical consequence. Little will the Ames or Dibdin of the year 2059 care, bibliographically speaking, for the works of Hallam and Macaulay, Scott and Wordsworth, the early editions of which will be obtainable, in dusty calf or abraded morocco, for ninepence a volume, at every bookstall; but fabulous prices will be realized by copies, unique or of excessive rarity, of a Cumming's *Apocalyptic Sketches*, or a Tupper's *Proverbial Philosophy*; a set of Playbills will fetch the price of a whole library of the classics; and an auction of the facetiæ of the middle of the nineteenth century will agitate the hearts of bibliomaniacs who have vainly endeavoured to possess themselves of an *editio princeps* of the *Ascent of Mont Blanc*, or *Mrs. Caudle's Lectures*. Although it may sound like a paradox, libraries are swelled to an enormous bulk, not so much by the treasures of literature, as by its dregs and its scum. A moderate apartment may receive all the noblest monuments of human thought and knowledge, though "the world itself could not contain all the books that should be written" for the varied intercourse of society. The great productions of literary genius are borne onwards with the stream and are imperishable; the whims and fashions of the hour sink to the bottom, and can only be rescued from total oblivion by those who have the courage to dive down to the accumulated rubbish of past ages.

"Despised books have a strange trick of revenging themselves, by becoming indispensable. Dr. Bandinel gave ten times its weight in gold for the 'riff-raff' condemned by Sir Thomas Bodley, who, on the repeated application of the first Bodleian librarian, Dr. James, to be allowed to purchase plays, replied, 'I can see no good reason to alter my opinion for excluding such books as almanacks, plays, and an infinite number that are daily printed, of very unworthy matter and handling.' A short time before the date of this letter, was printed Marlowe's *True Tragedie of Ricbarde, Duke of Yorke, and the Death of Good King Henrie the Sixt*, a copy of which was purchased a few years ago, by Mr. Rodd, for the Bodleian Library, for 13*l*.—being, we believe, the highest price ever, up to that time, given for a single play. It is recorded that one of the libraries, which had a copyright claim, rejected as worthless the first works of Walter Scott, Mrs. Opie, Wordsworth, Shelley, Lord Brougham, and M'Culloch. 'It is in the fragments,' writes M. Libri, 'of some alphabets, of some small grammars published for the use of schools, about the middle of the fifteenth century, or in the letters distributed in Germany by the religious bodies commissioned to collect alms, that bibliographers now seek to discover the first processes employed by the inventors of xylography and of typography. It is in a forgotten collection of indifferent plates, published at Venice, by Fausto Verantio, that an engineer may find the first diagram of iron suspension bridges.' "

BIRTHDAY OF SHAKSPEARE AND CERVANTES.[*]

As regards the day of Shakspeare's birth, what proof is there of the bard having been born in the month of April at all ? That the 23rd, at least, was not the day of his birth, is all but certain. Such was not the understanding of those relatives or friends under whose care his tomb was erected, and who may fairly be supposed to have had the best knowledge upon the subject. From the terms of the Stratford inscription—*Obiit ano. doi.* 1616, *ætatis* 53, *die* 23 *Apr.*—it is clear they never conceived his birth to have fallen upon the same day of the month as that of his death, he having gone at the time of the record some way at all events into his fifty-third year, instead of having exactly completed the exact annual cycle. The 23rd of April having been also usually given as the date of the death of Cervantes, not a little of puerile, half-mystical sentiment has been vented upon the supposed extinction of two such mighty luminaries of the firmament of genius on one and the same day. To Mr. Robert Chambers (in the *Book of Days*), seems to be due the credit of having, for the first time, exploded this fallacy—as follows: —" It has not heretofore been pointed out that, if Shakspeare died on the day reckoned the 23rd of April in England, and Cervantes on that reckoned the 23rd of April in Spain, these two great, and in some measure kindred geniuses, necessarily did not die on the same day. Spain had adopted the Gregorian calendar on its first promulgation ·in 1582, and consequently the 23rd day of April in Spain corresponded with the 13th in England; there being at that time ten days' difference between the new and old style."

MODERN MYTHOLOGY.

Professor Max Müller, in his learned lecture upon this branch of study, enters fully into the origin of the different stories about the

---

[*] In 1867, the German newspapers announced the death of a man who was so devoted an admirer of Cervantes that he spent nearly the whole of his life, and a considerable fortune, in collecting every edition of *Don Quixote* which had been published in Europe since its first appearance. There were found in the library of this curious bibliomaniac 400 editions of *Don Quixote* in the Spanish language, 168 in French, 200 in English, 87 in Portuguese, 96 in Italian, 70 in German, 4 in Russian, 4 in Greek, 8 in Polish, 6 in Danish, 13 in Swedish, and 5 in Latin.

Barnacle goose. He quotes from the *Philosophical Transactions* of 1678 a full account by Sir Robert Morray, who declared that he had seen within the barnacle shell, as through a concave or diminishing glass, the bill, eyes, head, neck, breast, wings, tail, feet, and feathers of the barnacle goose. The next witness was John Gerarde, Master in Chirurgerie, who, in 1597, declared that he had seen the actual metamorphosis of the mussel into the bird, describing how—

"The shell gapeth open, and the first thing that appeareth is the foresaid lace or string; next come the leg of the birde hanging out, and as it groweth greater, it openeth the shell by degrees, till at length it is all come forth, and hangeth only by the bill, and falleth into the sea, when it gathereth feathers and groweth to a foule, bigger than a mallart; for the truth hereof, if any doubt, may it please them to repair unto me, and I shall satisfie them by the testimonies of good witnesses."

As far back as the thirteenth century, the same story is traced in the writings of Giraldus Cambrensis. This great divine does not deny the truth of the miraculous origin of the barnacle geese, but he warns the Irish priests against dining off them during Lent on the plea that they were not flesh, but fish. For, he writes, "If a man during Lent were to dine off a leg of Adam, who was not born of flesh either, we should not consider him innocent of having eaten what is flesh." This modern myth, which, in spite of the protests of such men as Albertus Magnus, Æneas Sylvius, and others, maintained its ground for many centuries, and was defended, as late as 1629, in a book by Count Maier, *De volucri arborea*, with arguments, physical, metaphysical, and theological, owed its origin to a play of words. The mussel shells are called *Bernaculæ* from the Latin *perna*, the mediæval Latin *berna*; the birds are called *Hibernicæ* or *Hiberniculæ* abbreviated to *Berniculæ*. As their names seem one, the creatures are supposed to be one, and everything conspires to confirm the first mistake, and to invest what was originally a good Irish story—a mere *canard*—with all the dignity of scientific, and all the solemnity of theological truth. The myth continued to live until the age of Newton. Specimens of *Lepadidæ*, prepared by Professor Rolleston of Oxford, show how the outward appearance of the *Anatifera* could have supported the popular superstition which derived the *Bernicla*, the goose, from the *Bernicula*, the shell.

Professor Max Müller has also examined shortly the origin of some mediæval legends, such as the legend of St. Christopher, of St. Ignatius Theophorus, which owed their origin entirely to the misapprehension of a name. The story of the talking crucifix of Bonaventura is traced back to the saying of Bonaventura that it was the image which dictated all his works to him. The legends of saints fighting with dragons are explained as allegorical representations of their struggles with sin. St. Patrick, driving away every poisonous creature from Ireland, is explained as a missionary who had successfully driven out the venomous brood of heresy and idolatry; and the belief in martyrs walking about after their execution with their heads in their arms is traced back to sculptures in which martyrs, executed by the sword, were so represented. Another case of modern mythology is when an abstract term, expressive of a quality, or of a mode of existence, is raised into a substantial, real, and personal being. This tendency, which in ancient times led to the creation of gods and goddesses, such as Virtue and Peace, and to a belief in beings such as Kronos, Time, Eos, Dawn, Demeter, Earth, produces in our own times conceptions of a similar character, such as Nature, Force, Atoms, Imponderable substances, Ether, &c., which receive a passing worship in the successive schools of philosophy, and are at the bottom of most of the controversies which occupy the thoughts of each generation.—*Saturday Review.*

FATE OF AMBITIOUS RULERS.

In the historic page, you, of course, meet with hundreds of men celebrated for their victories; and amongst others, Alexander, Philip, Cæsar, Hannibal, Pompey, Anthony, Pyrrhus, Sylla, Seleucus; and in your own times, Napoleon. But it is equally true that in the same page you find it recorded, that in all these campaigns, the conduct of all and each of these individuals was governed by ambition, not patriotism—personal aggrandizement, not the good of their subjects or fellow countrymen. And, what were their several rewards? Alexander and Hannibal, a cup of poison; Anthony died the death of a suicide; Pyrrhus was killed by a brick thrown by a Spartan woman; Sylla was killed by vermin; Philip, Cæsar, Pompey, and Seleucus, were assassinated; and Napoleon died on the rock of St. Helena, an exile from his country.

Almost all great men, who have performed, or who are destined to perform, great things, are sparing of words. Their communing is with themselves rather than others. They feed upon their own thoughts, and in these inward musings brew those intellectual and active energies, the development of which constitutes the great character. Napoleon became a babbler only when his fate was accomplished, and his fortune was on the decline.—*Lamartine.*

THE STORY OF DIDO.

Virgil, like all the poets that aim at surpassing truth, history, and nature, has much rather injured than embellished the image of Dido. The Dido of history, widow of Sicheus, and faithful to the manes of her former spouse, causes her funeral pile to be prepared on the promontory of Carthage, and ascends it, the sublime and voluntary victim of a pure love, and of a faithfulness even unto death. This is somewhat finer, holier, and more pathetic than the cold gallantries which the Roman poet allows her with the ridiculous and pious Æneas, and her amorous despair, in which the reader cannot sympathize. But the *Anna Soror*, and the magnificent farewell, and the immortal imprecation that follow, will ever plead a pardon for Virgil.—*Lamartine.*

BURNING ALIVE

Was no more a reality than John Doe and Richard Roe; and the obstinate retention of the form of the sentence, for generations after it had ceased to be executed, proves, not the cruelty of our ancestors, but the extraordinary pedantry of our lawyers, who could not part with a fiction, whether revolting or childish, without suffering under the agony of a severe operation.—(*Notes and Queries*, 3rd S. No. 19.)

Mr. Phillimore, in his *History of England*, needlessly exaggerates in his references to the burning of women. He refers to this in three several places. In the first he states, quite correctly, "The law ordered women to be burnt alive in 1770; it is said the hangman generally strangled them first—*Jy consens.*" A few pages further on he declares that women were burnt alive; and yet again he returns to the charge in a little while, declaring that Elizabeth Hering was burnt alive in 1773, and that all the details are given in the *Annual Register*. His authority, however, does not bear him out, but distinctly declares that Elizabeth Hering was first strangled.

———

WHO'S WHO ?

Mr. Roebuck, M.P., in a speech at Salisbury in 1862, related the following anecdote :—"I recollect some years ago, being in Hampshire, I went out of my house in the morning, with the *Times* in my hand, and going into the garden, I found a labouring man whom I rather liked— a shrewd, clever fellow. He said, 'Any news, sir, this morning?' 'Yes,' I replied, 'rather bad news.' 'Bad news! what's that, sir?' 'Why,' I said, 'the Duke of Wellington is dead.' 'Ah, sir,' he remarked, 'I be very sorry for he; but who was he?' Now if I had not heard that I should not have believed it. The man who said it lived within one hundred miles of London; was a clever, shrewd fellow, and yet he wanted to know who was the Duke of Wellington. Could you have believed that within one hundred miles of London there was darkness so great that the name of Wellington was unknown to a man between fifty and sixty years of age? But so it was—'I'm very sorry for he, sir,' he said; 'but who was he?' "*

———

THE GREAT MOGUL.

Mr. Henry Mead, in his work on the *Sepoy Revolt*, gives the following very graphic picture of the "Great Mogul" and his offshoots:—

"It is little more than half a century since Lord Lake, whilst engaged in a campaign against the Mahrattas encamped near the city of Delhi, and making his way into the palace, found there the representative of the royal house of Timor in the person of an aged man, poor

———

* By this anecdote we are reminded that, although sixteen years have nearly elapsed since this great man was laid in his tomb, the erection of the National Monument voted to his memory has not been commenced !

helpless and blind, the plaything of fortune, the prize, by turns, of numerous adventurers. His ancestors had, by the law of force, at one time acquired the dominion of all India; and the rule which had raised them to the pinnacle of greatness had sunk him to the lowest depths of abasement. He had lived to see the dominions over which he had himself reigned, the prize of successive conquerors; his wealth scattered, his wives dishonoured, and had reached the climax of human misery, when a brutal soldier scooped his eyes out with a dagger, and left him without the hope of better days. The English general seated him again in the chair of royalty, and in return for a parchment gift of the countries which he had won, and intended to keep, by the sword, allotted to him the first rank in the long line of mockery-kings that once reigned, but now who merely live in India. In public and private the Padisha, as he was called, received the signs of homage which were considered to belong to his pre-eminent station. He had never forgiven the English since a governor-general insisted upon having a chair in his presence; and, until recently, the agent of the latter, when vouchsafed the honour of an audience, addressed him with folded hands, in the attitude of supplication. He never received letters, only petitions: and conferred an exalted favour on the government of British India by accepting a monthly present of 80,000 rupees. Merely as a mark of excessive condescension, he tacitly sanctioned all our acts, withdrew his royal approbation from each and all of our native enemies, and fired salutes upon every occasion of a victory achieved by our troops.

"Hitherto it would have been impossible to have found a royal ally more courteously disposed; and we believe it never entered the brain of the most suspicious diplomatist, that the treaties between the Great Mogul and the East India Company were in any danger of being violated by his majesty. To sweep away the house of Tamerlane would not have added one jot to our power. Outside the walls of his palace, the King of Delhi, as he was termed, had no more authority than the meanest of those whom he had been taught to consider his born vassals; but within that enclosure his will was fate, and there were 12,000 persons who lived subject to it. The universal voice of society ascribed to this population the habitual practice of crimes of which the very existence is unknown at home, except to the few who form the core of the corrupt civilization of great cities. Its princes lived without dignity, and its female aristocracy continued to exist without honour. The physical type of manhood was debased, whilst the intellectual qualifications of both sexes, with one or two exceptions, did not reach even the Mohammedan standard of merit, perhaps the lowest in the scale of modern humanity. But a 'Light of the World' could not exist even in these days without experiencing earthly troubles. His Majesty had no fear of Mahratta daggers, and his pension was paid far more punctually than were the revenues of his ancestors. Domestic troubles were more burdensome, perhaps, to his effulgent shoulders than would be the cares of the universe, and there were no less than 1200 little lights which radiated upon him from all parts of Hindostan, and required a great deal of oil to keep them burning. It was no uncommon thing for one of this celestial race to be obliged to live on fifty shillings a month, but in no case did he forget the dignity of his birth. A Mussulman is obliged to settle a dowry upon his wife, and a member of the *Soolatun* (plural for Sultan) never endows her with less than 50,000*l*. Their sole occupation was confined to playing on the Indian lute, and singing the king's verses. Too proud to work with their hands, too ignorant to be useful with their heads, they would have been content to continue for generations to come in their late miserable condition—forlorn mortals, empty alike in pocket and stomach, in heart and brain, and conscious only of the possession of unsatisfied appetites."

AN INGENIOUS FORGERY.

By far the most accomplished forger of modern times is M. Simonides. He comes from the Island of Syrene, opposite Caria, and made his first public appearance at Athens, where he offered some MSS. for sale which he said had been carried off secretly from Mount Athos. A commission which was engaged to examine them reported favourably, especially upon a MS. of Homer, which was accordingly purchased at a high price. Before very long it was discovered that the text of this ancient MS. was Wolf's, with all the *errata*. Next he appeared at Constantinople, where he tried hieroglyphics, cuneiform inscriptions, and Armenian history, but somewhat unsuccessfully. Nothing daunted, he tried a new device, and came out as another Dousterswivel. He declared that at a certain spot an Arabic MS. in Syriac characters would be discovered by digging. Workmen were accordingly employed, Simonides himself not being allowed to descend. By-and-by a pause was made for luncheon, and not long afterwards Simonides called out, "There it is; bring it up." The soil about it, however, was quite different from that of the ground. The workmen were grinning, and when interrogated confessed that during luncheon the Greek came out for a short time, jumped into the pit, and began to burrow. He next made his appearance in England with, amongst other wonderful treasures, a MS. of Homer on Serpent's skin, which professed to have been sent from Chios Hipparchus, son of Pisistratus. This and several others he persuaded Sir T. Phillips to purchase. Almost the only libraries which he failed in cheating were the British Museum and the Bodleian. On visiting the latter place he showed some fragments of MSS. to Mr. Coxe, who assented to their belonging to the twelfth century. "And these, Mr. Coxe, belong to the tenth or eleventh century?" "Yes, probably." "And now, Mr. Coxe, let me show you a very ancient and valuable MS. I have for sale, and which ought to be in your library. To what century do you consider this belongs?" "This, Mr. Simonides, I have no doubt," said Mr. Coxe, "belongs to the nineteenth century." The Greek and his MSS. disappeared. Some time afterwards a palimpsest manuscript was sent to Berlin, professing to be a history of the kings of Egypt in Greek, by Uranius of Alexandria. The Academy declared it genuine, and the Minister of Public Instruction was ordered to purchase it for 5000 thalers. Professor Dindorf offered the University of Oxford the honour of giving this valuable book to the world, and the work was accordingly begun under the editorship of the professor. Before many sheets, however, were struck off, notice came that the printing was to be stopped. Lepsius, naturally anxious to know how far Uranius supported or demolished some of the theories about Egyptian history, was disappointed as well as amused to find that the book was little more than a translation into very bad Greek of portions of the writings of Bunsen and himself. Ehrenberg then examined the manuscript with his microscope, and discovered that the palimpsest was really later than the more modern one—the old ink overlaid the new.—*Cornhill Magazine.*

HISTORICAL PHRASES.

A valuable feature in the work of Herr Büchmann* is the collection of Historical Phrases, with rectifications of many that are attributed to wrong parents, and anecdotes relating to others. The saying that "no one is a hero to his valet" is taken from Madame Cornuel, who had but one talent, and is given to Montaigne, who has ten talents. Louis XIV. may or may not have said, " *L'état c'est moi,*" but there is no good authority for it beyond the character of the monarch. " *La parole a été donnée à l'homme pour déguiser sa pensée*" is always ascribed to Talleyrand, but belongs really to Voltaire. It seems also that "the beginning of the end" is not Talleyrand's, though no other author has been discovered for it; and Talleyrand's " They have learnt nothing and forgotten nothing," occurs in a letter of the date of 1796, written to Mallet du Pan, and published in his correspondence. In like manner, Metternich's " *Après nous le déluge*" was the property of Madame de Pompadour. Nothing is more generally quoted among men of letters than Buffon's sentence, " *Le style c'est l'homme.*" And yet this sentence does not occur in Buffon ; nor does the moral which everybody draws from it belong to Buffon. What Buffon really says is something very different. After praising a careful style, and declaring that only well-written works will descend to posterity, he adds that knowledge, facts, even discoveries, do not ensure a long life to a work if it is not well written, because facts and discoveries can be easily transplanted into other works, and even gain by a more skilful treatment. *Ces choses sont hors de l'homme, le style est de l'homme même.*" This does not mean that a man's style is his character, but that his style is all he can contribute of himself—two very different things. It is not surprising that the Count of Artois did not utter the phrase, " *Il n'y a rien de changé, il n'y a qu'un Français de plus*" ; but we are amused at being introduced to the actual author in the throes of composition, and at hearing Talleyrand, who presided over the work,

---

* *Geflügelte Worte ; der Citatenschatz des Deutschen Volks.* Von Georg Büchmann. Berlin, 1864.

tell him that he had only to make a good speech, suitable to the time and the man, and the Prince would believe that he had actually spoken it. Napoleon is more fortunate, as he is left in undisturbed possession of the " one step from the sublime to the ridiculous."

The newest German phrases are derived almost exclusively from the late or present Ministers of Prussia. If the Bismark Cabinet has contributed little to the statesmanship or honour of the country, it has enriched the language by some popular expressions which are not unworthy of their authors. Von Roon started the "pleasing temperature" of the Upper Chamber; Bismark himself is the father of "Catilinist existences," " iron and blood ;" while others have contributed the common phrases of " moral conquests," and of " a promise not worth the paper on which it is written." The name of Philistines, which Mr. Arnold proposes for adoption in England, seems to have originated at Jena in 1693. After a fight between town and gown, in which a student was killed, the pastor of Jena preached upon the fray, and said it reminded him of the words, " The Philistines are upon thee, Samson." With this story we may couple another, which Herr Büchmann places under the head of Luther. The Germans have a phrase for anything that is at the last gasp, "that it is in the last of Matthew," this being Luther's way of referring to the last chapter of Matthew. A Catholic preacher, talking of Protestantism in his sermon, said that it was in the last of Matthew, and after church a Protestant came up and thanked the priest for his admirable sermon. " What," said the priest, " you, a Protestant, thank me !" " Why not ?" replied the other; " is it not written in the last of Matthew, 'Lo, I am with you always, even to the end of the world.' "—*Saturday Review.*

THE BOROUGH OF OLD SARUM.

In the *Cornhill Magazine*, September, 1868, is a paper entitled " Pocket Boroughs," containing a curious account of the decayed villages and collections of ruined sheds and barns which used to return members to Parliament in the old times, but which were disfranchised by the Reform Bill of 1832. Of the most corrupt instance of these " pocket boroughs" we here read :

" The case of Old Sarum is a very peculiar one. This place used always to be quoted as one of the most flagrant examples of the absurdity of the old system, and any allusion to the one inhabitant of that ancient borough, who was supposed to return its two members, was always thought a good joke. But the fact is, that, till about 120 years ago, there was not even one inhabitant of Old Sarum ; and I remember being puzzled at first how to reconcile this fact with the record of 'contested elections' which occurred there in the reign of Charles II., and again in the reign of Queen Anne. But on examining the point one sees that these were cases rather of disputed returns than of contests in the modern sense. Not but what there were materials for even these. It did not follow in those days that because there were no residents, therefore there were no voters. And on the site of Old Sarum still flourished fourteen freeholders, who were likewise ' burgage holders,' and who met periodically under the 'Election Elm'—a tree which I regarded with veneration—to choose their representatives in Parliament. Sarum *had* once been a place of great importance. Its castle was one of the chief barriers of the south-west against the incursions of the Welsh; and before the removal of its cathedral into the valley where it now stands, it must have been one of the finest cities in the kingdom. But when no longer required as a military post, it is easy to see that its inaccessible position, on the summit of a very steep and very lofty hill, would soon lead to its desertion. But as early as the reign of Henry VIII., the old town was in ruins, and not a single house in it inhabited. And we may suppose that by the end of the seventeenth century it had become just the bare mound that it is at present."

To this we may add that the burgage tenure of Old Sarum was pur·chased by Governor Pitt, who once owned " the Pitt Diamond ;" and here at Stratford House, at the foot of the fortress hill, lived Robert Pitt, the father of Lord Chatham, whom Miss Seward erroneously states to have been born here: the birthplace of the great Minister was, however, in the parish of St. James, Westminster.

WHAT IS BUNCOMBE?

What is the real meaning of that which the Americans have named Buncombe? What are the conditions favourable to this diseased growth? The social stratum most susceptible of Buncombe is that which forms the main substance of American society. Americans are almost universally educated to the point of admiring ornament, but not up to the point of distinguishing gold from tinsel. All Buncombe is a form of vulgarity which resembles most closely the ostentation of a man who has sprung suddenly into wealth. The gentleman who " strikes oil" in America covers his house and his dress with barbaric ornaments; and as the whole nation may be said to have struck oil metaphorically, it is not strange that they adorn their language with a similar mass of tinsel. The most extreme and offensive forms of Buncombe survive chiefly in the half-settled districts; and the really cultivated Americans—such men as Washington Irving or Hawthorne or Mr. Longfellow—write a style fully as pure as Englishmen of the same literary standing.

Buncombe, then, may be described, not as a necessary product of democracy, but rather of the rapidly changing state of society. When things have come to a state of equilibrium, each class will have its appropriate costume, both mental and physical. But when a large number of persons suddenly discover that they ought to be much wiser and more eloquent than is actually the case, they show all the awkwardness of a clown introduced into good society, by indulging in very grotesque and gorgeous ornaments. And the only way in which they can be thoroughly reformed is by receiving that amount of general education which will enable them to pay due respect to the best models. Perhaps it is a too sanguine expectation that within any moderate time the English shopkeeper will be able to distinguish between Buncombe and real eloquence, and to prefer simplicity to tinsel. It may be still longer before the gentlemen whose profession it is to flatter a mob will not seek to impose upon them by using the most many-syllabled words and the sentences most heavily weighted with epithets that they can discover. Only we may take some comfort from the fact, that side by side with inflated nonsense, good vigorous English is a most powerful weapon, and will end by establishing always its superiority over windy bombast.—Abridged from the *Saturday Review.*

APPENDIX.

LEADERS OF THE ENGLISH REBELLION.

The Rebellion was an outbreak of the democratic spirit, a movement from below, an uprising from the foundations, or as some will have it, the dregs of society. Cornet Joyce, who carried off Charles I., and who was highly respected in the army, had, however, been recently a common working tailor, or, as Clarendon describes him, "a fellow who had, two or three years before, served in a very inferior employment in Mr. Hollis's house." Colonel Pride, whose name is preserved in history as having purged the House of Commons of its malignants, was about on a level with Joyce, since his original occupation was that of a drayman; it is said that Cromwell, in ridicule of the old distinctions, conferred knighthood on him "with a faggot." But the tailor and the drayman were, in that age, strong enough to direct the course of public affairs, and to win for them a position in the state.

Of the Fifth Monarchy men, three principal and most distinguished members were Venner, Tufnel, and Okey. Venner, who was the leader, was a wine-cooper. Tufnel was a carpenter living in Gray's-inn-lane. And Okey, though he became a colonel, had been a stoker in a brewhouse at Islington, and next a most poor chandler, near Lion Key, in Thames-street. Cromwell himself was a brewer at Huntingdon, as stated by his own physician; and Colonel Jones, his brother-in-law, had been servant to a private gentleman. Deane was a servant to a toyman in Ipswich; but he became an admiral, and was made one of the Commissioners of the Navy. Colonel Goffe had been apprentice to a drysalter; Major General Whalley had been apprentice to a woollen-draper, but became "a broken clothier." Skipton, a common soldier, who had received no education, was appointed commander of the London Militia; he was declared commander-in-chief in Ireland; and he became one of the fourteen members of Cromwell's Council. Two of the lieutenants of the Tower were Berkstead and Tichborne. Berkstead had heretofore sold needles, bodkins, and thimbles, and would have run on any errand anywhere for a little money. Tichborne, who was a linendraper, not only received the lieutenancy of the Tower, but became a colonel, and a member of the Committee of State in 1655, and of the Council of State in 1659. Other traders were equally successful; the highest prizes being open to all men, provided they displayed the requisite capacity. Colonel Harvey was a decayed silkman, who got the Bishop of London's house and manor of Fulham. So was also Colonel Rowe; and Colonel Venn was a "broken silkman in Cheapside." Salway had been an apprentice to a grocer, but, being an able man, he rose to the rank of a major in the army; he received the King's Remembrancer's Office; and in 1659 he was appointed by Parliament a member of the Council of State. Around that council board were also gathered Bond, a woollen-draper at Dorchester, and Cawley, the brewer in Chichester; while by their side we find John Berner, who is said to have been a private servant, and Cornelius Holland, who had been a link-boy and a servant. Among others who were promoted to offices of trust, were Packe, the woollen-draper; Perry, the weaver; and Pemble, the tailor. The Parliament which was summoned in 1653 is still remembered as Barebones, who was a leatherseller in Fleet-street. Thus, too, Downing, though a poor charity-boy, became Teller of the Exchequer, and representative of England at the Hague. The common opinion is that he was the (illegitimate?) son of a clergyman at Hackney, though this is doubtful; and no one appears to know who his father was. To these we may add that Colonel Horton had been a gentleman's servant: Cromwell had a great regard for this remarkable man. Colonel Berry had been a woodmonger; Colonel Cooper a haberdasher; Major Rolfe a shoemaker; Colonel Fox a tinker; and Colonel Hewson a cobbler.

In the provinces, in 1647, Chelmsford was governed by a tinker, two cobblers, two tailors, and two pedlars; and at Cambridge most of the colonels and officers were mean tradesmen, brewers, tailors, goldsmiths, shoemakers, and the like. And, when Whitelocke was at Sweden, in 1653, the proctor of one of the towns abused the Parliament, saying that "they had killed their king, and were a company of taylors and cobblers."

Yet, some of the above classes were ostentatious enough; for Walker, who relates what he himself had witnessed, says, that about 1649, the army was commanded by "colonels and superior officers who lord it in their gilt coaches, rich apparel, costly feastings; though some of them led dray-horses, wore leather pelts, and were never able to name their own fathers and mothers."—Condensed from Buckle's *Hist. Civilisation in England*, vol. i., where the several authorities are quoted.

GENERAL INDEX.

THE END.

By the Author of the present Work.

NOTABLE THINGS OF OUR OWN TIME: a Supplementary Volume of "Things not Generally Known." With Frontispiece and Vignette. 3s. 6d.

Notable Things.

" You have not posted your books these ten years ; how should a man keep his affairs, even at this rate ?"—ARBUTHNOT.

Now ready, with Frontispiece and Vignette, 3s. 6d.

NOTABLE THINGS OF OUR OWN TIME;

A Supplementary Volume of " Things not Generally Known Familiarly Explained."

BY THE SAME AUTHOR,

JOHN TIMBS, F.S.A.

AUTHOR OF ''CURIOSITIES OF LONDON," ETC.

INTRODUCTORY.

A WRITER of strong common sense has declared the spirit of the time to require in every man not only a thorough knowledge of his own profession, but much general knowledge to enable him to keep pace with the rapid changes which are taking place around him. The truth of this remark was self-evident at the time it was made ; and every subsequent year has added to its corroboration, but with this change in opinion, that *to know one thing well, a man must know a little of all things ;* if we make good use of our lifetime, there is room enough to crowd almost every art and science into it. Dr. Arnold has emphatically said : " Depend upon it a mixed knowledge is not a superficial one: as far as it goes, the views that it gives are true."

VER.

It is to a conviction to the truth of these views that the present volume of "NOTABLE THINGS" owes its existence. Twelve years ago, first appeared *Things not Generally Known Familiarly Explained*, of which Ten Thousand Copies were sold within Ten Months; the sale has considerably exceeded 30,000. It has occurred to the author or compiler, as the case may be, that to keep the Reader POSTED UP in this Account-book of Information, a Supplementary Volume of Notable Things may be acceptable, provided the same attention be paid to the trustworthiness of its contents, and their variety and interest, as was devoted to its successful predecessor, *Things not Generally Known*, which, it may be recollected, has been described as "a book to take a bite of now and then, and always with a relish;" "a book as full of information as a pomegranate is of seed" (Douglas Jerrold); and "a little volume in which is more knowledge than is to be found in a hundred books that might be named" (*Athenæum.*)

This Volume of "NOTABLE THINGS" contains the leading *Novelties and New Views of the last Twelve Years*, or since the publication of *Things not Generally Known*, grouped conveniently for consecutive reading and ready reference.

From *The Bookseller*, May 1, 1868. — "*Notable Things of Our Own Time*, Mr. Timbs's new volume, like its predecessor, will be greedily devoured by every thinking reader to whom it may be presented, and will serve to set the dullest boy a-thinking. It is a record of progress, not in dull, dry, chronological order, but in detached pieces and subjects; here a little, and there a little; and eventually the well-informed man manages to pick up a good deal. To become a great astronomer is the work of a lifetime, but a little knowledge of astronomy, so far from being dangerous, is useful in the highest degree. The same may be said of geology, the antiquity of man, new countries, magnetic science, and the hundred other subjects touched upon in this useful volume."

From the *Publishers' Circular*, May 1, 1868. — "*Notable Things of Our Own Time*, a supplemental volume of *Things not Generally Known*. One of the pleasant gatherings of the curious, useful and entertaining, for the production of which Mr. Timbs has acquired a deserved celebrity."

From the *City Press*. — "Mr. Timbs's handy little volumes are each the results of some particularly happy thought; but it is quite clear that they cannot in all cases contain the latest intelligence; and so the compiler of *Things not Generally Known* has issued a sort of supplementary volume, which, under the title of *Notable Things of Our Own Time*, shall serve to keep everybody well *posted-up* in the most recent devices and discoveries. Of course the new venture will be a success."

LONDON: LOCKWOOD AND CO., STATIONERS' HALL COURT.

PRINCIPAL CONTENTS.

NOTABLE THINGS OF OUR OWN TIME.—CONTENTS.

Inventions anticipated — Spectrum Analysis—Antiquity of the Stereoscope —Photography applied to Astronomy — Revelations of the Microscope — —Adulteration of Food—Spectrum Microscope—Spontaneous Combustion —Leibig's Extract of Meat—Electric Lamp and Coal-gas—Oils and Paraffin —Drummond Light in Lighthouses— Lime and Magnesium Lights—Fuel from Water—Fire from Wood—Manufacture of Lucifer Matches—Warming St. Paul's Cathedral—How the Palace of Parliament is Ventilated—Nitroglycerine, new substitute for Gunpowder — Building Blackfriars Bridge — Metropolitan Main Drainage—Bank-note Library—Wonders of the Cotton Manufacture—Story of the Sewing-Machine —India Rubber Manufacture.

MINING AND WORKING IN METALS:— Recent Results of Mining—How to make Gold—Nicety of Machine-measuring—Air-hammers and Steam-hammers—Nasmyth, the Engineer—Calculation of Life by Machinery.

THE RAILWAY:—A Railway Journey Round the World—Building the Victoria Railway Bridge, Canada—Pneumatic and Subterranean Railways— Results of Railways.

THE ELECTRIC TELEGRAPH:—Magnetism and Electricity — Suspended between Heaven and Earth—Magnetic Mountain—Powerful Electro-magnetic Apparatus—The Electric Telegraph Data—"The Nerves of London"— Curiosities of Sound—Exhibition of Wilde's Electro-magnetic Light, at Burlington House—Sir Charles Wheatstone—Visible Speech.

OPERATIONS OF WAR:—Civil Engineering in Warfare—Enfield Rifles— Armour-plates and Great Guns — Armstrong and Whitworth — Naval Construction—Railways in Warfare— Story of the Needle-Gun—Iron Ships —"Great Eastern" Steam-ship—Destructive Conflict of Ironclads—Siege of Sebastopol — New Weapons at the French Exhibition.

DIAMONDS: — Diamond Cutting and Polishing — Koh-i-noor and Sancy Diamonds—"Regent of France" — Origin of Diamonds—Present Value of Diamonds—British Pearls.

LIFE, HEALTH, AND DEATH:—Brain of Man—How the Bedstead should be placed—Deaths by Lightning—Remedy for Poisoning—Alleged Influence of the Moon on the Insane—The Hour of Death —Death not Pain—Progress of Medicine —Medical Errors—New British Pharmacopœia—Chloroform, its History— What is Pepsine?—The Hammam, or Hot-air Bath—Faraday's Loss of Memory—Burial on the North Side— Beauty of Death.

HISTORIC JOTTINGS: — Columbus and the Egg—Chauvinisme—Black Monday—Luck of Crooked Money—December and the Napoleon Family—Results of War—Modern Battles—United Germany—England the Refuge of the World—Crises of History—The Protestant Church—The word "Altar" —Jewish and Christian Holidays— Marriages by Special Licence—Wars— Avebury a Burial-Circle?—Præ-historic Times.

GREAT EXHIBITION:—Origin of the Great Exhibition of 1851: Facts never yet published—The Alexandra Palace.

MISCELLANEOUS: — Gold Discoveries— Foreign Exchanges — Decimal and Metric System—Ascent of Mont Blanc —Prevention of Crime: Employment of the Destitute Poor—Tea-drinking in Russia—Restlessness and Enterprise.

LONDON: LOCKWOOD AND CO.,
STATIONERS' HALL COURT.